CW00516198

Mary T. P. Mann

Life of Horace Mann

Mary T. P. Mann

Life of Horace Mann

ISBN/EAN: 9783337849108

Printed in Europe, USA, Canada, Australia, Japan

Cover: Foto ©Raphael Reischuk / pixelio.de

More available books at **www.hansebooks.com**

OF

HORACE MANN.

By HIS WIFE.

SECOND EDITION.

BOSTON:

WALKER, FULLER, AND COMPANY,

245 WASHINGTON STREET.

M DCCC LXV.

DEDICATION.

I DEDICATE this work to THE YOUNG. Those who were young
when Mr. Mann first entered upon his educational work in Massachusetts, and who are now men and women, love to call themselves his
children. " My eighty thousand children" was a favorite expression
of his own; and those words alone expressed the sentiment he felt
towards them. They were to him the next generation, whose culture
must tell upon society for good or for evil; and it was a delightful
task to help them to a better one than was then enjoyed by the people
at large.

In his later life, other young people came under his direct personal
influence, who were old enough to love him with enthusiasm, and to
labor cordially to diffuse the views and purposes of life which he so
earnestly inculcated upon them. I know they will love to read the
record of his growth, of his affections, and of his success; and they
can also sympathize with his trials. If he had been less ardent, he
would have suspended the gigantic efforts he made for success in his
last enterprise to a period when he could have obtained more co-operation; but his zeal in the cause blinded him to the extent of his own
physical powers, and he fell as by a mortal blow.

M. M.

CONCORD, MASS.

INTRODUCTION.

It has been more difficult than was anticipated to write a memoir of a life from so near a point of view. I am conscious of my disabilities as well as of my advantages for the grateful task. One tends to idealize a character, which, during many years of the closest intimacy, was never swayed by unworthy motives, or acted upon secondary principles, and over which the beauty of sacred affections poured an indefinable charm. I am aware, that, where others see faults, I see only virtues. When his is called a " rugged nature," because he could not temporize, and because he made great requisitions of men upon whom were laid great duties, I see only his demand for perfection in others as well as in himself; and no man ever made greater requisitions of self. He could forget his own interests when he worked for great causes ; and he sometimes wished others, who had not his moral strength, to do likewise. But the very requisition often evolved self-respect to such a degree as to bring forth the power to do the duty, as many a man who has come under his influence can testify ; and what greater honor can we do to our fellow-man than to expect of him the very highest of which he is capable? It is true of him, that he had not much charity for those who sinned against the light ; but it is equally true, that his tenderness for the ignorant and the oppressed was never found wanting, and that the first motion of repentance in the erring melted his heart at once. Love of man was so essentially the impelling power in him, that it cost him no effort to exercise it ; but he had no self-appreciation which made him feel that he could do what others could not if they would. Perhaps the most remarkable trait in his character was his modest estimate of himself. He measured himself by the standard he wished to attain, and not by comparison with others ; and, when he was lauded for what he had accomplished, his unaffected humility made him uncomfortable because the act was not more worthily and adequately performed: for, at every stage of his progress, he was as far from his own ideal excellence as before. By nature, he craved the sympathy and approbation of his fellow-men, — not of the populace, but of those whom he respected and loved; yet even this craving did not deflect him from the path of rectitude, or blind him to the demands of duty. Principles were more to him than even friends; which is no light praise of one who loved so tenderly, and felt so keenly every suspicion of his motives. He rarely unbosomed himself; for his sensibilities were of exquisite delicacy: the musician who has the acutest ear for harmony is not more sensitive to a discord than he was to the slightest jar of feeling. He was too earnest a man to be able to sustain superficial relations with other men; and this often made him solitary when he would fain have been social, and made his intimate circle a small one. Friendship meant more to him than to most men: it implied not only pleasant social relations, but a oneness of sentiment and principle, without which the delicate links of the magic chain would soon part. He could not give his affections to those who did not share his love of humanity or his moral insight; for both his conscience and his intellect must consent before the bond could be cemented. But, when he did unfold his heart, the surrender was entire; and he became again a child in his confidence, and dependence upon affection. In those crises of his life when divergence of principle separated him, as was inevitable, from many whom he had loved, and of whom he had hoped all noble things, a woman could not weep bitterer tears over the disappointment. This tenderness of his character can only be equalled by the moral force with which he assailed whatever he saw to be wrong in the world. It was a conscientious act with him to battle with evil wherever he saw it. Man was endowed with his destructive and combative powers for this end alone, as he thought; his only legitimate enemy being evil. The men who were the victims of it were the objects of his solicitude; the men who made evil their good, the objects of his attacks, if only so could he lay the spirit that marred creation. Still, evil was, in his estimation, only relative; the absence of good, one of the conditions of imperfection and of growth.

"If I believed in total depravity, I must, of course, believe in everlasting punishment," he would say; "but I consider both unworthy of God." To hunt evil into its corner, therefore, was the first step towards turning it into food for growth. He could bear, for himself and others, present pain, however acute, in order to redeem as much of this life as possible for truth and heaven, whose enjoyment is entered whenever the spiritual element is made to take precedence of the earthly one in our double nature. Painful early impressions of his heavenly Father cast a cloud over much of his religious life; for persons of such delicate organization do not easily recover from impressions made upon their nerves in childhood. He could have said with another remarkable man who emerged from the gloom of Orthodoxy into the light and life of religious liberty, " My heart is Unitarian ; but my nerves are still Calvinistic." But his faith in endless progress grew stronger with every experience, till his very aspect was irradiated by it. All nature became full of revealings to him, — revealings of beneficent laws, of overflowing love : nothing in it seemed trivial to him ; for every thing had been an object of divine thought, from the humblest flower, or even stone, to the most distant star. And, while he loved with an unutterable love the beauty God had made, the revelations of science were scarcely less sacred to him than the revelations of moral truth ; and they were illustrative of each other in his teachings. This conception of the universe was not given to his childhood ; but he wished it to remain the birthright of all who came under his influence, rather than that it should be wrested from their experience as it had been from his own.

But not the less earnestly did he continue to labor to put the weapons of strength into the hands of the young, or less sturdily do battle against the enemies that assail us from within; and he learned to look with more pity than indignation upon those who abused God's gifts, when they should only have used them. In reproving the young, which it became his duty to do, he was often moved to tears ; and the more obdurate the subject, the more deeply he was affected. But one of those who responded most genially and naturally to his inspiring touch said of him, that " it was heaven to look into his face."

Those who loved him are consoled by the thought that he did not live to see the terrible struggle of his beloved country ; for he was keenly susceptible to every form of suffering, and had forelived it all by his realization of the relations of cause and effect. His clear moral convictions would have saved him from any doubt that this is a necessary war of purification; yet he had allowed himself to hope for a more peaceful solution of our national evil through the milder forms of industrial and commercial interests. Like the great souls of all times, he wished beneficent changes to come to pass through reflection rather than through violence.*

* Since the above was written, the glorious advance in public sentiment, which has resulted in the death-blow given to the cause of all our woe, might well make his friends wish that he could have lived to share the universal joy. Yet who can doubt that all is open vision to those who have vanished into other spheres from spheres below scarcely less divine?

CONTENTS.

CHAPTER I.

CHAPTER II.

CHAPTER III.

CHAPTER IV.

CHAPTER V.

CHAPTER VI.

APPENDIX.

A.

B.

C.

D.

LIFE OF HORACE MANN.

CHAPTER I.

HORACE MANN was born in Franklin, Mass., on the
4th of May, 1796. His father, who died when he
was thirteen, was a farmer, and a man who left in his
family a strong impression of moral worth, and love of
knowledge ; but he had not the means to give his children any better advantages of education than this inheritance. His mother, with whom Horace remained till he
was twenty years of age, was the object of his most profound respect and tender affection ; but, in those days, a
certain reserve and distance existed between parents and
children, which constituted a great barrier to freedom of
intercourse. His habits of reserve were such, that, by his
own account, he never told even his mother of personal
physical sufferings until they revealed themselves by their
own intensity ; and of his mental emotions he never
thought of any thing but to keep them to himself. In
our day, when enlightened parents make it such a point
to secure the personal confidence of their children by
sympathizing in their least joys and sorrows, we can
hardly reconcile a sterner rule with the idea of true affection, or estimate the depressing effect of such puritanical
manners upon a sensitive child. He was obliged to work
out all his problems alone, and retained only painful

recollections of the whole period which ought to be, with every child, a golden age to look back upon. But, even at that time, his lively affections and naturally joyous nature bubbled up irrepressibly when in company with those of his own age. He was full of practical fun and witty repartee; playing his native logic on all half-thinkers, but never unkindly. If any opportunity had been offered him for artistic culture, he might have excelled in it; for he sometimes tried his wings in secret. But there was a repressing influence upon all such "foolish waste of time;" and he said of himself, that, in his younger days, he was accustomed to regard the cultivation of the imagination in the light of a snare to virtue rather than as a legitimate enjoyment of God-given powers. It has been well said of him by a sagacious friend, that "his causality was an inspiration." It was all that saved him in those dark days, as may be seen by his own testimony. His modesty, however, being as striking a trait as his logical power, his heart was long influenced by the social views around him, even after he suspected their fallacy. In a letter to a friend, he says, —

I regard it as an irretrievable misfortune that my childhood was not a happy one. By nature I was exceedingly elastic and buoyant; but the poverty of my parents subjected me to continual privations. I believe in the rugged nursing of Toil; but she nursed me too much. In the winter time, I was employed in in-door and sedentary occupations, which confined me too strictly; and in summer, when I could work on the farm, the labor was too severe, and often encroached upon the hours of sleep. I do not remember the time when I began to work. Even my play-days — not play-days, for I never had any, but my play-hours — were earned by extra exertion, finishing tasks early to gain a little leisure for boyish sports. My parents sinned ignorantly; but God affixes the same physical penalties to the violation of his laws, whether that violation be wilful or ignorant. For wilful violation there is the added penalty of remorse; and that is the only difference. Here let me give you two pieces of advice which shall be *gratis* to you, though they cost me what is of more value than diamonds. Train your children to work, though not too hard ; and, unless they are grossly lymphatic, let them sleep as much as they will. I have derived one compensation, however, from the rigor of my early lot. Industry, or diligence, became my second nature ; and I think it would puzzle any psychologist to tell where it joined on to the first. Owing to these ingrained habits, work has always been to me what water is to a fish. I have wondered a thousand times to hear people say, " I don't like this business ; " or, " I wish I could exchange for that ; " for with me, whenever I have had any thing to do, I do not remember ever to have demurred, but have always set about it like a fatalist ; and it was as sure to be done as the sun is to set.

What was called the love of knowledge, was, in my time, necessarily cramped into a love of books ; because there was no such thing as oral instruction. Books designed for children were few, and their contents meagre and miserable. My teachers were very good people ; but they were very poor teachers. Looking back to the schoolboy-days of my mates and myself, I cannot adopt the line of Virgil, —

" O fortunatos nimium sua si bona norint ! "

I deny the *bona*. With the infinite universe around us, all ready to be daguerrotyped upon our souls, we were never placed at the right focus to receive its glorious images. I had an intense natural love of beauty, and of its expression in nature and in the fine arts. As " a poet was in Murray lost," so at least an amateur poet, if not an artist, was lost in me. How often when a boy did I stop, like Akenside's hind, to gaze at the glorious sunset, and lie down upon my back at night on the earth to look at the heavens ! Yet, with all our senses and our faculties glowing and receptive, how little were we taught ! or, rather, how much obstruction was thrust in between us and Nature's teachings ! Our eyes were never trained to distinguish forms and colors. Our ears were strangers to music. So far from being taught the art of drawing, which is a beautiful language by itself, I well remember that when the impulse to express in pictures what I could not express in words was so strong, that, as Cowper says, it tingled down to my fingers, then my knuckles were rapped with the heavy ruler of the teacher, or cut with his rod, so that an artificial tingling soon drove away the natural. Such youthful buoyancy as even severity could not repress was our only dancing-master. Of all our faculties, the memory for words was the only one specially appealed to. The most comprehensive generalizations of men were given us, instead of the facts from which those generalizations were formed. All ideas outside of the book were contraband articles, which the teacher confiscated, or rather flung overboard. Oh! when the intense and burning activity of youthful faculties shall find employment in salutary and pleasing studies or occupations, then will parents be able to judge better of the alleged proneness of children to mischief. Until then, children have not a fair trial before their judges.

Yet, with these obstructions, I had a love of knowledge which nothing could repress. An inward voice raised its plaint forever in my heart for something nobler and better; and, if my parents had not the means to give me knowledge, they intensified the love of it. They always spoke of learning and learned men with enthusiasm and a kind of reverence. I was taught to take care of the few books we had, as though there was something sacred about them. I never dogs-eared one in my life, nor profanely scribbled upon title-pages, margin, or fly-leaf; and would as soon have stuck a pin through my flesh as through the pages of a book. When very young, I remember a young lady came to our house on a visit, who was said to have studied Latin. I looked upon her as a sort of goddess. Years after, the idea that I could ever study Latin broke upon my mind with the wonder and bewilderment of a revelation. Until the age of fifteen, I had never been to school more than eight or ten weeks in a year.

I said we had but few books. The town, however, owned a small library. When incorporated, it was named after Dr. Franklin, whose reputation was then not only at its zenith, but, like the sun over Gibeon, was standing still there. As an acknowledgment of the compliment, he offered them a bell for their church; but afterwards, saying that, from what he had learned of the character of the people, he thought they would prefer sense to sound, he changed the gift into a library. Though this library consisted of old histories and theologies, suited, perhaps, to the taste of the "conscript fathers" of the town, but miserably adapted to the "proscript" children, yet I wasted my youthful ardor upon its martial pages, and learned to glory in war, which both reason and conscience have since taught me to consider' almost universally a crime. Oh! when will men learn to redeem that childhood in their offspring which was lost to themselves? We watch for the seedtime for our fields, and improve it; but neglect the mind until midsummer or even autumn comes, when all the *actinism* of the vernal sun of youth is gone. I have endeavored to do something to remedy this criminal defect. Had I the power, I would scatter libraries over the whole land, as the sower sows his wheat-field.

More than by toil, or by the privation of any natural taste, was the inward joy of my youth blighted by theological inculcations. The pastor of the church in Franklin was the somewhat celebrated Dr. Emmons, who not only preached to his people, but ruled them, for more than fifty years. He was an extra or hyper-Calvinist, — a man of pure intellect, whose logic was never softened in its severity by the infusion of any kindliness of sentiment. He expounded all the doctrines of total depravity, election, and reprobation, and not only the eternity, but the extremity, of hell-torments, unflinchingly and in their most terrible significance; while he rarely if ever descanted upon the joys of heaven, and never, to my recollection, upon the essential and necessary happiness of a virtuous life. Going to church on Sunday was a sort of religious ordinance in our family; and, during all my boyhood, I hardly ever remember staying at home. Hence, at ten years of age, I became familiar with the whole creed, and knew all the arts of theological fence by which objections to it were wont to be parried. It might be that I accepted the doctrines too literally, or did not temper them with the proper qualifications; but, in the way in which they came to my youthful mind, a certain number of souls were to be forever lost, and nothing — not powers, nor principalities, nor man, nor angel, nor Christ, nor the Holy Spirit, nay, not God himself — could save them; for he had sworn, before time was, to get eternal glory out of their eternal torment. But perhaps I might not be one of the lost! But my little sister might be, my mother might be, or others whom I loved ; and I felt, that, if they were in hell, it would make a hell of whatever other part of the universe I might inhabit ; for I could never get a glimpse of consolation from the idea that my own nature could be so transformed, and become so like what God's was said to be, that I could rejoice in their sufferings.

Like all children, I believed what I was taught. To my vivid imagination, a physical hell was a living reality, as much so as though I could have heard the shrieks of the tormented, or stretched out my hand to grasp their burning souls, in a vain endeavor for their rescue. Such a faith spread a pall of blackness over the whole heavens, shutting out every beautiful and glorious thing ; while beyond that curtain of darkness I could see the bottomless and seething lake filled with torments, and hear the wailing and agony of its victims. I am sure I felt all this a thousand times more than my teachers did ; and is not this a warning to teachers ?

What we phrenologists call causality, — the faculty of mind by which we see effects in causes, and causes in effects, and invest the future with a present reality, — this faculty was always intensely active in my mind. Hence the doom of the judgment-day was antedated : the torments which, as the doctrine taught me, were to begin with death, began immediately ; and each moment became a burning focus, on which were concentrated, as far as the finiteness of my nature would allow, the agonies of the coming eternity.

Had there been any possibility of escape, could penance, fasting, self-inflicted wounds, or the pains of a thousand martyr-deaths, have averted the fate, my agony of apprehension would have been alleviated ; but there, beyond effort, beyond virtue, beyond hope, was this irreversible decree of Jehovah, immutable, from everlasting to everlasting. The judgment had been made up and entered upon the eternal record millions of years before we, who were judged by it, had been born ; and there sat the Omnipotent upon his throne, with eyes and heart of stone to guard it ; and had all the beings in all the universe gathered themselves together before him to implore but the erasure of only a single name from the list of the doomed, their prayers would have been in vain.

I shall not now enter into any theological disquisition on these matters, infinitely momentous as they are. I shall not stop to inquire into the soundness of these doctrines, or whether I held the truth in error; my only object here being, according to your request, to speak of my youth biographically, or give you a sketch of some of my juvenile experiences. The consequences upon my mind and happiness were disastrous in the extreme. Often, on going to bel at night, did the objects of the day and the faces of friends give place to a vision of the awful throne, the inexorable Judge, and the hapless myriads, among whom I often seemed to see those whom I loved best; and there I wept and sobbed until Nature found that counterfeit repose in exhaustion whose genuine reality she should have found in freedom from care and the spontaneous happiness of childhood. What seems most deplorable in the retrospect, all these fears and sufferings, springing from a belief in the immutability of the decrees that had been made, never prompted me to a single good action, or had the slightest efficacy in deterring me from a bad one. I remained in this condition of mind until I was twelve years of age. I remember the day, the hour, the place, the circumstances, as well as though the event had happened but yesterday, when, in an agony, of despair, I broke the spell that had bound me. From that day, I began to construct the theory of Christian ethics and doctrine respecting virtue and vice, rewards and penalties, time and eternity, God and his providence, which, with such modifications as advancing age and a wider vision must impart, I still retain, and out of which my life has flowed. I have come round again to a belief in the eternity of rewards and punishments, as a fact necessarily resulting from the constitution of our nature; but how infinitely different, in its effects upon conduct, character, and happiness, is this belief from that which blasted and consumed the joy of my childhood!

As to my early habits, whatever may have been my shortcomings, I can still say that I have always been exempt from what may be called common vices. I was never intoxicated in my life; unless, perchance, with joy or anger. I never swore: indeed, profanity was always most disgusting and repulsive to me. And (I consider it always a climax) I never used the "vile weed" in any form. I early formed the resolution to be a slave to no habit. For the rest, my public life is almost as well known to others as to myself; and, as it commonly happens to public men, "*others know my motives a great deal better than I do.*"

A recent letter from a friend, touching upon the same topic, deepens the impression just given :—

. . . Yes, it is true that Mr. Mann spoke to me often of his boyhood, chiefly of its sorrows. One of these was the death of a brother, who was drowned at twelve years of age. He said he was a charming boy, and that his death immediately brought home to his heart the terribleness of the theological views in which he was educated. He had been in the habit of hearing logic chopped upon the scheme of the universe, the federation of the race in Adam, the plan of redemption by Christ's atonement, &c.; and there was a certain entertainment to his mind in this intellectual gymnastic, so that he became a very expert theologue himself, and could refute the Arminian and Arian theories with great acumen. But there were certain things that did not feel good to his heart which he often heard from the pulpit; such as, that "the smoke of the damned was the enjoyment of the blessed," and "the punishment of the wicked one of the special glories of God." He had none of the canonical evidences of being in a state of grace himself: and a strange fascination used to impel him, Sunday after Sunday, to find in Watts's hymn-book, and read over and over again, a certain verse, which must be eliminated from modern editions, for I cannot find it; but it depicted the desolation of a solitary soul in eternity, rudderless and homeless.

He had a strong impression, that, if he should die, he should personate the "*solitary soul*" therein depicted. But when his darling brother died, having not yet experienced the orthodox form of conversion, his agonized heart stimulated his imagination to clothe it in his brother's form and feature. He thought he could see in his mother's face a despair beyond the grief of losing the mortal life of her son; and when, at the funeral, Dr. Emmons, instead of suggesting a thought of a consoling character, improved the opportunity to address a crowd of young persons present on the topic of "dying unconverted," and he heard his mother groan, a crisis took place in his experience, similar to that described in Mrs. H. B. Stowe's story of the "Minister's Wooing," when Mrs. Marvin hears of her son James' death, without knowing whether he was converted or not. His whole being rose up against the idea of such a cruel Creator, and declared *hatred* to him! He would hate Infinite Malignity personified, if he must suffer eternally in consequence. The childish image, familiar to his mind, of a crystal floor covered with angels and saints playing on harps and enjoying the fruits of the tree of life, in the New Jerusalem, as described in the book of Revelation, — under which scene, in full sight, was the hell so often emphatically described by Dr. Emmons, — recurred to his imagination; and deliberately, with all the tremendous force of his will, he chose to suffer with the latter, rather than make one with the selfish immortals who found happiness in witnessing torture.

But to put himself at odds in this way with what he still thought was Infinite Power produced a fearful action upon his nerves. His imagination was possessed by the idea of a personal Devil, to whom he had no attractions, whatever was his repulsion from God; and he was yet too young to get behind all these forms, in which the depraved imagination of men had clothed the great realities of the spiritual life. Nature seemed to him but the specious veil in which demons clothed themselves. He expected the foul Fiend to appear from behind every hedge and tree to carry him off.

To escape from such misery, — which sometimes in the night amounted to such intensity that he saw fiends and other horrid shapes distinctly as with his bodily eyes, and was obliged to use the utmost force of his will to keep from screaming, — he did what he could to divert himself with study; but his early tastes for investigating and experimenting in science were all repressed by the impossibility of procuring books or any other materials to work upon.

Still the fund of humor, the sparkling wit, which all his sorrows could never quench, and the childlike playfulness into which he always fell with children, as if it were his element, could not but have made him a charming, merry child; and I have heard from his elder as well as from his younger sister and playfellow that he was such.

To me it was a marvel that so sensitive a boy, absolutely banished

2

from the bosom of a heavenly Father, grew up so sweet, so truthful, so faithful to the unknown God, whom he ignorantly worshipped, and who, unawares to himself, strengthened him for his protest against the popular theology.

The Unitarian sect was nearly unknown, and "everywhere spoken against," at the time he went to college; and he did not go where it prevailed, but to Brown University, where, while he was a scholar, there was what is called a "revival of religion."

He had now become acquainted with the classics, and had begun to read history and general literature; and he accepted the Deism of Cicero, and began to feel that true religion was the cultivation of social duty, and to feed his heart and imagination on the idea of making a heaven of society around him, with a home of his own for the Holy of Holies; though, as he said, he was not without occasional anxious glances towards the future life, of which he felt that he knew nothing.

The exercise of his great intellectual faculties, and of his pure and noble affections in philanthropy, gradually brought him into a healthier atmosphere of feeling and thought; and at last his happy marriage seemed to justify God's creation.

Such is the impression that he gave me of the general course of his experience, which I have expressed as well as I can. I did not know him until after he was a widower; and, in those first years of sorrow, all the gloom of his childhood returned upon him with terrible power. It was a relief to him to

> "Give sorrow words,
> Lest, whispering the o'erwrought heart, it break;"

and in such conversations he would detail his early life. I think I then obtained the deepest impressions I ever received from any mortal that the soul is a child of God, and that virtue has no element of self-love or self-seeking in it. He was good, and was willing good to others, and striving to confer it, although his heart's utterance as for a brief moment was that of Jesus of Nazareth: "My God, my God, why hast thou forsaken me?" I have, therefore, not been surprised, that since the stress of that bereavement grew lighter on his heart, and since he found himself in a home, and blessed with children, the radiance of religious light and love has flowed from his lips; nor that in the hour of his death he should seem never to think of himself, and to say no word except to uplift others into partaking the life and beneficence of God. Nothing in his life was more eminently characteristic than just such a death.

Yours,   ———.

But while some of the circumstances of his early life seemed thus adverse, others were favorable to the ripening of his strong yet gentle, brave yet tender, character. Perhaps they were all favorable; for those which directly hindered his intellectual progress may have tended indirectly to bring out in him his strong views and purposes of reform. The true soul transmutes all circumstances: only inferior natures are crushed by them.

In speaking of the influences which make a man a man, we must never lose sight of the truth, that only the highest natures are fully susceptible to the highest influences. The same motives may be operating upon different individuals; but only the well-poised soul will respond to them generously and faithfully. Emerson has truly said, " He is great who is what he is from nature, and who never reminds us of others; " and again, " Man is that noble endogenous plant which grows from within outward."

In speaking of his youthful longing for more education, he once said to a friend, " I know not how it was: its motive never took the form of wealth or fame. It was rather an instinct which impelled towards knowledge, as that of migratory birds impels them northward in spring-time. All my boyish castles in the air had reference to doing something for the benefit of mankind. The early precepts of benevolence, inculcated upon me by my parents, flowed out in this direction; and I had a conviction that knowledge was my needed instrument."

Reverence for knowledge as a means of good, had, indeed, prevailed in his father's family; and his only surviving sister, who devotes her life to more than one of the saddest charities of the world, basing her action upon both intellectual and moral culture, is but another proof of it.

Without any pride of pedigree, the family felt that it had an honorable, because a virtuous ancestry. All its traditions were of integrity and honor. The privations incident to the early settlement and growth of the New-England Colonies, following the sacrifices that necessarily pertained to the Pilgrim enterprise, strengthened sterling virtues, and transmitted them as a rich inheritance. Stern qualities, such as endurance, perseverance, toiling energy, and the might of self-sacrifice, were mixed with the more gentle traits of family affection, and devotion to the sentiments which had induced the forefathers to leave home and luxury for conscience' sake. The subject of our Memoir inherited his share of all these. All the family labored together for the common support; and toil was considered honorable, although it was sometimes, of necessity, excessive. Horace had earned his school-books, when a child, by braiding straw; and the habit of depending solely upon himself for the gratification of all his wants became such a second nature with him, that to the last day of his life a pecuniary favor was a painful burden, which could only be eased by a full requital in kind. One of the maxims he wished to have inculcated upon his children was, that they should "always pay their own expenses," and thus be able always to assert themselves independently, — the first element of true manhood. To afford them the means to do this, he denied his own life every luxury, and coined his very brain, as it were, into money.

A fine classical teacher at last crossed the young man's path, and a plan was formed by which he should pursue his studies. He prepared himself in six months from the time he began to study his Latin grammar, and entered the Sophomore class of Brown University in September, 1816. From that strain upon his health, and the still harder labors of his college-life, he never recovered. The rest of his life was one long battle with exhausted energies; but how valiantly he fought it! He struggled with it ignorantly at first, accomplishing all tasks as they presented themselves, until fairly laid upon his bed with illness; and, after he had learned the theory and art of health, leaving no effort untried to redeem his own. Those who watched over him were obliged to reason with him, however, even in his advanced years, when he laid out too much work for his strength; for he grew to be ashamed of ill health: and it must be confessed that he sometimes begged the question of duty to one's own health by saying that his life was not of so much consequence as the thing in hand to be accomplished.

Few young men leave home with so intense a sense of filial duty, or so thorough an acquaintance with mutual domestic sacrifices; and all his letters home breathe the spirit of devotion to his friends. Nor did any young man ever make smaller means answer his purposes. He did not complain of this, but often made comical representations of his pecuniary distresses.

In a letter to his sister, written soon after entering college, he says, —

If the children of Israel were pressed for "gear" half so hard as I have been, I do not wonder they were willing to worship a golden calf. It is a long, long time since my last ninepence bade good-by to its brethren; and I suspect the last two parted on no very friendly terms, for they have never since met together. Poor wretches! never did two souls stand in greater need of mutual support and consolation. . . . For several weeks past, I have been in a half-delirious state on account of receiving no intelligence from home; when this morning I met at the door of my boarding-house Mr. J. F. H——, only *two weeks* from Franklin! I would have shaken hands with the "foul fiend" himself if his last embassy had been to that place. For a good part of the time, I have been trying the experiment with respect to money which ended so tragically in the case of the old man's horse.

I wonder you do not write. You seem to treat it as though it were a task, like the pilgrimage to Mecca, and not to be performed but once in a lifetime. Perhaps you will say you have nothing to write about. Write about any thing. The whole universe is before you, and offers itself to your selection. Dr. Middleton wrote an octavo volume of seven or eight hundred pages on a Greek article, which article consisted of one syllable, which syllable consisted of one letter; and though I think such overflowing fecundity is not to be approved of, yet it cannot be so reprehensible as this lockjaw silence of yours. In your next letter, put in some sentences of mother's, just as she spoke them: let her say something to me, even if it be a repetition of those old saws, — I mean if it be a repetition of her good motherly advice and direction all about correct character, and proper behavior, and straight-forward, narrow-path conduct, such as young Timothy's in the primer. You know the sublime couplet, and the elegant wood-cut representing the whole affair in the margin. But I ought not to speak of any subject, which brings my mother's image to my mind, in any strain of levity. She deserves my love for her excellences, and my gratitude for the thousand nameless kindnesses which she has ever, in the fulness of parental affection, bestowed upon me. How often have I traced her features in that incomparable description of Irving's of the Widow and her Son: "Oh, there is an enduring tenderness in the love of a mother to her son!" &c.

Again, in allusion to his sister's attendance upon her mother during a long illness: —

I wish you to be careful of your health; but, as far as that will permit, continue to go on in the discharge of every office of filial tenderness and love. Never did a parent more richly deserve this requital. The ties of nature, the bonds of consanguinity, she has strengthened by all the innumerable and nameless deeds of maternal kindness and solicitude. Others may have been more ostentatious of their anxiety, may have spent more time in useless wishes or unavailing prayers, because it is much easier to desire and pray an hour that one may receive assistance, than to labor half that time to give it; but she has tested the sincerity of her affection by active and unceasing beneficence. When we have counted all her hours of care for us, and have cared as long and as deeply for her; when we have numbered all her days of toil, and have toiled as long; then, and not till then, can we commence the work of charity to her.

Many years after, writing to a friend during an alarming illness of his mother, he says, —

Principle, duty, gratitude, affection, have bound me so closely to that parent whom alone Heaven has spared me, that she seems to me rather a portion of my own existence than a separate and independent being. I can conceive no emotions more pure, more holy, more like those which glow in the bosom of a perfected being, than those which a virtuous son must feel towards an affectionate mother. She has little means of rendering him assistance in his projects of aggrandizement, or in the walks of ambition; so that his feelings are uncontaminated with any of those earth-born passions that sometimes mingle their alloy with his other attachments. How different is the regard which springs from benefits which we hope hereafter to enjoy, from that which arises from services rendered and kindnesses bestowed even before we were capable of knowing their value! It is this higher sentiment that a mother challenges in a son. For myself, I can truly say that the strongest and most abiding incentives to excellence, by which I was ever animated, sprang from that look of solicitude and hope, that heavenly expression of maternal tenderness, when, without the utterance of a single word, my mother has looked into my face, and silently told me that my life was freighted with a twofold being, for it bore her destiny as well as my own. And as truly can I say that the most exquisite delight that ever thrilled me was, when some flattering rumor of myself had found its way to her ear, to mark her readier smile, her lighter step, her disproportionate encomiums on things of trivial value, when I was secretly conscious that her altered mien was caused by the fountains of pleasure that were pouring their sweet waters over her heart.

His fears for the life of his mother were not realized at that time. This beloved parent lived many years longer to bless him and to be blessed by him. How radiant was her joy in his successes, not in the paths of ambition only, but of duty! When he achieved good for others, how her heart "ran o'er with bliss"! for she knew the high motives, the beneficent nature, from which his action sprang. Years after her death, when he was moved to tears by a testimonial of respect and affectionate regard for high services he had rendered to his State and to the world, how fervently he wished his mother had lived to enjoy it! How keen was his remembrance of her maternal joys!

This trait of filial piety is not dwelt upon here because it is exceptional, but simply because it was a trait in Mr. Mann's character. Good and devoted mothers are not so rare, that a great proportion of men who read this record of a son's affection will find it difficult to recognize in their own hearts the truth of the picture; but it is pleasing to know that the subject of our contemplation lost nothing out of his life from a neglect of or indifference to parental love, and that his appreciation of it was never wanting from his boyhood up.

From the home and good influences of this excellent mother, whose character he learned to reverence more and more as he grew older, and where, if he had not variety and means of great intellectual culture, he had the advantage of being kept in ignorance of much of the evil that is in the world during those years in which the young need to be guided over the quicksands of passion, and pointed to the heights of principle, and to the example of the great and good who have resisted temptation,—and who can doubt that the longer the youthful faith in goodness is fed by the ideal, the better?—Mr. Mann passed into the charmed circle of another holy fireside, with which many years of his future life were to be linked, and under whose influence his life-purposes grew and were matured. It was during his college-life in Brown University that he became acquainted with the lady whom he married long afterward, the daughter of the excellent President of that institution.

And here he slaked his burning thirst for knowledge at every fountain to which he could gain access. It is difficult for the young of the present time to estimate the advantages they enjoy in comparison with those of the generation to which Mr. Mann belonged. The young of this period begin where the young of that period arrived only after long study; for the knowledge of a thousand things then unknown is in the very air we breathe, and the very figures of daily speech are predicated upon scientific facts then sealed to most men. Freedom of thought is following swiftly upon the traces of improved scientific knowledge, and a giant stride is now making by the nations that have long slumbered. The great dead may almost be expected to walk amongst us to give an earnest of their joy at the awakening to which they in their earthly lives contributed.

Judge Barton, of Worcester, Mass., writes of him at this period:—

My acquaintance with Mr. Mann commenced in Providence in

the fall of 1816. We then both entered the sophomore class of Brown University, and soon contracted a friendship, which, on my part certainly, continued during his life. During the last two years of our college-life we were *chums*, occupying room No. — in University Hall. We were both of mature, and I believe about the same, age. Having been brought up in the country (he in Franklin, and I in Oxford, Mass.), it was perhaps rather due to our early education than otherwise that the dissipations of neither the college nor the city had any controlling attractions for us. During the three years of our college-life, I recollect not a single instance of impropriety on his part.

Perhaps I ought to confess one college sin, if sin it be deemed. The students had long been in the habit of celebrating the Fourth of July in the chapel. In our junior or senior year, arrangements were made for the accustomed celebration. The college government forbade it. A majority of the students went for resisting the government. I went for loyalty. But my chum, being a little the more impulsive, and having been chosen the orator for the occasion, went for independence and the celebration of it. The procession was formed in the college-yard. I concluded, that, if there must be rebellion, I had better rebel against the college government than against the majority of my fellow-students. I took the front rank in the procession ; helped to *open* the chapel door ; and chum went in, and delivered his oration amidst great applause. A trifling fine was imposed upon him ; but he lost no credit with either the students or the government. I believe your honored husband afterwards vindicated the principles of subordination in college government. But I trust that our Fourth-of-July rebellion never gave him any serious remorse of conscience : it certainly never troubled mine. There are cases when generous sentiment pleads strongly for an amnesty of the fault of violating strict discipline.

Notwithstanding Mr. Mann entered college under the disadvantage of going into an advanced class, he soon assumed the first place in it. He had been remarkably well fitted in the languages under an instructor of some note ; I think, by the name of Barrett. I never heard a student translate the Greek and Roman classics with greater facility, accuracy, and elegance. As we should expect, he was a fine writer; and, as we should *not* expect from that circumstance, he also excelled in the exact sciences.

My chum possessed qualities of a high order. By this means he attracted the attention and secured the respect, not only of the members of our own class, but of members of the other classes in college. Our room was the centre of much good company, except in study-hours; and I sometimes almost wished that I had not so interesting and attractive a room-mate. But I felt much more than compensated by his intelligence, and by the fact that the company his genial manners invited were from amongst the best young men in the college.

In connection with Mr. Mann, I always call to mind the late Rev. George Fisher of Harvard; a very respectable clergyman, who died a short time before him. He had been a member of the college a year before we entered; was then deservedly the candidate for the first part in the class, but eventually received the second part, while Mr. Mann had the first. You will excuse me for saying that I was not a competitor for either of these *parts*, so called; having in the space of nine months fitted for an advanced standing of one year in college, and being quite content with a position next subordinate to that of my friends.

The religious views of your husband and Fisher were not quite coincident; and their earnest, but I believe always courteous, disputes afforded much amusement, and perhaps some edification, to their fellow-students. I love to think of both of them as now tenants of the same happy land; and I trust they have learned that men may enter it through different channels of faith, provided that, in time, they avoid the broad way that leads to death.

After we graduated in 1819, our course diverged somewhat. Mr. Mann remained for some time at the college as tutor; while I pursued my professional studies principally in Massachusetts, at the Cambridge Law School. We met first in public life in our State Legislature in 1830; Mr. Mann as representative of the town of Dedham, and myself of the town of Oxford. He had been a member of the Legislature before I met him there, and remained some time after I left the Senate in 1834. He was President of the Senate in 1836. I found he enjoyed the same consideration and respect in the Legislature which was always accorded to him in the various public positions he occupied. We always agreed in our views as to public measures, and frequently co-operated in the committee-room, as well as in the ordinary routine of legislation. Among the most important measures that we instituted was the resolution of 1832 for a revision of the General Statutes of the Commonwealth. The resolution will be found in my handwriting : but Mr. Mann greatly aided in its passage ; and, after the revision had been made, he, with our learned friend Judge Metcalf, supervised the publication of the work in 1836.

Another and most beneficent subject of legislation, of which, as far as I know, Mr. Mann was the sole originator, is the State Lunatic Hospital.

I learn with much satisfaction that his friends are about to erect to his memory a bronze statue in front of the State House in Boston. That is well. But we have, my dear madam, in Worcester, a monument to his memory, literally " *ære perennius*," — our State Lunatic Hospital, — valuable not only in itself, but as the parent of those beneficent institutions throughout the country.

I might speak of your husband's valuable services as Secretary of the Board of Education in this State ; but those are well known to you and to all. I knew, if I could say any thing of interest to you, it must result from my early and intimate association with him in college-life. It is a green spot in my recollection, saddened, indeed, by the reflection that my friend is taken away before me, in the midst of his life's labor and usefulness. I shall always remain

Yours very truly and respectfully,

IRA M. BARTON.

Mr. Mann took the " First Part," as it is called, when he graduated. The subject of his oration was the "*Progressive Character of the Human Race.*" This was his favorite theme all through life, the basis of all his action in education and in politics. Another youthful production, of which no copy can now be found, was upon "*The Duty of every American to Posterity.*" It is said by one who remembers it, that he treated the subject with a depth of insight and breadth of comprehension that go far to elucidate the meaning of the Hebrew prophet, who entitled the Ideal Man he saw in the future the "*Father of Ages*."

He left college to enter the office of Hon. J. J. Fiske of Wrentham, Mass.; but was soon invited back to Brown University as tutor of Latin and Greek, where he was able to review carefully his classical studies and their collateral literature. He was very successful as teacher; noted for his fidelity and thoroughness, and the moral stimulus he gave to the pupils under his care.

He would have been glad to devote some time to scientific study, as his personal interest in it led him to see its superior advantages in the culture of the whole man; but facilities for it, so abundant now, were wanting then, and necessity obliged him to press on to the acquirement of a profession.

Mr. Mann had taken the highest honors of the college, and had been eminently successful as tutor; but, when he left the place where he had been so fortunate and so happy, more grateful to him than any honors were the tears shed at parting by his lovely young friend, who afterwards became his wife. Dr. Messer had soon marked him as a favorite, and admitted him to his domestic circle. His daughter was still but a child: but Mr. Mann carried her in his heart for the next ten years; and, as she grew and expanded into the most engaging womanhood, — for others as well as himself testify to her rare beauty of mind and character, — all his conceptions of excellence and all his hopes of happiness became identified with her image.

What condition of the human soul is so exalted as that in which the love, not merely of excellence, but of *the excellent*, purifies every sentiment, and rallies every power to make it worthy to love and to inspire love? What better guard-angelic over the character of a young man, especially over one already bent upon a noble career? Such it was to him: and many of the finer traits of his character were doubtless confirmed by this ennobling and purifying influence; for his native earnestness made it impossible for him to love lightly. The painful modesty which was one of his distinguishing traits, and which always, even after all his successes in life, made it so difficult for him to realize that he was worthy the highest estimation of his friends, rendered that period of his life one of intense anxiety as well as aspiration; and all tended to make the short period of his domestic happiness a consuming fire, whose extinction nearly deprived him of life and reason.

In 1821, Mr. Mann entered the Law School at Litchfield, presided over by the late Judge Gould.

A letter from J. W. Scott, Esq., now of Toledo, O., though bearing a recent date, is here given because it refers to that period: —

CASTLETON, N.Y.

MY DEAR MRS. MANN, —

. . . I first saw Mr. Mann in the summer of 1822, in the lecture-room of Judge Gould, at Litchfield, Conn. The law-school of Judge Gould was then in the zenith of its prosperity, having an attendance of about thirty students.

It was with a lively interest that I took my first observation of the young gentlemen with whom I expected to associate through a course of lectures. With no acquaintance or knowledge of any of the members, I took an interest in forming a judgment of their various characters and their comparative mental power by inspecting their persons. Phrenology had not then been taught in this country, and physiognomy was depended upon to show forth to the eye the characteristics of the person. Either through defect of my knowledge of it, or imperfection of the science, the conclusions deduced by me were quite incorrect. Mr. Mann's massive brow and high arching head did not then tell me what a great intellect was indicated; but the mild bright eye, and the pleasant expression of the eloquent mouth, told of geniality and mirthfulness.

It was therefore easy to believe what was told me by the students, that he was the best fellow and the best wit in the office; but not before I formed his acquaintance was it so credible to me (what I was also told) that he was the best whist-player, the best scholar, and the best lawyer of the school.

Several of the students had been admitted to the bar, and commenced practice before coming to Litchfield; and others had possessed superior advantages to obtain law knowledge, and had brought with them no little proficiency in the science.

Our lecturer, Judge Gould, was, *ex officio*, the bench of our moot court: the next office, that of attorney-general, was elective by the students. Mr. Mann had been elected to that office before my arrival. It was not until near the close of the season that I formed much personal acquaintance with him. I think our first intimacy was formed in the room of our fellow-student, James Sullivan of Boston, who was confined several weeks by acute inflammation of his eyes. The room of suffering was always, I believe, attractive to Mr. Mann; and Mr. Sullivan, by his excellent qualities, was especially entitled to sympathy and aid from all. In our moot courts, held weekly, the question of law to be discussed was proposed, the preceding week, by Judge Gould; and four students, two on each side, were detailed to discuss it; the judge, at the close of the arguments, summing up and giving the grounds of his judgment at length. The arguments of Mr. Mann were distinguished for the clearness — I might almost say the transparency — of the distinctions, and the fulness and pertinency of the analogies brought to the support of his position. On one occasion, when the side he sustained was opposed to the decision of the judge previously written out, it was the general opinion of the school that Mr. M. made out the best case. And of this opinion seemed to be the judge; for, after reading the arguments to sustain his decision, he proceeded to reply to some of the points of Mr.

Mann, and, as we thought, with some exhibition of improper feeling or wounded self-esteem.

Mr. Mann's mind was at this time, I think, more intensely engaged in metaphysical investigation than on any other subject; Brown being his favorite author.

I parted from Mr. Mann at Litchfield, with the full conviction that his was to be one of the great names of our time, whether his clear and fertile intellect should confine itself — as was not probable — to the law, or to any other one department of human knowledge. The only drawback to the realization of such a destiny seemed to be the lack of physical vigor compared with the immense development of his nervous system, especially his cerebral organs. His rich nervous temperament had, however, something of that wiry nature (such as I have heard Mr. Mann attribute to Mr. Choate) which gave the muscular and vital functions, as well as the mental, great capacity for endurance.

J. SCOTT.

Mr. Scott did not understand the theory of temperaments precisely as Mr. Mann and other modern physiologists do. Mr. Choate's temperament was undoubtedly a *fibrous* one, the most enduring and resisting of all; but Mr. Mann's endurance came from the force of his will, and was subject to terrible revulsions. He could not, like a man of fibrous temperament, turn from one long-sustained effort to another, and thus find rest; but utter prostration followed over-exertion, and many times in his life he has risen from such falls because his will never yielded the point. But this could not last always. Physiologists have assured him that there was but one mode of recovery for him under such circumstances. The only excesses he ever committed were those of brain-work; and *sleep*, not exercise, was his only restorative.

After leaving Litchfield, Mr. Mann went into the office of the Hon. James Richardson, of Dedham; and was admitted to the Norfolk bar in December, 1823.

He had studied law, as he did every thing else, exhaustively, and worked thenceforth eighteen hours a day. Mr. Livingston ably describes his " forensic practice " in these words : —

We believe the records of the courts will show, that, during the fourteen years of his forensic practice, he gained at least four out of five of all the contested cases in which he was engaged. The inflexible rule of his professional life was, never to undertake a case that he did not believe to be right. He held that an advocate loses his highest power when he loses the ever-conscious conviction that he is contending for the truth ; that though the fees or fame may be a stimulus, yet that a conviction of being right is itself *creative* of power, and renders its possessor more than a match for antagonists otherwise greatly his superior. He used to say that in this conscious conviction of right there was a magnetism ; and he only wanted an opportunity to be *put in communication* with a jury in order to impregnate them with his own belief. Beyond this, his aim always was, before leaving any head or topic in his argument, to condense its whole force into a vivid epigrammatic point, which the jury could not help remembering when they got into the jury-room ; and, by graphic illustration and simile, to fasten pictures upon their minds, which they would retain and reproduce after abstruse arguments were forgotten. He endeavored to give to each one of the jurors something to be " quoted " on his side, when they retired for consultation. He argued his cases as though he were in the jury-room itself, taking part in the deliberations that were to be held there. From the confidence in his honesty, and those pictures with which he filled the air of the jury-room, came his uncommon success.

In 1824, he was invited by the citizens of Dedham to deliver a fourth-of-July oration ; and it was of this production that Mr. John Quincy Adams used such warm words of confidence as to his future career.

In public life he was never a partisan ; and therefore,

3

though respected, could hardly be called popular. Nor did he ever let his feelings about men influence his public action. He advocated the right measures, and never allowed himself to be approached by motives of expediency; though, with all his ardor, he was eminently prudent and cautious. When State representative, to which office he was elected in 1827, his first speech was in defence of religious liberty, in opposition to a scheme by which close corporations could secure the income of given property forever to the support of particular creeds. His success was consummate: the bill was rejected; and no similar attempt was ever after made in Massachusetts. One of the first, if not the first, legislative speeches ever printed in the United States in favor of railroads, was made by him; and his whole public career of that period was marked by a devotion to the interests of public charities, of education, and of civil, political, and religious liberty, temperance, and public morals of every description. Mr. Livingston has ably described these labors in detail. No one who watched them, or carefully reviews them, can fail to see what a mighty power one man can exercise if actuated by noble motives, and with the conscientious feeling that he ought to do every thing he can which the powers he has been gifted with will enable him to do. Worldly ambition is an immense incentive to activity; but the activity so inspired does not run in the channel of love for the ignorant, the needy, and the oppressed. The patient, arduous labors which Mr. Mann performed in those years can never be estimated in the courts below; but they made him a world-moving power, and gained for future spheres of action a mass of experience and observation, which illuminated and indeed lightened his subsequent career, enabling him to accomplish that which would otherwise have been impossible.

Mr. Mann was not married until he had attained some eminence in his profession and in public life, paid the debts he had incurred for his education, and acquired a small competence. This he might have secured earlier, by his power at the bar, if he had yielded to the temptation the profession of the law holds out to the unworthy, — the *temptation to defend the wrong*. No lawyers are so popular with rogues — probably no lawyers receive such high fees from that class of men whose characters make the enactment of human laws necessary — as those who are facile upon this point. But Mr. Mann preferred to wait for his domestic happiness to yielding to great temptations that were offered to him. He had adopted the principle, from the beginning, never to put himself on the unjust side of any cause, even for intellectual gladiatorship and practice. The young who have been under his instruction and influence will remember how earnestly he inculcated upon them this duty to themselves.

Of Mr. Mann's marriage, and life in Dedham, an intimate friend of himself and wife writes : —

How brilliant he was in general conversation! with such sparkling repartee, such gushing wit, such a merry laugh, but never any nonsense. His droll sayings could never be recalled without exciting a hearty laugh at their originality. Even after the long life that has passed over me since those days of my youth, they are often suggested to my thoughts; but *I do not laugh now*.

His originality was so refreshing, so exciting, because he treated the most trifling subjects in a manner peculiar to himself.

And then how much power he had of drawing out other minds! The timid ones, who usually hardly dared express themselves on grave and weighty topics, would rise from a *tête-à-tête* with him, wondering at the amount of talent, thought, and feeling he had opened, and the chord of sympathy he had touched.

He was a *radiant man* then ; perhaps more so in the sprightliness and genuine mirthfulness of his nature than after the blight of sorrow fell so heavily upon him. In more intimate intercourse, in which his intellectual points were brought out, in the interchange of ideas and emotions suggested by mutual literary pursuits, we became cognizant of all the finer traits of his nature, as well as of the strong and brilliant ones. His exquisite tenderness and care for the feelings of others; his delicate appreciation of woman's nature, and his estimate of her capabilities, at the same time that he shrank from any assumption, on her part, of the place in social life for which she was by nature, and the evident design of Providence, unfitted; his love, too, for the beautiful; his quick eye for it in nature and art, in the inmost working of the human soul, and in its outward developments; and the truth and honor and disinterestedness and earnestness of his whole character, with his warmth of heart, and his love of his race, and the intensity which was so marked in every thing which he did and said, made themselves very apparent in familiar and easy talk on every imaginable topic. When in his intercourse with men, politically and otherwise, other aspects of his character were seen, and his intense expression of his sentiments was sometimes thought to be bitter and sarcastic and exaggerated, I always felt and said that those who so regarded him did not know what was in him.

His was too strong a nature not to come sometimes in collision with the opinions and prejudices, perhaps with the principles, of other individuals, by whom, consequently, his true character could not be appreciated.

When I knew his wife personally (I had long known her through him), I was indeed rejoiced that such an angelic being had been created to be his comfort, solace, joy, and happiness. She was extremely delicate in health, and called forth the tenderest care. This fostering, protecting, caressing care, she had, of course, in perfection. It was expressed in every tone of his voice when he addressed her. It seemed as if she were too ethereal to dwell long on earth, and was only permitted to taste of earth's most perfect bliss, and then was taken to her heavenly home. Then came that sundering which seemed so dark and mysterious, and which it required so much faith to acquiesce in. Was it necessary that his own heart should be broken before he could perform the work that was allotted to him ?

His most intimate letters of that period, which cannot be published, show with what a deep sense of responsibility and with what exalted aims he made that new home, — every such new home being a new test on earth of man's capacity for improvement. All his arduous labors were lightened by his young wife's sympathy, and his plans for the amelioration of the woes of society quickened and widened by her aid and approval ; for, though very young, he found in her not only all the womanly purity and sweetness that he had expected, but a wisdom and humanity rare at any age. And her religion was the breath of life : its mien was rejoicing and hopeful, and illumined instead of darkening life.

His short domestic happiness was to him the first perfect proof of the goodness and benignity of God ; but it was very brief. A little less than two years comprised the whole of their married life. Her delicate health had always given him great anxiety, and the sufferings of her last illness were very severe, but borne with such fortitude that he was not aware of its dangerous nature. She died in a sudden access of delirium, while he was watching by her side alone, with no one within call. The terrors of that dreadful night, spent alone with the dead, where he was found nearly insensible in the morning, revisited him with fearful power for many years at each recurring anniversary, and were never wholly dispelled.

In the season of grief which followed, the shadows of his early creed returned upon him, and darkened his soul ; for he could not reason then. When we suffer, no less than in the hour of death, we cannot go to find our religion : it must find us, and save us.

A few years afterwards, he wrote to a friend to whom he always loved to speak of his beloved wife : —

I spent the last Sabbath in Providence ; and when I visited the spot which had been to me, as it were, the central point of the universe, and spoke the name of her who was once so quick to hear every sound of my voice, but who never will answer it again upon earth, I think I was able to realize more fully than I had ever done before, that what I loved was not *there !* But what I still want is to be intimately penetrated with the feeling that she is in some region of blessedness. Were this a part of my consciousness, as the idea of our own existence is a part of our consciousness, whenever we reflect upon the things in which we have been engaged, I think I should soon find relief. It was on this account that I was more affected by that sermon of Dr. Channing's than by any thing I have ever heard before.

And again : —

Let me assure you that you have not pained me by adverting to a subject, which, as you truly suppose, does engross all my mind and heart, and forms the melancholy tissue of my life. My soul has gone over to the contemplation of one theme. Amid the current of conversation, in social intercourse or the avocations of business, in the daily walk of life, it is never but half forgotten ; and the sight of an object, the utterance of a word, the tone of a voice, re-opens upon me the mournful scene, and spreads around me, with electric quickness, a world of gloom. Perhaps even a nature composed of affection like yours cannot fully comprehend the condition of being through which I have passed. During that period, when, for me, there was a light upon earth brighter than any light of the sun, and a voice sweeter than any of Nature's harmonies, I did not think but that the happiness which was boundless in present enjoyment would be perpetual in duration. Do not blame my ungrateful heart for not looking beyond the boon with which Heaven had blessed me ; for you know not the potency of that enchantment. My life went out of myself. One after another, the feelings which had before been fastened upon other objects loosened their strong grasp, and went to dwell and rejoice in the sanctuary of her holy and beautiful nature. Ambition forgot the applause of the world for the more precious gratulations of that approving voice. Joy ceased its quests abroad; for at home there was an exhaustless fountain to slake its renewing thirst. There imagination built her palaces, and garnered her choicest treasures. She, too, supplied me with new strength for toil, and new motives for excellence. Within her influence there could be no contest for sordid passions or degrading appetites; for she sent a divine and overmastering strength into every generous sentiment, which I cannot describe. She purified my conceptions of purity, and beautified the ideal of every excellence. I never knew her to express a selfish or an envious thought; nor do I believe that the type of one was ever admitted to disturb the peacefulness of her bosom. Yet, in the passionate love she inspired, there was nothing of oblivion of the rest of mankind. Her teachings did not make one love others less, but differently and more aboundingly. Her sympathy with others' pain seemed to be quicker and stronger than the sensation of her own; and, with a sensibility that would sigh at a crushed flower, there was a spirit of endurance that would uphold a martyr. There was in her breast no scorn of vice, but a wonder and amazement that it could exist. To her it seemed almost a mystery; and, though she comprehended its deformity, it was more in pity than in indignation that she regarded it : but that hallowed joy with which she contemplated whatever tended to ameliorate the condition of mankind, to save them from pain or rescue them from guilt, was, in its manifestations, more like a vision from a brighter world, a divine illumination, than like the earthly sentiment of humanity. But I must forbear; for I should never end were I to depict that revelation of moral beauties which beamed from her daily life, or attempt to describe that grace of sentiment, that loveliness of feeling, which played perpetually, like lambent flame, around the solid adamant of her virtues.

It was not long after Mr. Mann's removal from Dedham to Boston in 1833, a change which was brought about by friends who loved him, and felt that it was essential to his continued life and usefulness, that distressing circum-

stances swept from him the hard-earned fruits of years of
toil, for which he had worked sixteen hours a day in his
profession, and subjected him to many privations of
common comforts that seemed necessary to his health,
then very precarious.   In the midst of this misfortune
occurred the death of his early and long-tried friend, Silas
Holbrook.

He wrote to a friend, of this event : —

A denser shade of gloom has come over the earth ; and my faint
heart bleeds anew.   There is no man living who loved me so well
as my friend Holbrook.   I have a thousand times comforted myself
with the thought, that if, amid the tempests of life, my character was
lost overboard, there was one man who would plunge in to save it.
As a friend, it is not enough to say of him, he was true : *he was
truth.*   At the time when the whole earth became to me a scene of
desolation, he was the first man that came to me across its boundless
wastes to support and uphold me.   I might never have again recognized Nature, or renewed my companionship with men, had he
not won me back.   Why should he be taken, and I left?   He who
rejoiced and improved every one here who knew him is snatched
away, and my sentence of exile and banishment is prolonged.
Where now is my best friend?   What and *whom* has he seen?
These thoughts overwhelm me ; and I can only say, that would to
Heaven I were as ready as I am willing to follow him !

The death of Dr. Messer soon followed, of which he
wrote to the same friend : —

Never was a more firmly linked circle broken.   There was in
that family such an intercommunity of thought and feeling, that the
result could never be otherwise expressed than by absolute unity.
Distrust was never banished from the house, for it never entered it.
There was, of course, a common consciousness, and a desire for
each other's welfare possessed all the energy of self-love with the
self-sacrifice of disinterested affection.   Of the effect of bereavement in such a family there can be no description.   I looked upon

the dead with envy, and pitied the living because they still lived. I administered consolations which I did not feel. I can speak to the heart-broken in language they can understand : I am versed in every dialect of sorrow. I know how this flattered and extolled world looks when it is seen from the side of the grave into which all its glory and beauty have gone down.

Dr. Messer, certainly, had inspired his children with the most entire confidence : he never inflicted upon them in his daily admin-istrations any painful sensations or emotions ; and hence to hear him, and see him, and obey him, became associated with the idea of gratification ; and pleasure and duty so harmonized, that they never knew from which motive they were acting. How rare it is to find that attachment which comes only from habits of agreeable inter-course, where no annoying or irritating acts are committed on either side, and where it has become a greater pleasure to yield or to har-monize than to be gratified by that which is displeasing to another !

A lovely mother also sanctified that home, of whom he said, that he never heard from her the expression of any other than a beautiful sentiment. Her love for him was so true, that there was always ample room in her heart for all that he loved and all that was his.

When his own mother died, he wrote : —

A memory full of proofs of the purest, strongest, wisest love is all that is left to me upon earth of a mother. So far as it regards this world, it is retrospection only in which I shall behold her, — the retrospection of a life in which she has always sought to make my comfort paramount to her own, and, amidst transient and casual cir-cumstances, has invariably kept her eye fixed upon my highest wel-fare. Death will not sanctify any of her precepts, her wise and judi-cious counsels ; for they were sanctified and hallowed before.

It is now years since I have felt as though I were on the isthmus between time and eternity. I have long ago left the earth, but have not yet entered the world beyond it. Standing in this solitude be-tween worlds, my mother has passed by me ; and how much the bal-ance of the universe has changed ! What weight of treasure is added to the scale of the future! A wife and a mother; and such a wife! In that heavenly world I cannot conceive of her lips as glowing with any diviner smile, nor her forehead as starred with a more glorious beauty. And such a mother! Were she now to return to earth, how, more devotedly than she has done, could she toil for the welfare of her children?

I go to-morrow morning to perform the last rites, and probably I am to have a day, the like of which will never come to me again.

Mr. Mann was subsequently associated with many minds whose high moral views coincided with his own, and whose happier religious associations aided his own efforts to put himself more in harmony with the universe, whose adaptations to the soul of man had been again lost sight of by his crushing sorrow. His quick sensibility to the sufferings of others, sharpened by his own grief, made him look upon life at that time as only a heritage of woe, to quote one of his own expressions. His native tenderness of heart had shown him before, that life becomes such to all who do not live conformably to the laws of their being; but he was now led to search more deeply into the remedies for it. For a long time, he felt as if motive itself were paralyzed: but others who saw his life, and its continued devotion to the highest aims and needs of humanity, saw that he was only temporarily benumbed; and his social and genial nature, at happy firesides where childhood and youth always recognized their friend, and where parents prized his influence, gradually became restored to cheerfulness. He often left such scenes abruptly when the contrast with his own lonely abode was felt too keenly; but he returned to them again, driven from his solitude by its terrors.

He was little interested in the exciting scenes of city life, where frivolity often reigns paramount; but he prized highly the pleasures of intercourse with cultivated minds.

Mere literary characters, who had no deep interest in ameliorating the evils of society, attracted him little. A certain golden thread of benevolence must be found in the texture of every work of art or literature, or it failed of an effect upon him; and it even seemed to him a perverted use of Heaven-bestowed powers. Where his heart did not find moral beauty, the external semblance was an empty shell. Perhaps he did not separate the work from its author sufficiently; for men "build better than they know," as our great poet tells us: but to him the work was vitiated if it did not spring from a pure source. He loved passionately the music of the human voice; but he often said, "It did not touch me: there was no benevolence in it." This peculiar criticism was always his test, and no instrumental music ever pleased him that did not touch tender chords of feeling. He used to say of himself, that he was born to sing; but the long repression of that as well as of every other artistic tendency left him only the power to enjoy, not execute. Music with appropriate words was his delight; but there were times when he could bear only the music, without the utterance of the sentiment in language.

When he returned to the world, it was rather as a spectator than a participator in its ordinary pleasures: but, baptized in the divine flame which sorrow lights in the soul, he was ready to do all he could to supply its needs; and it seemed to others that the period had passed when an unworthy thought or motive could influence him. His habits of indefatigable, inevitable labor stood him in excellent stead then.

Outward helps came to him from such souls as Dr. Channing's, Rev. E. Taylor's, Mr. J. Phillips's, Dr. George Combe's. Nothing could be more different than the modes in which the liberality of Dr. Channing and Mr.

Taylor had been nurtured. One was born into as dark
a faith as Mr. Mann himself, and had the misfortune, like
himself, to hear the doctrine preached by a powerful orator. Dr. Hopkins was to Dr. Channing's youth much
such an evil genius as Dr. Emmons was to Mr. Mann's:
but other influences were favorable to the emancipation
of Dr. Channing's mind; and by the help of these, and
of the highest culture, he had thought himself into the
happiest confidence in the divinity of human nature.

Mr. Taylor's youth was spent roughly, and reckless of
human creeds. Later in life, he fell among uncultured
enthusiasts, whose hearty religious enthusiasm he shared,
but whose bigotry and superstition he shed as the cater-
pillar sheds the skin from which it soars into life and
light and beauty. Bigotry could not retain or contain
the soul of "Father Taylor," as his sailor audience affectionately call him. Where he saw fidelity to duty, love
to man, allegiance to God, he gave his great heart. He
recognized the tie which binds man to God even in the
humblest form of piety in the simple and ignorant, and
no less in those who acknowledged it amidst the errors
and tyranny of human creeds. He knew the difference, and sharply discriminated between religion and
theology.

The cordial love and sympathy between these two great
men, who took the deepest interest in Mr. Mann, and saw
his value to humanity, gave the latter a practical assurance of freedom from bigotry, which opened his heart to
both; and he drew from their full urns the balm of consolation which strengthened his failing steps. They deepened his favorite thought, that love to man is the best
test of love to God, and *must precede it.*

Dr. S. G. Howe was an object of very tender affection
to him; and the reciprocation of the feeling was ever one

of his greatest enjoyments. The same uncompromising devotion to the great causes they together promoted strengthened this friendship. Both were disinterestedly benevolent, forgetful of self in duty, energetic and prompt in action, able to comprehend and act upon principle, and agreed that education must underlie all reforms.

Later in point of time, the Hon. Charles Sumner endeared himself to Mr. Mann by striking into the same vein of love of freedom, and unswerving allegiance to a high sense of duty. When Mr. Sumner first went to Congress, Mr. Mann said of him that he was " the greatest constitutional lawyer in the country, except Col. Benton." But that was not his highest title to the regard of good men. He could sacrifice popularity to principle, not from native indifference to the approbation of his fellowmen, but in defiance of a natural love of it and of the social pleasures it brings, that makes firmness in the path of rectitude a noble trait. Perhaps these three friends resembled each other more in this natural characteristic than in any other; and in withstanding its temptation lay their truest greatness, also kindred.

Another man, who has threaded New-England society like a beam of golden sunshine gleaming in dark places, was just then coming under the observation of those whose eyes were ever open to see goodness. Robert Waterston did not owe his original impulse to Mr. Mann, to whom he afterwards looked as a guide, or to any other than his own pure and noble nature, and to parents who knew how to cherish what was loveliest in their children. The death of a little only sister, whom the boy loved dearly, first drew his attention to other children; and he loved to gather them, and teach them to be good, when he was very young. When Mr. Mann first heard of him, he was a wonderfully successful Sunday-school teacher to a class of the most degraded Boston poor, and had drawn into the work many noble persons kindled by his enthusiasm ; and his father, in whose business employ he then was, gave him certain hours for visiting the families of the Sunday-school children he had assembled in Mr. Taylor's vestry, and with whom he kept up such close intercourse, that he knew which ran away from school, which told falsehoods, which stole, &c. Mr. Mann listened to the story of this young man with swimming eyes, and in subsequent years was anxious to secure his services for one of his beloved Normal schools, feeling that they were to be the nurseries of true teaching, and that in such hands the moral culture which he craved for his " eighty thousand children " might be found. Mr. Waterston loves to say now that he owes the continued consecration of his life to the mission — for which others can see that Heaven designed him — partly to the influence of Mr. Mann's career, which stimulated his native tendencies. When he had passed from that which, to some eyes, seemed a humble sphere, into a more prominent ministry, he was not corrupted by the worldly distinctions which gave him an opportunity to preach to the wealthy and the proud instead of to the lowly and ignorant ; for he still held so faithfully to his allegiance to the poor and oppressed, that he took Mr. Mann's part boldly and earnestly when many other friends dared not give him their countenance ; and this moral courage was the first step towards his separation from his society, where indeed many who had watched his more youthful career had always felt him to be out of place. It was as if Christ had left the fishermen of Galilee, and the multitude on the mountain, to preach common-places in the synagogue. Since Mr. Waterston's release from that bondage, he has had freedom to speak and act wherever a true man was most needed; and that is in all the unpopular places where a fearless word is to be spoken for the right, or wherever little children are to be blessed and instructed.

Another friend, whom Mr. Mann first met at a boarding-house, and who attracted him by singular nobleness of sentiment, was subsequently very dear to him, — Mr. Samuel Downer, always sagacious, independent, true to principle, unambitious, but full of insight into public men and measures, deep in heart, faithful in adversity.

Dr. Woodward, principal of the Worcester Hospital, — which Mr. Mann had projected and carried through the House of representatives with his one right arm, — and Dr. Todd of Hartford, also devoted to that benign charity, were a great delight to him, and objects of his enthusiastic love. Of Dr. Todd he once said, that he was " a man one wished to embrace if he only met him in the street." This gentleman had peculiar sympathies with him; for he, too, had lost a young wife of lovely character; and the mere knowledge of the fact which Dr. Todd communicated to him on one occasion, that drew his attention to Mr. Mann's domestic history, constituted a bond of union between them.

Mr. Mann looked upon his acquaintance with Mr. Combe and his works as an important epoch in his life. That wise philosopher cleared away forever the rubbish of false doctrine which had sometimes impeded its action, and presented a philosophy of mind that commended itself to his judgment: and yet there was not a servile surrender to his views; for, although he considered Mr. Combe his master. in reasoning power, he did not follow him to all his conclusions. Mr. Combe was rather devoid of imagination, and could believe nothing but what he could clearly understand. Mr. Mann had that "passport into Elysium;" and his reasoning power acted with it, arguing from the seen to the unseen, which is the object of faith. It was happiness enough for Mr. Combe to believe thoroughly in the improvability of the race; and his conception of its possible attainments in wisdom and virtue took the place, to him, of a future life of endless progress: but Mr. Mann had the assurance within himself that this life, with all its possible ameliorations and capabilities of earthly attainment, was but the vestibule of an existence which "the heart of man hath not conceived," and for which this condition, sometimes so mysteriously wretched, is but a preparation. He believed God to be too benevolent to have created one soul which was not eventually to find him, and understand him, so far as the finite can comprehend the Infinite. Present ignorance was but the reverse of a glorious future of ever-dawning intelligence. His own words often express this thought better than another's can do it for him.

I give a few letters of this period.

JULY, 1836.

MY DEAR SISTER, — I learnt from a letter which I received from ——, and still more from her own lips when I met her at ——, and with perfect fulness and distinctness from your letter to me, what apprehensions and anxiety about the condition of my mind had been disturbing the peace of yours. I know that it is, on your part, an act of the purest love and affection to communicate to me your alarms and your desires. Nor, if you have such feelings, would I on any account have you smother or conceal them. To each other let there be no hidden fold of the heart. If I act up to this principle, I cannot forbear to say that this knowledge of the state of *your* mind has given *me* serious disquietude. I should be false to all the feelings of a brother if I could, without pain, see you either pursuing a course of conduct, or adopting a system of opinions, the inevitable consequence of which must be to render you unhappy. I know there are minds which can contemplate the unutterable and eternal suffering — a suffering equally without limit in degree and in duration — of a large portion of the human race with feelings of indifference ; indeed, it sometimes seems as if they contemplated it with a kind of horrible complacency ; it always being understood that they themselves are to be spectators only, not sufferers.   But you, my dear sister, thank God, have no such humanity.   It would be impossible for you to know of any high degree of suffering in any large portion of your fellow-beings, whether they were on the other side of the ocean or on the other side of the grave, without your own conscious sympathy going forth and pervading that suffering, and feeling it as though it were inflicted on your own spirit, at least in a degree.   I see, in the adoption, by a mind like yours, of such doctrines as those to which you so plainly refer, the residue of life filled with anxiety and terror ; at least for your friends, if not for yourself. I know you can never break your mind into such a submission to the supposed will of God as not to tremble and agonize when you see the torture applied to others, whether you see it with the bodily or with the mental eye.   It is this knowledge of the inevitable effect of such a faith upon a nature like yours that gives me pain.   I claim no superior sensibility to the fate of others over the mass of my fellow-men ; but I know that, to my nature, there can be no compensation in the highest happiness, and that of the longest duration, for the endless and remediless misery of a single *sentient* thing.   No : though the whole offspring of the Creator, with the exception of one solitary being, were gathered into a heaven of unimaginable blessedness, while that one solitary being, wide apart in some region of immensity, however remote, were wedded to immortal pain, even then, just so soon as the holy principle of love sprung up in the hearts of that happy assembly, just so soon would they forget their joy, and forget their God, and the whole universe of them, as one spirit, gather round and weep over the sufferer.   My nature revolts at the idea of belonging to a universe in which there is to be never-ending anguish.   That nature never can be made to look on it with composure.   That nature may indeed be annihilated, and another of similar form be created, and receive a similar name, as I might remove one of the lamps by which I am now writing, and substitute a

4

similar one in its place; but *my nature, that which constitutes me,*
shrinks from an existence where any such thing is ever to come to
its consciousness.

You say that our love to man should arise or flow from supreme
love to God. I do not think you had a definite idea in your mind
when you wrote that sentence. If God be the greatest and the best
of beings, then, indeed, should we strive to expand and dilate our
conceptions of him, and love will rise in our hearts at once; but that
emotion, after all, is a very different one from what we must feel
towards our fellow-men. God needs none of our aid, — our fellow-
men need it constantly; he is infinitely superior to us, — our fellow-
men are our equals, sometimes our inferiors; to his happiness we
can add nothing, — to theirs much. We know it is the duty of the
powerful to give strength to the weak; of those who have abundance to impart to the needy; of the wise to instruct the inexperienced. It is against the whole analogy of nature, and against
every clear perception of duty, to despoil the destitute in order to
give to him who already has a redundance, and to make the feeble
perform not only their own tasks, but also the labors of the healthful
and vigorous. We are, to be sure, to love God; yet it is not for
his welfare, but for our own. The individual who does not feel that
love, is bereft of a source of unfailing happiness; but he may still
perform the first of duties towards his fellow-men : and much higher
do I believe he stands in the scale of moral being, who faithfully
devotes himself to the welfare of his kind, though his communion
with his Maker may be feeble and interrupted, than the man whose
contemplations are so fastened upon the Deity, that he forgets those
children of the Deity who require his aid. So far as we can derive
strength in the performance of our duties by contemplating the perfect nature of God, or by dwelling intently upon the example of
Jesus Christ, so far it is our duty to do it; and should we be translated to a world where our fellow-beings can no longer be benefited
by our efforts, then, indeed, it would be our duty and our pleasure
to regard the supreme perfection with supreme love. But, while we
are on earth, the burden of our duties is towards man. This is the
entire texture of the New Testament. Where else in the whole
book is there such anxious repetition as in one of the last injunctions

of Christ?—"Lovest thou me? If thou lovest me, *feed my lambs;*" and again, "If thou lovest me, *feed my sheep;*" and again, the third time, "*Feed my sheep.*"

My sister, I have looked at the world from the side of a grave that has swallowed up my happiness. For months afterward, I daily and hourly yearned for death as much as ever a famishing infant yearned for the breast of its mother. But, during all that time, I felt not a moment's remorse because I had not loved God more. I felt, indeed, that it was a great and irreparable misfortune that I had not been taught the existence of a God worthy of being loved. All the regrets I had were *that I had not acted differently towards mankind.* That was a condition of mind, if there can be any such condition upon earth, to reveal to a man the sources and the objects of duty. What we learn from books, even what we think we are taught in the Bible, may be mistake or misapprehension: but the lessons we learn from our own consciousness are the very voice of the Being that created us; and about it can there be any mistake? I would plead with you on this subject, not so much on my own account, for that would be selfish, but on your account, and especially on account of the children, so much of whose happiness will depend upon your teachings.

Dear sister, farewell.   H. M.

BOSTON, Dec. 9, 1836.

MY DEAR FRIEND,— How wofully long it is since I have heard from you! What have I done to deserve the chastisement of silence? . . .

I thought you would have an ocean of gladsome feelings to tell me of, after your visit to Concord. Mr. Emerson, I am sure, must be perpetually discovering richer worlds than those of Columbus or Herschel. He explores, too, not in the scanty and barren region of our physical firmament, but in a spiritual firmament of illimitable extent, and compacted of treasures. I heard his lecture last evening. It was to human life what Newton's "Principia" was to mathematics. He showed me what I have long thought of so much, — how much more can be accomplished by taking a true view than by great intellectual energy. Had Mr. Emerson been set down in a wrong place, it may be doubted whether he would ever have found his way to the right point of view ; but that he now certainly has done. As a man stationed in the sun would see all the planets moving round it in one direction and in perfect harmony, while to an eye on the earth their motions are full of crossings and retrogradations ; so he, from his central position in the spiritual world, discovers harmony and order when others can discern only confusion and irregularity. His lecture, last evening, was one of the most splendid manifestations of a truth-seeking and truth-developing mind I ever heard. (Dr. Walter Channing, who sat beside me, said it made his head ache.) Though his language was transparent, yet it was almost impossible to catch the great beauty and proportions of one truth before another was presented.

I have been to see your great Incarnation of the Good and True one evening since his return to the city. Allow me to say that I think the Dr.* endangers your salvation more than all other things united. That much-abused being who has such an unenviable reputation for planning and carrying on all the mischief of this world, and who, by the way, if he is half as bad as is alleged, must be highly delighted at the exalted opinions which are entertained of his success, — *he* knows better than to try to tempt you by any thing selfish or by any mercenary motives. I don't believe he will ever attempt to ply you with luxurious apathy, and ease, and a worldly indifference synonymous with a want of human sympathy. He knows his *woman* too well : you are assailed on the other side. He makes you acquainted with persons, who, upon a single point, may have a little more than such a scanty modicum of merit as belongs to the generality of people, and then he makes you believe they are models, paragons, angels. Then you render a sort of divine honor, and are forthwith accused and punished for idolatry. But this is a digression. I only meant to say that I broached my heresies about miracles to the Dr.; and by degrees, as fast as he can bear it, I mean to let him know how wicked I am. He preached last Sunday, and it was as though his urn had been freshly filled from a fountain of everlasting love.

Excuse this scrawl, written for the sole purpose of condemning and punishing you for so long a silence.

Yours affectionately,

H. M.

* Dr. William E. Channing.

Jan. 24, 1837.

My dear Friend, — . . .

Probably neither you nor our sister M. ever had so certain and sure a correspondent as I am, — that is so certain and sure not to write when he was bid to. I surely am a man, (so far as your and her letters are concerned,) who reaps without sowing much ; and I do not perceive that my harvests are any less abundant, and rich, and nourishing than if I had paid the price of previous culture.

At nine o'clock this very evening, I flung myself down in my chair, for the first time this year, with the feeling that I had any choice among the things I might do. The bird, which for a month has been struck from battledore to battledore, fell for the first time on the ground, where it will be suffered to lie, I hope, till to-morrow morning.

I came, at nine o'clock aforesaid, from Warren-street Chapel. The lecture is spilt, and nothing can gather it up again. Now, laying my hand on my left breast, I do asseverate that I did desire to send the lecture to you before one syllable of it should ever have struck any other mortal tympanum : but that was impossible ; for though I sat up almost all night, last night, I did not finish it until after six o'clock this evening ; and part of it I read for the first time *to the audience.*

By way of confession, let me tell you that never have I written any thing which cost me so much labor, and, perhaps I can say, produced so little effect. The truth is, as I have often told you, I am like a man overtaken by a premature night : he not only goes slower, but loses time by going circuitously. I should like to have you see the lecture, because I have faith that you would deal sincerely with me, and tell me to the uttermost point and pendicle what strikes you as too short or too long, too high or too low, therein ; and if you will prescribe any way by which I can despatch it, provided you can return it forthwith, — for I may deliver it again next week at Roxbury, — I will send it to you without delay.

You always make up such a face at the egotism, as you call it, of your own letters, I wonder what you will say of this.

I have no particular thing to tell you as to aught that has happened either outside or inside of me. One of the Sundays, when you wondered where I was, I was at my mother's, who was *very* ill, and still remains ill. She is now very old and infirm ; and strange, — horribly strange, as it seems to me, — I should not shrink were I to hear that she had escaped from this dreary prison-house. Indeed, that is the aspect in which the living or the dying of almost all now habitually strikes me. My first feeling is, not that ill, but that good fortune has overtaken the departed. I used to look at the dead as *going* out of the world : now my first impression is that they are *coming* out of it. . . .

To C. Sumner, Esq.

My dear Friend, — I found a note on my table, this evening, written in so deprecatory a style, that I fear I may have appeared to press the subject of your making an address indiscreetly. If I have so done, I hope you will pardon me.

My attention having been now for many years drawn to all that variety and enormity of evils which make up the hell of intemperance, I have acquired what the artists would call a *quick eye* in discovering them ; the consequence of which is, that, wherever I go, some species of that generic horror afflicts me : and who can see it, or a ten thousandth part of it, unmoved ?

Knowing too, as I do, that if the talented, respected, and influential young men of this city, even to the number of *one hundred*, would stand in the pass of Thermopylæ, that worst of evils might be excluded forever, I have sometimes felt as if I had a right, in the sacred name of humanity, to call upon every one to contribute his assistance in so beneficent a work ; and I am aware that I sometimes speak to my friends as if they must yield obedience to the highest law of their nature, and perform this duty. Believing too, as I do, that the infidel towards God is more open to recovery than the infidel towards man, — he, I mean, who does not believe in the recuperative power of the race, — I know I am liable to make use of strong expressions, which may seem very extravagant if taken without the general views which are in my mind ; and it is more than probable, that, in speaking to you on this subject, I have exposed myself to misconstruction. But all these things I hope you will be good enough to overlook. . . . Do not believe that I would interfere with the freedom of not-speaking any more than I would with the freedom of speech.

Yours very truly,

HORACE MANN.

APRIL 29, 1837.

MY DEAR FRIEND, — It is now long since I have written you. I opine that you may not be unwilling to hear from me ; therefore I write. That you are well, I hope ; that you are too good for your own comfort, I know ; that you will ever learn to put alloy enough into your gold to deprive it of its ductility, and give it a consistence adapted to human uses, I question. *Ilium fuit.* And so, to-morrow night, will be said of the present session of what, in the magniloquent style of our forefathers, used to be called the Great and General Court. The Senate Chamber will be deserted. Its seats will be vacant. Its vaults will echo to the lightest tread. And that vast, coliseum-like hall of the House, which to-day has been compacted with life, — fermenting, tossing, raging, — will be like the silent interior of a pyramid.

Now I must tell you some things that have come to pass during the " hundred days." We have passed a most excellent license-law, adapted, as I think, to the present state of the Temperance reform. It prohibits the sale of all intoxicating liquors on the Sabbath. That day has hitherto been profaned and desecrated above all other days in the week. There has been more intoxication that day than on the other six. If I may be allowed to call names, I think it has been the Devil's benefit! His curtain rose early, his acts were numerous, his scenes combined every variety of wretchedness and guilt : yet throughout the whole there reigned a dreadful unity, such as no other drama ever equalled ; and, at the horrid *dénouement*, the whole — *stage, proscenium,* and *cavea* — were covered with death.

The bill passed by crushing majorities on both sides, — in the House, about 240 to 17 ; and in the Senate, 23 to 6. It contains other provisions of a most salutary nature. When I signed the act to-day in my official capacity, [Mr. Mann was then President of the

Senate,] the whole history of the fierce contest which was waged five years ago this winter in the House, when I stood almost alone in the front of the battle, rose like a vision before me. At that time there were but two representatives from the city of Boston who voted with me: one was Dr. J. B. Flint; the other the venerable old Major Melville, "the last of the Cocked Hats," who was a member of the Boston Tea-party in ante-Revolutionary days.

You asked me, some time since, what I meant by the triumph of the Temperance reform, and whether we must not always see excess. What I meant by the triumph of the Temperance reform was the entire prohibition of the sale of ardent spirits as a drink, the abrogation of the laws authorizing the existence of public places for its use or sale; thus taking away those frequent temptations to men whose appetites now overcome their resolutions. There are thousands and tens of thousands of inebriates who never would have been so, had the tavern and the dram-shop been five miles off from their homes.

When I tell you what has been done for the hospital at Worcester, you will be superstitious, and exclaim, "It has had an angel." Dr. Woodward's salary has been raised six hundred dollars; which will be the means, I think, of securing his invaluable services for some time longer. The Legislature have appropriated ten thousand dollars (I write the words out instead of figures, lest you should think I have mistaken in the matter of a cipher) to finish the buildings, so that, when done, they will accommodate say two hundred and thirty; seven thousand dollars for the purchase of land, so that our inmates can enjoy the advantages of agricultural employment, which we regard very highly; and three thousand dollars for a chapel, where the oil of religion may be poured in a flood over the ocean of insanity; and eight thousand dollars to meet the current expenses of the institution. All this was done without a single audible murmur of opposition; nay, with the greatest apparent cordiality towards the hospital. Besides this, the Senate has empowered its clerk to republish all the reports of the institution in one volume, together with other papers, as he may see fit, with an *ad libitum* authority as to the number of the edition. Enough will be printed to be distributed liberally in every State, and also to send to Europe. Ah! I never thought of this when, in 1830, we stormed the dungeons of inhumanity. The outer gates are broken down; and some of the captives are coming forth every day to enjoy the light and the beauty of the physical, and the holier light and beauty of the moral universe: yet here in this midnight silence, as I write, I hear from their more interior cells, as audibly as if it were the voice of the thunder-cloud, the voices of many victims awaiting in unconsciousness the day of their deliverance.

Those who saw Mr. Mann at this time, when he felt that the cause so dear to him was firmly established in the hearts and consciences of the people, well remember the radiance of his presence. It seemed as if life, joy, and hope had rolled back upon him from the realm of darkness in which he had seen them swallowed up. The cause always continued to excite his deepest enthusiasm; and, as Miss Dix extended it from the borders of his native State — with all whose dungeons he at one time had made himself so familiar — to the borders of the civilized world, his worship of her divine prowess waxed, and became a part of his consciousness; he counting it happiness enough, as he has sometimes said, "to be the lackey to do her bidding in the work." He loved to picture her entering alone realms of darkness where man did not dare to set his foot, and reading words of cheer from the Book of Life, or with a hymn upon her lips, quelling the fiercest raging of madness.

After the chapel was added to the hospital at Worcester, when that large and motley assembly, many of whom needed confinement and watching at other times, sat quiet and orderly during divine service, with no other check than their own associations with the scene, and the calm, penetrating blue eye and majestic brow of Dr. Woodward, who always looked like Jupiter Benignus, as he sat or stood by the side of the clergyman, it was a great pleasure to Mr. Mann so to time his visits as to enjoy the wonderful spectacle, and feel the blessed reflex influence distil drop by drop upon his own heart. He was personally beloved there also, and his presence always had a salutary influence.

CHAPTER II.

THE SECRETARY OF THE BOARD OF EDUCATION.

IN speaking of Mr. Mann as an educator, I enter into his inmost life ; for that cause, of all others, roused into action all his powers. He had always been interested in reforms ; but no cause in which his duties as a citizen involved him held the same rank in his estimation as this. His interest and action in the cause of insane hospitals had deepened his insight into the primary causes and hinderances of human development ; and the study of " Combe's Constitution of Man," which he met with in 1837, added new fuel to the fire of his enthusiasm. Although life had lost its charms for him since the death of his beloved wife, his reserved power was, unconsciously to himself, lying ready to be evoked by some great aim. After the stunning effect of that blow had passed away in a limited degree, he began a private journal, which covers the first six years of his secretaryship ; and a few extracts from that will show in what spirit he undertook it. But his own words, even in a private journal, do no justice to the zeal and devotion with which he prosecuted the work. The first conviction of his early manhood had been the necessity of head and heart culture in the citizens of a republic ; and, through every period of his life, the conviction grew, till it culminated in a fervor of action, which obstacles could not cool, and which no selfish or personal considerations could abate. If I can well describe

59

the sentiment that animated him, I feel sure that I shall kindle in the young, to whom I have dedicated this work, a generous emulation to go and do likewise, aiding rather than contending with each other at every step. If I can make it apparent how he understood the central principle of our religion, " Do unto others as ye would that others should do unto you," I shall feel that I have succeeded in an endeavor which costs me too much to be made for any lesser motive. Only those who knew him vitally know how truly he lived to that end, and how hard he labored to improve the relations of the young and inexperienced with the older and more experienced. Only through the young could he work out reforms which must underlie society before the next step in human advancement can be taken ; for it is the effect of practical unbelief, such as pervades what is poetically called " the world," to deaden hope and generous resolve, and to dim the light of the ideal man which burns in every soul till it is covered up and quenched by false doctrine, and by the " rubbish and muddy waters of custom."

One must understand all ecclesiastical and sacerdotal history, or the *animus* of it, to estimate the full effect of the ages in which might constituted right, with those few exceptions which illuminate history and redeem the race from the stigma of a failure. Only a great soul can *see* that God has made no failure ; though happily the simple heart believes it, as we see exemplified by the filial trust and faith of the lowly and pious sufferers, who, in all times, have taught us that God speaks in the humble and waiting soul.

Education, religious and political freedom, then, were the watchwords of his life and action. All collateral evils would vanish if these things could be established. In one sense, he cannot be said to have sacrificed himself to them ;

for he identified himself with them, and cared little for any thing else. To work for them was his happiness. All culture, all living, that could be transmuted into material for their advancement, were dear to him, if they were not to be monopolized by the few at the expense of the many; for there was nothing beautiful or of good repute which was to be selfishly appropriated. He wished every child of God to be so situated as to lay hold of the means of self-improvement; and with sledge-hammer and battle-axe he would beat down the obstacles, if they did not yield to the arguments of love and truth and justice. He considered it the first duty of government to put these means within the reach of every one. He did not believe that men were created to minister to their own pleasures, or even to their own self-improvement merely; indeed, he did not believe that any self-improvement could be vital which did not consciously ally itself with the improvement of others. He believed that man was created for ends of which he only obtains a faint and far-off glimpse, his consciousness of the great destiny that awaits him gradually deepening as he advances; that for this great destiny he is endowed with faculties of indefinite progress; and that he is so allied socially, that the advance of one cannot go on successfully without the advance of the whole. When he looked upon the inequalities of human condition, he saw that it was the consequence of man's not using worthily his God-given gifts; and that the stimulus of acting for the good of each and all caused these gifts to become divine in their proportions.

Feeble in health, and still more feeble in animal spirits, there were times when the exhaustive nature of his labors, and of the way in which he performed them, made it impossible for him to write down his own purposes and emotions for his own perusal. His journal was written

rather as a relief from depression, than as a full exponent
of his thoughts. He was not himself aware, that, while
under that cloud, the calls of humanity often touched
him as with fire from heaven. Nevertheless, a man's own
words are always an expression of himself, if written in
sincerity and simplicity. If he had been as much animated and inspired by his own eloquence upon this subject as others were, we should have had brilliant paragraphs recording successful performances; but he never
appreciated justly his own efforts. No sooner had he
made an effort than he was tormented by a sense of its
inadequacy to the demands of the occasion; and especially
when ill health and sorrow held such sway over him,
his exactions of himself were fearful. He has sometimes
been called " pitiless" in his requisitions of others: he
was so in regard to himself, never counting his own ease,
comfort, or even life, as of any importance, if he thought
the sacrifice of them could further the ends of any cause
in which he had embarked with a disinterested purpose.
It was not that he imagined that the world could not get
on without him, but that he saw so much to be
done, and so few willing to do the work, that he took
more than his share upon himself. He was content to
work at the underpinnings of great interests, sure that, if
these were well laid, the superstructures would be safe.
This characterized his later as well as earlier efforts; for
when, in subsequent years, he transferred himself to a
field in which much less had been accomplished than in
Massachusetts, he was still content to begin at the beginning, and made new and deeper explorations into the
kingdom of ignorance than any he had before been led to
make.

But I will not anticipate.

In Massachusetts the common-school system had degenerated in practice from the original theoretic view of the early Pilgrim Fathers. Common and equal opportunities of education for all was the primitive idea of those men who had been so signally made to feel how unequally human rights were shared. The opportunities, unparalleled in the world's history, which the establishment of the Federal Union had opened to all classes of men to obtain wealth, had caused this idea to be nearly lost sight of; and the common schools had been allowed to degenerate into neglected schools for the poorer classes only, instead of becoming nurseries of democratic institutions for all classes. For, as wealthier and better educated citizens turned away from them, the best talent and education were not secured to carry them on.

The word "classes" is not a good democratic word. Under our institutions, there should be but two, — the educated and the ignorant; and the latter should be an ever-decreasing one, gradually merging into the other. Mr. Mann's wish was to restore the good old custom of having the rich and the poor educated together; and for that end he desired to make the public schools as good as schools could be made, so that the rich and the poor might not necessarily be coincident with the educated and the ignorant. As long as poverty necessitates ignorance, society will always be divided on a wrong principle. Poverty may in itself be honorable; and it is a well-observed fact, that out of its ranks have risen the most distinguished Americans. The self-reliance and self-denial consequent upon limited means is one of the finest elements of education. Education is the best security for that competence which holds the golden mean between riches and poverty, affording time and opportunity for cultivation of all the powers, while it does not preclude the necessity of industry and exertion. For the temporal and spiritual advancement of society, Mr. Mann felt that the vocation of educator was the highest possible one in a republic. He approached it with the deepest awe and a sense of the highest responsibility, gladly relinquishing senatorial honors and wealth for its arduous but interesting duties.

Very exhausting labors had preceded his acceptance of the office of Secretary of the Board of Education. He had found the practice of the law very onerous; for he regarded the legal profession as one by whose conscientious practice a man wields great power for truth and justice. But he was unable to leave it for more congenial pursuits until he had discharged certain obligations already alluded to. When he assumed the office, he was wholly free from debts thus incurred, but nearly penniless; and had passed three years of his sad lonely life in his law-office, without even the solace of a borrowed domestic life such as can be found in a boarding-house.

Most of his friends, who thought wealth, the position which it insures, and the prospects of political advancement that lay fairly before him, the most desirable objects of life, considered him foolish and visionary in making the change from a lucrative profession. A few, who knew the spirit he was of, rejoiced in his decision, although his present aim promised no worldly honors.

CHAPTER III.

JOURNAL.

I GIVE a few extracts from his journal, chiefly to show the rise and progress of the new measures taken to carry out the original idea of universal education. The sad tone that pervades it was natural to him under his circumstances: but his native buoyancy of spirit and strength of will carried him through his great labors triumphantly.

May 4, 1837. I have long had an inefficient desire to keep a journal. This desire has always been just at the most unlucky point,—so strong as to make me regret the omission, and yet too weak to induce me to supply it. According to a law of optics, the particular inconvenience because it was near has seemed larger than the general benefit because it was remote. This, however, is an illusion of the senses, which it is the duty of the reason to rectify; for, in the eye of *reason*, proximity and distance are alike discarded, and every thing is estimated at its intrinsic value.

I wish to keep some remembrancer (daily when I am able, less frequently when I must) of the states of my mind, and of the most important transactions in which I may be concerned. I can put that upon paper, which, if I were to whisper even to the best friend, might expose me to a suspicion of vanity; and I think I have honesty enough to record in a diary against myself what my pride might induce me to conceal even at the confessional of the closest friendship. Besides, in this world of mixed motives, may it not be right to avail myself of the reflection, that the night shall record the actions of the day, in order to give form and heart to good purposes, and to impose restraint upon bad ones? Is it wise to deny

any helps which can assist in ascending the eminences of virtue ?
In this attempt, I hope I may be sincere : for what motive have I to
assume to be what my own consciousness would deny ? and what possible fear can actuate me, save that fear which is the beginning of
wisdom ? My future days are, like the succeeding pages of this book,
untouched, alike receptive of good or evil.   There is this difference,
however, —that the record kept in the *mind* is necessarily a true record.   That cannot be forged, falsified, distorted, or discolored ; and
that is the record which I am hereafter to have spread open before
my eyes.   It is my belief that each individual will hereafter remember all that he has ever *done, said*, or *thought*. *That is the book*
of judgment.   May that volume be so filled, that it may in after-
periods of existence be unrolled and inspected with pleasure ! and
may this volume be a transcript of that !

May 5. I thought to-day would furnish me nothing to record : but,
this afternoon, I was most agreeably surprised in meeting my friend B.
Taft, jun., Esq., of Uxbridge, with whom I was for several years associated in the erection and direction of the Worcester Hospital ; and
all our intercourse has left nothing behind which I do not now recollect with pleasure.   How much was that commission indebted to his
skill and practical judgment !   His good sense saved money, saved
embarrassment, and, in so doing, saved reputation : better even than
that, I think it made some.   If ever I performed a disinterested act.
it was in my efforts to found that institution ; and I have been fully
rewarded therefor.   Indeed, I have observed that acts emanating
from worthy motives have almost invariably yielded me an ample
requital of pleasure ; while those which sprung from a selfish motive,
however intellectually judicious, have, at least in their connections
and remoter results, ended in annoyance or injury.   Is this fancy ?
or is there some mysterious, indissoluble connection between embryo
motive and physical result, just as there is between the invisible, im-
palpable quality of a germ, and the self-exposing, self-diffusing character of the fruit ? Surely it is not above or beyond the wisdom of the
Deity to ordain such a connection.   And physical science affords a
thousand instances where we discern causes, not by knowing the process, but only by witnessing the uniformity of results.   Will not the
time come to us all, by an adamantine law of necessity, when we shall

be compelled to analyze all our own former motives, and to trace them to their results, and when the present invisible continuity between beginning and end shall be made manifest? Surely there is much, very much, in the deductions of experience, to authorize this broad generalization. And does not the argument, *à priori*, from a knowledge of the Deity, lead to the same conclusion? These truths—for I believe they are truths—are to me *revelation*. This species of revelation cannot be gainsaid. It does not depend upon historic proof. It was not designed to be transmissible from one generation to another. It had a higher design, — that of being personal, and therefore indisputable, to each and all.

May 6. This morning I engaged and sent to Worcester an elegant two-horse carriage to be used at the hospital to give rides to the female patients. The exercise they will thereby attain will be directly beneficial to their physical health, there is no doubt; and the agreeable emotions excited by pleasant rides in a fine-looking carriage, will, in an indirect way, be not less promotive of mental health.

Dined to-day with Edmund Dwight, Esq , for the purpose of conferring with him on the late law authorizing the appointment of a Board of Education. Mr. Dwight had the civility, or the incivility (I do not doubt that his *motives* would place the act under the former category), to propose that *I* should be Secretary of the Board, — a most responsible and important office, bearing more effectually, if well executed, upon the coming welfare of the State, than any other office in it. For myself, I never had a sleeping nor a waking dream that I should ever think of myself, or be thought of by any other, in relation to that station. Query, therefore, could he have been sincere in his suggestion?

May 7. Sunday. This day has furnished me with no incident, nor excited any train of thought that I now remember, which would be available, if recorded, for future use. Have I lost a day?

> "Count that day lost whose low-declining sun
> Views at thy hand no worthy action done."

May 8. Have read to-day the first article in the 130th number of the "Edinburgh Review," upon Lord Brougham's "Discourse on Natural Theology;" a most deeply interesting paper, — elevated, tolerant, philosophical. I know it is thought by many, perhaps by most professing Christians, to be a fatal heresy, and worthy of being purged by fire; but, for myself, natural religion stands as pre-eminent over revealed religion as the deepest experience over the lightest hearsay. The power of natural religion is scarcely begun to be understood or appreciated. The force and cogency of the evidence, the intensity and irresistibleness of its power, are not known, because its elements are not developed and explained. It gives us more than an intellectual conviction, — it gives us a feeling of truth; and however much the lights of revealed religion may have guided the generations of men amid this darkness of mortality, yet I believe that the time is coming when the light of natural religion will be to that of revealed as the rising sun is to the day-star that preceded it.

May 9. I have been to-day to Worcester, and found the affairs of the hospital prospering. Oh! how should I be able to bear the burden of life, were I not sustained by the conviction of having done something for the alleviation of others? Surely Nature sends no such solace for our own sufferings as when she inspires us with a desire to relieve the sufferings of others. How wonderfully she has linked the feeling of self-restoration with an efficient desire for the restoration of others!

May 10. A day of drudgery without any particular pain, and with only a single pleasure. I called just at night to inform a poor old mother about her daughter, whom I yesterday saw at the hospital, that she already showed decided symptoms of relief and improvement: whereat the old motherly heart began to overflow with grateful garrulity; and, as I was the nearest object, she poured it out in floods upon me. Is it not a pretty good sign if one feels ashamed at receiving more praise than he deserves? If others hear it, it may gratify vanity or enhance reputation; but, when one hears it all alone, he has nothing to do but to think whether he does not know better than to believe it. However, if one has not sufficient moral sensibility to be ashamed of praise which he does not deserve, then I suppose he would enjoy it; and if he *is* ashamed of being extolled beyond his merits, then does not the justness of the feeling of shame argue a condition of mind of which he may feel proud ?

.   .   .   .

May 12.   This day I carried a female friend to see the Institution of the Blind, and was delighted with her delight.   Indeed, who can witness the natural privation of sight, and think of all its lamentable train of consequences, and then behold those successful acts of skill and benevolence by which that privation has been supplied, without deep and abiding gratification ?   If the powers of the human mind and the resources of wealth were directed to ameliorate the condition of the unfortunate and the afflicted, instead of being devoted to selfish and sensual gratifications, what a different world this would be ! and, in the quantity and quality of happiness possessed, those who bestowed the favors would be as great gainers as those who received them.

May 13.   To-day Deacon Grant and I concluded that it would be expedient to hold a consultation, with a few of the most judicious friends of temperance, upon the subject of the means most eligible and expedient for the enforcement of the late license-law, which prohibits the sale of any intoxicating drinks on the Sabbath.   Each of us, therefore, undertook to send out a few invitations to particular persons, inviting their attendance to-morrow (Sunday) evening at the office of the Visitors of the Poor, to devise measures to secure if possible, even in this city, the execution of the above-mentioned law.   How incalculable, how unimaginable, an amount of private happiness and public welfare depends upon the faithful administration of that law ! How little does that public think even of its existence !   When will the human mind be instructed to arrange things upon a scale according to their intrinsic value, so as for the future to refuse the precedence to trivial and transitory objects over universal and immortal interests ?

May 14.   A meeting has been held this evening, as contemplated yesterday ; and I have been appointed chairman of a committee to have an interview to-morrow with the Mayor of the city upon the subject of providing means for causing the late license-law to be observed in the city.

May 15.   Called on the Mayor in pursuance of yesterday's appointment. He speaks decidedly and encouragingly. May his words become things! Had an interesting conversation with Dr. Channing on *the times*. His perception of the moral aspect of subjects is so intense, that it becomes almost exclusive; but, as morality is the central point of this earthly universe, he who selects that portion, even though he does not see all, yet sees more than any one else. His is a noble ministry. Supposing, what is sometimes said to be true, that he is a man of one idea, yet is not one life well spent in developing one idea, especially if it be that great idea upon which he has expended his powers? Had each man, great and small, developed an idea, great or small, what a wise world we should have about this anno Domini 1837!

May 18. . . . Spent this evening with Mr. Dwight, who showed me a letter from the Governor, proposing my nomination, with his, as a member of the Board of Education, provided for by a law of the last session. Mr. Dwight again urged upon me a consideration of the subject of my being Secretary of the Board. Ought I to think of filling this high and responsible office? Can I adequately perform its duties? Will my greater zeal in the cause than that of others supply the deficiency in point of talent and information? Whoever shall undertake that task must encounter privation, labor, and an infinite annoyance from an infinite number of schemers. He must condense the steam of enthusiasts, and soften the rock of the incredulous. What toil in arriving at a true system himself! what toil in infusing that system into the minds of others! How many dead minds to be resuscitated! how many prurient ones to be soothed! How much of mingled truth and error to be decompounded and analyzed! What a spirit of perseverance would be needed to sustain him all the way between the inception and the accomplishment of his objects! But should he succeed; should he bring forth the germs of greatness and of happiness which Nature has scattered abroad, and expand them into maturity, and enrich them with fruit; should he be able to teach, to even a few of this generation, how mind is a god over matter; how, in arranging objects of desire, a subordination of the less valuable to the more is the great secret of individual happiness; how the whole of life depends upon the scale which we form of its relative values, — could he do this, what diffusion, what intensity, what perpetuity of blessings he would confer! How would his beneficial influence upon mankind widen and deepen as it descended forever!

May 21. This afternoon, heard a most excellent sermon from Mr. Taylor on the duty of nonconformity to the world. It was compact with graphic delineations of fashionable and customary vices. What a wonderful man! There is a natural language which communicates to one mind the state or condition of another mind. In this language, words and sentences are subordinate instruments. Soul speaks to soul. Over this language Mr. Taylor has power. It is not embarrassed by rules of syntax. It makes itself understood in spite of all violation of those rules.

May 23. Wrote to Dr. Woodward yesterday on the subject of receiving an insane woman of this city at the hospital. To-day, received answer that she could be admitted. To-day, also, made application in behalf of another woman, belonging to Weymouth. Scarce a day passes in which I have not some call in reference to that institution. They are all acceptable. These duties I perform with spontaneous alacrity and pleasure. Let me commune with myself, and see that no arrogant feeling of pride and self-complacency mingles with my emotions on these occasions. I cannot deny, indeed, that to have been instrumental in furnishing means for alleviating such unimaginable forms of suffering is one of the few sources of earthly gratification which the consuming calamities of my life have not dried up. Nay, had it not been for a few such subjects of reflection to call off my thoughts when they were concentrating into despair, I think that long ere this I should have been driven into insanity and suicide.

May 25. . . . To-day has been spent in reading that most valuable book, "Combe on the Constitution of Man." When will truth be the standard of value?

May 26. The annual meeting of the Massachusetts Temperance Society took place this evening. Pretty well attended, and some good speeches made. The cause progresses. I used to feel a faith in its ultimate triumph, as strong as a prophecy. The faith is now in a forward state of realization; and what a triumph it will be! not like a Roman triumph that made hearts bleed, and nations weep, and reduced armies to captivity, but one that heals hearts, and wipes tears from a nation's eyes, and sets captivity free.

May 27.   An official annunciation of the following gentlemen to constitute the Board of Education has this day been made ; viz., James G. Carter, Emerson Davis, Edmund Dwight, Horace Mann, Edward A. Newton, Robert Rantoul, jun., Thomas Robbins, and Jared Sparks.   Thus a portion of the duties of a most important office are devolved upon me.   This I believe to be like a spring, almost imperceptible, flowing from the highest table-land, between oceans, which is destined to deepen and widen as it descends, diffusing fertility and beauty in its course ; and nations shall dwell upon its banks.   It is the first great movement towards an organized system of common education, which shall at once be thorough and universal.   Every civilized State is as imperfectly organized, without a minister or secretary of instruction, as it would be without ministers or secretaries of State, Finance, War, or the Navy.   Every child should be educated : if not educated by its own father, the State should appoint a father to it.   I would much sooner surrender a portion of the territory of the Commonwealth to an ambitious and aggressive neighbor than I would surrender the minds of its children to the dominion of ignorance.

May 29.   This evening, met Mr. Briggs and a number of other temperance gentlemen at the temperance house of Deacon Grant, the embodiment of the law and the practice of temperance.   Father Taylor was there, with a world of beautiful material images corresponding with his world of beautiful spiritual ideas, — the noblest *man* I have ever known.

May 30.   An attempt this evening, about nine o'clock, to set fire to this building in the attic over the entry-way, between Mr. Loring's room and mine.   Fortunately it was discovered early, and extinguished.   A gang of incendiaries infest the city.   What a state of morals it reveals !   Is it possible that such things could be, if moral instruction were not infinitely below what it ought to be ?   That passion against an individual might be so inflamed as to lead to such atrocities from a spirit of revenge, is sufficiently wonderful ; but that an enormity of that description should be perpetrated from the wantonness of malignity, seems incredible. When will society, like a mother, take care of *all* her children?

May 31. General Election Day. How different it is to me from what it was when a boy! Not one particle of my boyish mind seems to remain to establish identity. How perfect the change that may be wrought in us by new fortunes, new circumstances, and new views, leading to new pursuits! What a topic of moralization is the change, of which I am now conscious, between my present and my former self! Memory alone connects the two together.

June 1. Visited the navy-yard of Charlestown this afternoon with a friend. What a magnificent product of human art and labor is a ship-of-war! Were an inhabitant of some other planet to see a ship and a man side by side, would not he think the ship had made the man, rather than the man the ship? Yet, after all, there are, in my conceptions, painful considerations clustering round such an object, which even its magnificence cannot dispel. With all its vastness, it is only a more powerful engine for the destruction of human life. With its power of locomotion, it is only the more capacitated to seek out the objects of that destruction, wherever they may be, in any part of the world washed by the all-embracing ocean. If a thousandth part of what has been expended in war, and in preparing its mighty engines, had been devoted to the development of reason and the diffusion of Christian principles, nothing would have been known for centuries past of its terrors, its sufferings, its impoverishment, and its demoralization, but what was learnt from history.

June 3. Have completed to-day a cursory examination of the Plymouth-Colony Laws. I feel some disappointment in their perusal. They do not seem to me to evince so much forethought, sagacity, and comprehension of principles, as I had anticipated. Providence for the future is not so far-sighted; and selfishness is less self-preserving and self-improving than I expected to find. Compared with the contemporary legislation in the Massachusetts Colony, the advantage is strongly in favor of the latter. Schools seem to have occupied very little of their attention. Learning was not a prominent object of ambition. Great virtues and talents would have shed a higher lustre upon office, and, one would suppose beforehand, would have superseded the necessity of enacting, that, "if a person chosen governor should refuse to serve, he should be fined £20 for his delin-quency"!

June 4. Sunday. If religion consists in going to meeting, I have been non-religious to-day. The truth is, that hearing common sermons gives my piety the consumption. Ministers seem to me not to care half so much about the salvation of mankind as I do about a justice's case. When I have a case before a justice of the peace, I can't help thinking of it beforehand, and perhaps feeling grieved too, afterward, if in any respect I might have conducted it better. If I am at a dinner, the merriment or the philosophy of the *table-talk* suggests something, which I put away into a pigeon-hole in my mind for the case; and when I read, be it poetry or prose, the case hangs over the page like a magnet, and attracts to itself whatever seems to be pertinent or applicable. Success or failure leaves a bright or a dark hue on my mind, often for days. But, judging from external indications, what do ministers care on Monday, at a dinner-party or a jam, which way souls are steering? Let me al-ways except in this city, however, Dr. Channing and good old Father Taylor.

June 11. Sunday. As I sit down to write, martial music is playing in the streets. A riot of almost unheard-of atrocity has raged for several hours this afternoon between the Irish population of Broad Street and its vicinity, on one side, and the engine-men and those who rallied to their assistance, on the other. It is said lives are lost: it is certain that great bodily injury has been inflicted. Different accounts are given, by the different parties, of the origin of the affray, each nation charging the aggression upon the other. It will, of course, be the subject of judicial investigation : but I have fears that antipathies will pursue the foreigners; that sympathies will protect the natives; and that punishment will be administered with an unequal hand.

No man can have observed the state of public opinion on the subject of insubordination and violence, for redress of supposed wrongs, for some time past, without painful forebodings in regard to the future. A resort to force, if it has not been openly approved by men of wealth, character, and influence, has been but feebly repre-hended. Physical resistance has been spoken of feebly as one of the modes of redress. Men's minds have been diverted from the remedy of a quiet and calm administration of the law, if they have not been taught, indeed, to look with some degree of contempt upon the slow processes of judicial proceedings. A reverence for law has not been inculcated. The public mind has become habituated to the contemplation of speedier modes of redress. The sentiment of insubordination has not been branded. Overt acts of interference with the rights of others have been almost applauded; for when strong condemnation is expected, and only feeble and timid disapproval is given, the offender feels as though he had been justified. If it had been the practice of all men, and all public organs for the expression of opinion, to place violence and civil commotion at its true point in the scale of guilt, that condition of the common mind would not have existed out of which a riot could spring. Under the influence of such expressions of the public voice, for some time past, as I have referred to, those general feelings have grown up in which a sudden and widely diffused provocation would generate violence. An occasion only was wanting for thoughts to become actions, for ideas to find arms, for the impulse to take the weapon. Those who form, or contribute to form, this public opinion, are the real culprits; nor are those exonerated from guilt who might have done much to reform, to enlighten, to correct, but who have preferred the private indulgence of their own ease and their own luxuries to the labor of moulding public opinion. In a government like ours, there will be a public opinion of almost uncontrollable power. The educated, the wealthy, the intelligent, may have a powerful and decisive voice in its formation; or they may live in their own selfish enjoyments, and suffer the ignorant, the vicious, the depraved, to form that public opinion. If they do the latter, they must expect that the course of events will be directed by the licentious impulse, and that history will take its character from the predominant motives of action; and that they will, at distant places and at distant times, be doomed to bear the ignominy they are now disposed to ascribe wholly to others.

June 14. All the leisure of this day has been spent in writing a long letter to E. Dwight, Esq., at his request, portraying the duties of the Secretary of the Board of Education, and informing him of the relation in which I must stand to his proposition to me to accept that office. I cannot think of that station, as regards myself, without feeling both hopes and fears, desires and apprehensions, multiplying in my mind, — so glorious a sphere, should it be crowned with success ; so heavy with disappointment and humiliation, should it fail through any avoidable misfortune. What a thought, to have the future minds of such multitudes dependent in any perceptible degree upon one's own exertions ! It is such a thought as must mightily energize or totally overpower any mind that can adequately comprehend it.

June 16.   Have seen nothing, heard nothing, done nothing. thought nothing, to-day, worthy of being recorded in this valueless journal.   The whole day has been spent in investigating a legal question, which, the farther I explore, seems more and more promising for my client.   But what is the reason of that increasing confidence ?   This is a most profound and interesting question.   Do my convictions gain strength because I discover new reasons for believing I am right ? or does the revolving of old reasons in my mind ten times over produce the same effect as the discovery of ten new reasons ?   Who can analyze his own belief into its elements, and determine how much of it has arisen from some predilection to one thing, or repulsion from another ?   An opinion is adopted without reflection, or any comparison with other views, expressed perhaps with heedlessness, then defended through pride, then rescued from refutation through sloth in examining other opinions, then consolidated into an article of the creed.   Of what infinite importance is it, that in the incipient stages of conviction, when the mind perceives that it has the elements of belief in it that have not yet found out their affinities, before it subsides and hardens into conviction, — how infinitely important is it to keep the eye steadfastly on truth ! — never to think whether it will be popular, profitable, pleasant to have the truth one thing or another, but to ask solely, exclusively, earnestly, incessantly, *What is truth?*   There is no such treasure as truth ; there is no such source of happiness as truth ; there is no such antidote against calamity as truth.   Truth will bear a man prosperously onward ; but error is a burden that has to be carried.

June 17.   One cannot see the date, " *June* 17," without an acceleration of the blood, and a certain emotion of feeling taller. I am not in a mood to moralize or fustianize on this topic. How else can we so worthily or sincerely show either gratitude or admiration for the deeds of our ancestors as by improving and transmitting to others the various blessings they achieved for us? In our day, things are to be done, though not such things as they did. They did what the circumstances of that age demanded: the exigencies of our age demand the performance of appropriate acts quite as imperatively as theirs did. Our imitation of their example, as adapted to our times, is the only legitimate proof of our admiration, or the true measure of our gratitude.

June 19. Employed the whole day in looking up a technical question of law. I have not, therefore, had any thing in my head but technical combinations of technicalities. This part of the law has a strong tendency to make the mind near-sighted. What Coleridge says generally, and very untruly, of the law, may be just when applied solely to this part of it, — that its operation upon the mind is like that of a grind-stone upon a knife; it narrows while it sharpens. And is it not true that every object of science, however grand or elevated, has its atoms, its minute and subtle divisions and discriminations? The degrees of longitude upon the earth's surface, the zones into which the globe has been divided, and their corresponding lines and compartments in the heavens, would show pretty well in the registry for county deeds; but yet, in surveying and affixing the bounds and limits to these vast tracts of space, what minute calculations must the geographer and astronomer make! what fractions, what decimals, what infinitesimals! So the natural philosopher, whose patrimony, bequeathed to him by science, is continents and oceans and suns, must deal also with globules and animalculæ, and points vanishing into nothingness. Who can have more subtle questions to settle than the casuist or the metaphysician? So of all. In one direction we lose every thing in magnificence, in vastness, in infinity: in the other direction we are equally lost in attempting to trace to their elements those substances, whatever they are, whose aggregate is earth, ocean, air, sky, immensity. Those who see nothing in the law but technicalities, *apices*, and *summa jura*, are about as wise as the child who mistook the infinite host of the stars for brass nails that fastened up the earth's ceiling.

June 20.   Another day in search of the technical rules of law. If the whole professional business of a lawyer consisted only in investigating and determining technical rules, one might almost be excused for attempting to reach justice summarily through the instrumentality of that monster, a mob.   Those who only have to *pay* for technical law are comparatively fortunate ; but this effort for two days in succession to keep the eye fixed upon the edge of a razor is apt to make one a little nervous.   I will, therefore, try to try the effect of "tired nature's sweet restorer, balmy sleep."   Ah ! sleep I can rarely woo ; "balmy sleep," never !   Calamity and misfortune and attendant ill-health have thrown my system into such disorder, that now I never sleep ; and, as a necessary consequence, am never awake.   The sleep and the being awake — the land and the water — are mingled together, and neither can be enjoyed.

June 22.   Spent half an hour to-day in the Athenæum Gallery. Some exquisite paintings.   What an art ! — to vivify canvas, to make colors express soul.   By means of language, we can, at best, only communicate ideas one by one.   It is as though the ocean were to be shown to a spectator by separate drops.   By painting and sculpture we see the whole soul at once : the great ocean of its thoughts and feelings is taken in at a glance.   No wonder the ancients called the arts "divine."   And if it costs the artist so much labor, such sleepless study, such vehement strivings, to draw the outline of form with such wonderful exactness, to color the space within the outline with such exquisite skill, so that a mere trembling of his hand in the delineation, the slightest failure in the touch of his pencil, would mar the beauty of his productions, — if all this toil and care and dexterity are requisite to make a dead image, a lifeless, thoughtless, soulless copy of a soul, how much more toil and care and judgment are demanded in those who have the formation of the soul itself !

June 28.   This morning, received a call from Mr. Dwight on the subject of the Secretaryship ; and as the meeting of the Board is appointed for to-morrow, and as he did not seem to have arrived at any certain conclusions in his own mind, I thought the time had already come when points should be stated explicitly. I therefore wrote to Mr. Dwight, saying that it would be better for the cause if the candidate who should be selected should appear to have been the first choice of the Board ; that I therefore should feel it to be a duty to decline the honor of being voted for, unless it was *bonâ fide* my intention to accept ; that I would accordingly regard the subject in its business aspects alone, and place the matter in a point of view not liable to be mistaken. I then stated, that, as I should have some professional business to close up, it had all along been my intention not to receive more than twenty-five hundred dollars for the first year ; that as to subsequent years, if the Legislature should add any thing to the one thousand they have now appropriated as the salary of the Secretary, half of that addition should be added to the sum of twenty-five hundred until it became three thousand, but should not go beyond the latter sum ; that by this it would become the interest of the Secretary so to discharge his duties as to gain the favor of the public ; and that it was quite well in all cases, and with regard to all, to make their interest and their duty draw in the same direction, if possible. This was the substance of my letter ; though it had the proper amount of interlardings and lubrifications. I tremble, however, at the idea of the task that possibly now lies before me. Yet I can now conscientiously say that here stands my purpose, ready to undergo the hardships and privations to which I must be subjected, and to encounter the jealousy, the misrepresentation, and the prejudice almost certain to arise ; here stands my mind, ready to meet them in the spirit of a martyr. To-morrow will probably prescribe for me a course of life. Let it come ! I know one thing, — if I stand by the principles of truth and duty, nothing can inflict upon me any permanent harm.'

June 29. I cannot say that this day is one to which I have not looked forward with deep anxiety. The chance of being offered a station which would change the whole course of my action, and consequently of my duties, through life, was not to be regarded with indifference. The deep feeling of interest was heightened by the reflection, that, in case of my receiving the appointment of Secretary of the Board of Education, my sphere of *possible* usefulness would be indefinitely enlarged, and that my failure would forever force into contrast the noble duty and the inadequate discharge of it. The day is past. I have received the offer. The path of usefulness is opened before me. My present purpose is to enter into it. Few undertakings, according to my appreciation of it, have been greater. I know of none which may be more fruitful in beneficent results.

God grant me an annihilation of selfishness, a mind of wisdom, a heart of benevolence! How many men I shall meet who are accessible only through a single motive, or who are incased in prejudice and jealousy, and need, not to be subdued, but to be remodelled! how many who will vociferate their devotion to the public, but whose thoughts will be intent on themselves! There is but one spirit in which these impediments can be met with success: it is the spirit of self-abandonment, the spirit of martyrdom. To this, I believe, there are but few, of all those who wear the form of humanity, who will not yield. I must not irritate, I must not humble, I must not degrade any one in his own eyes. I must not present myself as a solid body to oppose an iron barrier to any. I must be a fluid sort of a man, adapting myself to tastes, opinions, habits, manners, so far as this can be done without hypocrisy or insincerity, or a compromise of principle. In all this, there must be a higher object than to win personal esteem, or favor, or worldly applause. A new fountain may now be opened. Let me strive to direct its current in such a manner, that if, when I have departed from life, I may still be permitted to witness its course, I may behold it broadening and deepening in an everlasting progression of virtue and happiness.

June 30. This morning I communicated my acceptance of the Secretaryship of the Board of Education. Afterwards I sat with the Board until they adjourned without day. I then handed to the Governor the resignation of my membership of the Board. I now stand in a new relation to them; nor to them only: I stand in a new relation to the world. Obligations to labor in the former mode are removed; but a more elevated and weighty obligation to toil supplies the place of the former. Henceforth, so long as I hold this office, I devote myself to the supremest welfare of mankind upon earth. An inconceivably greater labor is undertaken. With the highest degree of prosperity, results will manifest themselves but slowly. The harvest is far distant from the seed-time. *Faith* is the only sustainer. I have faith in the improvability of the race, — in their accelerating improvability. This effort may do, apparently, but little. But mere beginning in a good cause is never little. If we can get this vast wheel into any perceptible motion, we shall have accomplished much. And more and higher qualities than mere labor and perseverance will be requisite. Art for applying will be no less necessary than science for combining and deducing. No object ever gave scope for higher powers, or exacted a more careful, sagacious use of them. At first, it will be better to err on the side of caution than of boldness. When walking over quagmires, we should never venture long steps. However, after all the advice which all the sages who ever lived could give, there is no such security against danger, and in favor of success, as to undertake it with a right spirit, — with a self-sacrificing spirit. Men can resist the influence of talent; they will deny demonstration, if need be: but few will combat goodness for any length of time. A spirit mildly devoting itself to a good cause is a certain conqueror. Love is a universal solvent. Wilfulness will maintain itself against persecution, torture, death, but will be fused and dissipated by kindness, forbearance, sympathy. Here is a clew given by God to lead us through the labyrinth of the world.

July 1. This day I consider the first on which my official character as Secretary of the Board commences. The acceptance was with an express condition, that I was to finish my professional business already commenced. That, however, will occupy but a small portion of my time, and it will be tapering off continually. I mean soon to commence reading and writing with express reference to the office. . . .

July 2. Sunday. I heard Mr. Taylor this afternoon. How wonderfully rare it is to hear a sentiment of toleration uttered by a man who cares aught about religion ! A sceptic may well indorse the right of private judgment on religious subjects; for it is only an error on a topic which at least he holds to be worthless. But for one whose heart yearns towards religion ; who believes it to be the " *all,*" — for such an one to avow, practise, feel, the noble sentiment of universal toleration, can proceed from nothing but a profound recognition of human rights and the conscientious obedience to all their requirements. Yet such is Mr. Taylor.

In my early life, I was accustomed to hear all doctrines, creeds, tenets, which did not exactly conform to the standard set up, denounced as heresies; their believers cast out from fellowship in this life, and coolly consigned to eternal perdition in the next. I think it would have made an immense difference, both in my happiness and character, had the genial, encouraging, ennobling spirit of liberality been infused into my mind when its sentiments were first capable of being excited on that subject. Then it would always have been a matter of ready impulse, of spontaneous feeling, instead of my being obliged to work out that problem of duty by the most painful efforts of the intellect.

Mr. Mann might have here recorded a fact which helped to let the light in upon his mind. The Universalists were denounced then even more than now as God-forsaken, deistical sinners, wolves in sheep's clothing, out of the pale of Christian fellowship; but within his neighborhood there lived a man of that much-maligned sect, who was remarkable for all the Christian virtues. Probably his love to God was not credited, even if he professed it: but his love for man was unquestionable; for it was proved by his beneficent deeds and his honorable dealings. It was heresy in the young Calvinists (who were the only ones likely to dare to think for themselves, — youth being naturally rebellious to tyranny) to look upon his virtues as any thing but godless works; but to a bold thinker it was a nucleus around which thoughts *would* cluster.

Boston, July 2, 1837.

My dear Friend, — How long it is since the light of your pen visited me! It really is long, and probably it seems longer than it is. In the mean time, what a change in externals has befallen me! I no longer write myself attorney, counsellor, or lawyer. My law-books are for sale. My office is "to let." The bar is no longer my forum. My jurisdiction is changed. I have abandoned jurisprudence, and betaken myself to the larger sphere of mind and morals. Having found the present generation composed of materials almost unmalleable, I am about transferring my efforts to the next. Men are cast-iron; but children are wax. Strength expended upon the latter may be effectual, which would make no impression upon the former.

But you will ask what is the interpretation of this oracular ambiguity. A law was passed last winter, constituting a Board of Education " consisting of the Governor and Lieut.-Governor, *ex officiis*, and eight other persons to be appointed by the Governor and Council;" which Board was authorized to appoint a Secretary, whose duty it should be " to collect information of the actual condition and efficiency of the common schools and other means of popular education, and to diffuse as widely as possible, throughout every part of the Commonwealth, information of the most approved and successful mode of instruction." I have accepted that office. If I do not succeed in it, I will lay claim at least to the benefit of the saying, that in great attempts it is glorious even to fail.

Thursday. I wrote thus far last Sunday, when I was interrupted, and have not had time since to finish this letter. . . . Although my mind is full of the subject of my new duties, yet my thoughts are almost chaotic; and they will continue, I suppose, for a long time, to fly round and round without order and harmony. I hope, however, that the time will come when they will subside, and cohere according to some law of intellectual and moral affinity. As yet, my task seems incomprehensibly great. I scarcely know where or in what manner to begin. I have, however, a faith as strong as prophecy, that much may be done.

My intention is to leave the city for perhaps a few weeks, and go into the country (probably to Franklin), carry some books, and endeavor to think out something worthy of being acted. Some time early in September, I shall probably commence a circuit through the State, inviting conventions of instructors, school committees, and all others interested in the cause of education, to be held in the different counties, and at such times avail myself of the opportunity to recommend some improvements, and generally to apply a flesh-brush to the back of the public. Now, out of your abundance, I shall expect you to contribute much to fill my small urn of experience and knowledge. I will be a conduit between you and the public for as much information as my gauge will enable me to convey. Do let me hear from you soon.

Yours affectionately,

H. MANN.

July 3. What strikes me as most extraordinary in relation to my new office is, that every man, with the single exception of Dr. Channing, inquires concerning the *salary*, or makes remarks that look wholly to the comparative *honor* of the station ; while no man seems to recognize its possible usefulness, or the dignity and elevation which is inwrought into beneficent action. Does not the community need to be educated half round the compass, until they shall cease to look upon that as the greatest good which is the smallest, and shall find the greatest good in what they now overlook, and by which their minds pass as unconsciously as though it had no existence?

July 4. Celebrations during the day ; parade of military companies ; people turned out of doors, and houses shut up ; this evening, fire-works on the Common, which was filled, crammed, — as a vintner would say, "a quart of spectators put into a pint of Common ;" and all day I have not seen one staggerer ! "Laus Deo, et societatibus temperantiæ !"

July 8. This week I have commenced in earnest, and with some degree of exclusive devotedness, a course of reading tending to qualify me for my new duties. I have long known that no man can apply himself to any worthy subject, either of thought or action, but he will forthwith find it develop into dimensions and qualities of which before he had no conception. If this be true of all subjects worthy of rational attention, how extensively true is it of the all-comprehending subject of education ! This expansion of any object to which our attention is systematically directed may be compared to the opening of a continent upon the eye of an approaching mariner. At first he descries some minute point, just ~~rging in the distance, — the lofty summit of some mountain. As he approaches, other elevated points seem to rise out of nothing, and stand up in the horizon ; then they are perceived to be connected together ; then hills, cities, towns, plains, rivers, which the eye cannot count for their numbers, nor embrace for their distance, fill up the admiring vision. So it is in approaching any of the intellectual or moral systems which Nature has established.

July 9. Sunday. Spent the main part of the day in reading James Simpson's work entitled " Necessity of Popular Education ; " and, as I read and think upon the subject, that point, that speck, that dot, of which I spoke last night, grows larger and larger. Let it grow. I hope I shall have strength to explore some of its most important parts.

July 10. Still following up the great labor of preparation. Have this day examined a great variety of articles designed for apparatus in instruction. Here, on this point of introducing apparatus into common use, and thus substituting *real* for *verbal* knowledge, I must endeavor to effect a lodgement in the public mind.

July 13. Another striking instance has come to my knowledge, of a gentleman, whom I should have expected fully to appreciate the importance and the *inherent dignity* of my new office, expressing surprise that I should forego other expectations for its sake, and regret that its title did not indicate more fully the duties to be performed. If the Lord prospers me in this great work, I hope to convict such persons of error ; and as to the title, of what consequence is that ? If the title is not sufficiently honorable now, then it is clearly left for me to elevate it ; and I had rather be creditor than debtor to the title.

July 14. My reading upon the subject of my new duties is very delightful. Nothing could be more congenial with all my tastes, feelings, and principles. What occupation more pure, more elevated, more directly tending to good, and hence more self-sustaining? So let it continue to appear to me, and it will make the residue of life more tolerable than I had ever supposed it could be.

July 15. Still looking upon the externals of the magnificent temple which I hope some day to be less unworthy to enter. Had a conversation with Judge —— upon the subject, in which he brought out in their fulness all his conservative and anti-movement notions. Is he not so much of a conservative that he is in great danger of conserving error? and, if error can only be conserved, how mightily will it grow of itself!

BOSTON, July 16, 1837.

MY DEAR SISTER, — You will be not a little surprised to learn how great a change has come over my course of business-life since I last saw you. I have quitted the profession of the law. I hope that no necessity will ever compel me to resume it again. But why, you would ask, and for what object? I will tell you. . . . I have accepted the office of Secretary of the Board; and, as it will occupy all my time (and is sufficient to occupy me in ten places at once if that were possible), I necessarily leave my profession in order to bestow upon it my undivided attention. Could I be assured that my efforts in this new field of labor would be crowned with success, I know of no occupation that would be more agreeable to me, — more congenial to my tastes and feelings. It presents duties entirely accordant with principle. . . . Some persons think it not wise to leave my profession, which has hitherto treated me quite as well as I have deserved: others profess to think that my prospects in political life were not to be bartered for a post whose returns for effort and privation must be postponed to another generation; and that my present position in the Senate would be far preferable to being a post-rider from county to county, looking after the welfare of children who will never know whence benefits may come, and encountering the jealousy and prejudice and misrepresentation of ignorant parents. But is it not better to do good than to be commended for having done it? If no seed were ever to be sown save that which would promise the requital of a full harvest before we die, how soon would mankind revert to barbarism! If I can be the means of ascertaining what is the best construction of houses, what are the best books, what is the best arrangement of studies, what are the best modes of instruction; if I can discover by what appliance of means a non-thinking, non-reflecting, non-speaking child can most surely be trained into a noble citizen ready to contend for the right and to die for the right, — if I can only obtain and diffuse throughout this State a few good ideas on these and similar subjects, may I not flatter myself that my ministry has not been wholly in vain? . . . The laws which sustain our system of common-school instruction are scarcely better than they have been for a century and a half. If schools have improved, it has not been in consequence of any impulse given to them by government. . . . I intend to go to Franklin soon, to stay a week or two, to read on the new subject, to write an address, &c.; and if you will write to me there, and say you will come and stay a week or a few days, I will go for you. . . . H. M.

July 22. Have entered slowly upon my lecture, though a dyspeptic obscuration of intellect baffles the will. Dulness never had a more copious subject. Indeed, its largeness, its infinity, embarrass me. It is like an attempt to lift the earth: the arms are too short to get hold of it. However, I hope to get hold of a few handfuls. . . .

Aug. 12. On Friday last, went to Boston, where I remained one week. . . . Accomplished considerable business in Boston. Prepared and issued circulars to the school committees of every town in the State, designating time and place for holding the proposed conventions in each of the counties. As yet, nothing transpires which indicates at all in what manner the new mission will be received by the public. All is left for me to do. At the best, perhaps, I can only hope that the community is on a poise, and ready to be swayed one way or the other, according to the manner of putting on the weight.

Sept. 15. . . . Northampton. This evening, had a long conversation with —— ——, who was on a visit to Northampton, on the subject of attempting to enlighten and elevate the masses; and have found him an infinite sceptic. He holds the British Government, of kings, lords, and commons, to be the best in the world, or that can be in it; that classes are essential, — one to work, the other to improve; laments that the good old days of the aristocracy have gone by, when no upstart could ever obtain ingress into their ranks; and thinks that one portion of mankind is to be refined and cultivated, the other to suffer, toil, and live and die in vulgarity. In the course of the conversation, he denied that the class he eulogized ever insulted those who started in life, as he would call it, below them; and yet he insulted me and all my relatives twice most outrageously. That is their way. Beginning with the principle that they are from their birth superior, they are constantly acting it out in life, embodying it in conduct, and yet profess to be ignorant that they are committing the grossest indignities. A powerless, conceited, haughty race, who have little or nothing besides adventitious merit, — what would the poor insects do if they were deprived of that? Therefore let them be pardoned; not for any repentance or improvement, — for of that they seem almost incapable, — but for their insignificance.

Sept. 17. Yesterday, saw Mr. Lyman, who seems much interested in the cause. The High School for Females is constituted substantially according to the free plan of Mr. Alcott, contained in one of the volumes of the American Institute of Instruction.

Sept. 27. Found on my return a most encouraging letter from Dr. Channing, full of a spirit communing with my spirit. How different from the views entertained and expressed to me at Northampton by Mr. ———! and how different must be the source from which such opposite sentiments flow! Many of our educated men need educating much more than the ignorant. When shall we bring them both up to the level of humanity? Perhaps never; but we will try.

Oct. 8. Sunday. Have been over to see the Chapoquiddic Indians. Called on a number with their guardian, Mr. Thaxter, who, I think, is improving the habits and condition of the tribe. They have a meetinghouse-schoolhouse, "one and indivisible;" have had a Sunday school up to to-day, but are to have no more through the winter. Have next to no school among them, except this Sunday school. They appear, I should think, pretty well for an Indian settlement; having about fifty inhabitants and one barn on their part of the island. A failing and white-man stricken race!

To-morrow is the day of the convention here.

Oct. 10. This is Nantucket. Hither I have come to-day, gazing and still gazing upon the ocean; while the feeling in my mind continually is, "I do not comprehend it yet." The mind is adapted to admire it as much as the web-foot of a sea-bird is to swim in it. A striking anecdote of intolerance was told me to-day.

Last Sunday, being at Edgartown, where there were *only* a Congregationalist, a Baptist, and a Methodist society, — all Orthodox, — I thought I would go over to Chapoquiddic and see the Indians; which I accordingly did, and availed myself as much as I could of my visit to exhibit an interest in their welfare, and to encourage them in well-doing. Monday, the next day, was the day for the convention at Edgartown, called to meet at ten o'clock, A.M. It met at that hour; and, after being in session an hour or two, adjourned for the afternoon. One Rev. —— (reverend by courtesy, and a Christian by assumption), who came that morning from Tisbury, — nine miles, — told a friend of mine that he had understood that I was in town the day preceding, and *did not go to meeting:* so that it seemed, forthwith, on the getting together of the godly, the question had been, whether I had the Congregationalist, Baptist, or Methodist ear-mark; and, it being found that I was guilty of not having either, I was forthwith condemned; and, moreover, the Rev. —— said, that "if Mr. Mann was in town, and did not go to meeting, he had as lief not hear him as to hear him;" and further, that, if I did not wish to show a preference for either sect, I might have gone to hear each during the day, — thus giving me the alternative to hear three Orthodox sermons in one day, or be burned. I confess I had rather be burned; at least, a little.

Oct. 14. The convention *has been:* yet not wholly; for the meeting was unable to get through this evening, and has adjourned to Tuesday evening next. On the whole, a pretty good meeting; and, if the *cause* has any reason to complain, I have not.

Oct. 17. . . . Barnstable. Went two and a half miles out of my way to see an Indian school on the Marshpee District, kept by a Mr. Perry. If one may judge by appearances, that man has a high aim, and appeared very well at school, — invited and rather insisted upon my going home with him to dine. I found he lived in an Indian house. His wife had the dinner ready, to which we sat down. It consisted of a piece of corned beef and vegetables, — potatoes, one carrot and one beet, and brown bread without butter, salt, or the slightest thing in the way of pickle, spice, or any condiment whatever. There was no dessert. His "grace before meat" was less hurried than is usual, when, the rich viands being close by, and God a great way off, the flavor of the meat prevails over the odor of the sanctity, and the thanksgiving hurries into the enjoyment.   There this man labors for the children during the day, visits the people at night, and preaches to them on Sundays ; and all the apparent reward is meat and vegetables without trimming, while the millionnaires go for the several varieties of sensuality, and cannot afford time even to have a religious garment fitted upon their backs.   But will not the time come when he will have the banquets of immortality, and they will have to gnaw the dry bones of the past for rations ?

I trust I have left an impression favorable to the cause on the old sandy cape.   But we will try whether the seed sown in such a soil will grow.   Just a notice is given in the paper here of the educational meeting for next Tuesday, — about a *square*, not *quite ;* while a whole column is devoted to the proceedings of a county *political* convention : the reason given, indeed, for not being able to publish more, that the paper was occupied with political matters ; and the relative spaces allowed show the relative importance of the two subjects in the public mind.

Oct. 22. . . . To-day I have visited some of the graves of the Pilgrims.   How little they saw, two centuries ago, of this present ! Who can fathom future time ?

Oct. 29. . . . Boston.   Yesterday I witnessed the ceremony of the reception by the Mayor, at Faneuil Hall, of about thirty Indians, fresh from the wilds of the West.   On the very spot where we live, how many of them have trod ! now how few their remnants ! Other men — nor other men only, but other forms of being — now exist where they existed.   May it be for the better !   As specimens of the human race, the whole interview was mournful, together with the subsequent dance on the Common, — almost sceptic-making ; but, in contrast with the vast powers of civilized man, it was full of encouragement and hope.   How closely the red and the white man were brought together, speaking to each other, shaking hands ! and yet how many centuries lie between them ! . . .

Nov. 3. . . . Have been engaged all the week at court in Dedham, arguing causes.   The interests of a client are small, compared with the interests of the next generation.   Let the next generation, then, be my client. . . .

Nov. 6.   Glad to find Dr. Channing in the city.   As I called on him to-day, he proposed that some gentlemen engaged in ameliorating this pessimum world should have a "re-union" somewhere this winter.   If we can devise any scheme to give it a hoist, I am willing to try the strength of my back.

Dined with C. Sumner to-day, who is going to Europe soon. When he goes, there will be one more good fellow on that side, and one less on this.

To-morrow for Salem, where I am not only to repeat my speech, but where I have engaged to lecture for the Lyceum.   And, certainly, never was a poor debtor so desirous to get well out of the hands of his creditor as I am to get well out of that engagement. I have been obliged to write it all on my last journey, and it has given me a waking nightmare all the time. . . .

Nov. 10.   Went to Salem as proposed.   Met the convention; though that is almost too great a word to apply to so small a number of men.   But few were there.   Mr. Rantoul did not come at all, Mr. Saltonstall but little.   Things had not been arranged beforehand, and every thing dragged and stuck, — one of the poorest conventions I have had.   I went to deliver a lecture before the Lyceum also, introductory to the course.   That was done last evening to a very good audience at the Tabernacle Church.   But it was not the lecture I had prepared for the occasion.   Some of those who heard the Educational Address called for a repetition of that: so they had it.   I have been indebted to my friend Mr. Webb for many civilities while at Salem, and to as much assistance as it was in his power to render; but there my debts stop, not because of payment, but because I received nothing to owe for.

A friend who was present at this convention says it was remarkable to see the apathy with which it opened. One gentleman, who made one of the first speeches, questioned the expediency of endeavoring to get the educated classes to patronize public schools.   He spoke, he said, in the interest of mothers who preferred private schools for their children; and he believed the reasons that they had for this would always prevail: they would have their children grow up in intimacies with those of their own class. No one spoke on the American side of this question; and the unanswered statement of this partial interest which the educated had in the public schools seemed to cast a chill over the meeting. No generous sentiment was touched.

Another gentleman said he thought, that, preliminary to all things else, the Secretary should go round the State, and pass a day in every public school in it, and then make a report of their condition.

After several sapient speeches like this had been made, Mr. Mann rose and said, that, if the gentleman who made the last proposition would take the trouble to do a short sum in arithmetic, he would find that it would take sixteen years for the Secretary to do this work, if he never intermitted one day. A general stir in the assembly intimated that suddenly the immensity of the work to be done struck their minds for the first time. It was also striking to others, though Mr. Mann did not recognize it, to see the effect of his remarkable address, which followed in the afternoon. The request made, that he should repeat it at the Lyceum in the evening, showed that it did not fall on unintelligent ears.

An interesting portrait of him now hangs in the noble building erected for the Essex Normal School.

To-day, returned to Boston. My great circuit is now completed. The point to which, three months ago, I looked forward with so much anxiety, is reached. The labor is done. With much weariness, with almost unbounded anxiety, with some thwartings, but, on the whole, with unexpected and extraordinary encouragement, the work is done. That, however, is but the beginning. I confess, life begins to assume a value which I have not felt for five years before.

Nov. 16. To-day I have examined the returns in the Secretary's office, of which an abstract is to be made; and find they look very formidable. What an ocean of work lies spread out before me! Well, I am ready to plunge into it.

Nov. 28. Shortly after accepting the office to whose duties I am now devoting my time and soul, I planned to give up my office-room, take one in some respectable place, and live in a manner more agreeable to my feelings than I can here in this lawyer's office, where I have slept about three years. Such an arrangement has now been made; and probably to-morrow I shall begin upon it, having taken rooms at Dr. H——'s, corner of Tremont and School Streets. This, therefore, may be the last night I may sleep in this room, where I have been so long, and labored so severely, and — perhaps I may write it here alone without blushing — brought some things to pass.

It is not stated, I believe, anywhere in these confessions, that after my irreparable loss, which made a far greater change in my soul than in my external condition, — though what of the kind could be greater than that? — a misfortune of a different character, but comparatively light, befell me. It was comparatively nothing; yet, operating through my health, it aggravated other ills to a degree seemingly incapable of extension. I had become liable for my brother to the amount of many thousand dollars beyond the value of every thing I could command. His pecuniary misfortunes thickened upon him, so that he not only left me to pay his debts, but became necessitous, and called upon me in various ways to supply him still more. This I did to some extent, as far as I was able. When I found in what condition as to liabilities I really was left, I was living very comfortably. I changed my course entirely. I left my boarding-house, and after a time got a bed here, and have for about three years taken care of it with my own hands, restricted my expenses in every possible way, and lived out the storm. For a period of nearly six months, I was unable to buy a dinner on half the days. Suffering from hunger and exhaustion, overworked, I fell ill, and so remained for about two months; my best friends not expecting my recovery, and some of them, I sincerely believe, deprecating it as the infliction of further suffering.

Since I have been here in this house of offices, a part of the time
with no other person in the whole building, it has been twice set on
fire by incendiaries right over my head, and several other attempts
have been made.   I have held my life as nought; for to me it has
seemed to be worth nothing.   I have toiled in despair, yet not com-
plaining.   Now that the debts are paid, and I can call my income
my own, I mean not to endure those removable evils as I have done.
Not a slight trouble in this accumulation has been the belief that
there were those who ought to have at least showed me so much
sympathy as to have *offered* to relieve me; but that has not been
done.   I confess it is not in my power to feel in that case just as I
should be glad to.   But perhaps I do not know all their views
upon the subject.   I pray God that these trials may now be over
and past.   Yet not that I would escape from them to fly into any
that affect internal character or outward reputation.   No: let come
what may upon the body; let come what may to crush the intellect:
my most earnest prayer is that the moral nature, the affections, the
sense of justice and of right, may never be impaired.   Let all tortures come, provided *they* are safe.

Nov. 29.   As I anticipated last night, I leave this office to-
night, and somewhat of an epoch occurs in my life.   May I not
hope that at least the privations of which I have been the subject in
this place may not continue to visit me at another residence?   May
I not also hope, and with some confidence trust, that no change in
external condition will weaken the strong purposes of my mind, or
shake my resolution to devote what talents and what length of life
I may have to some good purpose?

I now leave these walls, which have witnessed for the last three
years so many disconsolate days, and so many sleepless and tearful
nights.

Nov. 30.   Thanksgiving Day; but, oh, what days they are to
me! and what a day would a real Thanksgiving Day be to me!   But
it fills my heart too full; and fortunately I have been so busy to-
day, that I have very much escaped the corrosion of my mind on
itself. . . .

Dec 2.   Yesterday I went to Ipswich, and preached my preachment to a pretty full house. . . . On the whole, perhaps it is well that I went where I can make a favorable impression, if it is but upon one man : it is something, and may turn the scale.

Dec. 10. Last Friday I was at an anti-mob meeting in Faneuil Hall. Had I time, I would write out an account of the meeting, and of the views which such occurrences are bringing out. A—— made a speech so flagrantly wicked as to be imbecile. No part of it came up to the dignity of sophistry. Every part of it was what common indecency would blush at. How can a man either pervert himself so, or be so perverted ?

But it is approaching the " witching time of night ;" and, as I slept scarcely at all last night, I must try my luck to-night ; and should I write what I feel, and all I feel, of that *devil*-opment, it would either occupy me till morning, or it would give me an excitement equally incompatible with rest. So let me look forward to the children of the next generation, rather than around to the incorrigible men of this.

Dec. 15. On the evening of the 12th, the freshly elected Mayor gave a party which I attended ; though I confess I neither appetize the parties nor the partisans very much. Thenceforth, including to-day, I have been hard at work, excepting last evening, when a re-union of certain gentlemen was held at Mr. Jonathan Phillips's. Dr. Channing, Dr. Tuckerman, Mr. E. Peabody, Mr. Bartol, and a young, unfledged theologian, made up the clerical side of the house : Ellis G. Loring and myself represented the lay gents. Dr. Channing introduced the subject of the meeting, which he had been the chief agent in getting together, by saying that he was desirous of meeting some friends in a social way, for the purpose, among other objects, of knowing what might be the actual condition of the public mind on certain vital principles. He wanted to know better than he did what sort of a world it was he was living in ; what influences predominated in society ; what was wrong, and what means could be devised to set the wrong right. His remarks had that perspicuity and distinctness which his mind imparts to whatever it handles.

The conversation of the evening turned mainly upon the prevailing state of public opinion in this city respecting the Faneuil-Hall meeting against mobs : and it seemed to be a very general opinion, that the opposition was not directed against abolitionists ; that there was no settled determination or desire to debar them from the expression of their opinions ; but that their opinions were not the opinions of the people of the city, and therefore ought not to go out from Faneuil Hall, because the place whence they were sent might cause them to be mistaken abroad for Boston sentiments, and the authorities of the city would be understood as favoring and countenancing doctrines they discarded.

Dec. 16. To-day, Hon. Jonathan Phillips has sent me the sum of $500. He has submitted it wholly to my disposal, to be expended in the cause. It shall be expended in the cause, if I live ; and I hope to make it do something — a little, a very little — towards it.

Dec. 18. Last evening, spent an hour or so in conversation with Mr. —— on THE subject,* and this afternoon two hours more. On the whole, my cavern has not been so much lighted up by this luminous body as I had anticipated. He may have such practical notions as a man long engaged in the practice must be compelled to learn ; but his views certainly have not seemed to me very original or striking. This may be part guess-work, part inference, and all wrong ; but it is at present the state of my mind. I hope I shall be compelled to alter it hereafter.

Dec. 21. . . . To-night I heard Mr. Emerson's third lecture. Not so lucid, pellucid, as the other. He condensed the commandments, as it regards young men, into two : " Sit alone," and " Keep a journal." The first, I think, is about equivalent to the " Know thyself : " the last, perhaps, is a more direct injunction, " Improve thyself." My practice has, for a long time, adopted the first ; and this book speaks of the last. " Have a room by yourself," said he : " if you cannot without, sell your coat, and sit in a blanket."

Dec. 31. The close of the year. I have not made an entry in this book for ten days, having been so engrossed in the printing of the Abstract of school returns and in the preparation of my Report. The last has cost me considerable labor. The Board meet to-morrow,

---

* The educational enterprise.

when it is to be presented. I have just been writing its last paragraphs; and now, at the end of the day and of the year, shall try to get a little rest for this weary body and mind. One thing, however, is certain. Severe as this labor is, it is surrounded with the most delightful associations. I am sure I can perform much more in this than I could in any other cause. But to-morrow will probably give me some indications about my Report. I shall present it with fear and trembling.

It is not prudent to open my heart to the associations that would throng it if permission for their entrance were given. The year has gone: it has joined the past eternity. I shall go with some of them ere long. When will it be?

7

CHAPTER IV.

CONTINUATION OF JOURNAL.

Jan. 1, 1838. This morning, read my Report to the whole Board, and have been, not on the shallows, but in the deep water of the fidgets ever since. I cannot tell how it has squared with their notions; for that is their test of right or wrong. I left the room to give them opportunity to let their minds run whither they would, without fear of running against me. Whether I should have been run down or crushed, railroad-fashion, had I been there, I know not. Whereupon, as the writs say by way of conclusion, I have not had a happy new year; and at this time of the night it has passed, beyond change. The time that comes to us is soft, yielding: like wax, we can shape it as we please. We take it, or perhaps scarcely take it: as it passes we give it a touch, or a careful, prayerful moulding; and now it is adamant! Yes: it is beyond miracle-working power. Omnipotence cannot alter or modify it. How wonderful! Now, nothing so flowing, so ductile, so shapable; now, all that calls itself might on earth, or in or beyond the starry universe, cannot color it with a new tint, or give it a new attitude. It is eternal!

Jan. 2. This morning the Board met, and, after a discussion of an hour or two, referred certain propositions to the Executive Committee. A headache has extinguished me the rest of the day.

To-morrow the Legislature convenes. Till to-day the last General Court was prorogued. Till to-day my senatorial life lasts; to-day it ends. With good sleep, I shall wake up un-senatorial. So be it. I would not exchange this life, toilsome, anxious, doubtful as it is, and may be, to be at the head of the "grave and reverend" senators to-morrow. Probably I am breathing the few last political breaths I shall ever respire. This drives one's mind back a little to see how the political breaths have been breathed up to this time.

But I will not go deep into that, lest I should fail, through under or over estimate, of hitting the true mark.

Jan. 6.   Since my last entry, I am sorry to say, I have accomplished but little labor; being obstructed, from some cause, in my mental machinery.   I have, however, worried through with the Abstract; and, this very evening, have a copy of it complete. That work, therefore, which has been a most serious one, is completed.   To-day I go at my Schoolhouse Report, which I hope will prove to be beautiful schoolhouse-seed, or seed out of which beautiful schoolhouses will grow, — a whole crop of them.

Jan. 16.   To-day a meeting of the Executive Committee of the Board.   The Governor had a sort of embryo report, — two or three life-points here and there, as in one end of an egg, where here and there an organ is visible, and the chick hovers half this side of the line, half, as yet, in night.

Jan. 18.   Yesterday, received an invitation to preach a preachment, in the Hall of the House of Representatives, on my *hobby*; and, to-night, have preached it.   A pretty full house, though the weather was unpleasant: held them one hour and a half, stiller and stiller to the end.

Feb. 3.   This afternoon, have had a meeting, full of interest and promise, at Chauncey Hall, of all the teachers of the primary schools in the city.   The object is to bring them together, once a week, to hear a lecture; to converse on some topics relating to the subject in which they are all engaged; and not only to have a free communication and exchange of the views which are now entertained, but, by turning the minds of so many persons to the facts suggested by their own experience, to improve and extend the valuable information that may now be possessed by all.   The future meetings, it seems to me, promise very much in behalf of the children of the city.   Mr. Russell is to deliver a course of lectures on elocution; and all subjects connected with teaching are to have their share of attention, especially that of moral training.   Oh for success in this!

Feb. 7.   Last night, lectured at Warren-street Chapel to pretty good listeners.   To-morrow at Newton.   I go in ignorance; but I wait the results.   Do we not all reap exactly the harvest of which we have sown the seed? . . .

Feb. 10. This afternoon, attended the meeting of the primary-school teachers again, — all women ; and, after a lecture from Mr. Russell, Mr. C. Barnard and I addressed it in relation to modes of teaching. The meeting was very fully attended ; as many as a hundred, I think, being present. This argues well. Why may we not have the primary schools much improved — doubled in value — in a single year ? I believe it may be done ; I hope it will be done ; I intend it shall be done, if I live that length of time to attend to it. That I should call *making a mark.*

March 2. The lecture before the Diffusion Society is delivered. I had a small audience, but an attentive one. Many people who were attracted by Dr. Walker's name and subject, of course, would not come to hear me, as I have nothing like the first to attract them, and the subject of education attracts no fashion to listen to its claims. Well, how could I expect that a subject which the world knows so little and cares so little about would produce any interest ? It is left for some one to excite that interest. That is the work to be done. To that, in various ways and with all assidulity, I must address myself. If, after ten years of labor, people should remain as indifferent as at present, there may be reason for desponding ; but now this very indifference is my impulse. If any thing can be done to push away some things which are before the eyes of men, and to put some other things in their places, I think it no rashness to say, " I'll try." I do not think I *delivered* the lecture well, — I was too much disconcerted, — but hope I may feel better next time.

March 10. My second lecture was delivered last evening, with some evident hitchings on the seats now and then. Afterwards went to Mr. Dwight's, where a number of gentlemen were assembled to discuss the expediency of applying to the Legislature for a grant to aid in the establishment of Teachers' Seminaries. Considerable was said on both sides, but mostly on the *pro* side. But, after they had mainly dispersed, Mr. Dwight gave me authority to propose to the Legislature, in my own way, that $10,000 should be forthcoming from himself or others ; and that at any rate he would be responsible for that amount to accomplish the object, provided the Legislature would give the same amount for the same cause. On Monday, it is my intention to make a descent upon the two honorable bodies, and see if they cannot be so rubbed as to emit the requisite spark. This looks well.

March 13.   I had the satisfaction of sending the following communication to the Legislature : —

To the President of the Senate and the Speaker of the House of Representatives.

GENTLEMEN, — Private munificence has placed at my disposal the sum of $10,000 to promote the cause of popular education in Massachusetts.

The condition is, that the Commonwealth will contribute the same amount from unappropriated funds in aid of the same cause ; both sums to be drawn upon equally as needed, and to be disbursed, under the direction of the Board of Education, in qualifying teachers for our common schools.

As the proposal contemplates that the State in its collective capacity shall do no more than is here proffered to be done from private means, and as, with a high and enlightened disregard of all local, party, and sectional views, it comprehends the whole of the rising generation in its philanthropic plan, I cannot refrain from earnestly soliciting for it the favorable regards of the Legislature.

Very respectfully,

HORACE MANN,
Secretary of the Board of Education.

This appears to be glorious ! I think I feel pretty sublime ! Let the stars look out for my head ! . . .

April 4. . . . To-morrow evening, I have engaged to lecture at Lynn.   Query, how shall I hit the good shoemakers with my flights and gyrations ?

April 14.   To-morrow afternoon, I have engaged to speak to Mr. Waterston's Sunday-school children at the North Church. This is a new field, and comes pretty close to preaching ; but, when I preach, I hope I shall not forget, that, however near a live man may get to heaven, he still sustains the main part of his relations to the earth.

April 16. . . . My Schoolhouse Report came out last Thursday. I think it will make the community of children breathe easier. . . .

April 18. . . . To-day the Board of Education has been in session. Important business presents itself; among other things, the mode of disbursing the sum of $20,000, — half of which comes from Mr. Dwight, and half from the State. No definitive action can be had at this time; but "eyes open" are the words. It is a difficult subject. The Legislature have fixed my salary as Secretary of the Board at $1,500; which will probably leave about $500 for my ordinary expenses and services, after defraying the extraordinary expenses. Well, one thing is certain: if I live, and have health, I will be revenged on them; I will do them more than $1,500 worth of good. Lectured at Charlestown to a good audience.

April 28. . . . On Thursday afternoon, I went to Franklin to see my friends. Found my sister removed to another place with her family. The old home, the place where I was born, and spent the first sixteen years of my life, has passed into other hands. I have no ancestral pride about such things, which is generally little else than self-love flowing out copiously over connected objects; yet I shall never be able to pass the spot without deep emotions. There lived my father, of whom I remember little; and there, too, lived my mother, of whom I not only remember, but of whom, so far as I have any good in me, *I am*. That place, too, has been consecrated by the presence of the purest, sweetest, loveliest being, — my wife. You, my love, know nothing of the sufferings which belonged to these associations; or, if you do, you must have such knowledge and faith as to disarm them.

May 13. . . . Have been reading Miss Edgeworth's excellent work on "Practical Education." It is full of instruction. I have been delighted to find how often the views therein expressed had been written out on my own thinking. Had I ever read the book before, I should charge myself with unconscious plagiarism.

May 21. Returned from Boston to Franklin this evening with bones and muscles all in one harmonious state of aching, — *cum multis tossibus*. Wednesday, met a committee for the county of Plymouth, and a few other gentlemen, and made a pretty full and explicit statement to them of the supposed views of the Board in regard to a seminary for teachers, by way of offering an inducement to the county to assist in the establishment of one in that county. To-morrow I am to go to Wrentham to confer with them there on the same subject. If we get Teachers' Seminaries, it will not be because they are of spontaneous growth.

May 25. On Wednesday, held forth to the orthodox Procrustes of Franklin. A pretty good house, for the spring season, and for a country place. But in that house how few of those with whom, when a boy, I used to assemble! Of the whole family, but two remain. Others, indeed, fill their places ; and yet, even for them, there is not less of the pain of anxiety than of the pleasure of affection. What is in the unseen future for them? Towards what goal are they speeding? What cup of sweets or of bitterness is mingling for them? Solicitude asks these questions, and may ask them a thousand times. They will never be answered in season to win the good, or turn aside the evil. On the use alone of the proper means can any confidence of their safety be founded. And in how few points can I reach them, — older, and of a different sex ! If my wife were yet upon earth, she would give them such an example of loveliness and purity, that it would stand before them — full in their presence — alike in the light and in the darkness. That is gone, and can never be supplied. God save their innocence, their purity, their integrity !

May 27. . . . This week, the Board of Education meets. Much depends upon our movements to the cause directly, and still more to the cause indirectly. If we prosper in our institutions for teachers, education will be suddenly exalted ; if not, its progress will be onward still, but imperceptibly slow.

June 9. On Monday, the meeting of the Board of Education was held. . . . All the questions were decided in accordance with my views, and very much to my satisfaction. . . . My first labor is to prepare an address to be delivered on my fall circuit. This is a labor of incalculable importance. On the acceptability of my address will, in no considerable degree, depend the success of the cause. I can do nothing alone. No one can do any thing alone. Others will act with me according as they are pleased with me. How necessary, then, that they should be pleased, not with a flashy pleasure, a pleasure flashing, and instantly expiring, but with an abiding satisfaction ; one founded on just, generous, and elevated views ; one that will connect itself with the higher faculties, and, by being founded upon them, will partake somewhat of their grandeur and duration, and not on the lower propensities, that act so treacherously, and expire so quickly !

After lecturing on the circuit at Nantucket and Edgartown, where he was requested to repeat his lecture in the Orthodox church, after having delivered it once, and where a deputation of young men met him on his way to Holmes Hole, with a request to deliver it there, he lectured again at Falmouth, and finished the tour in that direction with a convention in Barnstable.   To others his progress seemed like a triumphal procession, though his foreboding fears threw over it all a pall of apprehension ; for it was one of his peculiarities, to be ashamed of his lectures until he had tested them by the interest of an audience.   He had no misgivings about the righteousness of his cause, and the general views he took of it, but the greatest doubt about his own ability to present them adequately.

Sept. 4.   In the morning, I lectured in Hanover.   In the afternoon, Mr. Rantoul spoke business-like on the subject of Normal schools.   Mr. Putnam followed him with a speech made up of equal parts of sound sense and good feeling.   The ex-president made a most admirable speech, and one Daniel Webster followed him ; and it was, indeed, a great day for the cause of common schools.

Sept. 5.   Have spent the day at the hospital in Worcester, administering the affairs of that institution.   The thing there sought for seems to be, not more happiness, but less suffering; and why is not the latter as high an object as the former? . . .

Sept. 11. To-day the meeting of the convention has been in Springfield; and, in point of numbers, a miserable meeting it has been. It is at once discouraging and impulsive; for if they, as yet, do so little, there is more — still more — need of effort.

Sept. 17. Pittsfield. Meeting not numerous, but the two or three individuals of themselves equal to a meeting; Miss Catherine Sedgewick, for instance.

Sept. 20. To-day I have attended a grand temperance convention in Northampton. That movement is most encouraging. If temperance prevails, then education can prevail; if temperance fails, then education must fail. To-morrow I must address the people in this town, where great expectations have been raised.

Sept. 21. The day has passed; and, just as the hour for attending my address arrived, a furious rain set in, which deterred many people, and left rather a sparse population in the great house where we assembled.

Sept. 27. Worcester. Attended the Common-school Association meeting yesterday; and to-day have had a benefit of my own. On the whole, I think a little dent has been made in this place.

Oct. 6. Went to Salem and to Topsfield, where the convention for Essex County was appointed. We had a most beautiful day, but a most pitiful convention in point of numbers. In point of respectability, very good, as they always are. . . . Ah! how much remains to be done!

Oct. 8. To-day I have had the pleasure of being introduced to George Combe, Esq., of Edinburgh, who has lately arrived in this country, the author of that extraordinary book, " The Constitution of Man," the doctrines of which, I believe, will work the same change in metaphysical science that Lord Bacon wrought in natural. . . .

Oct. 10. Last evening, went to Taunton. To-day, have had a grand convention there. Had the good fortune to be accompanied by George Combe, Esq., and lady, from Edinburgh. Found them most sensible people; and him, whom I saw most, full of philosophy and philanthropy. He has, this evening, delivered the first in his course of phrenological lectures in this city, — a good lecture to a good house. I am rejoiced at an opportunity to form an acquaintance with a man so worthy and so profound.

And thus ends my peregrinating for the current year. I may have a meeting in this city; and then the *conventions* will be over.

When I undertook the arduous labor of effecting improvements in our common-school system, up to a reasonable and practicable degree, I did so with a full conviction that it would require twenty or twenty-five years of the continued exertions of some one, accompanied with good fortune, to accomplish the work; and I think I took hold of it with a cordiality and resolution which would not be worn out in less than a quarter of a century. I am now of the opinion that one-twentieth part of the work has been done.

This is a fitting place in which to say, that, for one convention authorized to be held by the Secretary, he had during this year held four or five, the extra occasions being at his own expense. He continued to do this through his whole occupation of the office, and was occasionally assisted by the contributions of friends to a very small amount. The same may be said of the Teachers' Institutes, a sort of temporary Normal school afterwards established. In the Teachers' Institutes he often labored alone for days.

Oct. 12. Have heard Mr. Combe lecture again this evening. He considered the effects of *size* in organs, and of *temperaments*, — all very well. I hope, if I get no new ideas from him, I shall at least be able to give some definiteness and firmness to existing ones. He is a man of a clear, strong head, and a good heart.

Oct. 20. For the past week, have been principally engaged in preparing the first number of the " Common-school Journal," — a periodical, the publication of which I intend soon to commence. . . .

To-morrow evening I go to Brighton to lecture on my hobby-subject.

Oct. 27. The past week has not brought much to pass. . . . Have attended three excellent lectures by Mr. Combe. They are very interesting, drawing clear distinctions between the mixed-up virtues and vices of men.

Last Saturday there appeared in the "New-York Observer" the first of a series of articles against the Massachusetts Board of Education, and *probably* their Secretary, professing to inquire into the bearings of the action of the Board in regard to religious teaching in the schools. They are addressed to Dr. Humphreys. Probably they will have no difficulty in making out that the Board is irreligious; for with them religion is synonymous with Calvin's five points. As for St. James's definition of it, "Pure religion and undefiled is to visit the fatherless and widows in their affliction," &c.; and that other definition, "Do justly, love mercy, and walk humbly with thy God," — the Orthodox have quite outgrown these obsolete notions, and have got a religion which can at once gratify their self-esteem and destructiveness. They shall not unclinch me from my labors for mankind.

Oct. 29. . . . Have heard Mr. Combe again this evening. He is a lover of truth. If any man seeks for greatness, let him forget greatness, and ask for truth, and he will find both.

Nov. 10. It is a long time since I have made an entry here, because I have been deeply engaged, and have had nothing of permanent interest to record. To-day I have sent the last of my manuscript for the first number of the "Common-school Journal." It is an enterprise whose success I look forward to with great anxiety. It will cost me great labor. I hope to be repaid in the benefits it may produce. My reputation in no small degree rests upon it. Oh! give me good health, a clear head, and a heart overflowing with love to mankind.

Nov. 15. Constant engagements prevent my entering my thoughts lately so often as I would. Mr. Combe's course of lectures, which is just finished, has occupied me a good deal, and to-night a splendid entertainment has been given him. To-morrow evening, I lecture at Chelsea. And so the time flies; and every day I have to ask myself what impression I am making, what I am doing in the great cause I have in hand. God prosper it, and enable me to labor for it!

Nov. 17. To-day the first number of the "Common-school

Journal" has been issued. With this I hope to awaken some attention to the great subject I have in hand. It must be made an efficient auxiliary, if possible. I know it will involve great labor; but the results at the end, not the labor at the beginning, are the things to be regarded.

This periodical fully answered the purpose for which it was established. It was continued for ten years, and contains not only Mr. Mann's best thoughts upon all the topics treated in it, but all the Annual Reports made to the Board during his Secretaryship. Friends contributed valuable papers to it also. It is a work which has been sought by those interested in education all over the world, even in the heart of Asia; and the numbers left after the work stopped had a regular sale as long as complete sets could be made out from them. In looking forward to the probable condition of our country after the close of this war, when the whole extensive area of it will be opened to free institutions, of which public schools will be an inevitable feature, certainly following the occupation of any portion of its territory by Northern men. a republication of it may be desirable. It would be the best possible accompaniment of the introduction of a common-school system in any region where the political conditions of things make such a system possible. Mr. Mann had frequent correspondence with Southern gentlemen upon the subject; but it always ended in the conviction that there could be no common schools established in a region where equality before the law was not even desired for all classes of white men. In the rural districts it was simply impossible. New Orleans is the only city where an attempt was made; and there, under the judicious superintendence of Mr. J. Shaw, something very creditable was effected; though it could in no wise compare with the results to be obtained where justice was, to say the least, the prevailing *theory*.

Nov. 25. Since my last entry, I have suffered from severe indisposition, and been utterly unable to accomplish any of the labors upon my hands. This is most unfortunate; for time grows short, while labor is long. I am a perpetual memento to myself of the value of health, and therefore of the pains that should be bestowed in childhood and infancy in taking the necessary steps for its production, and in bestowing the habits, which, except under most adverse circumstances, will insure its enjoyment. Could I live my life over again, I think I should adapt the means for its better preservation and invigoration; and yet, if, with my present knowledge, I do not obey the laws upon which it is dependent, how can I be sure, that, were I permitted to re-enact the scenes of life, I should be more wise, though I might be more learned? But, though the past is gone, the future is, *to some extent*, my own.

If any assault was made upon the Board, it was Mr. Mann's habit to disarm opposition, if possible, privately; and the following is an attempt of that kind. The progress of the work was often impeded by such assaults, arising from private disappointments of book-makers or ambitious men. Mr. Storrs was ever afterwards a cordial friend.

BOSTON, Jan. 19, 1839.

REV. DR. STORRS.

DEAR SIR, — Three days ago, I met my friend Mr. Louis Dwight; when our conversation turned upon the strictures lately made in the "Boston Recorder" upon the Board of Education and myself.

I said to Mr. Dwight that those animadversions were without a shadow of foundation; that they were cruel; that they were making my labors, already greater than I feel able to perform, still more arduous and anxious. Yesterday, Mr. Dwight was kind enough to call on me with the editor. The latter opened the subject of the articles in a very proper spirit and manner, and professed a desire to have any misapprehension rectified. I referred him to the extraordinary meaning which had been forced upon the word "sectarianism " in the prospectus of the "Common-school Journal;" to the declaration of the existence of ground for suspicion that I had matured in my own mind and deliberately resolved on a plan for the "exclusion of the religion of the Bible from our schools;" to the further declaration, that a simple perusal of the documents of the Board had caused suspicions to spring up in all parts of the Commonwealth that such a plan was concerted; and that the "mere existence of the suspicions was strong presumptive evidence that they were not wholly without foundation;" and what was perhaps worst of all in its natural effects, an expression, made in an apparent spirit of charity, of a strong inclination to believe that the Secretary is *honest* in his belief that the Board of Education cannot, without violation of law, allow books that treat on religious subjects to be placed on the desks of our schoolrooms. I then stated to him that the Board had never published any document authorizing the slightest suspicion, either against themselves or against me, like the one here referred to; that, so far from my entertaining a belief that it would be illegal to have any books treating of religious subjects on the desks of the schoolrooms, the very contrary was one of the most prominent points in my Report of last year, wherein I had at once exposed and deplored the absence of moral and religious instruction in our schools, and had alleged the probable reason for it; viz., that school committees had not found books, expository of the doctrines of revealed religion, which were not also denominational, and therefore, in their view, within the law, and not that books which did not infringe the law should be excluded.

He then told me that you were the author of those articles; and both he and Mr. Dwight seemed desirous that I should address you a note on the subject, and send you a copy of the only document which has yet been published by the Board, — they supposing that you had been misled by some letters addressed to Dr. Humphreys, which letters were instigated by the fact that the Board and myself would not become instrumental in introducing the American Sunday-school Library into our common schools.

Allow me to say, sir, that, by an examination of the law, you will find that the Board have no authority, direct or indirect, over school-books; and that you will see, by a letter addressed to me by name, a week ago, through the columns of the "Recorder," that a jealousy exists among your religious friends, even of a recommendation of school-books by the Board. I will also state, that by the rules and regulations for the government of Normal schools, *where the Board has power*, they had decided, before the appearance of P——'s wicked pamphlet, that the principles of piety and morality common to all sects of Christians should be taught in every Normal school, and that a portion of the Scriptures should be daily read.

I hope, sir, that my motives in writing this letter may be justly appreciated. I loathe controversy, especially at a time when the efforts of every good man are necessary in the work of improvement. I have no spirit for controversy, nor time nor strength to devote to it. To exclude all chance of my being involved in it, I must beg you to consider this letter as confidential, except so far as it regards Mr. Willis and Mr. Dwight, at whose request it is written.

Yours very respectfully,

HORACE MANN.

P. S. — The "Trumpet" directly and repeatedly has charged the Board with the intention to introduce religion into the schools, from the same evidence which others interpret so differently.

BOSTON, Feb. 11, 1839.

GEORGE COMBE, ESQ. *My very dear Sir,* — . . . We are all very glad to hear of your success and acceptability where you have been. When any meeting occurs among the members of your class, you are always remembered. We see that there will be a new earth, at least, if not a new heaven, when your philosophical and moral doctrines prevail. It has been a part of my religion for many years that the earth is not to remain in its present condition forever. You are furnishing the means by which the body of society is to be healed of some of its wounds heretofore deemed irremediable. They are doctrines which cause a man's soul to expand beyond the circle of his visiting-cards; that recognize the race as beings capable of pleasure and pain, of elevation or debasement. Many men have no more realizing belief of the *human race* than they have of

> " Anthropophagi, and men
> Whose heads do grow beneath their shoulders ; "

and I have always thought that this practical disbelief in the existence of the creature had, at least, as bad an effect upon the character as a disbelief of the Creator.

You observe, in your letter, that your audiences fell off from eight to ten per cent in Boston, New York, and Philadelphia, when you lectured on the moral sentiment. Now, my dear sir, are you not mistaken in this statement, in regard to Boston? We all observed otherwise. We think there was an increase in your audience here, both in numbers, and in attention, and in pleasure too, if that were possible, when you expatiated upon the foundations of justice, reverence, and goodness. Pardon me for being a little sensitive on the subject; for we should think our character somewhat involved in it. We think, on this point, we could not defend ourselves by quoting from Dr. Franklin, who said that revivals in religion always made him think of a scarcity of grain : those who had enough said nothing about it, while those who were destitute made all the clamor. . . .

Please make my regards acceptable to Mrs. Combe ; and believe me when I say that I am a better man for having become acquainted with your mind and yourself. I hope all your leisure time will be spent in our neighborhood.

Yours very truly,

HORACE MANN.

BOSTON, March 25, 1839.

G. COMBE, ESQ., Philadelphia. *My very dear Sir,* — . . . There have been some striking conversions, since you were here, to the religious truths contained in your " Constitution of Man." Some of these have happened under my own ministry. A young graduate of one of our colleges wrote me, a few months since, to inquire in what manner he could best qualify himself for teaching. He had then been employed in teaching for two years, after having received a degree. I told him, that, in the absence of Normal schools, I thought he had better take up his residence in this city, visit the schools, make himself acquainted with all the various processes which various individuals adopt to accomplish the same thing, and read all the best books that can be found on the subject. He accordingly came ; and, when he applied to me for a list of books, I, of course, named your " Constitution " as the first in the series. After about a fortnight he called on me, and said he had read it through with great pleasure, but did not think he had mastered the whole philosophy. A few days after, he came again, not a little disturbed : he had read it again, comparing it with his former notions (for he was highly orthodox), and found that the glorious world of laws which you describe was inconsistent with the miserable world of expedients in which he had been accustomed to dwell. I spent an entire evening with him, and endeavored to explain to him that your system contained all there is of truth in orthodoxy ; that the animal nature of man is first developed ; that, if it continues to be the active and the only guiding power *through life*, it causes depravity enough to satisfy any one ; but if the moral nature, in due time, puts forth its energies, obtains ascendency, and controls and administers all the actions of life in obedience to the highest laws, there will be righteousness enough to satisfy any one ; that, if he chose, he might call the point, where the sentiments prevailed over the propensities, the hour of regeneration ; nor was the phrase — a second birth — too strong to express the change ; that this change might be wrought on the hearing of a sermon, or when suffering bereavement, or in the silence and secrecy of meditation, or on reading Mr. Combe's " Constitution of Man ; " and, as God operates upon our mental organization through means, these might be the means of sanctifying us. He adopted my views on the subject, and is now, I believe, a convert beyond the danger of apostasy. But, my dear sir, I have occupied so much space with this case of conversion, that I have little for other things I wished to say. . . .

Very truly yours,

HORACE MANN.

March —. This afternoon, attended the anniversary meeting of the Warren-street Chapel Association, and heard a very interesting report read by Rev. Charles Barnard.' No remarks were made. Fifteen hundred children have been connected with the institution since it was opened. Had Sir J. Herschel been here to tell of fifteen hundred new stars which he had catalogued in the southern hemisphere, would he not have excited a much deeper interest, and had many more hearers?

This institution seeks out those children who seem to be outside of all the favorable influences of civilization. As shadows are always deepest where the light is brightest, those who are in the shadow of the bright light of civilization are in the deepest darkness. Our institutions for moral, social, and religious improvement, seem to have, in most instances, answered their end, or fulfilled their promise, when the community have been brought within the circle of their action; but a portion of the community are outside that circle, and therefore are even worse situated, relatively, than they would be in a less advanced state of society. These need an institution like the chapel.

March 31. Engaged to lecture four times this week, at Lynn, Salem, and Newburyport. Oh my poor body!

June 13. . . . Went to Nantucket, saw Mr. Pierce, obtained the consent of the school committee for his discharge from his engagements to them, and returned yesterday worn down with fatigue. But, at last, I believe we have a competent principal for one of our Normal schools; and this is a subject for unbounded rejoicing.

June 21. Attended on Thursday a meeting of the Executive Committee of the Board to act upon a proposition from Prof. Newman. . . . Thus the two schools at Lexington and Barre are now provided for, and I am relieved of a weight of anxiety and care which has been almost too much for me.

The subject of Normal schools now became the one which Mr. Mann considered of the first importance, and Mr. Pierce proved to have qualifications for his vocation even beyond his expectations. He not only knew how to teach with precision, but he evoked from his pupils, for the reception of his teaching, such a force of conscience as insured thorough study and assimilation of whatever was taught. When Mr. Mann first visited his school in Nantucket, he was charmed by the evidence of power that the whole management and all the recitations of the school evinced; and, when he spoke of it afterward to gentlemen of the place, one of the most respectable citizens said to him that he had lived forty years on the South Shore, and could always tell Mr. Pierce's scholars, whenever he met them in the walks of life, by their mode of transacting business, and by all their mental habits, which were conscientious, exact, reliable. Mr. Pierce had taught in that vicinity the greater part of those years. From that time, Mr. Mann had his eye upon him; and he always felt that to Mr. Pierce was chiefly owing the very rapid and unquestionable value, in all eyes, of this new movement. Those who were conversant with his modes of instruction, and of appeal to the sense of intellectual and moral duty in his pupils, can pick them out, even now, from other teachers. This characteristic of the school was handed down many years through the influence of his early pupils, two of whom were professors in Antioch College.

June 14. Last evening and this, attended Mr. Espy's lectures on the *Law of Storms.* He certainly starts upon a fair philosophic basis, and seems to advance nothing visionary or extravagant. No doubt the motion of every particle both of wind and vapor has its law, and so of all particles in combination; and why should not observation and reflection discover what that law is? . . . So far as we know the operations of the Deity, he seems to work by fixed, invariable laws; and special interpositions give place, in the opinions of men, just as fast as science advances. This gives glorious augury.

July 2. To-morrow we go to Lexington to launch the first Normal school on this side the Atlantic. I cannot indulge at this late hour of the night, and in my present state of fatigue, in an expression of the train of thought which the contemplation of this event awakens in my mind. Much must come of it, either of good or of ill. I am sanguine in my faith that it will be the former. But the good will not come itself. That is the reward of effort, of toil, of wisdom. These, as far as possible, let me furnish. Neither time nor care, nor such thought as I am able to originate, shall be wanting to make this an era in the welfare and prosperity of our schools; and, if it is so, it will then be an era in the welfare of mankind.

July 3. The day opened with one of the most copious rains we have had this rainy season. Only three persons presented themselves for examination for the Normal School in Lexington. In point of numbers, this is not a promising commencement. How much of it is to be set down to the weather, how much to the fact that the opening of the school has been delayed so long, I cannot tell. What remains but more exertion, more and more, until it *must* succeed?

Aug. 11. Still at Cape Cottage (near Portland), where I have been enjoying the society of Mr. Combe, who is, on the whole, the completest philosopher I have ever known. Ideas so comprehensive and just, feelings so humane and so true, I think I have never known before combined in the same individual. It has indeed been a most agreeable, and I think instructive, visit to me. . . . Mr. Combe comprehends how he is made, and why he was made, and he acts as the laws of his nature indicate; and, by submitting to the limitations which the Deity has imposed on his nature, he is enabled to perform the duties which the Deity requires of it.

Aug. 19. Great Barrington. . . . To make an impression in Berkshire in regard to the schools is like attempting to batter down Gibraltar with one's fist. . . . My health fails. I may perish in the cause; but I will not abandon it, and will only increase my efforts as it needs them more.

Aug. 31. Greenfield. There was not encouragement at Northampton. Ah me! I have hold of so large a mountain, there is much danger that I shall break my own back in trying to lift it! I could not shake the dust, but only the mud, off my feet against them. But to have any ill feeling toward them would only turn apathy into hostility; and as for despondence, the cause is so glorious that it must dispel that. . . . I wish the county of Franklin could have the spirit of Franklin. In this town much has been done, though, I fear, not in the right way.

Sept. 1. Heard a sermon this morning from the Rev. —— of ——. I do not wonder that ministers produce so little effect upon their audiences. They attempt to write more than almost any mortal can accomplish. The consequence is, that, with all possible diligence and effort, they must write mainly their first thoughts. They have no time for culling, but must fill their baskets with whatever grows rankest and is first found. This induces a habit of writing not only without premeditation, but without meditation. All thoughts are made equally welcome. Out comes a stream of commonplaces. First, there is a simple want of excitement; then the sermons become sedative and soporific; then they supersede opium as a narcotic. Thus ends the minister's power. Thus are turned into weakness the mighty elements given them to use. Without continued effort, the mind loses its power to make effort. Eventually, therefore, even a strong mind, being compelled to write weak sermons, is reduced to the level of its own productions.

To-morrow the convention. In Berkshire, they explained and excused the thinness of the meeting because the day was fair; in Northampton, because it was stormy. The truth lies in the dearth, or death, of interest in the subject. That interest I have got to create. The edifice is not only to be reared, but the very materials out of which it is to be constituted are to be grown. Can I grow them? — that is the question. In part, perhaps, may be the answer. Some one else may arise to form them into a noble and everlasting temple. Mine may be the labor, and another's the honor. Well, if I knew the work would go on when my labors cease, I would not touch the question of ultimate honor. Give me the certainty that the cause shall prosper, and I will waive all question about honor; nay, even in the uncertainty whether it will succeed at all, it shall have my extremest exertions.

Sept. 5. . . . Spent the morning at Barre. Twelve young ladies and eight young gentlemen admitted to the Normal School. Shall undoubtedly have thirty by the end of the month. This is a fair beginning. May it go on prosperously! This afternoon, the Governor (Briggs) delivered a very acceptable address, touching upon

the origin, progress, advantages, and hopes of a Normal school. . .
In the midst of adverse events blowing on opposite sides of my
boat, it is my business to keep it in trim. . . .

BOSTON, Sept. 11, 1839.

G. COMBE, ESQ. *My very dear Sir,* — Since I had the pain
of parting with you and Mrs. Combe, I have been realizing
the existence of perpetual motion ; otherwise I would not have
allowed so much time to pass by without reminding myself, by
writing to you, of the pleasant and instructive visit which I made at
Portland. Never have I passed a week in my life more congenial
to my coronal region. The quiet cottage, and the half-earth, half-
ocean landscape, are vividly present to my view ; and the old rocks
upon the shore, where the philosopher sat and discoursed wisdom,
are as firmly fixed in my memory as they are in their own bed. It
will take a long time, and much beating by storms, to wear them
out. And when I think of the sail in the boat, and the rides in
the old chaise, I will not say that I grow sentimental ; but I regret
that I had any other brain-work to do, which prevented me from
enjoying them as I ought.

Since I left you, I have held six educational conventions in parts
of the State nearly two hundred miles from each other, and in the
intermediate places, besides being present and assisting in the
examinations and opening of the Normal School at Barre. The
opening of the two Normal schools, and the finding of two suitable
and acceptable individuals to take charge of them, cost me an
incredible amount of anxiety. I believe I counted over all the men
in New England by tale before I could find any who would take
the schools without a fair prospect of ruining them. But I trust
we have succeeded. At any rate, my nightmare begins to go
off. I will not trouble you by stating the difficulties of the
problem given to me for solution ; which was to do right, and not
offend the ultra-orthodox. I needed your philosophy, i.e. equanimity, for that task.

I have heard but the expression of one opinion on the subject of
your coming here for another course of lectures. . . .

I cannot express to you my sense of undeserved honor for the insertion of my name in the new edition of your lectures on education. The first aspect in which the fact presented itself to my mind, when the dedication was shown to me, was, that it might render the expression of my sincere opinions about the worth of your works a little suspicious, as people might think that those views, which were dictated by all the judgment I have, possibly came from my gratitude for your kindness and the expression of your good will. But I will try to manage it in such a way that you shall lose as little as possible for conferring upon me an honor I did not deserve. . . .

My kindest regards to yourself and Mrs. Combe.

HORACE MANN.

Sept. 14. On Thursday I went to Lexington, where I spent the whole day in Mr. Pierce's school; and a most pleasant day it was. Highly as I had appreciated his talent, he surpassed the ideas I had formed of his ability to teach, and in that prerequisite of all successful teaching, the power of winning the confidence of his pupils. This surpassed what I have ever seen before in any school. The exercises were conducted in the most thorough manner: the principle being stated, and then applied to various combinations of facts, so that the pupils were not only led to a clearer apprehension of the principle itself, but taught to look through combinations of facts, however different, to find the principle which underlies them all; and they were taught, too, that it is not the form of the fact which determines the principle, but the principle which gives character to the fact. . . .

Sept. 21. This morning, bade good-by to Nantucket. Did all parts of the State receive me as cordially, and pay half as much attention to my views, as the good people of Nantucket, there would soon be a common-school revolution in the State. But this is far from being the case: therefore I have so much the more to do. Many people kindly express sympathy with me in regard to the embarrassments which I encounter, and the obstacles thrown in my path; and are pleased to say that they have feared that I shall be discouraged. They do not know the stuff I am made of.

Sept. 23. To-morrow is Convention Day for Barnstable. The prospect is very unpromising. Those are absent, who, in former years, have contributed to the interest of the meetings. Barnstable does not seem to have felt any *tingle*, which, in other places, has begun an excitement. When the tool is dull, or the material tough, put on more strength!

Sept. 24. The day is over. As miserable a convention as can well be conceived. If the Lord will, I will; that is, I will work in this moral as well as physical sand-beach of a county until I can get some new things to grow out of it.

Sept. 29. Plymouth. The cause is getting ahead in Plymouth County, beyond question. A large house was well filled here all day.

I am surprised to hear people express their surprise that I do not tire of this business. Why should I tire of such a cause? If I meet with encouragement, can any thing be more congenial to my feelings than to contemplate the progress of so glorious a movement? If, on the other hand, obstacles are thrown in its way, what higher service can any one perform than to endeavor to remove them? The more opposition, the more need of effort.

Oct. 1. Dedham. To-day, have had what must be called the convention in Dedham, — a meagre, spiritless, discouraging affair. A few present, and all who were present chilled, — choked by their own fewness. Surely, if the schoolmaster is abroad in this county, I should be glad to meet him. So it is: but it must be otherwise; perhaps not in my day; but, while my day lasts, I will do something to have it otherwise.

Oct. 13. A tolerable week as to brains. I have made some little progress in digesting the form of a Report. . . . Heard, a short time since, of the destitute condition of many Irish children on the railroad between Springfield and the New-York line. To-day, wrote to Mr. —— that I would be responsible for the expense of their instruction, and that he might engage teachers, at least for three months from the 1st of November.

Oct. 27. . . . To-morrow I begin the great work of getting out the "Abstract of School Returns," — a gigantic labor; but I go into it "choke-full" of resolve. Come on, labor, if you will bring health in your company.

Nov. 17. Laboring at my Abstract and Report with unabated

vigor. How the granite mass gives way under the perpetual droppings of industry! Oh for continuance in a good degree of health! and then exertion in this glorious cause will be a pastime. Neglected, lightly esteemed among men, cast out, as it were, from the regards of society, I seem to myself to know that the time will come when education will be reverenced as the highest of earthly employments. That time I am never to see, except with the eye of faith; but I am to do something that others may see it, and realize it sooner than they otherwise would. Their enjoyment may be greater than mine; but if my duty hastens that enjoyment, then that duty is greater than theirs. And shall I shrink when called to the post of the higher duty?

The above passage is a strong proof of how little the public estimated the value of such labors as Mr. Mann was engaged in at that time. He was made to feel keenly that the President of the State Senate, and a lawyer in lucrative practice, held a very different place in society from the Secretary of the Board of Education on a small salary.

Dec. —. During the week, I had an informal proposition to go to Missouri, as president of a college, with a salary of three thousand a year, a splendid house, gardens, &c.; but, as far as my own preferences are concerned, I would rather remain here, and work for mere bread, than go there for the wealth of the great Valley of the Mississippi. Oh, may I prosper in this! I ask no other reward for all my labors. This is my only object of ambition; and, if this is lost, what tie will bind me to earth?

Dec. 29. The Board met and adjourned. Did the occasion of reading a Report to them occur often, I certainly could not survive it. But it has passed.

Those who know the estimation in which Mr. Mann was held by his friends will perceive that this fearful despondency was very much due to the utter prostration of strength, which, at this time, followed unusual labors.

Some of his friends would have been thankful beyond measure to have taken him into their families as guest, boarder, or on any terms he would prescribe; and urged him in the warmest terms to come to them: but he shrunk from any thing that interfered with his total independence, and was unwilling to carry his heavy heart and failing health into any happy circle. His solitary room, however, was forcibly invaded by those who loved him, when he disappeared from their view for any length of time.

Jan. 5, 1840. Sunday. With the close of the old year, and the incoming of the new, I had many thoughts in my mind, but no power to say them. The year 1839, from ill health, from opposition in the sacred cause which I have wholly at heart, and from being called upon to do impossible things by the Board of Education, has been the most painful year — save *the* year — that I have ever suffered. But it has passed. I have come out of it. The cause has come out of it, and is beginning to give signs of vitality. I enter upon another year not without some gloom and apprehension, for political madmen are raising voice and arm against the Board; but I enter it with a determination, that, I trust, will prove a match for *secondary* causes. If the First Cause has doomed our overthrow, I give it up; but, if any thing short of that, I hold on. Three lectures this week.

Jan. 26. This week, on Wednesday, Governor Morton gave his inaugural address. He cut the Board of Education entirely. *Probably he did not know of its existence.* He has got to know it. He has made a mistake on his own personal account, I believe. But time will make further developments.

Feb. 2. Some partisan men are making efforts to demolish the Board of Education; but all the jealousies which ignorance engenders cannot be entered and recorded here. It is my fortune to stand as the pioneer of this movement; and, like other pioneers, I cannot expect to escape unscathed. But it is a cause worth being sacrificed for: and, first, I will try to conquer; but, if conquest is impossible, then I will try to bear.

Feb. 16. Looked over the last proof-sheet of my Report on Friday. It will be distributed to-morrow. What fate awaits it, I must wait to see. It has caused me great anxiety; and, if it causes anxiety to my friends, we shall be a sorry company. But it has aimed at truth; and if it brings truth down, and allows all to participate in it and to enjoy it, the labor it has cost will be repaid with abounding joy. I have done my best in the circumstances, and must stiffen my back to take consequences.

BOSTON, Feb. 22, 1840.

G. COMBE, ESQ., New Haven. *My very dear Sir,* — It is now almost two months since I received your kind parting, and, as yet, unanswered note. It grieved me to be sick; but as a consequence of it was your departure from the city, without another interview, and another expression both of the benefits and the pleasure I had derived from your acquaintance, I was almost more sorry for the effect than for the cause. After that capsize, I righted pretty soon: and need enough of it there was; for the boat in which some of the interests of education seem to be embarked has been assailed by cross-currents, head-flaws, and some monsters of the deep. But Palinurus has not slept, and she will weather the storm. First came the Governor's Address, which committed that high treason to truth which consists in perverting great principles to selfish ends. Then the cry of expense has been raised; and, were an Englishman to hear it, he would think the Board of Education was trying to outvie the British national debt. But it will end in alienating a portion of the public mind from the cause, which it will cost us another year's labor to reclaim.

What an enemy to the human race is a party-man! To get ashore himself is his only object: he cares not who else sinks.

There are some good men in Albany; which proves that Nature will have some good souls, notwithstanding all efforts to baffle her. There was your friend Mr. Dean of Albany, and Mr. Barnard, now representative in Congress, and Gen. Dix, formerly Secretary of State, who are worthy to be remembered in any consultation about destroying the city.

I have just been listening to a course of lectures on geology. This is truly a magnificent science. It has kept my causality and veneration in a state of great activity. I never enjoyed but one course of lectures more than that. The fact that made it most delightful to me was, that many of our granite, felspar, hornblende, and mica State Orthodox attended; and before all these, the lecturer, who is known to be one of the *elect*, assaulted, bombarded, battered, and demolished the six-days' account of the creation, until I sometimes fancied I could hear Moses himself crying out, " Et tu, Brute ? " Probably they would not have heard the same thing from any other man extant. He not only enlarged the creation immensely, but he reduced the Deluge to a mere puddle. He said there was not an existing phenomenon on earth which could certainly be traced to it. All this broke up through the primary and secondary formations of bigotry, just as his own volcanic fires rushed up through the corresponding geological strata. When, in the last lecture but one, he came to the upheaving action of earthquakes and volcanoes, he only described in the physical world what I had seen going on every day, so far as his audience was concerned, in the moral. He attempted to reconcile himself to Moses; but that made one think of the two men (is it not in " Gil Blas "?) who shook hands, and were enemies ever afterwards. . . .

Farewell to you both, and believe me ever, with the greatest esteem,   Yours,

HORACE MANN.

March 15. This week has been wholly devoted to preparations to meet the atrocious attack upon the Board of Education. The question still pends; but I am too much exhausted and worn out to comment upon it. I am compelled to go to New York; and the chance is that I must be absent when the day of trial comes. This is bad, but inevitable. I must submit; but the cause shall not die, if I can sustain or resuscitate it. New modes may be found, if old ones fail. Perseverance, perseverance, and so on a thousand times, and ten thousand times ten thousand.

March 19. New York. Was obliged to leave Boston yesterday in the midst of the Report of the Education Committee for abolishing the Board. Of course, the question is undoubtedly decided; but I remain in ignorance, and must do so until to-morrow morning, when, on arrival of the mails, I shall learn its fate. Let it come. If the Board is abolished, it will show how much is to be done in this great cause; and I think it will only inspire me with new zeal to accomplish it. If, on the other hand, it triumphs, then its claim to public favor must be evidenced by the good it shall accomplish. In either case, I stand almost pledged, if right, to advance the right; if wrong, to repair the wrong.

March 21. Heard yesterday from Boston that the bigots and vandals had been signally defeated in their wicked attempts to destroy the Board of Education: 182 in favor of the attempt, 245 against it. I have not as yet been able to bring my mind into a state to describe the merits of the case. Perhaps I may do it some time; perhaps it is not worth doing: but the letters of congratulation over their defeat show how much others enjoy it.

Yesterday Mr. and Mrs. Combe arrived here from New Haven; and we soon struck up a bargain to travel together to the West. From this I promise myself great pleasure and advantage. To be able to enjoy for a month the society of that man will familiarize great truths to my mind, if it does not communicate many new ones. The *utile et dulce* could rarely be more happily united.

March 22. . . . Another huzza from Boston to-day on account of the defeat of our enemies.

March 28. Washington. . . . This is the first time I have ever seen the Capitol. This is the first day I ever set my foot upon soil polluted by slavery. This day, on witnessing groups of colored persons, such feelings have poured into my mind as I have no language to express. They are too strong to be formed into words. To-night, after many days of excitement, my mind is not in a condition to declare what is in it. At some future time, I hope these emotions may take body and life.

March 30. Yesterday attended meeting in the Capitol, and heard a *roaration*. It might, perhaps, be called a sermon; but it had not one idea calculated to give clearer views of truth or stronger feelings of duty. Oh! when will the world be free from the drag-chain of most of the clergy?

To-day I have been in the hall of the House of Representatives and in the Senate Chamber; have seen the rooms, and heard the magnates. My impression of the magnificence of the former has been increased more than that of the greatness of the latter. Oh! how much good might these men do, if they would forget the interests of party, and attend to the welfare of mankind! Civilization would bound forward with unwonted speed, if the tenth part of the talent or a hundredth part of the resources were devoted to the amelioration of the race, which are now neutralized by the conflicts of parties. Would each party strive for the whole, each would be vastly more benefited than it now is.

March 31. Baltimore. . . . Ascended the Washington Monument, 180 feet in height, and cost $200,000, — a great height and a great sum; but they were for a great man. He left his monument, however, in the improved condition of his country : that is the only noble monument.

April 5. Wheeling. . . . The Alleghanies are not stupendous to the perceptive, but only to the reflective, faculties. The geological characteristics were full of interest. As we rode toward their summit, the strata were almost uniformly inclining upward. We then passed on about fifty miles, surrounded only by hills of somewhat more than ordinary magnitude. Here the strata were more nearly horizontal : they were of trap. When we came to the very summit, they were of granite ; and, the moment we began to descend from the western brow, the trap re-appeared, and the dip was toward the west. I was lost in amazement in contemplating the vital forces that upheaved this ponderous mass. The vastness of the power, and the length of time that has elapsed since it was exerted. were too immense for my comprehension, and made me yield myself to a feeling of wonder and reverence. Bald Mountain is said to be the highest point on this road. Laurel Hill is the westernmost battlement. From this the descent is rapid ; so rapid, indeed, that, in half an hour, I think our thermometer must have risen ten or fifteen degrees. The woods hitherto had circumscribed our prospect to the narrowest limits; and, as the road wound around the sides of hills which it could not directly surmount. our view extended forward only a few rods. But at this point, all at once, as though a curtain had been withdrawn, the Great Valley of the West burst upon us. Away in the horizon, as far as the eye could reach, in every direction, we saw all that the convexity of the earth's surface would allow. It was like a glance from a lofty headland upon the outstretched plain of the ocean, which, though level, seems to rise in the distance. So here we seemed to see distant and gigantic mountains; and we only knew by reflection, that what seemed to be a circular wall of distant mountains was only an apparent elevation, owing to immense extent, where miles in length made only an inch in height. It was only in this way that we approximated to any adequate conception of the vastness of the region which we saw, and of that immeasurably vaster region which we could not see, — of that world of territory which lay beyond the reach of vision and below the line of light.

April 8. Cincinnati. . . . I was told by the pilot of the boat in which we came from Wheeling to this place, that, according to the best estimate he could form, the distance from Cincinnati to Pittsburg is about 470 miles, and that the River Monongahela is navigable by steamboats ninety miles above Pittsburg. I am satisfied that the only way to get an adequate idea of this country is to travel through it. No imagination can give the realizing sense of its vastness, which is caused by that deepening, day after day, of the impression made by actually seeing it. and by combining the two elements of rapidity and length of time in passing over it. The imagination may conceive of great extent in an hour, or even in a minute: but imagination cannot hold on day after day; and all her impressions upon the brain do not leave traces so vivid, deep, and strong as come from actual observation, and from being made to comprehend by seeing and feeling, suffering and enjoying.

April 11. Spent the evening of Thursday at the house of Mr. Nathan Guilford. He is the author of the school system of Ohio. He prepared the bill and carried it through the State Senate in 1825. What great results have followed from this measure! Here is an encouragement. Cannot I work in a faith that needs only to look as far forward as fifteen years?

April 20. . . . On Monday we went to the "North Bend" to see Gen. Harrison, as probable a candidate for the next Presidency as any man in the country. He had been ill, — pale, thin, his skin shrivelled, and his motions weak. He entered into conversation, however, and seemed to gain strength and vivacity as he proceeded. His conversation was sensible, without being learned or profound. His manners had the utmost simplicity. In the course of the visit, he spoke of the events in which he had borne a conspicuous part, without the slightest elation ; and referred to his own frugal and homely life, without a hint that his poverty was a thing either to be proud of or ashamed of. His dwelling is humble. It is surrounded by a large enclosure, all of which is a lawn, except that behind the house, which is a garden. The whole is enclosed by what is called in New England a " Virginia fence." We entered this enclosure by a gate large enough for carts or carriages. There was no small gate or turn-stile by the side of the principal one, as usual ; it hav ing been wisely inferred that whatever could enter through a small gate might enter through a large one. The gate was secured by a wooden latch and button ; and the only process necessary in order to open it was to put the arm between its different rails, move the button, raise the latch, press against the gate, and the feat was fully accomplished. I doubt much if Windsor Park has any such gate in all its avenues. The path leading from the gate aforesaid to the door was such as had been formed in the natural course of events by the wheels of vehicles, and the indiscriminate feet of bipeds and quadrupeds. Of walks gravelled below and arbored above we saw none. The greensward had not been disturbed to make way for flowers. The water had not been gathered into fountains, but sought its way, irrespective of *jets d'eau*, wherever the laws of gravitation inclined it. The statues had not yet left the quarry. The doorsteps were such laminæ of unhewn and undressed stone as Nature had provided. All that art had done was to put them in the right place.

The house was a building with two wings. Part of the central building was veritable logs, though now covered externally by clap-boards, and within by wainscoting. This covering and these wings have been added since the log nucleus was rolled together. The furniture of the parlor could not have drawn very largely upon any one's resources. The walls were ornamented with a few portraits, some in frames, some disembodied from a frame. The drawing-room was fitted up more in modern style; but the whole of the furniture and ornaments in three rooms might have cost two hundred or one hundred and fifty dollars.

I think that half the farmers and mechanics in Norfolk County, Mass., have a room quite as well furnished as the best room of Gen. William H. Harrison, the leading Whig candidate for the Presidency of the United States. The billiard-room of a certain gentleman in Boston would buy the general out of house and home.

But how, Mr. Traveller and Taker-of-notes, did all this act upon your contemplations? These were my lucubrations thereupon. From that homely gateway never went forth any armed band to do injustice. No blood of human victims was upon the portals of the door. If there were no flowers along the path, no tears had been transmuted into hue and odor by the taskmaster; and rather would I go out and in amid that rude carpentry, and sleep beneath a thatched roof on a bed of straw, with obtruding winds and storms for my lullaby, than dwell in princely palaces, in the midst of gardens like that of Eden, when the wealth that created the enchantments around me had been plundered in war, or wrung by oppression from toiling vassals.

The conversation and phrenological appearance of Gen. Harrison indicated a man of clear intellect, without any great strength. His superiority undoubtedly comes from the absence of disturbing forces, rather than from original energy. He said, that, when Mr. Webster came to see him a few years ago, he prepared such entertainment for him as his house afforded, but had no wine; and added, that he had had none in his house for, I think, twenty years. He told his guests on that occasion that he should be glad to give them some, as they were probably accustomed to it; but that, if he had bought any, he probably should not be able to pay for it. After Mr. Webster went away, he inquired of his fellow-guests if it were really true that the general did not keep wine; and remarked, that he thought he should have it, whether he could pay for it or not.

We were shown an eagle, which had been caught a few months since, and presented to the general at a public meeting. At the battle of Fort Meigs, an eagle was seen hovering over the armies in the midst of the engagement; and the orator, with a poet's license, had taken the liberty to presume that the eagle, which was then regarded as an omen of martial victory over the foreign enemies of the country, was the same which was now caught, and was to be the omen of a civil victory over its domestic foes; that is, in plain prose, of a triumph of the Whigs over the Van Buren party. When Mr. J. C. Vaughan, who accompanied us, said that he must keep the eagle, according to the trust, until that political victory could be achieved, — " Ah! " said the general very promptly, " there is another condition to that. If Mr. Van Buren will repent of his iniquities, then he may remain where he is, and I will remain where I am."

He has no predominant self-esteem, or love of approbation. Those organs are small. Combativeness is also small. Alimentiveness and acquisitiveness are almost wanting. The moral region is tolerably developed; but this absence of the great mischief-working propensities gives it fair play. This is the key to his character and history. . . .

I have never enjoyed and at the same time profited so much by the society of any individual with whom I have met as by that of Mr. Combe; so that, as a traveller, I can hardly have a greater misfortune than to miss him. I hope they will return from Cincinnati, therefore, that we may go up the river together.

This country has been created on a splendid scale of physical magnificence. Are its intellectual and moral proportions to be of a corresponding greatness? We trust in God they are; for, if such an energy of physical nature predominates, it will lead to extremes of licentiousness, of brutal indulgence of all kinds, such as the world has never yet exhibited.

April 24. No Mr. Combe. My desire to see him is so great, that I defer my departure till to-morrow. If he does not come by that time, I must bid adieu to the expectation of ever seeing him again. This will be most painful. . . .

BOSTON, May 9, 1840.

MY DEAR MR. AND MRS. COMBE, — I am suffering under a malady for which there is no prescription in the pharmacopœia, nor any skill in the professors of the healing art. It is an intellectual and moral atrophy. After being high fed for five or six weeks, I am suddenly put upon the teetotal system. How I long for the *noctes et dies deorum* again! For a renewal of this wise pleasure, or pleasant wisdom, I would sleep with a steam-boiler breathing in my face, or " lie over " in that odd caravansary where Jonah took lodgings for three days and nights ; or, if nothing else would procure it, I would again enter a canal-boat. I am reminded of what Lord Byron said, — that hearing Mrs. Siddons had disqualified him from enjoying the theatre forever. We came from Stonington to Providence, and from Providence to Boston, ninety miles, in three hours and fifty minutes. Had the ears bolted from the track, or butted upon it, no righteousness would have saved us. . . .

Territorially, how insignificant Massachusetts appears to me ! It is not large enough for a door-yard for the West. Rhode Island always seemed to me very minute, compared with Massachusetts ; and I remember that one of my brother-collegians at Providence, who was offended at something there, once threatened to *shovel* it into the ocean ! but, as compared with that trans-Alleghanie world (of which there is enough to make a planet), there is not much difference between the two. But, as you say, every thing is by comparison ; or, more classically, " smallness is as peoples thinks." . . . I found all things had subsided into accustomed quiet or torpor in relation to the Board of Education. The universal forces of society are all concentrated upon a revival in religion, or a change in the administration. Distant and foreign events are said to have charms for our people. If so, the cause of education should begin to have attractions for them ; for I hardly know of any thing more distant or foreign to them than that. . . .

Well, my dear friends, I must bid you farewell. Had I control over the laws of Nature, I should fill not only the month of June, but all the rest of your days, with special providences in your behalf. Farewell again ; and whatever words are the strongest to express my esteem and affection, consider me as saying them.

HORACE MANN.

May 10. I arrived in Boston a week since, after a journey of three thousand miles. In Philadelphia I parted with Mr. Combe, who seems to me to understand, far better than any other man I ever saw, the principles on which the human race has been formed, and by following which their most sure and rapid advancement would be secured. I have never been acquainted with a mind which handled such great subjects with such ease, and, as it appears to me, with such justness. · He has constantly gratified my strongest faculties. The world knows him not. In the next century, I have no doubt, he will be looked back upon as the greatest man of the present. But he has a mind fitted for this extensive range. I have no doubt it would cause him great pain, were he to believe that his name would never emerge into celebrity : but he has an extent of thought by which the next age is now present to him, and he sees that his persecuted and contemned views will then be triumphant ; and, with that assurance, he can forego contemporary applause. Let me, too, labor for something more enduring than myself.

May 23. Another Abstract of school returns to be prepared, and, of course, an enormous amount of labor to be done ; but to this I go with good heart, knowing the wonder-working power of diligence.

The Governor said that he had not been satisfied with the course of the Board in relation to the library. The act creating them was very general. It made it their duty to attend to education in all its parts. He did not know but that the act would authorize them to take measures for the military education of the people. The form of approval adopted by the Board seemed to carry us back a century or two. It approximates to a license. If it were a new question, he should be opposed. It looks like the old black-letter licenses. He could not sanction it without compromising his own rights. He professed not to wish to injure those who had embarked in it ; was willing it should continue, if it could be done without the names ; was very much in favor of libraries.

The second day, Mr. Hudson called him out by saying that it seemed useless to discuss questions about altering the form of the sanction of the Board, until it was known how far the objections of any member went, whether to the present form only, or to the whole plan. To this the Governor replied, that he doubted the right and the propriety of the Board giving any recommendation to books; and he read part of a letter which he had prepared to send to the publishers, which was as follows : " I must decline to give my official sanction to any book which has been or may be presented to the Board " !

After this, a modification became indispensable. Thus has the most excellent plan of the Board, in relation to this most important subject, been defeated.

WRENTHAM, June 11, 1840.

MY DEAR FRIEND, — I received your former letter while I was putting up lightning-conductors to draw off the electricity from that cloud that had been raised against the Board. For a few days, I assure you there was not much leisure; and finally, as you know, the moral paragreles drew off the elements of fanaticism and mammon with which it was bursting. . . . I should be glad if I could make you see that this cause is wholly a practical one, and that all advancement in it is to be accomplished by human means, and not by transcendentalism; but it is hard, after all, to correct any one's mistakes, when those mistakes come from having higher, purer, more disinterested feelings than belong to the rest of mankind.

I was much interested in the story you told me of the young lady at the Normal school. I rejoice that the motive to do right prevailed; though I think it was the absence of intellectual light that gave such an aspect to the subject. The higher sentiments run into mistakes almost as easily as the propensities. Intellect and knowledge are equally necessary for the guidance of both. You have adverted to another subject, on which, perhaps, I ought to say a word. You left it at my discretion to do as I thought best about presenting your note to the Board. I exercised that discretion, but said nothing to you at the time, because I felt it would be impossible to make you see all the inherent difficulties with which the subject was surrounded. I strained my head and heart for three months last spring, and almost brought on insanity or idiocy, to obviate the difficulties, to allay the prejudices, to harmonize the oppositions, which encompassed that enterprise. I had the assistance of no mortal in it all. Nay, some, who ought to have aided me, almost openly blamed me that I did not at once make a perfect man, as God made Adam, and set him over·the school, without any salary.

But the Normal School has "got to going," and will go at some time, though this attempt should fail: but it never would go without more or less of these obstacles; and I feel glad, therefore, that the *pioneering* has been done. . . . If you have leisure, a good use you can make of part of it would be in writing to me. I have much that I would say to you, had I time; but a printing-press is roaring behind me, and I must say good-by.

Affectionately as ever,

II. M.

Aug. 9. I have only to record that yesterday I had the last proof of the Abstract. That great work, therefore, with the exception of the Index, Report, &c., is done; a labor in which I have almost died within the last ten weeks. I now resolve never to undertake to do so much work in so short a time again. It is a violation of the natural and organic laws: these are wisely framed, and it is unwise to disregard them.

This kind of resolve was, perhaps, the only kind that Mr. Mann never kept. He always did the work that presented itself, let it cost him what it might; and was often so prostrated by his exertions, — which were always ardently made, and with his whole soul, — that his friends feared he would wholly disable himself. I proceed with extracts from his journal, that the world may know that his office was no sinecure. He continued to lecture several times a week from this date.

Aug. 29. Lectured extempore at Holmes Hole, owing to the peculiarities of the place; then at Nantucket, at New Bedford, at the convention. An extempore lecture at Westport to a small audience. A hundred citizens went from New Bedford to Westport to hear a political address a few evenings ago, which is exceedingly flattering to my self-esteem, and love of approbation. But I must take my pay, not out of those organs, but out of conscientiousness and benevolence : these are long-lived powers, and shall stand when the day of the others is passed away forever. This county is one of the dark spots of the earth. I would ·pray most heartily for the success of the convention to-morrow, but am satisfied that success, if it comes at all, must come from works, not prayers. Politics have absorbed every thing else here. The idea of effecting political reforms by reforming the sources whence all evils proceed seems not to have entered the minds of this people.

Sept. 10. Tuesday, the convention at Bridgewater ; which, considering all circumstances, was pretty fair. Wednesday, we launched the Bridgewater Normal School. How much depends upon its success ! Last evening, I returned to give the last touch to the Abstract. A better work on the subject never has appeared, as I believe, in any language. It cannot but do immense good ; and half a century hence, I predict, it will be looked upon as one of the most interesting documents of the age. Now it will excite no notice except in a few minds ; unless, indeed, some bad persons may seize upon it as a means of mischief.*

Sept. 15. Wellfleet: a miserable, contemptible, deplorable convention. This morning, on arriving, I found that not the slightest thing had been done by way of arrangement ; absolutely nothing. To-morrow I will shake the dust from off my feet in regard to this place. Thus far I have found things in a deplorable condition in this county. How will it be ten years hence ? Such a state of things was not to be anticipated anywhere in Massachusetts. But I see every day how much is to be done. On Wednesday, the 16th, I came, through Eastham, Orleans, and Brewster, to Dennis. Visited several schools and schoolhouses, and found both schools and schoolhouses very miserable. Lectured in the evening ; making four successive evenings of lecturing. Thursday, went to South Dennis to see if any interest could be found or inspired there. . . . Visited a school where the intellectual exercises were wretched in the extreme : returned, and visited another

* This Abstract was compiled from the written reports of every school committee in the State.

in the afternoon with but little more satisfaction. At evening came to Yarmouth : called on Mr. ———, with whom I did not feel very good-natured, on account of his want of interest in the schools. Thus ends the Cape tour, with all the good in prospect.

Sept. 30. Had a meagre convention last week at Barre. Politics are the idol which the people have gone after, and the true gods must go without worship. The President of the County Association, and of the American Institute of Instruction, saw fit to stay away. When those who heretofore have professed the greatest interest in the cause, and who seem bound to support it by their official relations, fall off, I must do so much the more, — both their part and my own.

Yesterday I closed up affairs for Franklin County by a convention most miserable in point of numbers ; almost all of the principal men of the village going out of it to attend a political convention at Deerfield. Surely, if I were not proof against slights, neglects, and mortifications, I should abandon this cause in despair. But it is this indifference which makes perseverance a virtue. Did I meet with universal encouragement and sympathy, the work would be so delightful as to repay exertions as fast as they were made. It is these neglects that put me to the proof ; and I will stand that proof. Yet who could have believed beforehand that such men as ———, ———, ———, ———, &c., would have left the Common-school Convention in their own town to go abroad to a political one ?

Oct. 1. Pittsfield. Visited a school in Lanesborough ; then came here, and visited two more. To-morrow is the day of the convention, when I am to appear before somebody perhaps, but probably very few. All causes prosper more than the greatest of all ; and everybody is more ready to hear of subordinate and temporary interests than of primary and permanent ones. If it is not my mission to change this state of things, it is to commence a change of proceedings which will one day result in a change.

Oct. 2. The day of shame is over. At ten o'clock, the time appointed for the convention, not an individual had come into the place. At half-past eleven, eight or ten made their appearance from other towns, who, with about a dozen on the spot, constituted the convention. This afternoon, I lectured to about a dozen women and some hundred men; and, immediately after I got through, the company dispersed like a flock of birds that have been shot into. To-morrow I shall shake the mud (it will probably be rainy) from off my feet, and leave this place, — so dark, that it puts light out before it reaches it. For Westfield to-morrow, where I have some hopes of a better time.

Oct 1, 1840.

MY DEAR MR. COMBE, — . . . You ask me to express my opinion about your "Moral Philosophy." I have no hesitation in saying it is worthy of you. That it should be equal to the "Constitution of Man" was impossible. There can be but one discovery of the circulation of the blood, or of the solar system, or of the identity of electricity and lightning; and so there can be but one author of the "Constitution of Man." He or others may apply its principles to facts, and to new combinations of facts; but the great discoverer must stand unequalled by himself or by others. Your applications of the subject to criminal legislation, jurisprudence, &c., will in time, I have no doubt, work revolutions in those departments, but not until the general mind has become imbued and saturated with the true philosophy.

The political excitement of this country is increasing in intensity beyond all former parallel. The air has become a non-conductor to all sounds except such as come from the politician's mouth, and the light ceases to be reflected except to the politician's eye; or rather, without accusing Nature of any departure from her established usages, there seems to be neither ear nor eye for any thing but politics. People are running to and fro; but I fear the great misfortune is that *knowledge does not increase.* I endeavored, with the use of all my previous knowledge, to appoint my school conventions so that I might pass between the drops; but, behold! the political conventions come, not in drops, but in a sheet which it is impossible to escape. All seems to indicate that Gen. Harrison will be our next President. . . . The consequence of so fierce a contest between the parties is, that they are ready to sacrifice any thing to gain a vote:

they seem not to look beyond the next election ; that is, to them, the day of judgment. For the sake of getting the Catholic votes in New York, the Governor of that State has suggested that the Catholic sect should have their proportion of the school-money distributed by the State, to expend under their own direction, and, of course, for the propagation, not of secular knowledge (so to call it), but of religious instruction ; and the Secretary of State, who in New York is, *ex officio*, superintendent of the common schools, is advocating the same cause.

You asked me to make suggestions in relation to subjects proper to be treated in your Journal. I know of nothing by which you will be likely to do more good, both here and at home, than by explaining at full length, so as to make it intelligible to all Americans, what obstacles the cause of general education has encountered, and is encountering, in Great Britain, especially in England, through the bigotry of the religionists (*lucus a non lucendo*) in resisting all measures which do not emanate from, or cannot be controlled by, them ; in showing how the spirit of our laws forbids this sectarian interference ; and commenting in proper terms upon the efforts of fanatics to infuse their peculiar dogmas into the great subject of education, and the iniquity of politicians who favor their schemes for political effect. . . .

Farewell, dear Mr. and Mrs. Combe ! If my prayers had any efficacy, the only bounds to your prosperity and happiness would be your power to possess and enjoy them.

Ever and affectionately yours,

HORACE MANN.

At this period, Mr. Mann's phraseology concerning mental operations underwent a striking change, due to his interest in the phrenological science and philosophy. It somewhat mars the gracefulness of his speech ; but there was a peculiar pleasure to him in giving a definite expression to his ideas upon a subject which he felt to be satisfactorily cleared up by that mental nomenclature. Some of his friends used to tease him a little for having adopted this mode of expression from his excellent friend Mr. Combe; but he would reply, that he had been so long bothered by metaphysicians and their systems, that he enjoyed speaking wide of them all. He did not come to all Mr. Combe's conclusions, nor was he bound by his limitations; but he enjoyed that philosophy which recognized the adaptation of every faculty to its appropriate object. It simplified to him the whole theory of mental phenomena.

BOSTON, Nov. 8, 1840.

G. COMBE, Esq., Slateford, Scotland. *My very dear Friend,* — . . . I come to a point which I never thought would arise in my intercourse with you. From my earliest acquaintance with you, our relations have been established upon the basis of friendship. I have felt, and still feel, all, and more than all that I have expressed; and now the occasion which tests sincere friendship, the real *casus fœderis*, as the diplomatists call it, has come. Both Dr. H. and myself are disappointed in your Journal. How much of it comes from our expectations being unduly raised, we are unable to say; but, on a careful review of the grounds of our opinion, we cannot change it. That yours is superior to the common class of journals, we might admit: but mere superiority is not what will be expected of you; nay, demanded; nay, what you will be punished by public opinion for not producing. The author of the "Constitution of Man" cannot write commonplaces and truisms, and give a description of the mere outside of society, with impunity. Public expectation is a hard taskmaster, and will punish him for omission as well as for commission. We ventured to surmise that you must have kept a note-book of your goings from place to place, and of daily events, and which you have, to a great extent, copied. The consequence is, that careless memoranda, made from day to day when the mind was absorbed in other things, came forth as the product of the greatest reasoning faculties, and impressions early received are left uncorrected by a greater extent of observation and more just deductions from it. . . . This leads also not only to the juxtaposition of the most heterogeneous things, but makes the transition from one to the other bewilderingly rapid. Where entries are so strikingly foreign to each other, each one must have some recommendation of its own. It is like a jest-book, where each witticism or epigram must commend itself, and seems only the worse for having a good one above and below it. Had you thrown all that relates to your course of phrenological lectures in Boston under one head, and all the public institutions, the manners of the people, &c., under different heads, there would have been not only a continuity of subject, but you could not now, in your leisure and retirement, bring all the facts under your causality and comparison at once, without valuable philosophizing or moralizing. But taking up these things in detail and by fragments excludes the very things in which your strength lies; and, like Samson, you are shorn of your locks. A volatile, pert, flippant traveller will describe everyday trivialities better than you; but when the machinery of the universe gets out of order, then comes the *dignus vindice nodus.* Now, where social institutions are not wisely established, or where the manners and customs, and the tone of feeling that pervades society, among a people whose law is public opinion, are wrong, then the machinery is out of order, and those who can both perceive how it is, and how it should be, are commissioned to set it right. But I will not dwell on this topic. I am sure you will pardon what I have stated, even if wrong, because of the motive from which it comes. A regard for yourself, and for the great good which your other works can do, if not obscured by this, has prompted what I have said.*

Gen. Harrison, as you will learn by this conveyance, if not before, is to be our next President. Our State Legislature is entirely different from the last. The author of the movement against the Board was dropped by common consent, as the reward of his malevolence. . . .

Give my best regards to Mrs. Combe. Oh! you cannot tell how much I wish to see and hear you again. Command my services to any extent; and believe me most truly and faithfully yours, HORACE MANN.

* See Mr. Combe's reply in Appendix.

Dec. 20. Have been engaged mainly this week with a long article for the first number of the third volume of the "Common-school Journal." It contains some truths which it is desirable to send abroad; but whether they will prove to be in an unexceptionable form, is the question. I shall submit them to their fate, believing them to be true, and to contain no just ground of offence.

In this introduction, Mr. Mann shows how forcibly his mind had been led, by the " wild roar of party politics " of that year, to look into the secret springs of public action ; and how futile is the attempt to " define truth by law, and to perpetuate it by power and wealth, instead of knowledge." He closes it in these words, which apply equally to our own times : — .

. To the patriot, then, who desires the well-being of his nation ; to the philanthropist, who labors for the happiness of his race ; to the Christian, who includes both worlds in his comprehensive survey, — is not the path of duty clear and radiant ? Is it not the duty of the wise and good of all parties to forget their personal animosities and contentions ; to strike the banners of party ; to unfurl a flag of truce ; to come together, and unite in rearing new institutions, or in giving new efficiency to old ones, for the diffusion of useful knowledge, for the creation of intellectual ability, for the cultivation of the spirit of concord ; for giving to those who are to come after us better means of discovering truth, higher powers of advocating it, stronger resolutions of obedience to it, than we have ever enjoyed, possessed, or felt ? For clamor and convulsion and persecution, for the " wind " and the " earthquake " and the " fire," in which the spirit of God does not dwell, may not the past suffice ? and for the future, can we not listen to the " still small voice " of reason and conscience ?

. . . By a rational and conscientious use of the means put into our hands, an era may be ushered in, when the appearance of such a spirit as animated a Howard, a Washington, and a Wilberforce, will no longer be deemed a prodigy, and to be accounted for only on supernatural principles.

If there must be institutions, associations, combinations, amongst men, whose tendency is to alienation and discord, to whet the angry feelings of individuals against each other, to transmit the contentions of the old to the young, and to make the enmities of the dead survive to the living, — if these things must continue to be in a land calling itself Christian, let there be one institution, at least, which shall be sacred from the ravages of the spirit of party, one spot in the wide land unblasted by the fiery breath of animosity. . . . Let there be one rallying-point for a peaceful and harmonious co-operation and fellowship, where all the good may join in the most beneficent of labors. The young do not come into life barbed and fanged against each other. . . .

The common school is the institution which can receive and train up children in the elements of all good knowledge and of virtue before they are subjected to the alienating competitions of life. This institution is the greatest discovery ever made by man : we repeat it, *the common school is the greatest discovery ever made by man.* In two grand, characteristic attributes, it is supereminent over all others : first, in its universality, for it is capacious enough to receive and cherish in its parental bosom every child that comes into the world ; and, second, in the timeliness of the aid it proffers, — its early, seasonable supplies of counsel and guidance making security antedate danger. Other social organizations are curative and remedial : this is a preventive and an antidote. They come to heal diseases and wounds ; this, to make the physical and moral frame invulnerable to them. Let the common school be expanded to its capabilities, let it be worked with the efficiency of which it is susceptible, and nine-tenths of the crimes in the penal code would become obsolete ; the long catalogue of human ills would be abridged ; men would walk more safely by day ; every pillow would be more inviolable by night ; property, life, and character held by a stronger tenure ; all rational hopes respecting the future brightened.

Do not these words apply as well to the changed circumstances of our country, when a new field is so suddenly and wonderfully opened for the benign influences

of education, and when the subjects of its beneficence
spring forward to meet its benefits with such intensity of
aspiration, — an aspiration that. it is true, sees only vague-
ly all the good that is to come from it, but with a faith
that will "remove mountains:" when the North seems
to be resolving itself, directly and indirectly, into one
great Educational Commission, to make up by enthusiasm, and efficiency of labor, the work of a century in our
country's annals?

After the establishment of the Board of Education in
Massachusetts, Mr. Mann was the constant recipient of
letters from philanthropic and enlightened individuals
of the South, inquiring of him what could be done to
extend the blessings of common-school education to that
benighted region, where a few aristocrats monopolized all
the advantages wealth and culture could give, leaving
wide-spread regions, inhabited by their own Anglo-Saxon
race, a prey to the night and misery of ignorance; but
neither he nor they, when they reasoned upon it, could
see any light to their path in that latitude. But the
day-spring has come; and, by one of those astounding
retorts of Nature before which the machinations of man
sometimes stand aghast, an oppressed and down-trodden
race, whose aspirations for knowledge have hitherto been
suppressed by legal enactments, bids fair to rise in its
might, and be the superiors and instructors of the enslaved white men of the South,— no less enslaved, because
indirectly so, than themselves. Before they have well
shaken off the gyves that bound them, the negroes rush to
the fountains of knowledge to slake that undying thirst
which the Creator has planted in every soul, and which
they appreciate as yet only because it has been forcibly
withheld from them. Can the youth of a generation have
a nobler work before them, or indeed a more grateful

task, than to answer with all their stores of culture to such a noble aspiration? Party politics, which are always subversive of the best interests of society, will in future have little basis left in our land, when all its interests are for advancement and freedom; and we may now reasonably look forward to the day when the best men will not feel themselves degraded by entering into the political arena, no longer the arena of slavery and ignorance against liberty and light, but that of generous emulation to discover the best modes of ameliorating human life. One necessary condition of perfection is imperfection; and there will be enough for man to do to emulate the creative spirit of God after the equal rights of all men before universal law are secured, as the first stepping-stone in the ascent from the babe to the archangel.

A fire has long been smouldering in the souls of good men, which is now consuming the stubble of selfishness and the monopoly of God-given rights. It raged fiercely within that of Mr. Mann, and kindled hope and faith in him that the earth would before long quake and swallow the oppressor, or purify him as fire only can. " Oh that I could live a hundred years ! " was his oft-repeated exclamation. He wished to see the breaking of the great seals with his own eyes, and to help in the breaking.

BOSTON, Jan. 1, 1841.

I wish you, my dear friends, Mr. and Mrs. Combe, a happy New Year; yea, many of them, and very happy. I received, by the "Acadia," your welcome letter of Dec. 1, and the accompanying packages. The one addressed to Mr. Hart was forwarded as soon as it could be obtained from the hands of Uncle Sam, who, considering the amount of his business and the number of his acquaintances, is certainly the greatest uncle I ever had.

Oh! how many times I have asked myself, What will the philosopher say when he reads the letter of Dr. H. and myself on his first volume? Will he not exclaim, not merely "*Et tu, Brute!*" but "*Et vos Bruti!*" the first exclamation being usually translated, you know, "Oh, you brute!" But, if you have the power of Cæsar, you also have his clemency. If it is the seal of friendship to speak out all one's thoughts of a friend to himself, did we not stamp the impression ineffaceably deep? I have read the second volume, and it is much superior to the first. You have emerged from the gastric and sensuous region of the common tourist, and the great light of Causality begins to shine. This volume has merits enough to be self-subsistent, though I can hardly say that it will also be able to sustain the first. If the third rises above the second, as the second does above the first, all nations will cry out, "Lord, give us a fourth, and take the first away!" I have marked some errors, but they are mostly trivial; though it is well to be perfect where we can. Massachusetts has not had a State lottery, I think, for twenty years. In our revised statutes, you will see how throughly we try to smoke the vermin out. They are forever prohibited by the New-York Constitution. . . . And now I am doubly glad that I have closed the list of exceptions, — glad because they are done, and glad because I have done them honestly and faithfully, as I trust you would do to me, if I were the philosopher, and you a humble disciple. I will only add, that, a few days ago, Dr. Channing spoke very cordially of you to Dr. Howe and myself, and referred with interest to the forthcoming books; saying, very decidedly, that he hoped they would not come in the form of a journal, for that you had great power to treat of this country in a philosophical way, but that he lacked confidence in your journalizing skill; and he earnestly entreated Dr. Howe and myself to dissuade you from adopting that form of presenting yourself to the public. We concurred with him, to some extent, in his general views, but kept *mum* as a deaf mute on the subject of our special enlightenment. A rumor is in circulation that you are preparing a book, and a late evening paper announced that it was now in the Philadelphia press. Whence it came we do not know; for we have been secretive as death.

I do not think you have any thing to fear from the general manner in which you have spoken of this country thus far. If your conscience is satisfied, our people ought to be. I have often been asked what opinion you formed of the United States. I have replied, with an idea which I think you can expand, that of our *possibilities* you think every thing; of our *actualities*, not very much. And it seems to me this is the true view of the subject. An expansion of the ideas contained in your last lecture in regard to this country would make a glorious chapter.

I cannot say that I think our Presidential contests tend to unite this wide-spread people by any useful bond of sympathy or practical improvement. In the last few years, our contests have resembled those at Rome between the partisans of Marius, Sylla, Cinna, &c.; only that our soldiers use votes instead of arms.

In regard to education, I want you to look as much as your time will allow into the Abstract which I sent you, especially at the Reports of Roxbury, Charlestown, Harvard, Brookfield, Grafton, and Northfield. Allow me also to remind you of what I have said, in my Second and Third Reports, as to the dependence of the prosperity of the schools on the public intelligence; that the people will sustain no better schools, and have no better education, than they personally see the need of; and therefore that the people are to be informed and elevated, as a preliminary step towards elevating the schools. And then, further, you will look at the machinery by which it is done. The Secretary, by travelling round the State, by correspondence and interviews, obtains all the knowledge he can respecting existing defects and practicable improvements. He communicates this information to the Board: from them it goes to the Legislature, by whom it is printed, and sent into every school district of the State. Then the committee of each town is obliged to make a Report to the town, a copy of which comes back into the hands of the Board; and from these Reports the Annual Abstract is made. See also two Reports prefixed to the Abstracts of 1838–9 and of 1839–40. This is the machinery; and such a forcing-pump was never invented before: it only wants to be used vigorously, and it will inject blood into every vein and artery of the body politic. A long article on the subject appears in the "North-American Review" to-day. If possible, I shall get a copy to send to you to-morrow by the "Acadia;" if not, you can find one in Edinburgh. It was written by our friend and your most earnest disciple, George B. Emerson.

I have read Guizot. It is a great book.

Mr. Pierpont's case is still *in fieri*. He has published another letter, every word of which is a porcupine's quill. . . .

Farewell, and blessings attend you both.

HORACE MANN.

Jan. 17. The Board of Education has met. I have read a very long Report, which, like all my others, has not been well received. I must suppose they are better judges than I am, and that the Reports have no merit. Some people, I find, are disposed to give them some credit. I hope they will do good, and that will supersede all other considerations. In two days, they will probably be sent to the Legislature. That makes them public property, to be treated as political men may desire.

Feb. 7. Still troubled by a strong congestion of blood in the head, which has now oppressed the brain and sense for several weeks, owing to too severe mental labor. I must obey the natural laws. The power which I resist in disregarding them is more than a match for me. Not one particle of punishment is foregone; and the only way, therefore, to avoid, is not to incur.

Feb. 21. A minority of the Committee on Education, in the House, have reported a bill to transfer the powers and duties of the Board of Education to the Governor and Council; and of the Secretary, to the Secretary of State. Thus another blow is aimed at our existence, and by men who would prefer that good. should not be done, rather than that it should be done by men whose views on religious subjects differ from their own. The validity of their claim to Christianity is in the inverse ratio to the claim itself: they claim the whole, but possess nothing.

Feb. 28. The bill to transfer the powers of the Board, &c., has not yet come up, but probably will to-morrow, when we shall see how many have any adequate appreciation of this great subject, and hence how much work is yet to be done: for the work is, to make all adequately appreciate it ; and, until that is accomplished, the work is *not* done.

MY DEAR MR. COMBE, — The third volume of your work is decidedly superior to the second ; and you already know my opinion of that, as compared with the first.   Your views on American civilization are sound and judicious, and written in a spirit of philosophic candor, which constitutes one of the great excellences of all your writings, and which will give you a greater power over antagonistic opinions than any previous philosopher has ever possessed.   There is but one striking departure from this rule ; and, indeed, it is the only important one, so far as I recollect, in all your works. . . . The address, also, will make a deep impression upon the public mind here.   I have always thought it was a most able view of the subject ; and it is conceived in a truly dignified and noble spirit, and expressed with great clearness and force. . . . There is much that is valuable in it, and that which we should all care most about, — there is that which will do great good.

Perhaps I ought, in a formal and explicit manner, to thank you for the mention you have so frequently made of me in the progress of the work ; but no selfish and personal regard which I can possibly have for you will ever bear any proportion to that general esteem and reverence which is founded on the imperishable basis of your mind and works.   Indeed, I have regretted to find myself the subject of such frequent commendation, because it will have the effect both to diminish my opportunities to speak of you as you deserve, and will impair the authority (if any) or the force of my encomiums when given, as people may say that I extol you because I have myself been praised.   But this is past.   You can yet help my mind, as you have hitherto done ; and whenever it is in my power to render you a service, remember, I am ready.

In regard to the Abstract, of which you speak so favorably, I entirely agree with those whose judgment is better than my own, that there is no such work extant ; nor do I believe there is more than one other community where men capable of preparing the materials of such a work could be found.

We have no "rural districts," independent of towns, each one of which is a body politic and corporate, with power to elect officers, levy taxes, &c. . . .

It is remarkable, that, at the very time that I am receiving your congratulations on the prosperity and security of my plans to improve our popular education, my friends in the General Court are preparing to fight another battle for their existence. D——, who was among the foremost in the attack last year, has returned to the assault again with as much virulence as ever. It so happens that retrenchment of expenses is the popular hobby this year; and both parties are running a race for the laurel of economy, and are willing to sacrifice all the laurels of the State to win it. The question will come on for discussion to-morrow or next day. We all think it cannot be carried through the Senate, if, unfortunately, it should pass the House. But are not reformers always persecuted?

It gives me pain to think, that, in a short time, another sea will roll between us; but there is that in our hearts that neither seas nor continents can sever. Please present my kindest regards to Mrs. Combe. I wish she could have enjoyed our winter, which has been unusually mild and delightful. Ever yours,

HORACE MANN.

March 28. . . . My health is rather gaining. How I long for a body of power to execute the purposes of the will! I intend to try an absence from the tumult and excitements of the city, and see if the lowering of the tone of the brain will not lead to improvement. My nervous is evidently predominating over all my other systems; losing in strength, but gaining in excitability. Oh, give me health! I have resolution enough of my own.

April 28. Attended the examination of the Normal School at Lexington, which was very satisfactory. The school is doing well, —very well. The experiment is succeeding. Whether it will have time to commend itself to the favorable opinion of the public, is what cannot now be determined.

It is a remarkable fact, which shows how society is divided into *strata*, that at this time, when the success of the Normal School was one day mentioned to a cultivated and wealthy Boston lady, she inquired what it meant, never having heard of it! This is mentioned to show how little many of the wealthier class of society, even in Boston, cared for any reforms or interests out of the circle of their visiting-cards; and makes more credible the apathy Mr. Mann found in all places in reference to an interest which he felt to be so vital to the Republic as thorough common-school education.

BOSTON, April 1, 1841.

GEORGE COMBE, ESQ. *My dear Mr. Combe,* — . . . Since I wrote you by the steamer on the 1st of March, your "Notes" have been published. What I have heard in private circles is commendatory; and, had they been written by one of less reputation, it would have been high praise. But your other works had created an expectation which it would require an extraordinary book to answer. The public is a hard taskmaster. It will not allow a man to fall below himself with impunity. Its demands run with extraordinary facility from the positive degree to the superlative. The exceptions are, however, more to the form than to the substance; the contents of the chapters being so very heterogeneous. There is no continuity, no attraction of cohesion: but it is thought to treat our institutions with a great degree of candor and fairness; and the two last chapters are regarded as very valuable, and in every respect worthy of the author. It is also thought to be a book highly appropriate and serviceable to the British public. . . .

In my last I stated that another attack was made upon the Board of Education in our House of Representatives. Its decision was postponed till very near the close of the session; and it came up in the afternoon, and before a very thin house, half the members being absent. Mr. Shaw made a few remarks in defence: when the bigot D—— followed in a speech of an hour's length, the whole intellectual part of which was made up of misrepresentations; and the whole emotive part, of aspersion. The previous question was then moved and sustained; many of the Whigs voting for it, in order to shorten the session (which has been the Whig hobby this year) : and, without one word being said in reply, the proposition was voted down, — 131 to 114. Never was any question taken under circumstances more disadvantageous to the prevailing party ; and I am inclined to think that it will be considered, in flash language, a *settler*. . . . My kindest regards to Mrs. Combe. If I had any influence in the councils above, I would pray most devoutly that God would bless you both.

Very truly and affectionately yours,

H. MANN.

June 13. On Thursday, after my return from a long absence, I commenced in good earnest the examination of the Reports of the School Committees, in order to make selections from them for the Abstract. So far, they are excellent, and will furnish materials for another glorious document. I read them with real delight. And thus has begun my summer's work, — reading reports, many of which are almost illegible; examining returns, all of which ought to balance, but many of which cannot be made to ; and, in the end, reading proofs of the whole, — a year's work, to be crowded into three months, — a pleasant prospect for hot days !

July 29. To-morrow will furnish me with the last proof of the Abstract. Thus perseverance is putting its seal of consummation on another great work. So let it be. Every one of these will raise a wave of feeling in favor of the cause of education, which will not subside till the end of time.

Sept. 14. To-day I have been to Lowell, and have had a very pleasant interview with Mr. Clark and Mr. Bartlett, superintendents of some of the largest establishments in that city, on the subject of the superiority of educated as contrasted with uneducated people, in the amount and value of their products of labor. My object is to show that education has a market value ; that it is so far an article of merchandise, that it may be turned to a pecuniary account : it may be minted, and will yield a larger amount of statutable coin than common bullion. It has a pecuniary value, a price current. Intellectual and moral education are powers not only insuring superior respectability and happiness, but yielding returns of silver and gold. This is my idea. Questions founded on these views I have put to them; and they have been answered in a way attesting this value of education, beyond my expectations.

To MISSES R. AND E. PENNELL (pupils of Normal School). *My dear Nieces*, — I shall enclose the money for your bills; and I do it most cheerfully, for I trust you will get a great deal more good from it than the mere money is worth. Indeed, as money merely, it is worth nothing; but, as a means of improvement, I hope it will produce a hundred, or at least sixty fold.

If you are reading "Brigham on Mental Excitement," you must take care of your own excitement. If you get much excited in studying how to prevent excitement, you will be as badly off as the man who put out his eyes studying optics. I shall never cease to give you admonitions about your health, having lost so many years of my own life through the want of a little knowledge and attention, which I could so easily have acquired and applied.

We were all very much pleased with the appearance of the school on the day when we visited you. Dr. Howe speaks of it often. We think you have the very best instructor,* — one who is worthy of all your confidence.

I do not think you need any impulse to greater diligence or effort. What young ladies usually lack most is self-possession, — the power of using and commanding their faculties on emergencies, or on occasions when inconstant minds will be thrown off their balance. Very many persons can do what they would when alone or with their friends; but, when exposed to observation, they are disconcerted and frustrated, and become ninnies, though it is the exact time when they most need calmness and equanimity. How unfortunate it would be, could you keep ever so good a school, if, as soon as the committee or strangers made their appearance, your senses should take French leave, throwing you into a cataleptic fit! This misfortune comes from having the organ of cautiousness, or of love of approbation, too much excited, so that they absorb the whole forces

---

* Rev. Cyrus Pierce, now deceased.

of the mind, and leave nothing by which the other faculties can be worked. But this, bad as it is, is *beauty* compared with the boldness which comes from self-esteem. You will find that to keep the balance of the faculties is the greatest of all desiderata. It is that which makes the perfect man. For the great object of self-possession, you ought always to be able to say to yourself, " I have done as well as I could. I know my motives are good. I believe that the world is so constituted, that good motives, with a moderate endowment of intellect, will enable their possessor to produce great benefits, and always to be worthy the esteem of good men. Where motives are right, and the intellect is clear (even though it be not very strong), there is no occasion for any very intense activity of cautiousness ; and therefore I will command my powers, and keep down too great anxiety." In this way you can learn to stand on your feet when there is nothing but the glance of a human eye to throw you off your poise. . . .

Yours very affectionately,

H. M.

Boston, Oct. 13, 1841.

My dear Mr. Combe, — Before I attempt to tell you how welcome and dear was your letter of July 16, to which Mrs. Combe was so kind as to add a postscript in her own hand, — beautiful gilt edging to massive silver plate, — I must first explain my own long silence. . . . During the month of September, I was absent from the city on my annual circuit ; but I expected to return in season to write you by the steamship which sailed on the 1st of this month. Before my return, however, an unusual confluence of fatigues, anxieties, and efforts overpowered all my strength ; and in that state some villanous tavern-keeper smuggled a little poisonous food into my port of entry, which immediately caused infinite mischief throughout the internal economy of my kingdom. If I were in a moralizing mood, I should say, How strange it is that this paragon of Nature, this lord of all below, this being whose thoughts wander up and down through eternity, can be extinguished, annihilated, by a slice of bad bread ! Now, I hope this account (having no flesh to lose, I was reduced to mere cellular tissue) will present me before you *rectus in curiâ* : although I am not without fear that your causality will compel you to look one step back in the order of events, and find my offence, not in the sickness, but in the causes that induced it ; just as the law holds an intoxicated man responsible for an act done in the state of intoxication, not because he knew better when he committed it, but because he knew better when he incurred the hazard of committing it ; he being, as my Lord Coke says, *voluntarius demon*. Well, if so, I can only say, I have now suffered the penalty ; and, thus having expiated the offence, I ought to be restored to my rights.

By the way, you know Graham, the author of the teetotal, anti-carnivorous system known by his name. He resides at Northampton, in this State. Last year he was dangerously ill ; and the first labor to which he devoted himself after his recovery was the writing of several long articles for a newspaper as an apology for his illness, in which he endeavored to vindicate his system from the odium of the malady, and himself from the guilt of being principal or accessory to its perpetration. It occasioned considerable quiet ridicule at the time ; but I confess I felt rather disposed to commend the course, believing it far more rational than the common mode of appealing to minister and congregation to offer public thanksgivings for a recovery from the consequences of misconduct, when not even a scant resolution of amendment enters into the public displays of gratitude.

Your account of the social manifestations of the German mind is most interesting. Though brief, yet it is an outline sketch from one standing on an eminence, and who sees outside and around the object he delineates. I availed myself of the liberty you gave to show your letter to many persons, to whom it has given great delight. At the time I read it, I was reading Miss Sedgewick's "Letters from Abroad," and that part of it in which she describes Godesberg, your then place of residence. The strong sympathy I have for her, and my affection for you, made the coincidence very pleasant. Have you seen her letters ? She is indeed a noble woman. Humanity exhales from her whole being. Her benevolence, conscientiousness, and reverence will not suffer any scene to be left, or any discussion to be closed, until they have expressed their reflections upon it. . . .

I perceive, with unbounded pleasure, that the "Constitution of Man" has had a sale wholly unprecedented in the history of scientific works. As demonstrating a spirit of inquiry on this class of subjects, and the adoption of the best means to gratify it, this fact is most cheering to those who wait for the coming of the intellectual Messiah. . . . Its views must be penetrating the whole mass of mind as silently and latently indeed as the heat, but as powerfully as that for productiveness and renovation. What constitutes a broader and deeper channel for the diffusion of these truths is that they are reproducing themselves in the minds of liberal clergymen, and hence are welling out from the pulpit, and overflowing the more barren portions of society. A Unitarian clergyman told me last week that he had just preached a sermon drawn from your "Moral Philosophy," and had been complimented for it by his parishioners. If once the doctrine of the natural laws can get possession of the minds of men, then causality will become a mighty ally in the contest for their deliverance from sin as well as from error. As yet, in the history of man, causality has been almost a supernumerary faculty : the idea of special providences or interventions, the idea that all the events of life, whether of individuals or of nations, have been directly produced by an arbitrary, capricious, whimsical Deity, alternating between arrogant displays of superiority on the one hand, and a doting, foolish fondness on the other, has left no scope for the exercise of that noble faculty. What a throng of calamities and follies it will banish from the world, as soon as it can be brought into exercise !

The article on the common-school system of Massachusetts appeared in the "Edinburgh Review" for July. It was received here by all the friends of the good cause with great delight. Conjecture has been active in divining its authorship ; but even our friend Dr. Howe is at fault. As it bore no resemblance to your ordinary style, and was untinctured even with a homœopathic dilution of phrenology, he thought it could not be yours. Mr. S. has given out that it was written by some member of Parliament, who was very anxious to become acquainted with our system, and whom he supplied with all our documents for that purpose. With others, the title to its authorship is ambulatory, migrating from Mr. Stimpson to Lord Brougham and yourself. To all, however, and especially to my friends, it is in the highest degree gratifying, — I mean, to all whom you would like to gratify, — for one of the authors of the report to abolish the Board is incensed against it, and asserts that it was written here, and sent to Edinburgh to be printed and sent back; but nobody believes him.

Howe is doing nobly for the cause. Indeed, I sometimes think we should have been wrecked before this but for his pilotage. The Normal schools are doing well. I have completed another Abstract of the Massachusetts school returns. It is even superior to its predecessors. The statistics show an advance over the preceding year in all the elements of prosperity belonging to our school-system.

Dr. Channing writes me, "I should be glad to see the letter to which you refer; for Mr. Combe is a wise observer, and Dr. Follen told me that he had met no foreigner who understood Germany better, or as well. That country is very interesting, and full of anomalies. Under despotism, there is much freedom of thought. To a plodding industry they join wildness of speculation and imagination; and, what is more striking, they are said to be licentious in the social relations, and a moral people in other respects. Their intellectual influence on Europe is greater than that of any other people. I wish Mr. Combe would help us to comprehend them."

I am exceedingly obliged to Mrs. Combe and yourself for all your kind wishes in regard to my health, and that I would join you while on the Continent. I should be most happy to do so, could I take Massachusetts with me. But it is too large for my pocket, though not for my heart.

I have read your brother's work on Infancy with much delight. While perusing it, I saw Death let go his gripe from more than ten thousand children. . . .

Farewell! Ever sincerely yours,

HORACE MANN.

Nov. 23. Came from Boston to Walpole yesterday, where I have had a meeting which must be called the County Meeting, though the smallest and most discouraging I have had in the State. If I could allow aught to break down my spirit and hope, it would be the manner in which these efforts to arouse public attention seem to fail. Words, counsels, exhortations, seem like substances thrown into an abyss. I hear no report giving assurance that somewhere there is a bottom upon which they strike. But continue to throw in I will. Perhaps it may be my own fortune, at some future day, to hear an echo from the depths. If I do not, some follower of mine in the glorious cause will do it; and at length the chasm shall be filled, and not only be filled, but, above, the superstructure shall rise as high from the surface as its depths now sink below, and that structure shall be the glory of the world.

BOSTON, Feb. 28, 1842.

GEORGE COMBE, ESQ. *My dear Mr. Combe,* — Your kind letter of Nov. 15 I did not receive till about the 10th of January. I should have said beforehand, that the intensity of my desire to hear from you would have been an attractive force sufficiently strong to draw it into my hands in a shorter time. But it seems to have been projected into space with great centrifugal velocity, and almost to have formed an orbit in which it might have revolved round me forever. New York was the point of its perihelion; but there the centripetal prevailed, and brought it to the centre at once. I could not write you by the steamer of the 1st of this month; for my engagements were so numerous, that I wanted not only the hundred hands of Briareus, but brains enough to keep them all at work. I was rejoiced, in common with your other friends here, to hear of your happy and quiet life. We wish our boisterous democracy could furnish you with a peaceful retreat; but in our political latitudes there reigns one storm, and that is endless. I have often thought there was the closest analogy between the geological theory and human history; a time for the wild commotion of all the human propensities, raging and battling with each other, and bursting upward through all the orders and classifications of society; just as, in the early geological eras, the action of internal fires broke through the primary formations: and, pursuing this comparison further, I have hoped that by and by these hostile forces of the social economy would subside, and lay the foundation of a state of society as much more propitious to human happiness than is the present, as the exuberance of the alluvial deposit is beyond the sterility of its granite substratum.   All I hope is, that my life may be as a single leaf cast off from this deciduous generation, whose decomposition may add a single particle to the mass of deep and rich marl on which the growth of some future age shall luxuriate, and gather nutriment for a glorious moral harvest.

You say nothing would give you greater pleasure than a republication of your works, but that you should be sorry if it were to injure the publishers.   Your sympathy for them is useless. Assignees administer upon their estate.   I shall undoubtedly lose by them.   But there is one consolation about this and other things that have been happening to me in a row, and, with small intervals, all my life : God created me without any love of money ; and, in all his works, there is no more striking instance of the adaptation of the thing made to its circumstances. . . .

Howe is absent, and has been so almost all the time for nearly three months.   Early in December, he went to Columbia, S. C., to visit the Legislature of that State, and obtain an appropriation for the education of their blind children.   Though they were cold, and at first almost repulsed him, yet, when they granted him an opportunity for an exhibition before the members, they surrendered themselves unconsciously into his hands.   His success was complete.   An annual grant of $1,200 was made ; and their blind children will be sent here this year.   He afterwards went to Georgia ; but could only obtain the good will and the promises of the people there, as the high-mightinesses of the State were not in session.   He then returned to Boston ; but did not stop more than a week, when, knight-errant like, he rushed forth again.   He went to Louisville, and from there to Frankfort, and gave an exhibition in the State House.   How well you must remember Frankfort, the quiet, sequestered little town, with its fountain of water playing in the yard, which you and I went to see ; the hill on the right bank of the river, which we climbed ; the tavern where we breakfasted so quietly, while you listened to the conversation of the revivalist minister with the impassive-souled judge about the praying governor !   All this seems like yesterday, — it seems like *now*.   Only I look up to catch your glad eye and voice, and to grasp your hand, and am reminded that there are four thousand miles between us.

Dr. Howe gave an exhibition to the Kentuckians, and carried them away as by enchantment. They voted, by acclamation, $10,000 in aid of an institution for the blind, on condition that some city should commence a school, and sustain it for a year. He then went to Louisville; and there such measures have been taken as will doubtless eventuate in raising the necessary funds, and insuring a permanent establishment for this noble object. The success of an appeal to the sympathies of our people in behalf of the blind may be now calculated upon as one of the *natural laws.* It has been tried in nearly half the States of the Union, and has never failed. At the painful sight of the deprivation of their unfortunate children, followed by the gladdening spectacle of the results of the wonderful art by which that deprivation can be supplied, avarice itself relents, and opens its coffers, and suffers the almoner of this bounty to thrust in his arm elbow-deep. We have just heard that he has left Louisville for New Orleans, that he may give sight to the blind in that God-forsaken region. Those who have eyes there seem to be more sightless than the blind. They are doing something, however, even in New Orleans, for education. Within the last year, one of the municipalities of the city has established a system of common schools; and my excellent friend, the Hon. John A. Shaw, — the man who prepared the minority report against the abolition of the Board of Education in 1840, — has gone out there to launch it. Indeed, there seems to be in several of the States a faint indication that there is but one remedy for our social ills, — the formation of minds whose intellectual vision can discern the laws by which social evils may be avoided, and whose well-trained sentiments pre-adapt and incline them to obedience.

I am carrying on the "Journal" for another year, although a labor which I am unable to perform. But, while I do all the work for nothing, it just pays its way, and is doing some good. I do not know but it would be going too far — and, if so, you will pay no attention to it — to ask you to furnish me, during your residence in Germany, with a series of letters in relation to the German schools, — their course of studies, modes of instruction, discipline, order, qualifications of teachers, attainments of scholars, results, &c.; any thing, in fact, which you could write without much labor, and

which would be most interesting to our people, and most beneficial
to our schools, whose condition and wants you well know. I think
your charity could not find a more useful channel to flow out in;
and it would be most delightful to me to spread your wise thoughts
abroad amongst this numerous people, — more numerous than
great.

I have got out my Fifth Annual Report. It is mainly addressed
to the organ of acquisitiveness, and therefore stands some chance
of being popular. In our Legislature, this winter, there is a very
good feeling towards the Board and its improvements. The Rev.
Dr. Palfrey, editor of the "North-American Review," has cut theology, and become a politician. He is Chairman of the Committee on
Education in the House. All the committees of both houses are
friendly to the cause; my two best friends there, Mr. Quincy, and
Mr. Kinnicut of Worcester, being respectively President of the
Senate, and Speaker of the House. If they could not give me good
committees, of what use would it be to have one's friends in these
offices? A bill is now pending before the Legislature to grant
further aid for the continuance of the Normal schools, and to encourage, by a small bonus, the respective districts of the State to
purchase a small school-library. We have pretty strong hopes that
it will pass. Mrs. Combe's parts of your "Notes" have been very
much and universally admired : they are golden threads interwoven
into the solid and enduring fabric of your own mind. I wish I had
power equal to my will to bless her, and then there should be no
room left for doubt as to quantity or quality. Some of my friends
have been trying to send me to England; but, while you are away,
the whole island seems to me empty. When it is inhabited again,
perhaps I may go to see it. Lord Morpeth and Dickens are both
in this country. Our political condition is very extraordinary; but
I have not time to describe it.

Most affectionately yours,

HORACE MANN.

Feb. 28.   To-morrow there is to be a grand celebration at Salem,
on account of the improvement and extension of their school-system.
A great change has been effected in that city, — a new body and

a new soul; new schoolhouses, and a new spirit among the teachers; and to-morrow is to be a *fête*-day. In the evening I am to lecture; and on Wednesday evening I am to endeavor, by a lecture in Brookline, to carry out a plan for the establishment of a high school there.

March 3. The brightest days which have ever shone upon our cause were yesterday and to-day. Yesterday, resolves passed the House for granting $6,000 per year for three years to the Normal schools; and fifteen dollars to each district for a school-library, on condition of its raising fifteen dollars for the same purpose.

Language cannot express the joy that pervades my soul at this vast accession of power to that machinery which is to carry the cause of education forward, not only more rapidly than it has ever moved, but to places which it has never yet reached. This will cause an ever-widening circle to spread amongst contemporaries, and will project influences into the future to distances which no calculations can follow.

But I am too much exhausted to raise a song of gratulation that shall express my feelings. Yesterday I breakfasted at Salem; came to the city; found that all possible exertion was necessary; worked all day; and at evening went to lecture at Brookline, to fulfil an engagement; and returned at half-past nine, having spent the day without another meal. To-day I have been hardly less busy. BUT THE GREAT WORK IS DONE! We must now use the power wisely with which we have been intrusted.

March 8. The joy I feel on account of the success of our plans for the schools has not begun to be exhausted. It keeps welling up into my mind, fresh and exhilarating as it was the first hour of its occurrence. I have no doubt it will have an effect on my health as well as my spirits. The wearisome, depressing labor of watchfulness which I have undergone for years has been a vampire to suck the blood out of my heart, and the marrow out of my bones. I should, however, have held on until death; for I felt my grasp all the time tightening, not loosening. I hope I may now have the power of performing more and better labor.

March 27. I am not well; but the success of the last session

11

is a perpetual spring of joy, throwing up continually sweet waters of satisfaction.

April 17. I have been busy with lecturing and my Report. Incredible pleasure and relief of mind are shed over my whole time by the glorious success of the cause in the Legislature.

April 24. I understand that eighteen thousand copies of my last Report to the Board have been printed in Albany, for distribution. This will carry it to many minds; and, if it does any good, I shall be paid for all my labor. It is also translated into German.

May 10. · Niagara Falls. . . . The convention at Utica lasted till Friday. I arrived about ten · o'clock this morning at Lockport, having travelled most uncomfortably in the canal-boat all night; thence to this place. I ran down to catch a hasty view of the Falls; but, being much exhausted, returned to dine. After dinner, I sallied forth, and have spent four hours on my feet, going from point to point, and gazing in astonishment and awe upon this great and varied work of Nature. The emotions it has excited I cannot now attempt to describe, — perhaps never; but commonplaces of amazement and admiration ill befit this unique wonder of the world.

May 17. Spent a day at Richmond, a border town of this State; and, so far as their interest in schools is concerned, they are on the borders, at least, of civilization, if not a little on the other side. When will Berkshire rise from her degradation?

May 22. Yesterday, commenced the great labor of another Abstract. This is an appalling undertaking; and were it not for its utility, which I see more plainly than ever seed-sower saw the future harvest, its very aspect would repel me from attempting to perform it. But I go into it with good heart and zeal; and, if my strength will only hold out, I shall count the toil more fondly than ever "a confined boy looked forward to his pastime."

Mr. Mann had no clerk, and no appropriation was made for one; and as he at this time spent all his salary, except what was sufficient for his bare necessities of board, lodging, and something to wear, in his office, he was obliged to do all his own writing and copying. He had no other assistance than what a friend occasionally insisted upon rendering him when his strength was seen to be nearly exhausted. But he worked now with pleasure, where formerly only hope illumined his efforts.

July 3. To-morrow is an eventful day for me. I find that expectations of my coming oration are raised high in some quarters; and it will be difficult, if not impossible, for me to satisfy them. But all that my strength and time enabled me to do I have done; and nothing remains but to submit it to the terrible ordeal of public opinion. Before twenty-four hours have passed, I shall know something of whether the great object I have in view — that of favorably influencing the public mind on this question of education — will be likely to be answered or not.

July 19. How weary a life this would be if my soul were not in it! but it is, and this renders the toil a pleasure. I see my efforts yielding their fruits; and God grant they may be so abundant that all mankind may be filled! Have been making a short visit at my friend Mr. Quincy's, in Quincy.

At this period, the Rev. Cyrus Pierce, who had so nobly fulfilled his part in the educational work, as Principal of the Normal School, failed in health, wholly in consequence of the too great labor he had performed. When the Normal School at Lexington was first opened, the means for its support were very scanty; and, during the time of its location there, Mr. Pierce not only did all the teaching, but superintended the interests of the boarding-house, and even rose every day at three o'clock to see that the fires were built; allowing himself, for a great part of the time, only three hours sleep. No one but a thoroughly conscientious teacher has any conception of the labor of keeping a good school. The exercises of school-hours form but a small part of that labor. The private study and preparation, especially in a school of advanced character like a Normal school, where not only things are to be taught, but the best modes of teaching are to be considered, compared, discussed, tried, and watched over in the model school in which the pupils of the higher school practise their art under close criticism of the principal (and, in that case, Mr. Pierce was principal of both schools, passing from one to the other daily, with every faculty stimulated to its keenest work, in order to do justice to both), — this study and preparation, I repeat, were almost beyond the power of man to endure: and Mr. Pierce, though of the firmest fibrous temperament, became the victim of intense neuralgic pain, which obliged him to relinquish his office. Mr. Mann's grief at this necessity was inexpressible: but he was obliged to look round, among the friends whom the progress of the cause had brought to his notice, for a successor. At this date, he wrote the following letter to Rev. S. J. May, who for the three succeeding years so ably filled the post vacated by Mr. Pierce : —

BOSTON, July 27, 1842.

REV. S. J. MAY. *My dear Sir,* — . . . The object of this note is to inquire, in an entirely confidential and unofficial manner, whether you will so far entertain the proposition as to allow me to present your name to the Board of Education for the Principalship of the Normal School at Lexington. . . .

My dear sir, neither my time nor my disposition allows me to indulge in compliment. You know something of what I think a Normal school-teacher should be. With such opinions as I have of the qualifications for that office, you need no words of assurance of my regard for and opinion of you. . . .

Very truly and sincerely yours, &c.,

HORACE MANN.

Aug. 14. The American Institute of Instruction is to meet at New Bedford this week, and I shall probably lecture there. The meeting is important, and in that part of the State there is much need of a revival in educational matters. The soil of Bristol County is so thirsty, that it would absorb all the dews which a dozen institutes could distil upon it; and even then I fear it would not be enriched to the point of vegetation.

Aug. 21. A good meeting at New Bedford. About seventeen thousand copies of my oration have been published, and another edition of three thousand is to be issued this week.

Aug. 28. Mr. Samuel J. May is probably to become principal of the school at Lexington. There will be at first an outcry on account of his abolition principles; but I believe he will be conscientious enough not to become a proselyter instead of a teacher.

Sept. 4. On Monday last, I went to Springfield to see if arrangements could be made for establishing a Normal school at that place. . . . The Abstract is now out, and will, I trust, shed a flood of light over the State on the greatest and darkest of all subjects. . . .

Oct. 20. I went to Springfield, as proposed; where I found all my expectations thwarted in relation to establishing a Normal school at that place. Mr. Calhoun will try to do something for the drooping cause there. . . .

I have not accomplished much during the last three weeks. Found my strength utterly prostrate from previous efforts. Hope to renew it, and go on rejoicing again.

Nov. 9. . . . I rejoice to find that evidences are everywhere springing up of the progress of the great work. A momentum has been given which will not soon be expended. Still I never felt so much like applying additional power, rather than relying upon the speed already attained.

Nov. 13. . . . To-morrow I go to Falmouth to attend a meeting of teachers. Thus may perpetual droppings wear away the stone of ignorance. One drop I expect to shed on this occasion, in the form of a lecture.

Dec. 11. Yesterday, attended a convention of school-teachers, and lectured before them. It is pleasant to see these proofs of interest on the part of teachers. They have a great deal yet to do; but these indications are not only performance, but promise for the future.

REV. S. J. MAY.

MY DEAR SIR, — . . . I shall be desirous to be present at your examination, but fear I shall not be able to. My Annual Report* is mainly at the bottom of my inkstand yet: and I fear that my two great organs will experience just the reverse of what they should under all my torments; that is, that I shall have a hardening of the heart, and a softening of the brain. . . .

Well, what is to become of us this winter? Are we to fall into the hands of the Philistines? If so, we must make friends of the mammon of party. I see a Democrat is to come from Lexington. Do you know him? Can you magnetize him? If so, infuse a fulness of the right spirit, though you faint in the operation. You know Mr. F——, of Nantucket. He worked well for us last winter. Cannot you secure him for the present? Mr. R——, of West Cambridge, also, was in favor of us last year. See him, if you can. If not, see his friends. Become all things to all men. Go, preach; and wherever you preach, speaking with a flaming tongue, miraculously convert. Let us carry the cause through one year more, and I think the young giant will be able to take care of himself.

Yours ever,

HORACE MANN.

Dec. 25. During the last week, an event highly favorable to the schools has taken place. Being filled with a desire (which might, perhaps, better be called a determination) to have the work of Messrs. Potter & Emerson, the " School and the Schoolmaster," distributed among the schools in the State of Massachusetts, as it has been among those of New York, by the liberality of Mr. Wadsworth, I ventured to make application to Mr. Brimmer, the Mayor elect of the city, to see if he would not take upon himself the expense of this benefaction. With a readiness and a propriety highly creditable to him, he signified not only his assent to the proposition, but his pleasure in embracing it; and he has authorized me to incur an expense not exceeding fifteen hundred dollars to carry out the plan. This will put an excellent work on the subject of education

---

* To be presented the 1st of January. — ED

in the hands of every teacher in the State, — a glorious thing! How many minds will be opened to a perception of the momentous work! how many will be stimulated! how many withdrawn from the transitory pleasures of frivolity and dissipation! What a harvest of blessings will be reaped from the sowing of this seed!

When I see what good may be done with money, I sometimes wish that I had some at my command.

Jan. 1, 1843. A new year! The past year is now beyond mortal or immortal control. To me, to the cause I have most at heart, it has been a most auspicious year. Event after event has occurred to give that cause an impulse; and I do not recollect any thing of an untoward character which is worthy to be mentioned. The grant for the libraries and for Normal schools, the increase of the town appropriations, the increasing interest felt in the subject by the people, and the well-timed donation of Mr. Brimmer of a work on education for all the schools in the State, attest the prosperity of the cause for the last year.

But another year now opens. The great subject of inquiry now is, What fortunes await the cause before it shall close? This inquiry I cannot answer, any further than to say, that what depends on human exertion shall not be wanting to its prosperity. I may die in the cause; but, while I live, I will uphold it to the utmost of my strength.

Jan. 22. . . . This week, Governor —— has come into power, and commenced his course by a most insidious and Jesuitical speech. He speaks of education; but not one word is said of the Board of Education or of the Normal School. There is no recognition of the existence of improvements effected by them. Six years of as severe labor as any mortal ever performed — labor, too, which has certainly been rewarded by great success — cannot procure a word of good will. This denial of justice, this *suppressio veri*, is of no consequence, only as it may prevent our doing as much as we otherwise might. But, if allowed to go on, a noble revenge shall be wrought, — that of making it apparent to the most prejudiced and unjust that much *has* been done.

The following letters are given to show the principle

upon which Mr. Mann conducted his educational labors. He thought it right and essential to keep them from all party influences; knowing that politics, in our country, vitiated every subject they touched. May we not hope now that that day is passing away?

Mr. May thinks it not judicious to publish the letters, as the public mind has undergone such a change upon this subject, that he fears it will injure Mr. Mann's reputation with some good men; but I am induced to do it, contrary to his advice, which I still respect for its motive, because Mr. Mann has been accused of timidity, and want of honorable openness and independence in his caution. His own rendering of the subject will show the fallacy of this: and his subsequent public course upon the subject of slavery shows plainly enough that he feared no man, and that he never renounced his principles for the sake of popularity. Nor did any one ever love the man, whom all his friends involuntarily call "dear Mr. May," better than he; and none the less, but all the more, because Mr. May is, by his nature and culture alike, so profound a hater of slavery. What a comment it is upon the torpid state of the national conscience at that time, that no public interest was safe that was associated with the desire to do away chattel slavery!

BOSTON, Jan. 27, 1843.

REV. S. J. MAY.

MY DEAR SIR, — I have been debating with myself for almost a fortnight whether I ought, or whether I ought not, to write you on a certain subject. At last, musing here, just before twelve o'clock, and warming my toes for bed, I have resolved to do so. Could you see my feelings just as they are, I should need no other apology. I can only assure you that it is from kindness alone that I do it.

I was at W—— a fortnight ago to-morrow evening, where I met a number of gentlemen at Dr. H——'s. The doctor and his family spoke very kindly of you, and expressed, with every appearance of sincerity, a great personal regard. But the doctor observed that you had lost a very fine girl from one of their most respectable families, in consequence of your having visited W—— a few evenings before, with a portion of your pupils, on the occasion of an anti-slavery meeting. Very little else was said ; but the obvious feeling was, that it was a pity that theoretical antislavery should prove to be practical anti-education, by depriving your school of a valuable pupil, and yourself, to some extent, of the respect of an influential citizen.

I write this in no unkindness, and in no spirit of fault-finding, but merely to apprise you of the consequences of your visit there on that occasion. I confess myself one of those who hold the maxim to be a damnable one, that " our actions are our own : the consequences belong to God." We cannot separate the action from the consequence ; and therefore the latter is as much our own as the former. Consequences *aid* us in determining the moral character of an action, as much as they do the physical properties of a body ; and, as it seems to me, I may as well adopt a theory that fire will not ignite gunpowder, and then flourish a torch round a magazine, and say, " Consequences belong to God," as to say it in reference to any thing else.

But I will not go on moralizing further. I have eased my conscience ; and I trust you will take this letter as it is intended, — perfectly in good part. . . .

Yours ever and truly,

HORACE MANN.

BOSTON, Feb. 6, 1843.

REV. S. J. MAY, — I had strong hopes of being able to see you to-day ; but the printers of my Report, after having worn my patience all out by delay, are now sending it to me so fast, that I cannot leave. If any one inquires why I am not there, please tell them the reason.

I have been anxious to reply to your last letter ever since I received it, but so much engaged that it has been impossible. Some things I think you have misunderstood, and others misrecollected.

For instance : I did not say that the young lady at W—— declined to go to Lexington because of the visit of yourself and pupils to the antislavery meeting. Yet you reply, that, if she were prevented from going for the reason assigned, " she must be inferior in mind and heart to many" whom you have. It was not the young lady : it was her father who refused to let her go, because he thought your going to an abolition meeting in term-time, and carrying the scholars, was aside from the purposes of the school, and of bad example. For aught I know, the young lady herself might have been an abolitionist, or good stuff from which to make one. Thus the school lost one pupil at least, and some friends. And this reminds me of what you say of your pupils, — that some of them were abolitionists when they came there, *or were made so by Father Pierce.* Father Pierce had no right to make them so, any more than he had to make them Unitarians, or Bank or anti-Bank in their politics. One was just as much a violation of his duty (if he did the act) as the other would be. We want good teachers of our common schools, and that is what the State and the patrons of the Normal schools have respectively given their money to prepare ; and any diversion of it to any other object is obviously a violation of the trust.

Pardon me for saying one word in reference to yourself. You certainly said that you did not mean to withdraw from the abolitionists, and that, by receiving more salary, you should be able to contribute more money to that cause ; but did you not also say that the school should have the *whole* of your energies? The extremest remark you ever made to me in regard to any active co-operation in abolition movements was, that if, in vacation. you happened to be at a place where an abolition meeting was held, you should not consider yourself debarred from attending it. This surely seems to me different from carrying your own pupils to such a meeting in term-time, and indulging in remarks which disaffected several very excellent friends of the school, and prevented one pupil from attending it.

I certainly say these things with no particle of unkindness to yourself. I think you will see, with me, which is the highest cause, or at least that the interests of the Normal School ought not to be impaired, nor its friends alienated, by active, public co-operation, not only by yourself, but with your pupils, and in term-time.

But I have time to write no more. I am sorry I cannot see you to-day. I hope I may soon. If in the city, do not fail to call. . . .

In a letter from Mr. Pierce, he says you are doing very well; but he does not think you make the pupils agonize quite so much as might be well for them.

Yours truly,

HORACE MANN.

BOSTON, Feb. 22, 1843.

REV. S. J. MAY.

MY DEAR SIR, — If, a few days ago, I overcame all doubt as to the propriety of addressing you on the subject of the actual loss which had occurred to your school in consequence of your zeal in another cause so alien from it, how can I forbear, at the present time, to point out consequences still more serious, which must result from pursuing the same course? If I believed you to have any doubt of the personal friendship and sincerity of my motives, I should first endeavor to convince you of that fact. But I must assume this, without a preamble. Pardon me, then, for saying that it is with inexpressible regret that I learn from the public newspapers that you are to be one of the lecturers for the abolition course about to be delivered in this city. Every friend of yours, and of the cause with which you hold so important a connection, is pained beyond measure at this annunciation. Three of your friends, ——, ——, ——, have spoken to me upon the subject with sincere grief.

In the first place, it is the middle of a term; so that the immediate accusation will be, by the opponents of the cause which you volunteer to espouse, that you are neglecting the duties of the school. I do not mean to say that I would make such a charge, but that it is too obvious not to be made.

In the second place, we have entertained great fears for the fate of the whole educational system during the present session; and these are not wholly dissipated. The Legislature is now in session, and we know there are many members of it who would rejoice in any pretext for making an attack upon the Board and the Normal schools. I cannot expect that the event announced in the papers can take effect without open or secret and extensive animadversions being made upon it. I have had a talk with your representative, and he is disposed to be reconciled ; but he expressly stated that his dissatisfaction with your appointment had arisen from his fears that you would more or less abandon the school to propagate your views on another subject, which fears he now hopes were groundless. Will you give occasion for the revival of those fears, and put an unanswerable argument in his mouth against all that I can say ? Being a Democrat, he could lead a great many of that party with him.

But a third consideration is perhaps still more important. A public interest and sympathy are now excited through the Commonwealth in behalf of the cause of education. With the exception of Mr. Dwight's donation, more has been given by rich men during the last year for its general promotion, probably, than ever before. . . . If I had not succeeded in producing a conviction, that, while I am engaged in administering the cause, it will be kept clear of all collateral subjects, of all which the world chooses to call fanaticisms or hobbies, I should never have obtained the co-operation of thousands who are now its friends. I have further plans for obtaining more aid ; but the moment it is known or supposed that the cause is to be perverted to, or connected with, any of the exciting party questions of the day, I shall never get another cent. I shall be bereft of all power in regard to individuals, if not in regard to the State.

And again: did you not tell me, again and again, that, if *the public would let you alone* in regard to your abolition views, you thought you could get along well enough with your friends? But how can you expect that the public will let you alone, if they find you, every term, making abolition speeches or delivering abolition lectures, and exhibiting yourself as a champion of the cause in a way and on occasions which so many will deem offensive ? The public is not wont to be so tolerant. You must not mistake my motives ; and, if you think I am speaking too plainly, you must pardon it for the zeal I have in the cause. . .   H. M.

Feb. 5. Last week, a libel was published against me in the " Mercantile Journal ; " and thus something is continually occurring to take away almost all the comfort of my life, except that which arises from the prosperity of the great cause. Well, then, I must make that prosperity my comfort.

Feb. 12. Were I to record all my thoughts, feelings, hopes, fears, for the week, they would make a volume. If I do not record them, I have little to say. I go to Manchester, N.H., on Wednesday, to lecture. To hope to accomplish any thing in New Hampshire by one lecture is as vain as to expect to make the ocean boil by throwing in one coal of fire.

Feb. 19. . . . Yesterday the whole question of the school-libraries was opened again in the House of Representatives, and was sustained by a *crushing* majority. So the cause has evidently advanced almost incredibly within two or three years. It now needs discreet and energetic management: it will then be able to take care of itself.

March 5. . . . Last night I read the last revise of my Report. So now, for good or for evil, it is done; and I trust it will eventually do good, but shall not be surprised if it is not well received.

CHAPTER V.

ON the 1st of May, 1843, Mr. Mann was again married, and sailed for Europe to visit European schools, especially in Germany, where he expected to derive most benefit. He hoped thus to do more for American schools than he could do, just at that juncture, by remaining at home. He thought the good cause was safely grounded in the estimation of the people; and now it only remained to improve methods of instruction, and to bring the subject of moral education more fully before the public. To this end, he had set in operation the most adequate means, — the Normal schools, — and placed them in the hands of men, who, as far as he could judge, saw the importance of that element in human culture.

The opposition he had been forced to encounter, and the double labor this had cost him, had seriously affected his health; and a change seemed absolutely necessary for his brain, which was in such a preternatural state of activity, that he could not sleep. As his friend Dr. Howe expressed it, "it went of itself."

The excursion did not prove so much of a recreation as his friends hoped it would. His time of absence was limited to six months; and his attention was so much absorbed in educational matters, that he had little strength or leisure to devote to mere amusement. It was his habit to spend the day, from seven till five o'clock, in visiting schools, prisons, and the men who were interested in these, and many of his evenings in reading documents which he gathered in his progress. He needed the suggestions of others even to see other things that he passed by the way. He read, but could not speak, the modern languages; but, with the help of an imperfect interpreter by his side, probably few men ever made such a visitation who gleaned more fruits. The "white-haired gentleman," as he was called, excited much interest in the schoolmasters, to whom he did not always give his name; for he wished to see the schools in undress, and therefore visited them unofficially, when that was possible, though always duly armed with credentials from the Ministers of Instruction. He was treated with much courtesy; though it is to be doubted whether the good men of the schools often underwent such a searching examination, not only into their proceedings, but into the theories and motives that impelled them. Probably not a few of them had glimpses of some aims of education they had not thought of before, — not through any formal instructions from the "white-haired gentleman," but simply from the questions he asked.

The main results of the tour were given to the public in his Seventh Annual Report to the Board of Education. In Germany alone he met with any true comprehension of what he regarded as moral and religious instruction. The effect of his Report of it at home was to shake some dry bones that had apparently become not only fossilized, but firmly embedded.

I give a few extracts from his journal.

LIVERPOOL, May, 1843.

On the 16th we visited Eaton Hall, one of the seats of the Marquis of Westminster. The income of this nobleman is said to be $5,000 per day. The avenues which lead to it from Chester are several miles in length, skirted with hedge and all varieties of forest trees. Herds of deer and cattle were grazing or ruminating in the grounds. Swans bedecked the quiet lakes. Trees to which each season for centuries had added bulk and loftiness stood around. At last, the massive pile opened upon our view. As we approached it, we saw some ten or dozen old women, with coarse features and a coarser garb, *carrying away upon their backs* the limbs of a large tree which had been felled; and around other parts of the premises, and in the pleasure-grounds, other groups of the same sex were busily employed weeding the walks, gathering in the new-mown hay, &c. The gardens and pleasure-grounds cover fifty-two acres, — about the size of Boston Common. Here was apparently every variety of flower and plant and fruit which could be found on the globe. Hot-houses were prepared for the productions of the South ; rocks, grottoes, and places adapted to the cultivation of the feeble and scanty growths of the North. Beds of pine-apples were ripening. Peach-trees were trained against the walls. Strawberries, cherries, &c., hung in luscious clusters. Vats of capacious dimensions were set under glass for the cultivation of the Egyptian lotus, &c. Long sheds, with bins upon the side, were constructed for the growth of the mushroom and potato sprouts. Artificial grottoes were scattered along winding passages ; the whole sometimes assuming the form of the most regularly laid out garden, and again winding away into labyrinths. But a description is impossible.

The house was constructed and furnished in a style of indescribable elegance. . . . The marble floor of the entrance hall was said to have cost 75,000 dollars. It was adorned with splendid pictures, coats of mail, magnificent tables, &c. The hall of communication (a miniature imitation of the cloistered aisles of Chester Cathedral) is 740 feet in length, lined with pictures and groups of statuary. When we came to a splendid piano in the library, the attendant, who was a lady dressed in violet-colored satin, adorned with heavy black lace, told us the young ladies played very well ; and in the garden we were afterwards shown " the young ladies' garden." Ah! was there no spot in the souls of these tenderly reared daughters where a brighter flower than any ever formed of rain and sunshine could have been cultivated, — the flower of sympathy for others' hearts, by Nature formed of as fine a mould, and, in the sight of God, of as high a price, as their own ? Was there no time when all the richest music wrought in the burning souls of the highest genius might have been bartered for the grateful voices of sorrow and poverty and crime which these daughters might have elicited? Well might all these accomplishments, and all this splendor and beauty, have been bartered for these; for heaven would have been given them as a requital.

I left in a state of mind which I cannot now express. I hope my feelings will find a form of utterance at some future time.

The next day, we visited Chester Cathedral. Of the antiquity of this there can be no doubt. No art can prepare a counterpart. Time puts a certain wrinkle and sallowness on its objects, that no common colorer can imitate, or graver etch. This cathedral is supposed to be twelve or thirteen centuries old. Its dimensions are vast. Here we saw a bit of a tomb of seven centuries. We went into rooms which were once occupied by nuns. Many old associations arose. These must always rise while the history of the secret deeds of monasteries and nunneries remains.

This ancient cathedral and splendid castle, and the *poor old women*, made an impression upon Mr. Mann that farther travel in England only deepened. Passing from high to low, from palace, castle, cathedral, to prison, school, and cottage, the glory and the shame of England were ever in sad and striking contrast. In a letter to his sister, written May 15, he says, —

I am here at a very interesting time, so far as the general question of education is concerned. A bill is now before Parliament for the establishment of a national system; but it is framed with such express reference to the promotion and extension of the Established Church, that it meets opposition from all the Dissenters. It originally gave all the power of appointing teachers and supervising the schools to the members of the church, and then it prohibited any manufacturer from employing any child who had not received a certificate from a school which the church approved; and therefore made the *bread*, as well as the intellect and morals, of all, dependent upon their will. But, if I begin to write on so prolific a theme, where shall I stop? . . .

In what did this bill differ from the persecutions of nonconformists, which drove the Puritans from England in days gone by?

May —. In passing from Liverpool to London on the railroad, we were struck with the exuberance of the vegetation. The fields were all so monotonously green, that at last I longed for a piece of Cape Cod for variety. . . . But we saw scarcely a large tree in the whole journey. . . . I was quite struck with the comparative amount of grazing and mowing land, compared with the tillage. More land sown to wheat, or planted with esculent roots, would very much increase the sustenance of man.

May 20. Visited Westminster Abbey. Here are deposited the truly great and the sham great. The truly great, however, are principally by themselves, in what is called the " Poets' Corner." The sham great are scattered about in the various chapels or niches. Here and there, however, a genuine man, such as Lord Mansfield, Wilberforce, Watt, was placed by the side of a king or queen, like gold pieces among copper pennies. . . . Here were deposited the remains of Ben Jonson, Milton, Dryden, Pope, Addison, &c. Among the kings and queens, there was a sprinkling of ladies of the bed-chamber, masters of the hounds, pimps, &c., who obtained this resting-place for their bones through favoritism. A statue of one of the kings had been covered with silver, with an entire head of the same metal. The head had been wrung off by some one at once acquisitive and unloyal, — probably done more from the acquisitive than the democratic instinct. A monument had been erected to one of Cromwell's generals, — Popham, — which was threatened with removal after the Restoration ; but at the intercession of his wife, and a proposition to have the whole inscription erased, it was suffered to remain. It is now a blank.

Cromwell himself was buried here ; but his remains were removed by his successor, and it is said they were hung at Tyburn.

The finest statue was that of Lord Mansfield.

The whole hardly impressed me so much as I expected.

May 23. Visited Smithfield Market, where John Rogers was burned. Is it not strange that the oddity of that ambiguous statement about the number of his children should almost universally have the effect of repressing all sympathy for the martyr, and all indignation against his tormentors?

Visited "Rag Fair," or the old-clothes market, which is a large open area, nearly square, all trodden to a mire, with coarse wooden booths on the side, prepared in the rudest manner, and so finished that there has been no waste of skill upon the material. When filled with old clothes, and wretched traffickers in them, what a scene it must present! Afterwards, taking a police-officer, I passed through covered markets for the same object, where sacks and bundles of old clothes were being opened and displayed, or had already been shaken out, and spread upon rough-board stalls, or counters. They were, probably, the joint product of the previous night's purchases and thefts. A more deplorable sight than the fetid, squalid wretches exhibited can hardly be imagined.

Went also through the Jews' quarter, where, from narrow, pent-up lanes, holes and caverns opening on either side, poured forth the foulest stench. The eye also was repelled that would penetrate to their loathsome recesses. What a place to lie in immediate proximity with so much luxury, voluptuousness, and superfluous wealth! From these dens of vice, debasement, and iniquity, we at length emerged, and passed through some respectable streets. One was that in which John Milton was born, — then named Grub Street. Onward we went through Billingsgate Fish Market, the sight of which added intensity to the meaning of the word, which had its origin in the foul language of that locality. In looking around, one could well imagine that he saw the genius of the place.

Went into the "long room" of the Custom House; and a long room it surely is. And why should not the room be long in which account is taken of the products of all the climes in the world, as they are borne to this spot by every wind that blows?

Visited Greenwich Hospital. Here reside seventeen or eighteen hundred sailors, mutilated, broken down, or decayed in the service of the nation, — the results of war. Who would not be a peace man after beholding such a spectacle? Hardly a battle has been fought by England within fifty years but here is one of its victims. Should each one of them tell his history, what a volume it would

make! Yet how few are these representatives, compared with the
constituency of the dead which they represent, — each one, perhaps,
representing a thousand! In the great painted hall of the hospital
are numerous and splendid paintings, commemorative of Britain's
naval glory, as it is called. Here the remembrance of all her
triumphs is perpetuated. Every child who visits this place is
taught to feel loyalty for the sovereign, a pride in his country, and
an ambition to distinguish himself in her service. In one glass
case was the very coat in which Nelson was shot at the battle of
the Nile; in another, the model of some celebrated ship, fraught
with historical associations; and so of all its garniture. Wherever
I go, this not only suggests itself to my mind, but forces itself upon
my senses. At Westminster Abbey, at St. Paul's, at all the public
buildings, there are monuments to honor the heroes of the nation,
whether on land or sea, and to embalm their memories. How deep
and energetic must be the effect of all this upon the national character! What the Roman Catholics do, by means of shrines and
pictures and images, to secure the blind devotion of their disciples,
the leading minds of Great Britain do to secure the feeling of
national pride.

The park belonging to the hospital is an object of great beauty.
The grounds rise to a considerable height, and overlook the country
for some distance. Here is the celebrated Observatory by which
time is regulated all round the globe. On the top of the dome,
and resting upon it, is a large ball, through which the spire of the
observatory passes up. At a minute before twelve o'clock every
day, this ball is made to rise half-way up the spire. An instant
before twelve. it rises to the top, and then suddenly falls. It is
now twelve o'clock at Greenwich, and a corresponding hour, wherever a British ship floats, all over the world.

From this we descended, strange emotions filling my breast, and
took our seats in the railway, built for about four miles on arches
sustaining it above the tops of the houses, so that it could not have
been necessary, for its construction, to remove any more dwellings
than enough to make room for the abutments.

On Monday, I spent the evening with Carlyle. What pleased
me most in Mr. Carlyle was the genuine, boyish, unrestrained

heartiness of his laugh. Made the acquaintance of Mr. Kay Shuttleworth, and of Edwin Chadwick, Esq., author of an "Inquiry into the Sanitary Condition of the Laboring Classes of Great Britain." With these men I am highly delighted.

May 25. Made the acquaintance of Leonard Horner, Esq.; a very sensible man, the chairman of the Factory Commission. Had much conversation with him on the subject of education in England and America.

He said, that, as factory commissioner, he had many times seen certificates of school-teachers given to children, to certify their attendance upon the master's school, signed by a cross, because the teachers were unable to write their own names. He also said he once saw some reason to doubt whether one of this class of teachers could read. He sent for him, and asked the question, whether he could read. "Summat," said he: "at any rate, I keeps ahead of the children."

Visited a Normal school, where we heard one of the teachers take passage after passage from the Liturgy, call upon his pupils for an exposition of its meaning, and then for passages from Scripture to prove it. Among these was cited, without a word of comment, that interpolated passage, that "there are three that bear record in heaven," &c. What a powerful machinery for sustaining the Church, whether its doctrines are right or wrong, and without any reference to their being right or wrong! The conductors or sustainers of the school do not approve this plan of upholding the doctrines of the Church by religious doctrinal instruction in the school, and would gladly modify its course to a very great extent : but they declare that they must have this education, or none at all; that, if they were to omit the doctrinal part of instruction, the whole influence of the Establishment would be directed against them, and would crush them immediately. They therefore submit to it as to an *inevitable* evil.

I afterwards went to the National Training College, Stanley Grove. This is a Normal school established by the National Society. The land, buildings, and fixtures have cost $103,000 ; and sixty pupils are the extent proposed to be educated here. How enormous an outlay for the object to be accomplished ! . . . In this

Normal school, not only the doctrines but the discipline of the Church are regularly taught; and Mr. Coleridge, the principal, says his hope is to raise up a class of teachers auxiliary to the Church, — a sort of half-clergymen, — and station them all over the land. Here, again, is power perpetuating itself.

May 29. Breakfasted with Mr. Whately, the Archbishop of Dublin, whom I found to be a very agreeable man, full of youthful vivacity and spirits, kindly in his feelings, and republican in his principles. He said a great many playful things, such as generally interest school-boys rather than theologians, — as, how can it be proved that there are many persons in the world having the same number of hairs on their heads; the old fable of the hare and the tortoise, &c.: and showed me the manner of constructing and throwing the boomerang, — a New-Holland weapon; also their method of forming a sling.

When I led him to speak on education, he evinced the most liberal spirit; eulogized the benefits of mere secular education; and said that the great and the only principle was to include as much of religious instruction as practicable, and to omit all the rest. There is no doubt of his being a great man; and I believe he is also a good one.

Visited a school in Sharp Alley, which is conducted on principles of toleration. It is called the " City of London Royal British School for Boys;" and one of its regulations is, " that the school be open to persons of every religious persuasion," and " that no book, commentary, or interpretation, tending to inculcate the peculiar tenets of any religious denomination, shall be admitted on any pretence whatever." The school is patronized almost equally by Churchmen and Dissenters, and both Roman Catholics and Jews attend it. The teacher told me that he was a Churchman, but that, as he was placed there to educate all the children without partiality or proselytism, he did not attempt the inculcation of his own peculiar opinions.

I was much pleased with the general method of instruction adopted in the school. *Res non verbâ* was the practical motto. Cards and prints were freely used, and every thing not understood was explained.

May 30. Visited St. Paul's, where there was a musical rehearsal of all the children belonging to the Sunday schools of London. It is said that on the anniversary celebration there are ten or twelve thousand collected together, and probably nearly as many adults attend as spectators. Galleries were fitted up under the dome of this immense edifice; and here the children were seated in the centre, while seats rising at each end in the form of an amphitheatre afforded accommodation for the vast audience. The view from the Whispering Gallery, to which we ascended, was most impressive. What a mass of human life, of human hopes and fears, of happiness and misery, was collected within that circle! Had there been a sudden revelation of all the future history of that company, who could have borne it? But these musings are useless, only as they stimulate one to greater exertions for the welfare of the young; and God knows I need no such stimulus. Nothing can ever alienate me from my sworn love of the young, nor divert my wishes and exertions from what I believe will best promote their welfare.

We then went to the Tower, where we saw how little and bad men could tyrannize over the great and good. We saw the style of the armor — and much of it was original — of more than twenty British kings; the frightful implements of war in use before the invention of gunpowder; the dungeon in which Sir Walter Raleigh was confined, and the stone room in which he slept for eight years. We saw the tower where the two children were murdered by the command of Richard, &c. We also saw the Regalia, or treasures of the crown, all of which a man might carry easily in his arms, and which are valued at three millions of pounds sterling: the crown alone, of the shape of a boy's cap without any visor, cost a million of pounds sterling. Three millions of pounds in the Regalia, and more than three millions of destitute, almost starving, subjects!

Visited the rooms, pictures, &c., of the Duke of Sutherland, at Stafford House, near Buckingham Palace. These are splendid beyond any thing I ever saw. . . . Were there no crime and no poverty in the world, how one would enjoy this!

Went to Windsor; and, having a ticket for special admission to the private apartments, we traversed them. To go to one end, that we might return through the suite, we traversed a corridor as long as Park Street, literally lined, almost as closely as they could be placed, with paintings, statues, &c., and the sides piled up with furniture, all the articles of which, as the Queen is not residing there now, had their covering, or night-clothes, on. From this we visited the plate-rooms, where the service of plate for the palace is kept. These are two rooms of very considerable size, with shelves behind glass doors, literally loaded down with plate. Most of the articles, we were told, were only silver gilt. There was nothing so poor as silver visible. Many articles were inlaid with diamonds. There was a lion's head of solid gold, as large as life, with cut crystal for teeth ; and a little bird, not so large as a pigeon, but intended to represent a peacock, its breast and plumes all inlaid with diamonds and precious stones, the value of which was thirty thousand pounds sterling. These two last-named articles were taken from Tippoo Saib. Are they mementoes of triumph, or of as wicked a plunder as ever one committed against another on Hounslow Heath?

Having sated our eyes with all these wonders, we returned by railroad as far as Hanwell, the celebrated Lunatic Asylum. It is a grand establishment, under the care of Dr. John Connolly.*

We had a delightful evening at Sir J—— C——'s, where we saw many admirable people, — Dr. Arnott, the author of " Physics ; " Dr. Reid, now employed by government in superintending the structure of the new Parliament House, and in regulating the heat, ventilation, &c., of the old one ; the Rev. P. Kelland, Professor of Mathematics in the University of Edinburgh ; Mr. James Simpson, the writer on education ; Mr. Chadwick, &c.

June 1. Called on Mr. Wyse, the author of the work on education, and had a very interesting conversation. . . . In the afternoon, visited the Home and Colonial Infant-school. This is a fine institution, conducted on the Pestalozzian system ; and I was told by Mr. John Reynolds, the principal, that nine-tenths of all the children in the kingdom get all the education they ever receive before they are nine years of age.

---

* This is one of the institutions for the insane, described in " Very Hard Cash."

June 2. Visited the Blue Coat School, or Christ's Hospital, as it is called. This school consists of about a thousand scholars. . . . The uniform or dress of the boys is peculiar. The school was founded in the time of Edward VI., and the dress remains the same now as it was originally. It consists of *no hat;* the boys going out in all weathers, at all seasons of the year, and to all parts of the city, bare-headed. I was told they never caught cold in the head. It would be well to inquire whether they ever have catarrhs, &c. About the neck, they wear a band, like a clergyman, not of lawn, but of coarse cotton. A long blue coat — coat above, but gown below — reaches to the feet, so full as to meet in front. The rest of the dress is small-clothes and coarse yellow stockings. The small-clothes button at the knee. The writing in this school is the most beautiful I ever saw. The method of instruction is very simple; the elements only of the letters being given, without any frame-work of lines by which to draw them. . . . I asked the head master, Dr. Rice, what instruction he gave his pupils in morality. He smiled, or rather sneered, and said he considered the teaching of morality a humbug: he taught religion, not morality. I asked him if he did not inculcate the duty and explain the obligation of truth, and the vice and turpitude of falsehood. He said that could be of little or no use; that Nature taught children to lie; that he explained to them from the Bible that the Devil was the father of lies; that, when a boy told a lie, he set him a copy, — such as, " Lying is a base and infamous offence," — and required him to write a quire of paper over with the sentence; that the offenders were generally submissive, for they well knew, that, if they showed any spirit of defiance, they would receive a sound flagellation. He added, that corporal punishment was much less used than formerly.

After this edifying conversation, I left him. How strange it is, that, on every other subject, the existence of reason is acknowledged: on that of religion, the most important of all, blind authority is appealed to !

After a survey of the premises where the Houses of Parliament are, and are to be, I went into the House of Commons, and sat three or four hours listening to an animated, though not very interesting, debate on the Canada Corn Bill. Here I heard Shiel (the

Irish orator), Lord Stanley, Mr. Hope, Mr. Woodhouse, Admiral Sir Charles Napier (the stormer of Beyroot) : and last a Lord N—— make a most violent and abusive speech against Mr. B—— ; to which the poor commoner, Mr. B——, only responded by a very servile speech, flinging sops where he ought to have flung daggers, and whining when he should have thundered. The abuse from the " noble lord " was heartily cheered.

Visited the Union Workhouse, Gray's Inn Lane. . . . The whole seemed to be well conducted, and impressed me very favorably with the measures that are taken to relieve people *after* they have become poor.

On Friday I visited Pentonville Prison. It is on the Pennsylvania system of solitary confinement; the intention being that no two prisoners shall have an opportunity to see each other while in prison, so that they may go out as great strangers as they come in. The arrangements to produce this result are certainly very curious ; but I doubt whether they fully accomplish it. Another professed object is never to let a prisoner see a stranger visitor, nor a stranger visitor a prisoner ; and yet I am certain, that, if I had desired it, I could have taken such a view of many of them as would have enabled me to recognize them after their discharge. Each prisoner, when out of his cell, wears a close woollen cap, coming down very low, with a long visor, or peak, which they are required to drop down over the face, and which nearly covers it all from view. Little eyelet-holes in this peak enable them to see any object immediately before them ; and, when they are marched out to the airing-yards or to the chapel, they are required to keep behind each other, and at some distance apart. The arrangements of the chapel and schoolroom (which are the same) are very ingenious. The tiers of seats rise behind each other, amphitheatre-fashion, very steep : the prisoners enter single file; and each one, as he takes his allotted seat, shuts his pew-door, which is high, and which effectually precludes him from seeing any other individual whatever except the minister or teacher. . . . The contrivance for watching the prisoners, when airing themselves in their yards, is equally ingenious. The yards radiate from a centre, separated from each other by a high brick wall. The occupants of the yards are watched from a centre.

Orifices in a brick wall surrounding the very centre command each yard. In another brick wall, within this, are similar smaller orifices, exactly opposite the larger ones in the outer wall. Between these two walls is a spiral staircase, from the top of which the superintendent can look into all the yards by a *coup d'œil*. . . .

The arrangements for a supply of water are admirable. The superintendent said no evil effects upon mind or body resulted from this system of confinement; but he did not seem to me very fully to have considered these important questions. It is generally averred that such confinement lowers the tone of the system, increases its susceptibility to impressions, makes the subject more yielding and pliable, and therefore seems to produce amendment, and redeem from the power of evil propensities; but that, when the system is re-invigorated by a return to society, when the force of the natural stimulants is again applied, the impressions made in a state of debility are effaced, the resolutions formed when the appetites were weak are broken, and the old identity of feeble self-restraint and vigorous passions is renewed.

At Pentonville, prisoners are retained but eighteen months. They are then sent to Australia; being divided into three classes, according to their behavior here. The first class (that is, those whose conduct has been most correct) are admitted to many privileges, and relieved from many restraints; the second class occupy an intermediate state as to privileges; the third or worst class are sent to work in chains. This holds out the strongest inducements to good behavior, and, with the strict surveillance that prevails, must make the order of the prison very good.

Prison discipline, and reformation, which is the highest object of prison discipline, was a subject of great interest to Mr. Mann, and one upon which he hoped to find time to write his views. It is a subject that involves the whole theory of morals and religion. If a criminal is led to believe — by education, or by the instructions he receives, when, for the first time perhaps, he has any opportunity of hearing any instruction (that is, after his imprisonment

for crime) — that his heinous sin is to make him the subject of eternal punishment, and that his relief from it is
only to be gained by his belief that another being has
taken upon himself the suffering due to the sinner, he
will not be likely to have sufficient vitality of faith to
secure his reformation under subsequent temptation;
but if he is made to realize the beneficent idea that in
each human soul is a recuperative power which he can at
will exercise for his own reformation, and that his Creator is ready to accept his sorrowful repentance at any
moment when it is sincere, and that he, as well as the
best educated and the most favored of fortune, has before
him a future life of endless progress, let his earthly fortunes be happy or not, a season of imprisonment might be
made indeed a golden hour for him. The first requisite
of a prison is, doubtless, such physical arrangements as will
secure health and comfort: the next is such instruction
as a parent would give to an erring child; and, in the
instructor's hands, there is no instrument so powerful as a
rational, earnest, and benign inculcation of the vital truths
of religion; these vital truths not being found in any creed
or dogmas, but in the proofs of the love of God shown to
man by the history of the soul, as exemplified chiefly in
the character of Christ, "a man tempted like as we are;"
for in this alone lies its true power. Instances could be
quoted from the experience of well-known clergymen
of our day, among whom I can, from personal knowledge,
cite the Rev. Edward T. Taylor of Boston, where men who
had never had an opportunity, because born and educated
at sea, to hear any religious truth inculcated, yielded very
soon, with all the strength of their strong natures, to the
convictions of duty evoked by such heart-preaching — informal, and without any of the paraphernalia of external
rites — as men like "Father Taylor" alone are capable of,

— men who through the form see the substance of religion, and understand the relations of the human soul to it. Father Taylor never addressed the sentiment of fear, but those of love and honor and self-respect: hence his success within the prison and in the still harder school of the world. Such men as Charles Reade (and there are doubtless others, though not yet organized for the work) see into the real difficulty of this great department of benevolence. Our own countrywoman, Miss Dix, has perhaps rendered as much service in this labor, though informally, as in the one by which she has openly moved the world. Her *leisure* hours, spent in penitentiaries, have been fruitful of good, which cannot be measured like her efforts for the insane. It is a work for woman; and, when chaplains for prisons are chosen from woman's ranks, we may look for a new era in prison-discipline. Is it not strange that Mrs. Frye has been so admired, yet so little imitated, in this respect? Mr. Mann often used to say, when he heard of women's complaints of having no career but the domestic one (which he thought a great sphere if well filled, and by no means limited to the care of one's own fireside), that, while the world was sown with jails and prisons, he could not understand the complaint, except by the fact that the practice of benevolence does not insure worldly distinction. In this connection, however, he always felt the difficulty thrown in the way by the common formulas of religious belief above referred to. A truly enlightened education of the people he knew to be the only permanent remedy in this as well as other neglected fields of human duty, and he also hoped for time to enter into such details. Any subject that involved popular theories of religion and morality, in their mutual relations, always looked to him like herculean labors; there was so much to be undone before a new beginning could be made. He was too conservative to pull down, without endeavoring to reconstruct something upon the ruins of fallen idols, yet too radical to leave error at peace.

In the evening, attended a fancy ball at Almack's, given for the benefit of the Poles; at which the company wore the same dresses which they wore at the Queen's masked ball. And such dresses! Such caricatures of humanity were enough to make a man call the baboons and kangaroos his brethren rather than these. Such an immense display of wealth, such pearls and diamonds, and cloth of silver and gold, — how would it all put to shame the pretensions of our displaying people! About twenty ladies were beautifully and tastefully dressed. The money of the others apparently did not hold out; for their dresses rose but just above the waist. Among the men there was not a single good head, — not one that argued strength and benevolence: among the women there were a few. About seven hundred persons were present.

June 6. Visited Norwood and Newgate. At Norwood there are more than a thousand children sent from London. They are the children of parents who are in the London poorhouses.

Visited Marylebone Workhouse. It contains about eighteen hundred inmates. They appeared very comfortably situated. Parts of the building have been constructed for a very long time, and without any knowledge of the importance of classification or ventilation. Some complaints have lately been made on this subject, and reforms ordered. Indeed, those who have the administration of the poor-laws of the kingdom — the poor-law commissioners, as they are called — seem duly to appreciate the importance of physical arrangements, and, in this particular, are effecting a great change throughout the kingdom.

The children are taught some of the elementary branches; the boys, some handicraft; the girls, sewing, knitting, &c. Eighteen hundred, — a population of paupers! Not half of the towns in Massachusetts have a population equal to this, inclusive of their whole numbers.

Dined in the evening with the Archbishop of Dublin, with whose noble liberality and catholicity of spirit I was more charmed than ever. He spoke again of Ireland, — of the means now in successful operation to educate her people ; more than 300,000 children being now in the schools which are under the superintendence of the National Board of Education. In alluding to the exclusive measures now insisted upon by the Established Church in regard to a national system of education in England, he said, "Suppose I should make a great feast, and among my numerous guests there should be a Jew : should I compel him to eat pork ? "

He was full of sportiveness and anecdote.

Lord Monteagle and lady were of the party. He is altogether the finest-looking nobleman I have seen, with a countenance full of the expression of benevolence, and a fair share of intellect, and therefore a gentleman with whom the archbishop would be likely to sympathize.

How good a man must have been, to remain so good after all the temptations and seductions to exclusiveness under which a high dignitary of the Church, like the Archbishop of Dublin, must have labored ! . . .

Visited the famous York Cathedral. . . . To me the sight of one child educated to understand something of his Maker, and of that Maker's works, is a far more glorious spectacle than all the cathedrals which the art of man has ever reared. . . .

After regaling our eyes on this great pile, we went to the wall around the town, said to have been built by the Romans. It is three or four miles in extent. It is now in excellent condition. We walked nearly round it, and went to the foot of the old castle, which has begun to crumble. . . .

June 10. We left Newcastle in a coach called "Chevy Chase." Thus are legends perpetuated. This is natural and agreeable. The county of Northumberland presents a very different appearance from the interior of England. We soon found the fields beginning to grow much larger, the hedges less frequent, the trees not one to ten : and at last we came to wide, open commons, where perhaps for miles there was no fence by the side of the road ; where there had been but very little cultivation, and most of the animals were sheep, the houses few, and collected into poor-looking villages.

This aspect of the country continued until we came to the Cheviot Hills, which divide England from Scotland. Beyond these, the cultivation very much improved. As we approached Jedburg, situated on the River Jed, the scenery was very picturesque, resembling in some degree that of Westfield River as seen from the Western Railroad or from the old Pontoosuck Turnpike. Jedburg itself is a romantic place. Here we saw the ruins of an old cathedral, and would most gladly have explored them; but they were at some distance, and only twenty minutes were allowed at dinner.

From Jedburg we went to Dryburg Abbey, the burial-place of Sir Walter Scott. Here we wished to stop, but could only enter Edinburgh by daylight by going on. From Dryburg to Melrose is about two miles. From Melrose to Abbotsford, the residence of the late Sir Walter, it is three miles. We saw the house which he built, the trees which he planted, and the grounds which he bought, — those fatal grounds! — and would gladly have made a pilgrimage to them: but we are looking to the future rather than to the past; and that, all things considered, seemed to have the most imperative demands upon us. I confess it was a sacrifice for which it is not probable that posterity will repay me.

We rode for many miles along the banks of the Tweed, which are full of beautiful scenery. On this day's journey we first saw the Scotch broom, a gaudy yellow flower; and the heath, which looked brown and lifeless, and had not a particle of beauty to ally it to poetry; and yet the Scotch make it the subject of poetical associations. This is pure *amor patriæ.* The heath looks as if it was dead when it came up.

On the way we saw the Duke of Buccleuch's dog-kennels, which were much better built, and had a far more comfortable air about them, than half the cottages we have seen in England and Scotland.

June 18.   During the last week, I have devoted almost my entire time to visiting the schools of Edinburgh. . . . It is said to be ascertained, from statistical returns, that not more than one-third of the children of Scotland are educated in the parochial schools: the rest depend upon private schools, or receive no schooling at all. . . . The office of teacher is substantially held for life.   He can be disciplined, however, for good cause. Teachers, in general, look for promotion to the Church. It is, as a general rule, only in default of such promotion that they continue in a school. Many, if not most of them, are educated for the Church, and then take a school until they can get a living. . . .

Of emulation, roused and inflamed to intensity in these schools, I have spoken on many occasions. However one might be disposed to regard it in matters purely of an intellectual character, it would seem beforehand as if there could be no difference of opinion respecting it when religious or moral emotions are to be enkindled in the mind. On those momentous themes, the very thought of which should make the heart quail and the eyes stream with tears, there is the same intellectual desire of responding as on a question of the multiplication-table, with no more consciousness of the solemnity of the subject treated in the one case than in the other. And when I asked the teacher of a school, in which every scholar had evidently committed to memory every verse of the Gospels and the book of Hebrews, to examine them on some point of social duty or morals, to bring out their ideas of conscience, &c., he did not seem fully to comprehend my meaning, and requested me to examine them myself. In this respect, they were not equal to a class of boys in a good school of our own.*

This teaching the bare doctrines or dogmas of theology, without awakening the conscience and purifying the affections, seems like teaching anatomy without physiology. It is as necessary that the application of the principles of religion to the duties of life, or morality, or natural theology, should be inculcated, as the principles of scriptural theology. . . .

The object which has called up the deepest and tenderest associations, far beyond those of any other object seen since I left home, was the lowly, humble cottage where Jeanie Deans is said to have been born. I have seen nothing that affected me so deeply as the sight of the residence, with the recollection of the story, of that noble girl.

On Thursday, passed Sterling Castle and the " banks and braes

* For details concerning Scotch schools, see Seventh Report of the Secretary of the Massachusetts Board of Education.

of bonnie Doon," and arrived at night at the east end of Loch Katrine. In the morning I rose at five, and ascended the beautiful hill behind our lodgings, near Loch Achray. Standing at any one point, there seemed no path by which the ascent was practicable : but seeking my way, step by step, I always found a spot where I could plant my foot ; and by diverging a little to the right here, and to the left there, — now descending apparently with a retrograde movement 'in order to turn a crag or reach a safer footing, — I at length stood upon the point which from below seemed inaccessible. And here I moralized. " It is in this way," thought I, " that great and difficult enterprises are accomplished. If one looks to the mighty evil to be overcome, or to the great moral renovation to be achieved, and thinks of these alone, he may lie down in despair at the apparent inadequacy of the means for the attainment of the end. But if he looks around and about him, and sees what good can be done, what is now within his reach and at his command, and addresses himself with all zeal and industry to do what can be done, to take the step next to the one just taken, he will gradually yet assuredly advance, and at last will find himself at the point of elevation which from below seemed unattainable."

We saw the launching of a little steamboat (the first ever launched here) that was intended to ply the waters of Loch Katrine, but we were ourselves taken over in a boat rowed by four men. In the course of the voyage, one of these said he was a teetotaler, and refused to drink any whiskey which was offered to him : so, when we stepped ashore, I gave him a double fee for his discipleship.

The scenery of Loch Lomond is at once beautiful and grand. (The scenery of Loch Katrine was obscured by a pelting, blinding shower.) It is a place in which to abandon one's self to the love of Nature, to become receptive of impressions, and to yield to the influence which they make upon the emotive part of our nature. Amidst all this, however, I confess my heart often turned to the fortunes of the rising generation at home ; and were it not that I hoped here to replenish my strength, to enter with renewed vigor into their service, I would have preferred to be closeted in narrow apartments, working for them, to all the joy of beholding this magnificent display.

Mr. Mann's heart turned to the "rising generation at home" too often during this short European excursion. Even the little recreation it afforded him to run up mountains, and sail all day occasionally upon a beautiful lake, gave his over-worked brain some relief, though never to the point of affording him much or quiet sleep, which was the restorer he needed. He "fought all his battles o'er again" in the night-watches; and not even the counsels of his wise friend Mr. Combe could persuade him to dismiss all thought of labor, even for a few weeks at a time, in view of the future advantage. He thought then that his hold of life might be very brief; and his wish to bring his plans for the common schools of his country to a certain maturity overmastered every consideration of prudence. When remonstrated with for thus violating the natural laws he so strenuously urged, his only reply was that he obeyed a higher law than he violated, and that the benefit of the experience he had gained must not be lost to the cause for any personal considerations. Finding remonstrances to be unavailing, his friends always felt the magnetic influence of his ardor such, that they yielded the point, and joined their efforts to his to accomplish the ends he had in view. But if he had occasionally given himself up to the healing influences of the nature he so much loved, and which is so admirably adapted to the wants of an exhausted system, he might have escaped another source of ill health which from this period distressed him for many years. It was the tic-douloureux, whose tortures rendered him nearly frantic, till at last he had a whole mouthful of apparently sound teeth extracted, which revealed the neuralgic sacs at the roots of three teeth, that had been the hidden cause of the malady. His health improved from that time, until the exhausting labors of the last few years of his life again prostrated him beyond recovery.

Thursday, June 22. Visited the Normal School at Glasgow. There is nothing peculiar in this school, except that Mr. Stowe, the principal, discards emulation as one of the incitements to study.

In the Royal Asylum for the Insane, the plan of common dormitories is introduced. One room is designed for four suicidal patients. It is said they will keep each other from committing an injury.

Dr. Hutchinson, the principal, says it answers an excellent purpose to place the melancholic and the boisterously gay in the same apartments : the excesses of each are counteracted by those of the other. This seems rational.

Under the protection of Capt. Miller, the Superintendent of Police, I visited some of the worst districts of Glasgow. The condition of the poor is inconceivably wretched in some of these quarters. In one place, we passed under an arch of ten or twelve feet ; then we came to a small open square, perhaps six feet, where all the refuse of many families was thrown. Through this we went up a narrow stairway into a room not more than ten feet square, where were three beds and two sick women, one groaning as if in agony. Here were all the furniture, goods, and chattels of the family.

In another place, we had to contract ourselves into a height of not more than four feet to enter the low door. We descended a long step for this, passed under a covered way where we could not stand upright by more than a foot, and entered a miserable room, about as large as the one just described, but not higher than my shoulders ; and on the front side was the only window, of six panes of glass of about six inches square. Along the street into which this window looked ran a brook, which sometimes rose and overflowed, and filled up these apartments almost to the ceiling. The water of the brook was exceedingly muddy and fetid. This district covered acres, in which there was nothing but a repetition of the same dreadful scenes. Children abounded here. Almost every female old enough to hold a child had one in her arms. This place of abomination was screened from public view by rows of fine houses and shops on some of the principal streets of the city.

Visited the old Cathedral of Glasgow, and heard the quota of legends that belongs to all such places.

Dr. Nicol, the astronomer, showed me very beautiful astronomical instruments. The transit instrument cost £800. Here, too, I saw a very beautiful anemometer, made by Mr. Osler of Birmingham. It records, or rather delineates, the course and intensity of the wind. A rain-gauge is also connected with it, by which not only the quantity of the fall of rain is ascertained, but exactly at what time it rained fastest, and how much the fastest. The cost of the whole is £40.

In the University of Glasgow is a statue of Sir James Watt. He was a native of Greenock, a poor boy, and at sixteen years of age came to Glasgow in search of his fortune. He used to stand at the great arched entrance to the square of the University, and sell toys of his own construction to the students. As he obtained means, he extended his traffic : but, being interfered with by members of the city corporation for exercising a trade, the university, which was also a corporation, took him under its protection ; and here his genius began to develop itself. An original model of a steam-engine — the very one on which he first exerted his inventive powers — stands by the side of his statue. How rude and feeble, compared with those beautiful and mighty instruments which have succeeded to it, this model appears !

In Scotland, there is a society, incorporated by act of Parliament, " for the relief of the widows and children of burgh or parochial schoolmasters." This society was incorporated early in the present century. All burgh and parochial schoolmasters are, *ex officio*, members of it. Each member is obliged to pay a certain sum annually towards the funds ; and, in consideration of this payment, his widow, if he leaves one, and her children, if children survive her, are entitled to draw an annuity from the funds. It is optional with the members to pay more or less within certain prescribed limits ; but the amount of the annuity to which these representatives are entitled is determined by the amount of the annual subscription.

There are many details of minor importance respecting this corporation, for which one must look to the act of Parliament and to the by-laws and regulations of the society. No widow or family can draw more than £25 a year.

The funds of this society are now rather more than £50,000:

total accumulated fund or capital on the 16th September, 1842, £54,297. 13s. 5d.

Taking a broad and statesmanlike view of the subject, it is clear that it would have been far better to give to schoolmasters such a competent salary, that each one, by prudence and good management, could not only support himself during his term of public service, but could also have a competency for his family. The whole scheme is an attempt to mitigate the evils of poverty, which the penuriousness of the schemers first inflicts. It is not, like a common insurance, a provision against casualties, or unforeseen or uncontrollable disasters; but it compels each one, however poor or unfortunate, or however small his salary may be, to contribute to a fund, the income of which is also to be divided among all, merely on the contingency of leaving a widow or an orphan, — not on the contingency of actual want, nor in case of actual want, on its happening through misfortune, or the sufferer's own improvidence.

HAMBURG. . . . This was once a fortress; and walls were erected all round the town, except on the side where it lies upon the Elbe. The ramparts are now demolished; and, where they once stood, beautiful winding walks are laid out, and the grounds are planted with various forest and flowering trees and garden-flowers of many kinds, stretching outward into the walks. The whole is open to the public, and the truant boy from the streets as well as the day laborer and the people of taste have free access here; and yet a tree or shrub is never injured, a flower is never plucked. Suppose the whole of Boston Common to be laid out like a gentleman's garden, the fences to be removed, and the whole thrown open to every one who might choose to enter, whether from the city or from the country: how long would the walks remain uninjured, the trees and plants unmutilated, the flowers unplucked? This is certainly a lesson to republican America.

Magdeburg is a walled city and fortified town. It contains about thirty thousand inhabitants. Its main street, called *Breite Weg*, runs through the city from north to south. At each end is one of the gates, or entrances; and before each gate are very extensive fortifications. Those at the south gate must cover five hundred acres or more. The fortifications are ramparts and moats, with covered ways, or subterranean passages, by which those on the outer walls, if driven in, can pass securely behind another and another; and there are still other barriers, I know not how many.

The sight of the whole produced a most painful impression on my mind. What a height of honor, of excellence, and of happiness, might mankind have attained, if a thousandth, or even a millionth, part of the wealth, and the time, and the talent, and the energy, which have been expended for their oppression and debasement, had been spent wisely in improving their condition!

BERLIN. — The institution for the deaf and dumb surpasses that at Magdeburg. . . . Almost all the public schools in Berlin were closed for the summer vacation the morning after our arrival. By the favor of some very kind people, we obtained access to several private schools; and here we saw excellent specimens of teaching.

The curiosities or "wonders" of Berlin are many and very interesting. The Museum, the collection of two thousand specimens of art from Pompeii and Herculaneum; the fountain in the Lust-garten; the Arsenal; the Palace, in which is the Kunst Cabinet; the library of five hundred thousand volumes; the Thier-garten, &c., — are certainly things well worthy the attention of any one who travels for sight-seeing.

July 16. At Potsdam we find the schools still open, and have seized with great avidity upon the opportunity of visiting them. With them all we are highly pleased.

We have visited Sans Souci, the palace built by Frederick the Great. In the New Palace* is one of the most tasteful and splendid of rooms, — a spacious apartment, more than a hundred feet in length and sixty in width, with pillars at each end so as to bring the central part into the form of a square. This room has a most beautifully variegated marble floor. Large and splendid figures are inlaid, radiating from the centre outward. But the most beautiful idea of the whole is the formation of the walls — which resemble stalactites — and the pillars. These are covered with shells of all kinds that fishes have ever lived in, or with specimens of mineralogy, tastefully arranged. The present castellan, who is

* This palace is said to have been built by Frederick after the seven-years' war, to prove that he had some money left.

an old gentleman of taste, has introduced this feature ; and kings and potentates, as well as lesser people, send him specimens from every part of the world, so that the collection is ever increasing. Large chandeliers are suspended from the ceiling ; and, when lighted up, the scene must be brilliant beyond the description of fable. . . . In the Old Palace at Potsdam, and in the new one near Sans Souci, we saw the favorite rooms of Frederick the Great, his library, tables, writing-desks, and various other paraphernalia.   Some of this has been preserved as nearly as possible in the same condition in which it was left by him.   It is said that a clock, which he had always wound up with his own hand, stopped at the very minute of his death ; and it has been left in that condition ever since.   Here, as in other palaces, was a perfect wilderness of pictures.   The rooms of state were as rich as gold and carving and painting could make them.   England's palaces do not compare with them.   In many instances, the eye was pained with the profusion of those things which were intended for its delight.

At Charlottenberg we saw a very beautiful mausoleum, or small temple, erected by the late king to the memory of his wife, the lamented Louise.   Here is a statue, — recumbent, — larger than life, of the queen, by Rauch.   The building was very simple in its architecture, and very rich in its materials ; and the only unpleasant circumstance pertaining to our visit there was that the keeper should be allowed to take money from visitors, for the king, for showing the monument of his deceased mother.

At Potsdam we became acquainted with Von Turk, a man long celebrated for his charitable deeds.   He has erected several orphan-houses ; and is now at the head of one, to the support of which he is said to appropriate his whole income.

One of the most interesting sights in Potsdam is that of the Royal Orphan House, founded by Frederick the Great.   It contains a thousand children, — all the children of soldiers.   They seem collected there as a monument of the havoc which war makes of men. They are instructed in all the rudiments of knowledge and in music, and are practised in gymnastic exercises to a remarkable point of perfection.   They performed feats which I have never seen equalled, except by a company of professed circus-riders or rope-dancers.

Here we saw a terrible array of feather-beds, a hundred and forty in one room; and no other covering, in summer weather, but a feather-bed weighing fifteen or twenty pounds!

HALLE, *July* 21. In the Franke Institute are three thousand children under the superintendence of Mr. Niemeyer. The orphans compose but a small part of this number. It was founded in the eighteenth century, and is said to be the father of all the orphan-houses which have been erected since in Germany. The teachers were all of a very high order, — intelligent, benevolent-looking men. The institute is a quarter of a mile long, six stories high, several apartments thick, built round an oblong court-yard. The statue of the founder stands in one of the courts before the director's house, with his hands on two children's heads, and the motto on the pedestal, "He trusted in God." . . . We also visited a poor-school, where the children behaved much better than they dressed (I have seen schools, in some countries, where the children dressed much better than they behaved); also a school for *very* poor children, where they are taken care of while their parents are at work; and a school of a dozen or fifteen large scholars, who had been examined for confirmation, but had failed in consequence of their ignorance of the Bible. Here they were collected, and put under the care of an instructor, who was endeavoring to give them, to *commit to memory*, so many verses of the Bible as would authorize their being confirmed, avowing their belief in the Lutheran creed, and partaking the sacrament of the Lord's Supper. They certainly were as desperate-looking subjects as I ever saw; but they could obtain no clerkship, apprenticeship, or other employment, unless *confirmed*. . . . All the inconveniences and physiological wrongs of German schools find a compensation in the character of the teachers. Those whom I have met in the schools, if assembled together, would form the finest collection of men I have ever seen, — full of intelligence, dignity, benevolence, kindness, and bearing in their countenances and demeanor the impress of conscientiousness and fidelity to their trust. In our own schools, the employment of female teachers has been frequently advocated; and one of the strong arguments in favor of their services has been, that they were more kind, affectionate, forbearing, and encouraging than the other sex. In Germany this argument would not be understood; or, rather, the fact on which the opinion is founded with us does not exist there. As yet, I have never seen an instance of harshness or severity : all is kind, encouraging, animating, sympathizing. This last is true to such a degree as would seem almost ludicrous with us. A German teacher evinces the greatest joy at the success of a pupil in answering a question; seems sorrowful, and even deeply moved with grief, if he fails. When a question has been put to a young scholar, which he strove and struggled to answer, I have seen a look of despair in the teacher ; but if the little wrestler with difficulties overcame them, and gave the right answer, the teacher would seize and shake him ardently by the hand to felicitate him upon his triumph; and where the difficulty has been really formidable, but the exertion on the scholar's part triumphant, I have seen the teacher seize the pupil in his arms and embrace him, and caress him with parental fondness, as if he were not able to contain the joy which a successful effort had given him. At another time, I have seen a teacher actually clap his hands with delight at a bright reply. And all this has been done so naturally, so unaffectedly, as to excite no other feeling in the residue of the children than that of a desire to win the same favor for themselves.

DRESDEN, *July* 29. . . . We have visited the gallery of paintings several times, and found a collection vastly superior to any thing seen since leaving England. Without being much of an amateur, I must say that there is true delight in looking at such *chefs d'œuvre* of genius ; and, if other things were as they should be, it would give unalloyed pleasure to see them. But when we reflect how the arts have flourished amid an immeasurable extent of misery, and that those who have cultivated them most munificently by their patronage and their wealth have been most regardless of the welfare of their fellow-men, it throws a cloud over the brightest pictures which the pencil of the artist ever painted.

Aug. 2. Visited the Green Rooms, as they are called, of the Palace. Here are collected the wonders of Art and the riches of Nature. . . . The regalia of the Saxon kings is one of the richest in the world. A few years ago, it was mortgaged for five million dollars ; and this was supposed to be only about half its value. Oh, how these look to a philanthropic eye, that knows at what an expense of human happiness they have been acquired!

Aug. 3. Saxony has a constitution, and a representative body of two houses. The constitution was granted by the king in 1831. The upper house, where the ministers have a seat, that they may answer questions and make explanations, &c., during the debates, seemed, when I visited it, to be really a deliberative and a dignified body. . . . A representative assembly in Saxony, with Austria on one side, and Prussia on the other, is like a bit of good ham in an otherwise miserable sandwich.

In a burgher school near Dresden, I heard, for the first time in Germany, a lesson on the constitution of the State. The teaching was extemporaneous ; and the teacher took occasion to contrast the excellence of their present condition, when they have laws made by representatives elected by themselves, not only with the condition of unlimited monarchies around them, but with their own condition in former times.

From Dresden we visited the tomb of Moreau. The monument is very cheap and simple. It marks the spot where he fell. At the great battle of Dresden, in 1813, between Bonaparte and the allies, it is related that Bonaparte saw a small body of men assembled on a little elevation, a mile and a half or two miles from his headquarters, and also that couriers were constantly passing to and from them. He immediately ordered one of his batteries, consisting of twelve guns, to load, and elevate for that spot, and, at the word of command, to fire simultaneously. This order was executed. The group at which the guns were directed consisted of Moreau, of the Emperor Alexander, the king, and others. The ball which struck Moreau took off his leg on one side, passed through the body of the horse, and took off the other leg. Bonaparte said if he had fired a single shot into such a company, as most men would have done, he should only have alarmed them, and committed no execution ; but something was to be hoped from a dozen guns.

In Leipsic, Mr. Mann and Mr. Combe had unexpectedly met. Mr. Combe had been peremptorily sent to Germany, and condemned to silence, by his physicians, on account of an attack upon his lungs; and the two friends were put under protest: but they disregarded every prohibition, and *pied à pied*, or on some pleasant excursion, they talked solidly from morning till night during the few weeks they remained together. In spite of the apprehensions of friends, Mr. Combe improved every day. Sometimes, taking one horse, one would literally " walk on the horse," as the French say, while the other walked on foot, still talking, till Mr. Combe had imparted all his observations on the country, with which he was familiar by frequent and long residences, and till they had talked far into the future as well as into the past. At last, time was no more for them; and they reluctantly parted, never to meet again on earth, except in the affections, and in such measure of intellectual companionship as correspondence by letter could give. Both were men capable of deep and abiding friendship; and the brilliancy of the one was a fine counterpoise to the gravity of the other, each being endowed with logical power to satisfy the other's demands for that quality of intellect, without which neither could enjoy interchange of thought with any one.

Aug. 4. We started, in company with Mr. and Mrs. Combe, on an excursion to Saxon Switzerland, as it is called, —a region about twenty-five miles east of Dresden.

We went first to Pirna to visit a lunatic asylum of great repute. It contains rather more than three hundred subjects. The building is most beautifully situated on a very high eminence rising abruptly from the right bank of the Elbe. It entirely overlooks the whole town, and would do so if it were a hundred feet lower. It was an ancient castle; and, having been built expressly for a garrison, it may well be supposed that the internal arrangement is ill adapted to the purposes of a hospital. We heard beautiful music, some pieces of which were performed by the inmates, who appeared to be well treated, and as happy as such sufferers can be. Apart from the main building is a separate establishment for the convalescent, — an excellent arrangement. The hospital was established in 1811, when the king had supreme power, and it was not necessary to enlighten the people to secure obedience to the commands of the State. How different is this from the case in Massachusetts! Our hospital depended for its support upon the good will of the people, and therefore it was necessary to enlighten the people. Annual reports are not published from this German hospital; but in Massachusetts the people were enlightened in various ways, particularly by the preparation and publication of extensive reports. These, being freely distributed, have produced an entire revolution in public opinion upon the subject of insanity. Probably far less has been done in the course of thirty years, in enlightening the minds of the people of Saxony on this subject, than has been done in Massachusetts within ten years.

When this country was occupied by Bonaparte, in 1813, he wished to station a detachment of soldiers at Pirna. Accordingly, he despatched orders to the superintendent to have the hospital cleared in eight hours. The insane were sent to the neighboring church, and the troops occupied their dwelling.

On our way to Schandau, we passed the Fortress of Königstein, — a fortress which has never yet been taken. On all sides but one, it is inaccessible to any thing that has gravity. Opposite to it is the Fortress of Lilienstein, which is *almost* inacessible on all sides. Yet Napoleon caused a road to be made for a considerable distance over a before impassable tract of country, and three cannons to be carried to the top of this bluff, in the hope of throwing his shot into Königstein; but the distance was too great, and therefore the attempt unsuccessful.

Lilienstein is a beautiful, symmetrical eminence, rising from the level of the surrounding country; and shot up through the centre of this is a tremendous mass of sandstone, leaving a surface, at a vast height from the region beneath, of an extraordinarily striking character. It is more than a hundred and fifty feet higher than its fellow, and is a more imposing object; but Königstein is situated immediately on the left bank of the Elbe, and serves to command that channel both into and out of the heart of the country.

On Saturday, the 5th, we set out for Saxon Switzerland; proceeding a number of miles in a carriage, when we were obliged to alight, and either be carried in a litter, ride on horseback, or go on foot. The scenery of this region of country is most peculiar. In one place, a perpendicular wall of rock from three to five hundred feet high encloses an area of two miles in diameter. The rock is sandstone, and generally appears in thin layers (from one to ten feet in thickness), although sometimes there is no visible division horizontally for a hundred feet; but vertically they are all split, as it were, into pillars, the rifts being generally very narrow; and sometimes the clefts cross each other at right angles, dividing the mass into small squares if we consider them horizontally, but into immense parallelograms when considered vertically. The summit of each pillar has been worn by time, so that it presents the form of a rounded cap, or dome. The highest point in this vicinity is that of the Winterwalde, seventeen hundred feet above the level of the sea, and commanding a view of the whole region; and when the grandeur of the features and the wild natural aspect are contrasted with the cultivated fields which lie to the east, and with the quiet flowing of the Elbe as it is seen towards the west, the scene is picturesque and imposing in the highest degree. For particulars of sites and wonders, the guide-books must be consulted; but no one can have any adequate idea of the face of Saxony, who does not visit this miniature of Switzerland. The best route is that from Chandau to the Kuhstall first, and back by the Elbe.

On Monday, the 7th, I visited the two Chambers again, and was struck with the order and sobriety of the members of each. The lower as well as the upper house sits uncovered, and the members all leave their hats and overcoats in an anteroom. In the lower house there is a democratic party, or a party contending for more privileges. Last winter, they made a strong effort to carry a measure for the publicity of criminal trials, and the removal of restrictions from the press.

To show how much the constitution is valued, it may be remarked, that in Leipsic the day of its anniversary is a holiday in all the public schools.

In the evening we were invited to the house of a Mr. de Krause, a pleasant gentleman, who, with his family, spoke very good English.

He told me that all the governments of Germany, excepting Austria and Prussia alone, had constitutions and representative assemblies.

We made the acquaintance to-day of a Mr. Noel, a cousin of Lady Byron. He is an English gentleman, who married a Bohemian lady, and lives at Ispilitz. He assured me that this country is working its way rapidly towards liberal institutions. Even in Bohemia, where a sort of parliament is assembled thrice a year to register the will of the king, — it being so much a matter of form, that the sessions last but a single day, — even here a spirit of inquiry is aroused, and for the last two years the right had been exercised of asking some questions in reference to the use of moneys granted to the king. At the coming session, he said he knew that this inquiry was to be renewed and insisted upon. Thus light is dawning upon the midnight of Austrian despotism.

He told me that education is very general in Austria, but that it is very inferior, and that government means to keep it within its present limits. A number of private gentlemen, last year, desired to contribute the means, and erect a school in Prague for the preparation of teachers; but, on making application to the government for liberty to do so, they were refused. Yet, even in Austria, a man is not allowed to teach until he has served an apprenticeship as an assistant school-teacher for a year or more.

To-day, also, I was introduced to the Hof-prediger *Ammon*, a Catholic priest, the keeper of the king's conscience. I found him a most delightful man; full of generosity; a noble figure, fine head, the most charming expression of countenance; and, when any thing was said that particularly interested or pleased him, he would seize the speaker by the hand, and evince the liveliness of his satisfaction by a hearty shake. He inquired very particularly about the Germans in America, —their civil, social, and political condition; and exhibited the warmest interest in every thing that concerned the welfare of man. If such a man can grow up under the influences of Catholicism, what would he be under a nobler dispensation? He spoke of Bohemia, which is Catholic, with great regard, and said that the school-teachers who came from there had more practical skill, though they were not so theoretically conversant with their duty as those of Prussia and Saxony.

We have met with but very few beggars in Prussia and Saxony; not so many in all as I have seen in a single day in London. But when, in making the tour of Saxon Switzerland, we entered Bohemia, we encountered more beggars in an hour than we had seen before in a month. Indeed, the road was almost thronged with them; and I think they must all have heard the story of the unfortunate woman who meant to succeed by perseverance, — by worrying, if not by exciting compassion.

Erfurt was formerly a Saxon city, but was transferred to Prussia by the Holy (or, more properly speaking, the Unholy) Alliance. We called immediately on Director Thilo, to whom we had an introduction. After visiting schools, we went to the monastery where Luther translated the New Testament; saw the pulpit where he preached, and the cell which he occupied. This is the celebrated cell of Luther at Erfurt. Here is shown the very inkstand out of which he wrote, — a large, coarse, wooden box about three inches long, five inches wide, and six inches deep. That *box* moved the world. How many sceptres must be added together to get the emblem or the remembrances of such power! We saw his first translation of the New Testament; specimens of his handwriting, as well as that of Melanchthon, which are preserved in a glass case, and are certainly not models of calligraphy. In this cell it was that Luther had those strivings which he held to be contests with the Devil; and so completely did his imagination triumph over his senses, that he supposed the Devil appeared to him, and tempted him, face to face. In the cell, upon the wall, is shown the spot made by his inkstand when he hurled it into the face of his Satanic Majesty. This was certainly a very intelligent hint to the intruder; and, if his complexion were a matter of any consequence to him, it may be presumed he did not expose himself a second time.

From Erfurt to Eisenach. Visited, with Director Schmid, the schoolhouses of Eisenach, one of which is new and quite elegant, but constructed without the slightest reference to its being inhabited by breathing animals. Mr. Schmid is a man of the highest nervous temperament, and of great mental activity. He took us to an examination of a private school, where two fine-looking teachers were in turn examining a class of about thirty girls. Here the idea recurred to me, but more forcibly than ever before, what a disproportion between the amount of *thought* and of *talent* devoted to the cause of education here and in America.

Visited the Schloss of Wartberg, where Luther hid himself when he fled from Worms, and where also, it is said, he translated his Bible. Here the cell which he occupied is shown, and another place on the wall where he flung his inkstand at the Devil. Which is the true scene of that rencounter, I have no means of knowing; but according to all traditions, wherever it might be, the Devil came off second-best.

Saw the cathedral where the emperors were formerly chosen and crowned, and the present Town House where they repaired to dine. In the great dining-hall of the Town House, at the ends and sides, there are forty-five niches, with pictures, in each, of the whole series of German emperors, from the tenth century down to the present, when the line came to an end. I was told that great care had been taken to obtain these likenesses; and a rascallier-looking set of fellows one would not desire to see out of a state prison.

While visiting the Cathedral, I fell in with my friend Dr. Howe, whom I was more glad to see than I can express. The meeting was purely accidental. I should like to have Babbage calculate the chances that two atoms like Dr. Howe and myself, floating about in the atmosphere of all Europe, would come in contact with each other.

Aug. 19. At Schwalbach we dined, and at Schlangen we remained over night. . . . These great watering-places are in the Duchy of Nassau. . . . The schools here seem to be very well managed, the teachers competent; and here, as elsewhere, nothing is wanting but freedom. But is it not a reproach to freedom when men who are free act less wisely for themselves than despots act for their subjects?

DARMSTADT. . . . In speaking with the director of the city schools here about the regularity of attendance, he said they did not know that there was any other way: the children were born with the innate idea of going to school. *Our* school registers and abstracts

14

will show that our children are very far from having any such instinct.

Aug. 26. Came to Carlsruhe, or Charles's Rest. It is said, that, in the early part of the last century, Prince Charles was travelling through this part of his dominions, when, sitting down to rest under a tree, he conceived the idea of founding a city from that centre. He laid out thirty-two roads from that point, like the radii of a circle, corresponding with the thirty-two points of the compass. One-half the area laid out is still forest. The only stream upon which the city is built is about large enough for one duck with her brood to swim in, and it has no natural advantages whatever. It stands here solely to gratify a selfish whim, and is upheld by being the residence of the Grand Duke and the garrison of a few thousand of his soldiers. At a short distance to the west flows the Rhine. Such are the effects of folly when united with power. Berlin is another example of the same thing. Carlsruhe has provided very liberally for the education of its children. There is a polytechnic school, in which the subjects taught are very interesting, and have a close relation with practical life.

Sept. 3. I remained at Baden during the whole of the past week, and tried to drown disease out of my system as people drown a woodchuck out of his hole; but I found that disease had a stronger hold than health, and, therefore, that I was daily drowning out the latter instead of the former. Finding that I was growing worse so fast that there would be small chance to grow worse much longer, I abandoned all hope and water at the same time, and hastened away.

At Baden I visited the remains of the old castle, which are stupendous. In its walls there is an *oublié* where prisoners were immured, to be forgotten by the world.

In the new castle I also visited some horrible dungeons, — a descent below the surface of the earth, and then winding passages through eight or ten cells of solid walls; and, last of all, a dungeon, into which those condemned, or those only suspected, were let down through a trap-door to receive a horrid punishment, perhaps to die a lingering death. In a passage-way adjoining the prison was a vault of unknown depth, over which was placed a trap-door, and by the side of the door an image of the Virgin Mary. This image the condemned prisoner was requested to kiss; but, the moment he approached it, the door fell, and he was precipitated to the bottom, where were placed large wheels stuck full of sharp-pointed and sharp-edged knives, that, by their revolutions, cut him to pieces. One would think that ghosts would dwell in such a house, if anywhere; and that no king could enjoy the honors of royalty who inherited blood from such ancestors. . . .

At Bingen, also, I saw an old castle which had its trap-door and dungeon *à la mode*. . . . From Bingen we came to Coblentz. Here the Rhine passes through what is called the Rhine-gau, — a kind of scenery which cannot be described; or, if describable, the best description may be found in " Childe Harold."

In Coblentz the greater part of the people are Catholics. I heard a priest of the Catholic Church give a religious lesson to the children. A part of it consisted of an explanation of the sacrament of the Lord's Supper, and particularly of transubstantiation. He said, if Christ could turn water into wine, then why not turn wine into blood, and bread into flesh? — and I am sure I could not tell him why one was not as easy as the other. The children were obliged to sit for an hour, with their hands placed together in front, and hear this nonsense. They seemed uneasy and miserable enough. I went into the church, heard the mummeries, saw the genuflexions, and the sprinkling with holy water. The quantity of water did not seem to be material; for, when two women went out together, I saw one of them dip the tip of her finger in the holy copper kettle, and the other then touched the tip of her finger to the tip of the wetted one, and both passed on. I am inclined to believe that such a homœopathic dose answered the same purpose as taking an entire bath.

COLOGNE. — The Dom Church is one of the grandest structures I ever saw. On the top of the great tower is still standing the huge crane by which the heavy blocks of stone were raised. The church not being completed when first built, this was left to be further used, and so remained since the thirteenth century. At one time it was taken down; but, soon after, the town was visited by a furious thunder-storm, by which the inhabitants were terribly frightened, and which they attributed to the removal of the crane aforesaid. Whereupon it was re-instated by acclamation; but whether it has since kept off all thunder-storms, as in duty bound, I know not.

This is all the notice of the Cathedral of Cologne, that miracle of art and beauty, which appears in Mr. Mann's hurried journal; but, although such structures generally awakened more painful than pleasurable feelings in him, he was overcome by this one so far as to linger round it, and revisit it, and do homage to its wondrous beauty and its miraculous proportions, as long as he staid in Cologne.

The Church of St. Ursula has nothing in its architecture to attract notice : but it is remarkable for being a place of more bones than Golgotha; for that, if we take the account strictly, was only a place of skulls, whereas St. Ursula has all the varieties in the whole skeleton. In building the church, large niches, or holes, were left in the walls; and these have been filled with dead women's bones, as the tradition goes: but probably no scientific physiologist or comparative anatomist has ever examined them to see whether they were not bones of men or monkeys. The tradition is, that ten thousand virgins were put to death for allegiance to their vows of chastity, and that these bones belong to the said virgins. In the choir, and around the altar, about fifteen feet from the floor, are twenty glass cases, set into the main wall of the building. These cases are divided into twenty-four compartments; and from behind each little pane of the glass looks out, or rather grins out, a skull. Twenty times twenty-four is four hundred and eighty. No doubt, some churchyard was robbed to obtain these. But here, also, is said to be the skull of St. Ursula herself; and in this church, or in some other in the same town, is also the skull of St. Peter, and the skulls of the three wise men who came from the east at the birth of the Saviour.

HOLLAND. — Here is a society for promoting the public good, whose headquarters are at Amsterdam, with branches in all the principal cities. It numbers forty thousand members. It was commenced in 1784 by a Baptist clergyman. It did a great deal for the public schools before the year 1806, when the government took them under its protection. Since that time, great improvements in the education of the people have taken place.

Holland is famous for its benevolent institutions. Amsterdam alone has twenty-three hospitals, alms-houses, and charitable foundations of various kinds. It is said that when some one, in conversation with Charles II., prognosticated speedy ruin to the city from the meditated attack of Louis XIV.'s armies, Charles, who was well acquainted with the country by a residence in it, replied, "I am of opinion that Providence will preserve Amsterdam, if it were only for its great charity to the poor." I called on a venerable old Quaker gentleman in Amsterdam, a member of a society for the improvement of prisons and prisoners. He said he could not introduce me to the prison, and would not if he could; *for it was too bad to be seen.*

A deputation from Holland is now in England, examining the Pentonville and other prisons, with a view to the erection of a new one. The Quaker gentleman is in favor of the Pennsylvania system, with some modifications of the rigors of that system.

In the evening, we came to Haarlem.

Sept. 12. Tuesday. By the politeness of M. Johannes Müller, we had a card for Mr. K. Sybrandi, a Baptist clergyman, who was as civil as possible to us. With him we visited many schools.

Mr. Sybrandi was once a religious teacher at the deaf and dumb school in Groningen. He told me that he had great difficulty in giving to the children any just apprehensions of God; that the ambiguities of the language were such that he was liable to give erroneous impressions, which he did not himself discover till afterwards, when it was too late to remove all the influences that had sprung from them. He told an anecdote of giving them a lesson in reference to the divine prerogative of pardon. The verb which, in the Dutch language, signifies "to pardon," has a double meaning, signifying also "to poison." He had told the children, that, under certain conditions, God *pardoned* all sinners; but one pupil understood him that the enumerated conditions were those under which God *poisoned* all sinners.

The pupils at Groningen are taught to speak with the lips; and signs are not only disused, but discouraged. As illustrative of the perfect manner in which they succeeded in speaking, he said an anecdote was told of a visitor who went through the institution, hearing the conversation between the teachers and the pupils, and when he had seen all the school, and his guide came to a pause, turned to him, and told him that it was not those, but the deaf and dumb, whom he had come to see. I cannot but believe that there is something of exaggeration in this. I have seen none who could not be easily and instantaneously distinguished from a perfectly organized individual; and yet it is not without foundation, for the deaf and dumb can be taught to speak in an intelligible manner.

. . . The children whom we have seen in the Dutch public schools have been very well behaved. Their organization is widely different from that of the German children. They have far more self-esteem and firmness, and I think also more destructiveness; and this seems to accord with the national character.

. . . We went to Leyden from the Hague. I felt a curiosity to see this town, because it was for a time the residence of some of the Pilgrim Fathers, who were driven from England by the persecutions of the church and government there.

I have often been at Plymouth, in my native State, and looked out from the shore eastward, as it were to see them coming, for freedom's sake, to a strange and inhospitable shore. Here I looked westward to see them departing; and it seemed as if my spirit could follow them on their desolate course, — a path which was illumined only by the light of duty, and in which they were upheld only by the love of truth. I found in this beautiful town no memorials of their residence. No monument marked the spot whence they departed, no antiquarian knew the place where they resided. Not even one of their descendants, whom I visited, knew any thing about them, or felt any interest in them. Even in Plymouth, art has obliterated all vestiges of their footsteps; for the spot on which they first trod is now ten feet below the surface of the wharf, where commerce plies its occupation. But what need have such men of monuments? A monument to their names is but an object placed near the eye to intercept the real vision of their greatness. Not the gates of the Leyden city, whence they departed from the Old World, nor the Rock of Plymouth, where they entered the New, are monuments of their glory; but the free institutions of America, the career and the capacities of human improvement opened throughout that boundless Western World, are the monuments and testimonials of their worth. Half the planet whose air we inhale has already been blessed by their godlike attributes; and the time is not far distant when the whole shall join in one acclaim to their praise.

At Leyden we saw Jussieu's botanical garden, as well as the Linnæan. They are said to be among the best in the world. The keeper said it contained twenty thousand individual plants. Australia was largely represented in a fine conservatory.

In some of the schools here was the most offensive proof I have yet witnessed, that the Dutch, like the Germans, have no noses.

When one large school opened, all the children placed themselves in a becoming attitude, and closed their eyes; then one of the boys, being appointed, read a short prayer. I have never seen in any schools, either abroad or at home, public or private, composed of older or younger scholars, such propriety and decorum, during devotional exercises, as in the Dutch schools. No religious dogmas are allowed to be taught in them.

We saw here the Japanese museum of Dr. Siebold. Although I was disappointed in this, yet perhaps it was because I had expected too much. There were many objects of curiosity, and some of a more rational interest. What pertained to the fine arts, however, was uniformly placed in the foreground; while specimens of the useful ones, on which the welfare and progress of mankind so much more directly depend, were thrown aside into obscure places, or even cast away like rubbish. The manner in which a nation makes a mill, or builds a house or a ship, is far more important than the manner in which they make japanned baskets or silk sandals.

The Town Hall of Leyden contains a number of pictures illustrative of the distinguished men of the olden time. A court of justice is also in this building.

The road from Leyden to Rotterdam, through the Hague, is a very delightful one. It lies, almost all the way, along the dike or embankment of one of the great canals. The waters of the canal are high above the level of the surrounding country; and this country is also above the surface of the numerous canals by which it is intersected. At brief intervals along the way, windmills are stationed, which raise the waters of the surrounding country, and pour them into this great canal, which is upheld by its embankments, and thereby preserves the whole land from inundation. I have not seen a single lock, from Ryswyk, where we left the Rhine, made necessary to accommodate a difference of level in the land. With a few exceptions, when we saw sand-hills in the distance, the whole area is almost one dead level, not only as far as the eye can reach, but as the traveller proceeds, day after day, stage after stage, it presents the same aspect. I have seen but very little tillage : it is almost all pasture-land.

At Rotterdam, we visited a prison for young offenders, — one hundred and forty-four, between the ages of ten and eighteen. They are confined for periods varying from a year to half a year. The principle of reform is constant occupation, either manual or mental. From eight, A.M., till twelve, the boys are in school, where they learn to read, write, cipher, &c. ; and some of them are taught to draw very beautifully. After dinner they work at various trades, —joinery, carpentry, tailoring, shoemaking, &c. The commandant was a very good man. The prison for those under arrest was on the old plan, in which there are only varieties of *bad*, without any good.

In Antwerp, we ascended to the top of the tower of Notre Dame before breakfast ; and after breakfast attended a school for girls, kept by a nun, where the children work and study alternately. The work is the manufacture of lace, which begins at six in the morning. It is a very curious operation, and well worth the trouble of seeing. In Brussels, where the richest lace is made, there are larger establishments. It is said the spinning of the thread is very injurious, and indeed sometimes fatal, to the eye. The finest lace is worth forty dollars a yard. But why should a queen or a duchess hesitate to wear lace which cost forty dollars a yard, because one class of people are worked to death to get the money, and another class destroy the eye in making the article ?

In Brussels, all the schools were in vacation, even those for the deaf, dumb, and blind. While we were there, the Queen of England made a visit to her uncle, which caused a great stir among the people. There was a vast crowd out on the occasion, and the city was beautifully decorated. But the people were very well behaved, and no disorder marred the harmony of the occasion. Here I saw many Catholics worshipping in the churches: and every thing which I have seen of them, here and elsewhere, impresses me more and more deeply with the baneful influence of the Catholic religion upon the human mind; and not upon the mind only, but even upon the body. The votaries are not degraded only, but distorted; not only debased, but deformed. Belgium has lately laid the foundation, by a fundamental law of the government, for a national system of instruction. The schools, which are for the whole kingdom, are to be under the civil authority as to their instruction, but under the ecclesiastical in reference to morals and religion; and religion and morals are proclaimed inseparable in the schools. This latter branch of instruction is to be given by clergymen of that denomination to which a majority of the children in the school belong; but the children of parents of a different denomination are not held to be present at the instruction. As, however, the population of Belgium is mainly Catholic, it is easy to see to whose benefit this law, though on its face impartial, will inure. Here the Catholics are giving to the Protestants a taste of what the Protestants, in some other places, are endeavoring to force upon them.

The same law which establishes a system of public instruction establishes two Normal schools.

PARIS, *Sept.* 20. . . . At the hall of the Louvre, the heads of several of the kings to whose hands the destinies of millions were committed were as rascally as their lives; and why should not the former correspond with the latter, as effect bears a relation to cause?

After visiting many hospitals and prisons in and around Paris, Mr. Mann says, —

On the whole, I think we are far ahead of any thing I have seen in Europe in regard to the treatment of the insane, especially if we take into consideration the material arrangements as well as the moral treatment of this class.

At Versailles, the Normal School of France occupies the buildings which were the dog-kennels of Louis XIV. and XV.; and a revolution which can turn a dog-kennel into a Normal school has at least one argument in its favor. . . .

The Jardin des Plantes is the embodiment of science. The Museums of Comparative Anatomy, of Mineralogy and Botany, are splendid collections. Even to the uninstructed eye, the number, variety, and beauty of the objects they contain are a source of high gratification. What, then, must they be to the well-prepared mind, which sees here such a profusion and diversity of beautiful and magnificent objects as would at first lead him to suppose that many a god, each powerful to create and bountiful to bestow, had here mingled the abundance of their gifts, until, on a profounder view, he discovers running through all this variety, and connecting its most dissimilar parts, such a unity of plan, and consistency in execution, as compels him to believe that all this disparity of parts and exuberance of detail proceeds from one and the same all-powerful and all-wise Creator!

The Foundling Hospital is a vast cesspool, where one portion of the vice of Paris, after passing for a long time in subterranean channels, is brought to light. The facts connected with it are appalling. For an average of ten years, the number of illegitimate children deposited here has amounted nearly to five thousand annually; a number many times greater than the whole number of births in the city of Boston. The total expense of this establishment in 1839 was three hundred thousand dollars. At the same date, the number of children belonging to the institution was fifteen thousand seven hundred and nineteen. All this must strike not only the moralist and the philanthropist, but even a political economist, — who might be neither moral nor philanthropic, — with terror. What a condition of society it comes out of! and what a condition it must soon plunge the best society into! All these are thoughts which would arise without any prompting in the mind of a reflecting man; but, to excite the appropriate emotions which appertain to these intellectual truths, one should see the place itself in all its details, and particularity of misery. Considered as history, how much crime does it reveal! Considered in its present connections with those wretched beings whose misfortune or guilt has filled it, what a living record of shame and woe is each deserted child! Considered as prophecy, considered in its necessary and indissoluble connection with the future degradation of these unhappy but innocent outcasts, of what an inconceivable amount of mortification, of secret grief, of crime, of despair that leads to crime, is it the certain herald! If one, standing in the midst of these five thousand guiltless but helpless beings, were suddenly gifted with the spirit of prophecy, if he could lift the veil which hides their future destiny, what forms of woe, of desperation, of madness, of suicide, of death, and of crimes that are worse than death, would start up and fill the air before him! How would the low and piteous wail, which strikes the ear as soon as one passes the threshold, rise to a tempest of groans! Oh, woe for humanity that it should contain these elements of misery and wrong! Oh, deeper woe for humanity, that, while it contains these elements, there should be so few among the great and powerful of the earth to seek for its amelioration!

Took a walk through the Place de la Concorde to the Champs Elysées, and up to l'Etoile, or Arch of Triumph, — a splendid work of art, commemorative of some of those remarkable events in the history of France for which she ought to feel remorse instead of pride.

On the whole, the prisons which I have seen in Paris were miserably constructed (with one exception, — that for the "Jeunes Détenues"), and under loose regulations; the prisoners associating together indiscriminately. Their keepers do not seem to me to be men of high character and principles; and therefore those elevating influences that should daily flow in upon them, as the surest means of their reformation, do not appear to exist. Nothing in the situation of the prisons, in the wisdom of the penal laws, in the conscientious administration of them by the courts, nor in the character of the head director or spiritual guide, can produce the legitimate effect of prison discipline upon the motives and character of the condemned, unless the assistants, who are continually brought into contact with the prisoners, be themselves of a character to transmit any good influences which may flow out from others, or to originate and exert such influences themselves.

Versailles was built by Louis XIV., who, it is said, expended two hundred million dollars upon it. In extent and splendor, it surpasses any thing I have yet seen in Europe. The front is a thousand eight hundred and fifty feet long : but this gives no idea of its capacity ; for its wings are nearly, if not quite, as capacious as its front. It has been placed in its present condition, as a pictorial history gallery of France, mainly by the present king (Louis Philippe). It contains pictures of all the great battles fought by Napoléon. These are arranged in chronological order ; a room, or suite of rooms, being devoted to the victories he gained in one year, another to those gained the next year, and so on. One suite of rooms is devoted to the marshals of France, another to the admirals, another to the kings, &c. But the spirit of the whole breathes of war. The canvas glows with martial fire. The whole scene is red with the blood of battle. It seems to be rather a temple dedicated to Mars than the work of a civilized nation in the eighteenth century, — of that era which we call *Christian*. Beforehand, one would say it is impossible that such a thing should be done. With a thorough knowledge of the French people, one may say that it is impossible such a thing should not be done. Here and there only, and scattered, with wide intervals between them, is there any memorial of sages, philosophers, or philanthropists. And this spot is visited more, perhaps, than any other in France. How must all these things cultivate that love of military renown, that passion for the criminal glories of war, which has worked such havoc upon the resources, the prosperity, and the lives of this people !

The water-works or fountains of Versailles admit of no description : they must be seen. In the Great Fountain of Poland, seventy-four separate fountains pour out their streams. The grotto — a structure of a semicircular form — is built of stones, terrace above terrace, eight in number ; and the water which flows into the upper one pours over its brink into the second, and so on until it reaches the lower terrace, the whole being on one side of a circle or area of beautifully ornamented ground. The Fountain of Columns is an area of some hundred feet in diameter, in the centre of which is a beautiful fountain, playing into a large basin, around whose circumference are twenty-four other fountains, throwing up beautiful jets of water, and altogether making a circle about the central one. Outside of all this are double rows of marble columns, with marble beams, as it were, extending from the top of one column to another, binding them all together. Then comes the Fountain of Apollo, which represents him, after the completion of his day's circuit through the heavens, resting from his labors, and receiving the homage and caresses of his nymphs. On each side of him are his horses, also reposing after the toils of the day. As a background to these groups, an artificial rock of huge dimensions rises up to a great height, now overgrown with trees. In the centre of this rock, and immediately behind the principal group of figures, is a cave, from which pours a copious stream of water; and, a little to the left of this, another stream gushes out, and descends, in short cascades, to the basin below.

Last and grandest of all is the Fountain of Neptune. The huge basin of this fountain is in the form of a half-circle. On the straight side or diameter spout up many fountains, the middle one being the highest, the others in regular gradation; so that a line drawn through the tops of the respective jets would describe an arc of a very large circle. At the corners, two immense lions spout vast quantities of water from their mouths. These jets are directed, at an angle of thirty or thirty-five degrees, towards a central point in the basin. On a parallel with the line of jets first described, rising out of the basin, are other jets, and again others; so that the whole number, considered simply as stationary objects, present a beautiful symmetry. Thousands of people were gathered around the circular side of the basin, enjoying the beautiful scene.

In addition to all that has been described (which, however, has not been described), these great basins are all so symmetrically located, and the avenues of tall trees that lead from one to the other so appositely opened, that every beauty in each is enhanced by its relation to the others and to the whole. The Great Fountains, as they are called, are played on the first Sunday of every month, when half Paris pours out to see the spectacle. At

Versailles are also the palaces of the Great Trianon and the Little Trianon. These have not much beauty or splendor, but are memorable for the fortunes and characters of the beings who have inhabited them. The latter was the favorite residence of Marie Antoinette. Here she sought to imitate humble and domestic life by having a group of Swiss cottages constructed, and to please her fancy by something quite the reverse of that life which she had always led. One of them was a dairy, where she and her ladies-in-waiting used to play dairy-women. It is a fact worth remarking, that while those who are in humble walks of life are perpetually striving to reach or to imitate the splendor of the opulent, and longing to exercise the authority of the powerful, here was an individual, born to power, educated amid the luxuries of a court, and resident in the most luxurious court in the world, who sought for novelty and gratification in the simple employments of the laborious poor.

After returning to London, I visited Oxford, the seat of the famous university. I had a seat in the cars, from London to Oxford, with a student or fellow of one of the colleges. I had much conversation with him; and when, at one time, it became necessary to explain to him that I was not an Englishman, he immediately replied, "Oh! then you must be a Russian, as you speak our language as none but an Englishman or a Russian can." . . . The professorships of Oxford go far to exhaust the various sciences, according to their usual grand division into subjects. But hardly any one attends upon these lectures. The professor of law advertises, several times a year, that at such a time he shall deliver a course of lectures on law; but no one appears to hear him, and he delivers no lectures. So of the other professors. Dr. Buckland occasionally has a few hearers in attendance upon his geological lectures; but this is an exception. Each college, in addition to the public professorships above mentioned, appoints a certain number of private tutors, who are taken from among the fellows of the college making the appointments, and these private tutors instruct in Greek and Latin. On these instructions all the pupils are compelled to attend; and Greek and Latin become the only secular subjects of study, with exceptions too insignificant to be mentioned. Theology is studied, as this is the aim of a large part of the students resorting to Oxford. The Latin grammar is still studied in the original language by the pupils of the preparatory schools. The average age of those entering these colleges is eighteen years. One might marvel at the folly of devoting four years, at this period of life, to the classics; but hardly any thing is marvellous which has habit, early education, and prescription on its side. All the old, who have the control, have been educated in this way; and all the young who aspire to honors in the university know they are to be obtained only by pursuing the same course. The old practice is still kept up, of having a sermon delivered in Latin the day before the commencement of the term. I was present during a part of this pedantic exercise, and heard an elderly man prosing off from a manuscript, from which he never raised his eyes, to about twenty younger men in gowns. . . .

The great Bodleian Library has become so vast, that no account is any longer taken of the number of its books, and the books of which are not arranged according to subjects, but sizes; a catalogue designating the place where they may be found. This has a very great disadvantage, especially for a young man, who may not know beforehand what particular book he wants, or what is its title; whereas, if they were arranged according to subjects, an inquirer could resort to the proper compartment, and find whatever the library might contain on that subject.

In the Bodleian Library, I had another amusing instance of the knowledge of one of the body of learned men at Oxford. The gentleman who took me round into the various rooms containing the immense piles of books, observed, when he saw me looking at some law-books that had just come in, that, three or four years ago, a young gentleman from America, who visited the library, told him, much to his surprise, that the English law-books, and especially the English reports, were used in American courts! My conductor was the professor of Arabic! Here was a professor of Arabic who did not know that the common law of America is the same as the common law of England!

On the whole, though I had not very elevated conceptions of the glories of Oxford before visiting it, I must confess that an inquiry into its organization, course of study, and especially the spirit that prevails there, took away most of the respect, such as it was, that I had. Dr. Buckland told me there was no intercourse between the officers and fellows of the college and the inhabitants of the city. They looked down upon all those not educated like themselves with disrespect or contempt; and no private worth, nothing but the most extraordinary genius or attainments in other departments, could atone for an ignorance of Greek and Latin.

Mr. Mann's visit to Europe may have saved his life at the time; but it could hardly be called a rest. He hardly waited till the exhaustion caused by a very stormy and sea-sick passage home had passed away before he again plunged into excessive toil. He sought the repose of the country to prepare his Seventh Report, which was upon education in Europe; and this was immediately followed by the long controversy with the Boston masters, as the public school-teachers of the city were called. These masters formed almost a close corporation, eager for each other's interests, and almost monopolizing, by the influence they exerted, the choice of who should form this very important body. But Mr. Mann's own account of the war they waged with him will give a more just view of it than any one else can do.

The following extract shows the tension of his nerves under this infliction: —

BOSTON, Feb. 10, 1844.

DR. E. JARVIS. *My dear Sir,* — . . . Can you do any thing for a brain that has not slept for three weeks? I can feel the flame in the centre of my cranium, blazing and flaring round just as you see that of a pile of brush burning on a distant heath in the wind. What can be done to extinguish it?

Yours truly,

H. M.

My DEAR MR. COMBE, — Would to Heaven that an ocean did not separate us, and that some mode of communication more quick and spiritual than that of correspondence by letter were left us! I long again for intercourse with your mind, in order to discover more and more of those laws of the universe that determine the order of Nature and regulate the affairs of men. It is only through a knowledge of these laws that the individual can be brought into harmony with the universe, and that the progress of the race can be placed upon a secure basis. . . .

Our history since I last wrote you, though full of toil, anxiety, and feeling, can be told in a few words. We suffered, from Dieppe to Brighton, from Milford Haven to Waterford, from Dublin to Liverpool, and from Liverpool to Boston, one of the worst passages that have been experienced since St. Paul's shipwreck. There were many ships lost the night we came across the English Channel; and, during the whole of our voyage home, we had a strong head wind, and of course encountered a heavy sea, which struck day after day, like a pugilist, directly into the nose of the vessel. I passed sixteen days and nights almost without food, and with as little sleep. Of course, all vitality was abstracted from me. At home, I found an immense mass of labor to be performed; and doubtless I commenced it before my system had recovered from its exhaustion. On the whole, therefore, I have not been able to accumulate any stock of health, but have lived upon what strength I could make from day to day. . . . My Report, generally speaking, has met with unusual favor; but there are owls, who, to adapt the world to their own eyes, would always keep the sun from rising. Most teachers amongst us have been animated to greater exertions by the account of the best schools abroad. Others are offended at being driven out of the paradise which their own self-esteem had erected for them.

The Episcopalians here have always borne me a grudge because I have condemned the spirit of the English Church in denying all education to the people, which they could not pervert to the purposes of proselytism. After the appearance of the first two numbers of my Journal this year, and of my Report, a regular attack was commenced upon me in a paper which is the organ of that sect, and was published in Boston.   Of course, they had too much craft to avow the real grounds of their hostility, but fabricated charges, in regard to which they excited the sympathy of others. Hence they were in the false position of a man who acts from one set of motives, while he avows another.   The reasons given in such cases never correspond with the feelings manifested or the charges made.   A man who lives in that way can never take good aim; and so, of course, misses the mark.   These attacks became so virulent, that I at last replied.   My first reply was admitted into the paper that had brought forward the accusation; and the editor accompanied it with remarks so weak and wicked, that I replied to those.   This last communication he refused to admit.   I then published it in another paper.   Both of my articles have been extensively copied into other papers; and, as far as I can learn, I have almost all the other denominations on my side, and even the great mass of the Episcopalians themselves.   Though I am considered as having kept down my temper pretty well, for one of the uncircumcised Philistines, yet some writers, who have espoused my cause in the newspapers, have opened all the batteries of destructiveness upon them.

On the whole, it is believed that this will be the last effort of orthodoxy to secure the admission of its doctrines into our schools. . . .

I have hardly left room for personal and domestic concerns.

I told you in my note that our boy was born on the 25th of February.   Your brother's book is our guide in all things.   We live alike in the light of his laws and in the admiration of his spirit. We have come out into the country to a place about twenty-five miles from Boston, on the old post-road to Providence, where we intend to pass the summer.   It will take a very long letter from you to tell us half what we want to know about you.   One thing, if you can, I wish you to do; and that is, to prepare for me four articles on the four temperaments, detailing the different manner of treatment that each of them should receive, especially in childhood.   This would be for my Journal, several volumes of which — enough, I believe, to make up your file — I have sent you.   Give our kindest regards to your brother's family (in whom we include Mr. and Miss

Cox), and all who inquire for us, or who, through you, have been led to take any interest in us. . . .

We go on with the cause very much as heretofore. Though we had a Whig Legislature, yet there was a strong infusion of hostile spirit in it. But they did not dare to attack our cause. We asked nothing of them; and our politicians will not give, except they expect to receive in return. Send me what educational news you can. I sent you a Report, not addressed. Give it to whom you please.

Ever truly yours,

HORACE MANN.

WRENTHAM, June 27, 1844.

REV. S. J. MAY. *My dear Sir,* — . . . I am six feet deep — that is, over head and ears — in the Abstract. It is going on well, and will come out bright. My heart is in the work, or fifteen hours a day would kill me. . . .

TO THE SAME.

BOSTON, Oct. 16, 1844.

MY DEAR SIR, — Troubles thicken; but that only makes me stiffen. On Friday, this week, at the Teachers' Convention in Ipswich, Mr. Swan is to lecture on reading-books. Of course, the plan of Mr. Pierce and myself is to be blown up. In the evening, F. Emerson is to lecture on the best modes of improving common schools. Of course, every thing which we care for and consider indispensable is to be assailed. I have so much to do, that I cannot go. Will you go and defend the cause, and save the Essex-County teachers from being carried over *en masse* into the ranks of our enemies? I shall insist on paying your expenses; but I want your time and influence there.

In the greatest possible haste, I am yours, &c.,

HORACE MANN.

In making extracts from Mr. Mann's letters to Mr. Cyrus Pierce, with whom his intercourse was like that of a brother, I shall not omit his own references to some slanders of the day which touched his honor, — a point upon which he was keenly sensitive.

C. PIERCE, ESQ. *My dear Sir,* — I am disappointed about the fitting-up of the schoolroom. I had set my heart upon having a Normal room for the Normal school. I feel unwilling to relinquish the beautiful vision I had in my mind. If you make the case known in Newton, cannot some further assistance be obtained? I will write to the postmaster about it. Why will you not see Prof. Sears?

I think he is so much interested, that he could engage to get a hundred dollars or so. Perhaps Mr. James would do the same. If Mr. Jackson has returned, see him. I cannot bear the thought of giving it up. In the last resort, you may run the Board in debt two hundred dollars; and, if they won't pay it, I will.

So far as what the Board owns at Lexington will not do for Newton, sell it, and use the money. You have said nothing about a bell. Perhaps some one will give one by and by. You must see Messrs. James and Sears. I do not believe Mr. Sears will let the thing go without an effort. Yours truly,

HORACE MANN.

P. S. — Put the rooms in good order.

JULY 30, 1844.

GEORGE COMBE, ESQ.

MY DEAR FRIEND, — It is now the last of July. Months and months have passed since we have heard from you. . . . As you are as punctual to your plans as the sun to the seasons, I have supposed you would be in Edinburgh in May; and accordingly directed two letters there, and sent you my last Report and some volumes of the " Common-school Journal," with other documents. One of the documents was entitled the " Common-school Controversy." If you have received it, you will see that we have been engaged in a struggle here on the question of *doctrinal* teaching in our public schools. The accounts, in my last Report, of how religion is forced down the throats, and thus introduced into the circulation of children abroad, has started some of our fanatical people, who think it is necessary first to put me down, that they may afterwards carry out their plans of introducing doctrines into our schools. What I said of religious teaching in the English, Scotch, and Prussian schools, would, as I thought, be an antidote against attempting the same things here. With the ultra-orthodox it has proved just the reverse. They say, " Why cannot we do here as they do there ? " They know by experience that the Bible never effects the teaching of their views, *unless they send an interpreter with it.* Therefore they are determined an interpreter shall accompany it; and, if this is not done forthwith, they think it will be too late. I speak advisedly, and from the best authority, when I say that an extensive conspiracy is now formed to break down the Board of Education, as a preliminary measure to teaching sectarianism in the schools. The latter they can never effect; but the former, it is not impossible, they will do. But it will not do to present this bold ground as the basis of the attack. They can have an understanding between themselves in regard to this, but make the charge on other pretences. One of the other means is to impugn the accuracy of my Report on certain points. I wrote you, heretofore, that I understood the Scotch delegation, who came out here to obtain funds in behalf of the Free Church, being ashamed of the religious aspect of some of their schools, as presented in my Report, had given out intimations adverse to its accuracy. These they are endeavoring to extend by public rumor, to make them cover more ground. Can you help me in these matters ? — remembering that, by so doing, you are helping the cause of religious freedom, not only in this country, but over all the world. What I shall want from Scotland is something I can use as authority to show that my description of their schools is correct as regards the manner of imparting secular as well as *religious* instruction. The school in Niddy Street, Edinburgh, and also a school kept by Mr. Carmichael, for giving classical education, will fully sustain every word I have said in regard to the vehement and rapid intercourse between teacher and pupils. I think, also, that you may hear such religious instruction as I have described in many of the schools of the common grade. I am sorry to trouble you even with these rumors of wars; but I most seriously apprehend we are to have a conflict. The best portion of the orthodox are with us, who may possibly ward off the impending danger; but you know how feeble is the control which reason can exercise over fanaticism.

Can you tell me, without any trouble, what is the supposed amount of rents drawn from the land in Ireland by absentee landlords, and what also is the value of tithes (commutations) paid for the support of the Protestant clergy. and taken out of the country annually?

I think Mr. Wyse told me the latter was six millions sterling; but I have forgotten, and have lost a few of the last sheets of my Journal.

What is the whole number of voters in the kingdom for members of Parliament? What is the number of union workhouses?

I am not going to write a book.*

   With much love and regard,
         HORACE MANN.

            BOSTON, Dec. 1, 1844.

MY DEAR MR. COMBE, — I owe you for three long, excellent, soul-cheering letters; and yet I am so circumstanced, that I can give you in return only one short and worthless one. We have been spending the summer in the country, about thirty miles from Boston, and came into winter quarters last evening. . . . The orthodox have hunted me this winter as though they were bloodhounds, and I a poor rabbit. They feel that they are losing strength, and that the period even for regaining it is fast passing out of their hands. Hence they are making a desperate struggle. They feel in respect to a free education, that opens the mind, develops the conscience, and cultivates reverence for whatever is good without the infusion of Calvinistic influence, as the old monks felt about printing, when they said, "If we do not put that down, it will put us down." My office, duties, labors, stand in their way. Hence my immediate destruction is for the glory of God. They have not done yet;

---

* Mr. Mann considered himself as still a servant of the State, and thought he had no right to write a book for his own interest. He had therefore embodied his observations of foreign schools in his Seventh Annual Report.

though from circumstances, which I will proceed to name, they have just now suspended hostilities.

There are two classes, — the one who are orthodox only by association, education, or personal condition. These may be good people, though they always suffer under that limitation of the faculties which orthodoxy imposes. The second class are those who are born orthodox, who are naturally or indigenously so; who, if they had had wit enough, would have invented orthodoxy, if Calvin had not. I never saw one of this class of men whom I could trust so long as a man can hold his breath. These are the men who are assailing me.

My Report caused a great stir among the Boston teachers: I mean those of the grammar-schools. The very things in the Report which made it acceptable to others made it hateful to them. The general reader was delighted with the idea of intelligent, gentlemanly teachers; of a mind-expanding education; of children governed by moral means. The leading men among the Boston grammar-school masters saw their own condemnation in this description of their European contemporaries, and resolved, as a matter of self-preservation, to keep out the infection of, so fatal an example as was afforded by the Prussian schools. The better members dissuaded, remonstrated, resisted; but they are combined together, and feel that in union is their only strength. The evil spirit prevailed. A committee was appointed to consider my Report. A part of the labor fell into the worst hands. After working at the task all summer, they sent forth, on the 1st of September, a pamphlet of a hundred and forty-four pages, which I send you, and leave you to judge of its character. I was then just finishing my Annual Abstract, a copy of which I send you, and which I commend to your attention for its extraordinary merits. As soon as the preparation of the Abstract was complete, which was my *recreation* during the hot days of summer, I wrote a "Reply to the Boston Masters." In this Reply, you will see of how much service your letter and others have been to me. Please make just as warm acknowledgments to Mr. Maclearan as ought to be made by me. His kind letter was most welcome.

I think the Reply is doing something in Boston. All except the ultra-orthodox papers are earnest, I may almost say vehement, against the masters. I ought to have said that one of the masters, William J. Adams, Esq., came out in the newspapers with a public retraction, and disavowal of his signature.

Our municipal election for mayor, school-committee men, &c., comes on a week from Monday; and, in some of the wards, a change has already been made in nominating school-committee men, the voters being determined to have better schools and less flogging. In ward number seven, the central and most intelligent ward in the city, strong resolutions were passed on the subject, evening before last. Others meet to-morrow evening, and are resolved to do the same. Mr. Quincy is the candidate for mayor; and he goes for reform, both as a friend of the cause, and as my strong personal friend. . . .

But things are coming to a crisis. The prevailing party will probably be left in possession of the field for some time to come. . . .
Ever and ever truly yours,
HORACE MANN.

P. S. — You will do me another great favor by either supplying me, or informing me how I can supply myself, with Capt. Maconochie's pamphlets, published at Hobart Town in 1838 and 1839, and also some account of his administration at Norfolk Island. I want all that I can turn to good account on the subject of school-discipline.

PORTLAND, *Sept.* 1, 1844. . . . Prof. Stowe's introductory lecture before the Institute was an admirable thing. It was on "Religious Instruction in Common Schools;" and he occupied and powerfully defended even broader ground than I have ever done. They have voted to print five thousand extra copies, and it will be circulated far and wide. The orthodox must now denounce him, or let me alone.

BOSTON, Dec. 14, 1844.

C. PIERCE, ESQ.

MY DEAR SIR, — I received your note, with the accompanying bills, yesterday. They have astounded me. As you say yourself, it is more than double the amount which I ever had an idea of expending upon the place, — more than double what we ever talked of. . . . The Board held its annual meeting on Tuesday and Wednesday last. In making the estimates for the current expenses, I proposed to Mr. James, the chairman of the visitors, the allowance of five hundred dollars for expenses of fitting up, beyond the Newton contributions. Even to that sum he seriously demurred, but finally put it in. It was handed to the Governor, as chairman and presiding officer, who expressed a doubt about its being presented to the Board, on account of its amount. Mr. Bates then sought an interview with me, and repeated the doubts of the Governor, confirmed by his own. I told him that five hundred dollars was as little as we could get along with in addition to the Newton contributions; and, if the Board did not see fit to make that allowance, I should pay it out of my own pocket. It was then allowed. But what will they say to a thousand eight hundred and fifty dollars ? I confess I know not, and see not what can be done.

When the purchase of the building was suggested to some of the members at fifteen hundred dollars, and before we got the money to buy it, an objection was made to the amount, that the Board had no right to expend so large a sum for a building. Yet here is between three and four hundred dollars more than the whole sum, for improvements only !

The whole strikes me as a very serious matter ; and I have not been so alarmed about any thing this long time. What measures can be devised for relief ?

Truly yours,

H. MANN.

The Board had not agreed to purchase the building; and Mr. Mann begged the money, and purchased it himself. But Mr. Mann may speak for himself in a letter written as late as 1852, when political opponents tried every means to undermine his reputation.

In 1850, some gentlemen who knew that he had fitted up the building at his own expense, and contributed something toward the erection of the two other Normal school-buildings, made a representation of the facts to the

Legislature of Massachusetts, and he was partially re-
munerated by the State; but it was done wholly without
his seeking. Mr. Livingstone published the proceedings,
which will be found in the Appendix to this work.

Dover, N.H., Oct. 30, 1852.

C. Pierce, Esq.

My dear Sir, — After speaking every evening this week from
an hour to two hours each, I feel a little *Monday-ish*, as you ministers say. Still, I am in good spirits, and have a faith undimmed
in our ultimate triumph.

Perhaps you have seen that the apprehension I expressed to you
about the enemy has been already fulfilled. The "Boston Post"
of Friday last, in one of those short *javelin* paragraphs by which
they mean to kill people from an ambush, asked, "What are the
facts in relation to the purchase of the Fuller Academy in West
Newton, by Hon. Horace Mann, for the Norm School?" — in-
tending thereby to make an insinuation against :

I wish I could have seen you after I saw that; but I was on my
way to preach the political gospel here in New Hampshire. Could
I have seen you, I would have asked you to tell the "Post" that
the facts were that I begged the money to buy the premises, instead
of asking the State to buy them; and then, that you and I spent
thirteen hundred dollars of our own money to fit them up; and
then ask the judgment of the "Post," whether, if there was any
thing dishonorable in that, it was on our side.

If I have any friends, they will find it necessary to be on the
lookout, especially this week.

In haste, yours very truly,

HORACE MANN.

Mr. Pierce immediately sent a notice of the facts, over
his own name, to the "Post;" but, at this remote time, I
cannot tell whether it was inserted. Probably not. It
was about that time that his political enemies sent an
emissary to search the archives of the State, hoping to

find some evidence of Mr. Mann's tampering with the public moneys. Of course, the record was clear, and they retired baffled.

In this connection, although equally out of date, I will subjoin part of a letter from Hon. J. Quincy, jr., in reference to another accusation of the same kind, — that of appropriating to his own use the proceeds of the building, when sold, on the removal of the school to Framingham.

FROM HON. JOSIAH QUINCY, JR.

Boston, Nov. 21, 1862.

My dear Mrs. Mann, — My donation of fifteen hundred dollars was made to your husband, to be used by him in promoting popular education.

The immediate cause of the donation was this : The Normal School, which was originally established at Lexington, had been, or was about to be, discontinued; and the project, ridiculed and opposed, was likely to be abandoned. At this time, your husband came into my office, and, in his very striking manner, said, —

"If you know any man who wants the highest seat in the kingdom of heaven, it is to be had for fifteen hundred dollars."

I asked what he meant. He replied that a schoolhouse at West Newton could be purchased for that sum; and this, if obtained, would enable the friends of education to convince the State of the importance of Normal schools, and insure their becoming an essential part of the common-school system of Massachusetts. I gave him the money, directing him *to take the deed in his own name.* He sold his library to fit up the building, giving more than I did to the cause. The result was that Normal schools have been introduced in many, and will be introduced in all the free States.[*]

In order to prevent any misunderstanding, I subsequently gave

---

[*] Mr. Quincy has inadvertently blended two transactions in this statement. The Law Library had been sold several years before to fit up the boarding-house of the Lexington Normal School; a promised donation for that purpose having been unexpectedly withdrawn. Other sacrifices were made to meet the demand for fitting up the West Newton house, which were made jointly by Mr. Mann and Mr. Pierce.

him a written authority to apply the proceeds of the building, when sold, to any purpose that he might judge most conducive to promote the interests of popular education.

The reward playfully offered for the donation is reserved for others. I ask no greater than the consciousness of having aided him in the noble and philanthropic purpose to which he devoted his life. I have the honor to have been the friend of Horace Mann.

Yours truly,

J. QUINCY, JR.

It was Mr. Mann's intention to use Mr. Quincy's donation to put a raised gutta-percha globe into all the common schools of Massachusetts. He projected one, and it was executed by some of his friends; but gutta-percha works were suspended in the country, owing to some difficulties in the way of working it cheaply and stably; and, after spending about five hundred dollars upon the project, it was necessary to give it up. Mr. Quincy's donation, however, was duly applied for the good of the State.

BOSTON, Feb. 28, 1845.

MY DEAR MR. COMBE, — For your long and interesting letter of Dec. 29 I can give you only a short and dull one. I have but a few moments to write.

. . . I have inquired of two of our best lawyers, and both are clear and decided that a war with Great Britain would *not* result in a forfeiture or confiscation of American debts due to British subjects, or of American stock owned by them. Mr. Loring said he would send me an abstract of the law on the subject; and, should it come in season, I will forward it. But have you not Chancellor Kent's "Commentaries" in your law-library? If so, examine vol. i. pp. 64, &c., and you will find the whole doctrine clearly and satisfactorily explained.

Heaven forefend that the case for a legal adjudication of the question should ever arise! I should look upon a war with Great Britain almost in the light of a civil war. In the Atlantic States, it would be deprecated with a depth and fervor that could not be described. It would bring ruin to thousands of business-men, and would shock the spirit of peace in the more moral and religious portion of the community. I am sorry, however, to say that I fear a different spirit prevails at the West. Combativeness and destructiveness occupy a larger portion of their brains, and are made more active by education. They are also removed far more from the restraints of direct interest, and feel far less the restraints of morality. God hasten the day when war between the great nations of the earth shall be impossible!

I received your two letters containing an account of the religious common-school controversy in Massachusetts. It was well drawn up, and I hope will do good. Ecclesiastical oppression is wearing away in Europe; but, alas! about as slowly as the disintegration of granite mountains by the seasons and elements. The paper of which you spoke, containing a review by a phrenologist of the "Vestiges," &c., I have not received.

I am sorry to say that my controversy with the Boston schoolmasters is not ended. They do not accept the propositions of peace which I made. I am told they now have a Rejoinder in press. I think it ought to be out soon, if ever. It is now nearly four months since my Reply was published. An old militia-officer in the country told me he guessed it took them some time to bring their forces into line. All this is very bad, as it makes me anxiety and labor. . . . Capt. Maconochie must be an extraordinary man. I learn, by a communication from him, that he is in favor of teaching a creed in school. He thinks it gives a good form of words, which, in a case of urgency in subsequent life, may have a resurrection, and be clothed with spiritual power and life. I shall enclose a note to him in this packet to you.

We expect this morning to hear the result of the Texas business. (It is now March 1.) Great anxiety prevails. On Tuesday next, President Polk will be inaugurated. I cannot write more, but remain as ever truly and devotedly yours and Mrs. Combe's.

HORACE MANN.

Concord, July 4, 1845.

Rev. S. J. May. *My dear Sir*, — . . . I hardly know whether I ought to hope that your situation is to your mind, or whether I ought to desire that you should have occasion to repent and return to Massachusetts, out of which you never should have gone. I cannot, however, but be good-natured enough to wish you *here* in the first place, but contented and happy wherever you may be.

My mind is wholly absorbed, as always, in school-matters. We have not yet succeeded in making arrangements for the new Normal schools. Delay after delay has interposed, and postponed action. It has, however, been decided that the one at Bridgewater shall be continued there. . . .

Probably you have seen that the "masters" are out in a "Rejoinder" against me. It has fallen dead-born from the press: very few read it. Two Orthodox newspapers have tried to indorse it; thinking, as they always do, that whatever is practised against a Unitarian is for the glory of God. The same man who wrote that carping review in the "Christian Examiner" has a short notice of it in the last number of the same periodical, which has some shameful slurs. I think my friends ought to protest to Dr. —— and Dr. —— against turning their batteries to the overthrow of their friends. It is only ——'s connection with the Boston schools which prompts him to this course. He has been so long on the committee, that he thinks a condemnation of them is a condemnation of himself.

The "masters" are in great trouble. Some of them went to the mayor, and besought him not to put Howe or Brigham on the committee of examination. He had some spirit, and put them both on, — Howe as chairman of the grammar-department, and Brigham of the writing. They have adopted a new mode of examination. A list of printed questions is prepared on each subject, which are given to all of the first section in the first class of each of the schools, so that all the scholars in each section can be compared together, and also all the first sections in all the schools. The same time is allowed to all for preparing and writing down their answers. This necessarily gives a transcript of the actual condition of the schools; and *rumor* reports that it is any thing but flattering. The results will be drawn off in a table; and eight thousand copies of the reports are ordered to be printed. We shall know what condition our boasted Boston schools are in.

There are suggestions for certain changes among the masters. Howe has asked me several times whether I thought you to be so devoted to the cause of practically improving the condition of the colored people, that you would come to Boston and take the Smith School;* for the general opinion is that F—— must go. I have told him that I presumed you were under engagements more or less binding at Syracuse. . . .

I see by an Albany paper that there is a State Convention called, at Syracuse, of common-school teachers, &c. Am I not right in divining that this is a movement *against* the county superintendents, and designed to promote conservatism or stand-still-ism throughout the State?' In the next number of the "Journal," I shall publish some of the proceedings of the late Syracuse Convention, with a very strong expression of good will towards the superintendents. My account will be taken from the "Onondaga Standard," which was much better than the one in the "Journal." I have long witnessed with very great satisfaction the course taken by the "Onondaga Standard" on the subject of common schools.

Being on the ground, you will have a chance to see and know the means and objects of the common-school convention. Is it not of great importance to moderate their antagonism against the system of county superintendents as far as possible, and, should they persist in passing any offensive resolutions, to make use, as far as possible, of the influence of the press in counteracting them? Of these things, however, you can judge better than I; and I have no doubt you will do whatever you can, both for the State of New York, and to prevent any unfortunate re-action against Massachusetts. Very truly yours, &c.,

HORACE MANN.

Boston, Sept. 25, 1845.

My dear Mr. Combe, — Since your letter of the 2d of June, I suppose you have visited your favorite spots upon the Rhine; and I hope that you and your party, particularly Mrs. Combe, have

* Colored school.

realized all the health and pleasure which you anticipated from the excursion. How happy would it have made me could I have been of your number! but, instead of that, I have been spending my dog-days in an agony of hard work. Nor have I been scorched and sweated by a natural Sirius only, but by a moral one. My doughty assailants, the Boston schoolmasters, thought best to collect their forces, and strive at least to make good their retreat. Whether they have done so, you will judge by the pamphlets I herewith enclose. About the last of May, after having taken six months to rally, they came out with a Rejoinder to my Reply. Our controversy was taking so obvious a turn in favor of improvement in the schools, that my regret at being called into the field again was very much modified: accordingly, on the first of August, I gave them an answer; and thus, as between ourselves, the matter now rests.

After the presentation of the Report, the conservatives and mas-ters' aides-de-camp insisted upon proceeding to an election before the charges proposed in the Report could be submitted to the public. The old members of the committee reasoned that the al-leged condition of the schools convicted them of negligence and re-missness in the discharge of their duties in former years; and there-fore they were to defend where they thought there was any hope, and to palliate and deprecate where they could not defend. An election of the masters was precipitated; and notwithstanding the most earnest efforts on the part of the conservatives, and those who wear their eyes in the posterior part of the head, so as to forever look backward, and not forward, — notwithstanding all this, *four* of the masters have been turned out; a work which, twelve months ago, would have been deemed as impossible as to turn four peers out of the British House of Lords.

Such is the present *status* of the matter. The Report will soon be in the hands of all; and there will be a vigorous contest at the ensuing city election between the young Boston and the *lauda-tores temporis acti*. But the change already effected in the public mind, and even in the schools themselves under the old heads, is immense. It is estimated that corporal punishment has fallen off twenty-five per cent; and the masters have gone to work this year with the idea that they are *to make their calling and election sure*.

But enough of this. Knowing the kind interest you take, not only in the welfare of the schools, but in whatever concerns me, I have ventured to give you this long narration. I have suffered severely in the conflict, so far as my feelings are concerned; and doubtless I have suffered considerably in my reputation. The masters constitute a strong body of men. They are thirty in number. They have immediately under them, and to a great extent dependent upon them, twice as many more ushers and assistants. Between all these there is a natural bond of union. Each one has his or her circle of relatives and friends; and the whole, acting in concert and through favorite pupils, are able to produce a great effect upon the public mind. But the old notion of perfection in the Boston grammar and writing schools is destroyed; the prescription by which the masters held their office, and appointed indirectly their successors, is at an end. There is a strong revulsion of feeling in the public mind, and the masters are hereafter to stand upon their good behavior rather than on the self-complacency of their employers; so that good will eventually come out of evil, in the old-fashioned way. . . .

Always your friend,

HORACE MANN.

CONCORD, Oct. 7, 1845.

CYRUS PIERCE, ESQ. *My dear Sir,* — Where are you? and what are you doing? I hear no more from you than if you belonged to a different planet; but I hope your affairs prosper. Have you seen the Report of the Boston School Committee of the Grammar and Writing Schools? What a pile of thunder-bolts! Jupiter never had more lying by his side, when he had ordered a fresh lot wherewith to punish the wicked. If the masters see fit to assail me again, I think I can answer them in such a way as to make it redound to the glory of God.

I have got up a new project for Massachusetts, — Teachers' Institutes. I am to have four of them, — one at Pittsfield, which, in the geography of common schools, lies in the arctic regions, above the line (hitherto) of perpetual congelation. I had obtained a promise from Gen. Oliver, formerly a distinguished teacher in Salem, to go to Pittsfield, and officiate as one of the teachers of the

16

school. Thinking that institute provided for, I have engaged all the available teachers whom I know to go to other places. But Gen. Oliver has disappointed me. I have tried several others since, and can secure none. I do not see but I must make a draft on you. I intend to take Pittsfield myself for three or four days, and teach by day, and lecture by night; but by that time my pond will be drawn down, and I shall also have to come away for the purpose of attending another, at Fitchburg. Now I am writing all this story to prepare the way for bespeaking the services of yourself or Miss Tilden * to go to Pittsfield, in case I do not succeed in getting any one else. I know it is a bad thing to take away any of your forces; but it is not a hundredth part so bad as it would be to have one of these institutes prove a failure at the very commencement of the experiment.

There are some reasons why I should prefer to have you go, and others why I should prefer to have Miss Tilden go. It would be *fun* to see her manage the great boys, and teach them their A, B, C's in arithmetic, and I think it would give them an intellectual spasm such as they never had before. There need not be the slightest objection on her part. Of course, all expenses will be defrayed; and there is no reason why either of you might not have as pleasant a time as is consistent with a good degree of hard work! Please answer as soon as convenient,

And believe me ever truly yours, &c.,

H. MANN.

When Mr. Mann arrived in Pittsfield, and entered the schoolroom assigned for the purpose (all the common schools were in vacation), at seven in the morning, to make arrangements, he found the room had been left unswept, and had not been put in order for his reception. A hundred pupils, the teachers of schools, were expected at nine o'clock. Gov. Briggs, then actual Executive of the State, who felt great interest in Mr. Mann's plans, and

---

* This lady was a very superior mathematical teacher of the West Newton Normal School.

had accompanied him to the schoolhouse, borrowed brooms in a neighboring house; and the two gentlemen swept and dusted the room, and had all things in order at the appointed hour.

Boston, Nov. 3, 1845.

C. Pierce, Esq. *My dear Sir,* — ... I have the most favorable accounts from Pittsfield. It was quite a stroke of policy to have Miss Tilden go there. She produced forty times more effect than you or I or any one else could have done, had we exhibited the same command of the subject that she did. I wish you could spare her for a day or two to go to Fitchburg; but I hardly dare ask it. Contrary to my expectations, I found myself alone there the first two days, with more than a hundred and thirty teachers about me; and you will of course say that I had to manage pretty shrewdly not to expose my ignorance.

On Thursday, A.M., I am to start for Nantucket. From there I must go to Chatham, on the Cape, where we are to have another institute; and from there to Bridgewater, where we wind up our fall musters, as the militia-men say. I hear you are working the young brains again very hard, making some ill. Remember, it is your duty to *give* power, not to *take it away.*

Yours ever and truly,

HORACE MANN.

In explanation of this last sentence, I must say that Mr. Pierce was so anxious for the fame of the school, that he inclined to press study too hard. He was a man of apparently iron nerves himself (though, alas! subsequent years proved that even iron nerves could not withstand such trials as he gave them); and his friend, whose more delicate organization gave him keen sympathy with over-excited brains, was obliged to stand as guard-angelic over the health of his beloved "Normalites." An equal zeal for the success of what they had undertaken — a project that was to have such far-reaching consequences — animated both, and was accompanied with an equal forget-fulness of self. They were not working consciously for their own fame; but they alike felt that they were laying the foundations of the only lasting basis of a free republic, as yet free only in name, but destined to outlive its own shortcomings, as surely as truth and humanity are loftier principles than gain and oppression. "Would that they could have lived to see the dawning of that day!" is the exclamation of our blind affection; but they doubtless see its progress in the future far more clearly than we can.

BOSTON, Nov. 21, 1845.

C. PIERCE, ESQ.

MY DEAR SIR, — I have this moment returned from a four-weeks' expedition, attending Teachers' Institutes. I write to request, to urge, and, if I only had authority, to *command* you to go to the great "Practical Teachers'" meeting at Worcester on Tuesday and Wednesday next. We know where it originated, and what the plans of *some* of the movers are. I am debarred from going. No member of the Board of Education can go; but you must go and watch the enemy.

Very truly yours,

H. MANN.

BOSTON, Dec. 2, 1845.

REV. S. J. MAY.

MY DEAR SIR, — I have long desired to write to you, and to acknowledge the receipt of your favors. But the old reason has still deterred me, — work, work, work. If Hood had known my case, he would have written the "Song of the 'Secretary,'" instead of the "Song of the Shirt."

I see you cannot silence the battery that is opened upon me in your neighborhood. My enemies here seem to have succeeded in saturating the minds of the New-York teachers with prejudice against me, and to a degree that is unaccountable; and your neighbor, the "Advocate," is made the vehicle of discharging their spleen. What have I done that has brought upon me this contumely and bitterness? What have I done that renders me thus worthy of the extreme of ridicule and opprobrium? . . . These personal attacks are very annoying; and I should like to prevent them, if it can be done. I hope I have written to him the soft words that turn away wrath; but perhaps his is a worse kind than Solomon referred to.

We are now in a state of excitement and anxiety on the subject of the school committee. The "thirty-one" are exerting every muscle against the reformers. Nothing can exceed their activity, or the baseness of the means that some of them resort to. I wish you to read the number of the "Journal" for Dec. 1, and see what resolutions have been taken on the subject of corporal punishment in our schools. . . .

We have had a State teachers' meeting here, originally designed as an attack upon the Board of Education; but the movers, like your Albanians, were not able to carry out all their plans.

It is late, and my sheet full : so good-night.

Ever yours,

HORACE MANN.

BOSTON, Feb. 13, 1846.

MY DEAR MR. AND MRS. COMBE, — Were I to stand upon ceremony, I should not write you at the present time. But ceremony, at the best, is vanity; and between us it would be mischief. Having an opportunity to send my last Report, I avail myself of it, and put in this note to say that we have another little son, born on the 27th of December. He is a fine, healthy little fellow, fat enough for an alderman, and has a head planned and executed on the principles of phrenology. His mother and I have been discussing the immensely important subject of his name. When I said to her that George is a pretty name, she said George Combe would be a glorious name; but we should not dare to call him so without your consent, indeed without your expressed desire, which I can hardly hope for. Our oldest boy, whom his mother calls after me, is well, and has a very active temperament and a very inquisitive mind. . . .

Yours ever and truly,

HORACE MANN.

Mr. Combe, who had no children, but whose love for them was very great, took much interest in his "name-son," as he called him; and was never weary of reading minute accounts of the doings and sayings of both the children of his friend.

APRIL 27, 1846.

My dear Mr. Combe, — I write you from Gardiner, Me., where I have come to spend a few days with some old friends of Mrs. Mann. I am partially resting from my labors; though Sisyphus never will be permitted to cease rolling his stone up hill. . . . What are you doing now for the good of the race? I trust you will not cease to use your brain for the right formation of other brains, as long as it has the power of operating. . . . My affairs are going on prosperously. The Boston masters have not attempted any reply to my "Answer." I think they never will; but I almost wish they would. One of the already ripened and gathered fruits of the controversy is, that it is admitted on all hands, that, since the controversy began, corporal punishment has diminished in the masters' schools at least eighty per cent!

I received, by one of the last steamers from England, a London edition of my Seventh Report, the very *causa malorum*. It was edited by Mr. Hodgson, who is at the head of the Mechanics' Institute, Liverpool; and it has copious running notes from beginning to end. It so happens, that, in regard to every one of the points in my Report which the masters questioned or denied, Mr. Hodgson, in his notes, has confirmed my statement. That is very gratifying, as he had never, I presume, seen one word of the controversy. . . .

As ever, yours,

H. MANN.

WEST NEWTON.

My dear Sumner, — After you went away last evening, the same reflection occurred to me which always occurs in relation to such bequests as Mr. Tuttle proposes to make; namely, why don't these benevolent men execute their good deeds while they are alive, and not wait till after they are dead, and so lose half the pleasure of it?

I was delighted at Mr. Tuttle's plan of spending his money *in solido*. It often requires all my charity not to accuse the men, who wish to leave a money-monument behind them, of expecting to hear people praise them as they lie in their graves. Let the generous give what money they have to give to be expended in blessing the world *immediately;* and, when that is used up, somebody will give more. But these mortmain funds keep others from giving more, because the want seems to be supplied. There is only one improvement on this; and that is, to give during life, and not wait till after death. How Girard got fleeced and balked, and his benevolence kept in abeyance for years!

I cannot forbear saying how much I was delighted with the *object* of Mr. Tuttle's charity. How I should love to administer such a benevolence! One year of it would be worth all the honors of Congress forever; that is, to me. Look at the last three verses of that little song of Whittier's, at the end of the number of the "Common-school Journal" I sent you. You can also point them out to Mr. Tuttle.*

I send you a number containing my letter to the children of

---

* The verses alluded to are these : —

> Yet who, thus looking backward o'er his years,
> Feels not his eyelids wet with grateful tears,
> If he hath been •
> Permitted, weak and sinful as he was,
> To cheer and aid in some ennobling cause
> His fellow-men?
>
> If he hath hidden the outcast, or let in
> A ray of sunshine to the cell of sin;
> If he hath lent
> Strength to the weak; and, in an hour of need,
> Over the suffering, mindless of his creed
> Or hue hath bent, —
>
> He hath not lived in vain; and, while he gives
> The praise to Him in whom he moves and lives,
> With thankful heart
> He gazes backward, and with hope before,
> Knowing that from his works he nevermore
> Can henceforth part.

Chatauque County, New York. It cannot shoot very wide of Mr. Tuttle's notions about children, I think. . . .

Yours very truly,

HORACE MANN.

Such letters as the following are given, in order to meet false accusations and misrepresentations : —

Boston, May 15, 1846.

Rev. S. J. May.

My dear Sir, — After a night's ride, I have just got back to Boston from the convention at Albany. I could hardly reconcile myself to the disappointment of not meeting you there. The convention treated me very civilly. I delivered the lecture which was pronounced so heretical in the "Advocate" some months ago. It was apparently well received; and Elder Knapp, of revival memory, said he would give any thing to see it in print. Mr. C—— complimented me by a special resolution, inviting me to deliver a speech on the subject of free schools; came and caused himself to be introduced to me, and gave me a long history of the influences which had been exerted, at the outset, to make his paper what it was; said that he had felt constrained to admit sentiments not his own, but that the end of such things had come. He spoke freely of and against the Albany clique. The amount of it was that he was disposed to be gracious; and though he did not do what I think the highest notions of duty would have prompted, yet I accepted it, and I trust it will be the commencement of a new era. . . . I am greatly fatigued to-day : I cannot write more.

Ever and truly yours,

H. MANN.

Wrentham, July 25, 1846.

Rev. S. J. May.

My dear Sir, — . . . We expect the new Normal School Building at Bridgewater will be dedicated on the 19th of August. It will add vastly to the pleasure of the occasion to see you there. Do come; do. The other, at Westfield, will be dedicated about the 1st of September. Then we shall have three. I think the cause will be anchored when those are completed, so that no storm which F. E. or the Boston schoolmasters can conjure up will drive it from its moorings.

I see that N—— has, in the "Teachers' Advocate," opened his small battery upon the Normal schools. The statement made in the first number, that one of the Normal schools in Massachusetts "has become extinct, and the State appropriations would have been cut off from the other two, had not a private individual offered to give a sum equal to that appropriated by the State," contains two errors, probably falsehoods. The school originally at Barre has not "become extinct." It was suspended for a short time, owing to the death of its principal. It is now removed to a more central and commodious place, where the State has assisted in erecting a building for it. The appropriation made for these schools, after they had been four years in operation, was made *wholly by the State.* No private individual gave a cent. The State was so well convinced of their merits from the experience it had had, that not only was there no aid, but there was no opposition to the grant.

Another statement, made in number two, shows the extreme ignorance of the writer. He says the members of the Normal schools in Prussia are graduates of the universities. Not one in a hundred, probably not one in five hundred, of them are so. These flagrant misstatements ought to be pointed out. . . . The examination of the Boston schools is conducted this year in the same way as last. The masters are submissive, and it seems already certain that a great improvement over last year has been made. . . .

Believe me very truly and sincerely yours,

HORACE MANN.

WRENTHAM, Aug. 6, 1846.

MY DEAR SUMNER, — The new Normal Schoolhouse at Bridgewater is to be dedicated on Wednesday, the 19th inst. Address by Hon. William G. Bates.

The active and leading agency you have had in executing measures which have led to this beneficial result would make your absence on that occasion a matter of great regret.

I know it will console you for your troubles in relation to the subject to be present on the day of jubilee, to gratify so many persons, and to participate in a joy which will be common and comprehensive.

Let me assure you, that, however it may seem beforehand, you will not be sorry afterwards for having made some exertion, and even some sacrifice, to be there. Probably there will be three hundred graduates of the school who will feel deeply disappointed if you are not present.

Do go! do go!

Ever and truly yours, &c.,

HORACE MANN.

BOSTON, May 7, 1846.

C. PIERCE, ESQ.

MY DEAR SIR, — I heard you were going to add another hour to study-time this term. I protest against this. Your love of approbation for the fame of the school must not be a Moloch, before which young virgins are sacrificed! . . .

Ever yours,

H. MANN.

WRENTHAM, May 24, 1846.

C. PIERCE, ESQ. ·

MY DEAR SIR, — . . . You acknowledge that you have really added one hour in a week to the period of study; and, including four Saturday hours, you have thus an hour each day for five days. Now, if you have any exercise or duty for Sunday, then I do not see but you plead guilty to the whole of the charge.

You say there is about as much truth in this as in the story of "flogging a model schoolboy in the barn, doubtless under distressing circumstances." Am I, then, to understand that there was as much truth in the flogging story as there is now acknowledged to be in the story about study-hours? . . .

Ever yours,

H. MANN.

WRENTHAM, Aug. 6, 1846.

REV. S. J. MAY.

MY DEAR SIR, — I have just received yours of the 29th ult. ; and, while I am pleased with all its contents, there is one thing in it which has so delighted me, that I cannot help thinking of it, and writing to you about it : I mean the mention of the purpose and possibility of your becoming the editor of the "Teachers' Advocate." That, indeed, is a "consummation devoutly to be wished ; " and I beg you to leave no pains spared to accomplish so desirable an object. How much you could help me, and how readily and heartily would I help you all in my power ! . . . Push the thing, therefore, with all the resources you can command. Few events would give me greater pleasure, both on your own account and on account of the cause, than to hear that you have succeeded.

Have you heard that the Legislature of Maine, at its present or late session, has established a Board of Education, and provided for the appointment of a Secretary at a salary of a thousand dollars a year ? This looks well.

Gov. Slade, of Vermont, has consented to become the agent of a society for the promotion of national education at the West, and will remove to Cincinnati as soon as his present official term expires. I think we will give the Devil one kick yet before we leave the world.

Yours ever and truly,

HORACE MANN.

WRENTHAM, Sept. 23, 1846.

REV. E. B. WILLSON.

MY DEAR SIR, — I have just received your desponding missive of yesterday. I see you are sensitive : you have not got case-hardened yet ; you have not been rebuffed and neglected, and seen every mountebank and hand-organist and monkey-shower and military company running away with your audience. I have been accustomed for years to yield precedence to every puppet-exhibition or hurdy-gurdy mendicant ; but I always transmute this discouragement into encouragement (or stimulus). If people are so indifferent to the highest of all earthly causes, it only shows how much we have yet to do ; and if it is to take a great while to do

what must be done, then it is time we were about it; and if it is
an arduous business, then our coats must go off, and we must address ourselves to the work with corresponding good will.   Let us
convert despair into courage.   If you cannot get seventy teachers
together at a Teachers' Institute in the great County of Worcester,
I know you will work harder for the cause of common schools as
long as you live.   I shall be grieved at such a spectacle, indeed;
but my heart has ached hundreds of times before, yet I have infinite faith.   It is a part of my religion to believe in the ultimate
success and triumph of the cause.   If it can come in my day, I
should like it; but a true disciple works with the same zeal for the
object of his faith, whether its glorious consummation is to be greeted
by his own eyes, or whether it is yet the embryon existence of some
distant century. . . . .

        In great haste, yours very truly,
                            HORACE MANN.

                     WEST NEWTON, Feb. 25, 1847.

MY DEAR FRIENDS, MR. AND MRS. COMBE, — All I can say in
defence of myself for being what you call a "naughty man" is
that I have had a *conflict of duties*, and that I have postponed the
performance of those which would have been most agreeable for the
sake of those which seemed to me most indispensable to the welfare
of the cause to which I am pledged.   "Strike, but hear."

    In the early part of the last season, I prepared another volume
of our Annual School Abstracts, containing nearly four hundred
pages.   Even before this was completed, I had to go away on a
tour of Teachers' Institutes (described in my Ninth Report), which
occupied me for seven or eight weeks.   On my return, in November,
I was obliged to sit down and write my Report, a hundred and
seventy pages, and carry that and the Report of the Board through
the press.   My correspondence equals all the labor I have enumerated.   I have had the general care and superintendence of the
erection of two Normal school-buildings, which have been built the
last season, and are now occupied; and, what I know will gladden
your hearts, I have built a house for myself at this place, which we
came into on Christmas Eve.   I have been a wanderer for twenty

years ; and, when any one asked me where I lived, I could say, in
the language of another, "I do not live anywhere ; I *board.*"
This Arab life I could bear while I was alone ; but, when I had
"wife and weans" to carry from place to place, it became intolerable. I should have preferred, on many accounts, to live in the
city ; but so small is my salary, and so considerable the demands
made upon it in order to carry forward the cause, that it was necessary to give up the idea of a city residence, or resign my office.
We have, therefore, put up a shelter at West Newton, ten miles
from Boston, and within a hundred rods of the West Newton Normal School. . . . Just as I was looking for a little relief from the
pressure of my labors, a child of sin and Satan came out with a
ferocious orthodox attack upon the Board of Education and myself,
which I felt moved to answer ; and here is another pretty job of
work of fifty-six pages. Now, I assure you, it would have been
vastly more pleasant to have been writing to you and Mrs. Combe,
and telling you about Mrs. Mann, and *little* Horace Mann (who is
three years old to-day), and *little-er* George Combe Mann, who has
a head that would satisfy the most fastidious and exacting phrenologist, — I say it would have been vastly more pleasant to do this than
to be fighting, like St. Paul, the wild beasts at Ephesus.

I received the "Phrenological Journal," containing your article,
which I read with great pleasure and profit. . . . I should like exceedingly well to be made acquainted, from time to time, with whatever promotes the progress of humanity, whether it comes in the
form of improved education or in any other. How horrible is the
condition of Ireland ! It pours a bitter ingredient into every meal
I eat. I had thought, owing to improvements in agriculture and
commerce, that famines were at an end ; but it seems that misgov-
ernment can more than cancel all the blessings of science and the
bounties of Heaven. The policy pursued towards Ireland for the
last few centuries will be one of the most appalling admonitions to
future governments to be found in the pages of all history. I hope
it may lead to such organic changes in the policy of the British
Government towards that people, as will, in part, compensate for the
terrible calamity they are suffering, and will prevent the possibility
of its repetition. Great commiseration is felt in this country for the

famishing people. A large committee is now engaged in the city of Boston in collecting subscriptions. No report of the amount obtained has been yet made; but I have no doubt it will be in some degree worthy of the city, though it must be immensely inadequate to the relief of the sufferers. Bennett Forbes, one of our wealthiest men, and a man whose heart is bigger than his purse, has offered to take charge of any ship that shall be freighted with relief.* Oh, if all the millions we are spending in this execrable Mexican war could be appropriated to the relief of suffering, the instruction of ignorance, and the reformation of the wicked, what a different world we might have! The money and the talent employed to barbarize mankind in war, if expended for education and the promotion of the arts of peace, would bring on the millennium at once.

You know, my dear friends, how incessantly I am engaged. Do not be punctilious about *return* letters. Write me when you can. I have no letters that are so acceptable as yours. Keep me advised of all that is important; for I have not time even to read English newspapers sufficiently to know what important things are going on.

Our present Congress closes its session on the 4th of next month. The next Congress will be a very different body of men. For the honor of humanity, they ought to be. My kindest regards to your brother, and to all who do me the honor to inquire after me.

Ever and truly yours,

HORACE MANN.

WEST NEWTON, April 25, 1847.

MY DEAR MR. COMBE, — Your kind letter of March 24 is before me. I learn from it that you were, at its date, without intelligence from me. You write, too, somewhat despairingly. But why should you lack faith? Do you not believe in my regard for you, as in a law of nature? While my nature and yours remain unchanged, I cannot but have the highest estimation of you, and I cannot cease to be grateful; for you have been my benefactor in the largest and best sense. By the steamer of March, I sent you not only a long letter, but a large parcel, and gave you some account of

---

* Mr. Forbes nobly redeemed his promise. — ED.

my year's work, so that you might see for yourself that idleness was not the cause of my omitting to write to you. . . . I sent you a mighty great Abstract of School Returns which I had got out, and also copies of a controversy, which, in the way of by-play, I had had with one of the wild beasts of Ephesus; and a more untamable hyena I do not believe St. Paul ever had to encounter, — once a preacher of the annihilation of the wicked, then a Universalist, and now a Calvinist of the Old-Testament stamp. In believing in total depravity, he only generalizes his own consciousness. . . . Since I wrote you before, he has come out with a "Reply," which is worse than the others, in a sort of geometrical progression. This I have answered in a "Letter" to him, and am now awaiting his next movement. I read, with great interest and profit, your article on education in the "Phrenological Journal;" and it is now somewhere in the circle of my friends, going about doing good. I have also just received the same in tract form. . . .

There has already been sent to Ireland, from Boston alone, money and provisions to the value of a hundred and twenty thousand dollars. Mr. Quincy told me he had no doubt it would soon amount to a hundred and fifty thousand dollars. This would look beautifully on the celestial records, if the Devil had not such a *per contra* of a hundred millions spent in this infernal Mexican war. Still, it is about the first item ever entered to the credit of a nation in the books above; and, as such, it is not only a fact, but a promise, — an augury not less than an entry. I wish you to inform me what is the estimated sum drawn annually from Ireland by the absentee landlords. How different is the character of the Irish peasantry or immigrants here from that of the English landlords! The former are sending home amounts of money which are so incredible that my memory cannot hold them, while the latter are drawing the heart's blood out of the country. Will you please also inform me what are the revenues of the Church derived from Ireland, and spent at home and elsewhere? I also want to obtain the best accounts I can of the "ragged schools" in London. I have access to the Reviews; but are there no tracts or pamphlets on the subject? I do not get at the present state of public sentiment in the United Kingdom on this all-important question of education. . . .

At our last Congressional election, Howe consented to be the candidate for Congress of the anti-slavery and anti-war party. I think in so doing he made a great mistake. Any other man would have served as a rallying-point as well as he; and such is the inexorableness of party discipline, that he at once lost a great portion of his well-earned popularity and extensive influence. He was proscribed, and, in a few days after, failed of being elected on the school committee, when he might have been but for that misstep.

I shall leave the babies for Mrs. Mann to write about. Please think how much I have to do, and never wait for a letter from me as an inducement to write one yourself.

With kindest regards to Mrs. Combe and all who inquire after me,

I am yours ever,

HORACE MANN.

WEST NEWTON, May 22, 1847.

REV. T. PARKER.

DEAR SIR, — Yours of the 15th inst. was not received until this evening. I shall be most happy to meet the friends of a true conservative reform anywhere, and particularly at your house, if my engagements will possibly permit.

The Board of Education, however, are to be met on Wednesday next, and may be in session two or three days. I have never been able to escape from them and their committees for an hour. If, therefore, I do not appear, you will infer that I cannot.

By a "conservative reform," I mean the removal of vile and rotten parts from the structure of society, just as far as salutary and sound ones can be prepared to take their places.

Yours very truly,

H. MANN.

WEST NEWTON, Nov. 14, 1847.

MY DEAR MR. COMBE, — I intended to write you by each of the last steamers, but was absent from home; and, when I attend Institutes, I have no time nor thought for any thing else. Our cause is flourishing. Other States are coming into the ranks of improvement. New Hampshire has appointed a school commissioner.

Public sentiment in Rhode Island, under the administration of Mr. Barnard as school commissioner, is revolutionized. Vermont has established a Board of Education; and even the democratic State of Maine has, within the last twelve months, organized a Board nearly on the same principles, and precisely with the same objects, as Massachusetts. All these are so many buttresses to hold our fabric firm. I feel great interest in the movement in Maine, and am going down there to spend a few days, to use a flesh-brush upon their long torpid backs. I trust we shall make this a revolution that will not go backward.

We have not heard from you since your return from the Continent. Our last letter was from Mr. Cox, announcing the death of your brother, that benefactor of mankind. How many people will be better and happier because he has lived! This is his noble monument. To go about doing good is religion. In ages yet to come, he will live upon earth; and his wise precepts, the representatives of himself which he has left upon earth, will "go about doing good." We have been greatly interested in your pamphlets, and in the additional matter contained in the new edition of the "Constitution of Man." The citadels of bigotry must eventually be crumbled under such missiles; but it is a long contest, and neither you nor I shall see the victory but by an eye of faith. But never mind. It is the evidence of a true disciple, that he can labor as faithfully, though triumph is a thousand years off, as though it were to be won to-morrow, and he already heard the note of preparation.

Please give me all practicable information about British affairs. The history of this age will hereafter stand out prominently in the annals of the race. I would that it were more worthy!

With undiminished affection for yourself and Mrs. Combe,

I am, as ever, truly yours,

HORACE MANN.

During all his educational life, Mr. Mann had never allowed himself one day of pure recreation. If he made a visit to a friend, some educational errand was sure to lie in ambush, or some plea to be entered for the furtherance

17

of his cherished plans. He had not the art of lying fallow, and thus gathering new strength for labor. His love of children was the only natural outlet for his native hilarity; and this blessed resource was all that saved him when the outside world seemed bent upon harassing him. He never could turn his back upon them: others had to defend him from their loving inroads, hunt them in his study, and pick them off his writing-desk, and out of the back of his chair, where they would be found perched. No play was so charming as that in which he partook. He did not know how to tell fairy-stories, nor approve of them, unless allegorically beautiful; but he could bring the wonders of Nature within the compass of their admiring little souls. It came to be necessary to make a rule about taking turns upon his knee: and they learned to watch for the occasions when he laid down his pen, or was alone in the often-sought study, to which all the schoolmasters and school-committee men, educators and would-be educators, earnest inquirers or malcontents, had free access. To "tell papa" became a necessity; for his sympathy was never wanting, whether in joy or sorrow. To cultivate the religious character of his children, irrespective of dogmas, was his aim, and he knew it could not be cultivated too early; but he so dreaded for them the painful impressions stamped upon his own young heart, and he was so sure that terror must be the first emotion excited by the knowledge of God, that it was long before he could consent that his eldest child should know of the existence of a higher Power. When the inevitable moment came, and the child's cravings for that knowledge could no longer be set aside; when he passionately demanded "who made him" or it (for every thing was a mystery without this solution), and would not be denied, — his father walked the room in the deepest

agitation : but when he perceived that immediately the
heart and intellect gave a recognizing consent to the conception of a loving heavenly Parent, who made father
and mother, and the *butterfly*, whose mysterious evolution
from the chrysalis was the special object of inquiry at
the moment ; and that the little boy needed no further explanation and no other satisfaction, — tears of joy relieved
him of his painful anxiety, and father and child had from
that time a never-ending topic of mutual interest in tra-
cing God through his love and works. It was the happiest
of thoughts to him, that his children could make God a
sharer of their joys, and an object of personal affection
and confidence.

Suddenly, owing to the death of Mr. John Quincy
Adams, came the demand for his services as representative to the National Congress. It was an important
crisis in the cause of liberty ; for slavery was then to be
stemmed, or allowed to extend itself indefinitely ; and a
champion as fearless and persistent as Mr. Adams was
needed in his place.

At first, Mr. Mann could hardly, by an effort of the
imagination, place himself in any other position than that
which he occupied: but, on reflection, he saw that the new
office had bearings upon the great cause, which allied it
closely to its interests ; and he allowed himself to be per-
suaded.

His hope of seeing a Department of Public Instruction in the National Government was, however, not realized.

His friends were glad to have him leave his educational
labors for a time ; for his plans were so large, and had so
expanded in his hands, that no man could execute them
without suicidal efforts. He could plead the necessity of
more assistance for his successor, but was not the man to

beg it for himself; feeling, as he did, that there was but a very partial appreciation of the work yet to be done.

During the first session, he did not gain much rest; for he still retained the office of Secretary of the Massachusetts Board of Education, pending the choice of a successor: and his friends, Dr. Howe and Mr. Sumner, urged him to undertake the defence of Drayton and Sayres, owners of the little sloop " Pearl," who had allowed some fugitives from the District to escape in their vessel.* They knew he would not make it a technical matter merely, but would improve the opportunity to enunciate great principles which he and they had at heart. They did not urge him, as men often did, to do that which they would not have done themselves. He felt the kindling influence of that spirit in them which burned within himself, — an unquenchable flame of patriotism, and love of justice; a desire to hold up his testimony against the great sin of his country. They all stood alike ready to sacrifice every personal consideration to the cause. Not even friends could urge selfish claims in the presence of such sentiments as animated their conferences upon these topics, though the domestic calamity was not to be lightly estimated. Indeed, the light of the house went out when he left it. One little boy planted himself upon the hall-stairs every day, for a month, to " wait for papa," and could hardly be torn from his post; and another would open the daguerrotyped likeness, and weep over it, saying, " How beautiful he is!" To be " little papas " to the new-born babe was the most grateful form of consolation; and the postscript to the boys in the daily letter home was seldom wanting. They were unwilling to see other people sit at his desk or in

---

* The particulars of this case and the argument to the jury will appear in a future volume.

his special chair. He had taken care of every one, instead of allowing himself to be taken care of. The house had been furnished by his taste, and he had had a special interest in all its arrangements. Even the flowerbeds knew his shaping hand, and it had trained the vines and rose-bushes over porch and summer-house. When his absence became intolerable, the children were told that he had gone to help make the laws that would make people do right; and, as they had never known him to do wrong, he remained ever to them a near providence, stimulating every aspiration, and feeding their hunger for knowledge and the means of knowledge.

WASHINGTON, April 26, 1848.

MY DEAR MR. COMBE, — . . . I write you this from a seat in Congress; a place which, a few weeks ago, it would have seemed as impossible for me to fill as to be the successor of Louis Philippe. Strange events have sent me here. I have time to-day to write but a single word more, to say, that, wherever I am, I shall never cease to be your friend and admirer, and to acknowledge my indebtedness to you for the great principles of thought which have helped me on in the world. . . . I am writing this during an earnest debate; and, if I delay, I shall fail of sending it off in season for the steamer which goes from Boston on Saturday. My best regards to Mrs. Combe, and believe me ever and truly yours,

HORACE MANN.

WASHINGTON, April 28, 1848.

REV. D. WIGHT, JUN.

DEAR SIR, — Your letter of the 25th inst., this day received, has found me in the midst of very pressing engagements; for, for a few weeks, I have assumed new duties, without being released from my old ones. This pressure of business, however, counsels me to promptness, instead of delay: I therefore give you a brief and perhaps a too hasty answer.

Some of the questions you have propounded, I regard as very simple and plain ; while some of them might lead to *theoretical* difficulties, if not to *practical* ones. I regard it as sufficient, at present, to take a practical view of the subject.

You ask whether "literary qualifications" alone are sufficient for a teacher. I answer, that, in my opinion, they are not. Moral qualifications, and ability to inculcate and enforce the Christian virtues, I consider to be even of greater moment than literary attainments.

You ask, again, whether school committees are bound to approve Roman Catholics. I do not touch the cases of "Jews, Mahometans, Pagans," &c. ; for I presume you have no such cases in hand. You also further ask what has been the practice in Massachusetts, so far as I know, on this point.

The city of Lowell presents the most striking case that has come to my knowledge. There, several years ago, a very intelligent committee, consisting of clergymen and laymen, entered into an arrangement with the Catholic priests and parents, by which it was agreed that the teachers of their children should be Catholics. They were, however, to be subject to examination, and their schools to visitation, by the committee, in the same manner as other teachers and schools. I have not time to enter into details ; but you may find a minute and interesting account of the whole proceeding, as prepared by one of the school committee of Lowell, in the last April number of the "New-Englander." I refer you to this as more particular and satisfactory than any account I can give in a letter.

But this was a case where Catholic teachers were provided for Catholic children. I know no case in Massachusetts where Catholics have been brought forward as teachers of Protestant schools.

But as to the true interest and meaning of the law, premising that I have no *authority* to declare what the law is, still, when asked by a gentleman, from proper motives, what my *opinion* of the law is, I am free to express it. It is but an opinion. The school committee have the sole authority in the matter ; and they must discharge their duty on their responsibilities, as I or any other man must do on ours.

I do not see how, according to our law, a man is to be disfranchised, or held to be disqualified for the office of a teacher, *merely because he is a Catholic.* If his manners and his attainments are good, if his conduct is exemplary, his character pure, and he has ability to inculcate justice, a sacred regard to truth, the principles of piety, and those other excellences which the Constitution enumerates, can you reject him because you understand him to be a Catholic? Would Père la Salle, Fénélon, or Bishop Cheverus, be disqualified, *by the fact of their faith alone,* to keep a school in Massachusetts?

In any case of this kind, however, there are some other points which I should think it lawful to consider and act upon. For instance, I have always and under all circumstances held that the Bible is a book which should be introduced into our schools. Protestant parents have an undoubted right to have their children read the Protestant version, and be instructed from it. If I had reason to suppose the candidate to be a Catholic, I should feel perfectly authorized to inquire, and to know, whether, if approved, he would use the Bible in school in such a way as the committee should direct; whether he would use the Protestant version for a Protestant school; and whether, also, he should not feel under obligation to abstain, on all occasions, from obtruding his peculiar or sectarian views upon the scholars. I should want security on these and similar points. I could not construe our law and constitution to say, that, because a man is a Catholic, therefore he cannot inculcate and simplify justice, virtue, the principles of piety, &c. And again: if the district (as you suggest in this instance) has been so grossly delinquent as to choose an immoral and profane man as prudential committee, I should not regret to see them punished in any way that would not harm the children.

These, my dear sir, are my general views. If I had more time, I might be more explicit and guarded, and perhaps suggest some further limitations or qualifications of my opinion; but, rather than delay, I have given you at once what, according to the best of my knowledge, is a true exposition of our law, without raising the question whether the law is right or wrong. If this opinion seems to you unsound, you had best go to some counsellor on the subject, or raise the question for the courts.

H. MANN.

WASHINGTON, June 9, 1848.

. . . We have just heard that Gen. Taylor has been nominated for President. If so, it has been done by the combined force of slavery and war. The principles on which all the best men of the North profess to act — the great principles for the advancement of civilization — have been sacrificed to sustain the war-fever and the slavery-grip. I do not feel as if I could stand this: at any rate, I trust there will be a movement at the North which shall look to other objects, which shall be led only by men who inscribe peace and liberty on their banners. I have almost ceased to have any of the feelings of a mere politician; and, situated as I am, — I mean, as I still fill the office of Secretary of the Board of Education, — if I come out at first, and take any leading or prominent part in politics, I shall be accused of political interference through the influence of my office; a thing which, as you know, I have for so many years tried to keep clear of. I feel, therefore, unpleasantly hampered at the present time. Were it not for the necessity thus laid upon me, I should be inclined to heroic measures.

WASHINGTON, June 10, 1848.

There will be great enthusiasm for Taylor at the South, and great coldness at the North, — in some instances, aversion. It will play mischief with Whig politics in Massachusetts. I have a difficult position. I shall try to keep my conscience; though, in so doing, I may lose my office.

WASHINGTON, June 13, 1848.

It is evident there will be great opposition to Gen. Taylor in the North. This will lead to a feud among the Whigs themselves; so that they will have to fight, not only the Democrats, but each other. Our district will doubtless be in trouble. I may lose my office; but I will try to preserve my integrity.

The ground on which the nomination for Taylor goes is not with-

out plausibility. They say we must turn out the present Administration at any rate ; that, if Taylor be not supported, there is a
worse evil. On the other hand, it is said we have yielded to the
demands of the South again and again ; that they always ask for
once more ; and that we may yield and yield forever, and still they
will require us to do it *once more.* This conflict will probably dis-
tract my district more than any other in the State ; and there is
no State that will suffer so much as Massachusetts.

WASHINGTON, June 24, 1848.

MY DEAR SUMNER, — I think you are rather the hardest taskmaster since Pharaoh ; and I am not sure I ought to stop with that old
Egyptian scamp.

You know I am not only Acting Secretary of the Massachusetts
Board of Education, and now keeper of a sort of intelligence-office
on certain subjects for the whole country (in which capacities I have
literally had *thirty* letters to open and answer in a day since I have
been here), but you also know that I came into the class here when
the other members of it had read the book half through ; so that I
had the back lessons all to make up. You also wanted me to undertake the defence of the "Pearl" prisoners, who will be arraigned next
week, probably on Wednesday, — on how many indictments, do you
think ? I expect 245 (two hundred and forty-five). I shall write
again when I am certain. You have been drumming me up for a
speech in the House, and now you want me to go to Worcester. Is
not all this a little too bad ?

Besides all this, if I am not greatly mistaken, you are calling me
to account for not plunging at once, with the toga of my secretaryship on, into the Taylor war. Now, I have written at length to
H—— about this latter point, and you may see the letter. Understanding this whole matter, I should like to know what you and
others think about it.

Truly yours,   HORACE MANN.

WASHINGTON, June 28, 1848.

The District Attorney is making ready for a fearful amount of
indictments against Drayton and Sayres, — so many, that, if the

prisoners should be convicted on all of them, it will require an imprisonment of hundreds of years to expiate the deed. . . . There must be a tremendous re-action at some time — perhaps not till after our time — against the oppression and abuses which are committed to uphold slavery.

WASHINGTON, D.C., April 24, 1848.

C. PIERCE, ESQ.

My DEAR SIR, — I assure you I was right glad to see the superscription of a letter in your beautiful handwriting. Now, do not laugh at my adjective; for beauty, you know, is in the eye of the beholder. . . .

I find myself as comfortably situated here as I could expect; but I have not the slightest expectation of ever feeling any attachment for the position. I have no idea that I can make my efforts tell on the body with which I am associated. From present appearances, I have not run away from correspondence on schools and education, but into it. I may have an opportunity to do an unseen work in this behalf, — even greater than I have ever done before. I have seen enough already to give me even a deeper conviction of the necessity and indispensableness of education than I ever had before. It is the only name whereby a republic can be saved. If I ever return to the field, as I hope to, I shall return with new motives for exertion and zeal.

We have had a great excitement here for a few days. The South are on fire. They like to sympathize with revolution so long as it will stay three thousand miles off; but revolution at home is to be decided by different principles. They have furnished some admirable texts for Northern men to preach from; and according to the gospel these promulgate will be the disciples they will make.

Love to madam.

Ever and truly yours,
HORACE MANN.

WASHINGTON, D.C., April 26, 1848

DR. JARVIS.

DEAR SIR, — I acknowledge with great pleasure the receipt of yours of the 22d instant; and what welcome news you impart respecting the progress of school-matters in Dorchester! An appropriation of $10,000 + 4,000 + 10,000 in a single year, when last year you raised but a little more than $6,000, if I remember rightly! This is triumph, and reward for all your labors. . . .

And now, my dear sir, you do not know how home-sick and State-sick I am; that is, how I long to get back among the boys and girls of the Massachusetts schools. One consideration only helps to reconcile me to the change. I am satisfied that I was on the point of breaking down remedilessly when I came away. If my heart was not growing hard, my brain was growing soft. I begin to feel a little better. If my health is restored, I shall be back in the *vineyard* again before long. The present crisis about our new territory, — is it not enough to wean anybody from home?

For all the kind things you are pleased to express, I can only say that they point to what I would do, rather than to any thing I have done: indeed, what I have done falls so far short of what should have been done, that I feel something of an emotion of shame whenever the subject is called to my mind. . . .

Believe me most truly and sincerely yours,

H. M.

WASHINGTON, July 18, 1848.

We are getting along very slowly. There is much business in the hopper, only a little of which will ever be ground out. It is impossible to tell what will be the fate of the territorial bills. The future welfare and greatness of the Territories has very little to do with the question. The fate of millions and millions is to be voted upon as it is thought the temporary and evanescent interests of politicians will be best subserved. "Who shall be President?" is deemed of more consequence than whether there shall be millions of slaves in the West in each generation, and a thousand or million generations of these. I see, every day, more and more, the necessity of the great work of education; and were I young, or had I my old strength again, nothing should keep me from that work of works. How different this Government would be if there were any coronal region belonging to its sensorium!

WASHINGTON, July 29, 1848.

The celebrated Compromise Bill, on the subject of slavery in the Territories, came to the House yesterday, and was laid upon the table — that is, to sleep forever — by a vote of 112 to 98. The majority represents the antislavery interest in the House. It was a scene of absorbing interest. The house was more full than at any other time since I have been here. Usually, when taking the yea and nays, the House is like Bedlam. No one cares for any thing but to give his own vote in turn. But yesterday it was still as a church. Every man wanted to know how every other man voted. The South has had a fiery dispensation this Congress. Speech is getting to be free here, and they have been coerced into some decency and deference.

WASHINGTON, Aug. 5, 1848.
Rev. S. J. MAY.

MY DEAR SIR, — I thank you for your letter of the 2d inst., in which I find so much new proof of your old partiality. The speech you so kindly refer to, I think has produced more effect than any other of my educational writings; which is to be attributed, not to its greater power (for I think it inferior to most of what I have said on this subject before), but solely to the fact that it was said *in Congress*, and by *a member of Congress*, whom I find to be a very different man, even though he be the same, from a mere Secretary of a Board of Education. It was very attentively listened to; and some members from slave States came to me immediately after, and from civility, or other motive, offered me their congratulations. I do not hear that it is doing any harm in the way of exasperation or otherwise. I have just received a note from an entire stranger, — a Virginian born, — in which he says he, *now and hereafter*, goes for "free soil" in new Territories, and for the annihilation of slavery where it exists. Excuse this appearance of egotism to an old and most valued friend.

You go to Buffalo, then. I have but one word to say. If you have any regard for the purity and moral strength of the *Great Party* that is to be, don't put such a corrupt man as Van Buren at the bead of it. Just so certain as you do, the cause itself is tainted and corrupted.

Ever and truly your friend,

HORACE MANN.

WASHINGTON, Aug. 5, 1848.

We had a verdict of "guilty" returned yesterday against Drayton. The jury were in consultation twenty-one hours. We understand that those who stood out for the prisoner were at last induced to surrender by the fear of losing all patronage and custom in the city if they refused to convict. But this is not the end of it. We shall try to set the verdict aside on what seem to us good grounds.

Aug. 7. Notwithstanding we have reverses, yet I think the law is on our side ; and we mean so far to get the principles on record, that, if we fail here, we can get the decision reversed in a higher court. I am in a good work; so do not feel uneasy about me. Maybe it will turn out to be a *great* one. . . .

I am told that public opinion in this District is undergoing a change.

Aug. 10. Ah! the verdict was against us again yesterday. It seems impossible here, at the present time, to have an impartial trial. No jury, in a free State, would have convicted Drayton in either of the cases. No jury would have remained in consultation half an hour, without acquitting him. We must struggle hard yet. They have not yet got him hopelessly in their clutches.

WASHINGTON, Aug. 11, 1848.

We began yesterday with the first case against Sayres. It looks better than the others; and I do not see how it is possible, even with the most prejudiced jury and afore-determined judges, to convict him. But I may not estimate the force of prejudice and predetermination aright. If we were in any *Christian* land, I should be sure of success.

But we have done a glorious work in the House to-day. A few days ago, we passed a bill for the establishment of a territorial government in Oregon. It went to the Senate, and they amended it by adding the Missouri-compromise provision to it; that is, that all territory north of 36° 30′ north latitude should be free territory, and all south of it slave territory, as they desired, — this line to extend to the Pacific Ocean.

When the bill came back to the House, we voted to non-concur in the amendment of the Senate; and, to the surprise of everybody, we had thirty-nine majority. All the Northern Democrats, so many of whom have heretofore voted with the Southern Democrats and Southern Whigs on slavery questions, — all excepting four, — voted with us. They can no longer stand the fiery furnace of public indignation on the subject of slavery. It is one of the most glorious events that has happened this century. All our discussions on the subject of slavery during this session have tended to it.

Saturday Morning. All ready for the fight. This case will go to the jury to-day. I do not know what will come next. If the Government tries another of these cases, we cannot get through till Tuesday, or perhaps Wednesday; so that we may be separated a day or two longer. But hereafter it may give us pleasure to remember all this.

Aug. 13. Verdict of "Not guilty!" The fight in Drayton's case helped this one very much.

We went back to the Senate to see if they would recede from their amendment to the Oregon Bill. They debated it a good part of the day yesterday, and *all night*, and took the question about nine this morning. There was a majority of *four* for receding. So the Oregon Territory will be established with the slavery restriction in it. Is not this worth coming to Washington to see? It is a great triumph, and the first upon which we can really rely. The days of each of the four members who voted against us in the House will probably be ended thereby, politically.

WASHINGTON, Aug. 14, 1848.

Drayton has a wife and children in Philadelphia. Sayres has a wife: I do not know whether he has children. I went yesterday to bid Drayton good-by in his jail. He was firm and collected, resolved to abide his fate. Sayres must remain till December, at any rate. Do I think *my* fate hard? Let me compare it with theirs. I feel in this case as if I were not working for Drayton and Sayres alone, but for the whole colored race. Is it not clearly right that I should stay and help these men, who have no chance of seeing *their* homes for months, and possibly not for years? I cannot believe. besides, but this trial is to have an important influence on the subject of slavery in this District. We are quietly and silently making thunderbolts, which will by and by be hurled at the heads of the proslavery men here.

Aug. 17. I hoped to be able to send you the verdict of the jury to-day; but I am disappointed in this.

Mr. Carlisle made a most complete and beautiful closing argument on our side yesterday. It was then the District Attorney's duty to address the jury, who would then retire to consult and give their verdict.

But Mr. *Key* asked for a few minutes' delay, and then said he had such a severe pain in his head, that he could not go on with the argument, and moved the court to postpone the trial till this morning. This the judge did; for he does every thing against the prisoner, and nothing in his favor. So we lost nearly the whole day. How painful this was to me, I cannot tell you. The truth is, as I believe, the District Attorney is getting sick of his infernal cases, and will make use of any pretext to get rid of them at the present time; that is, postpone them to another court.

WEST NEWTON, Sept. 22, 1848.

MY DEAR MR. MAY, — . . . I hope you do not despair of the race, though you write so despondingly. Probably I think quite as little of Congress, intellectually and morally, as you do: still I trust they will never repeat some of the wicked things they have done. I certainly agree with you, that schools will be found to be the way that God has chosen for the reformation of the world. Somebody has said. God is never in a hurry. We are; and therefore the ameliorations of society seem to go on so slowly. It is not by any one miraculous blaze of light that the dark paths of earth are to be at once illumined, but slowly will the day-star creep up, and the sun after the day-star. I think more progress was made during the last session of Congress, in favor of antislavery, than during any ten Congresses before; and it is not only progress, but momentum, or headway, which will help forward through another stage. There are many people among the Southerners who are all ready to become openly hostile to the institution. They have been made clamorous in its defence by the violence and denunciation of Northern abolitionists. The first thing is to get their ear, their attention; and this never can be done by railing. Anathema and vituperation make them brace themselves up against conviction; and they act as the chambermaid did, who said to her mistress, "The more you ring, the more I won't come."

As to my present position, you will probably see by the papers of this week that I am almost compelled to assume a new attitude. My intimation not to be again a candidate for Congress did not proceed upon the supposition of my continuing Secretary of the Board. I have come to the conclusion that it is best for me and for the cause that I should retire from that post, — not from my zeal or works in the cause itself, but from an official relation to it. My purpose was to be a free man next 4th of March. But my movement to get out of this office seems to threaten to get me into it; for both conventions this week, the "Free Soil" and the "Whig," have unanimously nominated me for re-election. So, if I am chosen, I must go again.

WASHINGTON, Dec. 2, 1848.

I had the most confident expectations that we should get through with Drayton's cases to-day; but yesterday, Mr. Bradley, a lawyer on the opposite side, spoke five mortal hours, and did not get through even then. I hope he will finish to-day, and then Mr. Carlisle will speak. I wish you could hear him! He is a young man, rather small, but beautiful, dignified, and gentlemanly; the best-natured fellow that ever was; of Irish descent, and full of Irish fire; polished in his diction; imaginative, poetic, and withal an excellent lawyer, — so much so, that there is always a solid *terra firma* of good sense for all his lofty flowers and magnolias to grow out of. He contests a point of law with the judges as if he had devoted himself wholly to law. He retorts upon an assailant as if he had spent his days among men of elegant conversation, and his nights in regaling his mind over the best literary works; and he is as quick in his susceptibility to generous sentiments as if he had been brought up by the Sisters of Charity.

WASHINGTON, Dec. 28, 1848.

I think the country is to witness, or rather experience, serious times. Interference with slavery will excite civil commotion at the South. Still it is best to interfere. Now, when we have a Southern man and a military man at the head of the Government, is the time to see whether the Union is a rope of sand, or a band of steel. It is not a life at all congenial to me. The great question of freedom or slavery is the only one that would keep me here.

WASHINGTON, Jan. 9, 1849.

Do you mean, by the " present doings of South Carolina," the measures which the Southern senators and representatives here are adopting to overawe and frighten the North from making free Territories and a free District of Columbia? If so, then you already must know what I think of them. I will not say those movements are treasonable; but they are quite as treasonable as the old Hartford Convention, which all friends to the country condemned. They are to have their adjourned meeting on Monday evening next; and I think the movement will be defeated. It will be embarrassed, at any rate. But to let you into the whole secret of the movement would be very much like telling little H. about the wickedness of men; and I have not time to do this to-day.

JAN. 15.

There is great commotion here in political matters. To-night the Southern Convention, called to see what measures the South will take on the subject of slavery, are to meet. An address has been prepared by Mr. Calhoun, which is said to be in the highest degree inflammatory. It is thought here, by many of the most intelligent men, that Mr. Calhoun is resolved on a dissolution of the Union. Many of the Democrats also are playing into the hands of the South, because they desire to break up the Whig party; that is, to dissever the Northern and Southern branches of it.

18

JAN. 16

I sat up last night to hear the result of the Convention, which did not break up till midnight. Mr. Calhoun's report was recommitted, which is equivalent to a defeat. The Southern Democrats went with him ; the Southern Whigs went against him : so that *politics* helped to modify the course of both, even in regard to slavery. It is considered a triumph for the friends of the Union, and a *quasi* triumph against the Southern machinations to protect slavery.

WASHINGTON, Feb. 4, 1849.

A supposed fraud on the part of the President, in relation to the treaty with Mexico, has been discovered ; and if it turns out as is apprehended, — that is, if he has not some answer which we cannot now conceive of, — he has been guilty of one of the most high-handed atrocities ever committed by any ruler of a civilized people. But I do not allow myself to form an opinion until I hear what the evidence is.

FEB. 5.

We are having a very interesting debate to-day on the subject of the treaty which the President ratified with Mexico. It is a very serious affair. The President is in a *tight place.* He will find it difficult to extricate himself. It will lead to much future action.

FEB. 7, 1849.

I rejoice that this Congress is drawing to a close. I shall breathe easier on the slavery question as the 4th of March draws nigh. A strong proslavery effort is making. The plan is to invite the inhabitants of the new Territory to form a State constitution. If this succeeds, then the argument will be, that Congress must receive them, let their constitution be what it will, whether prohibiting slavery or not. If California were to form a State constitution of her own will, she would doubtless put an antislavery restriction in it ; but, if we ask her to come, it will be expected that we shall take her as she comes. On this point, there will be a struggle before the close of the session. If we can weather this cape, we shall go out, apparently, into a comparatively tranquil sea.

WASHINGTON, Feb. 20, 1849.

We had a decision yesterday in court; and it was, as I expected it would be, in our favor. This gives Drayton and Sayres a new trial, and under much better circumstances than before. It was gratifying to have the court to which we appealed demolish, one after another, the abominable decisions by which the judge, in our trials last summer, decided against us, and sought to secure a conviction of the prisoner. I struggled against his nefarious conduct like a man struggling for his life; but it was in vain *then*. It is not in vain now.

FEB. 21.

It is just a year ago to-day since Mr. Adams fell in this House. . . . Yesterday and to-day we are striving to get at a bill, which is on the calendar, in favor of abolishing the slave-trade in the District of Columbia. The South are playing shy.

FEB. 22.

The President made a lame defence in regard to the treaty with Mexico. But nothing will be done about it, except to *scold:* for our people will never give up the gold; and, even if the gold were not there, they never would give up the land.

WASHINGTON, Feb. 27, 1849.

MY DEAR SUMNER, — Mr. Palfrey made a grand speech last night. About half of it was in answer to the speech of Gov. M'Dowell of Virginia, — the most elegant and captivating speech made during the session, but in which some questions were put to Massachusetts which it required a scholar and a Christian to answer. Mr. Palfrey answered them all most beautifully.

We are now taking the yeas and nays on the California Territorial Bill. There has been a vehement effort to defeat it, or rather to defeat the " Jefferson Proviso " in it. I will give you the result, if we ascertain it before the mail closes, which will be in a few minutes.

In great haste, yours as ever,

HORACE MANN.

Bill passed, — ayes, 126; noes, 87. GLORIOUS!

Before I write you again, the question of freedom or slavery for the Territories will be settled. There is a bare chance, if the decision is against us, that it may be recalled by the next Congress. I have great fears as to the result. We sat until between eleven and twelve last night. It is one to-night. We shall probably sit nearly all night to-night; and that winds up the concern for good or for ill. I am not without hope; but my fears preponderate. Most others would say, "God save us!" but I believe he will let us save or sink ourselves.

MARCH 4, 1849.

The Republic is safe. We commenced our session yesterday at eleven, and were adjourned this morning at seven. It was a tumultuous night, but it was fought bravely; and the victory is ours. The slave-party, and those of the Democrats who act with it, have wrought from the beginning of the session to provide the way for bringing in the new Territories as States, without any restriction as to slavery. Not succeeding in getting any of their regular bills for that purpose through Congress, they started the project, a week or two ago, of attaching a section to the Civil and Diplomatic Bill, — a bill that provides for defraying all the expenses of the civil departments of Government the current year. It was utterly incongruous in this bill: but they knew the bill must be passed, or the wheels of Government must stop; so they fastened it on to compel its opponents to vote for it. This was in the Senate. The House did not agree to it. A committee of conference was appointed. That committee could not agree: so the question came back to the House; and on that we had the contest. It is impossible to detail the manœuvres and tactics by which the respective parties conducted the strife. At last, however, at about two o'clock this morning, we succeeded in attaching an amendment which virtually took the *slavery* out of it. It was then sent to the Senate; and there, after two or three hours' hard fighting, they yielded; being satisfied that they could not bring the House to their terms, and being unwilling to take the responsibility of stopping the wheels of Government. There were two regular fist-fights in the House, in one of which blood flowed freely; and one in the Senate. Some of the members were fiercely exasperated; and had the North been as ferocious as the South, or the Whigs as violent as the Democrats, it is probable there would have been a general *mêlée*. But all this depends upon the *men*. I walked round the House a number of times; conversed with all the Southern slaveholders whom I knew, and, by introduction, with some I had not known; and had not an uncivil word. I never felt farther removed from the spirit of fighting in my life. At last, at seven this morning, Mr. Winthrop made an elegant farewell address in answer to a vote of thanks; and we all *ran*.

WEST NEWTON, April 12, 1849.

To GEORGE COMBE, ESQ.

MY DEAR MR. COMBE, — Silence is not forgetfulness. . . . On Feb. 23, 1848, Mr. J. Q. Adams died, struck down in his seat on the floor of Congress. Having recently moved into the Congressional District which he represented, I was nominated as his successor in the following March; and, on the third day of April, was elected.

Can I justify myself to you for having laid down an educational office, and taken up a political one? I can truly say, that, on my part, the change was an involuntary one. After the nomination was made, I prepared an answer, peremptorily declining it. But various collateral incidents and accidental causes led a council of my best friends to decide that I should reverse my purpose. Among other considerations, I think a regard for my health was the most decisive; and, if my health or life were worth any thing, they were right. I now verily believe that another year, without aid and without relaxation, would have closed my labors upon earth. On the 13th of April, I went to Washington. Soon after, I resigned my Secretaryship; but the Board, not being prepared to appoint a successor, requested me to continue to discharge its duties till the close of the year. This I consented to do, especially as it would afford me an opportunity to make a final Report, — a peroration to the rest. Thus, instead of being a relay, I was made to run double stages, — to perform the duties of a member in Congress, and by correspondence to carry on the Secretaryship. . . .

You may have heard of an attempt to carry off seventy-five slaves in one night, in a sloop from the city of Washington, which occurred last spring. It caused the fiercest excitement; and the prisoners, who were taken, three in number, were doomed to destruction. I was importuned and over-persuaded to undertake their defence. Not a lawyer in the city of Washington would argue the question of the constitutionality of slavery in the District of Columbia. I longed to do it. The trial came on in August; and for twelve successive days, in a Tophet called a court-room, with the thermometer seldom lower than ninety, I fought against as abominable a spirit as ever disgraced a Jeffrys or a Coke. The atmosphere was so impregnated by the excitement without, that it became, to a great extent, a non-conductor of humanity and reason to the jury within. One of the prisoners, however, escaped entirely ; one was convicted of an offence punishable by fine only, with imprisonment until paid ; and the third was convicted on the indictments, sentenced to ten years' imprisonment on each, while thirty-nine indictments for a similar offence were continued. Exceptions were taken to numerous rulings of the court, which were argued before the Appellate Court in November; and all the judgments were set aside. Now we are to begin *de novo*, but under much better auspices; for many of the abominable legal doctrines of the court below have been annulled. But I dwell too long on this.

After the 1st of September, on my return home, I had all my arrears of official business to bring up, institutes to attend, and my Report to make. I went to Washington in November to argue the questions of law, and again in December to attend the session. I returned home on the 5th of March, 1849. We had a fortnight of the worst possible weather before I left Washington, and three weeks of the same kind after I got home. Exposure to this, the fatigue of travelling, and being up all night, as we were some of the last nights of the session, *abolished me*. I have had no lungs, no stomach, no brains, or only had them as foes, and not as allies. Within a week past, we have had fine weather ; and my vital currents are once more beginning to flow. I avail myself of the first leisure hour, and use my first returning strength, to write to you. And now, have I not made my justification for this long omission? Will you not pardon me? I doubt not you will say the excuse I urge is sufficient for not writing; but what excuse, you will ask, can I render for so gross a violation of the natural laws? It is only this: That it seemed to me I had duties to perform which were of more importance than life itself; and therefore, in the conflict of laws, I obeyed the highest.

I have just begun to read the Memoir of Dr. Channing by his nephew, W. H. Channing. I am about half through the work, and about half through the life. And what a life! If inspiration is claimed for anybody, was not Dr. Channing inspired? How lovely, how true, how gloriously progressive! If you have not read it, I entreat you to read it forthwith. I never knew before how athletic and vigorous he was when a boy, and how, when at Richmond, Va., and striving to obey the highest moral and religious laws of God, he was, in this very act of supposed obedience, violating every physical law, and thereby almost cancelling the beneficent power of his spiritual attainments, by incurring bodily debility that lasted through life. What a divine desire to take care of his heart, with utter ignorance and heedlessness as to the condition of his stomach! Oh, if he had understood that God was the Creator of both organs, and that the value of either is reduced comparatively to nothing by the neglect of the other! Why was not this a proper case for a miracle? Why could not some spare angel, some loiterer, perhaps, about the courts of heaven, have been despatched to give him the substance of a certain book called the "Constitution of Man," or of "Combe on Digestion"? Modern theology cannot answer this question; but you and I can answer it reverently and philosophically, and in a way which will "vindicate the ways of God to man."

On political affairs, I cannot but remark how full of instruction they are in both hemispheres. What an upheaving in the Old World! What an expansion of life and vigor in the New! We are as yet too near to take a view of the Olympian vastness of these events. We cannot see their magnitude any more than an insect can measure the outline of a pyramid, on one side of which it is perched. To compass these events, we must stand at a distance of a hundred years, — a point at which you and I shall never stand in this life; though I am beginning to feel as Dr. Franklin did when he poured out a fly from an old bottle of wine, and re-animated it, and said that he would like to be bottled up for a century in the same way, and then be revived to take an observation of the progress of the world.

With sincere love, whether silent or garrulous, your abiding friend, HORACE MANN.

BOSTON, April 30, 1849.

HON. HORACE MANN.

DEAR SIR, — I thank you for sending me the Document of the House of Representatives in Boston. As for your conduct in the education-matter which it brings to light, I can only say, *It is just like you.* When I see such conduct, I thank God, and take courage.

I believe I have all of your printed speeches but the last; and, as one day or another I may have to "reckon" with you, I beg you to send me your last speech in Congress.

Yours truly, THEODORE PARKER.

May 11, 1849. When I added the postscript yesterday, with "Not guilty," I felt vast relief; for I did not think it possible that the attorney for the Government could be so ferocious and vengeful as to try Drayton still again. To the astonishment of every one, he this morning declared for another trial against him, on another indictment for stealing the slaves. He has called in one of the most eminent counsel to assist; thus stultifying himself, after he has lost one case, by employing aid to help him gain another.

It has taken all day to find a jury that had not made up or expressed an opinion respecting the merits of the case. One man was asked whether he had formed or expressed an opinion respecting the prisoner's guilt or innocence; and he spoke out boldly, before both court and jury and all the spectators in the court-house, saying, "Yes: my opinion is that he ought to be hung."

Another man who was summoned said the same thing to one of the officers of the court. This shows what a deadly hostility there is in some minds to the prisoners. Others earnestly desire their acquittal, but hardly dare to speak out. When I happen to be standing aside, they come along once in a while, and speak confidentially about it.

May 13. The cause came on yesterday in good earnest. It is very easy to see, that, in Gen. Jones, we are to have an antagonist vastly superior to Mr. Key. Indeed, with a jury composed of not more than two-thirds of knaves or fools, I should not have been afraid to try even such a kind of case as this against him. But the difference between a giant and a pygmy does not represent the difference between the great and the little man we are now contending against.

May 17. I spoke nearly three hours in the case yesterday. Mr. Carlisle now addresses the jury, and then Gen. Jones. No case ever looked better for a prisoner, if it were only on some other subject. But the spirit, or party-spirit, of the people here, is fierce and fanatical beyond expression. They are hardly in a state of mind to be reasoned with. We have some advantage with a jury; for they know they must sit still, and listen; and, by calming them and expostulating with them, one may at last make an impression. But, should it ever be my fortune to be tried by slaveholders, I should consider myself doomed as soon as I was accused.

BOSTON, Nov. 14, 1849.

HON. HORACE MANN.

MY DEAR SIR, — It is time to go to bed; but I cannot go to sleep without thanking you for the noble work you have done to-night. Of the magnificence and eloquence in thought and in speech, I shall not stop to speak: they were the smaller beauties of your sermon.

I must thank you for the magnificent morality you set before those young men.*

I think I can appreciate the heroism it required to do so, and to speak, as you have spoken, on such an occasion, in such a presence, when your words must seem *personal* to many; no, not to many,

* Lecture before the Mercantile-Library Association.

but to a *few*. I know well enough, and you know much more and better than I, how your oration will be received by the men who are looked upon as models, but whose baseness it exposed, whose littleness it scathed with terrible fire. But there were many true hearts, in bosoms younger than mine, which beat with yours, and echoed back your words.

I have often been thankful that you are in Congress, — one faithful man, not a slave to the instinct for office, more than a slave to the instinct for gold, but a representative of the instinct for justice and for truth.

There is one that will long be grateful to you for such words as you spoke to-night, and the life which makes them not words, but *deeds*. I beg you to accept my most hearty thanks, and believe me

Truly your friend,

THEODORE PARKER.

WASHINGTON, Dec. 11, 1849.

Half an hour ago, Mr. Clay came into the House, and took a seat near mine. I have been studying his head, — manipulating it with the mind's fingers. It is a head of very small dimensions. Benevolence is large ; self-esteem and love of approbation are large. The intellect, for the size of the brain, is well developed. His benevolence prevents his self-esteem from being offensive ; and his intellect controls the action of his love of approbation, and saves him from an excessive vanity. This vanity, however, has, at some periods of his life, led him into follies. He derives his whole strength from his temperament, which is supremely nervous, but with just as much of the sanguine as it was possible to put into it. Considering the volume of the brain, or size of the head, it has the best adjusted faculties I have ever seen. The skull, after death, will give no idea of his power, as he derives the whole of it from his temperament.

Dec. 13. A word about the proceedings of the House yesterday. The Southern men concentrated on William J. Brown of Indiana for Speaker. He is a Democrat. The Democratic portion of the regular Free-soil party thought, if they could get him to make pledges on the subject of free soil, they should get a Free-soil man and a Democrat too. So he gave them pledges that he would do the very opposite thing from what was expected of him by all the Southerners who had brought him forward and sustained him. He came within two votes of being elected. Five of the Free-soilers voted for him. This alarmed some of the extreme Southern men, who thought there must be mischief lying under "that white heap," as the rat said of the cat covered with meal. Three of them withdrew their votes from Brown, and he lacked two of a choice. This led to an inquiry, and the whole rascality came out. You will see, by the "Republic" I send you, how he got cursed. I feel like going into sackcloth and ashes for human nature.

Dec. 14. We had a terrible day yesterday. The most violent declamation, and almost a fight. But to-day has opened more calmly. The paper will show you what we have to witness. Oh, how it makes one yearn for the light of truth, which would save men from rushing violently against each other in their zeal to reach the true goal !

Dec. 22. I shrink from the praise that you say I receive in certain quarters. It is prompted, in part at least, by motives in which I do not at all participate. I have voted for Mr. Winthrop, and in that way have fulfilled the hopes of the Whigs. He was their first choice ; he is only my second or third : yet, as he is the best man we could possibly elect, I have supported him. Just so much undeserved credit as I get from the Whigs, just so much undeserved censure I shall get from the Free-soilers.

We have had the worst outbreak in the House this morning that we have ever had. It was infernal. The "Globe" will tell you all our proceedings.

Dec. 23. The Speaker was chosen at six o'clock last evening, after the stormiest day that even our tempestuous Congress ever experienced.

Howell Cobb is Speaker ; one of the fiercest, sternest, strongest proslavery men in all the South. He loves slavery. It is his politics and his patriotism, his political economy and his religion. And by whom was he allowed to be elevated to this important post? By the Free-soilers, who, at any time during the last three weeks, might have prevented it, and who permitted it last night when the fact stared them full in the face. Mr. Winthrop was not unexceptionable, it is true; but what a vast difference between him and a Southern, avowed champion of slavery, with all the South at his back to force him on, and at his ear to minister counsel! How strange is that hate of an evil thing which adopts the very means that secure its triumph! How strange that love of a good thing which destroys it! Now we shall have all proslavery committees. All the power of patronage of the Speaker, and it is great, will be on the wrong side; and this has been permitted by those who clamor most against all forbearance toward slavery, when by a breath they might have prevented it. Surely they must believe that God punishes only *commissioners*, not *omissioners*.

WASHINGTON, Jan. 5, 1850.

I went last evening with Mr. —— to hear Professor Johnson lecture. In walking home, we got into some discussion about the condition of the country, and the prospects of humanity in general. I found Mr. —— apparently sceptical about any amelioration of the condition of mankind, or that there is, in truth, "a good time coming." When I spoke of sloughing off the vices of mankind, he replied, that if men were to obey the laws of God, as I had been indicating, the *drain* of vices would be stopped, and the race would soon become so numerous as to lead of itself to infinite distress. I said, if men once understood their duty, and the means of happiness, no man would have any more children than he could support, educate, and leave in an eligible condition behind him, any more than a judicious farmer would have more stock on his farm than he could support with profit to himself, and with humanity to them. I told him, further, that the bringing of a human being into this world, with a moral certainty of his being unhappy and miserable, I regarded as a far greater crime, *in the abstract*, than sending a human being out of it. Both seemed to be entirely new ideas to him.

E. W. CLAP, ESQ.

DEAR SIR, — Mr. Thompson has been to see me. Of course, I was obliged to tell him there might be circumstances in which I would vote for a slaveholder. This, I suppose, has lost me a hundred votes; but I had better lose a hundred by honesty than gain one by dishonesty. . . . In great haste, very truly yours,

H. MANN.

WASHINGTON, Jan. 7, 1850.

. . . Mr. A. has infinitely slender cause to praise Mr. Cobb for putting Mr. Giddings on the Committee on Territories, and Mr. Allen on the District Committee, and Mr. King on the Judiciary; for he has so buried them up with Southern Democrats, that they cannot get their heads high up enough to breathe. With such a committee as Mr. Winthrop would have appointed, we should have met with no obstacles in getting our measures before the country and the House. Now we shall encounter the most serious of obstacles at every step; and, if it is possible for skill or power to bar out all antislavery measures, it will be done.

There is no end to the perversions of partisans. A partisan cannot be an honest man, whether he be a political or a religious partisan. How necessary it is to cultivate the seeds of truth in the young! Nothing can be, or can approach to be, a substitute for it. So of the great principle, that it is for the interest of every man to be a true man, and that by no possibility can perversion or error be useful. How the world needs to be educated!

Does H. get exact and complete ideas of things? Can he reproduce what you teach him? This is an all-important part of teaching. Has a lesson been so learned that the pupil can restate it in words, or exemplify it in act, or draw it on blackboards, &c.? This is the test to which learners should be early subjected. I am very glad about the music. We pity Laura Bridgeman for the privation of her physical powers; but how many of us need to be pitied for the privation of faculties whose absence deforms just as much as a loss of the senses! One of these is music.

WASHINGTON, Jan. 12, 1850.

E. W. CLAP, ESQ.

DEAR SIR, — If you do not pity a poor fellow who is condemned to stay here and vote day after day, doing no good, and perhaps some harm, then you are more hard-hearted than a slaveholder. . . . I hear the Free-soil men are very ferocious against me because I voted for Mr. Winthrop. Some discussion was had about getting up an indignation meeting to give me a special denunciation. But probably they will think they can do the same thing without exposing themselves to an answer. . . .

I am told that Mr. —— and others have got this notion in their heads, and speak of it freely, — that I am to be put forward next year as a candidate for Governor, in order to break down their party. *They want, therefore, to break me down first.* It is not what is past, but what they profess to apprehend for the future, that directs their course. They mean to put me in the wrong, at all events. Hence that article in the " Republican," a week or ten days ago, written, as I am told, by ——. I should like a good opportunity to set this matter right. . . .

Truly yours,

HORACE MANN.

JAN. 11, 1850.

We have been going the same rounds, in attempting to choose a Clerk, which occupied us three weeks before we chose a Speaker. It is most irksome business, and cuts away all the ties that bind me to office.

We have just this minute elected a Clerk from Tennessee. He is a Southerner, but as unobjectionable as any Southerner can be. He does not hold slaves ; but he was once a member of Congress, and voted with the slave-party through and through. I have not voted for him at all, though he is a Whig. We had an exciting time at the close of the voting, and before the vote was declared. The Southern Democrats, seeing how near he was to being elected, came over to him one after another, and at last gave him just enough. That is the way. They are always more true to slavery than to Democracy. It is a good result ; but I am rejoiced that I did not help to bring it about. During the whole voting, the Northern Whigs came round me, and some of our Massachusetts men too, and urged and besought me to change my vote. At one moment, when only one more vote was wanted, forty men turned beseechingly to my seat. I shook my head at them all; and at that moment a Southern man on the other side of the House jumped up, and changed his vote. This settled it.

JAN. 27, 1850.

My lecture in Albany was delivered in Dr. Campbell's church. He was not there to hear it; but on the list of lecturers were Mr. Parker, Mr. Peabody, Dr. Dewey. This list frightened Dr. Campbell; and, as I learn by a letter received from there yesterday, he has closed his church against the course. Isn't this beautiful?

JAN. 28, 1850.

I am sorry that dancing is made a standing amusement at the parties where the Normalists go. In the way in which it is generally *done*, it is of little benefit to health, and of little advantage to any part of man's nature; but my objection to it is the mischievous use which the enemies of the school will make of the custom. I can give up so much for peace!

JAN. 30.

Mr. Sears will not find it easy to sweep prudential committees out of existence. Reasons very different from what belong to the merits of the case will be present at the settling of that question.

As for the Abstract, it is a great mistake. If it is understood that such portions only are to be taken as belong to one topic, and, after being taken once, that topic is to be dismissed, the consequence will inevitably be, that the committees will ignore the topic which has received attention, and write on some one which they hope will receive attention.

I cannot but wish it were possible for some man or men to spread themselves over this great State of New York, and see that the children are as well taken care of as the pigs.

JAN. 29, 1850.

This morning I was introduced to ———, a gentleman from North Carolina, who wanted to have a talk with me about slavery. He is embedded in all the doctrines in its favor. He has been offering all commercial, economical, and pecuniary arguments to me in reference to slavery in the Territories. As to the moral and religious

aspect of the question, he is as firm for slavery as William Lloyd
Garrison is against it. He says he is willing to take up with any portion of the new territory which the South can accept, as a decent
pretext for surrendering the rest. I told him I would give the
South any money as an equivalent, any amount of the public lands
which they may turn into money; but one inch of territory for
slavery — never ! let what would come.

Dark clouds overhang the future : and that is not all; they are
full of lightning.

Feb. 4, 1850.

Gen. Taylor's Message is very good so far as it relates to California. He recommends that it be admitted as a State. But, in
the same message, he recommends *non-action* in regard to New
Mexico ; that is, to form no territorial government for New Mexico,
but to await its own motion on the subject. Now, the benefit of a
territorial government in New Mexico, with a prohibition of slavery
in it, is, that, while such a prohibition exists, no slaveholders will
dare go there, and therefore will not be there to infuse their views
into the people, and help form a constitution with slavery in it. If
there is no such government, and no such prohibition, the fear is
that slaveholders will go there, and exercise an influence in favor of
slavery, and help form a constitution which shall not prohibit it,
and, when they send that constitution to Congress, will get in, and
so slavery be ultimately established by reason of present neglect.
I approve, therefore, of the California part of the message, but
disapprove of the other.

Feb. 6.

I really think, if we insist upon passing the Wilmot Proviso for
the Territories, that the South — a part of them — will rebel. But
I would pass it, rebellion or not. I consider no evil so great as
that of the extension of slavery.

Feb. 7.

Yesterday, Mr. Clay concluded his speech upon his Compromise
resolutions. Its close was pathetic. There is hardly another slaveholder in all the South who would have perilled his popularity to
such an extent. It will be defeated : but, if we from the North are

still, it will be defeated by Southern votes and declamation ; and it is better for the cause that they should defeat it than that we should.

You were right in saying that I would not have asked Mr. Winthrop about putting me on a committee ; for I would not have answered such a question, had I been in his place, and had it been asked me. Still, I think I should have held an important place on an anti-slavery committee ; and, what is more, should have had a majority of colleagues who would act with me. Now every thing is in jeopardy.

I never said whom I would vote for, nor whom I would not. It would have been a bitter pill to be obliged to choose between the three candidates ; but, if I had been so obliged, I should have voted for the least evil.

Feb. 14.

You ejaculate a prayer for my protection. I do not feel in any personal danger. I mean to tell them what I think, and in such a way that they shall understand me. But I am principled against doing it offensively.

If Mr. Clay had demanded immunity for slavery in the States and in the District only, he would have demanded nothing more than the South claims as absolute right ; and so it would, in their eyes, have wanted the reciprocity of a compromise. Nobody but the abolitionists of the Garrison school pretends to interfere with slavery in the States ; and non-interference with slavery in the District, now only fifty square miles, would have seemed to them paltry. I think, *regarding the thing as a compromise*, Mr. Clay has done pretty well. But I do not concede their right to carry slavery into the Territories at all ; and therefore I will never yield to their claim to carry it there, come what will. I should prefer dissolution even, terrible as it would be, to slavery extension.

Washington, Feb. 6, 1850.

E. W. Clap, Esq.

My dear Sir, — . . . You must be entirely mistaken in your speculations. The Free-soil party, with the best principles to stand on that ever a political party had, well-nigh ruined themselves by

19

their injudicious conduct. But I am afraid the Whigs are behaving every whit as badly as they. Last Monday, a portion of the party gave the most insane votes that ever sane men gave. They voted down, or helped to vote down, not only the Wilmot Proviso, but the Declaration of Independence and the Ordinance of 1787. To be sure, they say they voted against these doctrines because they were brought forward by Root and Giddings for the mischievous purpose of embarrassment and party spite, and without any adequate cause. But I would not vote against such a measure if the Devil brought it forward. . . .

Yours very truly,

HORACE MANN.

WASHINGTON, Feb. 12, 1850.

. . . You remember what a hue and cry was raised among all the teachers and friends of the existing institutions of the deaf and dumb at my Report on the subject. Mr. P——, of the New-York Institution, wrote a libellous article, which he sent to the "North-American Review;" and which was so bad, that even Mr. B—— would not publish it until it was mitigated. Mr. Gallaudet chimed in; though he was more civil, and left his successor to do the offensive work. Afterwards, as you will remember, they sent an agent to examine European institutions, and make a report adverse to mine, — a work which he performed with zeal, and without scruple. The "thirty-one" took it up, and put it as an arrow into their quiver; and so poor I was rather put down, or thought to be so, by the public.

But, at the same time that that controversy was going on, a Dr. Dix of Boston, who was in Berlin, wrote home a letter, in which, without knowing at all what was going on here, he sustained my views in full. Afterwards, Mr. Willis, who had seen the wonder, ratified my statement; and James F. Austin, in a letter published in the "Boston Advocate," did the same thing. But nothing, I suppose, has ever removed a strong impression which was made on the public mind, that I was *romancing*. In the "Christian Register" of last Saturday, there is a long article, by an eye-witness of the Berlin *Anhalt*, which confirms my statement throughout. The author refers to me; says he did not believe me, but now is convinced by his own eye-sight; and his statements are stronger than mine.

I have written to Dr. Howe, hoping to get it published in some of the Boston papers: so that I hope the truth will work its way, though it may be slowly.

In regard to instructing the deaf and dumb in our country to speak as they speak in Germany, the difficulty is in our anomalous spelling, and the variety of the sounds of our vowels. But by phonetic means it may still be done: and perhaps that is the final reason why phonetics were invented; for, in every other respect, the system only obscures the origin and philological history of the language. It would be worth while, however, to have all literature published in it also, for the sake of the deaf and dumb, who are restored to society by means of speech.

FEB. 18, 1850.

In the House, this morning, a resolution was offered to direct the Committee on Territories to bring in a bill for the admission of California. The Southern men were foolish enough to commence an opposition, not merely to the measure, but to every thing; that is, to attempt to stop the wheels of Government, to prevent us from doing any thing, by a perpetual call for the yeas and nays; thus taking up all time, and suspending all business. It is a resolution on the part of the South to prevent the Government from doing any thing at all, if it attempts to do what they object to. It is a *revolutionary* proceeding, — revolution without force; but it may come to force elsewhere.

It shows what an excited state of feeling the South is in; and it furnishes us with an opportunity, which I trust we shall improve, to show our firmness. It was the worst possible issue for them to make, and one on which I do not believe they can defend themselves, even at home. Do not be alarmed for me. I shall take care of myself, and sleep and eat as usual.

FEB. 19.

The opposition, and the calling for yeas and nays, motions to adjourn, excusing men from voting, &c., continued till twelve o'clock at night; when the Speaker declared that Monday was at an end, and that the debate on the resolution ended with it. This allowed us to go home to bed. It was an exciting time. Members were very good-natured on the surface; but there was a deep feeling underneath.

FEB. 20.

You are mistaken in supposing the great majority of the South would rejoice if slavery were not extended; at least, this is true of the men who control public sentiment. Mr. Clay is almost a dictator in Kentucky. His personal popularity saves him.

We live a hurried and confused life here. So much labor to be performed, and such short days to work in; such mighty events to control and regulate, and so little of public spirit and intelligence to direct them! Life is quickened to an almost unconscious whirl. One thing alone makes it tolerable to me, — the possibility of doing something to favor the right or to check the wrong.

MARCH 1, 1850.

I dined at the President's to-day, and sat on his left, with only one lady between, and had considerable conversation with him. He really is a most simple-minded old man. He has the least show or pretension about him of any man I ever saw; talks as artlessly as a child about affairs of State, and does not seem to pretend to a knowledge of any thing of which he is ignorant. He is a remarkable man in some respects; and it is remarkable that such a man should be President of the United States. He said it was impossible to destroy the Union. "I have taken an oath to support it," said he; "and do you think I am going to commit perjury? Mr. Jefferson pointed out the way in which any resistance could be put down, — which was to send a fleet to blockade their harbors, levy duties on all goods going in, and prevent any goods from coming out. I can save the Union without shedding a drop of blood. It is not true, as was reported at the North, that I said I would march

an army and subdue them: there would be no need of any."
And thus he went on talking like a child about his cob-house, and
how he would keep the kittens from knocking it over.

March 4. To-day Mr. Calhoun's speech will be read in the
Senate, he being unable to deliver it. Mr. Webster is expected to
speak very soon. I do not believe he will compromise the great
question. He will have too much regard for his *historic* character
and for his consistency to do any such thing; at least, I *hope so.*

March 5. Mr. Calhoun's speech was given yesterday. It does
not give universal satisfaction, even at the South. This is good.

March 8. Mr. Webster spoke yesterday; and (can you believe
it?) he is a fallen star!—Lucifer descending from heaven! We
all had the greatest confidence in him. He has disappointed us all.
Within a week, I have said, many times, that he had an historic character to preserve and maintain, which must be more to him than
any temporary advantage. His intellectual life has been one great
epic, and now he has given a vile catastrophe to its closing pages.
He has walked for years among the gods, to descend from the empy-
rean heights, and mingle with mimes and apes! I am overwhelmed.
There is a very strong feeling here among the Whigs of the New-
England delegation; and we shall do what we can still to uphold
our cause. It is a terrible battle. Not balls of lead or copper
strike their victim down, but, I fear, those of gold, or what some
men value more than gold,—the possession of office. But Mr.
Webster never can be President of the United States; never, never!
He will lose two friends at the North where he will gain one at the
South.

March 10. I have read Mr. Webster's speech carefully. It has
all the marks of his mind,—clearness of style, weight of statement,
power of language; but nothing can, to my mind, atone for the
abandonment of the Territories to what he calls the law of Nature
for the exclusion of slavery. When so much of Delaware, Virginia, Kentucky, and Missouri, lies far north of a great part of New
Mexico, how can a man say that a law of Nature will keep slavery
out of the latter, when it has not kept it out of the former? The
existence or non-existence of slavery depends more upon conscience
than climate. Why should all the South be so anxious to pass this

law, if Nature has already passed one? Who knows but mines may yet be discovered in New Mexico? — and mining is the very kind of labor on which slaves can be most profitably employed.

I wish I had not made my speech. I should like to take up these topics, and set forth what seems to be the merit or the demerit of them. There is a very strong feeling here that Mr. Webster has played false to the North. Many of our men will speak, and we shall have an exhibition of Northern feeling yet.

March 14. Mr. Webster has not a favorable response from any Northern man of any influence. It is hard to believe that a man who has been so intellectually consistent should at once overthrow his grand reputation; but who can tell what an ambitious or disappointed man will not do to accomplish his object? Oh, how priceless is principle! . . . The delegate of Congress from Mexico (not yet received as such, because Congress has as yet established no Territorial Government over it) tells me the New-Mexicans are very averse to slavery, and that labor is too cheap, and the danger of slaves escaping too great, for any slaveholder to meet the risk of transferring his property there; that climate and soil are not adapted to it, &c. But the opening of mines, as I have said before, would create a demand for them; and all that is said of out-door labor in reference to the uncongeniality of the climate does not apply to menial service. Besides, though the Mexicans may be hostile to slavery, yet they are a feeble, effeminate, unprincipled race; and ten strong Southern men, with their energy and activity, with their domineering and overpowering manners, would be a full match for a hundred of the best Mexicans that could be found. There is no absolute security but in the proviso.

As soon as we had the President's message, in which he proposed non-action on the part of Congress, and that the Territories should be left to form their own institutions, I foresaw some defection from the spirit which had before governed Congress. I therefore wrote to some gentlemen in New York, advising first that they should send out a regular missionary, who should traverse all the settlements in that country, and pre-occupy the minds of the people against slavery; or at least that they should send out antislavery tracts in English and Spanish, and scatter them throughout the whole region. The first project was supposed to be too expensive; but the latter has been adopted, and an address to the inhabitants will be distributed there in both languages to every one who can read. We are determining mighty events; and the occasion, therefore, is worthy of a mighty struggle.

BOSTON, March 11, 1850.
Saturday Night.

HON. HORACE MANN.

DEAR SIR, — God bless you for your noble speech which I have just read in the "Boston Daily Journal." Send me a copy to keep as a monument of the age when the Websters did as they have done, and oblige

Yours truly,

THEODORE PARKER.

MARCH 13, 1850.

The hallucination that seizes the South on the subject of slavery, is, indeed, enough to excite our compassion; but an excuse of their conduct to themselves on this ground, would, perhaps, enrage them more than any thing else. I would be willing to offer them any pecuniary indemnity which they might desire. Indeed, I had thought of bringing forward some such idea in my speech; but I feared they would only scout it.

I do not think Mr. Webster can be honest in the views expressed in his speech. I would struggle against a belief in his treachery to the last minute; but this speech is in flagrant violation of all that he has ever said before.

You are in an error in supposing that the exclusion of slavery from the Territories will affect the growth of cotton or rice unfavorably. Slaves are in great demand now for the cotton and rice fields. No production of the Territories would come in competition with their great staples. It is a fear of losing the balance of power, as they call it; and no doubt, in some cases, a fear that this is only a beginning of a war upon slavery in the States themselves. On this latter point, they will not be pacified by any declarations made by the North. Then, again, on this subject they are not a reasoning people.

To recur to Mr. Webster again. He has said some things it was quite unnecessary to say, and some things not true. Look at his interpretation of the admission of Texas! The act was, as he has quoted in his speech, that four new States — no more — might be formed from Texas: those south of 36° 30' might be slave States, and those north *must* be free States. Now, he says we are bound to admit *four* slave States. But we are bound to admit only four in the whole. Why, then, admit all these four as slave States, and then others, *that is, if we get the consent of Texas,* as free States? No: we are to admit but four in the whole; and, as one or two of these are to be free, there must not be four slave. He therefore not only proposes to execute that ungodly bargain, but to give one or two slave States to the South as a gratuity.

So his offer to take the proceeds of the public lands to deport free blacks is of the greatest service to slavery. It is just what the South wants, — to get rid of its free blacks. It would enhance the value and the security of the slave property so called. Had he proposed to give the proceeds of the lands to deport *manumitted* slaves, that would encourage manumission, and be of real service to humanity. Indeed, the more I think of the speech, the worse I think of it.

WASHINGTON, March 21, 1850.

SAMUEL DOWNER, ESQ.

MY DEAR SIR, — I am glad to hear from you. I did not know but you would give me over to "hardness of heart and to a reprobate mind" after my votes for Speaker. But I am as well satisfied as I can be of any thing that it was the best course. If we must have one of two men for Speaker, you do nothing towards deterring me from supporting one of them, on the ground that he is a bad man, so long as I can prove the other to be a worse one. I have found that those who hold to the doctrine, that they will not take the least of two evils, forget that, by adding their own course to the number of evils, they make *three* of them, and then generally take the worst two of the three. I prefer the least one of two to the worst two of three. . . .

H. MANN.

MARCH, 1850.

To S. DOWNER.

MY DEAR FRIEND, — Mr. Webster astonished almost all Northern men here. We are recovering from the shock; but it was a severe one. It was as unexpected as it was astounding. It may seem egotistic in me; but I wish I had not spoken till after he did. I should have liked to ask him how he knows that God has Wilmot-provisoed New Mexico. Has he had any new revelation since the North-west Territory needed provisoing, since Wisconsin needed it, since Oregon needed it? Indiana came near being a slave State, proviso and all; and would have been so, if Congress had not rejected her petition, — John Randolph, of Virginia, making the report. Has God Wilmot-provisoed the whole belt of country from the eastern side of Delaware to the western side of Missouri, any more than he has New Mexico? and, if so, why has not his proviso taken effect? Is there not a vast region of those States that lies far north of the greater part of New Mexico? Has Mr. Webster any geological eyes by which he has discovered that there are no mines in New Mexico which could be profitably worked by slaves? If predial slavery cannot exist there, cannot menial? Does not slavery depend more on *conscience* than on *climate*? If individuals do not desire to carry slavery into New Mexico for personal profit, may not communities and States desire it for political aggrandizement?

As to fugitive slaves, I need say nothing. While Massachusetts citizens are imprisoned in Southern ports, I think fugitive slaves will be gentlemen at large in Massachusetts.

But the offer to give eighty millions received and a hundred and eighty millions expected to be received from the public lands to transport free negroes to Africa, and thereby to give increased value to slaves and increased security to slave property, is atrocious.

Now, would to God that you Free-soilers were not a separate organization! With what power such men as S. C. Phillips, G. Palfrey, William Jackson, and Sumner, could act upon the Whigs, if they were not alienated from them! For Heaven's sake, heal this breach, instead of widening it, and bring the whole force of the North to bear in favor of freedom!

With best love for your wife and your babes and yourself, I am very truly and sincerely yours,

H. MANN.

Mr. Calhoun died this morning. . . . The opinion is that the South will be relieved. He has carried his doctrines of disunion so far, that his political opponents have made capital out of his extravagances. He had done all the political thinking for South Carolina for twenty years. That State has known but one will, and that was his. It is the most oligarchical State in this Union, — perhaps in the world. The spirit of its people has rendered it so. I regret his death politically : I think it will tend to canonize him, and give a sort of sanctity to his enormities. Men will attack his seditious and treasonable doctrines with less earnestness than if he were alive ; for it always looks, or can be made to look, like cowardice to assail a dead man. His private life has been, I believe, unimpeachable ; but his public course has been one of the greatest disasters that has ever befallen the country. His errors have all originated in his disappointed aspirations for the Presidency. Oh, if we could only look a few years into the future, or, throwing ourselves forward a few years into the future, look back, what different motives of action would be suggested to our minds !

Mr. Calhoun's funeral, which took place to-day, was attended in the Senate Chamber at twelve o'clock. I did not wish to connect the thoughts I have with death with the thoughts which I have with him ; and therefore I did not attempt to be present. What a test of true greatness is death ! How it converts to vanity and nothingness all which is not intrinsically worthy ! How it magnifies and eternizes whatever is good ! The preacher who could carry men for an hour to the other side of the grave, whenever they have a prospect of worldly appetite or ambition or aggrandizement in view, and make them look back upon the objects of their desire from that point, would indeed be a minister of God.

April 6, 1850.

Public affairs are looking worse here, — more dangerous for the cause of liberty than ever. The defection of Mr. Webster is dreadful! The Whigs and Free-soilers in Massachusetts are so hostile to each other, that, though the great body of them think alike on the most important subjects, they cannot act together. They fly from each other with hard words, instead of laboring together for the cause of the country.

Since Mr. Webster's speech, the tide of things is changed. The South have taken courage, and are pressing their schemes with renewed energy. Their old *skill* can hardly be improved.

Being the last bid for the Presidency, this speech of Mr. Webster's was the heaviest; but the other aspirants for the same object do not wish to be outdone or outbid, and so they are taking a strong Southern ground. I fear the cause will be lost. God grant that I may be mistaken!

Many remarks upon Mr. Webster are published in these letters, because the spirit in which Mr. Mann held up his testimony against him is often misrepresented. In his subsequent life, he often said, that, if he had never done any thing else purely for the love of truth and his country, the course he had pursued in regard to Mr. Webster had' the sanction of his later conscience and judgment; that he acted consciously against his own immediate interests; and that society would finally justify him, though he never expected justice from the men who followed so closely in Mr. Webster's footsteps in sacrificing the cause of freedom and truth for party, or political or personal considerations.

On the day when he left home to take his first letter against Mr. Webster to the printer, he said, "I am going to do the most reckless thing, on my own account, which I have ever done, in publishing this letter. A thousand of the most prominent men in Massachusetts will never speak to me again. But I must do it; and I shall probably follow it up with more."

REV. T. PARKER.

DEAR SIR, — I have just returned from a visit of some days into the western part of New York, where I have seen our common friend, the Rev. Mr. May. He has written a letter to you, which I take pleasure in forwarding. I attended service in his church last Sunday morning, where he administered the communion, and spent at least half an hour in enforcing our duty to follow the example of Jesus Christ in our *conduct* rather than in our profession or creed. He pathetically lamented the apostasy of so many of the clergy at the present time, and their active agency on the side of wrong; and he said, what I and I doubt not many others were rejoiced to hear, that, while so many doctors of divinity were proving faithless to their highest trust, Theodore Parker, the man whom they denounced as an infidel, was more ably and conspicuously faithful to the cause of truth than any of their number. It produced a strong sensation, as home-truths always will. . . .

Yours very truly,

HORACE MANN.

BOSTON, May 6, 1850.
HON. HORACE MANN.

MY DEAR SIR, — Perhaps I ought not to trouble so busy a man as you are to read so unimportant a matter as a letter from me; but I cannot reasonably forbear telling you how thankful I am to you for writing such a noble letter to your friends and constituents. God bless you for it! I intended once, soon after Mr. Webster made his speech, to have written a public letter to you, and reviewed the whole matter before the country; but I am glad I did not, for then I should, perhaps, have prevented you from doing better than any one has done hitherto. A hundred and seventy years ago, John Locke wrote: " Slavery is so vile and miserable an estate of man, and so directly opposite to the generous temper and courage of our nation, that it is hardly to be conceived that an *Englishman*, much less a gentleman, should plead for it."

Yet think of Mr. Webster and his eight hundred "retainers," as the "Advertiser" calls them!

Accept my heartiest thanks for your many services, and believe me your friend and servant,

THEO. PARKER.

WASHINGTON, May 18, 1850.

. . . My letter is approved or disapproved a thousand times more for its bearing on party attachments than for its merits: so, though I do not accept as just all the criticisms made upon it, or the condemnations bestowed upon it, neither do I suffer myself to be elated by the extravagant praises which it receives in certain quarters. I hope there is nothing in it that I shall be sorry for or ashamed of hereafter: that is the greatest thing, after all. It pleases all people with whom antislavery is the first object. This is because antislavery is my first object. As you shade off with less and less antislavery, or more and more proslavery, and into attachment to party as a paramount motive of action, it is liked less and less, or disliked more and more: so that it has a perfect test.

I suppose Mr. Webster is in a very anxious state of mind. He has never known what it was to encounter general opposition before. I have most urgent letters from the North that I shall answer his Newburyport letter.

WASHINGTON, June 9, 1850.

Yesterday I read Prof. Stuart's pamphlet in defence of Mr. Webster. It is a most extraordinary production. He begins by proving biblically that slavery is a divine institution, permitted, recognized, regulated, by God himself; and therefore that it cannot be *malum in se*. The greater part of the work consists in maintaining this point both from the Old and New Testaments; but he spends a few pages at the close in showing that it is contrary to all the precepts and principles of the gospel, and is little better than all crimes concentrated in one. How it can be both of these things at the same time, we are not informed.

He says, with Mr. Webster, that we are bound to admit four slave States from Texas, although we were to admit but four in the whole; and one at least, if not two, of the four were to be free States. But he says it is to be by the consent of Texas; and Texas may give consent to only four slave States taken in succession. Now, the answer to this is so plain, that it is difficult to see why even an Old-Testament orthodox minister should not see it.

When a contract is *executory*, as the lawyers say (that is, to be executed in future), and it contains mutual stipulations in favor of each of the parties, then nothing can be more clear than that each of the successive steps for fulfilment must have reference to what is to be done afterwards. Neither party can claim that the contract shall be so fulfilled by the other party in any one particular as to render the fulfilment of the whole impossible. Each preceding act of execution must have reference to what, by its terms, is to be subsequently executed.

So he says the Wilmot Proviso for a Territory is in vain, because the Territory, as soon as it is transformed into a State, can establish slavery. But the Wilmot Proviso over a Territory defends it against that class of population that would establish slavery when it becomes a State. It attracts to it that class of population which will exclude slavery; and therefore such proviso is decisive of the fate of the State.

JUNE 17, 1850.

This is Bunker-Hill day; but, though the cause of human liberty is intrusted to us now, there is not much of the Bunker-Hill spirit here. Compared with our fathers, we have become a most mercenary race. With many, human freedom is a light affair, when placed in the scale against money; and Mars and Mammon are the greatest gods in the Pantheon.

We are just now taking a vote to give a portion of the public lands to the States, to be appropriated to the support of institutions for the insane, the deaf and dumb, blind, &c. Almost all the public lands have hitherto been given to the States in which they are situated; and, generally, more for business and economical purposes than for charitable ones. What a glorious fund it would be, if all the public lands, or their proceeds, could be consecrated to education and to the amelioration of human suffering! I had a dream of this sort once, but shall never be able to realize it. . . . The preliminary vote has passed by more than three to one!

JUNE 18, 1850.

Yesterday Mr. Webster made his last and special declaration. A motion was pending, that it should be no objection to the admission of any State hereafter to be formed out of the territory ceded by Mexico, — that is, California, Utah, or New Mexico, — that its constitution should recognize or provide for or establish slavery. The present Congress, it is admitted on all hands, has no power to act on that subject; but the movement was designed to give some moral power to the claims of slavery hereafter, should such claims be made. Mr. Webster took a retrospect of his whole course since the 7th of March speech, his Newburyport letter, &c., and declared that he had seen, heard, and reflected nothing which had not confirmed him in the soundness of his opinion; and so, in the most solemn manner, he declared his purpose to go for the bill. I think it will pass the Senate beyond all question. I fear it will also pass the House. It is said that Mr. Clay put in the provision about buying out the claims of Texas at some eight or ten or twelve millions of dollars, for the very purpose of securing a sufficient number of votes to carry it.

The Texan debt consists of bonds or scrip, which, at the time the Compromise Bill was brought in, was not worth more than four or five cents on the dollar: but the same stock is said to be now worth fifty per cent; and, should the bill pass, the stock will be worth a premium. Now, where so many persons are interested, will they not influence members? May not members themselves be influenced by becoming owners of this stock? It affords at least a chance for unrighteous proceedings; and, should the bill pass, there are members who will not escape imputation and suspicion.

A rumor has reached us from New Mexico, that the people are taking steps there to call a convention for the formation of a State Constitution. Should this prove authentic, as most people here think it will, and should they put a proviso against slavery in their constitution, would it not look like a godsend, — like a special providence, — notwithstanding all we say about that class of events? Oh, may it turn out to be so!

WASHINGTON, June 13, 1850.

S. DOWNER, ESQ.

MY DEAR SIR, — You must excuse me for not answering all your kind letters. I should be glad to do so, if it were possible, especially if it would be the means of getting more; for they are most acceptable to me.

I learn that Mr. Webster has written home, that, *if the North will give way on the subject of slavery*, THEY CAN HAVE A TARIFF IN SIX WEEKS; and I suppose the address now to be circulated is for signatures, calling upon the Massachusetts delegation to make " concession ;" that is, to surrender the Territories to slavery : then we may have " beneficent legislation," by which he means a tariff.

I am also told that the Hon. ——, a factory superintendent at Lowell, on a salary of four or five thousand dollars a year, was on here two or three weeks ago to see if some arrangement could not be made to barter human bodies and souls at the South for the sake of certain percentages on imported cottons at the North ; and that Mr. Foote of Mississippi, and Mangum of North Carolina, offered to become sureties for the arrangement : how many others, I do not know. I have no doubt of all this, *not a particle;* though I communicate it to you to give you the means of further inquiry, and of action after inquiry is made. . . .

The Whigs, with very few exceptions, appear to stand well in the House ; and I trust we shall be able to give a good account of ourselves. How I wish the Whigs now had all the Free-soilers in their ranks ! In great haste, yours ever and truly,

HORACE MANN.

WASHINGTON, June 28, 1850.

S. DOWNER, ESQ.

DEAR SIR, — The fate of the Compromise Bill is still doubtful in the Senate, though public opinion here is against its success. Nothing but the prowess of Clay could have kept the breath in it to this time.

The news from New Mexico, if confirmed, knocks the bottom all out of the compromise. If they organize a government there, choose a governor and a legislature, appoint judges, &c., it will present a very pretty anomaly for us to be sending governor, judges, &c., to them. But the great point is the presumed *proviso* in their constitution. With that, the longer the South keeps them out of the Union, the more antislavery they will become.

. . . Well, Downer, it is the greatest godsend in our times that Taylor was elected over Cass. It is the turning-point of the fortunes of all the new Territories. Had Cass been President, they would have all been slave, and a fair chance for Cuba into the bargain. I am not sorry because I did not vote for Taylor; but I am glad others did. I think he has designedly steered the ship so as to avoid slavery. . . .

Best regards to your wife. You know you always have them. Look out for the boy, and make a hero of him.

Ever and truly yours,
H. MANN.

WASHINGTON, July 1, 1850.

Webster said there were only two parts of the Constitution which had any bearing on the subject of the trial by jury; and that the Constitution, neither in its letter nor in its spirit, required the trial by jury for a fugitive slave.

I proved in my letter that the article in the Constitution about courts did have a bearing, and a most important one, on the subject of jury trial; because, on the strength of it, Congress provided jury trials for more than nine-tenths of all the cases that ever arise in the courts. I showed, that, under this article about courts, Congress had power to make provision for juries.

On the second point, I showed that the spirit of the Constitution did clearly require, that, in legislating on the subject of fugitive slaves, Congress should provide the jury trial.

Now, some one who has written an article in the " Christian Register," which no man at once honest and sensible could write, takes the second position of Mr. Webster, and applies my first answer to it; that is, when Mr. Webster says the trial by jury is not de-

20

manded, he applies my answer to the part of Mr. Webster's positions, that there was no clause having any bearing on the subject, or conferring any power.

The Compromise Bill drags along with various prophecies about its success. How I shall hallelujah if it is defeated in the Senate !

SEPT. 1, 1850.

" Oh that we could see the end of crime from the beginning ! " was the ejaculation that broke spontaneously from me on reading the account of ——'s last day. It has always struck me that the cultivation of causality would be a mighty aid to morals, because it would connect consequences with actions in our minds so indissolubly; and the least reflection would always show that there must be more suffering from unlawful indulgence than there can be enjoyment: so that every man would know that he would be the loser by not suppressing his passion. A starving man knows the difference between bread and a rock. Can any circumstances be supposed in which he would prefer the rock to the bread, when eager to gratify his appetite ? Suppose the conviction to be just as clear in the human mind, that all wrong-doing will bring pain, and vastly more pain, too, than it can bring pleasure, — because to suppose that a man can violate any law of God, and get more, or as much, from the enjoyment, as he must suffer from the punishment, would be to suppose that he could outwit or circumvent the All-knowing and All-powerful, — suppose, I say, this conviction to be perfectly clear and strong, and I cannot see how a man could deliberately choose the evil, and refuse the good. It may be replied, that most men, in their sober senses, will acknowledge that they must lose more by pain than they can gain by gratification for all transgressions of the divine law. Grant that they may do so in their sober moments; yet when the temptation comes, and passion arises, this conviction is darkened : it is, at last, temporarily lost sight of; and, in its oblivion, the evil triumphs. But no passion can make us love pain rather than pleasure ; and if we ever come to see that offences will bring pain and will destroy pleasure, as clearly as we see that two and two make four, or that fire will consume, or water will drown, then how can we choose to incur the pain by committing the wrong? In some things, we see this now. Why can we not in more? Why, eventually, can we not in all?

It is a sad hour. News has just come from the White House that the President is dying. If he dies, it will be a calamity that no man can measure. His being a Southern man, a slaveholder, and a hero, has been like the pressure of a hundred atmospheres upon the South. If he dies, they will feel that their strongest antagonist has been struck from the ranks of their opponents; and I fear there will not be firmness nor force enough in all the North to resist them. The future is indeed appalling.

July 10. Long before this reaches you, you will have heard that Gen. Taylor is gone. It is indeed a sad event for the country. Only one thing, at the time of his election, reconciled me to it, — the perfect political profligacy of his opponent. But the course of Gen. Taylor has been such as to conciliate me, and all whose opinions have coincided with mine, to a degree which we should have thought beforehand impossible. He had probably taken the wisest course that *he* could have taken. He poised himself between the North and the South. He knew it was utterly impossible for any prohibition of slavery to pass the present Senate; he supposed that no Territorial Government could possibly be passed by the House, without the proviso; and therefore he took things at first where he knew they could be left after the contest of a session. He went for no Territorial Government at all, leaving the Territories to form State Governments for themselves; being well convinced that they would form *free* constitutions. He relied upon this with more confidence than any of us did: but he had it in his power to procure the fulfilment of his own prophecy; and I am satisfied that it has been his purpose, from the beginning, that slavery should be extended no farther.

A dark hour is before us!

July 12. To-day the city is dressed in mourning. No one as yet seems to know what will be the policy of the new President, — whether it will be for freedom or for slavery, or whether he will not profess to adopt such a middle course as that slavery will be sure to get the advantage in the end. I look upon the movement in New Mexico — that of inserting the prohibition of slavery in their new constitution — as even more valuable than I did before. They will be far less likely to recede from this ground, having once adopted it.

I suppose the Cabinet work is done, and that Mr. Webster is to be Secretary of State. This is to be regretted for a thousand reasons; but there are some aspects of the case in which it may argue well for a settlement of the hostile questions which now agitate the country. Mr. Webster will be very acceptable to the South for the very reason that he has made himself offensive to the North. I only hope it will eventuate for the good of the country.

July 21. Four of the seven members who compose the cabinet are from the slaveholding States: so, if we consider Mr. Webster a proslavery man, they have five out of seven. But one thing is very observable, — though four are from the slaveholding States, yet one is from Missouri, one from Kentucky, one from Maryland, and one from North Carolina. All these are just south of Mason and Dixon's line; and they are from the States that hold slavery in its more mitigated forms, and not one of them is an intense proslavery State. The men selected are, I suppose, moderate men, comparatively, on this subject. Therefore, though the South have no confidence in Mr. Webster as an honest man, yet his late change of position on this subject renders him less offensive to the extreme men, and more acceptable to the moderate men.

If Mr. Fillmore has taken this course to conciliate the South in the first instance, and, with his Cabinet, eventually to subserve Northern feeling on this subject of slavery, then the whole may eventuate well; but if it is a concession to the South, on the surface, to be followed by an adoption of their views as to slavery ultimately, then it deserves all reprobation. For myself, I shall not give my confidence to this Administration, on this point, until it earns it. When it does earn it, then, as a matter of justice, I shall no longer withhold it; though, in the honesty of one of the members composing it, I have not, and probably never shall have, the slightest confidence. I therefore await developments. It has proved, so far, a godsend to Mr. Webster; for I do not believe he could have withstood the opposition against him in Massachusetts. Now, instead of being defeated, he escapes from the conflict. Still I can have no confidence in his ultimate success; for no one can safely prophesy success of a dishonest man.

JULY 23, 1850.

Yesterday Mr. Clay made his closing speech on the Compromise Bill. He spoke three hours and ten minutes, and seemed to retain his vigor and mental activity to the last. It is certainly very remarkable. He is now in his seventy-fourth year. For more than two months, he has sat in his seat every day, listening to the attacks made upon his favorite measures, occasionally replying when he thought it expedient, sometimes by a speech of half an hour, and always alive and on the alert; and now, at the end of this long and intense vigilance, he makes a speech of more than three hours, full of energy and skill, and comes out of it alive. He is certainly an extraordinary man, prepared by nature to do great and good things, but has not fulfilled his destiny in regard to the latter.

Every day of my life impresses the conviction upon me more and more, how important is the early direction given to the sentiments as well as to the intellect. There is now power enough among the educated men of the country to save it, if that power were rightly directed.

JULY 27, 1850.

One of our colleagues, Mr. Daniel P. King of Danvers, is dead. . . . What a series of startling events befall us! and yet how little they are heeded! As we sail along, the cry is raised, " A man overboard!" There is a momentary arrest; but soon the ship is on its way again as if nothing had happened. There is no place so good to die in as at the post of duty. When Smith O'Brien was on his trial for treason in Ireland, and while he was sitting in the dock, which is the criminal box, he was asked for his autograph; upon which he wrote, —

> " Whether on the gallows high,
> Or in the battle's van,
> The fittest place for man to die
> Is where he dies for man."

A noble sentiment, beautifully expressed!

July 29, .850.

We have just heard that Mr. Winthrop has been appointed senator to fill the place made vacant by Mr. Webster. Under the circumstances, the duty of appointing devolved upon Gov. Briggs. I am so certain, that I can almost say I know this appointment has been very disagreeable to Gov. Briggs, and that he has been forced into it by the Webster influence. The promotion, and therefore indorsement, of Mr. Webster by President Fillmore, has given the proslavery party a prodigious advantage in this contest. If the South, and their proslavery friends at the North, do not carry this measure, it will be almost like a miracle. But there is a goodly number of us who will stand firm. For my part, I would rather have the feeling of free thought and free speech within me than to have the highest office which the nation can bestow.

The Compromise Bill is coming to a crisis, and the contest becomes intense. Two tie-votes were taken yesterday in the Senate on important amendments, which shows how nearly parties are divided.

WASHINGTON, July 31, 1850.

My dear Downer, — You could not have given me any proof of your friendship so acceptable as in writing to me with the frankness you have done. I am astonished at the idea that my notes were unjustifiably severe in the apprehension of any reasonable man. It is, as it seems to me, nothing but *truth* that gives them an edge. In what might be called harshness or bitterness, or, to use a still harder word, vindictiveness, my references to Webster, compared with his contemptuous and supercilious manner to me, were as honey to vitriol.

However, if I have gone beyond the point, in attacking Mr. Webster, at which the sympathy of the public is on my side, then I have made a mistake ; but I do not feel that I have done a *wrong*. It cannot, however, be expected that my friends will attack him as his do me, or that mine will defend me as his do him. Besides, — and this, I think, accounts for the most of it, — since my notes were written, he has not only escaped the doom which awaited him as a Massachusetts senator, but has passed into a place of great power and influence. All are now looking at him as a man having almost the nation's patronage at his disposal, and as interested to carry out measures which will pay in gold. But I have no such prerogative, and therefore must suffer. This is my explanation of the matter. Could it have been possible that our fortunes could have been changed, I believe the result would have been changed also.

You speak of my not having written to you. It is too true. But I have been so worn down with what seemed indispensable to be done, that I have not found time, and could not. as I sometimes do, make it. . . . I wish you would write me often. Tell me in frankness every thing that will be of service to me, and all in which I feel interested, whether I reply or not. Your letters are always so welcome to me, that, if you could know how glad I am to receive them, it would be some compensation to you for writing them.

I have not time to go into political speculations. The Compromise Bill will probably pass the Senate to-day, or almost certainly to-morrow. . . . Yours truly,

H. MANN.

Aug. 5, 1850.

We are rejoiced at the defeat of the Omnibus Bill. It strengthens the chances of the Territories for freedom. All delay in admitting California, that comes from slavery, will intensify their hatred of it. However the questions may be decided in Congress, the chances are increasing, that the Territories, by their own action, will exclude it. This, too, is the best mode in which the work can be done; for there are many at the South who would all but rebel, if not actually do so, should Congress prohibit slavery, who would still allow it if the Territories themselves prohibit it. Several of the Southern States have actually resolved that they would resist if Congress should pass the proviso; but none have dared to utter a threat if the inhabitants of the Territories legislate it into existence.

Aug. 7, 1850.

The President's message, yesterday, on the subject of the Texan boundary, gives general satisfaction. The extreme Southern men, who are for the doctrine of States Rights, or nullification, or secession, of course denounce it. But the *Constitution men* from all parts of the country will, I think, uphold it. . . . Mr. Webster's letter to Gov. Bell is deprecatory in its tone, — a letter coaxing or fearful or timid. The prospect now is that there will be a settlement of the most exciting and alarming topics before Congress, and that the country will have peace out of the commotion in which it is now involved. It may postpone the close of the session for a few days, or even weeks; but this we must bear for the general good.

Aug. 15. The House is engaged in an earnest debate on the subject of the President's message about Texas; the North generally defending and upholding it, while the South is declaiming against it *con furore.* The South is becoming, to appearance, more desperate; and the men talk treason as they take their daily meals. We are to have warm times here before we leave. Calling the yeas and nays, and practising all manner of delays, will be resorted to, no doubt; and we shall have one or two night sessions. But it is thought we are strong enough to divide, and work by relays; that is, one half of us stay by for twelve hours, and the other half for the next twelve.

WASHINGTON, Aug. 9, 1850.

S. DOWNER, ESQ.

MY DEAR SIR, — Perhaps you will think my prophesying is not from above, because I said the Compromise Bill would pass on the very day that it didn't. But I was deceived, in common with almost everybody else. At the time I wrote you, I had not seen the "Morning Intelligencer" or "Union" of that day, but observed afterwards that both of them anticipated its passage almost certainly. It was a most extraordinary combination of circumstances that defeated it, — wholly unexpected by either friend or foe.

You have written me a most excellent letter — your last — full of wisdom and truth. I suppose the issue is made up in Boston, and that Websterism is to be triumphant. Of course, "outer darkness" must be the fate of all who do not bow down before the image that he sets up. You speak of my defying it and assailing it. I feel just as you speak; but it is not the time now. New events will develop themselves before the adjournment of Congress; and we shall not know where to plant ourselves until we see the results of present movements. If we were to take any ground to-day, the chance is that some new event would change the whole aspect of affairs, and render the application of the wisest counsels ineffectual. When the session is over, we shall see what is before us, and what is behind.

I shall not be surprised even if California is not admitted this session, or, if admitted, then admitted on such terms as would make us all prefer that it should remain where it is. . . .

Yours ever and truly,

H. MANN.

WASHINGTON, Aug. 11, 1850.

S. DOWNER, ESQ.

MY DEAR SIR, — Nothing is more agreeable to me than your letters. I feel, on seeing them, that the whole world has not abandoned me, which many other things that I see would almost make me believe.

In yours of the 8th inst., you suggest that I should present myself before the public again, and, as I understand you, without delay. But, in the first place, have I any chance to be heard in such a storm? I fear not. . . .

And again: the new leaves of the history of the country are turning over so fast, that comments upon the text on one leaf are almost superseded by what the next suggests. It is impossible to say what is to be the result of the session which must now be drawing to a close. Suppose, which is not impossible, that California should not be admitted: in that fact, there would be thunder enough to frighten Jupiter. Suppose, if California *should be* admitted, Territorial Governments should be formed without the proviso: that single fact would put more weapons of war into one's hands than Vulcan could forge in a twelvemonth. When the session closes, however, things will have, at least for a time, more of a fixed character.

Aug. 12. Since writing the above, I have seen the "Dedham Gazette" of Saturday, which has a very strong article against Webster and his body-guard, and therefore indirectly in my favor. There is one peculiarity about that editor's articles on this subject. He never approves my course or defends me, unless when, by so doing, he can put the Whigs in the wrong. Such defence is almost as bad as a direct condemnation; for when any Whig finds his own party placed in the wrong, and me in the right, for no other reason than because I differ from them, it prejudices him against me more than any thing else could. It turns out,'therefore, that my standing on independent ground, and not pledged to any party, leaves me without any support whatever arising from partisan feeling, and exposed to all the violence of opposition which can arise from that source. This is the political misfortune of my position; but conscience got me into the scrape, and conscience must sustain me through it.

The "Norfolk-County Journal" of Saturday contains a very pointed article on me. It says nothing about the future; but I should not be surprised if it meant as much as the "Courier" has expressed. . . . But this thing occupies my thoughts too much, and I am afraid it does yours. . . .

Very truly, as ever, yours,

H. MANN.

WASHINGTON, Aug. 15, 1850.

S. DOWNER, ESQ.

MY DEAR SIR, — I have yours of the 10th inst., in which you say, "I do not hear that any of your friends are hearing from you." If you had heard of any such thing, you would have heard of what does not exist. I have written to but one friend in my district since the first clap of thunder that opened the storm: that was to my friend Clap, of whom I spoke to you. To whom can I write, and what can I say? I hope I am not entirely without friends, personal at least, if not political. . . . But what can I write to them? They do not write to me; and my bump of self-esteem is not large enough to enable me to thrust myself before them, and intimate a desire of being defended by them. I should like very well, if not too much trouble, to have you introduce yourself to E. W. Clap. I think, if I have a zealous friend in the world, he is one. He lives out in the country, and sees many of the Boston men who go out into the country to sleep. The noisy, clamorous Whigs never had much political liking for me. I was not sufficiently subservient to party discipline. . . .

It seems a great pity now that I had not formally declined being a candidate before this outbreak. Then I could have stood my ground, and bade them defiance before the people; nor should I have any doubt, under such circumstances, what their decision would be. But now there is so much in what you say about my declining looking like fear, or, at any rate, being construed into fear, that, in the present condition of things, I hate to do it. Still, if it has got to be done before a nominating convention meets, perhaps it should be done before long. It will be hardly safe for any convention to act before the close of the session of Congress; for it will be impossible to tell how things are to be left at the end of it.

. . . Your friendship seems a thousand times more valuable now, in my need, than when, in former days, I knew it to be worth so much.

Yours most truly,

HORACE MANN.

Aug. 18, 1850.

. . We are now debating the Civil and Diplomatic Appropriation Bill in the House. It is quite uncertain when any one of the exciting questions will be taken up. On those questions, the old parties are greatly divided; and many members act upon their own judgment, or with reference to the wishes of their constituents at home. There is a party, however, which is determined to support the Administration, without further inquiry. The truth is, the slave-power of the South and the money-power of the North have struck hands. The one threatens the Union: the other yields, professing to be in fear of disunion, but really for the purpose of obtaining the profits of trade and of getting a new tariff. The whole mercantile press of Boston is under the influence of this power. They either come out decidedly, and denounce every thing and everybody that stands in the way of getting more money, at whatever sacrifice of human liberty, like the "Courier," "Advertiser," and "Post," or like the other papers, the "Traveller," the "Mercantile Journal," &c., they maintain silence on the subject while the enemy is at work. The "Courier" is the most spiteful and virulent against me. They cannot reason me down; so they try to ridicule me down. They copy from the "Springfield Republican."

Aug. 19. . . . We have no indications yet of what is likely to be done with the Texas Boundary Bill. The subject presents some points of real difficulty. Different views will be taken of the same facts, according to the party medium through which they are seen. We are in trying times; but I never felt my mind clearer and stronger to do the right, and defy consequences.

Aug. 20. Since the children of Mammon have opened their batteries upon me, Downer writes me frequently, and says the wisest things about political and personal affairs. He is so much ahead of the age, that very few will appreciate him. He seems not to have any power to lead or create a party; but he has more wisdom than four-fifths of those who constitute parties. He proves all the good things I have ever thought of him.

Aug. 23. I stay at home this morning to write to you. I long to be at home; but the time of our departure cannot be seen by any political astronomer. There is a probability that we shall come to some of the exciting questions this week. We are as ready now to meet them as we ever shall be. The great influence of Mr. Webster is brought with full force to bear against all security for freedom in the Territories. His name, his reputation for talent, and, above all, his power of patronage and influence in the Government, tell with prodigious force upon all measures. His going into the cabinet may be the salvation of Mr. Fillmore's administration; but it is even more likely that it will be fatal to the cause of freedom. See what comes of intellect without morality!

We had another furious storm last night. It reminded me of the last, — the one in which Sumner's brother and Margaret Fuller were lost; and, when I hear the winds howl and sweep so at night, my mind always goes out to watch along the seashore, and then I cannot but see what the next papers relate of disaster and death. I always had a special horror for a shipwreck. It seems to me the

most terrible form of death that is not ignominious. If, however,
— and I often have a vivid intellectual perception of this, — we
regarded death as we should, it would cease to be the dreadful
spectre that it now is. How much of this, in all after-life, must
depend upon education !

WASHINGTON, Aug. 21, 1850.

S. DOWNER, ESQ.

MY DEAR SIR, — The only question on which the sincere friends
of freedom here have any doubt is the Texas Boundary Bill. Most
of us, I think, will go against this as it now is ; but suppose it
could be amended so as to conform its northern line to that of the
Compromise Bill, and suppose also we could strike out the provision
which secures the right to Texas to bring forth *four slave States*,
what would then be your opinion about suffering it to pass, or helping to pass it ? This boundary properly settled, I think we could
count upon all the rest as free territory.

I see the "New-Bedford Standard," a Democratic Free-soil paper,
comes out for the boundary *as it is*. So does the "Nantucket
Inquirer." So, I am told, does the "Ploughman," a neutral paper:
Doubtless the Whig papers will generally come out for it.

There is to be a competition between the old Hunkers of both
parties for Southern support. On this Texan boundary question,
I prophesy they will carry the country with them. On the Terri-
torial questions, country or no country, I will never go with them.
Either no Territorial governments, or governments with the Wilmot
Proviso in them.

Please give me, as soon as you can, your opinion on the boundary matter, and I shall prepare myself for doing what, under all the
circumstances, seems to be best for the cause.

Your last letter was very gratifying. You seem to me to take
the most just, practical, as well as theoretical view of things.

In great haste, very truly yours,

HORACE MANN.

WASHINGTON, Aug. 25, 1850.

I must say, *my dear Downer*, for the friendliness of your letters
turns the esteem and regard which I have always had for you into
affection.

Your view of the difficulty of my case corresponds exactly with mine. The sentiment of the old catch, " I cares for nobody, and nobody cares for me," is perfectly true when applied to parties. No party has felt that I was in full communion with it. The " communication," as the magnetizers say, has not been established. They may have believed, what always was and always will be true, that, while ready to do any thing for their principles, I would not sell myself to their partisan schemes. Hence, in a crisis like this, they feel that I am not the man for them.

From all that I learn, I am led to suppose, that, while every thing is done against me that can be done in the lower part of the county, there is a state of entire quiescence in the upper. From those parts of the district which are in Plymouth and Middlesex Counties, I hear almost nothing. I have letters from different parts of the State which are as complimentary as my most partial friends could desire. They speak of the universal disaffection there is towards Webster, and of the sympathy there is for me. But these are away from commercial and manufacturing localities. In such resorts, and among men engaged in business, who are susceptible on the Mammon side of their nature, I suppose Webster is all-powerful. Never was a greater influence exerted than his friends are exerting now, here as well as at home; and I think that the Territories have as good a chance to come in without the proviso as California has to be admitted as a free State.

It is impossible for the friends of freedom at home to take any but the most general positions now.

Within the coming month, there will be developments which will have decisive influences upon parties and individuals. No conventions should be held till after the adjournment of Congress. We shall then see what foe we have to meet, and what weapons we have to fight with.

On the Texas Boundary Bill I may have an opportunity to say something, though not much at length. Texas has been allowed to slide or steal into possession of a great extent of territory to which she has no right, — all, or almost all, between the Nueces and the Rio Grande, from the Gulf up to New Mexico. The New-Mexicans, by fixing the boundary in their constitution at 32° on the east side of the Rio Grande, have cut their friends off from all attempt to give them any thing below. My impression is, that if the Texan Boundary Bill were amended so as to adopt the compromise line, — that is, starting from twenty miles above El Paso, and going north-east to the south-west corner of the Indian Territory, — and if the provision were stricken out which gives Texas a right to an additional *slave* State, it would be best to vote for it. Please to tell me what you think of this, as soon as convenient.

I do not know exactly on whom to rely in these times. . . . I will send you one or two letters, that you may see what people say to me. . . . Please return these letters to me. I receive any amount of this kind, — much more than the amount of the newspaper abuse.

Yours ever,

HORACE MANN.

WASHINGTON, Aug. 28, 1850.

MY DEAR DOWNER, — I received yours of the 26th to-day. We are at last at the hand-to-hand encounter. The Texas Boundary Bill is up. The Omnibus is to be reconstructed, or there will be an attempt to do it, and then the Devil is to be harnessed in to take it through by daylight. I tremble for the fate of freedom. I fear our only hope will repose at last on the Territories themselves. A motion is now pending to amend the Boundary Bill by adding substantially the New-Mexico and Utah Territorial Bills to it. Then another motion will be made to add California to that. This is the bait. It is hoped that the friends of freedom will not venture to vote against adding California, so that this amendment will be easily effected. But then, California being on the amendment, it is hoped that this will carry over a sufficient Northern force to sustain the whole ; that is, there are men who will not dare to vote for New Mexico and Utah without the proviso, who will venture to face their constituents, if, at the same time, they can say they have secured freedom to California. But while there is life there is hope.

The inference which you draw from the entire silence of every one of my acquaintances in the city is inevitable. However painful, it forces itself irresistibly upon my mind, *I have not a friend among them.* While I seemed prosperous, and had the leading men of the public on my side, they professed friendship; but now, when I am away, and when a most extraordinary conjuncture of circumstances has exposed me to the raking fire of all the sons of Mammon and all the sycophants of power, I see that they are as heedless of me, my character, my interests, my feelings, as though I were one of the slaves whom they are willing should be created. It is saddening, disheartening. I feel it for myself some : I feel it for human nature more. But will I ask them to come to my rescue, and fulfil the promise which years of intimacy and of professions have made? No : I will perish before I will beg. And as for this war in favor of liberty, and against its contemners, high or low, I will pray God for life and strength to carry it on while I live, and for the spirit that will bequeath it to my children when I die.

Yours ever and truly,

HORACE MANN.

AUG. 28.

The moneyed interest of the South protects slavery; and the moneyed interest at the North, especially in Massachusetts, or wherever cotton is manufactured, sympathizes with that at the South. One wants slaves to produce the cotton : the other wants many slaves to make cotton cheap. Hence they go together as far as they dare; and our friend —— said to somebody, he "didn't care a damn if there *was* another slave State," — so much has the love of money gangrened his generous soul !

At last the *cominus*, or hand-to-hand fight, has come. The Texas Boundary Bill is before us. A very good spirit seems to exist this morning; that is, there is a great deal of joking and laughing going on all over the house. Perhaps, however, it is on the principle that persons are prolific of *bon-mots* when about to be hung.

AUG. 29.

The first question about the Boundary Bill was, "Shall it be rejected?" This was decided in the negative by a very large vote; all its friends as it stands in its present shape, and all who thought it could be put by amendments into an acceptable shape, voting in the negative. Every one voted in the negative, except those who were determined to go against the bill at all events. Then came an amendment to attach the New-Mexico and Utah Bills. This is now pending. Should it prevail, then another amendment will be offered to attach the California Bill to it; and this will reconstruct the Omnibus.

An attempt will be made to manage the case, as by parliamentary tactics, to prevent us from taking a direct vote on the Wilmot Proviso, and thus save some of the Northern doughfaces from the odium which a direct adverse vote on that question would inflict. The Speaker, being in favor of the bills, will recognize the right men at the right time, so as to help forward the measure. I have the greatest fears that all is lost.

SEPT. 2.

You may expect, notwithstanding what Miss —— says, that Mr. E—— will vote with the Northern proslavery men, and help decide all the great questions now pending against us. He, like all the rest, will be artful; and, when he finds a chance to cast a vote against slavery which will do slavery no harm, he will be glad to improve it; but in the essentials he will go for them. . . . I have no doubt the time will come when Mr. Webster's course will be seen in the true light; but it will not be till after the mischief is done, and then only individuals will be vindicated, while the cause will be ruined.

SEPT. 4.

We had two or three proslavery speeches yesterday, and we have been taking some very interesting questions this morning. This whole question has become so complicated, that it is difficult to explain it. It cannot be done by letter. I hope I shall have a chance soon to do it orally. . . . I wish every night that you could see our sunsets. I get no time to read or to write. To keep up with the business of the House, to prepare myself so as to know how to vote conscientiously, occupies my whole time. If I would vote with the party, or vote without knowing any thing upon what I vote, it would save me a great deal of time. We have just voted to commit the Texas Boundary Bill to the Committee of the Whole on the State of the Union. This gives us a chance to amend it, and put

21

it in a better shape. The friends of freedom all voted for this; and many who do not care for freedom, but who must vote as they did, joined us, so that we prevailed by 101 to 99.

SEPT. 6.

I had no letter from you last night, nor eke this morning. I am so sure that you never fail, that I always convict the railroads or postmasters, and condemn them.

I had a sad day yesterday. The day before, Mr. Boyd's amendment, giving a Territorial Government to New Mexico, not only without a proviso against slavery, but with an express provision, that, when States are erected, they may be slave States if they wish, was voted down; but yesterday that vote was reconsidered. Then Massachusetts members went for it, although our Legislature, the last of last April, expressed the most decided opinions to the contrary, and although, before this new Administration, in which Mr. Webster takes so conspicuous a part, the whole North, with the exception of a part of the cities, was against it. Mr. E—— has voted steadily and uniformly for slavery. It is getting to be a fixed law, in my mind, to have no faith in men who make money their god. It is amazing into what forms the human mind may be shaped. Here are twenty, perhaps thirty, men from the North in this House, who, before Gen. Taylor's death, would have sworn, like St. Paul, not to eat nor drink until they had voted the proviso, who now, in the face of the world, turn about, defy the instructions of their States, take back their own declarations a thousand times uttered, and vote against it. It is amazing; it is heart-sickening. What shall be done? I know no other way but through the cause in which I have so long worked. May God save our children from being, in their day, the cause of such comments by others!

P. S. — It is two o'clock, and the infernal bill has just passed. Dough, if not infinite in quantity, is infinitely soft. The North is again disgracefully beaten, — most disgracefully.

SEPT. 8, 1850.

Texas has not a particle of rightful claim to all the north-western region this bill contends for; but she has passed a law claiming it, and threatens to make war upon the Union if her claim is not allowed. An extra session of her legislature is now in being. Her governor recommends that she should raise and equip men to march to Santa Fé, and subdue the people there to her control (who are Mexicans, and who hate her); and the legislature is now preparing means to carry, or rather to seem to carry, their threats into execution. Our great Presidency-seekers, Webster, Cass, Clay, &c., wish to succumb to her claims. They cannot afford to offend any party at the South, because they want the votes of the South. The South wants Texas to have all this territory, because Texas is one of the most atrocious proslavery States in the Union; and, if any part of the territory is set off to New Mexico, they say it may eventually be free. Those who think their party will gain something by yielding to this false claim of Texas go for it with their leaders. Texas would not relinquish an inch of it but for money: therefore · it is proposed to give her ten millions of dollars to buy her off. It is the most outrageous piece of swindling ever practised. In reality, we give her, by this boundary, a hundred thousand more square miles than she owns, and ten millions of dollars besides. President Taylor meant to maintain the rights of the country; and, if he had lived, we should have tried strength with the miserable braggarts of Texas: but, since his death, the whole policy of the Administration is changed, and with that, owing to their power and patronage, Congress is demoralized, and the bill has passed, and the Territories have governments without any prohibition of slavery. California is admitted as a free State; and that is all the compensation we have.

I am sick at heart, and disgusted at the wickedness of men.

SEPT. 9.

Eureka! Eureka! or at least *almost* Eureka! The House has passed a resolution this morning to adjourn three weeks from to-day. It must be acted upon in the Senate; but I think they are tired enough to go home, and that it will not be postponed longer. This will bring it to the very last day of the month, and I shall almost count the hours till it comes.

Read Mr. Underwood's speech on the Texas Boundary Bill, and understand it, and you need read nothing else on the subject.

The politicians and the Texas bond-holders had a sort of punlic frolic on Saturday evening, after the bill for the admission of California, and for the establishment of a Territorial Government for Utah, was passed. Texas stock, which, on the 1st of January last, was not worth more than five or six cents on the dollar, will now be worth one dollar and five or six cents! This bill appropriates ten millions of dollars. Think, then, what immense and corrupt influences have been brought to bear upon the decision of this freedom-or-slavery question! . . . One of the most extreme antislavery men in all the North, who had given the strongest pledges, made the most emphatic declarations, and defied all consequences in the most unreserved manner, went over as soon as Mr. Webster was appointed Secretary of State, and has voted on the proslavery side ever since. He has been talking for some time about going to California, and, this morning, has notified the House of his resignation, and started for New York. See if, before six months have elapsed, he does not have an office. It wrings my heart to see such venality.

West Roxbury, Sept. 9, 1850.

Dear Sir, — I suppose that any word of commendation which I could utter would seem to you as a very doubtful compliment; for, if it is a desirable thing *laudari a viro laudato*, it is undesirable to be praised by a *viro odioso*. Still, I cannot help saying to you how much I honor and esteem you for the services you have rendered to your country and mankind since you entered Congress. I thought, at the time you first went there, you would find more trouble there than with the Boston schoolmasters and such poor things as Matthew Hale Smith. It seems to me, not only that you have done a great service by your speeches on slavery, but by what you have done in opposition to Mr. Webster. Excuse me for saying so; but there are some things in your Notes which it grieved me to see there. They weakened your position; they gave your doubtful friends an opportunity to pass over to Webster's side; and to your real foes they gave an opportunity of making out a case before the public. Still, to candid men, it must be plain, from your Notes, that Mr. Webster is exceedingly base. In doing this, you have done a great service. Webster has often been attacked, but almost wholly by political rivals or mere partisans, neither of whom were sincere in the charges against him. You attack him on moral grounds. I think your attack must disturb him more than all ever written against him before now. But, in the mean time, you are continually or often attacked yourself, your language misinterpreted, your motives assailed. There is nobody to defend you. Some cannot; others dare not. Then some of the men you have relied upon were never worthy of your confidence, and will do nothing. You have crossed the path of some selfish men by your theories of benevolence, and mortified them by your own life; and they will pay you for both. Some men would gladly have written in your defence; but they would only bring you into trouble. You saw how "Codus Alexandrieus," in the "Advertiser," tried to couple you with me; and you doubtless appreciated the benevolence of the attempt. I write to you chiefly to suggest to you, whether it would not be a good plan for you to write another letter to your constituents, *on the state of the country, the conduct of public men* (above all, of Webster), and your own relations to the wicked measures of the past Congress. It seems to me you might, in this way, *orient* yourself before the public, and give them a good deal of information which they need and want. I suppose, of course, you knew the attempt made in Boston (and by a few in New York) to defeat your election this autumn. *Marshall P. Wilder* is thought of by some men for your successor. Such a letter as you might write would settle that matter.

I beg you not to answer this letter, which will only occupy your time; but believe me truly your friend and servant,

THEO. PARKER.

SEPT. 10.

This is Tuesday, my black-chalk day; for, on this day, I get no letter from home. The House is now discussing the question, whether the representatives from California shall be admitted as members of the House. They are objected to because they were chosen by the people long before California became a State. The bill to admit California was signed by the President yesterday, and these claimants were chosen nearly a year ago : so that they were chosen to represent a State before there was any such State.

What a mighty country ours is ! It has all the means of greatness but intelligence and integrity. In these how deficient it is ! I hope God will let us live through our youthful follies and vices, as he does some individuals ; and that, later in life, something may be done to atone for the follies of these early days.

The time for our adjournment is fixed. Then — oh then ! I will not think too much of what may lie between me and my hopes.

SEPT. 12.

What I wished to tell you yesterday was what Miss Dix had just told me about her hospital in New Jersey. One gentleman has given money enough — several hundred dollars — to place a fountain in the yard ; another to buy a magic lantern for the amusement of the patients ; and she had just asked a Mr. King, a member of the House, to give her money for a library, and he had given it. So she was all smiles and delight when I saw her. Think of her going round, first to establish hospitals ; then to fill them, and to take care of them ; and *then* to enrich them with libraries and apparatus, and beautify them with embellishments !

I have been writing so far while the clerk was calling the yeas and nays on the Fugitive-slave Bill, — an outrageous bill ; not so bad as the one I denounced in my second letter, but one which will make abolitionists by battalions and regiments.

It has just passed by a vote of 105 to 73, — an enormous majority. I think this bill will inflame the country more than the Territorial bills ; but I do not know but the nerve of the country has been so often excited, that it has lost its susceptibility. I cannot speak with any composure of this series of diabolical measures. What makes it all so terrible is, that these bills passed by treachery, — the grossest treachery of those who were chosen to do directly the opposite thing. I wish I had my former force with which to curse the measures, if not the men !

WASHINGTON, Sept. 10, 1850.

MY DEAR DOWNER, — . . . You see all is gone. The influence of the Administration became all-powerful   E—— voted in committee against the Wilmot Proviso, *direct*. D—— was swept away. He voted on the first day against the Texas Boundary Bill, when it was alone; and the next day in favor of it, with New Mexico attached. There will be the most vigorous efforts to wheel the Whigs into line. Will they wheel? All motives on the surface will prompt them to do so. Thousands will say, "What can we do better? It is past: it cannot be remedied. Abandon the past, and go for the future." This will be the superficial argument; but I mistake if the Whig party has not received a wound from which it will never recover. Good-by!

Ever yours,

HORACE MANN.

WASHINGTON, Sept. 13, 1850.

S. DOWNER, ESQ.

MY DEAR SIR, — Is it true that you say, or that you have been informed, that I have written any apologetic or any explanatory or deprecatory letter to the editor of the "Boston Bee," which he is privately showing?

It certainly shows native genius when men can build so large a superstructure of falsehood on so small a foundation of truth. I will tell you the whole story, so that you may see how big a bird can be hatched out of a small egg.

Some time during the present session, — I think, last winter, — one of the editors of the "Bee," Mr. R——, called on me here. I saw him several times, and he appeared friendly, and our interviews were agreeable; that is, to me. He asked some favor of me, which I gladly rendered. He then expressed his thanks, quite as warmly as I could have desired; told me that his paper had done me injustice formerly (during my controversy with the Boston schoolmasters); said he resisted it at the time, but was overcome by his partners; and then expressed to me, in strong terms, his regret for the injury that had been done me. I gave him to understand, that, at the time, I had felt the injustice, but that the occasion had passed away, and with it almost all recollection of it; and that I should be none the less ready to do him a favor when occasion should offer.

In July or August last, when the "Bee" published that gross

falsehood, that I (with others) had visited Mr. Fillmore, and had interfered to persuade him not to appoint Mr. Webster as a member of his Cabinet, the interviews which I had had with Mr. R——, his apology for the wrong done me by the "Bee," &c., came to my mind. At that period, the "Bee" had, for some time, been assailing me through what was called a "Washington correspondent." Under these circumstances, I thought I would write a letter to Mr. R——, remind him of our former intercourse, and put him upon his bearings as a man of honor and truth. I did not know his partners, and did not wish to write to them, or put myself in their hands in any way. I thought, if I had not entirely mistaken the character of Mr. R——, I would prevent further abuse and falsification by appealing to him. I therefore wrote him the letter marked *private*, or *confidential*, in which I referred to our former interview, reminded him of his apology, and remonstrated with him for the course taken in charging me with what I had not done. There was not a word in the letter which a gentleman might not write or receive ; nothing clandestine, nothing partisan ; no threats for anger, no intercessions for favor. Not knowing Mr. R——'s partners, and at the same time knowing how such things get distorted and misrepresented and falsified when they pass through a partisan medium, I wrote to him alone ; and I can hardly conceive that he should show the letter, even to his partners. Certainly, if I did not entirely mistake his character as a man of honor, he cannot have been showing that letter to the public or to individuals, or suggesting that there is one idea in it unworthy of me, as a man of truth and sincerity, to feel or to express.

I desire, therefore, that you would go to Mr. R——, and, if the letter is in being, ask him to show it to you (for which this is my permission), and learn for yourself whether it contains any thing which I might not write, or any thing which would authorize him to break the seal of silence by showing it.

Yours very truly,

HORACE MANN.

WASHINGTON, Sept. 13, 1850.

MY DEAR DOWNER, — I wrote you nothing about affairs; and how could I? The atmosphere is full of treachery. If what was done about New Mexico and Texas shocks every honest mind, what will be said of the Fugitive-slave Bill?

By the way, in the " Boston Courier " of Tuesday they pretend to give the Texas Boundary Bill; but they wholly omit the clause at the end, by which an additional slave State is given to Texas. So I see, in the " Union " of this morning, they profess to give the Fugitive-slave Bill, but leave out from the fifth section one of the most obnoxious and outrageous provisions which the bill contains. I have seen these bills quoted falsely in other Northern papers. Is this ignorance, or falsehood?

You do not tell me how this series of measures strikes the Northern mind. Are they all dead in Massachusetts? Will there be no re-action? or will the Whigs face about, and go for slavery in 1850, as the Democrats did for Texas in 1846? . . .

We had no chance to amend the Fugitive-slave Bill. It was hardly anticipated that not a moment's debate or chance for amendment would be allowed. . . .

If the friends of freedom do not rally on this, they are dead for half a century.

Does the " Atlas " lie down, and take it without one kick? Do all the Boston papers take command, as expressed by Byron?—

" Kiss the rod ;
For, if you don't, I'll lay it on, by God ! "

Yours ever and truly,

HORACE MANN.

SEPT. 13, 1850.

I wrote you word yesterday what an infernal day's work we did. The Fugitive-slave Bill was driven through under the gag. The floor was assigned to Mr. Thompson, a Pennsylvania Democrat, who made a speech of nearly an hour long, and then called for the previous question, which was sustained ; and so all possibility of debate or of amendment was precluded.

Sept. 14. . . . I do not think Mr. Webster has any chance for the Presidency. The South, having used him, will fling him away. But that he neither does nor will see. My own opinion is, that, notwithstanding all this billing and cooing of the heads of the hostile parties, there will be a deadly fight between them ere long. They have united to settle this question satisfactorily to the South, so that they might challenge Southern votes. It has been a competition for political power, stimulated, in regard to some of them, by the venality growing out of the Texas ten millions.

Sept. 15. There has been a very sharp debate in the Senate, in which the Southern men have rode and overrode Mr. Winthrop, and hunted up all the ugly things they could say about Massachusetts, and pitched them at him. I do not think Mr. Winthrop has sustained himself very well. He ought to have carried the war into Africa, or at least to have repelled the intruders from his own territory. When we speak of the South *as they are*, the first thing they do is to ransack our old history ; and whatever they can find either against the law of toleration as we now consider it, or the duties of humanity as a higher civilization exemplifies and expounds them, they bring forward. They have never yet been properly answered. If some such man as Sumner was in the seat, he would turn the tables upon them.

The South are more rampant than ever. They feel their triumph. Two or three times within the last week, the " Union," the Southern Democratic organ here, has declared, that, if such or such a thing is done, the Union will totter to its centre. Her interminable cry will now be, if she cannot have her own way, that the Union is tumbling to pieces. We are to have this idea of dissolution as the supplement for all argument, and the arsenal of all weapons. There is a momentary lull ; but the presidency-seekers will soon open a deadly fire upon each other.

SEPT. 16.

I have just come from the library, in one of whose alcoves sits Miss Dix, and fills the members that she calls about her with her divine magnetism. When I see her and some others, how I do long to have her portion of the human race rise to their true condition! I am for "woman's rights," in the highest sense of the word; not for her being made a politician, a soldier, a judge, or a president, but for her entering that glorious sphere of benevolence which Nature has opened, but which the selfishness and short-sightedness of men have hitherto closed up. . . . She is full of anxiety about her bill now before Congress. She reminds me of my old anxiety for some of my educational measures; and in this particularly, that I see, that, as soon as she can accomplish her present plans, she has others lying behind, and ready to be brought forward to take the place of the successful ones.

One fortnight from to-day, we close!

I hope to have but one more *black* Tuesday in this place. . . .

SEPT. 17.

There is a great rush here of the Tariff party. Mr. Webster has held out the idea all summer, that, if we would surrender liberty, the South would withhold their opposition to a tariff. This is the idea that has worked such a wonderful change in Boston, and in those parts of the State connected by business with it; and almost all parts of the State are so connected. It is the pecuniary sensorium, and the nerves reach to all the extremities; for it is within twelve hours of every part of the State by railroads, &c. This idea, therefore, that money is to be made by a settlement of the difficulties in favor of slavery, has been the corrupting idea of the year, and it has worked its way with prodigious efficacy. Several attempts have been made to get a tariff measure through; but, as yet, all have failed. I suppose this to be the reason why there is such a flocking here now from Lowell and Boston. How disgraceful it is! and yet, if these motives were exposed, they would first be denied, and then the author of the charge would be sacrificed. It is a corrupt state of affairs; but I think not all who are engaged in it either see or feel how base it is.

It is this class of people who are making the outcry against me.

WASHINGTON, Sept. 21, 1850.

REV. S. J. MAY.

MY DEAR SIR, — . . . You have seen how Websterism overrides every thing in Boston. A large portion of the voters in my district belong in Boston, and have no sympathies or interests but in Boston, and only come out into the country to sleep and vote. They are exciting an opposition to me, to the extent of their influence and Webster's money. Were it not for this, I should long ago have positively declined to be a candidate again. The posture of affairs may compel me to withhold the execution of this purpose. . . . I have no heart to write a word on the course of things in Congress this session. The slaveholders have overthrown principles, and put them to rout as Napoleon did armies.

Yours very truly,

HORACE MANN.

SEPT. 19, 1850.

A Mr. Venable, of North Carolina, is making a speech against any special efforts to colonize Liberia. He thinks the negro settlements there will fail ; that the settlers are incapable of civilization, and will soon relapse into barbarism. This is a fine commentary upon that view of the special providences which justifies the slave-trade and slavery in this country for these hundred years, in order to return the race to the land from which it came, and thus introduce or transfer our civilization into that region of the earth !

The days wear away beautifully. Ought any one to be placed in such a position as to desire the lapse of time ? . . .

SEPT. 20.

It is truly appalling to see the swarms of men who come on here from the North — and a full proportion of them are from Massachusetts — to re-enforce the interests of the manufacturers, — cotton, woollen, and iron particularly. Oh, if there were such alacrity, such zeal, such effort, for what is good ! But though I have no doubt such a state of society will come at some time, yet that time is a great way off. If it is, then why should we not try to bring it nearer, as we may do ?

. . . Last night I was taking my accustomed walk on the terrace, when there spread all over the western horizon one of the most gorgeous sunsets I ever beheld. Then I wanted more eyes than mine to see, and more sensibilities to feel what provision has been made to gratify sentiments whose use the mere utilitarian cannot perceive. The world needs educating up to the enjoyment of the pleasures which are strewn around them. So much beauty exists unknown and unperceived! So it is with truth; so it is with affection.

SEPT. 21.

The Fugitive-slave Bill is very much altered from what it was when originally offered. That bill made all postmasters in the United States judges, who might decide the question of freedom or slavery. As it stands, the courts of the United States are authorized to appoint as many commissioners as they may think fit; and these commissioners are also authorized to appoint marshals (whose duty it will be to serve legal process), as many as they see fit, for making arrests, &c.: so that there will be no deficiency of officers to carry out its nefarious purposes. It is a surrender complete and abject, like those which characterized the baseness of the courtiers in the time of the Charleses and the Jameses. Posterity will treat the conduct of our leading men as Macaulay has treated that of the sycophants and courtiers of the Stuarts.

SEPT. 23.

For four or five days, we have had as beautiful weather here as can be had anywhere out of Eden.

We shall have a crowded week; public business pressing, which can hardly be postponed without arresting the wheels of Government; private claims urging attention, and seeking any sleepy mood of the House to steal in and get something from the full pockets of Uncle Sam; and members, tired, disgusted, and homesick, deserting their seats, and going home. In some States, the elections will come on very soon; and such of the members as are candidates will feel too anxious about their own private political fortunes to stay longer and attend to the public business. It will be a most deplorable sight, such combinations of selfish interests, and such dissolving of combinations whenever new interests intervene. It is a sad spectacle, I assure you; but I am telling tales out of school.

It is twelve o'clock. One week from this hour, no matter what is going on, — an orator in the midst of a speech, or the Speaker himself with a vote but half declared, — as soon as twelve o'clock comes, down will come the hammer, and this session of Congress will be adjourned. Let it come!

Poor, dear Miss Dix! Her bill has failed this morning in the House; or, at least, it has been referred to the Committee of the Whole on the State of the Union, from which it cannot be returned should the session continue for a year. I went to carry her the news; but she has not come up to the library to-day.

Yesterday, when her bill came up, men were starting up on all sides with their objections; but to-day the point under discussion is, to pay an additional sum to the soldiers in the Mexican war for expenses of coming home, and almost all are in favor of it. It is amazing how war-mad all the South and South-west are. Conquest and numbers constitute their idea of glory. Christianity is nineteen hundred years distant from them.

I have not yet had time to read S——'s letter; but her letters have a charm for me always. I wonder how so much poetry as she has ever kept itself from flowing into rhyme. I am sure she might make her everlasting worldly fortune by writing songs for children, reasoning like a fairy on all the realities and moralities of life. Hasn't she the word-faculty? or what is the reason she doesn't do it?

I am glad Mr. Pierce has arrived.* How deep the feeling with which we look back upon perils escaped and the object of our labors secured! It must be a little more than a year since we had the *fête* that "welcomed" him away. I rather envied you your visit to him. I should really like to hail him again. Why could not the old soul transmigrate into another body? However, he has done his work, — a great work; one that can never be undone. What he has done is not the erection of a structure that will not increase, and will decay, but it is the planting and early culture of a seed which will grow, and cannot but grow, and must protect other trees of the same healthful influences in their growth. "Lame, cold, and

---

* Cyrus Pierce, of the West Newton Normal School.

numb " as he is, there are few young men that could equal him in the race.

It is very cool here, — " autumnal," as you say ; and to-day it is beginning to storm. I am always glad to hear of you "gardening;" and, when you are out, the children are out too.

WASHINGTON, Sept. 24, 1850.

MY DEAR DOWNER, — I have but time to say a word. . . .

There has just been another desperate attempt to get a tariff. Messrs. A—— and G—— were put forward to pioneer the measure. Mr. G—— moved to reconsider a bill from the Committee on Commerce, giving Canada vessels a right to lade and unlade in our ports, &c., so that it might be sent to the Committee of the Whole on the State of the Union, to be there amended by a tariff. So the motion prevailed. Then a motion to lay the subject on the table failed. Then came the question about committing with instructions, which failed by a large vote. So the whole thing slumped. We are surrounded by lobby members from Pennsylvania and New England. The men who have been ready to barter away liberty and blood and souls for profits have failed again miserably. Mr. Webster's promise made at the Revere House, that, if the North would go for conciliation (that is, the surrender of liberty), they could then have " beneficial legislation " (that is, a tariff), has not been fulfilled.

I regret as much as any one the suffering of our laboring classes ; but there is a retribution in all this which gratifies one's moral sense.

Good-by to you, my friend !

HORACE MANN.

WEST NEWTON, Nov. 15, 1850.

MY DEAR MR. AND MRS. COMBE, — I received your brief note from London, dated Sept. 15 ; and afterwards your letter from Edinburgh of Sept. 29. The letter gave me what I must call an unlawful pleasure : for it fully acquitted me of what my own conscience had long told me I was guilty of ; namely, neglect of you. Mary has often said to me, " Now, my dear, you *must* write to Mr. Combe;" and I had as often replied, "Yes, I must and will." But, like all other promises, these were made under the tacit and implied condition of possibility. But the possibility never came; and, before I get through, I must tell you why. I have received a copy of the Annual Report of your school; which Mary and I read together, as we always do every thing that comes from your pen. Your Life of Dr. Combe was sent here before I came home. Mary began to read it, but put it off that we might read it together. Since I came home, we have begun it, and advanced nearly half way in it; but other engagements of one kind and another have interrupted. I find it very minute in its details; so much so, perhaps, as to be objectionable to the general reader : but to me, who know the subject and the writer, and who have such a deep personal interest in every thing they have said or done, it never loses its interest. I should as soon complain of an absent friend for giving me all the incidents of his fortune, when, the more of each twenty-four hours he describes, the better. I like to read his letters. I delight, and profit too, in reading a book which never departs from the phrenological dialect, and refers every thing to phrenological principles. It is like a review of a delightful study.

When first offered the nomination for Congress, I had serious doubts about accepting it : but I was in my twelfth year as Secretary of the Board of Education; and, while acting in an official capacity, I was under the trammels of neutrality between all sects and parties. It was just at the crisis when the destiny of our new Territory of about six hundred thousand square miles in extent was about to be determined. All of human history that I ever knew respecting the contest for political and religious freedom, and my own twelve-years' struggle to imbue the public mind with an understanding not merely of the law but of the spirit of religious liberty, had so magnified in my mind the importance of free institutions, and so intensified my horror of all forms of slavery, that even the importance of education itself seemed for a moment to be eclipsed.

Besides, my fidelity to principles had made some enemies, who, to thwart me, would resist progress, but who, if I were out of the way, would be disarmed, and would co-operate where they had combated. . . . The commencement of the session in December last was full of excitement. We voted three weeks before we succeeded in making choice of a Speaker; the issue being between freedom and slavery, modified by its bearing upon the next Presidential election. In the Senate there were three men, Clay, Webster, and Cass, each one of whom had staked body, reputation, and soul on being the next President. In 1848, Gen. Cass had surrendered all that he could think of, as principle, for the sake of winning the Southern vote. Clay had just been returned to the Senate, and Webster had been thrown into the background, partly for his mighty advocacy of freedom, and partly because he had no skill in flattering the people. Clay devised a plan of indirect opposition to the policy of Gen. Taylor, which, should it be unsuccessful, would hardly injure its originator, but, if crowned with success, would place him high and conspicuous above the President himself.

Up to this time, at least ostensibly, Webster had maintained his integrity. But he supposed his final hour had come. Cass as a Democrat, and Clay as a Whig, had offered to immolate freedom to win the South. Webster must do more than either, or abandon hope. He consented to treachery, and, to make his reward sure, proposed to do more villanies than were asked of him. His 7th of March speech was an abandonment of all he had ever said in defence of the great principles of freedom. It was a surrender of the great interests of freedom in the new Territories then in issue, and it was wanton impiety against the very cause of liberty. We were not merely amazed, but astounded by it. He artfully connected the pecuniary interests of the North with this treachery to freedom. Our manufacturing interests were in a deplorable condition. He told the manufacturers, that, if they would surrender freedom, they could have a tariff. This assurance was repeated in a thousand covert forms. It brought out the whole force of Mammon. One of the Boston newspapers, the "Daily Advertiser," whose whole circulation was among the wealthy and aristocratic, took ground in his defence at once. Another of them, the "Courier," sold itself immediately for mere money to him and to his friends; and such an overbearing and threatening tone was assumed by his whole pretorian guard, that every other paper in the city, however clamorous it had been for freedom before (except the

22

" Liberator "), was silenced. The press in Boston, for the last six months, had been very much in the condition of the press of Paris.

I came home to visit my family in April on account of ill health in it, and staid a month. The public mind had not recovered from its shock ; and Mr. Webster's " retainers," as the " Advertiser " unluckily called them, were active in fastening their views upon the re-awakened consciousness of the public. I conversed with many very prominent individuals. I found they agreed with me fully in regard to Mr. Webster's treachery, and in private would speak freely, but in public would not commit themselves to a word. This was grievous, and reminded me of what you used to say so often, — that our people have not confidence enough in truth. I was invited by a respectable portion of my constituents to address them. I wrote them a letter instead. In that letter, I reviewed the course of the leading men, — Cass, Clay, and Webster. I pointed out Mr. Webster's inconsistencies and enormities in as searching a manner as I could, but in a very respectful tone. He and his friends swore vengeance against me at once.

When I returned to Washington, he *cut* me. He indulged in offensive remarks in private intercourse. In a letter written to some citizens who sought to uphold his course, he put in the most arrogant sneer that his talent could devise, and published it. That gave me a chance to review his letter, and to discuss the question of trial by jury for alleged fugitives. In another letter, he made another assault upon me. This, too, I answered. Just at this moment, Gen. Taylor died. The Vice-President, a weak and irresolute-minded man, succeeded. Mr. Webster was appointed Secretary of State ; and he thus became omnipotent, and almost omnipresent. The cause of freedom was doomed. Thousands saw what the event would be, and rushed to the conclusion. Three-fifths of all the Whig presses went over in a day. The word of command went forth to annihilate me ; and, if it was not done, it was for no want of good will or effort on the part of the hired executioners. From having been complimented on all sides, I was misrepresented, maligned, travestied, on all sides. Not a single Whig paper in Boston defended me. Most of them had an article or more against me every day. The convention to nominate my successor was packed by fraudulent means, and I was thrown overboard. . . . To bring the *odium theologicum* to crush me, an evangelical was taken as my opponent. I took the stump, and put the matter to my constituents face to face.

The election took place last Monday, and I have beaten them all by a handsome majority. This is something of a personal triumph. therefore; but, as a triumph of principle, it is of infinitely more value. Nothing can exceed the elation of my friends, or the mortification of my enemies. The latter feel like a man who has committed some roguery, and failed of obtaining his purpose in doing it.

This triumph of principle in Massachusetts gave indescribable pleasure to Mr. Mann. All the sanguine hopes of many friends, who were deeply interested in the result, for his sake as well as for that of the good cause, had failed to give him one ray of hope that the election would be carried in his favor. He was quite content to be the means of defeating the triumph of the other party, which would have been such a lasting disgrace to the State; but expected no more. He had been called up at night more than once by bands of his friends, who went from town to town in the district to attend the various conventions, to hear their assurances that his election was probable: but all their eloquence had failed to convince him of any greater success than this, so discouraged and heart-sick for his State had he become from the evidences of Mr. Webster's malign influence; and when a relative in his family went, late at night, to the village to count the votes, and brought back a favorable answer, he was equally incredulous, and coolly proposed to wait till he could count them himself when the newspaper should come in the morning. The young lady's ardor was quite cooled down; but, on descending the hill in the morning, she met the village omnibus on its way up, and the driver swung his hat with the announcement. She flew back to be the first to tell the news, but could not speak when she arrived. The carriage passed the gate, however; and the vociferous demonstrations assured Mr. Mann of the fact. He walked the floor some time without speaking, and at last, "Thank God for Massachusetts!" were the first words he could utter; and those who knew him best knew that the choked voice was not that of a selfish emotion. It had not been his intention to stand as candidate for a Congressional election again; for he felt that the odds against freedom had been so great, that it was a waste of his time, which could be better employed in the good work of bringing up the nation to the desired point, than by sitting in Congressional halls whose very atmosphere polluted the breath of freemen. But the state of affairs at that critical juncture forbade him to leave his post then, even though he were to have been sacrificed by remaining firm to it. A defeat at that time, and under the circumstances, would have been very disastrous to him; but he was not accustomed to make himself the first consideration. He really belonged to no party. The Whig party, which had elected him for certain purposes, had proved recreant to their own principles, and had left him standing just where they put him. He went to Congress the first time because his constituents thought him the best man, at that juncture, to carry out the principles of Mr. Adams in the cause of freedom: they had changed, but he had not changed; and it was not his fault if he stood without a party for a time.

In October, 1850, Mr. Webster, in a letter from Franklin, N. H., to a committee of gentlemen in New York, says, —

"I concur, gentlemen, in all the political principles contained in the resolutions, a copy of which has been sent to me; and I stand pledged to support those principles, publicly and privately, now and always, to the full extent of my influence, and by the exertion of every faculty which I possess."

Two of these resolutions were as follows : —

"*Resolved,* That we cordially approve of the recent measures of Congress for the adjustment of the dangerous questions arising out of the acquisition of territory under the treaty of Mexico, &c.

"*Resolved,* That the Fugitive-slave Bill is in accordance with the express stipulations of the Constitution of the United States ; . . . and that Congress, in passing a law which should be efficient for carrying out the stipulations, &c., acted in full accordance with the letter and spirit of that instrument ; and that we will sustain this law and the execution of it by all lawful means."

WASHINGTON, Dec. 14, 1850.

C. PIERCE, ESQ.

MY DEAR SIR, — I am glad to hear from you, and that you think of putting on the harness again. I guess the "old clock-work" will go well yet. Whatever I can do for you, I shall do with great alacrity. I doubt the expediency of establishing another Normal school yet a while in Massachusetts. Those already in existence must be filled and crowded before another will prosper. I do not know what sphere you intend to fill : the one you talked of with A—— would open a noble field for usefulness, though I should struggle against all secondary causes that should threaten to remove you from Massachusetts.

My journey to Washington was in some respects pleasant. I was greeted all along the way by many persons known and unknown to me ; and, on arriving here, I found the controversy between myself and Mr. Webster had really assumed a national notoriety and conspicuousness. Whigs and Democrats had a common exultation, though it was probably more for his defeat than for my victory. . . .

Yours very truly,

HORACE MANN.

WASHINGTON, Dec. 22, 1850.

MY DEAR DOWNER, — I see by the date of my letter that it is *Forefathers' Day;* and I cannot but ask myself what the stern old

Puritans would say, were they here to witness the degeneracy of their sons. Evil days have surely come upon us. There is a very considerable number here, it is true, who are still faithful to their principles; but they are embarrassed and oppressed with the palpable fact before them that they are in the hands of the Philistines, and that nothing can be done in behalf of the measures they have so steadfastly and earnestly contended for. The Administration has placed itself on open, avowed, proslavery ground. They will be proscriptive of enemies, and bountiful to friends; and I fear that what Mr. Webster once said will prove true, — that he had never known an Administration to set its heart upon any measure which it did not accomplish. There will be a giving-way somewhere; and all effective opposition will be frightened away or bought up.

But to what a pass has Northern recreancy brought us! You see the list of conditions which the South are everywhere laying down, upon compliance with which, in every item, the Union can alone be preserved, — no abolition of slavery in the District of Columbia; no imposition of a proviso on any Territory, — which looks to its future acquisition, and is meant to forestall its doom; no objection to the admission of any State, whether from Texas, New Mexico, Utah, *or from any new acquisitions*, on account of the proslavery constitution, &c. And now the Governor of Virginia, in a special message to the Legislature, has proposed the holding of a national convention, at which the North shall appear as suppliant, shall promise all that the South demands, and shall lie down on her belly, and eat as much dirt as she can hold. It is said there is no end to discoveries; and certainly there is no end to discoveries in humiliation. One would think that even the soulless instigators of Northern Union meetings would recoil on the brink of this abyss of degradation. But such is the progress of things; and, however low they go, a "lower deep" still opens before them. Even the "National Intelligencer," with all its proslavery instincts, shudders at this pit.

What shall we do here? I declare myself ready, for one, to do, to the utmost of my ability, whatever may appear under the circumstances to be advisable. I find it to be true, as I have always said, that there is no more chance of repealing or modifying the

Fugitive-slave Law than there is of making a free State out of South Carolina. Still, my own opinion is that we ought to make a demonstration upon it. My belief is that there never was so much need of contending against the slave-power as now. There is far more reason for a rally now than in 1848. Then a great prize was in imminent peril. Had Cass been made President in consequence of a diversion of Whigs into the Free-soil ranks, it is, to my mind, as certain as any unfulfilled event, that California would have been a slave State, and New Mexico and Utah would have had slavery had they desired it. This great interest was put in jeopardy by that movement; though, fortunately, God sent us a deliverance.

But now there is no such immediate and magnificent stake to be lost or won. We cannot lose any thing now, *because we have lost all.* Our dangers are prospective. Cuba, Mexico, Nicaragua, are the game now afoot. We must be prepared for the time when these shall be the subject of contest. We must see that we have Congresses that will stand their ground; and therefore the anti-slavery principle must not be suffered to sleep. . . .

Yours as ever,

H. M.

LETTER FROM GEO. E. BAKER, ESQ.

DEAR MRS. MANN, — I send herewith a copy of the letter alluded to in my note to W. W. & Co. The original I have bound with other valuable letters and autographs, and I cannot detach it without injury.

Your husband's memory is very dear to me. I was very early impressed by his character, and you know how durable early impressions are. While the admonitions of the other " committee men " — many of them able men — have faded away, the counsels he gave nearly forty years ago in the old schoolhouse are still alive with me. And then it was easy and natural for me, little boy as I was, to see whom my father esteemed above all other men, although Mr. Mann was then but a young lawyer, without any official position save that of " school-committee man." I remember well when he was first elected to the Legislature. About that time, the Tremont House was opened, and was the wonder of the people; and it was among the small-talk of our neighborhood, including several young ladies, that Horace Mann boarded there. My vivid recollection of this illustrates the adage, " Little pitchers have great ears." I think it was after I was a few years older that he astonished and captivated me by a most eloquent (volunteer) defence of a prisoner in court charged with theft. These words ring in my ears while I write: " I consider it as much my duty to defend this man as it would be to reach out my arm to a man floating down a stream and in danger of drowning." The prisoner was acquitted; the jury not even leaving their seats. Even the unrelenting prosecuting attorney confessed to the effect of Mr. Mann's argument.

Pardon me; but it is a delight to me thus to dwell on the recollections of my boyhood, and of so great and good a man.

Very respectfully,

GEO. E. BAKER.

WASHINGTON, Dec. 14, 1850.

GEO. E. BAKER, ESQ., *Member of Assembly, Albany, N. Y.*

DEAR SIR, — I remember you well as one of the little*st* boys on one of the lowest seats in the old schoolhouse at " Connecticut Corner," in Dedham.

I have a vivid recollection of how my heart used to exult in hope as I saw the " little fellows " in jacket and trousers, out of whom my imagination used to make *good and true men* for the country and the world. And if you can conceive how it must delight me to have those visions realized in a single case, then you may compute the pleasure which I enjoy in the receipt of many, many such remembrances as yours. Your father* was one of my best friends, and I have great respect for his memory. I am glad you are to go among the men who make laws, and, what is more efficacious than laws, public opinion, for the community. Nor am I less delighted to hear, that, in your political convictions, you are attracted towards Mr. Seward. I say attracted *towards* Mr. Seward; for I do not quite agree with him on some views which I consider ultra : and yet, in the main, he holds sound doctrines, and certainly supports them with ability.

* John Baker, Sheriff of Norfolk County.

As to your course of action, allow me to express the hope that you will connect yourself with educational, charitable, and philanthropic spheres of action, rather than with party combinations and schemes. As soon as it is understood in what direction your taste and predilections lead you, you will find yourself placed in those positions, or falling into them naturally, and as if by gravitation.

Two years ago, I revised the whole system of Massachusetts common schools; and if you have any desire to see my work, and will address our Secretary of State, asking for a copy of my revised Tenth Report, I doubt not he will send it to you.

May I suggest to you to purchase and read and study two volumes, just published, of Charles Sumner's orations? You will find them full of the most noble views and inspiring sentiments. I could wish a young man, just entering political life, to do nothing better than to form his conduct after the high models there presented.

Excuse the haste of this letter, written, as most of my correspondence is, in the midst of constant interruptions; and believe me very truly yours,

HORACE MANN.

WASHINGTON, Jan. 5, 1851.

To E. W. CLAP, *Walpole, Mass.*

MY DEAR SIR, — . . . After a week of factious opposition, we have at last, this morning, passed a vote, by a large majority, to do the handsome thing to Kossuth. The South and the "Old Hunkers" have been in a "tight place." How could they vote to honor one fugitive from slavery, and chain and send back another? If an Austrian "commissioner" should issue his warrant for Kossuth, and he should kill the marshal, would he, like the Christiana rioters, be guilty of treason?

You see my book* has been prosecuted, in the name of the publishers, for libel. If the greater the truth, the greater the libel, the book must plead guilty. Regards to you all.

As ever, very truly yours,

HORACE MANN.

---

* "Of Antislavery Documents and Speeches," which is to be republished with some additional matter.

WASHINGTON, Jan. 6, 1851.

My DEAR MR. COMBE, — . . . I have nothing to write on political subjects that can afford any gratification to a humanity-loving man. In 1848, there was a great inflowing of the sentiment of liberty, both in Europe and in this country. You have already experienced the ebbing of that tide in Europe, and it has receded as much relatively in this hemisphere as in yours. Notwithstanding the inherent and radical wickedness of some of the compromise measures, as they were called, yet the most strenuous efforts are making by the Administration to force the Whig party to their adoption and support. It is a concerted movement between those who are ready to sacrifice liberty for office and those who are ready to make the same sacrifice for money. From the day of Mr. Webster's open treachery and apostasy (if indeed he had political virtue enough to be an apostate), he has been urging the idea upon New-England Whigs, that, if they could give up freedom, they might have a tariff. This has wrought numberless conversions among those who think it a sin not to be rich. They say in their hearts, "The South wants cotton to sell, and must have negroes to produce it; we want cotton to manufacture, and so we must have negroes to raise it: slavery is equally indispensable to us both." So both are combining to uphold it. Before Texas was annexed, the whole Democratic party at the North denounced it. As soon as that was done, they wheeled round like a company of well-drilled soldiers at the word of command, and supported it. I fear the great body of the Whig party will do no better as regards these infamous proslavery measures. Party allegiance here has very much the effect of loyalty with you. *It has the power to change the nature of right and wrong.* I profess to belong to none of the parties. I have given in my adherence to certain great principles; and by them I stand, not only in independence, but in defiance of parties. I should like to send you a copy of my letters. I will do so as soon as I can find an opportunity. . . .

WASHINGTON, Feb. 10, 1851.

E. W. CLAP, ESQ.

My DEAR SIR, — . . . I was glad to hear from you, and should be much obliged for a more detailed account of proceedings at

home.   Things are looking bad for freedom there, and worse here.
There never was a greater effort on the part of any Administration
— not even in the most imperious days of Jackson or Polk — to
subdue all opposition, by fears or by rewards, than at present.
Webster is as corrupt a politician as ever lived.

What is the chance of Sumner's success ? . . .

Yours very truly,

HORACE MANN.

WASHINGTON, Feb. 14, 1851.

MY DEAR SUMNER, — Remember it is the darkest time just
before day.   I have long had very serious apprehensions about the
result this session; that is, the end of the beginning: but you
must now apply to yourself the counsel you gave last autumn to
me; that is, *you* must now take the field, and vindicate your cause
before the people; not *yourself*, — that I do not say, — but the
CAUSE.   If you do not prevail now, Massachusetts goes over to
Hunkerdom.   This may the gods avert! . . .

Yours ever,

HORACE MANN.

NEW YORK, March 1, 1851.

I had a call this morning from a man who wishes to get a grant
from Government, and so he is civil to me.   It gave me just the
feeling I used to have at the selfish civilities of many Boston men,
when I was in our Legislature, who used to coax and pet and
flatter me, and tell me what fine speeches I made, and make me
dine, and force me to drink their wine (for I had not then the full
grace of a teetotaler); but as soon as I left that presidency, and
became an educationist, they knew me no longer.

The ice on the Susquehanna seemed perfectly strong, and I was
not afraid to go where I saw the baggage-cars go.   I wished you
could have been clairvoyant enough to see me when I stepped on
the hither shore; but we suffer in this life for our short-sightedness.

SYRACUSE. — I trust you will now be at ease about me; for here I
am in Mr. May's home, and I am to remain here until Monday.

He came to the hotel yesterday morning, and, like a true Hopkinsian theologian, made his free grace irresistible, and took me up here. He has a beautiful place, — as beautiful as ours : so I feel quite restored to old comforts again.

We had about ten speeches, and at least six of them were very brilliant. There was an air of boldness, of defiance even, against the crime, and its abettors and promoters, which augurs well for the cause.

Neal Dow, the moral Columbus, was there, — a small, innocent-looking, modest man of middle age, who looks as though he must have felt infinitely surprised, when, as Byron says, he waked up one morning, and found himself famous.

A mighty audience last night, I was told, — not less than five thousand people. I had only a music-stand to put my lecture upon, and was obliged to stand one side of it, — a rascally arrangement ! Had I not had your plain handwriting, I could not have got along at all: so I thought of you continually, as you helped every sentence out of my mouth. I think of that cough of George's. Do I hear it ? or is it imagination ?

The temperance camp is all astir. I have just been invited to deliver *another* temperance lecture before I leave the city.

Dear H. and G., — did I hear my little boys speaking last night with singing voices like birds, and showing glad eyes and smiling faces ? or was it a dream ?

Washington, April, 1851.

My dear Sumner, — *Laus Deo !* Good, better, best, better yet ! By the necessity of the case, you are now to be a politician, — an honest one. Scores have asked whether you would be true. I have underwritten to the amount of forty reputations.

Yours truly,

HORACE MANN.*

* This note was written on occasion of Mr. Sumner's election to the Senate.

LETTER TO THE YOUNG MEN'S DEBATING SOCIETY, 111 BOWERY, NEW YORK, IN REPLY TO A COMMUNICATION ASKING HIS ADVICE IN RELATION TO THE BEST MANNER OF DEBATING.

WEST NEWTON, Monday, June 16, 1851.

I am very glad to be made acquainted with the existence of your society, and feel highly honored by your request for a word of encouragement and counsel.

I have an inexpressible interest in young men, and wish I could live my life over again, that I might cause less of evil and more of good than I have done. But life is a book of which we can have but one edition : as it is first prepared, it must stand forever. Let each day's action, as it adds another page to the indestructible volume, be such that we shall be willing to have an assembled world read it!

You say you constitute a debating society. Will you allow me, as a friend, to make one remark on the subject of the choice of subjects, and another upon your habit of treating them ?

I would recommend that you choose topics for discussion which are, as far as possible, both theoretic and practical. The theoretic will exercise your speculative faculties, which are essential to comprehensiveness, forethought, and invention ; and the practical will cause you to keep continually in view the uses which may be made of your combination of ideas. Both powers will make the man, so far as the intellect is concerned.

My other remark is, — and I am sure you will think more and more of it the longer you live, — never investigate nor debate for triumph, but always for truth. Never take the affirmative or negative side of a question till after you have mastered it according to the best of your ability, and then adopt the side which judgment and conscience assure you to be right.

The mind is not only the object to be improved, but it is the instrument to work with. How can you improve a moral instrument by forcing it to hide or obscure the truth, and espouse the side of falsehood ? If you succeed, you do but injure others by inducing them to adopt errors ; but you injure yourself more than any one else. The optician who beclouds the glass through which he looks is a wise man compared with the reasoner who beclouds his faculties. Keep one thing forever in view, — the truth; and if you do this, though it may seem to lead you away from the opinions of men, it will assuredly conduct you to the throne of God.

With sincere hopes for your welfare, I am, dear sir, very truly yours, &c.,

HORACE MANN.

WASHINGTON, July 13, 1851.

. . . A Virginian told me yesterday that he saw I kept preaching: and, upon my evincing some curiosity to know what he meant, he said he heard a discourse from me the day before, — Sunday; all which, being at last interpreted, meant that he had heard a street temperance-lecturer read my Letter to the Worcester Temperance Convention, to a large audience which he had collected. I see the letter itself is in Monday's "Commonwealth." . . .

I was glad to see in some paper yesterday a letter from Gen. Scott to Gen. Jackson, declining a challenge for a duel which the latter had sent him. It was well written, saying at the end that he, Gen. Jackson, could probably gratify his feelings by calling him, Scott, coward, &c., *till after the next war;* meaning thereby, that, in another war, he would have an opportunity to vindicate his courage, &c.

The general impression here is that Mr. Webster cares nothing for the Whig party, but will accept a nomination from any body of men not too contemptible to be noticed.

WEST NEWTON, Aug. 4, 1851.

REV. S. J. MAY, — . . . Webster has debauched the country, not only on the subject of slavery, but of all decency and truth. Well, I have no doubt who will come out right ten years hence.

Very truly yours, &c.,

H. MANN.

WEST NEWTON, Sept. 25, 1851.

REV. T. PARKER.

MY DEAR SIR, — . . . I wish to find a few of the best authorities, taken from as wide a range as possible among heathen and pagan writers, in favor of the higher law. Can you refer me to them? I wish to shame our Christians by a little pagan morality. . . .

Yours very truly,

HORACE MANN.

WASHINGTON, December, 1851.

My DEAR Mr. Combe, — . . . In this political wrangle, I, who before was, in some respects, very popular, have become very unpopular. But I look to futurity for my vindication. During the past summer and autumn, I have collected and revised all my leading speeches and letters on antislavery, and have published them in a volume, making nearly six hundred pages. They will be, in a good degree, historical as to my course on the great questions of freedom and slavery. For a time, I, and those with whom I have acted, may be under a cloud; but I have no doubt as to how we shall stand a quarter of a century hence. And hereafter, when some future Macaulay shall arise to announce the verdict of history in relation to these times, I can feel no doubt that he will condemn the statesmen and the judges who have upheld the infamous compromise measures and the Fugitive-slave Law, to stand forever by the side of, and to share the immortal reprobation which now, by the universal consent of mankind, is awarded to, the lawgivers and the courts of the Stuarts.

I came to Washington last Saturday, bringing the whole family, and a niece who is very dear to me, and who proposes spending the winter here. We are situated in a most pleasant part of the city, on Capitol Hill; and hope to have as agreeable a winter as one can have in the midst of these national immoralities. The business of the session will consist mainly in the manœuvres, intrigues, and competitions for the next Presidency. The only candidate yet named, whom I can support, is Gen. Scott. He will not mingle in the intrigue. I shall be a spectator of these questions, having no temptation even to participate in them.

—— ——.

I am exhibiting myself in a new character, — that of a school-book maker; and am preparing, in conjunction with a gentleman who is very competent to perform the labor, a series of arithmetical works based on a new principle. Instead of taking, as the data of the questions, the transactions of the shop, the market-house, the bank, &c., I explore the whole range of history, biography, geography, civil, commercial, financial, and educational statistics, science, &c., for the materials which form the basis of the questions: so that the pupil, in addition to a problem to be solved, shall always find an interesting or instructive fact to be delighted with. I can, however, give you but a meagre idea of my plan, which I have fully unfolded in my preface, and which I hope some time to send to you.*

I ask myself a thousand times, Shall I ever see you again? and the answer which probability returns makes me sad. With our best regards to yourself and Mrs. Combe, we are, as ever, most truly your friends.

HORACE MANN.

P. S. — There is something in your suggestion of having me for your posthumous editor that struck me as almost ridiculous. Your chance for being the survivor is probably better than mine. But that is no reason why your work should not proceed. *Put all your wisdom into it.*

WASHINGTON, Dec. 5, 1851.

MY DEAR FRIENDS MR. AND MRS. COMBE, — . . . Politics in this country do not, as they should, mean a science, but a controversy; and in this sense we are all involved in politics. When will the time come that politics can be taken from the domain of passion and propensity? I have no doubt that such a millennium is in the future. Nor will the whole world enter that millennium at the same time. Wise and sage individuals like Mr. George Combe must be the pioneers: then it must be colonized by a larger number, and then entered and dwelt in by all. But I fear the epochs and eras which will mark and measure these successive stages of consummations are to be *geological* in their distance and duration. Doubtless you have seen a book entitled the "Theory of Human

---

* This arithmetic was published in Philadelphia: but the publishers made little effort to forward it; and Mr. Mann was too much occupied, when he became aware of this, to take any measures upon the subject.

Progression," which, from internal evidence, is Scotch in its origin, and whose object is not only to prophesy, but to prove, the future triumph of peace and justice upon earth. I have read but part of the book. I am reading it to my wife at odd hours, when our chances of leisure come together. I have long believed in the whole doctrine; but it is delightful to see it argued out, not only to take the Q. E. D. on authority, but to feel the truth of the solution. All sciences, even the natural ones, have been the subjects of controversy and of persecution in their beginning: why, then, should not the science of politics? One truth after another will be slowly developed; and by and by truth, and not individual aggrandizement or advantage, will be the only legitimate object of inquiry. Then will *its* millennium come! — Doubtless you have through the public papers the political movements of the country at large. The old struggle for supremacy between the political parties goes on; but worse means are brought in to insure success than ever before entered into our contests. The North (or free States) comprises almost two-thirds of all our population; the South (or slave States) but about a third. The North is really divided into two great parties, Whigs and Democrats. These are arrayed against each other in hostile attitude; and, being nearly equal, they cancel each other. The South is Whig or Democratic only nominally. It is for slavery exclusively and intensely. Hence we now present the astonishing and revolting spectacle of a free people in the nineteenth century, of almost twofold power, not merely surrendering to a proslavery people one-half the power, but entering into the most vehement competition to join with them in trampling upon all the great principles of freedom. We have five prominent candidates for the next Presidency. All of them are from the North. The South does not put forward as yet a single man; for Mr. Clay can hardly be considered a candidate. Each one of the five candidates begins with abandoning every great principle of constitutional liberty, so far as the black race is concerned; and to this each one has saddled more and more proslavery gratuities and aggrandizements, as the propositions he advanced were made at a later period of time. All Whigs professed to be shocked when Gen. Cass offered in substance to open all our new

Territories to slavery. But Mr. Webster's accumulated proslavery bounties, as compared with those of Gen. Cass, were as "Pelion to a wart." Mr. Buchanan offers to run the line of 36° 30' through to the Pacific Ocean, and to surrender all on the south side of it to slavery. Mr. Dallas, late Vice-President under Mr. Polk, tells the South that the antislavery spirit of the North will never be quiet under the compromise measures and the Fugitive-slave Law; and so proposes *to embody this whole series into the Constitution by an amendment*, thus putting them beyond the reach of legislative action. And Mr. Douglas, a young senator from Illinois, who aspires to the White House, offers Cuba to the South in addition to all the rest. In the mean time, the South sets forth no candidate for the Executive chair. Some of their leading politicians avow the policy of taking a Northern man, because "a Northern man with Southern principles" can do more for them than any one of their own. All of them are virtually saying to Northern aspirants. "Proceed, gentlemen; give us your best terms: and, when you have submitted your proposals, we will make our election between you." Is it not indescribably painful to contemplate such a picture, — no, such a *reality?* You must feel it as a man: *I* feel it as an American, — you as a lover of mankind, I as a lover of republican institutions.

You will, of course, understand that such contests cannot be carried on without corresponding contests in the States. In Massachusetts, many collateral issues have mingled with the main question. Mr. Webster's apostasy on the 7th of March, 1850, had not at first a single open defender in our Commonwealth. Some pecuniary arrangements were made by which one or two papers soon devoted themselves to his cause. In a few days after the speech, he visited Boston; and, at a public meeting to receive him, he held out, in unmistakable language, the lure of a tariff, if they would abandon principle. This interested motive appealed to both parties. It was pressed upon them, both in public and in private, during the whole summer, and indeed until the approaching termination of the 31st Congress showed that it was only a delusion and a cheat.

During the summer, another pecuniary element was introduced. The merchants of New York sought a monopoly of Southern trade through a subserviency to Southern interests. The merchants of Philadelphia and Boston forthwith became competitors for the same profits through the same infamous means. In this way, within a twelvemonth, all the Atlantic cities were carried over to the side of Southern policy. I believe I told you of efforts made against myself, and their result, in the last year's election of a representative to Congress from my district. Since that time the process of defection has gone rapidly on, spreading outwards from the city, and contaminating the country. The great body of the *Whig* merchants and manufacturers in the Northern States now advocate Mr. Webster for the Presidency. This, of course, determines the character of the mercantile papers. A large meeting was held in Boston last week to nominate him for that office. He is expected soon to resign his secretaryship, and to travel South on an electioneering tour. His health is very much impaired; and that glorious physique, which should be in full vigor at the age of eighty, is now nearly broken down. He can do nothing but under the inspiration of brandy; and the tide of excitement also must be taken "at the flood;" for if a little too early, or a little too late, he is sure to fail.

In Massachusetts we have had a fierce contest for State offices. Mr. Winthrop was the Whig candidate for Governor; and his election would have been claimed as a Webster triumph, though not justly so. But he falls short of an election by about eight thousand votes. The Free-soilers and Democrats combined, and have obtained a majority in both the Senate and the House. This secures an anti-Whig Governor, and is a triumph of antislavery sentiment. We have never had a more fiercely contested election. I was "on the stump," as we say, about three weeks, speaking from two to two and a half hours almost every evening. Since the election, I have been delivering lyceum lectures; so that you may well suppose I am pretty much "used up." With this term in Congress, I hope to escape from political broils, and to live a life more in accordance with both natural and acquired tastes. . . .

H. M.

WASHINGTON, Jan. 3, 1852.

REV. S. J. MAY.

DEAR SIR, — It is now a long time since I have received any copies of your shots at Mr. C——. So I suppose the war is ended. I did not see his articles; but, from yours, I should suppose you had much the better of him, both in temper and logic. It is curious that you should propose to engage my professional services for your defence in a case arising out of the Fugitive-slave Law, and that so soon my own writings on the subject should require legal defence. I presume you have seen in the "Commonwealth" that Mr. Commissioner Curtis has commenced an action for libel against Mr. Muzzey, the publisher of my speeches, on account of that Lancaster exhibition of himself. What do you say now to being my counsel? Are you ready to do as you would be done by?

. . . I hope you see full debates of Congress — such as are published in the "Globe" — in relation to the reception of Kossuth. The whole opposition to him comes from the South, and from Northern Hunkers who are devoted to the South. The avowed opposition is based on the question of "intervention;" but the real motive is slavery. While they demand that one fugitive shall be fettered and sent home, they cannot bear to see another *feted* and honored. You see the cloven foot; indeed, you can see nothing else. With best regards for your family, I am

Very truly yours, &c.,

HORACE MANN.

WASHINGTON, Feb. 10, 1852.

MY DEAR DOWNER, — There is nothing of much moment transpiring here. Cabell of Florida, in the House, a few days ago laid down the Southern Whig platform, that no man should be supported for President who was not sound on the slavery question; and added, that though Scott, for every other reason, would be his first choice, yet he had not come out in favor of slavery to this time, and he feared it was even now too late. He was determined (Cabell) never to be caught by another Taylor. Murphy, from Georgia, followed on the Democratic side, and prescribed very much the same creed for the Democrats that Cabell had for the Whigs. So you see the bold stand the South is taking. They will *talk* up to it now. Next June, they will *act* up to it. Will not both parties at the North succumb?

Dismy of Ohio, in the same debate, on being taunted for voting against the Fugitive-slave Law, said he did it because it was not stringent enough!

DANSVILLE, N. Y., 1852.

I have seen only the most meagre account of D——'s and R——'s speeches. I do not see how D—— can come out without being battered and shattered to pieces. Nor ought he to. I think he has been false to great principles, though with such palliations as apostates always find. I think posterity does not look at crimes as the traitors themselves do. With the latter it may not be unmitigated and untempted crime. They have their excuses, their subterfuges, and their casuistry. Görgey doubtless disguised his treason to himself under some plea of benefit to his nation. It is a known fact, that Arnold stoutly contended that he desired to confer a benefit on his country as the motive of his treachery. Judas probably made himself believe that the interests of religion demanded the surrender of his Master. Even Mr. Webster talks to this day as if, in sacrificing the immortal principles of liberty, he had only the good of the Union in view. But when the occasion has passed by, when the event is far removed into the past, then the palliations and the pretexts are lost sight of; and only the black, fatal, damning guilt remains for the detestation and abhorrence of men.

WASHINGTON, D.C., Feb. 13, 1852.

C. PIERCE, ESQ.

MY DEAR SIR, — We heard from you authentically through our common friends, from whom we had a very pleasant visit; but directly we have not heard from you at all. We should be pleased to be remembered in your thoughts, and now and then to have an hour of your time; but the claims of old friendship perhaps belong to that class of imperfect obligations which cannot be enforced against the will of the party. Let me assure you, however, that

you have no truer friends, no warmer admirers, than Mrs. M——
and R——, to say nothing of the gentleman who first knew you
when your fame was *insular*, and who adhered to you through all
seasons and at all times, until it became continental, ay, co-exten-
sive with civilization. . . .

To say that the political aspect of things here is not the worst
possible, is about all the praise you can give it.   A politician does
not sneeze without reference to the next Presidency.   All things
are carried to that tribunal for decision.   The greatest interests and
the worst passions are assayed for this end, and their value determined accordingly.   The next canvass will doubtless be the most
corrupt and corrupting one ever witnessed in this country.   It is
the general opinion here that there is but one Whig who can by any
possibility be elected, — Gen. Scott.   The Democrats will triumph
over every one else, whoever their candidate may be, — perhaps
over him, should he be nominated.   I believe Gen. Scott to be a
very honorable, high-minded man, — a man of rare talents and attainments.   On the other hand, I believe the man whom the people
universally call "Old Sam Houston," alias "Old San Jacinto,"
to be a man of incomparably more character, honesty, and resolution than any other of the Democratic candidates.

Unwell as I am here, — for we made a very respectable hospital
here for the last twelve weeks, — I am going to try a little rustica-
tion at the North.

I hope to attend the great Temperance Banquet at New York on
Wednesday evening next.   I am also engaged to deliver a temperance lecture in the same city on Tuesday evening.   Indeed, I am
to speak four successive evenings, from Tuesday to Friday inclusive;
hoping by that means to improve my digestion.   After that, I have
some idea of going up to see brother May at Syracuse, and congratulate him for the hundredth time that he was not hung in Massachusetts with that dreadful malefactor who included three capital
crimes in one act.   I think I have told you that story, and have
seen you laugh at the predicament in which your brother May
might have been placed.   It is sometimes very strange how serious
people will laugh at serious things.   I wish you could meet me at
New York or Syracuse, or elsewhere on the way, and let me look

again upon that good old horologue whose machinery keeps such excellent time, however much the case may have been battered.

You must see Kossuth, at any expense of ribs or toes; for he will warm your heart. Many of his admirers think him perfect. His enemies will probably succeed in finding foibles enough in his character to prove him human.

Your sincere friend,

HORACE MANN.

BLOOMING GROVE, N.Y., Feb. 22, 1852.

. . . This is a mere rural region; but they have had a course of lectures this winter, and the audience is gathered from all the surrounding country. How came the people, you will ask, to be of this inquisitive and intelligence-loving character?

Their former minister, Mr. Arbuckle, was a strong-minded and honest man, whose mind, by its natural operation, reasoned out some points of dissent from the Presbyterian creed: whereupon his brethren arraigned and excommunicated him. This disengaged his mind from their creed; and he went on growing into truth, — the people of his congregation for the most part adhering to him. After Mr. Arbuckle left them, some natural affinity led them in their search to find their present man, Mr. Austin Craig. He is now about twenty-eight years of age, and a most extraordinary young man. He was led to invite me here by seeing my "Thoughts for a Young Man." He devotes himself very much to the young. He is very earnest and sincere; has a fine cerebral development, though small in the lungs. His introductory remarks this morning, and also his sermon, were exceedingly beautiful in spirit and in manner, all based on phrenology, and full of most delightful religious spirit. His people are sensible enough to have but one service a day: so we have spent the afternoon together, in company, too, with a college-educated farmer; and I find them full of a love of truth, entirely emancipated from old theological dogmas, and sympathizing hereby with all progress. Aside from Howe and Downer, I hardly know another such a lover of the true, and yet so young He wrote to me a long time ago for liberty to publish an edition of my "Thoughts for a Young Man," for gratuitous distribution.

I was put into a chamber last night with no sign of a fireplace; air like the inside of a cavern made in a snow-drift; and, as if that were not enough, the three doors of the room — one of which leads into the entry — were cut off at the top, so as to leave an opening five or six inches all round the house. Then I had a feather-bed and a comforter, and it was a dismal prospect; but I put a shawl round my head, leaving only a spiracle, or breathing-place, and really had a very good night's sleep, and came out this morning free from a cold. All this makes me want to get home again. It is some compensation, however, to find such a man and such a people. It shows what the people would be if Orthodoxy would let them alone. I wish I were clairvoyant enough to see how you all are, but must submit to the conditions of my nature. Perhaps the time will come when this will cease to be one of its conditions.

Washington, March 27, 1852.

C. Pierce, Esq.

Dear Sir, — . . . I found I was doing no good here, and that it seemed impossible for me to effect any; and therefore I took a short excursion into the State of New York, in hopes to redeem a little of my time from worthlessness by preaching the gospel of temperance and education. I spoke on these themes to willing or unwilling ears for about twenty-five successive nights, and returned in better health.

I find people in the western part of the State of New York more alive to the importance of thorough female education than we are in Massachusetts. They are seeking to reach the true point, however, not by public and free institutions for all, but by private institutions for those who can afford it. I spoke on this point to some social parties, not in the way of a lecture, but of a private conversation, with liberty of catechism. At Rochester, a meeting was held for the establishment of a female college whose curriculum of studies should be equal to that of other colleges; and some very sensible and energetic women are engaged in the enterprise. At Lima, about twenty miles from Rochester, they have a college for both sexes; and I was invited and present at two or three social parties where the young lady-students composed a part of the company. They have here a preparatory school of some six hundred or seven hundred pupils, whom I addressed. At M'Grawville, a little farther in the interior, is another college, whose doors are open not only for both sexes, but avowedly for all colors. Another college, already largely endowed,* is about to be opened at Yellow Springs, Ohio. Sixty thousand dollars are to be expended the ensuing summer for buildings. This is established with especial reference to the education of females. (Confidentially, what should you think of your humble servant's complying with a request to preside over this?) I think the young ladies of the West are stronger, larger, and better developed in every way, than those in Boston and its vicinity. A few miles out of Rochester, I attended an examination of a boarding-school, kept by Mrs. Brewster, formerly Miss Bloss, the historian; and I think I never saw twenty young ladies together to be compared to that number in her first class. There was not an ordinary-looking person among them; and twenty such foreheads I never beheld before "all in a row." I saw a great many intelligent and earnest people. Doubtless the character of my mission selected this class from among the masses as a magnet will pick out steel filings from sand, and brought them around me; but their existence and their affinities were the main thing to rejoice at. I advocated the Maine Law with the zeal of one crying in the wilderness.

I felt very deeply indebted to you for the pains you took to set me right in the matter of the Normal schoolhouse and premises. I was so much disturbed by the *apparent* course of ——, that I wrote him a letter of inquiry, putting the thing in a not unfriendly and uncomplaining manner, and making no reference to any sources of information. He replied at some length, solemnly declaring that he had never given any impression that the property belonged to the school, the Board, or the State; but, on the other hand, had showed Mr. Quincy's letter to all the people of West Newton and elsewhere who had any interest in knowing the facts. What think you of this? If his letter were by me, I would send it to you, that you might know how broad his denials are. It is enough to say they are as broad as language can make them.

---

* Mr. Mann proved to be mistaken about the endowment of this college. — ED.

As to politics, I do not know as there is any thing here that you do not know as well as we do. Congress does little else but intrigue for the respective candidates. The partisans are now so zealously at work for their respective favorites, that they have little time for assailing their opponents. As soon, however, as the nominations are made, the battle will be set in array, and the batteries will be played with Napoleon-like energy. I did not go to the North at all on a political mission; but still, where there was so much said, I could not but hear some of it. The hostility to Mr. Fillmore, throughout the northern and western parts of New York, is very intense. It is not merely an opposition of principle for his abandonment of all the great doctrines of freedom, but it is personal. The objections to Mr. Webster, so far as principle is concerned, are very much the same as those urged against Mr. Fillmore. As to the candidates of the other party, all you can say is, that one is as bad as possible, and the other a good deal worse. Any idea of getting a man who is as he should be is out of the question. I fear the only resource left us will be to get rid of the worst. But here you will say I touch on the expediency doctrine, which I shall not now attempt to discuss. . . .

M. sends very much love to you both. If R. were here, I know she would do the same; for she has it in her heart. So has

H. MANN.

WASHINGTON, April 24, 1852.

DR. JARVIS.

DEAR SIR, — I have just received your favor of the 19th instant, and the accompanying volumes; for which I am greatly obliged to you. If, as Adam Smith said, a man who makes two blades of grass grow where but one grew before be a "public benefactor," of what honor is he worthy who diffuses ideas regarding health and life among the people? The doctrines of human physiology have come in just in season to save the race from destruction. Had their advent been delayed much longer, it is doubtful whether men would have been able to discover them at all. They might have gone, like our Western Indians, beyond the gravitating point. You have done your part to save them.

Political parties here seem crystallizing about Fillmore and Scott. Our debates lately are mostly on the Presidential question ; but I don't think Mr. Webster's name has been mentioned for three weeks in reference to the matter.

What are you doing at home? From what I hear, the coalition is not making headway. If they are not, then I suppose Hunker Whiggery is. When Mr. Webster is dead, will Hunkerism die? I hope so.

You must see Kossuth. He has the best sort of greatness; that is, goodness. . . .

Yours very truly,

HORACE MANN.

WASHINGTON, May 8, 1852.

MY DEAR MR. COMBE, — We are on the verge of a Presidential election. Our political caldron is beginning to seethe vehemently. Macbeth's witches had nothing in theirs so baneful as that which gives character to ours. The political leaders desired to make it palatable to the South ; and hence they have saturated its contents with proslavery. Even under the application of the three-fifths basis of the Constitution in regard to the slave-representation in Congress, we can give nearly two-thirds of the Presidential votes. Could we only unite for freedom as the South do for slavery, all would be well ; but the lower and hinder half of the brain rules, and we do not. The acquisition of our new territory from Mexico, by robbery under the form of a treaty, gave opportunity for competition between our leaders for Southern support. . . . Mr. Fillmore, the present President, goes for what is called the " finality " of the compromises, and makes himself acceptable to the South by issuing proclamations, and giving instructions to marshals and prosecuting attorneys to enforce the Fugitive-slave Law. Mr. Webster tries to get some new popularity in the same quarter by lauding the same accursed law, and by maintaining that it is not only constitutional, but " proper " in itself. The only Whig candidate who is not fully committed on all these proslavery measures is Gen. Scott ; and towards him, therefore, the antislavery part of the Whigs are looking as their only hope. Portions, indeed, of the antislavery men, —

the abolitionists and no-government men, who vote nowhere ; the Liberty-party men, who will vote for no one who does not represent their views in full ; and the extreme men, perhaps, of the Free-soil party, — are as violent against Gen. Scott as against Gen. Cass. This repellency of bigots and partisans seems to act on the law of the "inverse ratio of the squares of the distances;" for they are much more violent against those who *almost* agree with them than against those who are at the opposite moral pole. How the contest will eventuate, it is impossible to foresee. Should the Whigs indorse the "compromise measures" of 1850, or should they nominate Mr. Fillmore or Mr. Webster, or should Gen. Cass, if nominated, come out in favor of the "compromise measures," the Democrats will certainly prevail. There seems to be but one chance for the Whigs to succeed ; namely, the contingency of their nominating Gen. Scott, and then of his non-indorsement of the "compromises." Of course, the greater portion of the antislavery people are hoping for this result.

Another great moral question is profoundly agitating the people of the Northern and Eastern States : it is the question of temperance. Between one and two years ago, such a concentration and pressure of influence was brought to bear upon the Legislature of the State of Maine, that though it is said that body was principally composed of anti-temperance men, yet it passed what has now become famous, and will forever be famous in the moral history of mankind, — the Maine Liquor Law. Its grand features are the search for and the seizure of all intoxicating liquors, and their destruction when adjudicated to have been kept for sale. It goes upon the ground that the Government cannot knock a human passion or a depraved and diseased appetite upon the head, but it can knock a barrel of whiskey or rum upon the head, and thus prevent the gratification of the passion or appetite ; and after a time the unfed appetite or passion will die out. The author of this law was Neal Dow, the mayor of the city of Portland. He enforced it, and it has worked wonders. The alms-house ceased to be replenished with inmates ; assaults and batteries became rare ; the jail-doors stood open ; and the police officers held almost sinecures. The success was so great, that the temperance party in other States have made it an element in popular elections; and though in most instances they have been defeated at the first trial, yet they are resolved to return again to the contest. The Legislature of the Territory of Minnesota passed the law, but provided that it should be submitted to the people for ratification; and it has been ratified by a popular vote! And, what is still more important, the Legislature of Massachusetts, now in session, has this very week, after one of the most earnest and protracted contests ever waged, passed a similar law. It is to be submitted to the people next month. If a majority vote for it, it is forthwith to become the law of the State. If a majority vote against it, then it is to be suspended in its operation, and we will agitate anew. But this, perhaps you will say, is an heroic remedy for the evils of intemperance. I acknowledge it. But, when a disease becomes so desperate, I go for heroic remedies. I would resort to surgical practice, and lose a limb to save a life, or deplete the whole body to reduce a topical inflammation that threatens to be fatal. When I saw you, I believe I used occasionally to take a very little wine; and I sometimes, though rarely, drank tea. I believe I had left off coffee long before. But, for many years past, I have abjured wine, coffee, tea, and every thing of a stimulating nature. I confine my beverage to the " pure element," and am a great deal better in health for the practice.

My whole family has been in Washington since the commencement of the session. . . . How I wish you could come here and see them! for then one of the greatest desires of my life would be answered; that is, I should see you.

How goes on the work of educating in your island? I had a printed account of an examination in your school; but how is it for the million? . . .

Your friend and disciple,   HORACE MANN.

WASHINGTON, May 13, 1852.

REV. E. FAY.

MY DEAR SIR, — No event in my life has ever caused me more deep and solemn anxiety than the application to become a candidate for the presidency of your proposed college at Yellow Springs, Ohio. At first, the impression made upon my mind by your proposal was not deep; and nothing but the habit which I have always had, never to decide important questions until after the fullest deliberation, prevented me from declining it at once. But I must now confess, that, from the day when I first had the pleasure of meeting you at Lima, the importance and attractiveness of the work proposed have not ceased to gain strength in my mind.

The two great ideas which win me toward your plan are, —

First, That of redressing the long-inflicted wrongs of woman by giving her equal advantages of education — I do not say in all respects an identical education, but equal advantages of education — with men; and, second, The idea of maintaining a non-sectarian college.

I have always had the deepest aversion to sectarianism, and to all systems of proselytism among Christian sects. I would enlighten the human mind with all true knowledge and with science; I would repress the growth of all evil propensities and desires; and, in doing this work, I would take the gospel of Jesus Christ as my text-book, and the life of Jesus Christ as my example. In this way, I would endeavor to train up children in the way they should go.

As far as possible, I would prepare every human being for that most important of all duties, the determining of his religious belief for himself. It seems to me that a generation so trained would have an infinitely better chance of getting at the truth than the present generation has had. I always look upon my own conclusions on questions of faith with a measure of distrust, lest I may have landed in possible error on one side, from the vigor of the spring which I gave to escape from what seemed certain error on the other.

These, sir, are my general views, with which you have a right to be acquainted before making your relations with me any more special or intimate.

Again: so strong, in order to that high degree of success at which I should aim, would be the necessity, not only of public and official co-operation, but of private and personal cordiality also, on the part of the faculty with whom I should be associated, that I should ask the privilege of nominating two of its members, subject, of course, to any reasonable objection of any kind which could be alleged against them. One of these would be a young gentleman, the other a young lady. You see, by this, that I should propose to introduce females into the corps of instructors. I do this, not only because I think they would make as good teachers as men, but because, when young ladies are assembled together for instruction, I think they need maternal as well as paternal counsel and guidance. As they do not leave their sex behind them, they should find mothers as well as fathers at the institutions where they reside. The claims of sex and sentiment are not to be thrust aside for those of intellect.

And one thing more. Recognizing the possibility of contingencies that cannot be foreseen, I think it would be best, should an appointment be tendered me, to accept of it at first as only a *pro tempore* one ; that is, to organize the institution, to stamp certain great features upon it, and to give it its direction and momentum. In this the greatness of the work would consist. When plans are settled, when instrumentalities are arranged and put in operation, the acquired impetus supplies, to a great extent, the place of original vigor; the obstacles are overcome, and the direction becomes a habit instead of a foresight. It is the " marshalling of affairs," as Lord Bacon expresses it, that demands the faculty of seeing results in initiatory processes, or effects in causes. In all this I should deem it no indignity to be held inferior, so far as natural capacity is concerned, to numerous or numberless others ; and the only advantage which could be claimed for me would be my life of experience on various and important theatres of action. It is the beautiful attributes of your enterprise that attract me toward it. Should I see these attributes organized, embodied, and in living operation, I might well claim the right to retire from its further administration.

The time at which we might look for such an event would be uncertain ; probably not less than two or three, nor more than five or six years. The graduation of the first class from the institution at the end of four years would seem a natural period ; but this might be shortened or prolonged by intervening circumstances.

The future would still be left open to any such arrangement as its own circumstances should counsel.

In the light of a mere worldly or pecuniary transaction, and as between parties, one of whom asks for wages, and the other promises to pay them, your proposition in regard to a salary is by no means satisfactory. Were that the only or the chief consideration, I should only send you the briefest words of declining; but it is very far from being so: and I assure you that your proposition looks now to my mind far more inviting than it did when you broached the subject, and spoke to me of a probable salary of $3,000. The moral side of the question has gone up more than the pecuniary has fallen down.

I do not make any serious account of this difference. A little yielding on both sides, either directly or indirectly, might probably bring us upon common and acceptable ground.

I have now touched upon the leading topics which occur to my mind as proper to be understood in this preliminary state of proceedings. The above seem to me the only conditions on which I could comply with the request you have so flatteringly urged. Whether acceptable or not, your institution will always have my best wishes; and you have the present tender of any unofficial services which at any time I may be able to render you.

Very truly and sincerely yours, &c.,

HORACE MANN.

WEST NEWTON, May 31, 1852.

REV. E. FAY.

MY DEAR SIR, — I had no sooner arrived at West Newton than I was unexpectedly summoned back to Washington to attend to indispensable business. I have just reached home again, and found your letter of the 26th inst.

I regret that I had not understood some features of your plan before, as it might have terminated negotiations at once. Please inform me if I am to understand that each "scholarship owner" is entitled to a vote in choosing the Faculty, and also in dismissing them. If so, I fear you will find it impracticable to obtain a complement of suitable officers. Supposing you have twelve or eighteen hundred entitled to vote. On any sudden clamor against any officer, however unfounded, a sufficient number of these might be assembled to eject him. Dissatisfied students might disaffect their patrons. Enmities are more active than friendships. Most people will go farther to gratify a grudge than to reward merit. The malcontents, therefore, might easily be assembled, while the contents would remain at home, and thus a man's fate be determined, and his reputation sacrificed, without any of the guaranties of innocence. I make these remarks without any suggestion or suspicion that your contributors are not as fair and honorable as any body of men so constituted can be. Doubtless they are even pre-eminently fair and honorable. I do it also with the hope, not to say confidence, that I myself, and those appointed to act with me, could get along as well as the average of men under such circumstances. My point refers to the very nature of such a relation. I think I could refer to several crises in all our New-England colleges, when all the officers, or at least a majority of them, would have been swept away under such an organization. If not right in this understanding of your plan, please inform me ; and, if you can obviate the force of the above suggestions, I shall be happy to hear your arguments.

Your remarks in relation to the appointment of those personal friends of mine have much force in the abstract; but they apply only partially. The young gentleman and lady to whom I referred are a nephew and niece of mine, whose education and the formation of whose character I have watched over, and in a good degree directed, from their childhood. He has now been engaged in teaching for fifteen or eighteen years with unvaried success, and the lady for ten or twelve. She is now a teacher in one of our Normal schools. Both are of the very highest grade of character ; have large attainments, and the habits of industry which are a promise of continued acquisition. He is a Baptist; she is a Unitarian. The religious life of both would be acceptable to all good men.

I do not think of any "Orthodox" man at the West for the station you mention ; but I know one here who would, as I believe, be admirably qualified for the department of mathematics, especially *applied* mathematics. He was for many years a teacher in an academy, and has since been a practical engineer and machinist ;

24

and, in the value of the instruction he would impart, has probably no superior in the country.

May I have the pleasure of hearing from you soon?

Very truly yours, &c.,

HORACE MANN.

WASHINGTON, June 24, 1852.

E. W. CLAP, ESQ.

MY DEAR SIR, — I left home on Saturday, stopped over Sunday in New York, and came on on Monday. At Philadelphia I heard the news of the nomination; and, when I arrived at Baltimore, the first men I saw were some of our Massachusetts Hunker delegates. Sadder-looking men away from a funeral I never saw. The Fill more and Webster men composed a majority of the convention, and therefore had every thing their own way in the organization; in the Committee on Credentials, by which they let in all their friends, and shut out all their enemies, without reference to the fairness or unfairness of their election — just as the Democrats did Rantoul; and also in the Committee on Resolutions.

But, when they came to the nomination, the antislavery and anti-compromise portion of the convention prevailed; and, if they did not win a full triumph, their enemies suffered a terrible defeat. They withstood not only the Southern slavery phalanx, but all the influence of the Government, and all the mammon Hunkerism of State Street, Wall Street, and Walnut Street. . . .

H. M.

WASHINGTON, June 24, 1852.

. . . When the Whig Convention nominated Scott, they killed off those who had been most clamorous for slavery, and therefore did a great work. Though not a triumph of antislavery sentiment, there-fore, it was a defeat of Hunkerism at the North, and of slavery domination at the South. It was the first antislavery stand in a National Convention that has ever been successful. So far it is matter for thanksgiving and hallelujah. But it adopted the pro-slavery platform. This was effected by the union of the slavery men of the South, and the Hunkers or Fillmore and Webster men of the North. These together made a large majority ; one hundred and forty-nine being a majority. All these men worked together in the organization for the Committee on Credentials and for the Platform Committee, and were, of course, successful. But, when they came to candidates, they split. Nothing could carry enough of the Webster men over to Fillmore, or enough of the Fillmore men over to Webster, to make a majority. A portion of each knew of the other, — what all sensible and unbiassed men knew, — that the nomination of the other would be death to the party ; and they would not defeat the party, even for the nomination of a favorite. Thus it was done, and thus it was not done.

There is such an infinite difference between Scott and Pierce, that all true antislavery men must desire the success of the former. About ten or a dozen Whigs from the South, and about the same number of Fillmore men, went over for Scott. This is all that could be meant by the South's supporting Scott or abandoning the compromises. They have got them *in form*, but not much more. The reason why they say Scott adopts the Southern platform is, that he accepts the nomination of the party that adopts the platform ; and, indeed, his telegraphic despatch to the convention was, that he accepted the nomination with the platform. But as many interpretations can be given to the platform as to the Thirty-nine Articles. And, besides, the Whig Platform, though disgraceful to human nature, is not so black by many hues as the Democratic.

I read this morning the greater part of Kossuth's speech at the Tabernacle, New York. Is it not his *greatest speech?*

We are now taking the question, by yeas and nays, on the passage of a bill to give a certain quantity of the public lands to the old States for educational purposes ; and it looks as if it would go through the House. I hope so with all my organ of hope.

WASHINGTON, June 29, 1852.

Mr. Clay is dead : he expired between eleven and twelve o'clock this morning. . . . Probably no public man ever had more ardent or more numerous friends. He was a man of great nobleness of heart. He has impressed his mind upon the policy of the country ; an impress, however, which is becoming fainter every year. On the

slavery question, he has always been far in advance of the people
among whom he lived.   Had he belonged to the North, he would
have become an antislavery man, and not a treacherous or perfidious
one like Mr. Webster.   He has lived to see Webster die a moral
death, and Webster sees him die a natural one.   I have no doubt,
such has been the secret hostility between them, that each is rejoiced
at the fortune of the other.   Rivals for public favor for so many
years, their competition is now at an end   Both have failed in the
supreme object of their ambition.   Would that all politicians and
all men would learn a lesson from so instructive an example !

WASHINGTON, July 1, 1852.

MY DEAR MR. COMBE, — . . . My friend Henry Barnard, Esq.,
who for many years was Secretary of the Board of Education, either
in Connecticut or in Rhode Island, is about to visit England and
Scotland, partly on account of his health, and partly to see your
schools.   You have always been partial enough to affix a higher
value to my services on the subject of education than I could honestly claim or fairly expect.   If you will put double all the credit
you have ever given to me, and pass it to Mr. Barnard's account,
you will hardly do his extraordinary services more than justice.
His mind is full of wisdom, and his life has been full of devotion on
this subject.

You will have learned, before receiving this, the event of our party
Presidential nomination.   What an awful moral has been derived from
the fate of those who have been false to freedom !   Every one of
those Northern men, who, for the last half-dozen years, have devoted
themselves to slavery, have been set aside ; and those men who
suffered and indirectly promoted all the atrocities of the Mexican
war, though against all their own professions, did, by that very
dereliction from duty, raise up two warriors to come in and pluck
away the honors they had forfeited their integrity to obtain.   Was
it not a just retribution ?

There is all the difference between the candidates that there is
between a hero and his *valet de chambre*.   Scott, too, is an antislavery man.   Pierce will be the merest tool of slavery.   The

Democratic Convention was almost *in toto* a proslavery body, and the ultra proslavery portion of it prevailed in the selection of Pierce. In the Whig Convention, the antislavery element prevailed; so that, though the contest is implicated with other matters, and its real issues are somewhat obscured, yet, if Scott is elected, it will be a great antislavery triumph. It was the first time that the antislavery element ever prevailed in *any* national convention.

Mrs. Mann and the children have gone home. I live here alone, and, of course, forlorn. I hear from them every day, and they are well. With kindest regards to yourself and Mrs. Combe,

I remain, as ever, yours truly,

HORACE MANN.

The long and tender friendship which existed between Mr. Mann and Mr. Barnard, beginning in their common duties in the educational field, finds little record in these pages, for the want of letters which have been lost. They always took counsel together, and, though men of different theological views, were equally liberal and universal in their administration of schools; feeling alike that it was the vital and not the speculative part of religion that should be taught in them.

JULY 8, 1852.

. . . I see by the telegraphic report, that at a meeting of the Native-American party at Trenton, N. J., this week, Mr. Webster was nominated for the Presidency. This makes his position supremely ridiculous. It is an insignificant party, founded on the narrow basis of being born *in* America or *out* of it. If Mr. Webster does not notice it, there stands the nomination to show his power. If he declines it, everybody will laugh at him.

WASHINGTON, Aug. 10, 1852.

REV. THEO. PARKER.

MY DEAR SIR, — I hope you did not think the two queries which I put to Mrs. Mann imposed any necessity on you to write an answer; though I am so glad to hear from you, that I might be tempted to use means a little irregular for that end.

I sent the question about Gen. Scott's supposititious policy because I think *justice* to be the *highest policy.* I know you think so too. It being my belief that Scott is an anti-war man and an anti-annexation man, I think it wrong, or rather it would be very wrong in me, to intimate the contrary. Besides, the tendency of all such statements is to put the two Presidential candidates, Scott and Pierce, upon the same ground; whereas I think their principles, desires, and purposes are very diverse. I know there is little if any difference in the platforms; but there may be all the difference there is between life and death in two pilots, though both profess to steer by the same chart. One may wreck you, while the other may get you safely into port.

A strong effort is made, by men who care more for democracy than for antislavery, to make it out that freedom has more to hope from the success of Pierce than from that of Scott; but this I believe to be a great mistake, and I do not think the argument ingenuous.

As to the amount of the Free-soil vote, it must be remembered, that, in 1848, New York alone gave one hundred and twenty thousand votes for Van Buren. Now, if she gives fifty thousand, I shall be agreeably disappointed.

Our loss of Rantoul is very great. I am also struck with exceeding sadness, because this is the second blow that our cause has received. Taylor's death let in the whole pack of slavery bloodhounds, and they have wantoned in their power ever since. Will not Rantoul's death unleash another pack? I fear so. Nothing but my faith in God saves me from despair; for just now I can hardly " walk by sight."　　　　　　　　　　　　　　　H. M.

WASHINGTON, July 15, 1852.

I walked an hour yesterday, including sunset-time, on the southeast terrace; and a greater variety and variegation of the " fields of air " I never saw. There was no wind; so that the changes were merely atmospheric and chemical. But such rapidity of scene-shifting I never before saw. At every turn I took, a new celestial tapestry was displayed. There was no noise of ropes and pulleys: but the change was complete. The Gobelins could make nothing finer; but oh! for extent and rapidity of production, what are the Gobelins to the great Manufacturer? How I longed for you and the children!

I see that Mr. Tallmadge of New York comes into direct collision with Mr. Webster's "retainers" in Boston. He made a public speech in New-York City the evening of the day that Mr. Webster passed through there. In that speech, he said he had seen Mr. Webster that day, who told him there was nothing to be done but to support the regular nominations. This statement the "Boston Journal" says it is "authorized directly and authoritatively to deny." This brings out Mr. Tallmadge, who re-affirms his statement. The truth is, Webster is so deeply wounded he cannot get cured. He would rather defeat everybody than be thus set aside himself.

JULY 16.

. . . Miss Beecher prays, if I want any more comfort in this life, that I will not try to build up a college at the West, and says Mr. Stowe held up his hands in deprecation at the thought. So you see what persons who *know* about things think our prospect would be.

I should like to see Father Pierce anywhere, even in a picture; but still think that he and I, and such looking people, ought to let those who don't know us inquire how we look, rather than show our faces.

I see that some one, in a Maine paper, says he wanted to nominate Ralph Waldo Emerson for President, and Nathaniel Hawthorne for Vice-President; but, seeing they have such good men as Scott and Graham up, he concludes not to do any thing more about it. Wit ought not to run its head against a stump of any kind. That man forgot that both President and Vice-President cannot come from the same State.

I do feel homesick here. When I was here in the summer of '48, I had so much to do, that I had no time to think how I felt: I was still Secretary then. The next summer I spent here (1850) was the year of the slavery controversy; and I was too much alive to the immense interests at stake to have any consciousness of my own personal pleasures or sufferings. But this summer there is nothing to engross me, and my thoughts fly home, morning, noon. and night. I see nobody, and live a lonely life, and, I fear, an unprofitable one. I am thinking all the time that it is the last summer I shall ever spend in Washington.

JULY 27.

. . . I should like to see Rev. Theodore Parker move a table without touching it, directly or indirectly. Suppose what we call electricity is the motive power of the universe, embracing magnetism, caloric, gravitation, &c.; suppose the vital principle in us — at least the principle of mere physical life — is electricity too: may not an organized possessor of this principle be able to exert a force stronger than that which operates upon unorganized bodies, or one organized being be able to exert a controlling influence over another organized being? If so, why may not the battery in a man's brain overcome the natural gravitation of a table? I have seen a magnet, that could lift but a few pounds when acting alone, lift seventeen hundred-weight when a current of magnetism was poured through it. Now, if the brain could evolve this amount, why should not that lift according to its size, structure, &c.? This is all I have to say on the subject.

Kossuth designed to leave, as I suppose, in a way to secure privacy. As for his going *incog.* for any bad purpose, I do not believe a word of it; nor have I heard a lisp, to prove it, of any credible testimony. A report was sent abroad that he had gone without paying his debts. There could not have been a word of truth in it: a regular Hunker lie.

I agree with you that history is bad reading for children. What, then, must be thought of a great part of the Old Testament, which records as terrible crimes as any to be found on record? It is too terrible a world to make children acquainted with. It is said we must look back to get wisdom to direct us when going forward. I hope we shall soon get wisdom elsewhere, or be so far advanced as to need no past warning. Biography *of the right sort of lives* is the better reading for children. And science, and the elements of science, — what can be better than that, where we do see God in his works? Here the mind will find its true discipline.

I send you a "Liberator," which has a communication from the *reformed* John Wesley, on the last page; also a speech of Mr. T. Parker's, on the inside. What can Mr. Parker mean by saying, that, if Gen. Scott is elected, we shall probably have an annexation of a "large slice" of Mexico during the next four years? Will the good gained by making a man out worse than he is repay the evil? Mr. Parker has been so much wronged himself, that he should be careful about wronging others.

In 1837, in a speech delivered in New York by Mr. Webster, he said, —

"On the general question of slavery, a great portion of the community is already strongly excited. The subject has not only attracted attention as a question of politics, but it has struck a far deeper-toned chord. It has arrested the religious feelings of the country; it has taken strong hold on the consciences of men. He is a rash man indeed, little conversant with human nature, and especially has he a very erroneous estimate of the character of the people of this country, who supposes that a feeling of this kind is to be trifled with or despised. It will assuredly cause itself to be respected. It may be reasoned with; it may be made willing — I believe it is entirely willing — to fulfil all existing engagements and all existing ties; to uphold and defend the Constitution as it is established, with whatever regrets about some provisions which it does actually contain : but to coerce it into silence, to endeavor to restrain its free expression, to seek to compress and confine it, warm as it is, and more heated as such endeavors would inevitably render it, — should all this be attempted, I know nothing, even in the Constitution or in the Union itself, which would not be endangered by the explosion which might follow."

What an apostasy has his been!

WASHINGTON, July 27, 1852.

MY DEAR DOWNER, — What is said about the Pittsburg Convention? From what I see and hear, I apprehend the current of feeling in Massachusetts sets in favor of nominating Hale, rather than Chase. For any genuine Free-soiler this would be the worst policy. That nomination should be such as to cut into the Demo-

cratic party.   Notwithstanding all that some of the Free-soil papers
say about the equal proslaveryism of Scott and Pierce, it is not at
all improbable there is the whole difference between the annexation and the *un*-annexation of Cuba, between the division and the
non-division of California, in these candidates.   How, then, can any
real lover of liberty fail to give the scales such a turn as shall check
slavery, and hold it at bay ?   Are not our Free-soil friends, in their
zeal to help the fortunes of the coalition, misled on this point ?
You, who have great influence with them, ought to make that
influence felt.   I wish you were to be at Pittsburg.   The nomination there made may bar slavery, or help it on.   To-morrow,
Summer means to speak.   He needs combativeness, which he has
not got.   Don't you think I could spare him a little of mine,
with advantage to us both ?   He will make a great speech, be assured of that.   He has all the material of all who have hitherto
argued the question ; and, besides, the greatest speech can always
be made on the right side.

I am awfully homesick.   The summer is dull : nothing is upon
the *tapis* in which I take any special interest, and my heart is with
my family.

    With affectionate regards to you and yours,

                    I am, as ever, your friend,

                                HORACE MANN.

Aug. 8.   I have sad news for you to-day ; which, however, you
will have heard before this reaches you.

Mr. Rantoul is dead.

I have been spending the morning about him, and the arrangements to be made on his account.   It will devolve on me to announce his death in the House to-morrow : so I can write you no
more to-day.

Aug. 9.   The melancholy duty is done. . . . Poor Mrs. Rantoul !
Of course it is a case where there is no language of external signs.
The heart alone knows it.   She arrived in the morning : he died
that night.   Every thing was done that could be done.   Funeral
services were performed at his lodgings.   At four o'clock, Mrs.

Rantoul, accompanied by several friends, took the cars for home. What a sad meeting !

WASHINGTON, Aug. 12, 1852.

I never had the slightest doubt that the "old Hunkers" of Massachusetts would rejoice over Rantoul's death. The Hunkers rejoice in his removal, just as the proslavery men rejoiced in Gen. Taylor's death, some of whom said they believed it to be an express interposition of Providence to defeat his work !

Drayton and Sayres are pardoned through Sumner's influence, and off in free territory. This was done last evening. The marshal of the district, who has the control of the jail, received the order for their enlargement last evening. He called on Sumner to go to the jail with him, but learned from the jailer that Mr. Stuart, the Secretary of the Interior, a Virginia man, had sent to him to delay their enlargement till this morning. Sumner saw at once what his object was, — that is, to get a requisition from the Governor of Virginia to take them into Virginia for trial; for some of the slaves whom they took in their schooner were from Virginia. He therefore insisted on the marshal's executing the order of the President for their release immediately ; and, as the marshal had no responsible excuse for not complying, they went to the jail, and the men were enlarged. Sumner took them up into the street, and then made arrangements at once for taking them to Baltimore last night, which was done ; and this morning they started from Baltimore for a free State, and are *safe*. He was afraid some sham process would be got up to hold them here until notice could be given to the Governor of Virginia. They are safe. Sumner has done well in this : but it could not have been done until *now;* that is, until the nominations had been made.

AUG. 15.

I have not gone the journey yet, and do not know that I shall. If a little bit of a speech which I am thinking of, but not talking about, were off my hands, I might ; but I do not know when it will be, if at all. . . .

I had encouragement for the floor when I wrote to you: but the House passed a resolution stopping debate ; so the promise was worth nothing. The next time we go into " Committee of the Whole," &c., we, of course, shall have a new chairman, and then I shall be as far off as ever.

Aug. 17.

Miss Dix's bill is now up. We are calling the yeas and nays upon it. It will pass, I think, without doubt; but I shall let you know before I seal this.

Miss Dix finds new work all the time. This District has about forty lunatics, which it supports at the Institution of Maryland, near Baltimore. These are all to be turned out in a few days; and she is trying to get a bill passed for a hospital in this District. . . .

The bill for a hospital has passed the House ! . . .

I thought I was to have the floor just now, and my heart went pit-a-pat; for I have never yet been able to speak anywhere without trepidation. But the chairman gave it to another man. At ten minutes to three, I shall try again.

Miss Dix's bill passed by yeas 98, nays 54. It always took two-thirds to get it up: so a majority did not help us.

Miss Dix is alarmed about her land-bill in the Senate; but I think it will go through there. She wishes to get through here, so that she can go to Nova Scotia, where they have made an appropriation for a hospital. . . .

I had rather a boisterous time for half an hour with my speech. It blew hard; but I weathered the storm.

Don't be alarmed when you see what Polk said about my not holding myself responsible; that is, according to the laws of the *duello*. He is a poor drunken fellow from Tennessee, for whom no one has any respect, though he is brother of the former President. They tried to choke me down: but they might as well have tried to roar down old Boreas; for, when I " gets *up* " a little, I am quite as hard to be subdued as the more noisy ones.

I hope to have it all printed, and perhaps in your hands, this week.

You will see what an attack Polk made on Parson Fowler yesterday, — not violent and furious, but annoying. He said to the parson coseyly, while speaking, " You know we two are Christians."

Polk is drunk every day. But it is now said that it will be honorably arranged, and there will be no " coffee and pistols " between them.

Aug. 27, 1852.

Sumner spoke about four hours yesterday; and it was a very finished and able speech, sustaining in every point his high reputation as a jurist and a scholar. It was delivered in a very elegant and finished manner. To speak in full, the 26th of August, 1852, redeemed the 7th of March, 1850.

Webster came into the Senate very early in the speech. He took a seat not far from Sumner, and about eight feet from me ; so situated that I must look into his face, or turn my head. I looked at him fascinatingly. I think he felt the magnetism streaming out of me. In about two minutes, his countenance fell : he got up and walked round to the other side of the Senate Chamber, staid a while, and went off. Sumner, during all the time he was there, was in the least solid part of his speech. It was one of his best orations, well studied and well delivered, and will tell on the country, and be a speech for a book and for history.

That drunken Clemens of Alabama jumped up *instanter*, and said, —

" Mr. President, it is proper sometimes to take notice of the ravings of a lunatic ; but the yelpings of a puppy are not to be regarded."

Miss Dix's bill has gone over to the next session. She sent for me yesterday afternoon in despair. But she has got an appropriation of a hundred thousand dollars for a hospital in this District ; and it is thought that her land-bill can be carried next session. It has passed the House, and, unless some amendments are made to it, will not have to come back here again.

Aug. 28.

. . . I got off a speech yesterday ; but it was too late to let you know by yesterday's mail. The Southern men tried to stop me by starting points of order. But it was always without reason : so I went on, and gave them a pretty strong blast. I think it best to show them that they can't stop debate; that, the more they try, the more it won't stop.

I wish I could be at home to behold the flowers and their beholders; but it is of no use to talk about that at present.

WASHINGTON, Aug. 28, 1852.

REV. A. CRAIG.

MY DEAR SIR, — I heard of a fact to-day which gave me temporary pleasure and permanent pain. It was that you had been applied to to become a member of the Faculty of Antioch College, and had declined. When the idea of your being connected with that institution flashed through my mind, it awakened every thing of hope, and turned hope into certainty. It was a revulsion of feeling, that carried my blood with it, to hear you had declined.

A man like you will do good anywhere; but how can you do so much good anywhere else on this earth as before children and with children, and transfusing your spirit into young men and women?

Had it ever occurred to me that you were a candidate with the committee, I do not know that I should not have made your acceptance a *sine qua non*. I know of no man in the world whose daily co-operation in such a work I should so much delight in as in yours. I do not expect, even on the contingency of my appointment, to remain connected with the institution for many years. My health and age denote this. How delightful the idea of leaving it in the hands of such a man as yourself! — able to work, willing to work, and qualified to work in the best spirit, and, of course, with the best results.

I have not time to write you at any length. I send you this *lament* from the midst of the roar and din of our Babel; and can only add, that I do most vehemently hope, that, if a professorship is tendered you, you will accept it.

Can you not come and see us this autumn at West Newton?

Yours most truly,

HORACE MANN.

CHAPTER VI.

ON the 15th of September, 1852, Mr. Mann was nominated for Governor of Massachusetts by a convention of the Free Democracy of the State assembled at Lowell. On the same day, he was chosen President of Antioch College, at Yellow Springs, Greene County, Ohio. He accepted the latter office. I give one or two paragraphs from speeches of his friends in regard to the former nomination. In the State Convention of the Free Democracy in 1852, the Hon. Anson Burlingame said, after the nomination of Mr. Mann for Governor, —

" As to the candidate we have nominated, I shall say nothing but that his fame is as wide as the universe. It was my fortune to be, some time since, in Guildhall, London, when a debate was going on. The question was, whether they should instruct their representatives in favor of secular education. They voted that they would not do it. But a gentleman then rose, and read some statistics from one of the Reports of the Hon. Horace Mann. That extract reversed the vote in the Common Council of London. I never felt prouder of my country. I call upon the young men of the Commonwealth, who have grown up under the inspiration of his free schools, to sustain their champion, and to carry his name over the hills and through the pleasant valleys of Massachusetts during the present canvass, with that enthusiasm which shall result in a glorious victory."

Seth Webb, Esq., at the same convention, said, —

" Two years ago, in spite of her old resistance to tyrants and her Anglo-Saxon devotion to the indestructible rights of all, Massachusetts was forced, under the lead of her chosen and mighty but apostate champion, to draggle her imperial wings in the bloody tears of a slave. From that day of horror, the statue of Liberty has been veiled among us; and the veil is not yet quite, though partially, withdrawn. The deed of shame will not be perfectly effaced until we place in the executive chair of Massachusetts a governor who is for liberty, and nothing but liberty, from the crown of his head to the sole of his foot; who will guard the personal security of the humblest and weakest individual on her soil with all the civil and military force in the Commonwealth; and who, if the feeblest infant were carried from her limits in violation of eternal rights and the laws of the State, would bring it back, if need be, at the head of an army, or resign his office for shame. Such a man, we believe, is Horace Mann. On the 5th day of April, 1851, Thomas Simms was carried away. On the 25th of April, 1851, Charles Sumner was elected senator of the United States. That was our first answer to the act. If we can follow it with the election of Horace Mann as Governor, I think we may rest somewhat content."

And Hon. Henry Wilson, at the same convention, said, —

" Gentlemen, you have selected, as your standard-bearer in the coming contest, one of the ablest men of Massachusetts and of the country. For six years he has on the floor of Congress, with fidelity, maintained the principles of the ' old man eloquent,' whose successor he is. The Whigs in convention assembled, a few days after the death of Mr. Adams, whose closing years were devoted to freedom and humanity, resolved that they wished their representative to follow in the track of Mr. Adams, and to be true to liberty. Mr. Mann was the nominee of that convention. And to-day there is not a man, here or in Massachusetts, that does not know, that at all times, and on all occasions, he has been true to the vote of the Whig party in the year that they put him in nomination, and true to the cause of freedom. And though, gentlemen, after being thus true, he was sacrificed, or the attempt was made to sacrifice him, by the Webster retainers of the Eighth Congressional District, yet the people, the Free Democracy, hundreds of Democrats of that district, and, to their honor be it said, many Whigs who could not bow to slavery, took him and sustained him, and all together returned him to Congress by an overwhelming expression of popular approbation. Within a few days he has uttered, on the floor of Congress, one of the most brilliant speeches for liberty that ever fell from human lips in our own or any other country. Over the struggles of the future it will exert an influence perhaps unequalled by any effort of our time."

WEST NEWTON, Sept. 10, 1852.

REV. S. J. MAY.

MY DEAR SIR, — You say so many kind things of my speech, that I am *nonplussed*. It really seems to me a very moderate affair, and was so far below what I wanted to say, that I had actually come to the conclusion not to speak. But some of my friends said I *must* speak, even if I did not print: so you have it. *Valeat quantum*, &c.

Does it not seem as if the Lord was not on our side? Think of losing Rantoul, who held many a bad man under his hand, who will now run riot; and Mr. Fowler, who was a real Free-soil Whig, and stood very much as I stood in 1848! . . .

Yours very truly,

HORACE MANN.

WEST NEWTON, Oct. 20, 1852.

REV. THEODORE PARKER.

MY DEAR SIR, — I am afraid you will be "sorry you 'listed," so many requests for service are appended thereto.

The enclosed correspondence explains itself, as they say; only that my letter is so misprinted, from the middle onwards, as to make worse nonsense than I did.

You will see that the New-Bedford people are in a rage. I have allowed the colored race superiority of the affections and sentiments, — the upper end of man's nature; but they want the intellect too. As for their "demon" of colonization, I did not hint at it; but so Richertson tries to understand me.

Now, they have requested the "Liberator" to publish the correspondence; and, if my friend P—— could get hold of such a thing,

my experience teaches me that nothing would delight his pious soul
more than to make the worst of it.   The colored people of Boston
are, at present, very well disposed towards me and our cause ; but
it would be in the power of the "Liberator" to turn all their sac-
charine into acetous by the infusion of one phial-full of innuendo or
suspicion about California.   Can you stop the chemical operation ?
You can, if any man can ; and therefore I take the liberty to trouble
you with the enclosed and this clumsy explanation, and remain, as
ever, yours most truly,

HORACE MANN.

WEST NEWTON, Nov. 8, 1852.

REV. A. CRAIG.

MY DEAR SIR, — I owe you certainly as much as one apology a
day for all the time your late excellent and beautiful letters have
lain before me unanswered.   But I have only to mention the word
"business" or "engagements," and you will understand all the
rest, and forgive me.

Last week, the first Faculty meeting of Antioch College was held
at my house.   They were here two whole days, and parts of the
preceding and following.   We had a very full and free discussion
on a great variety of points, and came most harmoniously to unanimous conclusions.   We have sketched a *provisional*, not *final*,
course of preparatory and undergraduate studies, which I intend to
copy and send to you for your revision and suggestions.

I found a most remarkable coincidence of opinion and sentiment
among the persons present, not only as to theory, but in practical
matters. . . . We were all teetotalers ; all anti-tobacco men ; all
antislavery men ; a majority of us believers in phrenology ; all anti-
emulation men, — that is, all against any system of rewards and
prizes designed to withdraw the mind from a comparison of itself
with a standard of excellence, and to substitute a rival for that
standard.   We agreed entirely in regard to religious and chapel
exercises, &c.   The meeting was very satisfactory, and has raised
my hopes very much as to the ultimate success of the enterprise.   I
can never, however, sufficiently regret that you are not of our
number.   I hope you will be ere long.

I read to the persons present a part of your letter of Oct. 14, in which you speak of a *magazine* for the place. We all exclaimed that you were the person to carry out your own idea. You must leave your limited circle at Blooming Grove, and speak to them, and to all good men from Yellow Springs. What a wide sphere for your improving influence !

You speak of lectures and of my lecturing. We have no Orthodox lecturers of any great celebrity amongst us. Emerson, Whipple, Parker, T. S. King, Sumner, Pierpont, &c., are all heretics of a very malignant type when tried by the Orthodox standard. The truth is, the iron bars of Orthodoxy do not allow a man to expand into the qualities indispensable for touching the common heart of men. Witness Beecher and Bushnell, who reach the public soul only because they have broken from their cage. . . .

Yours most truly,

HORACE MANN.

The meeting in question proved to be no true test of the opinions of several members present, one of whom afterwards ripened into the most deadly enemy of Mr. Mann and of the college ; and another of whom, not a member of the Faculty proper, almost shipwrecked the institution by mismanagement of its financial affairs. Indeed, its final pecuniary ruin may be largely traced to this cause.

WEST NEWTON, Nov. 22, 1852.

REV. A. CRAIG.

MY DEAR SIR, — . . . I have a strong desire to see you, and will try to be with you on the 8th of December next. My hesitation has arisen only from the fact of my having a cold ; or, what is worse, my extreme sensibility to colds. I need very much to be put into a better body. My health was ruined before I knew how to take care of it. My own house has a genial, summer temperature all winter ; and, on a lecturing expedition last week, I was obliged to sleep in a kind of barn-chamber, where I contracted a terrible cold. I have thawed it out of me to some extent, and hope to get over it wholly. In making an engagement for the 8th of December, I must express, what is always implied, sickness excepted. It is but right, however, to add, that, with all my engagements for the last twenty years, I have never failed in but one of them; and then the doctors forbade my getting up from my bed to meet it.

Your little tract is admirable. How it would suit George Combe! When I go to you, you must give me some for distribution.

My subject will be "Great Britain," unless you can have all your teachers present from the region round about; in which case, if preferred, I would deliver a lecture to teachers. The latter I should personally prefer; but I should want a sufficient number of teachers, besides the *ex-officio* teachers, fathers and mothers, to feel sure that I had some special sympathizers.

Yours as ever, very truly,
HORACE MANN.

SALEM, Nov. 25, 1852.

. . . By the papers which I see this morning, I think it is almost certain that the coalition is defeated. Rum and proslavery have done it. And, though I hope they will not yet triumph in Massachusetts, the opposite principles are not likely to be in the ascendant. We must fall back again upon our unfailing support, that God is just; and rely upon the future, since we have so little encouragement in the present. It is disastrous. As for my personal relations to the result, they are not worth a thought. I was prepared for it, so far as I am concerned, but could have rejoiced heartily in the triumph of our cause, or rather causes. This opens to me the prospect of a year of comparative leisure, which I need. I have a great deal of work to do with my brain, and now see some prospect that it may be done. Personally it may be all for the best, and for the Western enterprise *better yet*.

CINCINNATI, Dec. 1, 1852.

Here I am. I wish you could know it before this can reach you. . . . While in the boat on the Ohio (by the way, I think I shall never venture to commit any offence, and then run away for impunity), sitting quietly reading, a gentleman came up, and asked if this was Mr. Mann. Of course, I had to confess. He said he believed I knew a sister of his; and after a pause added, "Grace Greenwood." It was her brother, who lives in Cincinnati. Soon he introduced me to his mother; and there stood revealed the whole mystery of Grace's genius. She is a beautiful old lady; must be seventy or seventy-five (for married ladies, especially if they have nine children, *may* be so old). She says she was brought up after the strictest sect of the Orthodox, but she has wandered very far from them now. She went to visit her friends in Connecticut many years ago. Divisions had broken the old society in pieces; and a Unitarian had been settled, and was preaching in the meeting-house where she sat when a child. There was to be a meeting; and she tried to persuade her relatives to accompany her, but they would not countenance so bad a man. She went, and was delighted. She went on and described the minister, but could not remember his name. I said, "Mr. May?" — "Oh, yes!" she replied.

She talks excellent sense in good language. She is a good woman to be born of.

Washington, Dec. 5, 1852.

Here I am in slave-land again. It is the charmingest of days. The eastern sky, as seen from my window, is all golden with the morning light. What a world, if it only had *fit* inhabitants!

I hope you will keep the children out as much as possible this winter. I long to have them healthy, and inured to hardships. What a blessing it is to be able to endure physical exposures! It is next to being able to endure moral ones.

The Baileys more than hinted to me that Mrs. Stowe is getting a second park of artillery ready, which will be more formidable to the South than all the metal of "Uncle Tom's Cabin." You know, throughout the South, the answer made to her first work is, that it is an exaggeration, a caricature; so strong an over-statement, that it is not merely valueless, but mischievous. This view the Northern Hunkers adopt; and the English, so far as they dare. Now, her *recalcitration* is to collect facts, and accumulate them, from

Southern authorities, proving all, and more than all, the abominations she has described, out of their own mouths. Won't this be a
stiffener? God bless her! I think I will write to her to-day, and
put her on the track of some enormities which will help to deepen
the damnation of her accusers.

CLEVELAND, Dec. 13, 1852.

A striking development came out here yesterday respecting the
course of Andrew Jackson Davis, who is here lecturing on the
" spiritual world" matters. To give the whole force of the incident,
I must go back a little. When Mr. Parker was out here a few
weeks ago, he was advertised to lecture on a certain evening; but
the train of cars was delayed by some accident, and he did not
arrive in season. The audience being all assembled, Davis, who
was present, walked upon the platform, and told them he would
occupy a portion of the time. He said he could give them what
Parker's lecture would be; but he had some get-off to excuse himself for not doing it. He was afterwards *badgered* for saying he
could do it, and not doing it; and was told it would have been an
excellent chance for demonstrating, in an irrefutable manner, the
soundness of his claims to a knowledge of the absent and future.

Yesterday afternoon, he was lecturing again; and now was presented the opportunity he had so foolishly lost before. So he said
Mr. Horace Mann was to lecture here on Tuesday evening next,
on woman; and he would communicate to his audience some things
that I should say. He went on to detail some parts of what my
lecture would be; when a Mr. Morton, who had read a report of it,
in Davis's own words, in the " New-York Tribune," rose, and asked
him if he had not seen the self-same statements in that paper.
Whereupon the prophetic candle by which this seer looked into
the future suddenly went out.

WASHINGTON, Jan. 29, 1853.

. . . I went to see the Aztec children this morning. What
ninnies they are! They call the boy sixteen or eighteen years of
age, and the girl ten or twelve. The first is thirty-three inches
high, the second twenty-nine, of a swarthy color, or, as I should
suppose, an ultra-Creole complexion. The boy has no head, or

almost none, — about as large as a very large apple, and almost wholly behind his ears. The girl's is much better shaped, and she seems to be very much his superior. What can such brains do with the problem of the solar system, or with conic sections, or with the tough problems of ethics and jurisprudence? Who has brains large enough to answer these questions?

There was an advertisement in the "National Intelligencer" to-day of the sale of a slave at an auction-room. I was on the spot in season to buy; but some private arrangement had been made, and the parties did not appear. I wanted to see how I could manage such an argument for atheism as the sale of a human being would be.

One of our members died this morning. It seems as if the *fact* of death and our *views* of death could not belong to the same system, and that one or the other must be changed, or else what a contradiction and what sorrows! . . . Of your mother's eternal weal I can have no doubt, if any mortal has eternal weal; but my early associations with death are too much for my reason.

PHILADELPHIA, Feb. 4.

I had a house jammed and squeezed last night. Mrs. —— was there, and mourned over my heresies most grievously. Why is it, that when one of the Gentiles comes almost over to what these "Zion's people" think to be right (or know, for they *know* every thing), but still, if there is the least interstice left, — why is it, I say, that they pounce upon him more ferociously, and maltreat him worse, than they do those who still remain in the "outer darkness"? Can you explain this?

Feb. 6. I have your letter of Thursday. When will mankind, especially womankind, have a declaration of independence against fashion? If its government were a wise and paternal one, we could bear it; but it is as capricious and arbitrary as Queen Elizabeth, and even more cruel than that old hag.

Feb. 10. . . . I dined out to-day, at ——, and sat next to a lady, who, when she heard Mr. G. T. Davis speak of R——'s being a professor in Antioch College, said she thought women had enough to do without being professors, and she hoped it was not going to be any rule for others. I told her young ladies were to be educated there. She didn't know what young ladies wanted of a college education. She did not wish to study any thing but the piano and drawing: she had no leisure for it. There could not be too much drawing; for she never was tired of that. . . . She had some smartness, and would captivate many a young man, I have no doubt. It was about an inch and a half from the top of her nose to the place where benevolence should have been; and that was the whole space she had for perceptive faculties, which were good, and for causality and comparison.

I found the "woman's-rights" spirit very intense in Philadelphia, and also a counter-spirit quite as strong. Of course, those women whose notions I approach, but do not coincide with, are the most violent. I do not think I said a single thing that they had any right to be offended at, but am not at all surprised that they took offence. I told Mrs. Mott she was too ambitious, because she claimed for woman all the highest things in all departments. I concede her the highest in more than half; yet she cannot be satisfied. But she is a good woman, and I must love her.

Feb. 13. I have your letter about the children to-day. Your accounts of them always interest me, and, when they develop the fair side of their natures, always delight me. Oh that an untainted human being should be brought into so foul a world as this! I am getting to be entirely reconciled to the theologic idea of the old deluge; and, if I were counsellor, I am not sure but I should propose another.

Feb. 15. . . . Venable has just got the floor, and is going to give a *talk* on public corruption. If I had more faith in his own purity, I should like to hear him better. However, it is bad enough; and I don't think he will make his indictment much too comprehensive. There is great iniquity here, beyond all question, — increased immensely since the compromise measures, and made respectable (if any such thing can be made respectable) by Webster's known corruptions. It is as —— says it is in Boston, where a general demoralization has invaded all departments of life. How is a remedy to be found? I trust God knows. I don't, unless it be in the continued persevering and energetic efforts of all good men for reform.

Feb. 17. I went to hear Thackeray again last evening. I did
not like the lecture so well as the preceding one. It had much
quiet humor, which keeps a pleasant expression on the face ; but there
was not a high sentiment in either lecture, and he spoke of the
intemperate habits of the wits of Queen Anne's time as if he would
like to have drunk with them. Not a word of moralizing, from
beginning to end; not a *caveat* entered in behalf of youth : and I
think a young man would go away with the idea that there is a
natural affinity between genius and intemperance. I used to observe
in Miss Catherine Sedgwick's works, that she could never let a subject go until her benevolence had had its chance to dilate upon it.
Thackeray goes over this whole field of intellect most wide and
beautiful ; but neither benevolence, conscientiousness, or veneration
seem permitted or desirous to say a word. He appreciated Pope's
power, and made it stand out wonderfully ; but he found some
traits of meanness in him. His redeeming point, so far as his affections and sympathies were concerned, was his love of his mother ;
and this Thackeray *did* expand and adorn as if he loved his own
mother.

WASHINGTON, Feb. 13, 1853.

MY DEAR DOWNER, — I heard Thackeray last evening, whom I
suppose you heard in Boston. I am every day getting more in love
with the viscera, thoracic and abdominal. I reverence a good cerebral cavity ; but a good chest and a good " refectory " below it
are hardly less important. I never understood the full meaning of
the favorite English word " pluck " until I took it in its literal
sense : now I know exactly what it means, and believe in it. Our
Southern men are vastly more developed in that region than our
Northern, and therefore they override us. High moral developments are the only adequate antagonists to this vigor and valor of
the " lower organs ; " but, alas ! how little of this there is !

I was a good deal excited as well as wearied by my Western trip.
As the drunken man said to his minister, when he met him in the
highway, and wished to conceal from him the fact of intoxication by
a striking remark, " There seems to be considerable land round
here," so I say in regard to the West. What a vast framework

it is! With what, in the providence of God, is it to be filled up? Ay, that depends upon who shall fill it. They need such men as you and Howe out there. This is true; but where on God's earth, too, do they need such men more than in Massachusetts?

I went to Yellow Springs. It is a beautiful place. What thoughts rush into the mind when we survey the scenes of anticipated labor, or look upon those of the past! — not thoughts; for they are molten into feelings, and, by expansion, swell and dilate the bosom almost to bursting. When I went to my present home, I looked upon it as the place where I hoped to live, and expected to die. If thoughts were a graver's tool, what records would be inscribed upon all its trees and its rocks! But I will not sentimentalize. . . .

I have nothing new to say of affairs here. The telegraph makes you as well acquainted in Boston with all national matters as the morning papers do us. I am pleased with the turn which Cuban matters are taking. On this subject, and at this time, the slightest breeze of opposition to Cuban annexation from the South is worth more than any blast that can be made to blow from Northern hills.

I am to be at home four weeks from yesterday. I hope to see you here, still more to see you there; but here, there, or anywhere,

I am always yours,

HORACE MANN.

It was early in this year that a controversy took place between Mr. Mann and Mr. Wendell Phillips upon the point, whether a moral and Christian man could vote or hold office under our governments, State and National, because of the clause in the Constitution that seemed to favor slavery. The excitements of the time made it a very personal one; and few, even of their friends, read it all, because it was painful to read a dispute between two men whose action tended toward the same good end, — human liberty. It was characterized by Mr. Phillips's usual want of insight into character, and lack of justice towards those who differ from him.

Mr. Mann subsequently wrote a letter to Mr. Garrison, which covered the whole ground, and which was published in the "Liberator" of July 3, 1853. It will be republished in its proper place.

WASHINGTON, Feb. 23, 1853.

Yesterday I dined with Mr. Everett, with the Massachusetts delegation. What an accomplished man he is! Coming home after nine o'clock, I stopped at the President's levee. It was jammed and crammed, — east room, green-room, hall, passages, everywhere. I took one turn round the east room, and came out and away. It was probably the last time that I shall ever be in that house; and there is something *solemn-choly* in looking for the last time upon a place, even when one has little attachment to it. I have not been through Mr. Fillmore's room this winter. I cannot touch the hand that signed the Fugitive-slave Law.

FEB. 24, 1853.

. . . I saw Miss Dix this morning. She is an angel. She has got two or three hundred dollars out of the Government for a library for the penitentiary in this District. She has induced Mr. Corcoran to give a bit of land, fifteen thousand dollars for a building, and ten thousand for a library, to be called the " Apprentices' Library," here. Mr. Corcoran came to her the other day, and said he was overwhelmed with solicitations for money. " But you," said he, " have *carte-blanche*." Isn't she a " woman's-rights" woman worth having ? — going for their rights in the right way.

Our whole force at Antioch will have to be educated anew, and Calvin and R—— will have to do it. Mr. —— knows nothing about school-keeping.

As I look upon the Normal-school girls as part of my thunder, though they have R——'s lightning in them to make them shine, I thought I would stop last evening for a moment's call on Miss G——. I took her to hear Thackeray. It was an interesting lecture on Sterne and Goldsmith, with this difference in the manner of treating them, — that he brought all Sterne's faults and vices out into the boldest relief, and was most assiduous in covering all Goldsmith's vanities up. He did speak once of Goldsmith's "vanities and follies," and said he died two thousand pounds in debt; but that was all he had to say on the negative side of his character. But Sterne's amours and hypocrisies, his sentimentalizing and moralizing, while he was decrying his own wife and making love to other married women, and his flattering one married woman while he ridiculed her to another of his pretended loves, Thackeray did bring out, so that no one can ever forget it. Poor Laurence's bones will be in no hurry for the resurrection after such disclosures.

What a warning it is, — these dead things coming to life !

I went to Dr. Bailey's Saturday-evening party last night. Thackeray was there, and some notables among the ladies, — among the rest a splendid woman* from New York, originally from Nantucket, who scraped acquaintance with me going to Nantucket nearly twenty years ago. She looks young as Hebe, and has a son twenty-one years old. That is the way the women ought to be, and would be if God's laws were their higher law.

WASHINGTON, Feb. 26, 1853.

MY DEAR MR. CRAIG, — Can a clergyman, located sixty miles out of a city, sitting in his manse, with hardly a sound about him save the pleasant ones of waving trees or flowing waters, understand the hounded, badgered, tormented, fragmentary life of an M. C. in Washington ? If he can, then I need make no apology for so long delaying to answer your late letter. If he cannot, then, though innocent, I must be convicted.

The course of preparatory and undergraduate studies for the college has not yet been definitely determined. I sent you a provisional one. A meeting is called, at my house in West Newton, for the 23d of next month. . . .

I have no idea that our "terms and conditions" will involve regulations as to dress. Boys "dressing in girls'" clothes, and girls "dressing in boys'" clothes, had better be left, as the old Romans left the crime of parricide, unprohibited, presuming it would never be committed. I regard the fashions of dress as among the accidents and non-essentials of life; and when points of minor importance are made to take precedence of the "weightier matters of the law, — judgment and justice and mercy," — or health, influence, and character, it is a misfortune and a weakness. A well-balanced mind graduates all the affairs and interests of life on a scale according to their relative importance ; and though young people and imperfectly educated people put some things high up on this scale which ought to be low down, and *vice versâ*, yet, as they grow wiser, they are constantly re-arranging them, and conforming the order of caprice or mis-education to the standard of Nature. A well-developed mind and heart is the only remedy for youthful vagaries of fancy. . . .

On your third point, let me say that I presume no one will be compelled to board at the common table. . . . My observation, however, has convinced me that serious evils are likely to grow out of the self-subsisting method. It is usually adopted by those in straitened circumstances.

The desire of economy, added to the inconveniences of preparing food, make too strong a temptation to live meagrely. Now, the philosophy of living, as you know, is to make strength out of food. What can poor Nature do when her supplies are cut off; when, like the inhabitants of a besieged city, or mariners on a wreck, she is put on the shortest living allowance? There is a fatal seduction about this, too, to the ambitious temperaments. It gives a preternatural vivacity and activity to the faculties, which the deluded victim mistakes for strength. But its end is weakness, exhaustion, and premature decay. I know some temperaments will bear this much better than others. Unfortunately, those to whom it would be most injurious are most readily decoyed into it. As I grow older (may I hope wiser), I find my former contempt and neglect of the thoracic and abdominal viscera — or, to speak it plainly, of lungs and belly — gradually changing into a kind of respect, not to say homage ; not, however, as I certainly need not tell you, as the *dii majores* of my regard, but as the *dii minores*, — without whose help the upper deities of the brain are as helpless as a commodore without crew to work his ship. The calamity is, that there is such infinite ignorance about the rules of health and life among our people, that the kind, the quality, and the amount of food which people consume are determined by every conceivable consideration except the right ones.

Of course, the very object of the preparatory school is to fit its attendants for admission into the college. At first, this preparatory school will be our stock in trade, — the only thing out of which we can make capital. With our Eastern teachers, the Pennells, brother and sister, if we do not have an unusual kind of school for that latitude, I shall be disappointed.

And so you recur again (and I like to read what you so wisely and with such simplicity say) to the subject of a press. One thing only you omit. You speak admirably of an *effect ;* but where is your *cause ?* — of a paper ; but where is your editor? A glorious invention, you know, the Frenchman had for preventing the ravages of city fires ; but, when the conflagration came, he had only a specimen of it in a phial.

Where is the man to conduct such a paper? That is the " main question," by a higher title than any parliamentary law. I have pleaded with you to go. Oh, no! you are too well situated with the young people whom you love, and with the old people who love you. As for myself, if there are half as many pupils there as some of your sanguine coadjutors expect, I shall need a hundred heads, as well as a hundred hands, to meet the daily demand upon labor and thought.

When, in my younger legislative days, I projected a hospital for the insane, and carried it through our Legislature unassisted, and against great opposition, the Governor, on whom devolved the appointment of commissioners, sent for me, and told me he should appoint me (young as I then was) chairman of the Board. I remonstrated. "No," said he: "you have got us into this scrape, and you must get us out." What shall I say to the Rev. Austin Craig of Blooming Grove, New York?

And now, my dear sir, to whom have I given so much time as to you? And if anybody upbraids me for this, have I not full justification in being able to say, no one deserves it so much as you?

As ever, most truly yours,

HORACE MANN

WASHINGTON, Feb. 28, 1853.

MY DEAR MR. PARKER, — . . . It is generally understood that the Chief Joiner has settled every piece that is to go into his Cabinet. Marcy will be Premier; Cushing, Attorney-General; Davis, the worst of fire-eaters, for War, — the most exacting, proud, egotistic of Southern disunionists, taken both for his own sake, and as a compliment to the most scandalous and rascally of States. This gives the Cabinet not merely a Southern aspect, but even worse, — a kind of Mississippi, repudiating aspect.

WASHINGTON, March 1, 1853.

We sat nine or ten hours yesterday. I suppose the great Cabinet-maker has selected all the boards to make his Cabinet. Mr. Marcy, of New York, is expected to be Premier; that is, Secretary of State. Probably Caleb Cushing will be Attorney-General. Jefferson Davis, that self-absorbed egotist, a Southern fire-eater and disunionist, is to be Secretary of War, — a double compliment, I suppose, to the strongest proslavery man and to the repudiating State of Mississippi. It has a Southern aspect. I see no chance that Pierce will not adopt the Baltimore Platform, extol the Union, and those who have saved it. Three days will tell the truth or error of these prophecies.

March 3. This morning I went to see the colored school. I felt bound to pay my respects to the cause and the color; and that was my last chance. What a deep interest that school excites! — so many human beings within reach of varied forms of social enjoyment, and yet separated from them all by an impassable barrier. My mind was profoundly moved; and it was not until long after I got back into the whirl of business that other things effaced the impression.

March 5. I rejoice to-day that I am one hundred and forty miles nearer you, and farther from Washington. You will doubtless have seen Pierce's inaugural before you see this, — filibustering for Cuba, and giving notice that he is for the Compromise Measures and the Fugitive-slave Law! It is hardly creditable to his head, and most disgraceful to his heart. Those who voted for him, under the delusion that he would be antislavery, now see that he quotes their support as a proof that they, too, are in favor of slavery! . . .

I am a free man again. What a Congressional life I have had! But I have fought a good fight, and come out with a clear conscience.

How deeply the contrast in the state of the country was impressed upon my mind yesterday between the position on the subject of slavery which it occupies now and which it did occupy four years ago!

WASHINGTON, March 15, 1853.

To REV. THEO. PARKER.

DEAR MR. PARKER, — The first trial of Drayton and Sayres lasted twenty-one successive days. It was in the depth of a Washington summer. For the first days of the trial, the court-room was packed like a slave-ship. Within springing distance of me, on my left hand, planted himself regularly the man who drew his pistol on Drayton when he was marched from the river to the jail, and who was supposed to come armed into court every day, and to be ready to preserve order, — *à la Warsaw.*

On the second trial, I went to Washington on purpose. It lasted about a fortnight. Here we had the old verdicts set aside, and new trials ordered. The third time I also went on purpose. The trials lasted about ten days. The accused were saved from a penitentiary offence, and were only fined for a misdemeanor. For particulars, see my volume.

My expenses were paid; but I never received a cent of a fee, nor asked nor expected it. . . .

H. MANN.

BOSTON, March 17, 1853.

DEAR MR. MANN, — I saw Mr. B. B. Muzzey yesterday. He would like to see you when in town. His adviser on the law-question is a snob, one of the vulgarest in town ; crawling upwards, and would not like to slip down along his slimy track : so he must not offend Curtis and Choate and the rest of that tribe. As I understand it, this is the dodge just now, — to make the matter of libel a technical law-question for the sole consideration of the "judges:" then there will be left for the jury the *matter of fact* as to publication, and the *matter of penalty* as to damages. If they succeed, then Judge L. Shaw will decide "as he will decide," and such a precedent be established as will delight the central muscle (*in loco cordis*) of all the snobs who are growing into Hunkers, and of all the Hunkers who have grown out of snobs. Mr. Muzzey is not disposed to submit tamely. We ought to have a *ship-money quarrel* on this matter, with Muzzey for a John Hampden. I think he would like to have you of his counsel, but feels delicate about asking you. He thinks of Hale and Dana for the matter of fact.

Good-by !

THEODORE PARKER.

WEST NEWTON, May 22, 1853.

MY DEAR DOWNER, — You left the programme of our "Antioch:" but I mean you shall see what I say about the natural and moral laws; and so I send it after you.

The men under whose auspices the institution is founded are poor in this world's goods, but they are earnest; and you must see, that, by taking such a heretic as I am from the world's people, they have very different views from our evangelicals.

Now, my dear friend, if you have any deposit of "filthy lucre" to make in the *Upper Exchequer*, I wish you to remit the same, for the benefit of Antioch College, through my hands, — more or less, thousands or hundreds, — and I will see that it is entered to your credit above. Do you know of any better chance for investment ? . . .

Yours as ever,

HORACE MANN.

WEST NEWTON, June 15, 1853.

MY DEAR MR. COMBE, — I should have written to you some time ago; only I hoped to have something to send to you, and a friend to send it by. In both I have been, so far, disappointed : otherwise I should earlier have thanked you for your much-valued present of one hundred dollars, which I mean shall be better than a common monument of you; not a dumb and barren one, but a living, radiating one, diffusing instruction and delight. I mean to expend it, mainly at least, for phrenological works, yours heading the list, and in such duplicates as will allow you to be speaking all the time to many persons. In the new college, I am to occupy (I dare not say fill) the chair of Natural Theology. It is something of an advance (is it not?) to look outside the clerical ranks in America for the president of a college, where with the fewest exceptions, from time immemorial, not only have the clergy had a monopoly of this office, but the Orthodox clergy. I am inclined to think this is the first instance, in all the West, in which a layman has ever been elected to it. Succeed or not, I do not think it will be the last. The faculty has three clergymen and three laymen in it, besides one female professor, as it is to educate young ladies as well as young men ; and I intend to have it so arranged that the Sunday exercises of the chapel shall be performed alternately by the male members. In this way I hope to get something of philosophy, as well as theology, before the minds of the youth who are bold enough to resort there.

Mr. Mann left New England for the West early in September of this year. He was unable to dispose of his homestead, except temporarily ; and therefore realized with less force than he otherwise might have done the fact that he was changing his home permanently. All was uncertain as to the future, except that an untried enterprise was before him, insuring great labors ; but he was animated by a strong hope that he should be able to put into action many long-cherished and favorite views. It was surely a virgin soil that his educational plough-share was to break, and his enthusiasm figured a fair prospect of success.

His journey was not unattended with public evidences of sympathy from those who had concurred in the principles that had actuated his Congressional career. At Portland (for he took a Northern route), a deputation of friends, who had sympathized with his nomination by the Free-soil party to the office of Governor of Massachusetts, arrested him at the station to bid him a kindly farewell. Though he was peculiarly backward in seeking the sympathy he valued, he enjoyed the expression of it none the less when it was spontaneous and sincere. But when he parted with the last friend who accompanied him on the way, and felt that he had cut loose from all further participation in scenes not only of honest triumph but of much wounded feeling, the strong man gave way, and he wept like a child. Massachusetts was not all he wished her to be, and that he had hoped she would prove; but he had worked lovingly for her, and her very rocks and shores were dear to him. The friends who had been true to him, and the supposed friends who had deserted him, were remembered with almost equal tenderness; but it was difficult to convince him that his place in their memories would be kept green after he had passed away from their sight. When he arrived upon the new scene of labor, he threw himself, with all the ardor of his temperament, into the enterprise he had undertaken; for it seemed as if he was to make a new world: and it was only when the inconsiderate question was asked, " Which do you like best, the East or the West? " that he allowed himself to dwell with acute pain upon what he had lost.

" I must not think of my *brain relations*," he would sometimes say. " I shall realize the loss too much."

Several of his near relatives were around him; and the new home was gilded with a halo of hope, — hope of usefulness and successful exertion. The poetry of the broad prairies, which to other hearts spoke only of desolation, was to his exalted state of mind, as he passed over them, freedom, — freedom from all that fettered or darkened the human soul through the agency of man. Were they not yet to be wrought? Their future vegetation surely depended upon what seed was sown. He had been an eminently practical man; but his dreams had always stood before him, and they were of the fruits of knowledge and the "liberty of the sons of God." How sadly these hopes of a serene and successful field of labor were disappointed, only those can ever know who were inspired by his enthusiasm to share them, and who felt the disappointment with him.

Several years after, when driving one day over one of those broad wastes where occasionally a solitary log-house showed that human interests were beginning to be linked with Nature, his companion remarked, "I should not like to be a pioneer."—"Are we not pioneers?" he answered, not bitterly, but sadly; for he had already been made to feel that the borders of civilization are, in their social aspects, but a short remove from barbarism.

The ambitious brick towers of Antioch College were the first objects to be seen on approaching the spot; and its unfinished aspect was symbolical of the unripe condition of all its affairs. Mr. Mann once tried to describe it by saying, that, "supposing creation had lately issued out of chaos, it might be about as late in the week as Wednesday!" It was situated on a table-land, which, two years previously, had been despoiled of a magnificent forest to make way for that source of Western wealth,— wheat. The stumps of the trees still remained standing at the very threshold of the college. Eastern energy, starting upon the basis of Western promises, had projected it thus far into being; but its location was too near Slave-land not to feel the influence of its tardy fulfilments of all purposes. There was not even any one standing ready to receive the new president, except one of his own relatives who had arrived three days before him. No house had been built for his accommodation, as had been promised; nor had he received any intimation of the fact. No provision had even been made for a temporary residence of ten persons; but, happily, a large boarding-house, whose summer residents had left but a few weeks before, was by much persuasion opened to him at the moment. There were not many comforts in it: but he and his friends were strung up to a high tension of nervous energy, and contempt of trifles, having been forewarned, by one who knew something of Western life, that " the change from the quiet comforts of a New-England home would be found a matter both for laughter and for tears; " and the party took possession of the deserted rooms, which they were allowed to arrange for themselves, and which, by dint of a few old stoves, were made habitable for a fall residence. The college-buildings were far from being completed; and it was only by means of the most strenuous exertions, even by sabbath-day labors, that the chapel was made ready for the reception of the large number of guests who were expected to be present on the day of inauguration. The committee did not dare to proclaim the day too extensively; for it was feared that there were not accommodations enough in the village for so large a company as would probably come. But, in spite of their caution, when the day came, three thousand persons assembled, many of whom brought comforters and provisions, and slept in their carriages and carioles. Only one boarding-house belonging to the college-buildings, and designed for the accommodation of the students, was even partially completed; and the dining-hall of this was still to be made, except the framework. Boards were laid upon joists for the dinner-party of the day. One hundred and fifty students entered on the afternoon of the inauguration ceremony. The boards were swept, and the examination-papers laid upon them: and these alternate ceremonies of eating and examining went on for two or three days; and the company of young people took possession of the unfinished building, as far as windows were glazed and doors hung, a partition having been thrown up in the middle of it to divide the young men from the maidens, and two of the professors taking up their abode in the building previous to the occupation of Mr. Mann, who was to take possession of certain rooms in it as soon as they were in habitable condition.

The classes were opened at once, and the preparatory school commenced, the whole corps of professors throwing themselves into it. Out of the whole mass of applicants, representing every stage of human ignorance, eight were found qualified upon the whole, though with some conditions, to form a freshman-class. The rest, old and young, married and unmarried, some of them ministers who had given up their parishes to take a college course of study, were obliged to drop into the preparatory school, simple as were its requisitions. The teaching, fortunately, was of a high order ; the teaching corps invincible in resolution, patient, sympathizing with the universal aspiration, while lamenting the low stage of intellectual development; and the professors' corps, aided by a few intelligent and well-educated young ladies from the East, who went out prepared to take a college course, and before whom stood in amazement men of twice their age as humble pupils, soon evoked some order out of the chaos.

It was a wonderful spectacle then, — and grows more wonderful when regarded from a distant period of time, — the enthusiasm of those young people, who kept together under circumstances that might excuse almost any lapse from resolution to endure privations. It was long before the building was put into comfortable order. It was a year before any provision was made to furnish fresh water to the students, who were obliged to walk a quarter of a mile with their pitchers to procure a draught of the clear article; all the water furnished being brought from a distance, and poured into a huge vat of ten feet diameter, which stood upon a raised platform near the door of the Ladies' Hall. The water was often carted to it in cast-off oil-barrels that had been superficially cleansed; the hydraulic rams that originally supplied the vat having got out of order, with no Yankee promptness at hand to repair injuries.

The young ladies were obliged to fill their own bed-room pitchers at this vat, no domestic service being allowed by the superintendent. Early one morning, in the ensuing winter, a stranger who was visiting the institution, and had risen betimes to take the cars, found a delicate young lady struggling with a huge stream that was pouring from the vat. She had inadvertently pulled out the faucet; and knowing that the supply of water for all purposes, cooking included, would be lost if she did not replace it, was endeavoring to do so, standing upon the wet snow, and drenched to the skin by the stream. He rescued her from it; but she was ill for a long time in consequence of the wetting. Mr. Mann often ascended the ladder, to ascertain, by probing the vat with his cane, how much gravel was *not* held in solution.

A wealthy gentleman in the neighborhood, who owned several hundred springs of delicious water oozing from the brink of a gorge in the vicinity, and but one of which he could use himself, had loaned the use of *one* for the two previous years of college-building; but no entreaties could induce him to lend, rent, or sell the use of it any longer.

The next year, another person interested in the college purchased a distant tract of the gorge containing a spring of water, and it was brought up by hydraulic rams.

No appropriation was made for digging wells, either

for the college or the college manse, for many years; and then the enterprise only partially succeeded. To finish the history of the water question, which may be taken as a representative one of much of the spirit that actuated the community: the pipes for these rams had to be laid partially under another person's territory; and, though they interfered in no way with the tillage or pasturage of the same, the owner, being disaffected because he could not on one occasion make some money out of the college, threatened to cut them off. This calamity, however, was averted by much negotiation.

Many cold weeks elapsed, after the opening of the college on the 5th of October, before the stoves arrived which were to warm either the main college-building or the close dormitories of the students (ventilation having been entirely ignored in the structure). A change of plan in the superintendent's mind in regard to the stoves caused this delay. Some of the professors took possession of their apartments in the college-building before the plaster was dry, while it was still impossible to make a fire; thereby incurring maladies, which, in one instance at least, promised to be life-long. There was no remedy; for the village did not afford accommodations for the sudden influx of population.

Mr. Mann was unable to take possession of his apartments for many weeks after the opening of the college; for his household effects had been thrown in a storm upon some portion of the shore of Lake Erie not connected with any railroad, and were long supposed, indeed, to have gone to the bottom. When they were at last found, the carpets for the college-parlors, one of which the president was to inhabit, still remained untouched, till the ladies of the faculty unrolled and cut them out, and put them down; and they were also obliged to stand sentinels over their boxes of furniture out of doors, hatchet and screw-driver in hand, waiting for the appearance of some friendly professor or other dignitary to open them, no workmen being spared from the hurried preparations to aid in such small matters. The amiable superintendent decreed that no domestic's broom or mop should ever touch the stairs that led to the president's apartments; and said ladies took turns during that year in making them passable, for their own credit's sake, and for that of the institution. All offers made by the lady teachers to arrange the tables tastefully, with a view of cultivating good manners, were rejected by the superintendent and the stewardess as an invidious criticism upon themselves. It was even difficult to introduce the refinement of table-napkins, a set of which was presented by a friend. It was necessary to make a by-law to oblige the students to sit at table half an hour, such were their rough and uncultured habits. These things, however, were not to be allowed to daunt pioneers. The question sometimes came up, "Shall we laugh, or shall we cry?" The verdict was uniformly in favor of the former, when the subject was looked upon merely as a matter of personal comfort; but it was painful to Mr. Mann to be thwarted in his pleasant plans for even the outward improvement of his new disciples. Many projects were entertained of future dramas of "Antioch in the Bud;" but too sad associations linger around it now for the fulfilment of such playful threats.

Mr. Mann persisted in presiding over the common table, hoping by his presence to give a better tone to the manners of the young people, which, by all indications, would otherwise have disfigured the establishment. But no power to ameliorate the annoyances that all felt was given him by the acting superintendent, who soon became disaffected because not allowed by the faculty to rule the scholastic as well as the culinary department. One fruit of this disaffection was a cessation of work upon the college manse for several months.

During that year, Mr. Mann devoted much time to the cure of many habits in the students common to Western society, among which the indiscriminate use of tobacco was very prominent, even in boys of twelve years of age. Mr. Mann has been thought unduly severe upon this subject; which is not surprising, when we consider that it is a point of minor morals not yet recognized by the world in general. But perhaps even such critics would have sympathized with him there; for recitation-rooms and even parlors were rendered almost uninhabitable by the vile accompaniments of chewing and smoking. For several months, he spent every evening he could command in using his moral and persuasive influence to induce the students to renounce the practice; and succeeded so far, that, before the end of the first college-year, there were but three students who had not with apparent willingness signed a pledge to discontinue it, and to use their influence to make others do likewise. In some cases, the reform was very striking; for young men who had been addicted to the habit from youth up were changed from sallow, nerveless, irritable, stupid individuals, painful to behold, to fair, strong, cheerful seekers after knowledge and happiness. One young man, thus redeemed from apparent ruin, came to Mr. Mann every day, for two or three weeks, to report his resolution held since the day previous, hoping to achieve his emancipation by such slow stages; and every day received the encouragement and sympathy requisite to carry him on, till at last he announced himself able as well as willing to sign the pledge.

He appealed to the common sense of some, to the moral sense of others. Some who came into the class-rooms ragged, and pleading poverty, he ridiculed, assuring them that the money saved would at least pay for mending the coat-sleeve or the shirt-bosom. Some he pleaded with as fathers do with their erring children. But these admonitions were all private; for he always avoided destroying self-respect by public fault-finding, if possible. The same three who refused were finally ejected from the institution on account of the kindred vice of drunkenness. New students brought new cases to deal with; but, when public opinion was on the right side, half the battle was gained.

In view of the graver trials that came after, it would seem trivial to mention many which wore upon his nerves at that time. But he considered it a matter of great importance to cultivate the manners as well as the minds of the young people around him. His previous plans had been, to afford in his own house the proprieties and even elegances of social culture to those who had never enjoyed them elsewhere; but he was obliged to do the best he could with what appliances were at hand. His presence insured order and decency at the public tables; and for this end he continued to deprive himself and family, for the first year, of the luxury of any private life, a measure of which he might have enjoyed through the privilege of a private table.

But he could not prevent the Ohio pigs from walking through the dining-room, as there were no fences around the college-buildings, no doors to the hall, and no appointed homes for the animals. Water stood over shoes between the main college-building and the dining-hall (where there is a covered arcade in the picture), so deep that boards floated on it. One day a professor (a lady) was arrested, on her entrance to the hall, by a hog of unusual dimensions, which had made his watery bed where a doorstep should have been. She looked at it in dismay a moment, and then, being light of foot, tripped over it as if it had been a bridge, and sprang over a board which had been inserted where the door should have been hung, the board having been placed there by some friendly hand to prevent the intrusion of *living* bridges.

The ladies of the faculty and teaching corps arranged themselves in fine linen and gloves when Mr. Mann held levees in the parlors of the only hall then erected, hoping to suggest the refinement of re-arranging the hair, taking off the apron, and putting on a clean collar, for such occasions; and these improvements *did* grow, so that, by the time he could hold levees in the college manse, they presented the agreeable spectacle of a company of ladies and gentlemen in becoming dress and clean shoes. In the early college-days, when the whole area of twenty acres was one vast quagmire of clayey soil, in which plank walks sank below the surface, and in rainy weather floated upon it, this last refinement was simply impossible. It was necessary, in walking, to arm one's self with a shingle or other implement, to remove the mass which adhered to the shoe when it accumulated sufficiently to prevent farther locomotion.

In the later days, strangers often asked, with a semblance of incredulity, " Do you mean to tell me that these intelligent, agreeable, lovely young people are students of the college ? " Such was the effect of culture when the mind and heart were wakened to receive it.

Twice Mr. Mann's garden was stocked with valuable fruit from the East, and twice destroyed by cattle and pigs for want of enclosure : and, to the last days of his residence, the unsightly heap of broken brick, mortar, and stone, lay untouched before his door; but he had learned to look *over* it. It was impossible to ask for appropriations for such purposes, when it was difficult to obtain them for the commissariat of the boarding-house; and his own loose moneys, and all the contributions he could gather, were devoted to the relief of indigent students. A friend from Massachusetts, who visited him, wrote word, after his return, that he found every thing at home *painfully neat.*

Many serious difficulties soon arose in regard to the appointment of teachers, who were selected by the superintendent without consultation with the president. Finances failed; and then a sufficient number could not be employed, for want of money to pay them. This threw too great burdens on the few. Some failed for want of adaptation to the places they were called to fill: jealousies were fostered among others. The disaffection of the superintendent still delayed the building of the college manse: and his uncomfortable quarters, the self-denial he practised about personal comforts (for only in the privacy of his own bed-chamber would he partake of a little food that he could digest, furtively prepared in an inconvenient manner), the absorption of every moment of his time (for no waking hour was his own), and the anxiety he began to feel lest the institution would become bankrupt, proved too much for Mr. Mann; and, towards the end of the first year, he was laid upon a bed of suffering, from which only his iron resolution finally roused him; and he actually did remain upon his feet until vacation came, thus rendering the subsequent prostration still more fearful.

The question may naturally be asked here, " Could not

the president of the institution regulate the preparation of food upon his own table, even if it stood in the Commons' Hall?" The answer is, that the *raw* democratic principle, if the expression may be allowed, is very levelling in the regions of border civilization. He saw the jealousy entertained of men of Eastern culture by the rough denizens of the prairies, and knew that it was fed in this particular instance by the personal ill-will of the superintendent. He constantly feared a revolt in the dining-room, where all his plans were systematically thwarted; and it is but an additional proof of the enthusiasm of his young aspirants for knowledge that such a revolt did not take place, considering all the discomforts. The seats at the tables were round, four-legged stools; and Mr. Mann would not have a chair for himself, even after some ladies of the teaching corps ventured upon that innovation for their own accommodation and at their own expense. No one there, who estimated his services even approximately, can now review the history of these petty yet serious evils without a measure of indignation that baffles speech. The students of that period, who knew the whole, utter it with tongues of fire; but he never uttered a word of complaint, or would allow it in his hearing. " I can endure any thing for these young people," he would say. At last, others were convinced that only heroic measures could avail; and friends who advanced moneys, with no securities but the banks of faith and hope, stopped supplies until the obnoxious superintendent was dismissed. He did not fail, however, to infuse his spirit into others who succeeded, making dissatisfaction a tradition. He had much influence, having been largely concerned in getting up the institution. His successors, happily, were less powerful to contend with the giant will that would endure all things for the noble ends he sought. Mr. Mann's mode of resist-

ance, however, was chiefly to disarm hostile influences as
well as to endure.

After one occasion of exhausting fatigue, Mr. Mann
was himself startled, and the friends who were with him
painfully shocked, by a partial paralysis of speech, which
made him utter words inadvertently, and so irrelevant that
they struck his own ear. He was never reminded of it by
others, and never referred to it himself, even to those who
administered relief to him at the time; but the sword of
Damocles that hung over him was ever visible to the eyes
that knew and loved him best.

After his removal to a private residence, he had
some repose; for he was exempt from the unceasing
hum and confusion of a closely packed building: but all
responsibility for the discipline of the institution remained in his hands, and of this he could only be relieved
by the occasional fortunate chance of coadjutors who
could manage their own departments without friction.
In such an institution, a necessary officer is a matron
whose duties are combined neither with those of house-
keeper nor teacher; but for this there never were funds
enough, and constant difficulties occurred and recurred.
A mother's parlor, with the mother in it ready for all exigencies, should be represented, and the illusion should be
entire, in a house filled with young ladies of all ages
needing motherly suggestions and care. But that aid
was denied him to the end by circumstances beyond his
control. Even in his little cabinet, perfect unanimity did
not exist, nor even unalloyed good feeling. But the
power to form the cabinet was not given to him; and he
had to wait for the day when the evils consequent upon
this state of things should work themselves off, and
when all would come to look as he did upon the great
importance of their charge, rather than upon their own

private interest and ambition. Those who looked on and saw what he encountered, and what he bore patiently and hopefully, and how self-forgettingly and bravely he rose above all obstacles; how radiant his countenance was when he saw, that, in spite of all difficulties, the young people improved, and responded genially to his touch,— were inspired also to hope every thing, and fear nothing, and dwell only upon the great issues involved in the marked progress of several hundred aspiring youth, animated to intense enthusiasm by the magnetism of his presence and love : for he moved amongst them like a father among his children, most ready to spend his time and energies with the least hopeful. He truly believed that the germ of every thing good was to be found in each one, and that this only needed the sun of culture to grow and blossom, and bear fruit. All the previous training and experience of his life were brought into requisition to meet the demand; and he could hardly understand why all others did not feel as willing to offer themselves a sacrifice to the work as he did. He had hoped that only the devotion and not the sacrifice of any one would be required; for he had no question, when he undertook the charge of the institution, that means would be furnished to carry it on. When he found that these were not at hand, his only thought was to stand in the breach till succor came. He had expected to encounter ignorance in the greater portion of the Christian denomination, which had only of late thought worldly knowledge consistent with religion, and, like the Methodists of old, waited for " a call " before they attempted to instruct others; but a few noble and cultured minds among them had made him feel that the idea of true religious freedom had dawned upon them, and was destined to become a great and shining light. It was to this idea that he attached himself, and openly and freely gave his allegiance. That the light did not come more rapidly out of the present darkness, he mourned over as truly as any man : but he knew that the bud was grafted upon thrifty stocks ; and, when he was obliged to withdraw his respect from the fathers, he did not lose his confidence in the sons and daughters, but recognized in them so clear an acceptance of the great truth involved in the principles of toleration and free thought, that he loved to identify himself with the noble platform to the very last.

Perhaps no man, brought up in the very hot-bed of intolerance and spiritual pride, ever so utterly renounced every vestige of both. We sometimes see even the freest thinkers — those who have helped to break the bonds of others — as intolerant of difference of opinion in those whom they would fain lead as were the bigots from whom they broke away. But Mr. Mann was too conscious of this tendency in mankind to trust himself to indoctrinate others. He confined himself to clearing away the obstructions to free thought, and was not afraid to trust truth to the pure in heart, and to the intellectual integrity of those who sought it humbly. He has been called distrustful of men ; but he was not distrustful of human nature, although he looked carefully after the motives of special people. He thought human nature needed educating, and had been much maligned; and that it was only where circumstances had cultivated the earthly side of it unduly that the divine element was temporarily obscured. Education was, in his view, a word of far higher import than that popularly given to it. Its function was to call out from within all that was divinely planted there in the proportions requisite to make a noble being. He knew that man could not create in others what God had not created ; but he had a generous and noble faith in the

27

indefinite capacities of the human race for improvement. The fact of the humanity was all-sufficient to call out his efforts for the culture of any of God's children ; but in the aspiring youth of our Great West he saw with pro- phetic eye a glorious promise, whose fulfilment bid fair to release society from the bondage of error. The grand sweep of the horizon enlarged his own sense of power : and he unconsciously transplanted his own expanded thought into the breast of every one he saw intent upon the search after knowledge.

Many laughable incidents, growing out of the primitive simplicity of log-cabin life at the West, made the Eastern residents in this hitherto uncultured region realize the difference between the two states of society. Mr. Mann, in his Western lecturing tours, had often slept in the one apartment of a log-cabin (the owner worth, perhaps, a hundred thousand dollars) in which a row of beds were turned down at night to accommodate the household, guest and all : therefore he was not alarmed when a very demure young lady — not particularly young, but a student of the college — came to make the request that she might make up a bed on the floor of her apartment for her brother-in-law, who had come to visit her. Mr. Mann reminded her of the regulation, that no gentleman, except the fathers of the students, should go into the dormitory halls of the young ladies' department, even to make a passing call. She said she knew that was a regulation. but thought the case of a brother-in-law might be an ex- ception. Without hurting her feelings, he made her understand that such customs, although allowable under the sanction of parental presence in homes, would not answer in an institution of learning, where the discretion of young people could not always be trusted. however much their goodness might be confided in. But these

customs often gave him trouble. An old gentleman, who
was an itinerant preacher, brought two of his daughters
to him, and said they were afraid to be left at home alone
since the death of their mother ; and so he brought them
to the college, which was " as cheap a place as any other,
and girls were not of much account any way." The girls
were as uncultured as one might expect from such a view
of the subject. They conversed in the precise phraseology
of Aunt Dinah in " Uncle Tom's Cabin," which Mr. Mann
did not know till then to be the vernacular of the West
as well as of the South. But they knew how to read,
and had begun to learn to write ; and they were docile,
and could easily have been managed. The father, however, was a more difficult subject. He often came to visit
his daughters (having shut up his house), and would
bring to their chamber hampers of mince-pies, roast turkey,
&c., and stay a week or two. This was submitted to for
a while, although he necessarily turned his daughters out
of their narrow bed to seek sleeping-places for themselves
in other students' rooms, or on the floor. But at last he
brought a cousin to stay with him ; and, when the young
gentleman appeared, the occasion was seized for earnest
remonstrance and prohibition. The old preacher was
sore offended, and left with his daughters at once.

On one occasion, during a short vacation, a party of
gay young ladies thought they would amuse themselves
by visiting a fellow-student, a young man, who was at the
time engaged in a neighboring town in keeping a district
school, which he had playfully invited them to come and
see. The president was absent ; and, when they applied
for permission to visit a friend for a few days, their plans
were not so thoroughly investigated as they would have
been by his vigilant care ; and a delegated permission was
granted, on the ground that he always took pleasure in

promoting innocent recreations at such times, and, indeed, took pains to provide entertainment. The young ladies proceeded on their foolish frolic ; but, unluckily, the gentleman had also taken a few days' vacation, and was not to be found. They knew no one else in the place, and had relied upon him to find an abode during their stay ; and, as they suddenly realized the ludicrousness of their position, they wandered about the precincts till picked up by another fellow-student residing on a neighboring farm, who took them home, and entertained them until the evening train arrived. They returned under cover of the shades, and disposed of themselves among their friends in the village for a few days, too much mortified to re-appear at their boarding-house, and afraid of being found out and laughed at. They did not escape, however ; and they were brought to tears and dismay by the exhortation they received upon the subject of proprieties.

Another party of young people, innocent of any design to infringe these same proprieties, had laid all their plans, on a similar occasion, to spend a few weeks rambling about the country, and camping out ; but a word of appeal from Mr. Mann to consider what might be the effect on the public mind of so wild an expedition from a college surrounded by enemies and persecutors, who would be glad of an occasion to find fault, deterred them at once. In his assumed character of parent, he could not sanction that which, under other circumstances, might have been perfectly unobjectionable. The cheerfulness with which the students also gave up dancing as a recreation — a resource which would have been healthful as well as hilarious, and which Mr. Mann approved when pursued under proper regulations — showed how genuine was his influence over them. This amusement is a source of so much evil among the uncultivated, that a large proportion of the religious people of the Western communities looked upon it with a prejudice that would have induced them to remove their children from an institution where it was allowed; and, on the ground that it would deprive many of their companions of the advantages of education, it was cheerfully given up. After a few years, however, they were allowed to accept invitations to private houses where dancing occurred at seasonable hours.

In view of the various discomforts attending the premature opening of the college and its boarding-house, Mr. Mann sometimes allowed students to board in the village. He permitted it only in individual cases, and then under the restriction, that they should board in no family whose heads would not pledge themselves not to take young men and maidens together; for this would almost insure intimacies which might result in connections for life: and he wished to throw guards around the young ladies, which should preclude any precipitate steps of this kind, as careful parents would do. In his Inaugural Address, he had fairly met the question of the probability that marriages would frequently grow out of the intimacies of college-life; but there was a by-law of the institution to the effect that they should not take place there. The pledge given by housekeepers was violated in one or two instances; but they were parents who had daughters, and were foolish enough to take young men to board, and were alone responsible when their children chose to be married rather than to pursue their college education to the end. When Mr. Mann was consulted by the regents of another university at the West, in which there was a question of admitting both sexes, he advised against it, because there was to be no college-family, no superintendence of any description, but the young people were to seek their homes at tleir discretion in a city where no eye could be held over them. He considered the moral dangers to impulsive youth so great, when left without parental or other supervision, that he thought it better to forego the literary education than to incur them.

Enemies slandered the institution, and the slanders doubtless spread where the refutations have not always followed them; but no one conversant with the daily life and walk of Antioch College can deny that the purity and high tone of its morals and manners, in both departments, were unequalled by those of any other known institution. There are many colleges at the West, in whose neighborhood schools for young ladies have sprung up, in order that the services of teachers and professors in the former may be made available in the latter; and in such cases there have always been regulations prohibiting any intercourse whatever between the two. But it is the universal testimony of those acquainted with the subject, that loss of reputation, and even of character, are not unfrequent in such places, growing out of clandestine correspondences and meetings. Mr. Mann thought the monkish error of repressing natural sentiments should be swept away with other errors of the same nature, and a generous culture should enlist them in the interests of purity. Young people are thoughtless rather than vicious; and it is cruel to put them into circumstances where they can learn wisdom only from a fatal experience. Even at Oberlin, as was testified to not only by pupils, but by teachers of the institution afterwards employed at Antioch, the students, though dining at the same tables, were not allowed to speak at meal-times. At Antioch College, the dining-hall, which was, as at Oberlin, the commons of both sexes, was a charming scene of social enjoyment and innocent hilarity,—a scene which Mr. Mann specially enjoyed for its beneficent influences upon manners and happiness. On Thanksgiving days he liked to be a guest of this large family, which he regarded with true parental affection. The spoiler entered it more than once, and tried to alienate the affections of his students, but with very slight success. Disappointed ambition and disappointed greed did succeed in alienating the confidence of the Western public to a great degree : hence the failure of all their flattering promises to sustain the institution, which they might have done with perfect ease if deposed professors, and disappointed sharpers. and religious bigotry, had not aspersed it.

Mr. Mann was not the only individual who went into this enterprise with lofty aims and liberal and disinterested views, certainly with a very creditable degree of them : but only two or three had had sufficient experience even to share all his views, or form a just conception of what his purposes were ; and a far different spirit animated others with whom its destiny was involved, — not inextricably, perhaps, for it had already begun to slough off extraneous matter before he was cut off from it ; but at what a cost that was done, only those who were kindled by his enthusiasm, and who acted with him, know, or ever can know, adequately.

I would dwell a little longer upon one feature of this institution which interested Mr. Mann as deeply in it as its unsectarian basis. Colleges for women, or rather colleges frequented by women as well as by men, presented some objections at first view, which had their foundation in a delicate appreciation of feminine character. He had at one time felt them himself ; but his experience of the joint education in the Massachusetts Normal schools, two of which had this feature, had dispelled that doubt, in view of the advantages to be gained. He had never been pleased with any desire on woman's part to shine in public; but it was his opinion that the divinely appointed mission of woman is to teach, and it was his wish to introduce her into every department of instruction as soon as it could be done with good effect. He had watched teaching long enough to know that woman's teaching, other things being equal, is more patient, persistent, and thorough than man's; and that to equal intellectual advantages, that of moral culture, which should never be divorced from these, is more surely added thereby; and that this grows out of the domestic traits, which are not marred by this use, but only thus directed to the noblest ends. Nor does it interfere in any degree with the peculiarly appointed sphere of woman. She is better fitted for the duties of wife and mother for having first used her faculties in imparting knowledge under circumstances that are free from distracting cares. He had no desire to shut out men from the enjoyment of the same privilege; but he hoped, by the union of the two in the vocation of teaching, to annihilate as it were, certainly to banish, all brutalities of growth in young men, and frivolities in young women, and this without checking the hilarity or interfering with the simplicity of youth. He was rewarded signally by success, so far as he had the opportunity to test his views.

He knew that the preparation for such change must be very gradual; for there were as yet but few women to be found capable of filling the higher walks of instruction. The power to do it had been gained, previously to the establishment of Normal schools, only by unaided practice, which sacrifices many victims in the process. He had the satisfaction of placing in professorships in Antioch College two ladies, who, in addition to other opportuni-

ties of culture, had enjoyed the advantages of thorough
training, first as pupils, and then as teachers, in the best
Normal schools of Massachusetts; thus connecting his
early and his later labors.

After restoring the common school to its full function,
as conceived by its founders, or its discoverers, as he
called them, it remained for him to connect it by an electric chain with that advanced educational course represented by the college or university, and which wields such
mighty influence over society by its prestige. Indeed, he
had been able to add the culture of a later period of time
to that original conception whose *principle* shone so
purely to the minds of the early fathers, that no advance
upon that was possible, — principles having nothing to do
with time, and often gleaming through a dark age as a
prophecy of the future. He also felt that college education itself was to take a broader and higher stand than
the old scholastic method. No link of that chain of connection was wanting in his mind. The only obstacle to
the perfecting of his early work had been the want of
thorough and complete scholars to carry it on. He
wished accomplished men and women to have the charge
of Normal-school training, that the instruction in them
might fit teachers who could meet every requirement
of society: but the higher institutions of learning had
showed little interest in the work; and, as long as that
was the case, it would necessarily be of an inferior quality.
One year's course at a Normal school did not prepare
teachers, who entered it ignorant, to go into the high
schools, and train young men for college. He wished
graduates of the colleges to take such lively interest in
educational work as to add the Normal-school training
to their other acquirements, and make of it a profession,
like law, medicine, and theology. He hoped, in process

of time, to add such a department to Antioch College
itself; making the preparatory school of the college a
model school, after the pattern of that which is an
integral element at present of all good Normal schools
proper. The preparatory school of Antioch College
never proved to be what he wished it to be, simply because he could not command any one to superintend it
aright. Its first principal could not speak or write the
English language correctly; and no one who ever took
hold of it understood discipline in his sense of the word.
His hands were tied in that as well as in other directions,
as long as the institution was dependent upon the community in which it was located. All this he hoped to remedy, if it could be set upon an independent basis, and be
governed by intelligent men. The Western trustees had
good will; but most of them had not a conception of the
needs or the functions of an institution of learning. They
were supposed to hold the purse-strings; and if they had
been content to do that, and to let better educated men
do the rest, Mr. Mann could have accomplished thrice
what he was able to do with all the drawbacks in his
way.

The duties of one of his lady professors included instruction in a variety of branches; and her experience as
assistant teacher in a Normal school enabled her to be a
very great aid in arranging the general programme of
studies. The other took the chair of mathematics, after
the dismissal of the original occupant, and taught its
highest branches without book in hand, and in a manner
that was pronounced unsurpassed by those who were
conversant with our first American institutions; for she
united to an entire comprehension of her subject the
finest power of imparting that comprehension to others.
In all feminine traits of character, this lady was as rare

as in her intellectual cultivation. Her native grace of manner imparted instruction in beauty as it radiates from a flower, when she stood before her classes solving the most difficult problems as if she had discovered them, and as if books had not yet been invented. Mr. Mann knew this need not be a remarkable case, and that the few instances in which women have attained eminence in the learned world need not be remarkable cases; that they were not due to original genius so much as to happy opportunity, such as he meant to multiply and offer to the many.

In the early settlement of States in this country, it is impossible to diffuse educational advantages of the highest kind very widely. The pioneers, though usually men of energy who go from cultivated communities, are not often men of literary culture; and therefore the home-life is not so cultivated a one as a republic needs. The next generation is still less cultivated, of course; and the young people must be sent from home to secure education, or go without it. The question is not, therefore, whether to be educated away from the restraints of parental care is the best thing, theoretically, for daughters, but whether they shall have instruction at all. Since a university in every village, as suggested by Thoreau, is not practicable or possible in the present condition of the world's learning or with the present value placed upon education, the important point is to furnish the best kind of institutions, — those most nearly resembling families, — as well as seats of learning, and where there is a concentration of learned forces. Every thing must be provided for, — not only instruction, but a supervision that partakes of the parental character, and a degree of freedom compatible with the preservation of refinement, or the inculcation of it when found wanting. In American society, the freedom of intercourse between the young has ever been found compatible with virtue, in striking contrast to the system of repression that exists in the older societies of the world, even of modern Europe.

Such was the fair temple of Learning that stood before Mr. Mann's inward vision. He could see all the elements of it; and he felt confident that he could combine them aright, if the means were only in his hands.

To most of the young women who frequented Antioch College, intellectual life was a new life. In Eastern communities, in the average of public schools, especially in the country, the superiority of scholarship is unquestionably on the side of girls. Evidence of this was found in the statistics of the Normal schools. It was precisely the contrary at the West. In many cases, they had been absolutely cut off from instruction. There was no common stock of knowledge. They did not even know the history of the settlement of the country by white men. Of the Pilgrim Fathers many had never heard. Still less had they had access to that literary culture so delightful to woman. An occasional exception only made this more striking. One family from Indiana had been so remote from schools, that the daughters, who were deficient in technical education of all sorts, had been furnished with books of fine quality by their father, a man of taste and talent, though of limited education; and had so fructified in mind by this privilege, that they immediately took high rank as superior minds in the college by their written essays, so misspelled that they could hardly be deciphered; the words, indeed, often running together to the length of half a line.

Many found that within themselves which they had not dreamed to exist; and their enthusiasm became equal to the joyfulness of the discovery. It is astonishing how rapidly young people ripen under favorable circumstances; and they carried a new life back to the homes from which they had come. Nor did the accurate knowledge gained by close and systematic study, and by intercourse with other minds, come amiss or unneeded to many to whom intellectual life was not wholly new. The general defect in woman's education is its want of systematic precision. In the best educated, the taste is often cultivated while the logical powers are neglected ; and critical knowledge is left to what are called the " liberally educated," which means the college-educated. The Normal schools are the only public institutions, probably, where women have found this want supplied. The model schools for practice, under experienced teachers, have been powerful auxiliaries to this end ; for no acquirements can be so thoroughly tested in any other way as by teaching them. To teach well, one must learn accurately ; and it has been well said that " no one can teach well who does not teach out of a mine." The critical examinations of Antioch College also made accurate knowledge indispensable.

Mr. Mann wished to have as much of his teaching force as possible of the best quality of Normal-school pupils. The superiority of their work was a constant subject of gratification to him. He was particularly pleased on one occasion when he heard the services of a young lady spoken of who was employed as assistant to the teacher of music, himself a pupil of Lowell Mason, the distinguished teacher of vocal music in Massachusetts. The young lady taught the piano ; and the peculiarity of her instruction was not only its quality, but the fact that she not only gave the lessons, but saw that they were faithfully practised. The appointed hours for which her service was due were but a small part of duty performed. She kept guard over the practising, and no pupil escaped her vigilance.   The remark was made in Mr. Mann's presence by one who knew what she was speaking of, " She teaches like one of Father Pierce's pupils."—" She *was* one of Father Pierce's pupils," was the reply.   Instrumental music was not taught in the Normal schools.   But it mattered not what Father Pierce's pupils taught : their teaching had a uniform characteristic.   I know nothing, personally, of the teaching in the Normal schools of the present day ; but that which was practised under the critical oversight of Mr. Mann was of the highest order. In Mr. Pierce and Mr. Tillinghast, the first preceptors of those schools, he found spirits kindred to his own ; and I can also speak from personal knowledge of Mr. Conant, one of the successors.   The components of the instruction Mr. Mann designed for Antioch College were the drill of West Point, and the conscience of the Normal schools of Massachusetts.   Unhappily, there were not resources to meet the demands for the physiological training by which he meant to build up bodies ; and jealousies in regard to the choice of teachers from the East (where were the Western teachers ?) interfered with the perfecting of his plans for intellectual and moral culture.   The latter, however, was not wholly dependent upon material aid ; and with the help of five ladies and one gentleman of the requisite training as well as of good natural ability, and of many others of equal good-will and ability though not so well fitted, it prospered to a remarkable extent, in spite of all drawbacks, even those of malice and envy.   One of the proofs of inferiority is envy of superiority.   Humble ignorance is, unfortunately, the exception rather than the rule.   This is partly due to the nature of ignorance, and is one of the difficulties that cannot easily be solved.

In some respects, another world lies beyond the gentle slopes of the dividing mountains which separate the East from the West. The general interests of all mankind are the same, and the bonds between the different sections of our country are indissoluble; for it is all one civilization, flowing from one centre, originally organized by a great and overmastering sentiment of progress, destined to leaven the whole body politic with civil, religious, and political liberty. But no one can have lived long in both without perceiving that such widely separated sections of country have local differences and interests, as well as motives of action, which only a cosmopolitan spirit can identify as one at heart. It is certain that the East does not wholly comprehend the needs of the West, or such an interest as this one would have made itself felt to better purpose among those whose helping hand could easily have lifted it from the shoals on which it stranded. There were noble exceptions to this.

The aid which the Unitarians gave to the institution was given with their characteristic liberality. The charter provided that two-thirds of the trustees and of the faculty should always be of the "Christian denomination." The Unitarians, whose speculative opinions are substantially the same, were perfectly willing to give assistance, notwithstanding this illiberal clause. They had no wish to have the control of the college. They wished to aid liberal and unsectarian education. They alone had an approximate conception of the needs of that section of the land, and of the great part it was to play in the future destinies of the country. They saw, as Mr. Mann did, that this "Christian" sect was the only conduit through which unsectarian education could flow into the West; for other religious sects were too exclusive to work cordially for any such end. The Universalists had as bad a reputation among the Orthodox as the Unitarians, and therefore could not be thus used so safely. The idea that

God in his love and mercy would finally bring all men into his fold, however much they might have sinned in this world, was one step in advance even of the ordinary belief of Unitarians: therefore they must be atheists. Even many Unitarians were afraid of such latitudinarianism as that, and set bounds to the love of God. But they were perfectly disinterested toward the Christians, and magnanimous enough to pour out their money without receiving even courtesy at their hands, so they would but improve by the use of it; and they were willing to trust that to Mr. Mann's judgment, capacity, and experience. But Pegasus cannot work in harness. The more liberal and disinterested they were, the more they were suspected of secret designs. This suspicion was artfully made use of by disappointed men, whose want of character, not whose religious opinions, as they pretended, led to their dismissal from the faculty. The good and true men bore every indignity; were long-suffering under contumely; sacrificed portions of their salaries; waited uncomplainingly for their just dues (and *still wait*); and endeavored in every way to disarm ill-will, and to justify the motives of the truly generous sect that threw their thousands into an abyss, hoping one day to bridge it over. The men of the East alone knew the quality of the man who had undertaken the enterprise. How could the ignorant and the bigoted conceive of his plans, or comprehend their wisdom? To the very last, and even after the experienced head and heart that gave it its first impulse, and watched over it with the affection of a father, was irrevocably lost, the "Christian denomination" had every advantage of priority in action, plurality of vote, and repeated opportunities to rise from their own ashes. At last, the proposition came from themselves to deal more justly by their long-tried friends; and now there is hope of future success, if men can be found to labor in so arduous a field. The charter has been altered by excluding the obnoxious restriction. The unsectarian feature of the original plan has been practically realized. " It is no part of Christian charity to be imposed upon," has been well said. The Unitarians have vindicated their unsectarian spirit nobly. They are even beginning to feel that they do not stand quite firmly enough upon their own opinions to act always with energy. The re-action in them from the other hateful extreme had been so great as almost to become a weakness. They have made themselves liable to Fort-Sumter treacheries by their candor and benevolence, and begin to reproach one another for not defending themselves more manfully. The ground has been broken for them at the West. The blood of martyrdom waters the spot. If they have the pecuniary means, they can take an independent stand, and be no longer at the mercy of an ignorant and unappreciative public. Let them hang out their banner of Unitarianism, not defiantly, but invitingly, and crowds will come to enjoy the blessings they will diffuse. Many noble spirits, first kindled by Mr. Mann's labors, can give the best aid to any efforts now made. Time has winnowed the surrounding community of many characters that disfigured it, and marred all generous effort. It is not yet too late to enlist the enthusiasm of many who personally knew the spirit in which Mr. Mann worked upon the underpinnings, and who knew something of the experience he gained which should not be lost, and which they shared with him.

The body of the Christian denomination was represented by men of limited education and narrow views, but a little in advance of the general ignorance, and who cared more for the advancement of their sect than for the advancement of learning and virtue. Mr. Mann accepted ignorance as one of the evils he must necessarily combat. He did not despise it: he only pitied it, and bent every energy to removing it. But he had no respect for bigotry. The bigot may truly be said to be the only enemy that always baffled him. The influences of bigotry had clouded his childhood, taken the blue out of his sky in his early manhood, and haunted his imagination all his life. He encountered it in all his endeavors to promote the cause of education at the East as well as at the West. He hoped to drive it before him over the prairies, though he could not always hunt it out of its hiding-places in more conservative communities; but, where ignorance reigns, bigotry and superstition will be sure to dwell with it. He could exorcise it from the young; but it had become a part of the very vitality of the risen generation. Another demon, equally subtle, even more universal, the demon of selfishness, met him on every side. The two combined have ever baffled the influence of Christianity itself. They were linked together against all his efforts there. It would be an ungrateful task to enter into the details of the strife he waged with them. Perhaps he had conquered them at last. He thought he had driven them at bay at least, and hoped to deal a final blow by *success*, after outward obstacles to the prosperity of the institution were overcome. But his strength was spent in the conflict, in consequence of the great labors imposed upon him; and the venom which had been diffused by the crafty, the bigoted, and the selfish, had so far poisoned the atmosphere, that none have been found strong enough since his death to extract the poison.

The circumstance of his joining the Christian denomination, of which he speaks himself in one of his letters, has been made the occasion of traducing his character for truth and openness. Any man can be accused of insinecrity by those who disagree with him. He has been accused of it in politics by those who were angry with him for not adopting their views, and because he chose to make his own discriminations, and reserve to himself the right of breaking away from party when he thought parties forgot great principles in their partisan zeal; and he has been accused of it in religious matters both by those whose latitudinarian views went beyond all the freedom of thought that he had attained, and by those who feared *all* freedom of thought. He was a man who earnestly enforced his own convictions of duty, but who modestly estimated the value of speculative opinions, and wished to impose them upon no one, not even his own children. He had that confidence in truth that made him trust it to enforce itself upon a truly sincere and inquiring mind. In short, his faith in God, and God's adaptation of means to ends, was a vital faith. He broke away from the dogmas that were inculcated upon his youth by the force of this faith, when he was driven to the alternative of believing God an unjust God, or of doubting the interpretations of the Christian record that were imposed upon him. A truly logical intellect like his could not hesitate which to reject, until further light dawned upon him.

In the Bible-class at Antioch College, which he held for such members as volunteered to attend, it was his object to make a fair statement of the various interpretations, by different sects, of all disputed portions of the Scriptures, and then leave his hearers to adopt that which seemed to them most correct. On these occasions, his appeals to the conscience and the affections were as unique as his biblical criticisms. The latter he prepared with the aid of all the authorities he could find. For the former he appealed to the consciousness of each one of his hearers; for in love and good works all men can unite, whatever

tricks their intellects may play upon them. There are
no two interpretations of the precepts, " Love one another," and " Do unto others as you would that others
should do unto you."

He has been called Utopian in his theory of the relation
that should exist between young people in colleges. He
thought the time had come when a higher principle than
emulation should actuate those who were striving for intellectual and moral excellence, and when young people
in colleges should be taught to live together as brethren,
and upon a higher code of honor than that by which
rogues protect each other in evil-doing. Stupid people
looked on, and thought, that, if dogmatic religion were not
taught, no religion could exist, and that there was no
higher law than that of the rogue's creed, — " Defend me,
and I will defend you." Indeed, the community in general know no other religion, and do not understand the
principle of brotherly love; but he felt sure that he could
evoke a generous and Christian sympathy for each other in
the young, if he had a chance to address them. And the
event proved that he was right. Emulation was exorcised
under his influence. Mutual furtherance and interest in
each other's progress, intellectual and moral, took the
place of it. The contrary was the exception. He inculcated the precept, that the position of students created in
them serious duties and responsibilities toward each
other; that, if the good among them could not influence
the viciously inclined, it became their duty to seek the
assistance of those who had assumed the parental relation
towards them, not for purposes of chastisement, but for
more powerful influence.

A college was set fairly in operation, disfigured by no
traditional barbarisms or meannesses, such as some of
the institutions of the country have derived from their

foreign prototypes. Mr. Mann frowned down the first symptoms of riotous conduct, and by meeting in fair encounter, and battling with, what is called and also what is yielded to as " youthful indiscretion," taught young people coming to years of discretion to put aside the idle pranks of boys, and live together a dignified life of mutual respect and respectability. The presence of young ladies in the institution doubtless made this work easier. A public meeting was soon called by the students, and a vote taken to uphold obedience to law and order. A paper dated 1859, found in his desk, is a fair sample of such resolutions as were voluntarily drawn up by successive classes from the very beginning : —

At a meeting of the senior class of Antioch College, March 16, 1859, the following preamble and resolutions were *unanimously* adopted : —

Whereas we, the senior class of 1859, believe in the necessity of laws for the regulation of any literary institution, and have full confidence in the ability of the faculty of our institution to make such laws ; therefore

Resolved, That we will endeavor to obey the laws enacted by the faculty for the promotion of good morals and good order.

Resolved, That our influence should be such as to induce our fellow-students to observe these laws, and such as shall promote the general welfare of the institution.

This paper was duly signed by the chairman and the secretary of the meeting, and the words were not idle words. They implied far more than at first seems obvious; for this promise to use their influence for public order was resolutely acted upon. The higher classes did not exercise a spirit of mean and petty annoyance towards the lower classes, as is the case in most colleges, but stood in the relation of elder brothers and sisters to them. The first senior class was small, but every member of it was a gem; and those eight members, constituting the first class that graduated,—swelled to fifteen in the third year by a deputation from Oberlin College in the same State,— were a better force in the moral regulation of the institution than the faculty set over them. Each one of the former proved an efficient aid in the discipline; while many of the latter threw apples of discord not only into their own ranks, but among the students. Mr. Mann found it easier to induce the young people to take brotherly care of each other's welfare than to infuse his own spirit into the already demoralized characters of some of his coadjutors in government. This remark applies only to three of the faculty, well known to those familiar with the short annals of Antioch College, and who were got rid of at the first opportunity. But Mr. Mann felt strong in his young battalions. It was not long before they understood that he looked to them to be their own police: and when a tutor, who had resided in the gentlemen's dormitory to keep order, was exchanged for a lady teacher, he appealed to the senior class, one day after chapel service, to know if they were not sufficiently strong in moral force to take care of the building without such supervision. They rose to their feet simultaneously, accepted the trust joyfully and confidently, kept the promise well, and transmitted its spirit to their successors. It was Mr. Mann's pride and delight ever after to walk through the gentlemen's hall at any hour of the day or night, and to take visitors with him, to convince them that a true spirit of honor and fidelity could be evoked from the young, if they were properly addressed. But this had not been achieved slumbering. It was a work he had delegated to no man; for, though there were others who shared his faith, it required a de-

votion, a vigilance, a judgment, and a spirit of love, which
were untiring, and knew no secondary interests. Often
he sprang from his bed at dead of night to know personally the secret of an unwonted sound, or to satisfy himself
whether any suspicion of wrong-doing were well founded;
but he was so happy as never to have cause to repent of
the confidence he had reposed in his young friends. So
truly did he infuse his own spirit of guardianship into the
hearts of his best students, that they often came to him
to consult upon the measures to be pursued with a delinquent brother, that he might be saved from a summons
before the faculty. Such petitions as the following were
not infrequent, though they were not always drawn up in
writing : —

" We the undersigned, classmates of ——, from our long and
intimate acquaintance with him, believe that he will pursue a
course of life honorable to himself, and useful to society; and we
do hereby express our earnest desire that he may be permitted to
graduate with us."

Can it be doubted that one so petitioned for, though
in danger at the moment of losing his standing, kept
faith with his companions, and walked in the strait path ?
Such petitions were offered before Mr. Mann had by his
baccalaureate publicly proclaimed to the world that he
would give no diploma to an unworthy character; but
his students understood his principle very early. Far
worse cases than this one, over which Mr. Mann and his
students worked together in true filial and fraternal love,
would disprove the slur that has been cast upon him by
those who have said that he was not fit to guide young
men because he " could not shut his eyes." He was
principled against shutting his eyes. He would hunt a
lie or a vice into its own corner, and bring it to light, if

he spent months in the work, if he found he could not disarm it or bring it to confession by milder means; but it is not true that he could not forgive a delinquent. He asked only for repentance, and was severe upon those only who sinned against light. To the weakly erring his tenderness was unbounded, and his patience measureless. In these labors of love he was often so spent and prostrated, that he needed to be soothed as if a father's heart and hope had been wounded ; but his joy in success was so great, that, when he was thrown to the ground, he would rise from it Antæus-like, and go on rejoicing to new conflicts. Many a student was dismissed from his institution for the vice of persistent lying, — not always publicly, but removed by private communication with friends ; for that was the most hopeless form of youthful vice in his eyes, and he did not think it right to allow its contaminating influence in such a community. Our national vice of intemperance he treated like a physician, and shared with his students the vigils held over the few cases that came to an alarming crisis in the institution. But that vice never made headway there : a healthy public opinion made it impossible. This was his first object, to winnow out inveterate sinners of all kinds, and establish a public opinion that should soon frown down all excesses. To this end he was no respecter of persons ; and it is true that the children of some of the most prominent patrons of the institution were sent away from it on this ground, — that reckless and irresponsible persons must not be allowed there to corrupt the unwary, and spread demoralizing influences which no disciplinary or precautionary measures could counteract. The result of this care was that fine moral tone which distinguished the institution, and at last made it possible to receive difficult cases and effect reforms without injury to others. Before long, the college community ranked far higher than the outside community; and it was this success which induced Mr. Mann to remain in it, even after he himself felt that his strength was giving way. He was confident that he had proved the position he had taken in the beginning; and he knew that an influence had gone out, and would continue to go out, into the schools and homes of the West, as far as his students might be scattered, that would make the institution one, as he once expressed it, " where men would send their children to save them." In conferences with other college faculties, he obtained expressions of concurrence with his views; but, as far as I have learned, the concurrence ended with the expression. He thought something was gained, however, by winning over the intellectual sympathies of the elder generation so far that they could not in decency controvert them or deny their wisdom. He knew what advantage he had over older institutions which had been transplanted from the Old World with all their brutalities of custom; but he did not relinquish the hope that even they might be brought to shame and reformation.

A noble moralist, after sitting nine years in the Massachusetts Legislature, where he never lost sight of the highest aspects of public life, said he had left it with a better opinion of human nature than he had when he entered it. How heartily Mr. Mann sympathized in this opinion, after seeing some of his young pupils, fully possessed with the noble Christian sentiment of brotherly love, lift some of their companions out of the deepest mire of sensuality and intemperance into the light of a new life!

But one complaint of depredation was ever made; and that was the robbery of an Irishman's poultry-yard. This was treated by a short history, after morning prayers (an occasion which Mr. Mann often seized for any disciplinary remarks he wished to make in public), of the oppressions and disabilities which induced that unfortunate population to emigrate to a country better governed than their own, where their very consciences were made the means of oppressing them; and an appeal to the better feelings of the youth around him to live up to the theory of their country's hospitality, and show the fruits of a superior culture by good behavior. It was well done, and it was the last occasion for such an exhortation.

No accidental or adventitious circumstances can account for this. It was made a point of honor from the beginning to be gentlemanly and trustworthy in all relations with the community. A lady walking in the village of Yellow Springs, or its outskirts, felt protected by the sight of any student of the college. Was not this a result worthy to die for?

When Mr. Hill was invited to be Mr. Mann's successor, the remark was made to him that he would hardly be required to carry out Mr. Mann's Utopian views as exemplified in his "Code of Honor." Mr. Hill replied that he had watched Mr. Mann's course with the greatest interest, and it was that special feature of it which made him wish to be his successor.

There is no doubt that Mr. Mann's principle and resolution in regard to refusing admittance to no one on account of their color was a temporary disadvantage to the college, and alienated many who would. otherwise have contributed to its support. He would have been very glad if such applications had not been made until pecuniary difficulties were past; but he would never for a moment listen to the refusal of such applicants, if suitably prepared to enter. I remember but two instances in which the presence of two lovely young ladies of talent and refinement, who were slightly tinged in complexion, lost any actual scholars to the institution. One was of a young man from Delaware, whose father professed to be opposed to slavery; but, when he learned from his son that he was in the same classes with these young ladies, he ordered him to leave the institution at once. By the time the command reached him, the son had discovered that the scholarship and standing of these classmates were far above his own, and that they were highly regarded, and treated with as much respect as others: and he would fain have disobeyed the parental injunction; but it was peremptorily repeated, and he left with great but unavailing regret.

The other instance was that of a wealthy gentleman in the neighborhood, at the time President of the Board of Trustees. When his own daughter was of suitable age, and qualified to enter the preparatory school, he ordered the steward not to renew the entrance-tickets of those young ladies of color. The steward refused to comply, except by a vote of the Teaching Committee (Mr. Mann was one of these); which being refused, the gentleman threw up his office and all interest in the institution, and sent his daughter elsewhere. If the college is ever opened again, it is to be hoped that the great change of sentiment upon this subject, which has resolved some of the best and noblest of our Northern men and women into an educational commission for the instruction of the colored race, will make such circumstances as the above forever impossible.

Mr. Mann's own letters will be the most satisfactory history of this last, best portion of his life; and they will show how gradually, and almost unconsciously to himself (for he never admitted it), his hope of success faded.

MY DEAR DOWNER, — It is a long time since I have daily said to myself, "Now I must write to my friend Downer;" but the day has brought its engagements and occupations, and so the letter to you, not the remembrance of you, has been postponed. Probably I have suffered more from the delay than you have. . . . We are comfortably situated at last. Ohio growths are rapid growths; but this does not hold true of our house, which has not yet grown up to the chamber-floor. Another year, if we live, will probably find us in better condition. . . .

As to my daily life, it is a life of being busy rather than a life of hard labor. We have two hundred students, and should have had more if our dormitories had been ready to receive them. This is considered here rather an extraordinary beginning. If they should call on "Mr. President," on an average, only once apiece in ten days, it would make twenty calls a day; and so you see what my liabilities to be interrupted are. When the main building is done, I shall have a room in it; and then I shall have particular hours for receiving applications and visits. But you ask "how I like." Well, in few words, I think the moulding of youthful mind and manners is the noblest work that man or angels could do; and I ought to be content to fill even a subordinate sphere in such work. I have now a course of lectures, mainly physiological, which I am delivering on Friday evenings this term; and I have constant opportunities to say a word which may serve to shape opinion and character.

I preached, Sunday before last, to a large audience of students and villagers, and got through, perhaps, as well as I had any right to expect for a beginner.

Last Sunday, Mrs. M——, R——, and I joined the Christian Church. We thought our influence for good over the students would be increased. We had no ceremony of baptism; we subscribed to no creed. We assented to taking the Bible for the "man of our counsel," as it was expressed, with the liberty of interpretation for ourselves; and we acknowledged Christian character to be the only true test of Christian fellowship. This is all.

I was requested to speak for myself before the church. I said, that, ever since I had known the theological views of the Christian denomination, I had found them to be more coincident with my own than those of any other denomination; that I believed the whole duty of man consisted in knowing and doing the will of God; that I desired to express this belief, and to show my regard for those who held it by uniting with them; that my views for years had undergone no change. And then I entered an explicit *caveat* against the idea that belonging to any visible church organization was essential to salvation, quoting the case of Cornelius the centurion. I was unanimously voted in; and so of the others, without their saying any thing, except through me, that they also wished to join. . . .

Yours ever and truly,

HORACE MANN.

NOVEMBER, ALL-SAINTS' DAY, 1853.

MY DEAR MR. MANN, — "All Saints" is a good day to write to you, who sympathize with them all, and some of the sinners too, I trust. I concede to you the 29th for your lecture, with no meritorious self-denial; for I had written and asked for a different day for myself.

I have heard from you indirectly twice, — by the Howlands, good souls that they are; and Downer, great noble heart that he is. Sorry that your *impedimenta* got impeded. The "Boston Courier" praised your Inaugural highly. What have you been doing to deserve that? We go on nicely here. Sumner is stumping the State: if he had done it last year, you would not have gone to Yellow Springs till January. Mr. Palfrey, you see, kicks at the new combination. He is good, conscientious as a saint, but not progressive. I respect his *sacredness of individualism* He will not be mixed up with other men's messes, and so is a perpetual mar-plan, but always with most conscientious motives.

Love from all to ditto. Truly,

THEO. PARKER.

YELLOW SPRINGS, OHIO, Nov. 29, 1853.

MY DEAR MR. COMBE, — . . . M—— acknowledges that she has been egotistic; and I must be egotistic too, if talking about our own affairs constitutes egotism. I am wholly absorbed in my new work. I want to transfer the more improved methods of instruction and discipline and the advanced ideas of education from the East to the West. I am well aware that the seed which I hope to sow will hardly come up in my day; but my causality is so strong, that what *is to be at any time* has a semblance of being immediately present. Faith without causality must be a tough problem. Oh, how I wish and yearn that you could be here, so that we might spend the remainder of our days together, and that, whoever of us should die first, the survivor might close his eyes!

Farewell!

HORACE MANN.

YELLOW SPRINGS, OHIO, Dec. 5, 1853.

MY DEAR MR. COMBE, — I do not know that we have any thing new in this country of which you would not be likely to hear in England through the ordinary channels of communication. Our new President is a thorough party man, who has been obliged to pass through a fiery ordeal, or rather to run a terrible gantlet, in the distribution of his patronage. The "New-York Evening Post," a Free-soil, Democratic paper (which, however, strenuously supported Mr. Pierce during the late campaign), commends him in a left-handed way for filling all our foreign missions with persons who can leave the country for the next four years without being missed at home. It is thought that the nominations to office have almost exclusive reference to the highest good of the country and of mankind, — that is, assuming that the President's re-election at the end of the four years will be more promotive of the well-being of mankind than all other things, — for these nominations are made with reference to that event.

What do you think of France? . . .

Frivolity, sensuality, and the Catholic religion, — what will they not do for the debasement of mankind?

Howe remains very much as heretofore, — rather broken in health, but glorious in spirit. When he goes, it will be almost like taking the pilot from the helm. I should miss him more than it is possible for me to describe. . . .

Since writing the above, I have received your note of the 27th of May. If your health depended upon my volition, how strong you should be!

I am, as ever, most truly your friend,

HORACE MANN.

YELLOW SPRINGS, OHIO, April 24, 1854.

MY DEAR MR. CRAIG, — What will you think of Mr. Horace Mann? What can Mr. Horace Mann expect that you will think of him? Though you have written to me several times since I came to sojourn this side of Jordan, and made only the most reasonable requests, yet I must confess that I have not replied at all. Now, rather than bear the whole offence of this *apparent* neglect and unkindness, I must charge something to Nature, or circumstances, or fate.

Let me say that I have either had too much to do, or Nature did not give me strength enough to perform what she threw into my hands, or circumstances baffled me in the fulfilment of events that I counted on as certain. In short, it is hardly too much to say that I have thought of you continually, have retained all my admiration of you, have praised you with earnest and sincere words, and have all the time — that is, from week to week for three months past — intended to avail myself of the occasion of sending you my Inaugural, to write you a letter of explanations and thanks and hopes. For three months past, I have been constantly deluded with the promise that my address would be ready for me, and as constantly disappointed. I now send you a copy of it, invoking your kindness, but deprecating your criticism.

My dear Mr. Craig, when are you coming out here? It seems as though almost any thing desirable could be done if you were with us. Much must long remain to be done, if you are not. I want once more to see you and converse with you on this subject

Shall you not attend the Unitarian convention next May in Louisville? When you do come, you must calculate to spend two or three sabbaths with us, and preach in our chapel.

We are prospering as to numbers. All places for lodging in the college and in the village have been crowded from the beginning. We now have almost three hundred. More than a thousand have applied, but could not obtain accommodations. We are, however, filling up fast enough. I should not desire a very large quantity of this raw material all at once. We had better have it and manipulate it by degrees. Do let me hear from you; do let me see you. When you come, come with the idea in your mind of an *ultimate* change of residence.

Yours as ever, with great regard,

HORACE MANN.

The following letter was addressed to the acting superintendent of the institution, and shows by its tenor how little Mr. Mann and the other members of the faculty were consulted upon the important point of selecting teachers. In this instance, as in many others, the selections were made without reference to the instruction required, but to satisfy denominational demands; a consideration quite at variance with the declared spirit of the institution. One such appointee could neither spell nor use English correctly, and yet he had been set over the preparatory school.

YELLOW SPRINGS, April 27, 1854.

A. M. MERRIFIELD, ESQ.

DEAR SIR, — At the beginning of our present session, in order to meet the promises of our original prospectus and the requests of a large class of our students, we included book-keeping among the studies to be taught during this term. This was inserted in the programme, which has been posted in our halls ever since.

Inquiries have been constantly made, since our present term commenced, when the class in book-keeping would be organized. To these inquiries we have replied, that we were only awaiting the arrival of a new teacher, whom, for four weeks, we have now been daily expecting.

After you introduced Mr. K—— to me yesterday, and I informed him that book-keeping was one of the studies he was desired to teach, he replied that he had never studied it, was unacquainted with it, and, had he been informed by you that he was expected to do so, he should not have engaged to come here.*

At a meeting of the faculty, held to-day, the members instructed me to address the trustees through you, and inform them that they deem it indispensable, in order to redeem our promises on the one side, and to meet the justly raised expectations of the students on the other, that some teacher be immediately appointed who can teach book-keeping.

All the members of the faculty expressed the opinion, that, had any one of them been inquired of as to the qualifications expected in or the duties required of the new teacher, book-keeping would have been the first item mentioned after the necessary executive or disciplinary power.

In compliance with the direction of the faculty, I transmit to you this statement, and remain

Very truly yours, &c.,

HORACE MANN.

The chapter of difficulties opened up by this letter might be continued by innumerable details. Suffice it to say, for the present, that it had no end. Jealousy of Unitarian influence predominated in all the college councils, from its commencement to its sale under the sheriff's hammer in 1859. Many high-minded men were temporarily alienated from its interests by the industrious circulation of this sectarian jealousy. It prevented the appointment of some able teachers, as well as saddled incompe-

---

* This very estimable gentleman was selected by the superintendent, without any consultation with Mr. Mann as to what was required in the department. He could teach Latin admirably, however.

29

tent ones upon the institution. In some departments, this evil was never fully remedied ; and it was only amazing that so many students clung to it so long ; for many came and went disappointed of their just expectations, especially in regard to modern languages, which disappointment was due to no other cause. It is true that the want of funds came to be a serious obstacle to securing the services of distinguished men whose names might have given *éclat* to the college ; but, for all purposes of thorough instruction, Mr. Mann could have found enough persons who would have worked under him for a pittance, if he could have had any freedom of choice. But the first qualification of a candidate came to be, in the eyes of the trustees. "*Does he agree* sufficiently with us in religious opinions ? " instead of "*Has he the attainments to fit him for the position ?*" Yet how the brave, indomitable heart plodded on, hoping continually for better things, till the burden was no longer to be borne !

NEWARK, OHIO, Jan. 1, 1854.

MY DEAR MR. PARKER, — I wish you a happy New Year; ay, a great many of them. I came down to this pleasant village to lecture, from Cleveland. There I heard your name announced, and it has been ringing in my ears ever since. How I want to hear you ! how I want to see you ! When I have time to think of it, what a feeling of loneliness and far-offness comes over me at the idea of being separated from you and Howe and Downer, and others whom I so much love, not only benevolently, but selfishly ! for how necessary a part of all personal hopes and plans, as well as all my more public duties, you had become. But, when I think of what was once my home and my sphere, a feeling which I suppose must be like Turkish fatalism comes over me, and I say to myself. " Here you are, and here you must remain. Fate has you in its grip, and resistance is impossible. No secondary cause can release you, at least for a time. Go on, and transmute your evil into good as far as you can." So I submit, and try to make sunrises and sunsets look as when I could see my friends in the horizon.

I have nothing to say which can be of any special interest to you. I write to beseech you, if possible, to come and see us when you are in our neighborhood. If you go to Cincinnati, you are, when at Xenia, but nine miles from this place; even at Sandusky or Toledo, only a day's ride. What a different hue you would give to the sunlight! I had a most delightful visit from Downer. I felt a new emotion. I enjoyed his presence so much as to make me taciturn. Did you ever have that feeling beside a friend? I have not for years, and supposed it belonged to lovers.

I am working in faith. I don't know as I see any results, or ever shall see them; but I think that causes must produce effects. and so strive to put the causes in motion. I know that such things as I try to say to the young would have influenced me when I was young; and so I hope they may not all fall upon stony ground. But our sphere of action is so limited, and our foresight so short, that we must draw our encouragement more from faith and our philosophy than from realization. My position here has brought me into practical outward religious exercises; and I assure you I have enjoyed them very much.

Before I came from Massachusetts, I asked several of our authors and poets to give me each a copy of their published works for our library. I should have asked you too; only, when I saw you, you excluded all else from my thoughts. Let me ask you now. Please send them to me from home; or, if you can, bring them with you to our place, or to the point where you approach it nearest.

I wish you would also procure for me Dr. Hitchcock's "Discourse on the Resurrection:" I mean the one in which he holds that the "new body" may have no relation of identity with the "old body," but may only be the same number of pounds of oxygen, hydrogen, and carbon, got together in the same way! or at least so nearly the same way that no one will ever detect the difference. which I suppose would be just as well.

If Mrs. Mann were here, I know she would join me in most loving messages to Mrs. Parker and Miss Stevenson and other friends.

Yours as ever, most truly, HORACE MANN.

These familiar words to his friend show a trait in Mr. Mann's character, — the ever-recurring doubt, whether he was doing all that ought to be done in whatever sphere of duty he might be engaged. How often, when he had been wrought to great fervor of thought and speech on some topic of paramount interest to his own mind and heart, would he wonder and wish to know whether the fire kindled in other breasts! A little more confidence in his own power to execute his conceptions would have added much to his happiness; but, as results do not come immediately, he had to take refuge in his causality for encouragement. What a blessing his logic was to his heart! over what seas of difficulty and opposition and ingratitude it bore him!

One of his most appreciative pupils,[*] writing to a friend of the impression he made in his class-room, says, " His mode of teaching was suggestive and stimulating; not so holding his flock to the dusty, travel-worn path as to forbid their free access to every inviting meadow or spring by the way. It was his wont to hear us recite a few hours each week, assigning special lessons to special pupils, giving each some question, some theory, some matter-of-fact inquiry, on which each could pursue investigations at leisure, and prepare a paper to be read before the whole class, and be commented upon by himself. The range of these topics (when political economy was the subject) — taking in questions of agriculture and soil-fertilization, of canals and railroads, of commerce, of cotton-gins or steam-ploughs, of population, of schools and churches and public charities in their economic relations, and of those rising civilizations which bear up art and foster science, both necessitating and making possible greater civil and spiritual freedom, yet having their roots

* Rev. H. C. Badger.

among these lower material conditions — illustrates the comprehensiveness of Mr. Mann's favorite methods of educating and instructing our minds.

"But even this was not so peculiar to him as a certain personal impulse he imparted to all who came in contact with him, — the *impetus* with which his mind smote our minds, rousing us, and kindling a heat of enthusiasm, as it were, by the very power of that spiritual percussion. It was in this that he was so incomparable. A man might as well hope to dwell near the sun unmoved as not to glow when brought to feel his fervid love of truth and heartfelt zeal in its quest. The fresh delight of childhood seemed miraculously prolonged through his life: truth never palled upon his mind; the world never wore a sickly light. And this cheerful spirit, which was at bottom nothing but the most living faith in God and man, was so contagious, that indifference, misanthropy, despair of attaining truth, gave way before it, or were transformed into a like hearty enthusiasm.

"Then, in guiding the new-roused impulse, he was so conscientious and candid, so careful not to trench on the borders of individuality, nor to let our loving respect for him so fix our eyes on his opinion that we should lose the beckon of some proximate truth, that we felt him as gentle to guide as he was powerful to inspire."

Another answer to this question, to which he could hear no response at the time, is in the words of one who grew under him as only noble germs can grow, who saw him in all his later trials, and who watched over his last days with the tenderness of a son; and of whom the sufferer said, "His touch is as delicate as that of a woman." He now devotes himself and his rare gifts of heart and mind to the noble charity of guardian of the Soldiers' Home at Memphis, Miss.*

* C. W. Christy, guardian of the Soldiers' Home at Memphis, Miss.

With Horace Mann it is eminently true that religion was central: it was the core of his life. Four years ago, I did not say so; but in the depths of experience I have since learned that morality, as he saw it, includes what is usually called religion. He did not translate the moral law of the universe as too many of us translate it, who are satisfied to say that "honesty is the best policy;" that it is better to do right than wrong: but he found, and he said boldly, that the moral law is in the imperative. We ought to do and feel right because it is right, not because God commands, or that we shall get our reward in the future. If there be any moral perfection possible for us in this life, it is to have come to so love and desire right and virtue simply as right and virtue, that we shall not need to elect or choose them, but shall unconsciously and spontaneously cleave to and follow after them. To my own mind, I am wont to symbolize the life of Mr. Mann by the figure of an ardent and strong youth begirt with the perils and temptations of life, with these four sentences engraved around him in characters of fire : —

What is the moral law of the universe, — the highest I know, or can know? and what does it teach?

That moral law ought to be obeyed.

That moral law can be obeyed.

That moral law I will obey, *ruat cœlum*.

And when I add that no press or allurement of circumstances was able to entice or force him from his loyalty to this moral law, I have completed the statement of the central and organizing fact of his entire life. From this point we easily trace outward through his external life the influence of what thus lay at the centre of his being. All those angularities, those Gibraltar points, which so foiled and annihilated his adversaries, were doubled in power by his fidelity to the right. I said, his angularities; for thus certain traits in him appeared to some minds: but the clearer vision of another world will show us that his character was not angular, save as it was a mighty and loyal will crystallized.

Does it seem strange to any that such a character as his, as the world saw it, should have religion as its basis and organizing principle? . . . He tells us himself that he early came to grapple with the highest and yet fearfulest problems of human existence. Is not here proof enough that Religion, in some form, must be the primal conscious force of his life? The world dealt sternly with him : she brought him to the armories of power ; she trained him to industry or diligence, until, as he himself says, it became his second nature. And who shall trace the secret foundations of wisdom and power laid in that theologic or religious orphanage which brings one face to face with despair and with God ; which fills one's being with such an unutterable sense of aloneness and captivity, that life reveals itself as a flight through time to the bosom of the infinite Father? Who shall tell us what magazines of will are gained, of grim, earnest force, direct, persistent, affirmative, swift ; what clearness and length of vision? We are everywhere called upon to adulterate our life. It is considered a fine thing to have a little virtue, a homœopathic pellet of piety, in solution, in social and business life ; but, as the point of saturation is neared, the man is regarded as less and less likely to succeed in the world : every thing is spoiled if there be a precipitation. We forget that to be truly religious is to love as the soul says, without compromise, without hesitancy, without evasion, and without idleness ; with a rugged and angular energy, it may be, scorning consequences ; or possibly with a lamb-like, retiring temper, which works without friction ; which stays at home, or, if it goes abroad, goes as the angel of mercy and inevitable love, so evacuated of passion as to be unable to lift the axe of the reformer. Is there not need of both the lion and the lamb? And is it our place to say that God should send here none but lambs? If Nature makes up her material into a lion, the breath of life which God breathes into him does not transform him into a lamb, but he becomes one of God's lions. . . .

There are men who seem to front an infinite background of law, justice, and power : in their presence, the reverences natural to the soul rise up to assert themselves. All who came into the presence of Mr. Mann, especially in his hours of work, when the lion within him rose up and fought, felt that awe and reverence which power, genius, and virtue inspire. Few persons, if any, were so abandoned as to dare to be trivial or vicious in his presence. Some of us here know how he grappled with the apostle of free love : others can tell better than I of his conflict with the " great giant " of New England; of his short but earnest career in Congress; of his holy war upon intemperance, tobacco-using, and slavery. At such times, from every nerve of his being there seemed to come forth a whole park of Jove's artillery. It was this same religiousness that gave him such an inevitable directness in all he said and did. He gravitated as straight and as surely to the right as the stone gravitates to the earth. He seemed to travel the highway of power. He had courage and persistency because he had faith enough to do duty. We all know how present to him was the future. Immortality was one of the most familiar words upon his lips; and there seemed never to be absent from his thought the living sense of the truth, that the future flows out of the present. Virtue is moral victory, — is an infinite series of moral victories: hence constancy of purpose and of labor is indispensable. Labor to him was a sacrament. As Cecil said of Sir Walter Raleigh, "We know that he could and did *toil terribly.*" I find no other character which so illustrates to me that saying of Novalis as Mr. Mann: "By enlargement and cultivation of our activity, we change ourselves into fate."

Character and motives seemed almost transparent beneath his look. Cecil says, "I could write down twenty cases wherein I wished God had done otherwise than he did, but which I now see, had I had my own will, would have led to extensive mischief." Thus I think we may say of Mr. Mann's administration of this college. How many of us at the time thought some of his measures needlessly severe? Some persons, perhaps, thought them unjust. We were sure our own way would have been better. But now, after a little time, can we put our finger upon a case where we think our way would have been better? How much of his wisdom, how much of any man's wisdom, comes to him as a result of his love of virtue, and of his obedience to the moral law? Those are not hyperboles of the heart, beside itself with enthusiasm, which we read in the Scriptures: "The fear of the Lord is the beginning of wisdom;" "Commit thy ways unto the Lord, and he shall bring forth thy righteousness and thy judgment as the noonday." Do we not think, that, the purer and more transparent the medium, the farther and more copiously enters the light? and is not the good man the medium through which God shines down into humanity?

One of the great benefits of such a man is that his life forces men to take sides decisively; to be black or white : for it is yet true that the least tolerable of all human beings are those who are neither hot nor cold. His speech and his manner constantly made the appeal, " How long halt ye between two opinions ? " I often saw in him the old Hebrew earnestness, sternness, clear far-sightedness, that sees things as God sees them. And then he had the rarest of all qualities, — that of living as he believed. That is the highest praise of any man. Let him be solid; of one piece through and through; a man upon whom you can make observations, and of whom you can compute the future with just as great certainty as the astronomer calculates the movements of the sun and stars for centuries ahead.

I find no discrepancy between this deep religiousness of his character, and that fierce, unevadable vigor with which he pursued vice and its confirmed votaries. Where virtue and right were assailed, he acted with the rapidity and intensity of the lightning-stroke. The delusion has fallen upon men in these days, that every thing is to be done by compromise; by compounding with God, so as to let the Devil have matters partly his own way. It is expected that the attrition of our life will abrade and remove not only the social angles, but also the moral angles, of a man's character. Hence it is regarded as in some degree a fault in a man to act in the presence of vice as natural forces act when the conditions of their action are met. Truth, we ought to know, has a natural divine right; and whether it lives and acts in a man, or in the thunderbolt from God's own hand, it has a normal right to resist, to crush, to annihilate. The common parlor prudence of our day, the custom of lying, and betraying one's self to the Devil, which we have baptized and admitted not only into conversation and business, but even into the church and into morals, under the name of expediency and good policy, — this custom of trying to serve God and Mammon, Mr. Mann defied, and boldly put under his feet. His life was a constant negation to that shameful maxim of worldly policy, that every man has his price.

For five years he went out and in among us, our teacher and adviser, our reproof and encouragement; a Christian, and, as it were,

our father.   He came to many before me to-day as the spring sun
comes to northern groves and hillsides, the bringer and free-giver
of life and beauty.   He rose upon our educational world like a
star out of the east.   And yet the very depth and blood-heat
of my reverence and affection for him would forbid me to open my
lips in the presence of those less wrought upon by his heroic life
and death.   As yet, we are unused to his absence.   If his lithe form,
with its elastic, resilient step and dignified bearing, radiant with
the strength of self-conquest and impregnable virtue, were to walk
among us again to-day, and we were to hear once more his well-
weighed, living speech, it would be as if our dearest friend had returned to us after a short absence, rather than as the appearing of
the dead among the living.   The world saw him as the stern, lion-
hearted worker.   We who dwelt with him as his pupils knew him
as the kind adviser, as tender and solicitous of our welfare as our
own parents.   Those who knew him in the bosom of his family,
where he unbent, and let all the genialness and affection of his
deep nature come forth, tell us that in none did they find such
richness and tenderness of heart, — richness and tenderness as of
a mother.

Numerous other testimonials of similar interest could
be given from the reminiscences of students; but the
limits of this work cannot contain them.

Boston, Jan. 8, 1854.

My dear Mr. Mann, — Many a Christmas and New-Year's good
wish did we all send after you as the old year drew nigh its end.
You do not know how often Howe and Downer and I want to see
you, and strengthen ourselves in your great might and high purpose.   But it is a noble post that you occupy.   I am glad that you
are there, — sad enough for my own sake; sympathizing, too, for the
heartache which I know often comes over the homesick man.   But
I think of the generations which will rise up and call you blessed.
I think New England had no seed in her granary which the West
needed so much as yourself.   Now God has sown you in Ohio, I
look for great harvests which mankind shall one day reap there·

from. I know what energy you will bring to the work, what power to conceive and to organize your thought. I am glad you have also taken to preaching, trusting that you will preach the great natural religion whereof the revelations of old time are but a small part. God made the universe ; man made the Bible ; and poor Christian ministers say to the people, "Hush! don't listen to the universe, only to the Bible : the universe is Nature ; the Bible is grace ; it is God." . . . God bless you !

Yours truly,

THEODORE PARKER.

YELLOW SPRINGS, Feb. 28, 1854.

MY DEAR DOWNER, — . . . What do the Webster men say now ? The Nebraska Bill is the first upas-tree that grows out of his grave. . . .

Yours ever and truly,

HORACE MANN.

YELLOW SPRINGS, March 13, 1854.

MY DEAR SUMNER, — . . . I cannot describe my feelings to you on the Nebraska Bill. I seem like one who is dragged by fiery devils or Douglasses — it don't matter which — into Tophet, from which, for the next five hundred years, I see no escape. It is a case of desperation. It so encompasses me about, that nothing but the power and wisdom of God seems capable of reaching outside of it. Have you any hope ?

Very truly yours, &c.,

HORACE MANN.

NEW YORK, May 13, 1854.

MY DEAR MR. MANN, — How long it is since I have written you a line, or read one from you ! But I hear from you often by Downer and various others ; and I find that you are doing the same great work for Ohio which you did for Massachusetts. Well, God bless you ! But I fear that your excessive labors, as well voluntary as official, will break you down. Remember that it is a new country to you that you are now in. Do be wise ; for we cannot spare you yet. I fear the good God will wait some time before he gives us another Horace Mann. I thank you heartily for your long-looked-for "Inaugural." It will give pleasure to more than one of the household. . . . We have an antislavery convention from all the free States at Buffalo on July 4. "*Voilà le commencement du fin!*" Love to all.

Good-by !

T. PARKER.

YELLOW SPRINGS, May 30, 1854.

MY DEAR MR. PARKER, — You ought to know, that, "outside barbarians" as we are, your "Nebraska Sermon" and your "Discourse of Old Age," &c., are on the counters of our village book-stores. But none the less did I prize those sent under your own autograph, which (though not always unattended with difficulties) is always delightful to eyes and heart.

When your note of the 23d reached me, I was *pronus*, but am now getting *erect*. I have talked with Judge Mills about a rally of Northern forces, in defence of liberty, on the "Theatre of Words." Here we are great and glorious. Only give us some question where virtue and duty and piety can all be satisfied by fine speeches, and there never was such valor; but, beyond that, what cowards and cravens and shirks!

If the men who would go to such a convention would expend the same amount of time and means in converting or in rousing their own neighborhoods, now or before the next elections, something might be done; but I confess that latterly, at temperance meetings, antislavery meetings, &c., I have felt somewhat sheepish. I have heard a voice saying to me, "Why are you here, and not elsewhere? why are you talking, and not acting? why do you launch the thunderbolts of Salmoneus, and not of Jupiter?"

The North, in 1850, vested its capital in slavery. The Kansas-Nebraska Bill is the first payment of interest.

The papers this morning tell us of your commotion in Boston. Oh, how I burn to see it! I know you will be brave; and therefore will only say, Be prudent. When Boston was besieged in the Revolution, liberty was far less in danger than now. Why should I say, as is customarily said, "God help us!" I think he retorts, "Help yourselves!" . . .

With best regards of all of us to all of you,

HORACE MANN.

YELLOW SPRINGS, June 5, 1854.

MY DEAR DOWNER, — . . . What is the real state of the public mind and the Boston mind in regard to the practical beauties of the Fugitive-slave Law?* I get nothing worth a pin, except through the "New-York Tribune" and "Evening Post." Is Massachusetts any more worth living in than it was? Is there to be a time when I can speak of it without blushing? I know there are glorious men in it, as excellent as ever lived; but are they still under suppression? How I am mortified to think of L——! and yet it is only Websterism come to a head. . . . What glorious resolutions those were of Howe's! I bear this new outbreak from hell with a sort of sullen composure. When others display their excitement, and talk vengeance, I tell them that I went through all that experience in 1850; that they are now only where I was then; and that, if they had been *there at that time*, none of us would be here to witness what we now see. Can any thing be more true?

Off here a thousand miles, it looks as though the thing had not been well managed. Reasoning on the side of the rioters, and for the object of the riot, it was either folly to kill one man, or it was folly not to kill enough to answer the purpose. Do let me hear from you; and, oh, how glad I shall be to see you! . . .

Yours as ever,

HORACE MANN.

YELLOW SPRINGS, June 16, 1854.

MY DEAR MR. CRAIG, — I received, in due course of mail, yours of May 7. To that part of it which related to your health, let me say that I am rejoiced to know that a clergyman is recognizing and obeying the laws of health, and performing the first steps in the regeneration of the race; that is, their physical reformation. You

---

* Anthony Burns had just been surrendered.

honor philosophy and religion alike by so doing, and enroll yourself in the new school and among the new lights.*

I ought not entirely to omit, and yet how can I properly notice, that part of your letter in which you refer to the "Inaugural"? I never wrote any thing that seemed to me to fall so far short of what should be said on the theme therein discussed. Your partiality alone makes you speak of it kindly : and yet I love to be commended, even for such a reason ; that is, by such a man.

But, my dear sir, I sat down this time to make love to you ! Do not be alarmed. I am serious and literal ! I must woo you ; and nobody could woo who did not hope to win.

The Rev. Mr. Ladley, who has preached to the Christian Church in this village for the last few years, has just resigned. They are looking for a successor. Yesterday the committee called on me to make inquiry. Whom could I speak or think of but you? . . . If your right ear did not burn, there is no truth in signs.

And now, my dear sir, you want to do good. That is your divinely appointed mission. Where else can you reach and help to fashion three, four, five, or perhaps six hundred growing minds. and fashion them after your idea of the image of Christ? There never was such an opening for you ; there may never be such another. Were I a believer in special providences, I should think this had all the signatures of genuineness. We have a paper here, the "Gospel Herald :" where else can you better write? We shall have a library : where else can you better study? We are students of earthly lore : will you not infuse the heavenly? We are among a money-loving people : will you not make them sanctify money in its uses?

Re-preaching your sermons will give you a great deal of time for other services. Every thing says, "Come." "The Spirit and the Bride say, Come."

The people here are favorable to *extempore* sermons ; that is, when, as Mirabeau said, they have been fully thought out beforehand. I believe you preach so mainly. . . .

Yours as ever,

HORACE MANN.

---

* Mr. Mann here refers to the new philosophy growing out of the principles of phrenological science, for which this was his favorite designation.

YELLOW SPRINGS, July 1, 1854.

REV. THEODORE PARKER.

MY DEAR SIR, — Will you give us a lecture during the ensuing lecture season? I am most anxious that our students should hear you, — the young men that they may see the combined effect of talent and culture, and the young women that they may know the difference between men and butterflies. . . .

With best regards to all,

HORACE MANN.

To this Mr. Parker replied, when he was ready to visit the West : —

MY DEAR MR. MANN, — I hope to be in the place where "the disciples were first called Christians," on Saturday, the 14th instant. But as it would be very improper for such a heretic as I am to preach at Antioch on Sunday, and as I fear there is small chance for my hearing yourself, and as I doubt the worth of listening to the Rev. ——, I wish to know if there is not some place in its neighborhood, say Dayton e.g., where so wicked a man could hold forth and be welcome. If so, can you set the thing agoing in such a manner that I may ride thither on the following day?

Yours faithfully,

THEO. PARKER.

Mr. Parker was listened to with deep interest at Antioch; and many a petition was brought in, backed by earnest entreaties, and also in some cases by the expression of almost angry disappointment when refused, that Mr. Parker should be invited to preach. But Mr. Mann had but one vote in the faculty on that subject ; and both he and Mr. Parker thought it not best even to make the proposition, which would surely have failed to succeed, and might have added threefold bitterness to the existing jealousy of what was supposed to be Unitarian encroachment.

Mr. Mann's caution was not founded on any fear of

uttering truth : but he did not quite approve the spirit in which Mr. Parker uttered what he conscientiously thought, truth; neither did he think, from his experience there, that Mr. Parker would be understood or appreciated for his real worth by men upon whose breath the whole existence of the institution depended. For such measure of light as he thought Mr. Parker to have attained, — and he was of opinion that no other man was doing an equal work for the rights of private judgment and free speech, — that community was not ripe.

Instead of shocking religious sensibility and life-long associations by rude assaults upon the drapery in which such faith as they had was clothed, he would have echoed the words of John Robinson at Leyden : " The Lord has more truth yet to break forth out of his holy word. . . . Luther and Calvin were great and shining lights in their times ; yet they penetrated not the whole counsel of God. I beseech you, remember, 'tis an article of your church covenant that you be ready to receive whatever truth shall be made known to you from the written word of God." Nor did he forget the more ancient words : " I have yet many things to say unto you ; but ye cannot bear them now ; " which, unhappily, are as applicable now as then to many regions, even where the light of truth has dawned. It was in this spirit, and not in that of hypocrisy, with which he has been charged even by Mr. Parker, because he did not follow the method that seemed to the latter good, that he met and disarmed opposition, while he expressed his sympathy with all that was gained of freedom.

The following letter is inserted for its hearty expression of sympathy : —

HON. HORACE MANN.

MY DEAR SIR, — Your letter of the 3d has just reached me by the sea-side. If you will promise to stay away from the lecture-room, I will pledge myself to visit Yellow Springs, if I am invited to any neighboring cities of Ohio. It would afford me the greatest pleasure to see you and your institution; and I should jump at the naked hook, unbiassed by the offer of your hospitality or any lecture fee. I know you will be generous enough not to compel me to utter my sleazy thoughts before the prince of lecturers. . . . I ought to tell you with what admiration I read your "Inaugural," a few days ago, in the shadow of the rocks by the sea-shore. There is vitality enough in it to make a college thrive in Sahara. One would like to know the details of the diet that floods the brain with such impetuous electricity for the service of truth, making the sentences tingle the eye when they are read. Do you have a Leyden jar for a sauce-box upon your table?

Doubtless our Nebraska bills are fed at the root by tobacco-juice, brandy, and the weak liquor that trickles into the public mind from most of the sacrificial churches of the country; and it does the inmost soul good to read such hearty and vivid religious appeals as your "Inaugural" makes in favor of obedience to the hidden gospel in the constitution of body, mind, and soul.

Believe me sincerely yours,

T. STARR KING.

YELLOW SPRINGS, Sept. 10, 1854.

REV. AUSTIN CRAIG.

MY DEAR SIR, — I received your letter of the 4th inst. on Saturday, and have kept it two days, hoping to discover by reflection the wisest way of answering it. But my reflections have done me no good. The letter has filled me with sadness. It is contagious. You were sad when you wrote it, — morbidly so; and I am sad when I read it or think of it. You magnify your duties; and then you change the telescope, end for end, to look at your ability to perform them.

The idea that it was possible and probable that you would come here has occupied my mind very much for several weeks past.

30

The anticipated influence you would exert on our young men and maidens has filled me with joy; and when, last week, they came together at the beginning of our term, to the number of about four hundred, I assure you it was with very vivid delight that I looked forward to the influence of your spirit among them. Was there ever a more inviting field? With your eager desire to stamp the spirit of Christ upon the human heart, were there ever, or will there ever be, more hearts, or more susceptible ones, than these, on which to make the impress? . . .

I thought, too, that your duties would be light here. You could turn the old barrel of sermons over, and begin at the other end. I think the people here would want to see you pretty often in the church; but one of your sermons would make *forty* such as they have been accustomed to hear.

My dear friend, I fear the wind was east when you wrote that letter. Do not disappoint us. Prof. Holmes is delighted at the idea of your coming; so are others. As to external attractions, we have but few; but for one who lives so much as you do in the region of the heart, and who wishes to enlarge that region, I know of no place for you so suitable as this.

Farewell, my friend!

HORACE MANN.

These letters, urging Mr. Craig's removal to Yellow Springs, are given for the purpose of showing more clearly than the words of another can do the principles on which Mr. Mann wished to form the religious tone of the new institution. Mr. Craig's influence was as peculiar as his own religious character. It was not dogmatical, but exhortatory. It flowed out of his own religious experience with rare eloquence and simplicity, enlisting the sympathy and vivifying the answering sentiment in his audience with wonderful fervor. Mr. Mann held it in the highest estimation; and his importunity, which might otherwise seem unreasonable, can only be thus explained. But the bond between Mr. Craig and his own society was one that could hardly be sundered. In arranging the religious exercises of the institution, Mr. Mann had endeavored to make them acceptable as well as useful to the students. When this subject was discussed in an early meeting of the faculty at his house in West Newton, a long time before his removal to the West, one of the gentlemen who had been educated at an Orthodox institution in a community where only Orthodox families were encouraged to settle, and where all the influences, social and educational, were of consequence in one direction, and where it can be substantiated by facts that the students were ·actually persecuted into Orthodoxy, or had to flee from its borders, as many subsequently did flee to Antioch College, reported that it was the custom there to have a prayer before each recitation. When asked if such a practice might not tend to make young people weary of the observance, and even of religion itself, his good sense and candor induced him to express a doubt of its wisdom; and he was willing to accede to the more rational plans of Mr. Mann, who wished to enlist the good-will and sympathy of the young in all public religious exercises. He proposed that daily prayers should take place half an hour before entering upon the recitations of the day, in order that what he considered the religious rites of health, bathing and exercise, might not be neglected, and that no one might be inconvenienced by rising at untimely hours, or associating cold and discomfort with a rite which should have every pleasing association. The wisdom of these arrangements was manifested in the result. Absence from prayers was very unusual. Monitors appointed for the purpose for each class of the college and the preparatory school made memoranda, which were brought to Mr. Mann every Friday. If the absentees marked did not bring in their excuses or explanations before that day, their

names were read out after prayers on Saturday morning.
No penalty was attached to the violation; but, as Mr.
Mann collated the memoranda himself, he had his eye
upon delinquents, and the loving fear in which his disapproval was held was the strongest incentive to compliance with all rules. It was decidedly respectable in the
eyes of the young community not to violate any arrangement made for the good of all, and this healthy public
opinion worked wonders. To give vitality to the morning
exercises, they were administered in turn by the members of the faculty, who in turn took charge of the preaching. But Mr. Mann often took the opportunity to give a
word of counsel, reprimand, or exhortation, a few moments
after prayers; and on peculiar occasions he thought no
time so favorable as when the relations between religious
duty and the culture of their minds had been strongly
brought before them, in order that knowledge, which is .
power, might not be abused.

Many students have been heard to say that the prayers
offered in that chapel by the president were the first
prayers uttered by another that had ever excited their devotional feelings. No student was obliged to attend either
the devotional exercises of the day or the sabbath who
gave conscientious reasons for not so doing. The Quaker
or the Catholic had a permanent excuse, which would
have been extended to the Jew if occasion had required.
How else could it have been an unsectarian institution?
The Quakers, thus disarmed, often preferred to give their
voluntary attendance.

YELLOW SPRINGS, Oct. 26, 1854.

MY DEAR MR. CRAIG, — . . . There is something ludicrous in
your asking me to suggest the " pithy " books or trains of thought
on " prodigal sons " or any other wanderers. I read nothing but
the monitors' lists of absences, and think of nothing but to keep the

team in harness. Was not Mithridates celebrated for driving thirty-two horses in his chariot at once? What would he have said of four hundred? I can hardly be said to make any explorations into the regions of thought; and, when I do, the elements close behind me as behind a fish or an eagle, and leave no traces of their pathway.

I cannot tell you, my dear friend, how much all the more reflecting people here were delighted with your visit. I think you gave many of them a new idea of the function of an ambassador of Jesus Christ. But a plot was formed against you, which may be temporarily successful. Mr. —— wished to obtain an invitation himself. The last evening you were here, when you met company at my house, a regular conspiracy was set on foot to preach up revivals, and preach down other means of attaining Christian character.* There were several speeches, and they grew worse and worse to the end of the meeting; so that, as I was told, the more considerate of them were ashamed of the wildfire they had kindled. The whole of it was understood to be aimed at you, and designed to show the people that they needed such a man as Mr. —— professed to be. Your friends, seeing what a turn things were taking, have thought it not best to urge their preferences at present; and your friend Mr. H—— is engaged there temporarily, — which probably will mean all winter.

But those whose hearts are earnest for the religious growth of the place, and the most subduing influences upon the untamed spirits of the youth who resort here for education, will never surrender the hope of having you here. I exhort you, therefore, to hold yourself in readiness, that, when the time comes, you may be translated here as quickly as Elijah was into heaven. . . .

Yours as ever, most truly,
HORACE MANN.

After a while, it was thought desirable for Mr. Mann to accept some of the invitations to lecture which poured in upon him, with a view to interesting the Western pub-

---

* Great disappointment had been experienced in the Christian denomination because Mr. Mann did not allow revival meetings in the college for the purpose of swelling the village church.

lic still more in the institution, which showed symptoms of dying out for want of the means to live. Not being built and endowed with money, but only with promises and hopes, the prospects of the faculty in a pecuniary point of view grew more and more alarming. Agents failed to raise the requisite sums ; notes were protested ; enmities began to arise among the neighboring landholders, whose promised benevolence to the institution proved to be dependent upon the gains they made ; and a check was given to the influx of population, which had set so strongly into the village after the college was fairly opened, because whispers of bankruptcy were heard from time to time. It was made a cause of complaint against him in after-time, by enemies of the institution and of his presence in it, that he was absent on lecturing engagements ; but he never went without consideration for the institution, and his absence was almost always in vacation-time. In regard to the fortunes of the college, it was a tale of alternate hopes and fears, wearing to the strongest nerves, and endured at great expense of vitality.

PITTSBURG, Dec. 9, 1854.

It is as hard to keep clean in the physical atmosphere of Pittsburg as to retain one's integrity in the moral atmosphere of an Atlantic city.

DEC. 19, 1854.

This Scranton, where I now am, is near the poetic Valley of Wyoming, but is really the valley of stone coal and of iron manufactories, — a new place, grown up out of the mineral riches of the earth, just as soon as there was knowledge enough to discover them.

So it will be with all riches, as soon as they are combined with intelligence and skill. This doctrine I apply to our boys. If they really have common sense, and we can give them a good education, — in which I include a good moral character, — I have no fears about a good share of success for them in the world. I desire that they should have the very best education this age of the world can supply; and then, if I leave them this, and integrity and truth, and nothing else, I shall go out of the world thinking my duty in this respect not ill done. I cannot bear to think of them so cramped and straitened for means as I was: but even that is a thousand times better than ignorance; and ignorance is a calamity ten thousand times less to be depreated than any form of vice.

YELLOW SPRINGS, April 3, 1855.

MY DEAR MR. CRAIG, — I wish to write a long letter to you, but have hardly time to write a short one. The absence of Mr. H—— you know. All our thoughts turned at once to you. But I knew your engagements at your place with the beautiful name. We tried Dr. Siedhoff: he cannot come. We have made arrangements for the current term, not in all respects satisfactory. One class in Greek is postponed, which I do not like; and Mr. B—— takes one. We want a teacher for next September. It is *almost* six months.* You can fill that place. Your general culture, your acquaintance with Greek thought, your etymology, your Greek philology indeed, fit you admirably for the post. . . . I cannot tell you how delighted I should be. I would take you, for a time at least, into my house. We would build you up *bodily* almost as much as you would us *spiritually.*

This letter is not official; but you know how my heart yearns towards you. . . . Ever and truly yours, ,

HORACE MANN.

YELLOW SPRINGS, April 17, 1855.

MY DEAR MR. CRAIG, — If I thought you had at last taken the position of a final, irrevocable denial and refusal ever to join your fortunes with ours, and help us to carry on the great work here begun, I should submit to my sad fate as well as I could, abate a

* This was the amount of time necessary for Mr. Craig to give warning to his parish.

great portion of my hopes, and labor with my might for the fulfilment of the rest.

In reference to the arguments for remaining where you are, or coming here, you say that I may hold the scales while you put in the weights. But, my dear sir, may I not also see whether the weights are correctly or erroneously marked? If you put in platinum, and call it feathers, or feathers, and call it platinum, may I not point out the mistake, and remonstrate against it? Otherwise how am I better than any peg or hook from which to suspend them?

Now, have you not made a mistake something like this — quite like it — in relation to the "weights"?

In regard to health, would not our milder climate be more congenial to your lungs than the butcherly blasts of the Highlands?

In regard to society, you know that your nature yearns towards the young; that, reckoning from fossil old age down to indurated manhood and to irrepressible youth, the fervor of your affections, the vivacity of your love, increase far more than in the ratio that the squares of the distance diminish.

In regard to intellectual companionship, you know that you are now just as solitary as you would be on the top of Mont Blanc. Nobody comes up to your altitude intellectually. You may pursue your studies there; you may become very learned and wise: but it will not be that better sort of wisdom which is found by study and contemplation, blended with communion with men. The wisdom of the recluse is a very different thing from that of the practical moralist or statesman. Now, although we cannot supply you with many intellectual companions here at present, yet by and by I hope it will be otherwise.

In regard to the good that you can do, I must protest that I never saw such false weights used in all my life before. Why, seriously and solemnly, had you done this in old times, when barbarous punishments were resorted to, I should have been afraid of your ears; that is, your *metaphysical* ears. You must know, and do know, that whatever wisdom you have, or have not, you do retain more of the purity and simplicity and innocence of childhood than almost any other man, and therefore are divinely fitted to sympathize with the young while you instruct them, — to go down to the lowliness where they dwell in order to lift them to your height. I defy your modesty to deny this.

As for labor, — ministerial labor, — you have now a great storehouse of thoughts, more or less perfected : what better could you do, either for yourself or for others, than to review them, and give them, with the improvements of a second edition ? — thus lightening labor and enhancing benefits.

But what we want now in the college is a teacher in Greek for the coming year. Where shall we find him ? Was there ever such an opening? All the circumstances point to you ; every thing connected with the case shouts, " AUSTIN CRAIG ! " You can come for this year : if then health should fail, or repulsions spring up, or the social atmosphere become an east wind, or you should lose your interest in children, then you could return. There is no doubt, on the least intimation of that kind, your people would keep your place open for you. Why, then, will you not come and help us for this one year at least?

I must go and look after a class : so good-by, and God bless you, *and us* through you.

Very truly as ever,

HORACE MANN.

YELLOW SPRINGS, April 30, 1855.

MY DEAR MR. CRAIG, — By your letter of the 22d instant, I see I am required to sit down and compute the tables of an almanac, showing the declination, right ascension, &c., of your orb for the coming year, and for a somewhat indefinite future afterwards. We cannot, as yet, calculate the orbit of a *human*, astronomically, quite as well as we can that of Mercury or Neptune. Still, I will do my best. At any rate, I will put you in possession of facts from which you can cast a horoscope. . . .

The committee on the subject of teachers is authorized to employ a teacher of Greek. . . . There has also been a good deal said among the faculty about a chaplain for the college ; and, could we get the right man, the feeling amongst those of us who now supply the place of one would be unanimous in favor of the demand. They have been deterred, as yet, from bringing forward the subject by the condition of the college finances, which, we have reason to hope, will be improved before another year rolls round.

Both the chaplaincy and the Greek would furnish easy occupation to a man so equipped as you are. . . . The Christian society in this place is still without a pastor. The very favorable impression you made here last autumn, I believe, would have secured you an invitation, but for the eager efforts of some who hoped for an invitation for themselves if you did not succeed, and who based their opposition to you on the ground that you were not evangelical enough in regard to the agency of the Holy Spirit in the conversion of men. If you could associate with the people here for one year, I feel morally sure that a great majority would be for settling you here, and the society would receive great accessions. I cannot believe, that, once here, you would be allowed to go away until you went *the upper way.* I have now stated the facts conscientiously. I will not offer any new considerations about your health, your growth, your very much enlarged sphere of usefulness, &c., but remain, as ever, Yours affectionately,

HORACE MANN.

YELLOW SPRINGS, June 27, 1855.

REV. A. CRAIG.

MY DEAR SIR, — I am not dead; though, from my silence, you may think so.

Our last term and year closed yesterday; and now I can breathe a little easier.

When I received your letter some weeks ago, I thought I would not reply till I had official notice of your acceptance. But, though I have written on the subject several times, I can extort nothing. I hear, however, in other ways, that all is settled, and that we are to have the blessing of your presence next year. . . . Since I had your last letter, I have been so busy with our examination, that I could not get a splinter of time anywhere to float away upon: so you must forgive me. It has been said that God never will ask what a man has done, but what he has done *under the circumstances.*

And now, my dear friend, it makes my heart glad that you are to be here.   Let us make you as comfortable, bodily, as you can be. . . .

Yours as ever,

HORACE MANN.

YELLOW SPRINGS, July 24, 1855.

MY DEAR DOWNER, — We have not had one word from you since you left.   It would have been an act of benevolence native to your heart to tell us you got home well; but I suppose we must all give place to coup oil for a time.   If it is always to employ your thoughts, I shall place it in my anathemas with rum and tobacco. . . .

Tell me all the Massachusetts news of whatever I feel interested in.   Was it not good that E—— got stung in the tenderest place for his infamous vote?   I cannot but think the tide is turning. How the whole present political controversy is going to stand in history, I have no more doubt than I have of the progress of time. To say that slavery is to be triumphant, and its advocates honored, is to say that Judas and Jesus will change places. . . .

Yours as ever, most truly,

H. MANN.

ALBANY, Nov. 18, 1855.

I had a delightful visit to Mr. May.   I found an invitation there from Dr. Wilbur, who is the superintendent of the new establishment of the State of New York for idiots.   We went out there to dinner.   It is quite a magnificent place, — cost about seventy thousand dollars.   He has now about eighty idiotic children under his care.   After dinner, he took us over the whole establishment. I have a certain sort of pleasure in viewing such a scene; but it is not an unmingled one. . . .

Mr. May had invited Mr. Gerritt Smith to meet me; and, when we came back from dinner, we found him waiting for our return. We had quite an exhibition of souls to each other.   I do not wonder that he should be a popular man in spite of some of his unpopular views.   The next day, we three sat and talked "divine philosophy," or something else, which, in the present state of the world, I should rather call *divine heresy;* and then he went with me a dozen miles on his way home. I omitted to say, that, when I arrived at ——, a lady came to see me. This always puts me in a tremor. I feel like the cat in Mother Goose's melodies, or somewhere else, who describes so pathetically her *terrorification* when a bad boy set a dog on her.

"And while I stood trembling, and all of a shake," &c.

It proved to be ——. She is a person of good manners and address, and, what is quite as important, good dress.

BOSTON, Nov. 21, 1855.

. . . Early this morning, both Howe and Downer called on me; and it was pleasant to see them again. Downer has just been laid up for a week with an over-strained brain. I always feel very sorrowful when I think of his lame brain, because you know it was in my behalf that he first disabled it. How much he lost for his fidelity to me! How different would his loss have been regarded if he had sacrificed his fidelity, and saved his brain!* I have two letters from you, and one from Craig. How does the good man's head do? I wish it were as well as his heart.

BOSTON, Nov. 21, 1855.

MY DEAR MR. CRAIG, — I had a brief note from you; but it said nothing about what I care most for, — yourself. You have made us all love you so much, that a new obligation is upon you. You must take care of yourself for our sakes as well as for your own. The fame of your popularity among the students has reached here, and I am congratulated upon it.

I am on familiar ground again. If Massachusetts is compared with most other places, how much there is to admire! if with the ideal, how much to lament! However much we may advance, shall we not always be impatient at the contrast between the actual and the ideal?

Yours affectionately,

HORACE MANN.

---

* This allusion is made in reference to Mr. Downer's exertions in the political campaign for and against Mr. Mann, which was followed by a severe brain-fever.

ANTIOCH COLLEGE, Dec. 24, 1855.

MY DEAR MR. PARKER, — You, of course, are aware that a project is on foot by the " Bible Union," so called, for a new translation of the Scriptures. I believe the headquarters of this enterprise are at Louisville, Ky. At any rate, the " Bible Union Reporter," a periodical devoted to the cause, is published there ; I believe also at New York. It was started under the auspices of the following denominations. — Church of England, Old-school Presbyterians, Disciples or Reformers, Methodist-Episcopal Church, Associated Reformed Presbyterians, Seventh-day Baptists, Baptists, German Reformed Church, — all Trinitarians. But they want the indorsement of the Unitarians and " Christians ;" and they have sent to inquire of me who there is in this country or in Europe whose knowledge of Greek, Hebrew, Sanscrit, Syriac, &c., qualifies him for the work. I believe they will pay a liberal salary for such an indorsement.

I recommended you. They would like to know of some European also on whose knowledge and integrity they can rely. If any one can name to me such a man, or such men, you can. Will you please do it at your earliest convenience ? and much oblige

Yours very truly,

HORACE MANN.

P. S. — I was sorry to see so little of you during my recent visit to the East. I had, in some respects, a pleasant, in others a sad, time. Many of the houses in Boston appeared to me like living tombs containing the dishonored dead. Our affairs are looking somewhat precarious. Oh, if I could have one half-day's expenditure of the Crimean war, what a glorious use I would make of it !

ANTIOCH COLLEGE, Jan. 1, 1856.

HON. GERRITT SMITH.

MY DEAR SIR, — After assuring you of my very pleasant recollections of our late interview at the house of our common friend Mr. May, I wish to say that there is reason to fear the last sands of Antioch College are running out. The whole field of the Christian denomination has been traversed ; and it is now pretty apparent to my mind, that, unless we can have some *wholesale* instead of *retail* donations, our institution sinks. Our students — about three hundred on an average since we have been here — are dispersed ; and the cause of Liberal Christianity and a free-thoughted education expires for an indefinite time for all this Valley of the West. One of the most grievous of my regrets at this sad prospect is the apprehension that the experiment (as the world will still call it) of educating the sexes together will be rudely interrupted, to be revived only in some indefinite future.

It is now nearly three years since I have been here, all the time at a pecuniary loss to myself; and the professor of Latin, Mr. Pennell, whom I stipulated to have in that chair, and who came and who remains here solely from his personal relations to me, could any day have doubled the salary he is receiving here. We are willing, however, to remain. We can do so much as this in behalf of the institution ; but we cannot pluck it from the abyss into which it threatens to fall.

I sincerely believe there has seldom, if ever, been an occasion where a deed of pecuniary munificence would be so munificently rewarded by the highest and most precious kind of blessings ; where a great power might not only be saved to the cause of virtue and the progress of truth, but saved *from* the cause of bigotry, sectarianism, and all uncharitableness.

But I am not the judge of other men's responsibilities. They are the rightful judges of what shall be saved, and what shall be suffered to perish. If they understand the facts, I am bound to believe they will judge aright. These facts are, that, if help does not come to Antioch College, its fate will be decided in thirty days, and the end of this term will find its walls empty, its halls echoing only to the solitary tread of some stranger who comes to inquire where the spirit of the Christian denomination is gone ; or, what is far more painful to contemplate, echoing to the crowd that will frequent its apartments to revile the names of those who once held possession of it, and to counterwork all their efforts for a truly liberal education and a truly liberal Christianity. With the highest personal regard, I remain yours most truly,

HORACE MANN.

DANSVILLE, Jan. 24, 1856.

. . . I wish I had more disposition to look at the ludicrous side of personal matters. Perhaps it would save repining and querulousness. There are some things for which *fun*, not philosophy, was intended as a remedy. He is a wise physician who knows how to administer it; he is a wise man who gathers it copiously into his pharmacopœia. . . . My causality works actively on the children when I am away; and I am constantly foreshadowing what they are to be from what they are. Life is such a unity, that, if we could truly see what people are, we should see what they would become. . . .

BOSTON, (probably) January, 1856.

MY DEAR MR. CRAIG, — As I am writing home to Mrs. Mann, I must write a word to you, because you are now associated with all my ideas of home, — an object standing in the foreground of the picture. One of the pleasures of home is that you are there : one of the regrets of absence is to be away from you. Your spiritual-mindedness is the complement of my nature, — of what I have failed to be, though I was fit to be, and ought to have been. But Calvinism blasphemed all that part of me ; and, if it did not destroy the germ, it checked its development. I have something, I hope, of the other side, — the intellectual-religious side. What I have, I rejoice in ; but it constantly reminds me of what else I ought to have. I desire its possession more fully. I do not feel too old to cultivate its growth. I am only made to feel and to see how much was lost to my nature, because all was done that could be done, when I was a child, to educate the love of a heavenly-Father out of me, instead of educating it into me. This want I feel and deplore. You supply its place in me. You call to mind, better than any other *man* I have ever known, what Plato would hold to be the "recollections" of a previous state of being. Think, then, how dear you are to me ; because I feel, if I could incorporate your soul into mine, it would make me whole ; *i.e.*, a whole man.

I feel constantly, and more and more deeply, what an unspeakable calamity a Calvinistic education is. What a dreadful thing it was to me ! If it did not succeed in making me that horrible thing, a Calvinist, it did succeed in depriving me of that filial love for God, that tenderness, that sweetness, that intimacy, that desiring, nestling love, which I say it is natural the child should feel towards a Father who combines all excellence. I see him to be so, logically, intellectually, demonstratively; but when I would embrace him, when I would rush into his arms and breathe out unspeakable love and adoration, then the grim old Calvinistic spectre thrusts itself before me. I am as a frightened child, whose eye, knowledge, experience, belief even, are not sufficient to obliterate the image which an early fright burnt in upon his soul. I have to reason the old image away, and replace it with the loveliness and beauty of another; and in that process, the zeal, the alacrity, the fervor, the spontaneousness, are, partially at least, lost. You help me to recover it, and fix the true image; and thus you help my spiritual life. I would not part with one idea, one conviction, on the other side of my moral life; but I feel as though I should be a better man, and a vastly happier man, if I could add your side to mine. And as you have opportunity, my dear friend, let me entreat you to impart this loving side of religion to my little boys. Above all treasures, I long that they should have this. There can be no such chasm in their being as to be without it. For the trials of life, it is the best philosophy. For the joys of existence, it is the greatest magnifier; for it magnifies in the line of direction as well as of quantity.

But I am interrupted by company; and what will my wife say if I write but one sheet to her, and two to you to send in her letter? Good-by, my dear friend.

HORACE MANN.

Mr. Craig had been compelled by ill health to resign the professorship of Greek a few months before, but had remained at Yellow Springs, at Mr. Mann's urgent request, as a guest. After his return to Blooming Grove, he was invited to a new position in and near the institution, as will be seen by the following letters: —

MY DEAR MR. CRAIG, — I put a single word into Mrs. Mann's letter, more for the sake of telling you how Horace Mann loves Austin Craig than for any other reason. I had a dolorous journey to Meadville, hardly surpassed in perils and tribulations since the days of St. Paul. We missed every connection both in going and coming. My passage from Erie to Meadville was thrown into the night; and such a night! The thermometer of Meadville, shortly after I arrived there, stood at 31° on the wrong side of zero. I labored with Dr. S—— until about twelve o'clock the next night, and then started to return at three in the morning. Our driver froze ears, hands, and feet, dreadfully. Now, think of something twice as bad, and let that stand for the residue of the journey. Mr. P—— has sent word, that, if Dr. S—— does not raise the $28,000, some one else will.

The strongest desire is expressed for your return. . . . Our trustee meeting is on the 12th of March. If we can have your affirmative reply before that date, the proper measures can be taken by the Board of Trustees for giving you a *status* in the college as College Chaplain, and Lecturer on the Evidences of Christianity, Professor of Moral Philosophy, or something of that kind. This ought to be ; for you should have an official relation to the students as the basis of your moral one. Good-by, dear Mr. Craig; and, if my invocation were worth any thing, I would say, God bless you ! HORACE MANN.

ANTIOCH COLLEGE, April 7, 1856.

MY DEAR MR. CRAIG, — Herewith I send you the invitation of the Christian Society in this place to become their pastor. I need not tell you how much pleasure it affords me to do it.

The circumstances attending the call were such as you could hardly wish modified, were they at the full disposal of vanity or self-esteem. After your name was introduced at the meeting, it was said that you had been elected College Chaplain; and the inquiry was made, how you could be College Chaplain, and pastor of the Christian Church also. Omitting what I said about Mr.

31

Craig as a man, it was said that the relation which I wished to see you fill was that of officiating at the college one-half the day on Sundays, when the whole society would be invited to attend there; and the other half of the day at the church, when the college would attend there. Your morning duties at the chapel would never interfere with any thing at the church, and your evening services at the church would never interfere with any thing at the chapel. We * could take your morning duties at the chapel whenever desirable. I said that there was a natural alienation between the students of a college and the villagers where it was situated; that there was less of it here than usually happens; but that I wanted none of it: on the contrary, I wished to cultivate harmony, cordiality, identity of spirit, between us; and that you were the man to do it.

After the statement had been fully made and understood, the vote was taken, and it was unanimous with a single exception, — Mr. C——, who spoke highly of you, but gave as a reason for his vote afterwards, that you were opposed to church organization.

So flattering a call few men have ever had; and so fair an opening for usefulness rarely falls to the lot of ministers. I can now see nothing of a public or general nature which can stand in the way of a noble mission to the people of this place, college and village; and I do not believe that you will suffer any thing of a personal or private nature to do so. I know not what secrets futurity may have behind the curtain; but I never saw so fair a prospect for any man's filling his worldly stomach with the honey of success, and his Christian heart with the rewards of faithful ministrations in divine things, as now opens before you.

The church will be completed about the first of May. Do not, I beseech you, allow the ceremony of dedication to pass by without your presence. Let all future associations connected with the house be seen through the medium of that beautiful light. Even if you must go back for any period, longer or shorter, — though I sincerely hope not, at least during our present term, — come and be present, be installed, at the time of the dedication of the house; and

---

* The faculty. There was only one Sunday service at the chapel. — ED.

then, if absolutely necessary, I doubt not you can obtain leave of absence. But I want that radiant point in the sky at that place, where it will forever be so conspicuous.

. . . We are all well, thanks to the good laws of God which we are trying to worship him by obeying. We have about sixty new students this term, notwithstanding all the efforts of the ungodly to keep them away. . . .

I am, as ever, yours devotedly,

HORACE MANN.

P. S. — You cannot possibly forget where your home is when you come.

YELLOW SPRINGS, April 30, 1856.

REV. AUSTIN CRAIG.

MY DEAR SIR, — You have apparent reason, at least, to think the committee inexcusably tardy in answering your letter of the 12th inst. . . . One of the committee has been unwell; and accident has again and again prevented our meeting according to appointment. Yesterday afternoon we were together, and came unanimously to the following conclusions. . . . These are the three points presented to our consideration by your letter; and we think that our propositions correspond with your expressed wishes.

The committee strongly desire that you should be present at the dedication of the house. Its completion has been delayed longer than was expected. It will now probably be ready in two or three weeks; but we would rather wait a month, perhaps even more, than not to have you participate in those services, which will be so interesting to us.

Hoping that these propositions may be acceptable to you, and that an arrangement will be effected mutually promotive of the highest moral and religious welfare of both pastor and people,

I remain, as ever, most truly your friend,

HORACE MANN, *for the Committee.*

ANTIOCH COLLEGE, YELLOW SPRINGS, May 4, 1856.

MY DEAR MR. COMBE, — What will you do with a man who repents and sins again, and repents and sins again? Christ's rule is to forgive him seventy times seven times. And now, as I have not done this more than half seventy times seven, I have still somewhat of a margin left for continued offending. My dear friend, you must come and watch me a day, and see what I have to do; and then you would not only grant amnesty for all the past, but free Popish indulgences as to the future. But from all this how can you infer forgetfulness? How can I forget you, who have done my mind more good than any other living man, — a hundred times more? I not only think of you, remembering you, but, in a very important and extensive sense, *I am you.* You are reproduced in my views of life (though not in my views of death), and in that understanding of the wisdom and ways of Providence which vindicates God to man. I received your letter of April 4 two or three days ago; and my first impulse was to answer it *instanter*, and dispel any approaching shadow of a suspicion that I can ever lose my regard, my affection, for you. But I thought I would wait till to-day; because to-day, according to the old family Bible, I am sixty years old. This event excites in my mind a strangely mingled feeling, made up of joy and pain, to say nothing of a readiness or unreadiness to die. I am too intensely interested in the great questions of human progress, of humanity itself, to be willing to quit the field in this stage of the conflict. The vital questions of pauperism, temperance, slavery, peace, and education, covering as they do many digits of the orb of human happiness, I cannot relinquish, I cannot leave, without a feeling of the description of breaking heart-strings from objects which they have intwined. You may tell me the work will go on, and perhaps it will; but I want it should go on in my day. I long to see it. I want to help it, to expend myself upon it; and life seems bereaved of its noblest functions and faculties if it fails in this. I feel for these causes as a fond father feels for his children, whom he dreads to leave till they are out of moral danger, and have the common securities and guaranties for future safety and welfare. But I cannot stop the earth in its orbit, and that is bearing me round to the point where my participation in its struggles must come to an end. From all this, there is but one moral to be drawn, — to redeem the time that still remains, be it longer or shorter. But, oh! if with my present views I could be set back again to the age of twenty, how gladly would I release all that Divine Goodness, in the exercise of his highest prerogative of love, can bestow upon me elsewhere!

Our college is most prosperous in all respects but the want of money. By a great want of wisdom, if not by something worse, we were involved in great debts at the very outset; and the books and papers were in such a condition, that our embarrassment was not known. Revelation after revelation first startled, then astonished, then overwhelmed us. As time revealed deeper and deeper difficulties, the fair-weather friends of the institution, one after another, dropped off, or were turned into antagonists and maligners. Within the last three months, however, a rally has been made; and we now have hopes that the college will be lifted out of the slough of insolvency. When I feel our wants, and see to what beneficent uses we could appropriate money, it makes me desire wealth, and it gives me feelings of intenser condemnation for the manner in which so much wealth is spent. What untold blessings for the present and the future could be secured here by a hundred thousand dollars! and yet there is not a day in which many times a hundred thousand dollars are not uselessly, nay injuriously, spent in all the great cities of the world.

. . . We are politically in a very excited condition. The step about Kansas, and the approaching Presidential election, will probably create a fiercer contest than any yet known to our political annals. In Kansas, the attempt will be made, and probably enforced by arms, to maintain the fraudulent government of the "Border Ruffians." On the other hand, it seems impossible to avoid resistance. Yesterday's telegraph informs us that the sheriff of the usurping government was shot. The United-States army will doubtless be called in. The President will use his utmost prerogative to maintain the tyranny; for, should he omit a single effort, his nomination for re-election would be lost; and he is a man who would sacrifice a state or a country, a zone or a zodiac, for selfishness.

What a ridiculous ado they make in France about six pounds of baby! Our births are of human liberty or bondage! . . .

MY DEAR MR. CRAIG, — We have concluded to dedicate the church on the second Sunday in June, — the eighth day of that month. It is the unanimous wish of the committee that you should preach the Dedication Sermon; and you are hereby invited to do it. . . .

And now, my dear friend, how could you write me so incomplete a letter as yours of the 7th instant? The people here are all agony to know "whether Mr. Craig accepts the invitation to settle with us." I told them, that, by the middle of this week, we should undoubtedly hear from you. That time came, and your letter, but not a word about any thing beyond being present at the dedication. That, of course, would be most agreeable, but is not *the* thing. . . . The flock is without a head. What wolves will invade the fold, if left in this condition for six months, who can tell? . . .

My dear friend, let me exhort you to do two things. Come and speak for us in the chapel, Sunday, June 1; dedicate the new house, and be installed as pastor of the church here the next sabbath; and, having got released from what you call "home," let us make you another, and, for the good you can do, a better home. I hope to hear from you soon. With best regards from all,

I am, as ever, most sincerely yours,

HORACE MANN.

MY DEAR SUMNER, — I have just returned from an educational visit to St. Louis, Mo., — the eastern, not the western, end of the State.

We are all not only shocked at the outrage committed upon you, but we are wounded in your wounds, and bleed in your bleeding.

Since I left Washington, March 4, 1853, I do not know as I have ever felt a desire to be there again till now. But I suppose, if God meant to save my life, he found it necessary to keep me away.

I have only seen the newspaper accounts of your speech. I long to see the full report. Altogether the thing has produced a great sensation, — as great for good as Webster's 7th of March speech for evil. How the diabolical consequences of that speech are developing themselves! How every year vindicates our course at that time! The years are our avengers, and will continue to be.

In your full report, why will you not quote the very Memorial of South Carolina to the Continental Congress, asking to be relieved from furnishing her quota of men, because of her dangerous population at home? . . .

Yours most truly,

HORACE MANN.

ANTIOCH COLLEGE, June 16, 1856.

MY DEAR MR. PARKER, — I hear of you occasionally through the newspapers, when, like old Thor, you seize a Norway pine, and smite the wicked therewith; but I hear from you in no other way.

I will not intimate that you have forgotten me or *ours*, because I know how many men's work you have to do. It would give me great pleasure to hear from you. Working here, as it were, in solitude, and with a settled conviction that my labors and sacrifices will not be appreciated until I am removed from the scene of action, it would give me great satisfaction to hear a friendly voice from my old home.

Now the political Christ is crucified, what do the Judases who betrayed him say for themselves? I fear they have not even the one merit of their prototype, — repentance.

I have a strong presentiment that an excursion up the Lakes would be good for what little of mortality is left me, and that it would be far better if I could get some "glorious fellow" to go with me. Have you a curiosity, or a health-hoping policy, which would lead you in the same direction? I wrote to Downer to ask you; but he replies that he has not seen you. I hope you feel a disposition to see the great works of God in the Great Lakes.

Very truly, as ever,

HORACE MANN.

ANTIOCH COLLEGE, YELLOW SPRINGS, June 18, 1856.

REV. DANIEL AUSTIN.

MY DEAR SIR, — With much surprise and pleasure I have received from Mr. O. P. T—— of Salisbury, Mass., the sum of five dollars, placed in his hands by you, to be forwarded to me to be invested in some token of remembrance.

To be remembered by any one on whom we have conferred obligations is very grateful to our feelings; but to be remembered without obligation by a gentleman of your character and standing, seems, indeed, an instance of the *laudari a uno laudato*.

First, Please accept my very sincere thanks for your flattering remembrance; and,

Second, Let me tell you what I have ventured to do with the money.

We have many poor students here who are working their passage through college by the greatest frugality, industry, and effort. The condition of some of them, manfully struggling against adverse circumstances, makes strong appeals to my sympathy; and I cannot refrain from giving a considerable amount, every year, for the relief and reward of such noble exertions. We are now about closing the year, and my means for this purpose were really exhausted.

The day I received your letter, a young man came to me, saying he had found the bottom of his pocket, and must absolutely leave. Five dollars would carry him through this term; but five dollars were as impossible to him as world-making. I ventured to give him your five dollars. I thought it would give us both more pleasure than to put it in any book or other token or memorial. I thought it would *sanctify* it. If you do not approve, I will still do as proposed.

And now, my dear sir, I wish you knew more of our institution here, and of our plans. I wish I could have the pleasure of seeing you here. In all this Great West, ours is the only institution, of a first-class character, which is not, directly or indirectly, under the influence of the old-school theology; and though the mass of the people here are more liberal-minded and free-thoughted, more open and receptive and less cast-irony, than the corresponding classes in the East, yet the ministers are more narrow and bigoted. Our college, therefore, is really like breaking a hole in the Chinese Wall. It lets in the light of religious civilization where it never shone before. Think of this great State, with more than two millions of inhabitants, and only one Unitarian society! The Christians, however, are the best medium through which to introduce a more liberal Christianity.

I am, dear sir, in great haste, very truly yours,

HORACE MANN.

BOSTON, June 27, 1856.

MY DEAR MR. MANN, — Don't think that your labors are obscure, or likely to be forgotten in this generation, or for many that are to come. Your works are written all over the Commonwealth of Massachusetts, and are in no danger of being forgotten. I know how arduous your position is ; also how unpleasant much of the work must be. I fancy you now and then feel a little longing after the well-cultivated men and women whom you left behind at the East, and find none to supply in Ohio. But the fresh presence of young people is a compensation.

What a state of things we have now in politics ! —the beginning of the end. I take it we can elect Frémont : if so, the battle is fought, and the worst part of the contest is over. If Buchanan is chosen, see what follows ! The principles of the administration will be the same as now ; the measures the same ; the mode of applying the principles and executing the measures will be slightly altered, — no more. It is plain that another such administration would ruin the country for men like those of Middlesex County, Mass. I don't think the people will see themselves conquered by three hundred and fifty thousand slaveholders, headed by an old bachelor. If Buchanan is elected, I don't believe the Union holds out three years. I shall go for *dissolution*.

I wish I could go to the Lakes with *you*. But a family of intimate friends will sail for Europe the 25th of August, to be absent for three years. I want to see them all I can this summer: so we shall all go to Newton Corner, and live near by ; else I should do up my "unpretending luggage," and be off to Lake Superior with you.

I sent you a little sermon for the Sunday after Mr. Brooks struck Sumner; and have another pamphlet in press, containing two speeches made at New York a month ago; which please accept.

On the 6th July, I shall preach on *The Prospect with Us*, and perhaps print. July 8 I go to New-York Central University, at *Macgrawville*, somewhere in New York, and deliver an address on *The Function of the Scholar in a Democracy*.

I wish I was where I could see you often, but am glad to know that you are well. So are we all. With best regards from all to all, believe me   Yours ever truly,

THEODORE PARKER.

YELLOW SPRINGS, July 3, 1856.

My DEAR MR. CRAIG, — I received yours of June 23 a week ago, and have been most anxiously awaiting intelligence from your society. To-day it has come, and is, as doubtless you both know and knew, in the negative!

Is this irreversible? If so, my first impulse is to resign at once, and leave. I know the consequences: not that my withdrawing would be of any account; but, if I should go, Mr. Pennell and R——, of course, would not remain a day. This would be fatal to the concern.

I should regard this result more than I can express. I think I can sacrifice my own ease and emolument for the sake of success in accomplishing the great enterprise for which I came out here; but if no one else will make any sacrifice for the welfare of the college, and if we are to have Mr. —— as pastor of the church, or any one like him, then I feel as though the success of the college itself, at least under my administration, is jeoparded, and the only motive which I have for staying here is gone. *You* supplied all conditions. Your refusal to come leaves all conditions unsupplied. I write in haste and sadness, but am, as ever,   Truly yours,

HORACE MANN.

P. S. — If the refusal of the society is peremptory, is it peremptory after six months from the time you notify? I shall await with great anxiety an answer to *this* inquiry.

To Mrs. MANN, in Boston. — It is Wednesday, and already your going seems like some far-off event away in the dim distance. Should the boys come back full grown into manhood, and you gray, tottering, and decrepit, it would hardly seem longer. It seems long from morning till night, and from night till morning; only I seem to do nothing, and this makes it like a blank.

—— wrote me about a Mr. Mathematical H——, or an H—— of mathematics; saying it was rumored that our mathematical Magnus did not give satisfaction, and proposing this German in his place. What a howl there would be through all Zion if the glimmering of a suggestion were made that he were not *princeps inter mathematicos*, and that his place should be supplied by one of the world's people! . . . One man " driven into exile," one woman " forbidden the use of fire and water," another " discharged," another " abused and sent off; " and now the mathematical pyramid, the very Cheops of the cause, to be supplanted by that German-sounding name, probably, doubtless, undoubtedly, certainly, the very incarnate of German rationalism, neology, atheism! — ay, worse than atheism; for who knows but he is an unbeliever in the Devil? Consider the rest of the sheet filled with exclamation-points. I do not dare to sign my name to this sheet, though it mentions treason only to rebuke it.

My DEAR Mr. CRAIG, — Yours of July 20 has been forwarded to me at this place, whither I have come in search of the fugitive, health; at least, to escape from the debilitations of our summer heats. I wish you were here. It is a fortnight to-day since we arrived; and such paradisiacal weather as we have had! just warm enough not to be cold, and just cold enough not to be warm. Only one thing is wanting to me, and I should thrive like a green bay-tree; and that is the home diet.

Last night we had some commotion among the elements; and to-day it is cloudy, and a fire is comfortable. But a few whiffs of this air would make your lungs give a hygienic laugh. I am sorry to hear there are any symptoms in your throat or elsewhere which give you present discomfort or forebodings. I am afraid of that Eastern climate for your lungs. I do not believe that air will ever agree with you. It requires a Boreas to blow it, and none but a Boreas can breathe it. You are an exotic in it; and even hothouses will not save you, I fear. . . .

My dear friend, you must answer me one question ; for it will be an element in coming to conclusions that now impend. It is no other than the question I put you before : Suppose the six months during which you feel yourself bound to the Blooming-Grove Society to be at an end, would you, or would you not, come to Yellow Springs ? That is the question. Why should you not answer it ? It is an important element at least, if not a decisive one, in regard to ulterior things. I came here with great hopes, ready to put forth my best efforts, ready to make any sacrifices probably resulting in success. If I am to fail, I have already sacrificed too much ; and the sooner I stop, the more strength I shall have for something else. Let me hear from you by the time I get home, which I hope will be about the 20th inst.

Yours lovingly,

HORACE MANN.

Mr. Mann's visit to Mackinaw, owing to bad living and much depression of spirits while absent from his family, and with the care of an invalid relative instead of cheerful companions, was not productive of as much benefit as he had hoped ; and an unfortunate fall just after his return, which produced violent effects at the moment, and whose consequences reduced him for a time in flesh and strength before his family could reach him from a visit to the East, cancelled what little benefit remained from the cooler atmosphere, and absence from painful scenes. He entered upon the great labors of the next college-year weary and unrefreshed, and with added duties which did not legitimately belong to his office as president.

ANTIOCH COLLEGE, YELLOW SPRINGS, Aug. 25, 1856.

REV. D. AUSTIN.

MY DEAR SIR, — Your letter, full of kind expressions, of which I desire to be worthy, rather than flatter myself that I am so, is just received. Among life's draughts of vinegar, it is very pleasant now and then to get a sip of honey.

I believed you would ratify the use I made of your kind remembrancer, and I am glad to have you do so. I assure you it is transmuted into better material than any other thing I could have changed it for. I think I could make a glorious financiering business of it, could I be allowed, by a divine alchemy, to transmute into knowledge that gold which is now worse than lost in pampering vanity and pride, and thus change that knowledge into wisdom and virtue.

Our college is founded on scholarships, — a very common method at the West, but not a very sound one; at least, without some additional support. Each owner of a scholarship is entitled to a vote in electing the College Board of Trustees, and to keep one pupil at college free from tuition-charges. This may answer where the number of scholarships sold is very large, and only a small portion of them represented by pupils; for then we should have the income of the several unrepresented scholarships to support the one pupil who claims tuition under one. But if the number of scholarships sold is small, and the institution is popular, then most of the scholarships will be represented. Whence, in that case, is the fund to support the institution to be derived? It is obvious, that, unless it can have some endowment to repair to, it must fail.

I am greatly obliged to you for your kind offer to give the sum of fifty dollars annually for five years to students at once deserving and indigent. But, my dear sir, will you pardon me for making a suggestion or two here? We have many students who are poor; and I suppose I have given at least two hundred dollars a year, since I have been here, to aid this class. But I invariably do it in such a manner, that no one but the recipient knows, and sometimes not he or she, where it comes from.

We have nothing, in our whole institution, of the nature of prizes, honors, parts, medals, or any apparatus or artificial system of means which stirs up in the bosoms of the members of our family the unholy fires of emulation.

I hold and always have held it to be unchristian to place two children or youth in such relation to each other, that, if one wins, the other must lose. So placed, what scholars gain in intellect, yea, and a thousand times more, they lose in virtue. We rely on the love of knowledge, and the natural advantages which its possession confers; and we find that enough. I have occasion to use the curb quite as often as the spur.

Now, what could be done with our whole system, should your idea of a *bonus*, or of any competition, be adopted? Fifty dollars too, which would pay the whole tuition of only four students, might, if distributed in sums of five or ten dollars according to circumstances, help more. Put enough of the vitalizing oxygen into the lungs of each swimmer to buoy him up, and let him swim the rest. Let me, then, suggest that you put your fifty dollars into the hands of some member of our faculty, or of our Board of Trustees, many of whom would hardly be less judicious than yourself; and let it be distributed, according to exigencies as they arise, without the knowledge of any one but the recipient, and with none of the heart-burnings and jealousies and surmises of favoritism which every other method involves. I have been almoner in one or two such cases with great effect. When a poor student receives a small sum of money unexpectedly, just enough to meet a dreaded emergency, it seems a thousand times more as if it came straight from God than if he had been wrestling for it in the ring, and had won it as a trophy. I confess I have seen so many dismal forebodings removed, so much joy occasioned, even by a small amount of money, — tears of apprehension suddenly changed into tears of joy, — that I have envied the rich their powers of beneficence, with all its *reflected* happiness. . . .

You speak of remembering Antioch in your will. I sincerely hope so; yet I am about to interpose a caution. Antioch is now the only first-class college in all the West that is really an unsectarian institution; where truth, and nobody's or party's *ism*, is the object. There are, it is true, some State institutions which profess to be free from proselyting instrumentalities; but I believe, that, without exception, they are all under the control of men who hold as truth *something which they have prejudged to be true.* I do not believe, that, in all the West, there is such a Sunday-school class as I teach here. We believe the elements of truth are in the Bible, in the Gospels, in the life of Jesus Christ ; and we mean to find them there.

This freedom from proselytism our college recognizes and avows : and I trust it will always be able to live up to its doctrines. But how frail is human nature ! how weak to execute the good resolutions it had strength enough only to form ! With all my love for Antioch College, — and its prosperity is now the ambition of my life, — I would not give it any very large donation, one after the Lawrence standard of magnitude, absolutely and outright. I would put it into the hands of trustees, or a trustee, to be given to the college if it held on to its avowals of non-sectarian, non-prose-lyting administration.

One thing we want now and severely, — an exercising hall or gymnasium, especially for our young ladies. We pay far more attention to physical education than any other institution (except military ones) that I know of in the world. Oh, if some good man — so much the better if it were a good woman — would give me two or three thousand dollars ! I know it would make the bones in their own graves rest easier, and sleep a serener sleep, could they but feel how much health and happiness, how much physical, intellectual, and moral power, such a structure would create. But pardon me, my dear sir. I am running on unconsciously and unendingly. Your kind letter, amid my many cares and labors and trials, has opened my heart and loosed my tongue. You see this letter, from its very nature, is private ; but I am hereafter publicly your friend,

HORACE MANN.

YELLOW SPRINGS, Sept. 9, 1856.

My very dear Sumner, — I have to-day the great pleasure of hearing from you under your own hand. May God surround you with healing influences, and bless them ! It is impossible to tell you how much we have felt for you, — sorrow, admiration, hope, affection, for you ; grief, indignation, contempt, abhorrence, for the malefactor. Mrs. Mann read one account of the outrage, and could never read another. She said she felt the concussion of the blows all through her brain. I have not written you, because I felt that keeping myself away from all claim to your time or attention was the greatest kindness I could do to you. I am glad to be restored to the privilege of writing to you again.

Now comes your danger, — the danger of getting well too fast, — of not patiently awaiting the slow recuperative processes of Nature. Your brain must all be made over again. It took nine months to make it the first time ; and then it was not worth much until it had been some years in ripening and maturing. Do not, then, I beseech you, think that it can be made all over again and set to work in a hurry. *Festina lente.* I can hardly believe that the cause in Massachusetts needs your efforts. Pennsylvania is the battle-ground, the Flanders between North and South. I wish you could stand on one of the peaks of the Alleghanies, and make your voice heard from the Ohio to the Delaware.

O Sumner, how good it feels to hear the tramp of this army of freemen ! Every new battalion, as it comes into line, every shout of its aroused and cheering columns, heals a wound which the atrocities of 1850 inflicted upon my soul. Sweet is the anodyne after such torture !

When the healing influences of time have given you permission to buckle on your armor again, then do it ; but do not anticipate your hour. Seek the noblest revenge, which is strength.

My work is different from yours ; but, in some humble way, it conduces to the same end. Principles are the seeds to be sown in this field of time. The order of Nature, which is God's providence, will mature the fruit. I feel as if I were never doing more of this work than now.

. . . Come and stay with us a month. We will nurse you like a baby, on pap ; or feed you like a hero, on lion.

With best regards from Mrs. Mann, I am yours ever,

HORACE MANN.

ANTIOCH COLLEGE, Sept. 29, 1856.

REV. D. AUSTIN.

MY DEAR SIR, — Your favor of the 17th instant I received on Saturday last. I am greatly obliged to you for it. In the midst of the obstacles which I have to encounter here, I may be supposed to need the encouraging words of friends as much as the most indigent student needs the "material aid;" one instalment of which your letter contained, and others promised. I hope you will give me credit for being wise enough not to consider any thing "small" which can do good. I have undoubting confidence in your wise apportionment of your means, and I think I can assure you that what you may scatter here will be sown on good ground.

You intimate an intention of remembering the college by bequest, provided it shall continue to be administered "without *isms* (especially sectarianism, I trust) and without prizes;" and you ask me to name a person or persons to be invested with power to decide the question, whether, at the time the bequest may fall due, the college is entitled to receive it. I thank you sincerely for this wise provision. In the illiberality of sects, and in the partisan contests for superiority, no sect is beyond the need of such salutary restraints. It is most agreeable to me also to learn that we agree in opinion respecting the immoral tendency of prizes, honors, &c. I do not believe that such stimulants are the best, even for making philosophers: I am sure they are not for making Christians.

In compliance with your request, I give you the names of Dr. S. G. Howe of Boston, and Rev. Henry W. Bellows of New York, as suitable persons to determine whether this institution is faithful or faithless to its avowals.

I fear I may have said too much to you on the subject of a gymnasium. I am so anxious to obtain one, that I may be tempted to overstep the limits of propriety in regard to the means. If I have done so in this case, the motive must make what atonement it can for the act. I thank you for the generous and confiding tone of your letter. I will endeavor to prove to you that your confidence has not been misplaced.

With best regards, I remain very truly yours, &c.,

HORACE MANN.

YELLOW SPRINGS, Oct. 20, 1856.

MY DEAR MR. CRAIG, — Your having been here, and being gone, and being going to be gone, seem to me like a sad and doleful dream. Then comes the consciousness that it is not a dream, but a reality. . . . Mr. Doherty got the Christian Church together on Sunday a week ago, and told them, that, if they would raise four hundred dollars, he would see the pulpit supplied for a year. Nearly five hundred dollars were promptly raised ; and so he stands responsible for the *facit per alium aut facit per se* for the next twelvemonth.

We have a large entering class, but not so many young ladies in proportion as heretofore ; doubtless owing to the repellent power of the infernal Nichols.* Mr. Pennell starts for St. Louis tomorrow : so you hear another sound of disintegration. . . .

Your admirers here have been to me several times to know what they should do with that money. One of the committee introduced the subject to me again since the receipt of your last letter. I said I thought it would be most agreeable to you to have it expended for some permanent object of ornament or utility, to be attached to the college as a remembrance of you ; and I mentioned a chandelier. How emblematic of you would a great lighted chandelier be ! Shall the money be so expended ? If Mrs. Mann were here, she would send her regards along with mine. As she is not, I send double.

HORACE MANN.

YELLOW SPRINGS, Dec. 10, 1856.

MY DEAR DOWNER, — . . . We closed our fall term yesterday. We have had a prosperous term. We are getting more and more of an *esprit de corps* of the right sort among our young people. High hopes and high aims are, I think, gradually supplanting low ones. I can never get the institution, I suppose, fully up to my ideal ; but I can say it is advancing towards it.

With kindest regards from all to all, I remain yours as ever,

H. MANN.

---

* Dr. Gove Nichols, who established himself for a time in the neighborhood.

ANTIOCH COLLEGE, YELLOW SPRINGS, Dec. 10, 1856.

To REV. CYRUS PIERCE.

MY DEAR MR. PIERCE, — Were I to sit down to write you all I want to say, I must secure much time and much paper. But be assured I think of you often, and always with affection. My unbroken round of engagements, however, forces me to commit the almost impious act of sacrificing the demands of friendship. I desire exceedingly to see you, and have that opportunity to pour out and to take in which a personal interview alone can give.

I hear you have discontinued your relations to the school at West Newton. I am glad of it. If any person ought to stand on the "Emeritus" roll, it is Cyrus Pierce. Now you are floating, why cannot you suffer the gales of affection to blow you and Mrs. Pierce hitherward? I think we are doing something of a work here : it cannot in all respects come up to your high standard ; but, compared with the standard that has existed here hitherto, it is respectable. I have few things to look back upon with complacency during my past life ; but I do really think I have as much reason to hope for good from my present labors as from any in which I was ever engaged. I have a difficult navigation, as difficult as the first few years of my Secretaryship. Whether I shall have such help as to be able to ride out the storm, remains to be seen ; but, if that can be the case, I feel fully convinced that a glorious voyage awaits the craft, and that she will scatter rich freight upon a thousand shores long after the stone has been fastened to my feet, and I have been thrown overboard. But there is one gloomy idea that haunts my mind, and it is one which can find no remedy or hope. I feel every day more and more keenly that I must soon retire from the field of action, while at the same time my zeal grows and glows to continue the contest with evil. I love the good causes more than ever ; more than ever I want to fight for them : and the most painful idea connected with death is that I must be at most a looker-on, and cannot be a participator. How do you feel? Are you willing to retire? Are you patient under the long delays of Providence? Some one says, "God is never in a hurry." Well, if with him a thousand years are as one day, he can afford to wait. But we — how can we be expected to wait? I know it is in vain to struggle with destiny. It seems to me just as vain to struggle against this vehement desire to see the contest out.

Mr. Pennell has left us, — a great loss to us. He has gone into the high school at St. Louis at a salary of $2,500 a year! "The world does move, though." I went out there last spring to attend a State Educational Convention, and form a State Teachers' Association. I found the city teachers, who are mostly Eastern men, all alive on the subject. They were like dry fuel, fitly laid, and only needing a breath to kindle them. It was my good luck to be that breath, and they are now shining brilliantly. The city have not only voted this $2,500 for the principal of their high school, but the same sum for the salary of a principal of a Normal school; and they gave me *carte blanche* to appoint both. Whom can I find for the Normal school?

I am writing to Mr. —— probably for the last time. Since his prosperity, he has changed his whole manner and relationship to me. I exerted myself as a brother to help him up. *Up*, he forgets me. So goes the world, — at least many persons in it. God help us to make the world better!

With best love from Mrs. Mann and myself to Mrs. Pierce and the Nestor of schoolmasters,

I am, as ever, yours,

HORACE MANN.

YELLOW SPRINGS, Sept. 5, 1856.

MY DEAR MR. CRAIG, — I have received your late letter extinguishing all my hopes. I have no doubt of your being able to justify to your own conscience the conclusion to which you have come. It would, indeed, be most lamentable, if, to the indescribable evils consequent upon your decision, that of any conscious interference of choice with duty were added.

I will now say in strictest confidence to you what I have never said to any living being before, not even to my wife, — that the probability of my continuing for any length of time in my present position is very slight.

Mr. Pennell is about to leave us; and there goes one of the

corner-stones of the college. He came here from a salary of $1,300, with an assurance that it should soon be raised to $1,500. He afterwards had an offer of $1,600, which he refused. Last spring he had an offer of $2,000; which also, for the sake of the cause here and for my sake, he declined. And now he yields to an offer of $2,500 from St. Louis. Things were assuming such a desperate aspect here, that I did not think he ought to hazard the means of supporting his family longer, either for his personal friendship for me, or for the sake of our doubtful enterprise here.

The trustees have just closed their annual meeting. Mr. Zachos is turned out; Mr. B—— put in his place, — one of the best men we could have giving place to — another. Clandestine measures had been most extensively and thoroughly taken to prejudice the minds of the trustees against Mr. Zachos; and they came with a resolution which no arguments or expostulations that I, or those of us who were on the ground, could overcome. They could hardly have found a more objectionable man than their appointee. It would have the appearance of rashness, and perhaps of passion, had I resigned at once; and I shall do nothing which will tend to prejudice the institution after I leave it.

On the other hand, there is now a chance that our debts will all be paid by the first of next January. [This hope proved fallacious. — ED.] . . .

Prospects before us, or rather before me, lower as with vengeance. I know not what will come; but one thing I mean, at all events, to do, — to keep a conscience void of offence towards God and man.   Your always friend,

HORACE MANN.

YELLOW SPRINGS, Jan. 24, 1857.

MY DEAR SUMNER, — I read with avidity every thing I see about you; but, while all that pertains to your enduring interests exceeds what even a sanguine friendship would dare to hope, I grieve that your health and physical resources remain as they are. You must be careful. Should Boreas get into a shepherd's pipe, would he not rend it into a thousand splinters? Heal your body, and your soul will do well enough. . . .

When you have time and strength, do write to me ; and meanwhile believe me, as ever,

Most truly yours,   HORACE MANN.

APRIL 6, 1857.

MY DEAR, EVER DEAR MR. CRAIG, — Your letter from Cairo reached us the day our term opened.   Since then, the number and character of my duties in launching our craft for another term have crowded me half way to insanity.   But to-day we are under sail, and all posts are manned or womaned. . . .

I should have written you on some points; but Mrs. Mann has said them better than I could.   Ponder them, — for Antioch's sake, for humanity's sake, for God's sake, ponder them.   The bird's wing was not made for the air, nor our eye for the light, any more than you for Antioch College.   Why will you keep things apart that were made for each other ?

If I could feel that you would be my successor here, I should be ready at any time to say with old Simeon, " Now, Lord, lettest thou thy servant depart in peace."

May God bless and let me direct you !   Is that wicked ?

As ever, yours,   HORACE MANN.

YELLOW SPRINGS, July 3, 1857.

MY DEAR MR. CRAIG, — A new crisis has come to our affairs.

First, however, let me say that we have had a glorious Commencement.*   Governor Chase was here, and he says it surpassed any thing he ever saw in Ohio.   Rev. Dr. Gannett was here from Boston ; and he says, that, in all the particulars that affect a moral and accountable being, they never have had any thing to compare with it at the East.

. . . The Board has met, and elected a new Board.   Antioch College has " failed."   All its property is assigned for the payment of its debts.   The whole scholarship system will be abolished.   All the professors, including your humble servant, were decapitated by

---

* The Commencement of the first class that was graduated from the college.

the old Board   The new one, however, did replace the president's head before the flesh and nerves had become wholly cold and lifeless; so that, with care, they may stick together once more.

A new faculty is to be formed.   Doherty and Allen are very sure not to be re-appointed; and this will leave the cabinet a *unit* in sentiment and purpose.

Always much, but now more than ever, must the Rev. Austin Craig come to the rescue.   His services are indispensable, — first, as chaplain, to preach half the day on Sunday, having no connection with the village but that of cordiality and reciprocity of good works; and second, that of teaching, more or less as health may permit.

Now, my dear friend, we have a chance for a college such as was never known before.   In my "Baccalaureate," on Wednesday, I laid down the great doctrine, that the power of knowledge ought never to be added to the power of vice; that, up to the time of entering a college-class, the most vicious and abandoned should be educated; and the more so, the more so.   But, after that, none but the virtuous, the earnest, those who give confident promise of righteousness or right-doing, should be invested with the prerogatives and enchantments of knowledge.

Now, my dear friend, I feel God-authorized to say you must come and work with us, and, when my mantle falls off, take it upon your shoulders.   I see no alternative but this.   Blooming Grove, compared with this, is but the tiniest islet to the Western continent. . . .

Yours in the Lord and Antioch,
HORACE MANN.

YELLOW SPRINGS, June 7, 1857.

MY DEAR MR. CRAIG, — The vision forever flits before my mind, that, if I am to be at Antioch College, you are to be here too.   It cannot be selfishness.   It is genuine heart-belief that nowhere else can you do so much good as here . . . Now be a good boy!   Don't be over-modest.   Trust in God some, in Austin Craig also, and listen to this request, and make it prophecy now, and history hereafter.   Yours as ever, most truly,

HORACE MANN.

ANTIOCH COLLEGE, July 4, 1857.

MY DEAR MR. CRAIG, — Although the ink is hardly dry on the last letter I wrote you, yet, having a chance to send by your friends, I improve it.

I hardly know what I wrote you before; yet I know I wrote what was nearest my heart, and therefore it must have been about your coming here. If you would do so, I know it would be the turning-point in the history of this institution. It will make a difference of many students; and, what is better, it will make a difference in the moral and religious character of all. How gladly would I help you work here! how rejoicingly I would leave you here when I am called away! I know we have a chance for an institution here such as exists in no other part of the earth, — one founded on the love of truth and righteousness. We have the power of saying, and of maintaining the doctrine, equally new and great, that we will graduate none but true, exemplary youth; and this will push the world along half a century at one impulse. But, to all the good things I plan, you appear in the foreground of the picture. . . .

Pray let me hear from you soon. . . . These matters must be settled without delay.

Yours as ever, and more so,

HORACE MANN.

It was the moral superiority of the college rather than a literary one to which Mr. Mann looked forward with so much hope and confidence. He felt, indeed, that where study was pursued conscientiously, and with higher motives than the principle of emulation (which he considered an unholy one), it would secure superiority there; but he had fed his imagination with the conception of a practical religious life to be inspired into or evolved out of the young, to which he thought the generous heart of youth would respond warmly, if it could be disconnected from a religionism whose features make the young turn away, — not because the natural heart is altogether evil, but because it is a narrow rather than a broad religious culture which is inculcated. His young friend whom he so long and earnestly importuned to come to his assistance was to him the type of what all the young might be; and the fruits of his experiment during the last few years had satisfied him that his plans were not Utopian, as many of his friends wished to make him believe. He saw that the young could work together for their own and each other's improvement without the stimulus of rivalry or any base motive, but in true brotherly love.

MACKINAW, MICH., Aug. 6, 1857.

MY DEAR DOWNER, — Here we all are in Mackinaw, and enjoying ourselves too well not to tell you about it, and to wish you were with us. The climate, the air, &c., perform the promise made last year; and, as all the family are with me, I enjoy it vastly more than I did last year. I never breathed such air before; and this must be some that was clear out of Eden, and did not get cursed. I sleep every night under sheet, blanket, and coverlet; and no day is too warm for smart walking and vigorous bowling. The children are crazy with animal spirits, and eat in such a way as to demonstrate the epigastric paradox, that the quantity contained may be greater than the container. I verily believe, if you would spend one summer here, — say from about the middle of July to the middle of September, — it would make your brain as good as Samuel Downer's brain ever was since it occupied its present cranium; and that is saying a great deal.

In the first place, you would analyze, and, morally speaking, pulverize and sift, the whole island in four days.

In the second place, you could not get a mail but once a week. And,

Thirdly, you would then have nothing to do but to use your senses on the beauties of water and sky, and see that you had daily food for two or three common rations.

I am getting more weaned from Boston every day, and wish you did not love it so well. . . . I shall want the dividends promptly;

for I am in very close quarters as to money. The breaking-up of
the college as it did, without paying me a cent on about half a
year's salary (besides the general indebtedness to me on the old
score), has left me a sort of beggar. . . .

I want a good long letter from you, — long enough to let me
know all about your health, and how much you are released from
the weight and care of business, and how deeply you are still involved in it; because these things have the directest bearing upon
your health. Tell me all the news. . . .

Yours as ever, most truly,

HORACE MANN.

The climate of Mackinaw proved to Mr. Mann's temperament the most delicious one he ever enjoyed. With his
family around him, including even a faithful, devoted, and
well-trained cook; with the beautiful lake at his feet, its
plashing waters soothing his wearied nerves to sleep every
night, the golden beach enlivened every morning by the
tents of the Indians who came at daybreak from the opposite shore with their fish and fruits; with quiet boating
with his children, long walks with them in the lovely
woods, — he seemed almost to renew his youth. He knew
terrific labors awaited him on his return; but, for the first
time in his life, he turned his thoughts away, and went to
sleep on Mother Nature's bosom. He perhaps, of all persons on the island, was glad when the mail-boats did *not*
arrive; for they brought echoes of past and elements of
future toil to him. He read aloud heart-inspiring books,
— Whittier's poems, and other works which he had only
known before by their titles; and actually wrote a lecture
he had in his head in *verse*. On one side of the island, a
luxurious wood covers a declivity of one or two hundred
feet. He found a steep path through this wood, across
which ran a gigantic root, which he forthwith made his
study. Thither he escaped every morning with his port-

folio and pencils, challenging his children to find him, which they did at last; but they were not often allowed to invade his quiet there. Their turn came later in the day. With nothing in view but the beautiful lake and sky, and the music of the pines and the birds in his ear, he actually rested. A noble friend, Mr. Ward of Detroit, proposed to build a house upon the island, in which he invited him to spend all his summer vacations; and he felt as if, with such repose as that would be, he might yet work many years: for temporary rest in which to recruit for more labor was all that ever dwelt in his imagination.

On his return, he was required, as a condition of future existence to the college, to take the financial affairs into his own keeping. Every thing was to be organized anew, as it were. But there were some encouraging circumstances in the prospect, that promised to lighten the burden, as his letters will show.

ANTIOCH COLLEGE, July 18, 1857.

MY DEAR MR. CRAIG, — Yours of the 11th instant has reached me to-day. The delay has given me restless sleep and horrid dreams; but your letter promises a pleasant morning after a dreary night.

First, I send you a catalogue: second, I am afraid you want more exactness of detail than it will be possible for me, in our present disorganized state, to give; but I can make one assurance sure, — that we love you too well, and believe that the Lord has too much for you to do hereafter for Antioch College, to allow us to put your health in peril.

I feel as though I could yet, in desperate circumstances, perform a great amount of labor, and so does R——; and what you can't do, I hope we can. What is wanted is, that you, temporarily, should fill Mr. ——'s place. The college and school are so utterly dissatisfied with him, that it is said the *whole* of our to be seniors would leave if he is retained, and at least half of all the other college-classes. The case, therefore, is desperate.

. . . Six thousand dollars are to be raised by subscription, which, with the expected income from tuition and rooms, is thought to be sufficient to pay the teachers at about the same rate as heretofore ; and I think you should be paid according to the proportion of your labors. But on this point, my dear friend, you must trust to the Lord a little, and, while you are reasonably careful about earthly treasure, lay up something in the upper treasury, whose officers never embezzle or defalcate. You will be worth ten thousand dollars to the moral interests of the college ; and all this will, I have no doubt, be transferred to your account in the book of life. As to the future, you know what I hope and intend for you.

Yours as ever,

HORACE MANN.

Mr. Craig yielded to the demand made upon him at this time, and came to share the labors of the new college, as it in effect was, though there was little outward change. The absence of two members of the faculty, who had made its meetings a scene of unhappy feeling so long, lightened the hearts of all the little cabinet : indeed, the members had refused to serve with one of the ejected parties any longer, since he had not only falsified the record of which he had unfortunately been made secretary, but had broken faith with them as a body repeatedly, and, regardless of their honor as a faculty, voted one way at their meetings, and reported his votes falsely outside, — secure in the knowledge that the rest would keep their word to let the final vote upon any subject stand as a unanimous one. Mr. Mann often said no words could describe the changed feeling with which he stood upon the platform of the chapel, and *did not* encounter that face in his audience. But he was not destined to enjoy that immunity long. Although rejected from the faculty with every token of moral disgrace, the obnoxious ex-member returned after two months' absence, obtruded himself into all the gatherings of the students in the chapel, and often in the recitation-rooms even of his own successor (although she was a lady, and a stranger to him) ; and, "squat like a toad," remained there through the greater part of the year, sowing dissension among students and villagers, interrupting the harmony that existed between the college and the village church, and at last. actually, by the most violent, dishonorable, and unscrupulous proceedings, causing a schism in the latter, whose wounds were never again healed during Mr. Mann's life. At the end of the year, he published a slanderous and most false account of college and church affairs in a large octavo volume, which he spent a part of the next year in circulating, and in some cases peddling, through the "Christian" churches of the West. The effect of this was to alienate the interest of that denomination so far as to stop nearly all the supplies which earnest and self-sacrificing agents had been promised for the final redemption of the institution ; the sale having been postponed for two years, in order to give time for its friends to rally. Mr. Mann and other members of the faculty decided, after a time, that it was best to answer this libellous production ; and each one wrote his own defence, and published them together in a small volume. It is doubtful if the reply ever reached a tithe of the persons upon whom the libel was assiduously forced ; and therefore the influence of the latter remains this day to prejudice many of the so-called "Christians" against the college, future as well as past. The expense as well as labor involved fell chiefly upon Mr. Mann. The labor was one of the drops too much that filled his last cup of life.

ANTIOCH COLLEGE, YELLOW SPRINGS, Sept. 17, 1857.

E. CONANT, ESQ.

MY DEAR SIR, — It is not a pleasant task to answer the letter which your grandson put into my hands yesterday. Nevertheless,

I will do it frankly and directly, and, I trust, in a manner satisfactory to you.

The college was founded upon a rotten basis. By no possibility can a student be educated here for six dollars a year, or for six times that sum. It was intended to obtain four or five times as many scholarships as there would be scholars; but that, though intended, was never effected.

The consequence was, that the college has been running deeper and deeper into debt ever since it was opened. There was the most deplorable mismanagement in the building of it, as has since been ascertained, on the part of Mr. M——, so that it ran in debt greatly; and, since it opened, those debts have been increasing. Effort after effort has been made to pay off the debts; but they have all failed. We have thought from time to time that they would succeed; but we have been deplorably disappointed. At last it became apparent that the indebtedness of the college would not only require all the scholarship-fund for its payment, but would render every scholarship-holder liable for an additional amount beyond his scholarship, and equal to it; that is, every owner of a scholarship would not only lose his scholarship, but be liable for a hundred dollars besides. This, of course, would never do. The only alternative, therefore, was to transfer the college property for the payment of its debts, and begin anew on the basis of tuition. I say there was no alternative but this, or an entire breaking-up of the school, and an abandonment of the property to the creditors. The friends of the institution chose the former; and, though a misfortune, it was the least of the misfortunes before them. This they have done. Members of the Board of Trustees and others have subscribed six thousand dollars to help carry on the school this year; and we hope to meet the residue of the expense from tuition-fees and other resources. I have made the above statement as that of the trustees; in which, however, I fully concur. I have not yet stated, that, every year since I have been here, I have made more sacrifice for the college than the sum which you have paid. I am willing to make more if it can be saved for education, and a liberal, unsectarian Christianity. Are you not ready, my dear sir, to do the same? What better use can we make of our means? We now know the worst of it. This assignment cancels all the debts. Now we can start anew. Should a company be formed to buy in the college, and carry it on on the new basis (say to be owned in shares of five hundred dollars each), would you not still, for so great an object, take one of the shares? The college has done immense good already. I trust the Lord has friends enough to sustain it for the still greater good it may do hereafter.

Yours most truly,

HORACE MANN

MACKINAW, MICH., Aug. 7, 1857.

MY DEAR MR. CRAIG, — A steamboat which carries the mail lies at the wharf, but will start in a few minutes. I seize the moment to say that I have seen your letter to Mr. Fay. . . . I look upon your assistance as almost, or rather I ought to say absolutely, essential to carry out the plans in regard to Antioch which have now been announced. After all that has been said and done, it will be an immense affair to hold the college up to that standard of moral elevation which has now been officially promulgated. For that grand purpose, the highest and noblest practical enterprise which any man in the country can undertake, I know that you would be the best instrument the good God has yet made. Is it not an object in which all merely personal considerations should be merged? You must break through all ordinary impediments, therefore, to meet this God-appointed exigency. . . .

Farewell, and God bless you! Remember you are Heaven and not committee appointed to such a work for education as was never undertaken before.

HORACE MANN.

ANTIOCH COLLEGE, Sept. 17, 1857.

MY DEAR MR. CRAIG, — I saved the college by going to Blooming Grove, and securing your services in it; but I came near losing myself. For thirty-six hours after I left you, I was more ill than I have been for years. I lay by at Dunkirk over Sunday; and was just able to reach home, *semi animus*, on Monday. Well, I had this to console myself with, — if I got you, though I killed myself, I had made a great bargain.

Our school opens grandly with about a hundred new students, and a better-looking class of students than we have ever had before. These students have all been brought here by our reputation : they have not come to save six dollars a year on a scholarship. They evidently come from the more intelligent class in the community, and thereby show where our strength is growing. I have great expectations from your connection with the college. I understand there is great jubilation among the students, — a double jubilation indeed, — one for those who are to come to help us, and one on account of those who *are not.* Your presence is looked for most anxiously. The contrast between you and your predecessor in this branch will be immense. . . .

We are all well. I have had a dreadfully hard time since I returned. I want to tell you how the ungodly were caught in their own snare ; but this must be when you get here. Our arms are all open to receive you. . . .

Your friend, HORACE MANN.

YELLOW SPRINGS, Oct. 16, 1857.

MY DEAR DOWNER, — . . . We are going on grandly with the college. Notwithstanding the abolition of the scholarship system, which many thought would extinguish us, we have nearly three hundred students to-day, and more in the college-classes than ever before. There must be some reason that draws so many students here, notwithstanding the horrid pecuniary death we have been dying for four years, and notwithstanding every student who came was not without some reason to believe that the college would tumble down on his head.

. . . I am living on short allowance ; have not had a cent from the college for a year and a half ; and it costs me about $2,000 a year to keep up my " public house." . . .

Love from all to all, HORACE MANN.

ANTIOCH COLLEGE, YELLOW SPRINGS, Oct. 23, 1857.

REV. DANIEL AUSTIN.

MY DEAR SIR, — I acknowledge with many thanks the receipt of yours of the 15th inst., enclosing a check for fifty dollars. It is most timely. I have been called upon to the full extent of my means; and yet we have meritorious young people here whom it is a great delight to assist. Your gift will give many joyous hours.

Our college has been revolutionized within the last three months. The scholarship system has been abolished, and a system of tuition substituted. The one was almost free: the other is somewhat expensive. Yet we have lost very few in point of numbers. That so many should resort here while there is a chance that the college will tumble down over their heads; that so many should become members of our college-classes while there is any chance that the institution will have no name or existence ten years hence, — proves, as it seems to me, the reputation we have acquired for scholarship and discipline. Indeed, I think it is now acknowledged on all hands that we have the best institution for learning and good morals this side the mountains. The bigots are saying all manner of evil things about us; but we hope to survive their anathemas.

Have you seen Dr. Gannett's article about us in the last number of the "Unitarian Quarterly Journal"? He came out here Saul: he went back Paul. . . .   Yours most truly,

H. MANN.

YELLOW SPRINGS, Jan. 13, 1858.

REV. O. J. WAIT.

MY DEAR SIR. . . . With many thanks for your proposed attentions and civilities, permit me to say that all my feelings and habits would be far more gratified to be allowed, on my arrival at Cincinnati, to go quietly to a hotel, than to be surrounded with all the pomp and circumstance belonging to a king. I propose to stop at my usual place when in the city, — the Burnet House. There, when it is convenient, I shall be most happy to see you and your friends, and my friends if I have any. . . .

In the mean time, I remain very truly yours,

HORACE MANN.

My DEAR Mr. MAY, — I was many times glad to hear that you had so far recovered your health as to return to your home and your duties again. Has that terrible fellow they call Old Age got hold of you yet? Occasionally I think I hear the sound of his footsteps. I dread him greatly; not so much, however, for what he does, as for what he will prevent me from doing. There are a few causes — such as universal peace and universal freedom, and *education, the parent of them all* — in which I have become intensely interested, and want to fight in their ranks at least a hundred years before being summoned away. I fear the chances are against me.

During the ensuing fortnight's vacation, I propose to recreate myself on a lecturing tour this side and the other side of the Mississippi.

Internally our establishment goes on beautifully; but abroad the trump of doom is sounding in our ears. Some of our Eastern friends are anxious for us; but it is impossible for them to comprehend the significance of such an institution here : and so a great calamity may come upon the world, which the possession of one idea would have averted. This Great West has been conquered, religiously speaking, from Black Hawk to John Calvin. So far as the religious dogmas are concerned, I would rather it would be Black Hawk's again. The people of the West are open, receptive, mouldable. The ministers have a cast-iron epidermis, — so opaque and impervious, that no sunlight can get into them; so absorbent, that none is reflected from them, or all that strikes upon them is swallowed up and lost. The stronger minds, which break away from Orthodoxy as the common rule, find no stopping-place this side of general scepticism. In this great State of Ohio, with nearly three millions of people, there are but three Unitarian societies; and these are small. All the colleges of a first-class character have a strong infusion of Calvinism mingled with their daily food.

Although our first commencement was held last year, we graduated more than the average of the first eleven colleges in Ohio; and our numbers exceed those of any other, with the exception of Oberlin, and we have a far larger number than that had at our age. More than a thousand students, either from the collegiate or the proparatory department, have left us; and among them all, scarcely one who had been with us long enough to imbibe the spirit of the place has left us a dogmatizer or a bigot. Many have left for the ministry; but it is the ministry of truth, and not of a sect. There is a strong but a sober spirit of attention to religious interests among our students. Their moral character and conduct correspond.

On the east side of our grounds, and immediately adjoining them, is a farm of four hundred acres, with garden, vineyard, and orchard of twenty or thirty in addition. On the north-west, Judge Mills has a large flower and fruit garden.* On the south-west, a hundred and fifty rods from our doors, a Frenchman raises choice fruits for the market. Not one of these for two years has lost an apple or peach or grape. . . . Our dormitory, nearly filled with male students, has no tutor or proctor or overseer. In study-hours, it is as quiet as your house. We have no rowdyism, no drinking of intoxicating liquors, no gambling or card-playing; and we have nearly succeeded, notwithstanding the inveteracy of these habits at the West, in exorcising profanity and tobacco.

You know my views of emulation. It may make bright scholars; but it makes rascally politicians and knavish merchants.

All of our faculty now, except myself, are young (and I feel so), and are well qualified for their places, and filled with a generous enthusiasm. Five of them are members of the Christian Church, two of the Unitarian Church. Two of our professors are ladies. *Audi alteram partem.*

The whole college property is advertised to be sold at auction on the second day of June next! The Presbyterians have been contemplating the erection of a college for some years, and have collected funds for the purpose. A year ago, they located one at West Liberty, about forty miles north from here. Hearing of our disasters, they suspended all preparations for building; and, this present week, a body of them, or committee rather, made us a visit of examination. It is said all around that they will give sixty thousand dollars for this, — some say eighty thousand. No doubt they would be willing to give a few thousands extra for the sake of the omen.

---

* The students had at all times the privilege of crossing his domains in every direction.

What a chance for any one who stands at the door of wealth to say, " *Open sesame!* " Would not the very gates of heaven stand wider forever afterwards? Let this chance pass by, when will such an institution, in such a working condition, re-appear? You may have the brick and the mortar; but

" Where is the Promethean fire that will that light relume ? "

Excuse this long outpouring. My heart is full of the subject, — not at all, be assured, for any selfish reason; for I have not received money enough from the institution, since I came here, to pay my family expenses : but that " man cannot live by bread alone " is as true of your old and dearly loving friend, Horace Mann, as of anybody else.

Mr. Mann now threw himself into the final effort to save the institution to liberal education, secular and religious, with a zeal and intensity that alarmed those who watched over him, whose eyes were not holden by their own selfish aims. He was involved in a perfect network of the latter. Men who had pretended enthusiasm for him and for learning at first, fell away and became hostile when the failing fortunes of the college disappointed their desire to coin gold out of their unsold lands. They cared not who occupied the ground if these could be sold. Many dishonest men took refuge in the excuse that they were involved in college debts. Some men pretended to be in his confidence who were not so, and used his good name to cover up their evil deeds. Mutual animosities between parties connected with the college prejudiced the minds of those who looked on from without, and could not understand the complications thus entailed upon its interests. There seemed to be but one possible way in which to extricate it even from outward difficulties: this was for its friends to purchase it outright, and set it upon an independent basis, freed from all previous entanglements. A few more letters describing the labors of a few more months will bring the sad narrative to a close.

Yellow Springs, March 3, 1858.

My dear Mr. Craig, — You have not yet been gone two days, and we are all homesick for you already. My ears tingle to know what you are saying and doing at Stafford to-day.

. . . Doubtless it will be given you in that selfsame hour what you shall say: but, among the things which you do say, I trust you will not omit to dwell with earnest, apostolic unction upon the character of our students; their freedom from almost all the vices and evil habits which are commonplace in other colleges; the security of gardens and orchards and vineyards *wholly* from any depredations of theirs; on the fact that both the men and women of the village have been watching the past season for offenders against the temperance laws, yet never has suspicion rested on one of our students of having so much as visited a drinking-saloon or other similar resort; the feeling with which the young men are regarded by the ladies of the place; the high, elevated, and often religious tone of their exercises, whether for exhibition or class compositions; and what I think will strike your audience very forcibly, — the fact that, among all who have gone out from here from all the classes, J—— J—— is the only bigot I know of.[*] They go out, generally, deeply impressed with the importance of religious truth, but inquirers, not dogmatizers.

And now, my dear, very dear friend, may peace and blessing attend you all the days of your life!

I know Mrs. Mann would send indefinite quantities of love if she were here, and so would the childers.

Ever and truly yours,

HORACE MANN.

Yellow Springs, May 18, 1858.

My dear Mr. Combe, — I received your letter of March 18 about a week ago; and it would have given me unmingled satisfac-

---

[*] The man here alluded to entered with hostile feelings and bigoted views deeply rooted.

tion but for an expression at the close. In this you intimate that we have become forgetful or unmindful of you, and say you are unconscious of having done any thing to forfeit our esteem. My dear friend, I am exceedingly sorry that any such suspicion or suggestion should ever have come consciously into your mind. I assure you it represents no truth. My consciousness affirms this. There is no man of whom I think so often; there is no man of whom I write so often; there is no man who has done me so much good as you have. I see many of the most valuable truths as I never should have seen them but for you, and all truths better than I should otherwise have done. If I could do it, I would make a pilgrimage to see you; and, if you would come to America, I would take care of you till one or the other of us should die. You must find, and I can give, other and unanswerable reasons why I do not write to you so often as I would. The administration of the college is very engrossing. I teach political economy, intellectual philosophy, moral philosophy, and natural theology, one class all the year, and, one-third of the year, two classes. I take the whole charge of the Sunday school, which almost all our mature scholars attend voluntarily; and, with their eager and inquisitive minds, they demand substance, and will not be satisfied with form. The entire discipline of the institution devolves upon me. With such of our young people as need the curbing of the propensities, and to have their energies withdrawn from their present channels and directed into new ones, I spend a great deal of time privately. I cannot get at the heart in social addresses as I can in private appeals. When I have an interview with a reckless or perverse student, and pass into his consciousness, and try to make him see mine, I always shed tears; I cannot help it: and there is a force in honest tears not to be found in logic. This labor is diminishing as the spirit of the school, its *animus*, improves. And we really have the most orderly, sober, diligent, and exemplary institution in the country. We passed through the last term, and are more than half through the present; and I have not had occasion to make a single entry of any misdemeanor in our record-book, — not a case for any serious discipline.

There is no rowdyism in the village, no nocturnal rambles making night hideous. All is quiet, peaceful; and the women of the village feel the presence of our students, when met in the streets in the evening, to be a protection rather than an exposure. It is now almost five years since I came here, and as yet I have had no "practical joke" or "college prank," as they are called, played upon me, — not in a single instance. Think you it has not required some labor to superinduce this state of things on the free and easy manners of the West?

We are in the midst of a great community, ferociously Orthodox. In this great State of Ohio, already having a population of more than two millions and a half, there are but four Unitarian churches. Calvinism has terrible sway, and its whole artillery is levied against us. We take it broadsides, and work on. If we can go on, we will make a breach in the Chinese Wall, and let in the light.

But here the question arises, Can we go on? Our institution was begun when money was superabundant, when everybody felt rich and generous. The time for opening was proclaimed a year in advance. Then came disaster. All materials, labor, stock, rose from thirty-three to fifty per cent. Interest became exorbitant. The accounts were not well kept; and when I came, though it was not known to me for more than a year afterwards, the college was bankrupt, and has been bankrupt ever since. From time to time, new plans have been devised for raising money: they have failed. And now, unless help comes from some quarter, we shall disband, and leave the old schools and the old theology to take our place on the first of July next. Oh, if we had a tithe of the wealth that the world is squandering every day, what unspeakable good we could do with it! I know, if you could find and send us $100,000, it would be the happiest act in your long and useful life.

My dear Mr. and Mrs. Combe, good-by!

HORACE MANN.

It was not long after this letter was written that the intelligence of Mr. Combe's death came. Mr. Mann was hardly prepared for it even by Mr. Combe's own anticipation. The greatest consolation for the loss was in the feeling of joyful sympathy with that great consciousness which he had the happiness of believing would open his vision in another sphere of progress in a way which he did not himself anticipate. All Mr. Combe's imagination had been able to compass was the future progress of the human race on earth; and glorious and inspiring that imagination was, for glorious and inspiring was his conception of its capacities for earthly improvement. Mr. Mann enjoyed both. He, too, believed its destiny in this world was scarcely yet comprehended by the loftiest earthly conceptions: but he looked upon this world in its best estate as but a school for the cultivation of faculties which were to ripen in nearer consciousness of God, in spheres where fuller conceptions of his omnipotence would be vouchsafed to the soul that had been faithful to its earthly trust, and where the search into causes would be forever prosecuted without the drawbacks imposed by the earthly body.

YELLOW SPRINGS, OHIO, July 3, 1858.

D. CROMYER, ESQ. — . . . I often tell our young people, that, if they can be equipped for the business of life at thirty, they have done well. Let two young people enter upon the active stage of life, one at *twenty* years of age and the other at *thirty*, in every other respect alike, save that the latter has spent his ten years in preparation, and, at the age of forty-five, the latter will be ahead of the former in wealth, position, character, and all the means of happiness.

I hate debt as badly as Dr. Franklin did; and yet there are two things for which I would not hesitate a moment to incur it, — to save my life and to get an education, and for the latter as soon as the former.

A year after graduating is worth two years before. It is therefore a saving of fifty per cent of life. Is not this a good as well as an honest speculation? This favors borrowing.

But school-keeping and manual labor offer themselves as means of support. Many of the young men in our college support themselves wholly or partially in one of these ways. The most menial services about our buildings are performed by our students; and they are not respected less, but more, on this account.*

There is a great demand also in this vicinity for well-qualified teachers. After all, I should be governed more by the spirit of the young man you refer to than by his external circumstances all put together. Has he an irrepressible desire for knowledge, and for the uses of knowledge in benefiting his fellow-men? Is he prompted by a selfish and ignoble, or by a generous and lofty ambition? Does he think of the world which he can benefit by his own attainments and talents? or does he desire attainments and talents that he may make the world, through their influence, benefit him? . . .

These, and such things as these, are the data I should ask for, — the premises on which I should form my conclusions, far more than on circumstances of age or poverty.

Yours very truly,

H. M.

YELLOW SPRINGS, July 10, 1858.

MY DEAR DOWNER, — I suppose you will call me a fool; but we shall see better how that is when we get to the "new Jerusalem."

It was absolutely necessary to raise about twenty-one thousand dollars here by subscription, or else the college was remedilessly lost. We got all its friends to be present at commencement whom we could prevail upon to come, hoping to make a strong rally. But those who were most bound to step into the breach shrunk and skulked, and would do nothing. The thing looked utterly irretrievable. I then did what I suppose you will blame me for: but it really was a question, whether this one liberal institution in the

---

* In more than one instance, when talented and estimable young men feared not to be able to remain in the institution as long as they wished, from being unable to command the employment that would give them the means, purses were secretly made up by other pupils better off in this respect, and put into the president's hands for their relief; while the object of it was spared the pain of a dependent feeling by not knowing the individuals. In some instances, the stimulus of this testimony to their worth was very ennobling as well as animating to the subjects of it. — ED.

midst of a world of intolerance ; whether this one institution open
for the equal education of woman ; whether this one institution,
where alone the doctrine is promulgated and sustained in practice,
that no immoral young man shall add the attractions of learning to
the seductions of profligacy, — it was, I say, a question, whether this
institution should be sacrificed, or whether I should be.   I chose
the latter ; in consequence of which it is necessary for me to raise
four thousand dollars by the first of August next.   I hope I can
make some turn out here for the whole, or at least for a part of it.
My security here will avail if I can find the money ; but, if I cannot, then I shall have to put my property at the East into the market
or under the hammer. . . . Out of some of these resources I must
raise the money there, if I cannot here.   I shall know in a few days
just how much I must have ; and then I want to rely upon you to
raise it out of some of my means at any sacrifice.*

We have passed and are passing through hard times ; but, the
Lord willing, I think we will make something out of our opportunities yet.   I shall be detained here all summer, looking after college
affairs.   I am worked down, but am otherwise very well, and hope
to fight the Devil for some years yet.   With love from all to all, I
remain, as ever,

Yours most truly,

HORACE MANN.

P. S. — Oh, if some of those old fellows, who are rich to the
peril of their souls, only knew what was good for them !

The subject of the peculiar discipline of the college has
often been adverted to in these pages ; but the opportunity
to speak of Mr. Mann's efforts to bring the youngest class
of boys in the preparatory school to a sense of their duties
toward each other and to themselves should not be lost.
Several very bad children had been sent to his care by
parents who had found themselves baffled by their per-
versity; and one or two of them had introduced specifically, and enforced with much plausibility in the opinion of

---

* Mr. Mann concluded to subscribe five thousand dollars.   Mr. Downer had lost
hope about the success of the institution.

some of their companions, ideas of rebellion against
parents and the constituted authorities, secret associations,
signals for gathering together, places of meeting, &c.
Mr. Mann's suspicions became strongly excited. He lost
no time in investigating the matter. He knew the
influence for evil that one or two talented and unscrupulous boys could exercise, and thought heroic measures
were called for. He·invited the boys to his room in the
college, and also the parents of those who lived in the
town, the professors, and the teachers of the preparatory
school. Quite a large party assembled; and Mr. Mann
thoroughly explained his views of the relations the pupils
of a school should hold to each other and to their teachers.
He found it far easier to make an impression upon the
boys than he had formerly been able to do upon the young
men of the older classes, the better portion of whom had
finally coincided with and acted upon his views; for
the boys had not become so possessed with the current
notion, that it is honorable, under all circumstances, to
stand up for one's companions, right or wrong. He asked
them if they should not think it their duty to tell their
parents if their brothers were indulging in any wrong-
doing which was injurious to themselves or others, when
they knew that they could be kept from evil by timely
warning. Loving childhood answered, "Yes." Could
they not look upon their teachers as if they were parents,
and upon all their companions as brothers? He told them
he took the place of a parent when he undertook the care of
a boy whose parents were absent; and did not their position
as companions impose a kindred duty upon them? Would
it be true friendship to let one of their number perish,
when he might be saved by the influence of those in whose
care he was placed? and was he not in their care as well
as in his? and, if they could not persuade him to desist

from wrong-doing, would it not be right to come to him, or to some other teacher who might persuade him ? Before he demanded a response, he made it perfectly clear to them that he did not approve of tale-bearers; that it was only in the spirit of love that he wished them ever to speak to him of the faults of another; that, if they did it, they must not do it secretly, but openly, towards the faulty companion, who would then know that it was done out of good-will, and not out of ill-will, — out of true friendship, and not out of enmity. He also enforced the duty of answering inquiries truthfully when he or the other teachers felt it to be their duty to investigate cases of wrong-doing; showing them that scholars were bound by responsibilities toward their teachers as truly as teachers were so bound to their scholars, on the ground that all men are bound to help others to do right when they can, and especially when thrown together for purposes of education. If they did not feel willing, or were not strong enough in moral courage, to come unbidden for advice in such cases, they could surely see the obligation to tell the truth when asked. So strongly, so movingly, in behalf of the erring and the weak, did he enunciate to them the Christian duty of saving souls, that every breath was hushed, and many a lip quivered.

He then proposed to take a vote. Many hands went up, but not all. For the moment, at least, the appeal was almost irresistible.

He told them he understood the doubt. Some good boys whom he saw there doubted. He did not condemn them. He knew it might seem ungenerous at the first thought; but he had little doubt they would all say they were willing to be told of. He would take a vote upon that.

Every hand went up but those of the three bad boys, whom he well knew.

After a repetition of some of his former arguments, he proposed a vote upon the previous question again. Every hand went up but one besides the three delinquents'. He invited this one to come and talk with him again privately; telling him he knew him to be a good boy, and he thought he could convince him.

He then addressed the culprits; told them he knew them, knew their habits, knew the evil influences they had tried to exert, which he analyzed and scathed as demoralizing to character, and then forbade them to have any thing to do with the boys who wished to do their duty; forbade them to go to their rooms, or to play with them at recreation-hours, but designated them as " rotten sheep," who must not be allowed to infect the flock. They were only fit for the society of each other.

The faults of these boys had been gross indecency and profanity; falsehood; combinations against college-rules; secret societies for rebellious purposes, sustained by pledges, and penalties for their violation; the introduction of bad books, and even intemperance, young as they were.

Old and young went home with the feeling that a new view of duty had been taken; for it had been long since the public opinion of the college in regard to this matter had been established among older classes, and there had been no occasion for a re-enunciation of the principle, except in some individual cases.

The immediate effect was the breaking-up of all combinations; and the parents who resided in the village kept their children more at home in recreation-hours, not allowing them to mix so freely with the strangers. Renewed vigilance was exercised in regard to the regulations about study-hours, at which times no students were allowed, except by special permission, to go into each other's rooms. The " rotten sheep " kept out of everybody's way

for a time, and were soon withdrawn from the college by
their friends.

One cause of peculiar annoyance to Mr. Mann may
easily be understood to have flowed out of the peculiar
nature of the college, which was more liberal in its views
of female education, even, than others of the same kind.

A class of women was attracted to the institution who
would fain have set at nought all regulations conducive
to propriety of deportment as conceived by Mr. Mann.
They were not vicious, but wanting in what he considered womanliness, so far as to think, for instance, that, if a
young man could be allowed to walk down into the village
alone to do a little necessary shopping in the evening, a
young woman might do the same, although the village
shops were filled with idle and rude men and boys at that
time, and with many who would have been glad to fix a
stigma upon a liberal institution; or that the young ladies
might be allowed to exercise on the gymnastic apparatus
that stood near the gentlemen's hall. One of these young
women tried the experiment of taking her books to a gentleman's apartment one evening " to study with him," by
which she nearly lost her chance of further residence on
the premises; but she was saved by Mr. Mann's conviction
that it was in support of a theory rather than with any
evil intent. In that case, the other party or parties (for
there were two), were gentlemen not only in name, but
in reality: they understood the young lady's fanaticism,
but were candid enough to express their dissent from her
views in a friendly spirit, and prevent the recurrence of
the act.

Mr. Mann made the way of such transgressors hard,
and was always glad when they turned their backs upon
the college with disgust, as was sometimes the case.
Outside, " women's-rights " women of an ultra stamp

increased the difficulties for him by coming upon the premises, and promulgating their heresies against good manners.

On one occasion, when the faculty had decided that it was best that the young ladies and gentlemen of the literary societies should no longer hold their ordinary meetings together, but should meet separately, except on their public days, some women of this class felt that their rights were denied them, — "rights" being sometimes interpreted to mean, *just what I choose to do.* To avenge their wrongs, they induced the whole society to appear dressed in deep mourning on a very public occasion, when their united literary societies were addressed by a stranger. The faculty took no notice of it except by a good-natured smile, thinking the most salutary punishment would be to leave them to the public ridicule, without giving them the solace of being martyrs. The most prominent offender soon concluded to leave an institution where she was subject to such *oppression.*

As an attempt has been made to give a true history of Antioch College, it is fitting to give what few exceptions occurred to mar the beauty of its ordinary good behavior. It is remarkable how few of these there were. The only one that gave Mr. Mann any real and permanent pain took place towards the close of his administration of it. On the day of commencement in 1858, a very impertinent and even scurrilous paper was scattered broadcast in every one's path. It lampooned some of the faculty, though not Mr. Mann himself. It had been instigated and carried through by a young man who had been under severe censure; and a few others, who had also offended and been reprimanded, aided him. After much falsification, in the vain hope of defending or screening themselves, they were expelled. They refused to leave the

hall.   After being several times told to go, the superintendent, then a very worthy man, proceeded to remove
their furniture.   Mr. Mann happened to be in the college
premises, and heard there were threats of violence toward
this official.   He and another member of the faculty
walked over into the gentlemen's hall, and stood quietly by
while the furniture was carried out.   In the evening, at
the close of a lecture, Mr. Mann was publicly arrested in
his chapel by order of those young men, and held to bail
for violating the rights of domicile !   He succeeded in
putting off the trial for a few weeks, thinking it best to
make it an occasion for establishing the principle, that the
faculty of a college had a right to enforce the by-law, that
no persons not connected with the college should remain
on the premises, or, in other words, should have the control
of the college-buildings.   The Hon. Thomas Corwin was
retained for counsel, and did the work ably and wittily.
But the circumstance was a very painful one to Mr. Mann,
especially as it occurred at the same period as the libellous
attack of the discomfited ex-professor.   Undoubtedly, the
disrespectful and impertinent act was aided and abetted
— it certainly was sympathized with — by the aggrieved
literary ladies and their champions.   At such times all
malecontents take courage, and strengthen each other.
Mr. Mann could no longer say that there were none of
these in his little kingdom; and this grieved his fatherly
heart.

YELLOW SPRINGS, Aug. 18, 1858.

E. CONANT, ESQ.

MY DEAR SIR, — I acknowledge the receipt of your favor of the
15th inst., enclosing a bank draft for one hundred dollars on behalf of all those connected with the administration of the college.   I
assure you, it will be gratefully received.

You speak of a draft for two hundred and fifty dollars, sent to
me (as you say) about two years ago.   That was not sent to me;

but I find it entered on the college-books on the 8th of September, 1856.

In all institutions like ours, there must be two departments, — the educational and the financial. In ours, the educational has prospered beyond any thing that I have ever known or heard of. The financial has been as disastrous as it could be. I have had as much heretofore as I could possibly do in attending to the educational: I have now taken hold of the other. If its affairs are not greatly improved, and that, too, without much delay, I shall leave both.

The college was bankrupt on the day it opened, — miserably bankrupt: but its moneyed accounts had been kept in such a manner, that the fact of its utter bankruptcy was not then known, and could not be to any but its agent; and, if he knew it, he kept it to himself.

The scholarship system as here undertaken was a ruinous and suicidal system. It undertook to give a college education perpetually, without interruption, for six dollars a year! The children learning A B C in this town have paid that sum *per quarter* since I have been here.

The only scholarship system that possibly can be successful would be one where the capital or price of the scholarship is five or six hundred dollars, or where the scholarships are so numerous that not more than one of them in four or five is represented by students at the same time. Then the ones unused would help to support the ones used.

Now, the college being bankrupt, secretly so, when it was opened, and the scholarships being too few in number to bear one-half its expenses, the trustees administered it for four years, hoping that donations, &c., would rescue it, but running in debt all the time. At last, all plans for its relief having failed, and the public having lost all confidence in its pecuniary management, so that all donations ceased, there seemed to be no alternative but to assign the property for the payment of its debts.

This, of course, was a failure. It was just like the failure of any railroad or bank or manufacturing company. The stockholders lost their shares: that was the whole of it. But you know

34

that honest creditors must have their pay, though stockholders do lose all their stock. This is all that has been done. I, being one of the creditors, am a great loser by the failure. While it has cost me every cent of my salary to live here in the expensive though economical way in which I live, yet I have received but about half of that salary. Must I refund what I have received, that stockholders may get back what they have paid on their scholarship-notes? Will other *bonâ-fide* creditors do this? It is a bad speculation, as everybody knows; but, in such a case, must the honest creditors of a company lose, or the shareholders in the company? If the company had been successful, it would have been their gain. If unsuccessful, must it not be their loss? That there has been bad management, there is no doubt; but the radical defect was the viciousness of the plan of scholarships, and the irresponsibility of the men or man originally employed to carry on the work.

But, my dear sir, we have hopes of a change. A company is now being formed, consisting of the friends of the college, and the " Christian "* friends of those under whose auspices it was erected, to purchase it, and put it upon a new financial basis. The shares will be five hundred dollars each. Such is the plan. We should be very glad if you would become the proprietor of a share. The new company will have no *legal* connection with the old. They expect to pay for the property as much as anybody will pay. They expect to administer it under the same moral and religious auspices. They mean to take precautions that it shall be better managed in its pecuniary affairs than the old one has been. A gift of five hundred dollars will entitle you and your successor indefinitely to take part in its management.

Excuse this long letter. I feel an interest that you should see these pecuniary relations as they really are, and have no unkind feelings towards those who do not deserve them.

I am, dear sir, yours very truly,

HORACE MANN.

The following letters to the Rev. O. J. Wait, a clergyman of the " Christian denomination," so called, are in

---

* This term is here used denominationally.

reply to one from that gentleman informing Mr. Mann that the time had come when the support of Antioch College by that denomination depended upon his personal views upon the subject of religious conversion and regeneration. He therefore begged him to make a statement of those views, to be presented at a " Christian " convention soon to be assembled. It may well be asked, How could Mr. Mann retain any further connection with so bigoted and inquisitorial a people ? The answer is, That he considered himself placed there to repel precisely such assaults upon freedom of thought. He knew, that, if he left the place, it would fall into the hands of those who had no conception of what unsectarian education meant; and he was too deeply interested in its furtherance to give it up lightly. He had had abundant proof that the young people who were enjoying the advantages his persistent stay afforded them appreciated them, and would make noble use of them. He well knew, too, that no pains had been spared by malignant enemies to throw this firebrand in his path. It is heart-sickening to read the evidence of this in the voluminous correspondence of college-agents, friends, enemies, and victims; but it is the history of bigotry the world over.

Mr. Mann was one of those men, who, like the Christianized Brahmin, Rammohun Roy, believed in Christianity on other grounds than through the miracles recorded of it. Rammohun Roy translated only the precepts of Jesus for the conversion of his countrymen : for, as he said, the Christian miracles did not compare in marvellousness with those recorded of Pagan deities ; and the Godhead of three persons in one, preached by the Christian missionaries, was, in principle, the same with the thirty thousand in one of the Indian religion. He wished his students to look at the precepts of him who first promulgated the Fatherhood of God as the principle of ethics; for it was this truth which he believed distinguished Christianity from all other systems, — a truth conveyed in no form of metaphysical abstraction, but in the winged words of an unspoiled human being, whose first recorded utterance is, "Wist ye not that I must be about my Father's business?"

Mr. Mann labored ever to make this thought the inspiration of all who came under his religious instruction; for to act upon it he felt sure would criticise in the legitimate manner all the creeds among which they were educated, and preclude narrowness of mind, and bigotry of feeling, while it would engage all the energies of the heart and imagination. For what is "the Father's business"? The universe answers with all the sciences, and history with all the arts, rising through the mechanical and æsthetic and social to the art of arts, which has for its end the salvation of man, not only as an individual, but as nations and as a race. With such an ideal as this as manifest destiny, he knew that the interest of every sect would fade into nonentity.

Religion in its widest and most all-embracing sense was the native atmosphere of Mr. Mann's soul. Sometimes he had worshipped darkly, and then the universe was clouded. It often takes the whole of life to solve the problem of why we suffer. Gradually, as it solves itself to an eye open to the subject, the desire becomes more and more intense to help others in their analysis. "Why I suffer" at last grows clearer; and those minds that reach the solution gain the peace that it brings: but most souls only approach this, so easily is the vision dimmed and the mind swayed by the circumstances immediately surrounding us. The "mists of the affections," though they may be compared to the beneficent dews that sustain the otherwise parched and withered earth, often make all things loom to the intellectual sight; and we must wait till they are dispelled by the sun of truth before we can reason clearly. Gradually man learns to wait for this illuminating process, distrusting his own heart meanwhile. The universe became all alight to Mr. Mann at last. There remained no dark, inexplicable evils. His subtle causality penetrated one after another, and a flame of enthusiasm was kindled within him to point out the light; and the might of self-sacrifice which is born out of love carried him through labors that would otherwise have been intolerable.

YELLOW SPRINGS, Sept. 22, 1858.

REV. O. J. WAIT.

MY DEAR SIR, — Though I owe you many apologies for so late a reply, yet I am rich in all the best materials for an apology.

For the last fortnight, my engagements have not left me an hour of leisure. The commencement of a term is always a very busy time with me; but this year, owing to the changes which have been made, and to the fact that we have an entering-class larger than ever before, I have had more than enough to fill hands and head.

First, I thank you for the kind and friendly spirit in which your letter appears to have been written.

Your first two questions are substantially this: whether there has been any opposition, open or secret, direct or indirect, on the part of myself, or to my knowledge on the part of any member of the faculty, against Rev. Mr. Doherty or Prof. Allen, on account of their supposed religious views; and whether they have not, for some such reason, been left out of the present faculty.

I answer this inquiry in every form in which it can be put, in whole or in part, generically and specifically, with the most decided negative. I deny the imputation for myself, and, so far as I have ever known, for every other member of the faculty; and, if I knew of any other more positive or comprehensive way of denying it, I would use that way. There are many here who would not regret to be constrained to give the true reasons why those professors left.

Your next question relates to Prof. H—— and his leave of absence.

To this I answer, That though I advised Prof. H—— to go abroad, and study for the duties of his chair, yet that I did it with none but the most friendly feelings and motives; and that the idea of his religious views never came into my mind in that connection. The personal relations between Prof. H—— and myself, up to the time when he requested me to present his application for leave of absence, were of the most intimate and agreeable kind. There had never been any coldness between us for any reason. We conversed frequently together on religious subjects, and there was much sympathy between us. If inquired of, he will ratify this statement, I doubt not.

Your next four questions so run into each other, that I can express my opinion on the whole subject more briefly, more intelligibly, and, I trust, more satisfactorily to you, by a general statement, than by a specific *yes* or *no*. This I do as follows : —

I repudiate the Trinitarian's view of the Holy Spirit. I do not believe it to be a third person in, or a third part of, the Deity.

In my opinion, God's Holy Spirit is his will, his influence, an emanation proceeding from him, and pervading every part of the moral universe, in the same manner as his omnipotent power pervades all space.

I do not believe that God's Spirit acts spasmodically or convulsively, but that it is as strong, steady, and immutable as its Author, universally surrounding every moral agent, just as the atmosphere surrounds our bodies, yet not in such a way as to destroy our free agency.

We are born with natural appetites and passions which have no relation whatever to God's holy law, to religion, or to duty. This is the " carnal heart " of the Scriptures. This is the " carnal mind," which, as St. Paul says to the Romans, and through them to all mankind, is "enmity against God ; for it is not subject to his law, neither can be."

Afterwards our rational and moral powers are developed : " That is not first which is spiritual, but that which is natural, and afterwards that which is spiritual." By these rational and moral powers, and such other instrumentalities as God gives us, — parents, schools, the gospel and its ministrations, &c., — we learn something of what God is; and, just in proportion to our correct ideas of his nature and attributes, we see and feel that we ought to love and obey him. But this " carnal mind " does not love and obey him. Now comes the struggle. On the one side are all our animal and worldly desires, propensities, lusts; on the other, our reason and conscience, with all the persuasions, appeals, urgencies, of God's character, influence, or spirit, forever surrounding our souls, and acting upon them, as the sea surrounds the creatures that inhabit it. If the former prevails, then, at the end of every struggle, we become more hardened in sin, more callous to the entreaties of the gospel, more alienated from God, and defiant of his power and judgment. But if the latter prevails, then the will or determining power of the mind ranges itself on the side of Jehovah, resolves to seek for and to obey his will, and begins in heavenly earnestness to subdue and control all the natural impulses which lead to disobedience and sin; and not only so, but from day to day to conform ourselves, that is, our thoughts, wishes, lives, more and more " unto the measure of the stature of the fulness of Christ."

The manner in which I have often expressed myself is this : We are to imitate the painter or sculptor, who seeks first to become acquainted with the most perfect model; and he then strives to copy or transfer that model, feature by feature, lineament by lineament, expression by expression, to his canvas or his marble. So we, having decided, under the influences above mentioned, that it is our duty, and our highest interest, and our only freedom, to love God with all our heart and understanding and mind and strength, and our neighbor as ourself, should strive to grow up into the likeness of God and Christ, eradicating something here, supplying something there ; moulding, shaping, conforming, until it may be said without blasphemy, that man is in the image of God.

The occasions of this first resolve or determination to live a righteous life, and to dedicate ourselves to the service of our Maker, may be as various as all the events of our outward life, or as all the conscious mental experiences of our inward souls. It may be a funeral or a bridal, a birth or a death-bed, a prayer or a sermon, a lonely walk in the woods or a crowded religious meeting. It may be a remembered word uttered by a mother to our childhood; or it may be a blasphemous oath uttered by ourselves, which God hurls back to rive the heart that conceived it, as the lightning rives the oak. God is not confined to one method: yet I believe some methods are far more likely to be successful than others; and we must learn which are the best methods of doing these holy things, just as men have learned the best methods of doing natural things.

Sometimes the change is sudden, as in the case of St. Paul. Sometimes the change is so gradual, that the subject of it can himself fix no point of time when he said (to quote your expression), "Self is wrong, and Christ is right," as was the case with Dr. Chalmers and many other pious men.

You ask me, whether, "if my lectures should move the whole school to devotion and tender solicitude for their salvation, I would oppose such results." Well do you say that you "do not hesitate at my answer." Had you not added this, I should have exclaimed, "May God pardon you for such a question!" The most rapturous moments of my life are when young people come to me in private, or write to me, saying that their whole view and plan of life, their ideas of duty and of destiny, have been changed by what they have heard from me. Thanks be to God, the occasions of this kind are not few, but many; and there is scarcely a week in my life, when, by letter or otherwise, I have not some such assurance.

I have now, my dear sir, attempted to answer, not merely your inquiries, but your inquiring mind. I believe I have covered every point, and made a wide margin besides. I may not have used your technical expressions; but my expressions grow out of my system of belief, and belong to it. I have a great desire that what I have said may be satisfactory to you, because I believe you to be a candid, honest, and sincere man.

But, having now endeavored to reply to your inquiries because I respect your motives, I have something to add on my own account.

I think no man, or body of men, has a right to propound such questions to me. My life belongs to the world; and I hold myself at all times answerable to it for my conduct: but my opinions are between God and myself, and, except so far as I wish to avow them, are sacred and inviolable. The old inquisitorial torture does not differ one whit *in kind*, but only *in degree*, if a man can be held to answer anybody's questions in religious matters, under penalty of loss, whether of money or character or position.

While, therefore, I am rather glad of an opportunity to say thus much to you, and have no objection against this letter's being seen and scanned by proper persons, — that is, persons actuated by a right motive, — yet can you suppose for a moment, my dear sir, that I am going to place myself on a public stand for such men as Mr. M—— or Mr. L—— or Parson L—— to catechise, or those who may keep out of sight, but instigate them to inquiry? I am not for sale. I am not in quest of any political office. I have a duty to perform in maintaining the inviolability of religious opinions; and, if I yield to the "question," I set the example by which others may be coerced into yielding. I occupy my present position at great personal and social sacrifice. Released from this, I can earn, during three months in the year, at least a thousand dollars more than my salary, and have the other nine months to myself. I am here an exile from all the personal friends of my youth and life, and deprived of almost all those abundant means of literary and scientific delight, which, until four years ago, constituted so important a part of my legitimate and laudable enjoyments. I had learned from books, and was told when I was invited to come here, that the "Christian connection" looked at *life*, and not at *creeds*. Confiding in the truth of this statement, I was requested to write some account of the plan and scope of this institution, to be published in its first prospectus. I did so. I sent copies of it in manuscript to Mr. Merrifield, to Mr. Holmes, to Mr. Edmunds of Boston, and to Mr. How of New Bedford, &c. It received their unanimous approval. It was afterwards published, — a large edition, — and was sent throughout the whole "connection." If any exception was taken to it by any one, I never heard of it. Herewith I send you a copy of it, that you may see in its closing pages what was said in regard to sectarian teaching and to dogmatic theology. But, when I came, I soon found that I was never among a more sectarian people in my life than no inconsiderable number of these were. The whole interest which some of them manifested in the school was, whether I would say their religious *hic, hæc, hoc,* after them. One man wanted to know if *all* the teachers belonged to the Christian denomination; and on being answered, " More than half, but not all," he wished to know if his child could not be taught by those only who did belong to it.

Mr. Merrifield gave me the fullest assurance that the school was not to be a sectarian school; yet, after I came here, I found he had been at work, for months before those assurances were given me, to ingraft a biblical school — that is, a theological school — on it at *this place.* In February, 1854, Dr. Bellows came out here, and met the then Board of Trustees; and the whole matter was opened and discussed. He promised the contributions of the Unitarians if the sectarian character or idea of the theological school should be abandoned; and it was explicitly renounced by a vote. In consequence of this, the New-York Unitarians gave twenty-five thousand dollars; which the college has accepted and used, and now demands that it shall be *denominational,* — not merely denominational, but metaphysically and transcendentally so. You heard the question put by Mr. L—— to Mr. J——, when, at the conference, the latter was testifying from personal knowledge and observation to the religious character and highly favorable religious influence of the school: " Whether the religious teachings at the college did not tend to make the students live pure and virtuous lives, and do good to their fellow-men, rather than to love God through faith in Jesus Christ, as applied by the Holy Spirit?" Can any thing in " Punch" beat this?

Yet, on a moment's reflection, you cannot but see that you are asking me to appear in a newspaper conducted by one of this combination of men, and there surrender myself to the confessional.

You heard some of their alleged causes of offence at the late conference. One was that they had not been invited to the commencement-dinner given in part by the graduating class. Another was that I did not go to Mr. L——, and reconcile him to our course at the college (against which he took exceptions), instead of waiting to let him come to me.

But I have said enough to show you, I trust, that it would be unworthy of me to submit myself to the public in the manner proposed, and that the time necessarily occupied in answering questions respecting the agency of the Holy Spirit in the conversion of men, respecting the atonement, the resurrection, &c., is time that I ought rather to devote to the manners, morals, and literary progress of our students. This is not a theological school; and therefore theological questions do not come within the scope of its administration. I trust, that, on reflection, you will give an affirmative answer to this view of the subject.

One word on another subject, and I will relieve your patience.

It is said we have no revivals here. The reason of this is the serious and thoughtful character of our students on religious subjects. Take a set of drinking, gambling, swearing, blaspheming, and godless students, come upon them suddenly, make them see their sinful condition, and they will be frightened into as vehement a demonstration of their alarms as they had before given of their profligacies and revellings. But this effect can never be produced upon a company of thoughtful, serious young people, whose minds have been systematically turned in the direction of their religious condition, and to whom the ideas of their duty and their destiny are familiar, and who have led an exemplary life. This is precisely the case with our students. They do not receive religious excitements like savages, but like men of intelligence and morals, and generally pure and correct purposes. This is the true explanation of the complaint made against us.

I mourn that this most unjust and unwise movement will tend to alienate more or less of the "Christians" from us, and thus deprive them of advantages they so much need. I pray God that the folly of men may no longer stand in the way of the improvement of their children.

With great personal regard, yours very truly,

HORACE MANN.

YELLOW SPRINGS, Sept. 28.

REV. O. J. WAIT.

MY DEAR SIR, — I thank you for your kind, frank, whole-souled letter. Having had the pleasure of only a very slight personal acquaintance with you, I had no indications whatever of the character of your religious views on the points suggested. I had made up my mind, therefore, to the probability that I was, by my own act and my own statement, building up a wall of partition between us, which, so far as the interests of the college are concerned, might array you against its present administration forever.

But I had no alternative. You seemed entitled to know the truth; and I took the risk of giving it. Truth never yet failed to stand by my conscience; and I hope I never shall fail to stand by that.

I have read your letter again and again, and thought it all through many times again. I have the greatest desire to comply with your wishes. They prevail upon me so strongly, that I have several times been brought up at least *within sight of consent*. But the combined operation of all my faculties, the conclusions of my judgment, interpose a negative. I find the following points coming out in large stature and with a clear outline in my mind: —

1. The grounds suggested by you, and urged by them, are not the true grounds of opposition. I should, therefore, be just as far from satisfying their minds afterwards as before. If not invited to the next college-dinner, or if Mr. L——'s skin should be ruffled, and I should not leave my three hundred pupils to go and smooth it, I should have my peace all to make over again. Mr. S——'s first, and so far only, cause of complaint against me (as he afterwards told me himself in an interview which I sought) was, that, when I was to perform the chapel-services on Sunday, I did not go down and give him a special invitation to attend. You speak well about a class of men not competent to have the direction of a potato-patch. My dear sir, there are souls so small, that, if a million of them were sprinkled on the polished surface of a diamond, they would not make it dusty. As this imputation is not the real point of the objection, I shall not answer the objection by answering this.

2. If I answer this, I shall have a battery of others to answer. I shall have set the example of answering, and shall, with some plausibility, be held to follow it. Should I indorse in any satisfactory manner up to any point, and stop there, *there* would be the beginning of my heresy. I cannot well carry on a theological discussion or controversy and Antioch College at the same time.

3. Was there ever such a thing required or expected of any other president of a college? What would be thought of such a course at Amherst, at Williams, at Harvard, or at Yale? The very publication of the thing would inflame and arouse the jealousy of hundreds, which jealousy is now asleep.

4. I feel, and cannot get the feeling out of my bones, as though I should always be exposed to the unworthy imputation of having answered in order to retain my place. Though nothing would be farther .from the truth, yet how would that truth be made to appear?*

To those who may have read in Weiss's Life of Theodore Parker the letter to Dr. Howe written from Europe on occasion of Mr. Mann's death, — a letter which betrays all those traits of mind and heart which Mr. Parker's friends least like to remember, — the foregoing letters to Mr. Wait will be very satisfactory. They are a complete answer to the charge of having concealed from the leading members of the " Christian " sect his differences of opinion from them; on which assumption, Mr. Parker proceeds to draw the inference that " Mr. Mann did not know that a straight line is the shortest way between two points in morals as well as in mathematics." They are but a sample of his plain dealing with them all on proper occasions. To that extraordinary letter, so self-contradictory, as well as so inconsistent with the tone of all Mr. Parker's letters to Mr. Mann, many of which have been inserted in these pages, this whole volume is an answer more forcible than any special pleading could be. The last letter Mr. Mann wrote to Mr. Parker is the following introduction of a " Christian " minister: —

MARCH 1, 1858.

To Rev. Theodore Parker.

My dear Mr. Parker, — I take great pleasure in introducing to your acquaintance one of my dearest friends, and one of the best and truest of men, — the Rev. Austin Craig.

* The manuscript letter is incomplete.

You and he may not agree in *exegesis ;* but I know no two men, who in all matters of duty to man, or love to God, would be more in unison.

I commend him to your fellowship ; and remain, as ever,

Most truly yours,

HORACE MANN.

Its generous confidence and comprehensive charity are in very striking contrast with the letter of Mr. Parker. But it is perhaps fair to remember, that, when Mr. Parker wrote his chaotic letter, he was so enfeebled in mind by illness, as to be scarcely responsible.

At this juncture, Mr. Mann was urged to go to New York to attend a meeting held in the interest of the college.

NEW YORK, Oct. 7, 1858.

The Christian Convention has been in session to-day, and I have been present almost all day. This afternoon, Antioch has been up for discussion, and we have had a good time. . . . Mr. Fay and Mr. Haley made speeches ; and certainly they were received with a degree of favor for which I was not at all prepared. The discussion is not closed yet, and in the morning we mean to have Dr. Bellows himself present and *speechifying.* Mr. S——, who used to be at Yellow Springs, was present, and as full of evil as the first original serpent ; but as yet he has made no impression.

Oct. 10. . . . We had a capital convention so far as results were concerned. I think all opposition was quenched. Mr. Holmes came out very fervently for Antioch. Mr. S—— did his prettiest against us, but dared to do nothing openly, and was balked at every point. He found no party to co-operate with him.

ANTIOCH COLLEGE, YELLOW SPRINGS, Oct. 20, 1858.

REV. DANIEL AUSTIN.

DEAR SIR, — I have the pleasure of acknowledging the receipt, this day, of a check on the Rockingham Bank, Portsmouth, N.H., for fifty dollars ; for which please accept my thanks.

I wish I could respond as you desire to your friendly suggestion about my health. I have been and am still doing the work of two men, — a necessity occasioned by the lowness of our finances. All my vital organs are in good working order, except my brain. That is overtasked, and threatens to give way before its time ; and I may yet be an example of a violation of the laws I have so much sought to expound. Do you ask me how I can reconcile this to my sense of duty ? I answer, Only because I am engaged in a work worth more than a thousand such men as I am ; and I must not lose that to save myself.

Yours in great haste,

HORACE MANN.

YELLOW SPRINGS, Nov. 8, 1858.

MY DEAR DOWNER, — I have just received yours. . . .

I am rejoiced to hear that you have at last found a " pocket." Perhaps I should prefer that you should open this rich vein rather than any other man *after myself*. I do not think it is " foolish," as you say, to make money : the folly generally consists in spending it.

I am very sorry to hear of Parker's illness. If his great head breaks down, why should not my small one ? . . .

Don't be alarmed if you hear great reverberations about us. We expelled four of the boys engaged in the paper, and suspended two. . . . I presume it will make a great show in Orthodox papers. My brain is, I fear, worse than yours. The last year's work, with last vacation's work on the back of it, was too much ; and I am suffering severely.

Yours most truly,

H. M.

From this time, the tired brain knew no more respite. Labors accumulated, because a failure of the funds that had been privately subscribed to pay the faculty and teachers obliged some of them to leave their duties for employment that would pay their current expenses ; and this threw more work upon those who were left. Again Mr. Mann implored Mr. Craig to stand by the institution, and sustain it with his valuable influence as long as it floated upon the waves of uncertainty, which were rendered more boisterous than ever by contending elements. But Mr. Craig had lost hope, and would fain have plucked his friend away. He felt that he was working at too great a disadvantage, and that either the community around him must be more sympathetic with the movement, or the college must be sustained by ample funds, to enable it to act independently of the evil influences that abounded. He heartily approved of Mr. Mann's measures, but did not like to see him sacrificing himself so utterly. It seemed, indeed, like " casting pearls before swine " to throw so rich an experience into the midst of a people who could not see the difference between a great and a small man, and who did not know a good man when they saw one. But Mr. Mann resisted every entreaty to turn his back upon an enterprise from which he had hoped such great results. If he had not been influenced by his own purity of motive in this persistence to believe that the motives of others who wished to cling to him and to the institution were as pure as his own, he might have seen clearly that the hour had come when renunciation of the long-cherished hope would be the path of wisdom for himself, unless he felt ready to fall a sacrifice to it. He was reminded of the warning given him by his friend Mr. Combe, who begged him on a former occasion to save himself for a watchman in the march of improvement, that the fruits of his experience might not be lost prematurely ; but, although he was not without fears that his strength was failing, he fondly hoped success would restore his energies. He had of late been obliged to withdraw, more than he had previously allowed himself to do, even for purposes of rest, from social intercourse with his coadjutors, although he was aware that outside influences were plied to estrange them. Even his children had to be guarded from disturbing his short intervals of rest; for they still retained their love for their wonted place upon his knee, and he still extended his arms for them when they appeared ready to pour out their confidences and their questions. He would say, " Let me have the house quiet; " " I must go and hide in the glen, for I am not able to see company " (and at last he could not bear even the children's company in such walks); " Soothe me, for I am too tired; " and he would fall asleep the moment the pressure of engagements was lifted. He shrank from contact with persons who pained him, whether by their own depression or apprehension, or by their association with painful circumstances. He found repose in not seeing faces. Yet he did not yield: he would breast the possible wave that was to break over the institution, and was always ready to spring to the rescue when any call to act in its interests came to him.

The magnetism of his own zeal and devotion to a cause he thought to be so important had stimulated his Eastern friends, who rallied nobly, headed by the venerable Josiah Quincy; and they nobly redeemed their pledges when the hour came; but the West had failed. One last effort was made by his family to induce him to resign, but in vain. He felt that the experience he had gained in these laborious years, added to earlier experience so dearly bought, would enable him to effect what no other man, even of superior ability, could do so well in that place and under the circumstances. Some friends, who knew what would be the consequences if he must still bear the burden of the pecuniary difficulties of other years of debt and anxiety, were firm in the conviction that the college should not be purchased by those who remained true to it under such disadvantageous prospects; there being not a dollar in the exchequer to carry it on after purchase. In consequence of their remonstrances, temporary provision for its support was made; but it was not money deposited in the bank, and no one who subscribed to it was responsible to any tribunal but his own conscience. The promissory notes, however, some of which proved as good as bullion, were put into Mr. Mann's hands, to be paid on his demand. The Rev. Mr. Fay, for one, hazarded all he was worth upon the hope of future success. The college was bought in June, at the appraisement price; there being not one bid from any other quarter. Circumstances were now so far changed, that an independent body of men, a close corporation, owned the premises. This was so much more respectable a basis than the former one, which had not a single feature to recommend it, that, to Mr. Mann's mind, all other obstacles promised to vanish. It was, in reality, to be a new birth. The sectarian feature of the charter, that two-thirds of the trustees and two-thirds of the college faculty should be of the " Christian " denomination, still remained in it, it is true; but the present owners were disposed to be liberal, and he hoped further consideration might lead to a change in this illiberal charter.

The discussion, the purchase, and all the collateral exciting circumstances, were followed in a few days by the commencement exercises of the graduating class of that year. It has already been said that the three months previous to this meeting of the trustees, which caused such an unwonted excitement of feeling, had been a period of extraordinary toil as well as anxiety. Two of the professors were still absent; one ill, the other preaching for his daily bread. The whole care of the graduating class was left upon Mr. Mann's hands. They wanted subjects for their graduating exercises; they wanted criticisms upon their productions.

No members were chosen from the class, as in other colleges, to receive special honors; but as many speakers as the time would allow took part, and all who chose to prepare had equal claims to attention. Many of them were very far from home, or from any other literary aid; and Mr. Mann attended to them all. Unfortunately, all his children were ill, one at a great distance, the other two at home, requiring constant care and attendance: therefore he was not only left unwatched, when, as it afterward proved, he most needed watching, but he was anxiously watching others.

On the appointed day of public exercises and jubilation, he sat down early in the morning to finish the " Baccalaureate," which he had hastily prepared for the occasion, and which he carried to chapel, without having had time to read it over himself.

He could not preside over such a scene unmoved. He knew all that had been hoped, dreaded, and suffered by many. He would fain have been silent with his joy, and have found his rest in it. But no: he must be the most active participant in the common rejoicing, after so many weary days and restless nights. He was described to the invalids at home as looking " too happy, but very tired." The festivities of the day, commencing at seven in the morning, lasted twelve hours; and the public adjourned in heavy numbers from the college-dinner to his house, where a crowded *levée* was held till late at night.

The next day he was nearly speechless with fatigue; but instead of being laid quietly away in a darkened chamber, and all sounds shut out, an important committee meeting was pending, which lasted substantially two days longer. It was feared that paralysis would follow such a strain as this had been: but, instead of that, a burning fever raged in his veins, which there seemed not then coolness enough on earth to assuage; and sleep, his only restorative, was no more for him in this world. He struggled with it several weeks, fighting it at every step, instead of yielding to it, — not consciously perhaps, not deliberately, but feverishly. The weather was intensely hot. The very soil was turned into burning sand. Only hot winds blew. He roamed about the house, extending himself, now on the sofa, now on the floors, praying for rain, mourning over the time he was losing for preparation of duties to come, but conscious only of suffering, not of near death. How could such vitality cease? Ill as he was, he did not resign himself a prisoner to his apartment but three days; and, when he could no longer rise, he saw grouped before him the things to be done. His last expression of interest in the world, outside his immediate sphere, was his desire to hear what Kossuth was doing in Italy. When he heard the treaty of Villa-Franca read, he made a sign that he could hear no more. It excited him too deeply, sending the blood surging to his brain. It was well; for the next sentence would have produced a revulsion of feeling more dangerous to bear than any joy could be; and he was never told the sad reverse.

Nature began to give way more perceptibly. At last he begged for profound silence, "except George's humming: do not stop that." He loved music from the human voice; it soothed and diverted his busy and fevered thoughts from affairs. But he could not listen to words even when sung: they wakened too many associations. One day, while thus soothed, he heard drops fall thick and fast upon the tin roof of the piazza. It was a month since a rain-drop had fallen. He said, " Stop a moment, and let me listen to that music!" — "It is heavenly music," one replied. " Yes!" he said very emphatically; and after a long pause, during which his countenance beamed with a delighted smile, as he listened to a copious shower, he whispered, " I am making agricultural calculations: I cannot help it." The rain did not last long, and then he wanted the earthly strain again.

For many days, no food passed his lips but a little strained gooseberry-juice. He could not swallow a drop of water without pain: but relays of devoted students brought him fresh draughts every hour from the only cool well in the neighborhood; and the only physical pleasure left to him was rinsing his mouth with it, and letting it " percolate over his lips." It seemed strange that no special revelation occurred to show what would quench such internal fires as consumed him. He had no confidence in any medical treatment that was at hand, and his brain was morbidly active upon the subject; but when told that he must resign all care, even of himself, he tried to obey. At last a flash of lightning pain passed over him, which, he was sure, had disorganized his very substance. It was too true. But, after the rest of his frame could suffer no more, the brain continued preternaturally active for two days; and all his former life passed in review before him, — its joys, its sorrows, and its trials.

Loving and devoted students had watched over him and his sick children all the nights of many weeks. Where so many served lovingly, no one can be mentioned with prominence, without doing injustice to others. But the Rev. Mr. Fay, upon whom the coming calamity was already doing fearful work, allowed himself neither sleep nor respite; forgetting that he, too, was mortal. To no other individual out of his own family did the death of Mr. Mann so alter the world. Indeed, such was the effect of his inconsolable grief and anxious watching, that his own health, both of body and mind, was long after hanging upon a thread; and even now he shrinks from a review of those painful hours of alternate hope and dread. If the imparting of his own vitality would have availed to snatch his friend from his doom, he could not have given it more freely; but not even his assiduous magnetism could meet the case. All arts of man seemed unavailing.

Dr. Pulte arrived the evening before the last day. He gave but faint hope. Mr. Mann had not expected him; and, when he went to his bedside, he looked at him penetratingly, and begged him to let him feel his head, which he playfully examined with his hands, in his own sprightly way pronouncing it good and able, and then resigned himself to the examination. Dr. Pulte did not express his fears to him, but was obliged to return immediately to Cincinnati, after giving directions for a last attempt to save him.

The next morning, after a restless and troubled night, he begged for quiet in earnest but gentle words.

" Let the college gate be fastened open, that I may not hear it swing; let there be no step, no rustling dress, no face, but your own; communicate with others, not by words, but by slips of paper. Let me rest."

All was hushed for a little while. But he could not sleep. Could such a man be allowed to die unawares? Pain was soothed: he was evidently unconscious that his hours were numbered.

When he was told, he opened his eyes quickly; but his countenance only changed to an illuminated expression, that made it difficult not to rejoice with him that he was soon to tread the glorious path which so often kindled his imagination, instead of the thorny one of this world.

"Ask Dr. C. how long," he said.

"Three hours at most," was the answer.

"I do not feel it to be so," he replied; "but, if it is so, I have something to say. Send for B——" (a student who had given much anxiety). The head which had long been covered with the damps of death became hot as a cannon-ball as he roused himself. After speaking a few tender words to his family, he turned to the young man as he entered the room, followed by others who had heard the sad rumor, till the apartment was filled with people, some of whom, in the fashion of that country, were strangers. He spoke earnestly to his young friend, and called one after another of his students and his friends to him, and for two hours poured forth his great heart and soul in inspired words, with a depth of voice, and vigor of muscle, wonderful to behold in one lately so prostrate. It was as if he drew strength from the fountain of future life into which he was about to plunge. He abode ever in the palace of Truth; and from its portals he now said to each one an appropriate word, tenderly but sincerely, and so discriminatingly, that one trembled to listen. The hours can never be forgotten, either by those who were warned not to abuse, but only righteously to use, the exceeding riches of God's goodness, or by those over whom he poured his unbounded love and blessing.

Many saw duty in a new light as he again and again uttered the words, "Man, duty, God!" and prefigured by his appeals to them what they might do with such powers as he described them to possess. But no repetition of his words can convey the fervor of his spirit, the tenderness of his love, as expressed to all around him.

At last he said to Mr. Fay, "I should like to have Mr.

Fay make a short prayer, low, peaceful, grateful!" after which he again addressed those who stood round him, and sent affectionate messages to the absent, — to his son, to his sister, to Mr. Craig, and to other old friends. Prominent among those he remembered was Prof. Cary.*

"Dear Cary! — solid, steadfast, well-balanced, always wise, always right, always firm, — tell him how much I loved him!" And again he murmured, "Good, reliable, judicious, firm, gentle, beautiful Mr. Cary!" his voice gaining energy again as he went on. "And those good young men, Mr. Fay, who have always done their duty, — how I love them! Tell them how I love them. No words can express how I love them!"

When asked if he was not exhausting himself, he said, "No: it rests me."

More than once he exclaimed, "Oh, my beautiful plans for the college! I meant that Mr. Fay should prepare himself to be the president of this college; for I know no man living who will take it, who will carry it on as well as he." To Mr. Fay, who did not hear this, he said, "Preach God's laws, Mr. Fay; *preach them*, PREACH THEM!"—his voice rising each time he repeated the words, his trembling arm raised aloft as if to invoke Heaven's blessing upon him, his whole frame quivering with emotion. "You have more power over the public mind of the West than any man I know," he added after a pause. Then most energetically he repeated his entreaty that he would use it; for the world needed it.

---

* This gentleman had taken the place in the college of his beloved nephew, Calvin Pennell. Mr. Cary soon filled Mr. Pennell's place of appreciative co-operator and counsellor. He never needed to be told what were the peculiar requisites of a professor in an institution founded on the plan of educating young men and women together. His presence created order: his manners precluded opposition, and inspired the right sentiment for the occasion, without word or remonstrance. It would be difficult to describe his value to Mr. Mann or to the institution.

"O God! may he preach them till the light drive out the darkness!"

To his children he said, "When you wish to know what to do, ask yourselves what Christ would have done in the same circumstances."

It is impossible to record all his words, uttered in a clear, musical voice, that rang out strong as in his best days, now to his family, now to his students, now in memory of the absent. At last he again asked for quiet, and thought he could sleep. Motioning gently with his hand, he said, "Will not the friends fall back?" He wanted air and repose; but the crowd inconsiderately lingered, rendering the close of his noble life a struggle for breath instead of a peaceful slumber. He could not even speak to his much-loved nephew, Mr. Pennell, who arrived at that moment.

The chills of death shook him painfully; and he asked for blankets, which were heated and wrapped round him. Stimulants were administered, which brought no relief, but gave him temporary delirium, in which he uttered exclamations that showed how deeply he felt, and how keenly he remembered, some of the heart-trials that had been instrumental in cutting him off thus prematurely.

The strong brain found it hard to die. At last, God mercifully gave him rest; but "death" is not the word for such a translation.

It was on the 2d of August, 1859, that he left us; and his earthly form now reposes in the North Burial-ground of the city of Providence, where his family and friends have erected a monument modelled after the beautiful "Obelisk of the Vatican."

I close this Memoir with his own last words spoken in public, which no one can read without feeling that they were unconsciously prophetic: —

BACCALAUREATE ADDRESS OF 1859.

Young Ladies and Gentlemen of the Graduating Class, —

After journeying together for so many years on our passage through life, we are about to part. Another day, ay, another hour, and we separate. Would to God I could continue this journey with you through all its future course! There is no suffering of a physical nature which I could survive, that I would not gladly bear, if thereby I could be set back to your starting-point, — to the stage of life where you are now standing. When I think, after the experience of one life, what I could and would do in an amended edition of it; what I could and would do, more and better than I have done, for the cause of humanity, of temperance, and of peace; for breaking the rod of the oppressor; for the higher education of the world, and especially for the higher education of the best part of it, — woman: when I think of these things, I feel the Phœnix-spirit glowing within me; I pant, I yearn, for another warfare in behalf of right, in hostility to wrong, where, without furlough, and without going into winter-quarters, I would enlist for another fifty-years' campaign, and fight it out for the glory of God and the welfare of man. I would volunteer to join a "forlorn hope" to assault the very citadel of Satan, and carry it by storm, and bind the old heresiarch (he is the worst heresiarch who does wrong) for a thousand years; and if in that time he would not repent, of which I confess myself not without hope, then to give him his final quietus.

But alas! that cannot be; for, while the Phœnix-spirit burns within, the body becomes ashes. Not only would the sword fall from my hand; my hand would fall from the sword.

I cannot go with you. You must pursue your conquering march alone.

What, then, can I do? Can I enshrine my spirit in your hearts, so that when I fall in the ranks (as I hope to fall in the very front ranks of this contest), and when my arm shall no longer strike, and my voice no longer cheer, you may pursue the conflict, and win the victory? — the victory of righteousness under the banner of Jesus Christ. This transferrence of my enthusiasm, of the results of all my experience and study, into your young and athletic frames, is what I desire to do ; what, as far as my enfeebled strength allows, I shall now attempt to do.

But, first, the new circumstances under which we assemble to-day ; the new men whom I see on this stage occupying the seats of official dignity and honor ; or, where the individual men are not new, the new functions they have come here to execute ; in fine, the new auspices under which this commencement is held, — demand a word.

This is Antioch College still, the same as we have known and loved it heretofore ; but, according to the doctrine of metempsychosis, it is by the transmigration of the old soul into a new body. The old body, with its works (that is, its scholarships and its debts, and its promises to pay without paying), is dead ; and in its stead we have the resurrection of a new and glorified body, — a body without scholarships, without debts or pecuniary trespasses of any kind.

But this beneficent change has not been accomplished without a great struggle. In contests where the antagonist powers of good and evil come into collision, especially where the conflict is waged on a conspicuous arena, the respective combatants will summon their auxiliaries from above and below. We feel as if, during the last two years, our enemies had enlisted their most potent allies against us, but such as bore no tokens of coming from above. We feel as if the cause of right and truth had at last triumphed ; and therefore, though ready to forget and forgive, we feel as if we have a right to congratulate ourselves, and as if it were a duty to thank Heaven for our success.

Our opponents remind me of a half-crazed Italian philosopher, who, many years ago, invented a seismometer (a seismometer is an instrument for measuring the force of earthquakes) ; and, when Vesuvius was in blast, he went up its sides, thinking to measure the intensity when the mountain shook, just as a physician feels a sick man's pulse. The concussion and the lava and the thunder came, but a little harder than had been expected ; and experimenter, seismometer, and all, were exhaled into everlasting deliquium.

In one of the old Latin authors, of which my young friends here will be likely to have a fresher recollection than I, I remember the story of one C. Flavius Fimbria, who stabbed Q. Scævola at the funeral of Marius. But Scævola recovered of his stabbing: whereupon the assassin commenced a prosecution against him in the Roman courts because he did not die of his wounds. To make the cases parallel, we must expect a prosecution against Antioch College for not having died when it was poisoned by calumny and falsehood.

But I return to my purpose of striving to transfuse into your bosoms, for the life-work that is before you, some of the thoughts and emotions that have animated me.

Answer these questions! O youth just starting on your earthly and your immortal career: —

What are the sources of my welfare? What, also, are the sources of my misery?

There are two sources of human happiness. There are two also of human misery.

There is the happiness that alights upon us without any agency or forethought of our own. It comes to us, or wells up within us, ready-made and complete; and our first consciousness of it is in the joy it bestows. Such is the spontaneous, unbought happiness of infancy and childhood; the happiness which a mother's beaming face sends thrilling through the frame of a babe; the happiness which is felt when a father's strong arm rescues a child from danger and from fear; the happiness which we have in the natural gratification of all our senses and faculties.

The other kind of happiness is that which comes through our own procurement or co-operation, where, while God does his part, he leaves us to do our part; and so our gratification is the joint product of both divine and human agencies.

Hence, of human happiness, there are two sources, the Heaven-derived and the self-derived, — Heaven supplying us with the means: or, what is far more common, our happiness is the result of the interflow and commingling of both, — Heaven's bounty and our effort or instrumentality; the first performing the incomparably larger share of the work, though the latter an indispensable share.

So there are two sources of human misery. One kind befalls us.

It comes upon us as an aerolite might fall out of the skies upon a man's head; as the tortoise which the eagle carried aloft in its talons, and dropped upon the bald cranium of Æschylus, and cracked it; as hereditary diseases come upon children; or as all the curses of a bad government or a false religion descend upon innocent generations; or as Adam's fall, whether we understand it literally or allegorically, plunged the human race into unmeasured depths of woe. A child is born blind, or deaf and dumb, or shallow-pated, or with faculties more askew than limbs and features can be: unspeakable misery results; but it comes in the course of Providence, and the victim must submit and endure, trusting to the remunerations of eternity.

> "For God hath marked each anguished day,
> And numbered every secret tear;
> And heaven's long age of bliss shall pay
> For all his children suffer here."

The second source of misery is, like the second source of happiness, self-derived. It is the result of voluntary ignorance or crime; though in regard to misery, as in regard to happiness, vastly the larger portion results from an admixture of the two causes, — the providential and the personal. Now, both for such results of happiness and misery as spring from our own character and conduct, we must take care of our own character and conduct. By so doing, we can obtain a maximum of the one, and avoid all but a minimum of the other. For such results as are exclusively of divine origin, we must learn to obey God's laws; for a perfect knowledge and a perfect obedience of God's laws would introduce all possible happiness into the world, and eliminate all possible misery from it.

And, for this purpose, it is among our highest privileges to know that God operates by uniform rules. No matter if theologians and metaphysicians do divide God's providential dealings with men into the natural and the supernatural: each must fall under the domain of law. This is so, because it is impossible to conceive of a being, possessed of such glorious attributes as we ascribe to the Almighty, who should act otherwise than uniformly; because he must always act out of his own unchangeableness. Hence fixedness and certainty must pervade the supernatural not less than the natural domain. This fixedness and uniformity of operation are all that is meant by *law*. Hence a knowledge of his laws is attainable by man; and if a knowledge of, then also a conformity to them. To an intelligent apprehension, the Deity seems moving onward from everlasting to everlasting, not with devious, zig-zag motions, but in one right line; not with mutability and fluctuation of purpose, but upon one vast plan, so perfect in the beginning, that it needs no revision, addition, or expurgation.

To those who regard either the natural or the supernatural as not regulated by law, the Deity must seem adroit only, and not wise; as rescuing his own system from ruin by expedients and make-shifts, such as a bungling craftsman resorts to to operate a bungling machine.

But why any evil or misery in the world at all? Why not universal impassibility to pain? Why not man necessitated to be happy?—every nerve of his sensitive nature pervaded by delight, as every corpuscle of his body is by gravitation. Why not his soul a compound of spiritual joys as his body is of chemical ingredients? Nay, why not happiness, passive and spontaneous, congenital, anti-natal, eternal, without effort or wish for good, or resistance of evil, on our part, and man made virtuous and saintly in this life, and carried into immortality and transcendent bliss in another, as a dead-head, and all the saints only so many spiritual lazzaroni?

Had not God begun at zero in creating the race, where should he have begun? Should he not have bestowed language on children at birth, so that they might have told their mothers the seat of their pains, and thus have taken only one medicine, instead of all in the pharmacopœia? Should not children have had enough knowledge of metals to abstain from eating arsenic for its sweetness? Should they not have possessed enough knowledge to keep out of fire and water, and to count a hundred, and thus have fallen outside of Blackstone's definition of a fool?

But suppose all men to be born at a certain advanced point of development, at a certain height in the scale above zero, would they not then be encompassed with a new circle of inconveniences and privations, quite as serious and annoying, and quite as earnestly demanding the *manus emendatrix*, tho "amending hand," as Sir Isaac Newton called it? And so, at whatever degree along the ascending scale man might be launched into being, he would, at that point, feel an apparent necessity of having been started at a higher point, until nothing could satisfy his demands but to have been created with the infinite perfections of a God. Surely this is as strong as the mathematicians' *reductio ad absurdum*. The only uncomplaining point to begin at is to begin so low, that there is no ability to complain. Hence man is created at the point of blank ignorance, that he may have the felicity and the glory of ascending *the whole way*. Had he been set up any number of steps in the stairway of ascension, so much as he rose to higher elevations would have been lost from the perceptions of contrast and the emotions of sublimity. A mountain can never appear so grand to one born on its top as to one who was cradled in the vale, but has climbed to its summit.

Here, then, we see how evil comes upon our race. We are created with numerous appetences; all like so many eyes to desire, and like so many hands to seize, their related objects in the external world. The external world superabounds with objects fitted to gratify and inflame these internal appetences. And now these beings, fervid and aflame with these desires, are turned loose among these objects, without any knowledge of what kind, in what quantity, at what time, they are to be taken and enjoyed, but with free agency to take what, when, and as much as they please. Bring these four elements into juxtaposition, — the thousand objects around, the inward desire for them, the free will to take them, and complete ignorance of consequences, — and how is it possible to avoid mistakes, injuries, errors, crimes? With only one radius in which to go right, with the whole circumference of three hundred and sixty degrees in which to go wrong, and without innate knowledge of what is right and what wrong, — for a being so circumstanced never to err is just as impossible as for an infinite number of dice to be thrown an infinite number of times, and always to come up sixes. Take any one man out of the thousand millions of men now on the earth, and his appetite for food and drink is not adapted merely to one aliquot thousand-milliouth part of all the viands and fruits and beverages upon the earth : it is adapted to all edibles and drinkables alike ; and without knowledge, and something more than knowledge, he will seize them where he can find them.

Consider all the property of the world — gold, gems, palaces, realities, personalties — as aggregated in one mass. Our natural love of this property is not confined to one quotient, using all mankind as a divisor; but it is adapted to the whole dividend, and without knowledge, and something more than knowledge, will demand it. " Male and female created He them." One man to one woman, one woman to one man, is the law.   But each of one sex to all of the other is the adaptation ; and without knowledge, and something more than knowledge, chemistry has no affinities, mathematics have no demonstrations, more certain than that polygamy, Mormonism, Freeloveism, with all their kindred abominations, will be the result. . Among all the young sparrows ever hatched, shall " never one of them fall to the ground without your Father."   And, because one does fall, shall we say God's system is imperfect ? Does not the Preacher say, " Shall those who remove stones not be hurt therewith, and they who cleave wood not be endangered thereby ? " Who could foreknow that nettles would sting, until some person made a very sudden and perhaps improperly worded report of the fact ?   Shall all mankind use edge-tools, and no man's fingers ever be cut ?   How is an ignorant colony to avoid a malarious district until the fever shall have scorched and the ague shall have shaken enough witnesses to swear that region in open court to be the putative father of quotidian, tertian, or quartan ?   Why shall the convenience of lead service-pipes be abandoned, until the poisoned water shall have been caught, *flagrante delicto*, scattering colics and paralyses? After seeing the hardening effect of fire on clay, how can a man tell, without experience, that it will not produce the same effect on wax?   That is, in physical matters, how shall an agent, free to do what he *will*, and ignorant of what he *ought*, escape error, and consequent damage?   With an impelling force behind and no guiding light before, and with one only goal to be reached, how shall the engineer avoid fatal deviations right or left, or a no less fatal crash against obstacles in his path? How should the first builder of houses, as a defence against cold and storm, foresee disease through loss of ventilation?

In matters of pure intellect, how could the first generations understand all astronomy by looking into the heavens, or all geography and geology by seeing the surface of the earth? Why should they not accredit the evidence of their own senses in regard to the diameter of the sun and moon, and therefore believe that a man could carry one of them under one arm, and the other under the other arm to balance it? Why not explain eclipses of sun and moon by saying that a great dragon had swallowed them? Why not believe in all the chimeras and absurdities of astrology? Why not believe that the whole framework of the heavens rotates daily about the earth, as it seems to do? If a man cannot see around the curvature or rotundity of the globe, nor penetrate downward through its numerous strata, why not believe it to be flat and thin, and to have four corners, and to have been made, with all its appendages, in six secular days? And, if the muscles of man grow weary by labor, why not suppose that the Deity grew weary also, and ordained a sabbath for bodily rest? And when the passions flash their intense light of love or hate, of admiration or of disgust, upon the objects around us, can reason be always achromatic, and blend the whole emotional prism of rays into that white light through which alone the divine complexion and features of truth can be truly seen?

Still less in divine affairs could it be expected that a new-born being, occupying but a point in space, should fathom the depths of immensity; or, occupying but a point in time, should comprehend the eternities before and after. And when this frail child of an hour hears the thunder's roar, and sees the heavens ablaze, and feels the earth shake, and the forests bend, and oceans toss, and he is unable to form a conception of a spiritual God, why should he not fall down and worship the first thing which his own ignorance makes mysterious?

Oh beautiful idolatry, when it springs from a devout and reverent soul as yet unilluminated by knowledge! for, when the true God shall be revealed to such souls, they will cover the earth with the beauty of holiness, and fill the heavens with the fragrance of worship. Polytheism grew up because men had not minds large enough to conceive of one God capable of all these terrestrial and celestial marvels, and therefore they had to divide his attributes among thousands, even millions, of deities.

And, with all the numerous appetites and propensities innate in every man, how shall he maintain an equilibrium of exercise and of indulgence between them, and how a subordination of the lower to the higher, until the errors and miseries of the wrong paths, rising up before him like fire, shall have turned him back again and again to seek the right one? How should a man know, until some one shall have tried the experiment, that fire will burn, or water drown, or that alcohol will intoxicate, and opium narcotize, or that the only difference between a filthy tobacco-user and a vile green tobacco-worm is, that, while the worm never comes up towards the man, the man constantly goes down towards the worm? How, before trial or experiment, could it be known that dyspepsia is a non-conductor of knowledge, and that next to the calamity of being *non compos* in the brain is that of being *non pos* in the stomach? How, before observation, could it be known that avarice, among the worldly passions, is the most destructive to every sentiment of honor and nobleness in the heart of man, and that bigotry, beyond all other spiritual crimes, destroys most thoroughly all mercy and godliness in the soul; that a man may be a thief, and yet, according to the proverb, have some vestige of honor; that he may be a robber, and not despoiled of all generosity; that he may be a libertine, and yet have some filial or social affections; that an epicure can be generous after dinner, and a conqueror have a circle of favorites? And again: we know that the heathen pagans and savages open their heaven to the good man, come whencesoever he will; but a miser would keep the Omnipotent at work through all eternity creating wealth for himself, and the bigot would harry him with prayers to invent new tortures for heretics, and both remain surly with disappointment.

This combination then, I say, of inward appetites reaching outward, of innumerable outward objects adapted to the inward appetites, with free will and with ignorance of consequences before trial, necessitates mistakes which are physical evil, necessitates errors which are intellectual evil, and necessitates these violations of God's law which are moral evil. This theory vindicates the providence of God in the creation and government of man for the existence of what we call evil, by showing that, with beings at once finite and free, it was inevitable.

But, if evil is inevitable, how is man accountable for it? If moral evil *must be*, is it not absurd to call men wicked? Nay, is it not monstrous forcibly to set a man down in a certain place, or to put him in a given state of mind, and then pronounce him sinful for being there?

This is our solution of that Sphinx riddle : *Though evil be inevitable, it is remediable also ; it is removable, expugnable.* Nor does it at all follow, because evil necessarily now is, that it must necessarily always be ; nor because it must continue for a given period, longer or shorter, that it must continue forever. Most of the evils of mortals are terminable because they are exterminable. A farmer can rotate his crops : he can root out brier and thorn, and cultivate wheat. Legislatures make laws to prevent the recurrence of evils, to bar them out, to abolish them. Satirists lash the evil-doer with their terrific thong, and force him to desist from shame when he will not from principle. Oppressed nations invoke God, and dethrone the oppressor. Pioneers hunt out wild beasts.

Nor is it with great evils only, such as threaten life or limb, wealth or good name, that men combat. They take cognizance of the smallest annoyances, and remove or remedy them. They assuage hunger and thirst: in heat they seek the shade ; in cold, the fire. Every man seeks to take a mote out of his eye, or to banish a fly from his nose ; and, if his soul were large enough, he could just as well remove or abolish the evils of war, intemperance, bigotry, oppression, as to drive a snake from his path.

This, then, is the conclusion of the matter : Men are not responsible for the evils they have not caused, and cannot cure ; *but they are responsible for the evils they consciously cause, or have power to cure.* I am no more responsible for what Cotton Mather and his coadjutors did at the time of the Salem witchcraft, or for what Pharaoh did at the time of the Israelitish exodus, or for what my very much respected but unfortunate great grandparents,

Adam and Eve, did in the Garden of Eden at the time of the interview with a distinguished stranger in disguise, — I am no more responsible for any of these things than I am for the law of mathematics, by which, if unequals be added to equals, the results will be unequal, or by which, if the dividend is not a multiple of the divisor, you must have a fraction in the quotient.

But our power to diminish evils, to extirpate evils, one after another, creates the *obligation* to diminish and to extirpate. This duty is oftentimes coincident with selfishness or self-love ; that is, it is both our duty and our desire to gratify some natural appetite or propensity. But sometimes our duty conflicts with the appetites or propensities of the lower nature. In either case, the duty is no less sovereign. In either case, obedience is indispensable to our permanent well-being. In all cases, God commands the performance of duty at all hazards and all sacrifices. As, if matter is to exist, there must be extension and solidity ; so, if rational happiness is to exist, there must be a knowledge of God's laws, and an obedience to them. Whenever one perceives a law in Nature or in Providence, it is as though the heavens opened, and a voice from the Most High came audibly down, calling us by name, and saying, *"Do!"* or *"Forbear!"* Not the children of Israel only, but every man, stands at the foot of Sinai, and must hear the commandments of the Lord ; not ten only, but ten thousand ; not Decalogue only, but Myrialogue ; and must obey them, or die. For God's law is omnipotent as well as eternal, and we are co-eternal subjects of it. Nor is it to be supposed that he has one law of cause and effect for this world, and another law of cause and effect for the next world, but that there is no law of cause and effect between the two worlds. Better and far nearer the truth would it be to say that this world is cause, and the next world effect. Shall the acts of a man — great virtues or great crimes — live forever upon earth in their good or evil consequences, but shall the actor, the man himself, perish ? Shall a grain of wheat buried in the integuments of an Egyptian mummy two thousand years ago, if now exhumed and planted, germinate, and connect the reign of Sesostris with the nineteenth century, but shall the soul of him whose body was buried with that kernel of wheat pass into nonentity ? Shall a diamond adorning the shroud of some ancient king of Persia be restored to the light in our day, and again flash and blaze in the sunbeams, but shall the soul of the king himself live no more forever? God's laws abide forever, and we abide forever under them; and hence it is our highest conceivable interest as well as duty to conform, to inosculate our lives, our characters, ourselves, to them. In many things, the average of human knowledge shows this to be true already: additional enlightenment will demonstrate its truth in all things. A man inherits houses or lands. If his estate needs rounding out at any point, he adds to it, and symmetrizes its boundaries; and, if disproportioned in its kinds of production, he turns forest into tillage, or tillage into forest: if his house offends taste, or frustrates convenience, he modernizes it into beauty and fitness. So if a man, on waking up to conscious comparisons, finds himself abnormal, or distorted from the common type, — afflicted, for instance, with *strabismus*, or non-coincidence of the optic axes, — he applies to the surgeon, has the contracted muscle cut, and he no longer squints: so, if club-footed, or suffering under any other pedal malformation, he goes to an orthopedist, who, by the wonders of his art, reshapes the foot into simulation to the common pattern. If we have an unsightly or distorted feature, does not the smallest modicum of common sense teach us to cure or at least to palliate it? If wounded or diseased in body, do we not seek to be healed or cured, and submit to privation and pain to be made whole? See one of America's noblest and brightest sons, for an injury to the brain, which mad brutality in the council-halls of the nation had sacrilegiously inflicted on him, — see him seeking restoration in foreign lands, and going to the terrific *moxa*, the fire-cure, as to his daily meals; and why? Because he hoped, from these fire-thrills through all his nerves, for a rehabitation of the brain, and then for that other and hallowed fire in the cause of freedom and humanity such as touched Isaiah's lips. And if all this is done and borne for intellectual recuperation, nay, for the body that perishes, what ought not the scholar, — he who is indoctrinated into the knowledge of cause and effect, into the wondrous and saving knowledge of God's laws, — that knowledge which fuses the two worlds into one, and makes death only an event in life, — what ought not he to do or dare for the exaltation and grandeur of the soul?

And this brings me to the second stage of my inquiry: How shall we obtain happiness, how avoid misery?

I answer, in the briefest and most comprehensive formula, By knowing and obeying the law of God; for, in regard to all the higher forms of happiness, his plan seems to be to make men earn their own; he furnishing them with an outfit of capital and implements, or, as a business-man would express it, stock and tools.

The babe recognizes God's laws. Before it has any conception of divine attributes or a Divine Being, before it can articulate the Holy Name, it recognizes one of the most central of all laws, — that by which, under like circumstances, like causes will produce like effects. One well-executed burning of its fingers in a taper's blaze is sufficient: it needs no second lesson in that liturgy forever. Let a morsel of delicious food stimulate the papillæ of its tongue, and old age cannot obliterate its memory. So, but contrariwise, of the caustic or bitter. How soon the infant learns to call for water when it is thirsty, or to turn to the fire when it is cold! The boy learns the law of his sports. Sir Isaac Newton did not understand the law of resistance better than the slinger. A *ninny* farmer knows that, though he should sow the sea with acorns, and harrow them in with the north wind, he could not raise a forest of oaks upon its surface. A man may own all the coal-fields of Pennsylvania, or all the wood of the Hartz Mountains; but, without oxygen, he will freeze in the midst of them all. If a man will turn his bars of railroad iron into natural magnets, his road must run north and south. It may lie east and west to all eternity without their polarization. To create a visual image, the light must come to a focus on the retina of the eye, and not on the tympanum of the ear. Shadows are not projected towards the illuminating body, nor does an echo precede the sound that awakes it.

Not less true is it, that if a man will enjoy health, strength, and longevity, he must know and observe the hygienic conditions of diet, air, exercise, and cleanliness. A sound brain *cannot* be elaborated from a hypochondriac or valetudinarian body, nor systems of sound philosophy be constructed in an unsound brain. Good digestion is part and parcel of a good man; though it does not follow from this that pigs are Christians. Rum-blasted or tobacco-blasted nerves become non-conductors of volition; and a porous and spongy brain can no more generate mental fire than a feather can beget lightning. Weak parents can no more be blessed with strong children than wrens can hatch eagles; and it is as impossible for a child to detach himself from the qualities of his ancestry, as impossible wholly to break the entail of hereditary qualities, as it would be in a court of law to prove, at the time of his birth, the *alibi* of himself or his mother. Ezekiel notwithstanding, personal qualities are descendible; and, if the fathers will eat sour grapes, the children's teeth will be set on edge. It has been objected to Swedenborg, that he once introduced the Divine Being on an unworthy occasion. He says, that, when once dining in his chamber, the Adorable Majesty appeared before him, and said, "Swedenborg, do not eat so much." Was this an unworthy occasion? — *a dignus non vindice nodus?* I deny the justness of the criticism. It is one of the wisest revelations which that coffee-inspired prophet ever had. If a company of one hundred families would set themselves to-day profoundly and devotedly to the work of exemplifying God's physiological laws, they would, in five generations of continued fidelity to them, govern the world.

These conditions of prosperity, of achieving good and avoiding evil, pervade the intellectual and moral world. A man must know his faculties; he must know the subordination of the lower to the higher, and his practice must accord with his knowledge.

There are two grand laws respecting mind-growth, more important than the laws of Kepler. The first is the law of symmetry. The faculties should be developed in proportion. Their circumference should be round, not polygonal; they should be balanced, not tilted. Every faculty is firmer set when it receives support from *all* the others. Every faculty acts with indefinitely more vigor when the other faculties sympathize and co-operate. A man who has one arm spliced to the other, giving him the length of both in one, while the armless fingers are attached to the scapula; a man who is Daniel Lambert on one side, weighing seven hundred pounds, and Calvin Edson, weighing only forty pounds, on the other, — is not more deformed than a man who is all intellect and no sentiment, or all sentiment and no intellect. Heretofore the kingdom of knowledge may have been enlarged by a distortion of the faculties, — by concentrating a sufficient energy upon one power and in one direction to achieve a discovery which could not have been achieved had that energy been equally distributed among all. But hereafter an entire realm of new discoveries will be opened and the errors of former discoverers rectified by that brighter illumination, when the rays of all the faculties shall converge to a focus upon the object of inquiry, — as in that remarkable case which occurred in Boston as but yesterday, where the laws of music and of electricity were invoked to solve an acoustic problem in the heart's beatings which had baffled all the science of Europe.

It is this relative disproportion of the faculties which has given rise to so many of the errors and even the crimes of the race, individual and national. If a body of seventy-two city brokers were now appointed to publish a septuagint edition of the New Testament, they would leave out the four Gospels, and insert in their stead the last best edition of the most approved interest tables. It is this accumulation of all excellence around one egotistic idea which makes an Englishman believe that Divine Providence always operates in subserviency to the British Constitution. It is this same exaggeration of a national sentiment which leads the French nation to look forward to a judgment-day, when men will be separated to the right hand and to the left, not because they have or have not given food or drink or clothes to the needy, not because they have visited or failed to visit the sick or the imprisoned, but according as they have been or have not been soldiers in the Grand Army. The descendant of the Puritan is disposed to believe in the doctrine of vicarious atonement, because this getting every thing and giving nothing is such a sharp bargain, — very much the same plan on which the Puritan ancestor treated the Indians. So the national foible or infirmity of our people — its over-grown vanity and pride — stands on a parallel with the haughtiness of the Spaniard, the vainglory of the Frenchman, and the egotism of the Englishman.

The first grand law of the faculties, as a whole, then, is the law of symmetry. An obedience to this law will yield immense happiness, and avoid immense misery.

The next law is as important as the first. It is that all our faculties grow in power and in skill by use, and that they dwarf in both by non-use. By growth, I mean that they pass out of one state into another, as a grain of corn grows or passes from the embryo germ to the plumule, from the plumule to the stalk, to the flowering tassel, to the bountiful ear.

What was Benjamin Franklin at birth? Would he have sold for any thing in any Christian market? Could he have been forced upon a debtor as a legal tender, even for the smallest charge in the debt? Would any artist have purchased him for his studio, or any philosopher for his cabinet of natural history? No chemist could have turned him to any account in his retorts. He was destined for far other retorts than theirs. But he grew. From being a lump of flesh weighing so many pounds avoirdupois, he took on other qualities and attributes, each transcendent, culminating over the preceding. By and by he became Benjamin Franklin *plus* the English alphabet, then Benjamin Franklin *plus* the multiplication-table. By industrious days and laborious nights, by observation and reflection, by noble abstinence from foul excesses, by divine energy of will in temperance, in diligence, in perseverance (better than the theologic perseverance of the saints, because it was his own), he gathered knowledge, accumulated stores of experience, grew wise on observation and lucubration, until soon he became that Benjamin Franklin whose name the lightning blazons from one part of the heavens unto the other, and to whom every summer cloud in all the zones and to the end of time shall thunder applause. See the offshoots of this growing man at this point of his development! Morse, House, Field, are his own brain-begotten children. The lightning is nimbly at work to-day in the shops of ten thousand artificers. It strikes alarm-bells, and warns sleeping cities that conflagration and a fiery death are at their doors. It measures longitudes as no geometer or astronomer could ever measure them ; and before another twelvemonth shall have passed, by a new application of that elemental force which ran along Franklin's kite-string, a cable shall unite the

Eastern and Western Hemispheres, along whose electric threads shall fly to and fro such "winged words" as Homer never dreamed of. Then he grew into that Benjamin Franklin who signed the Declaration of American Independence ; then into that Benjamin Franklin who signed the treaty of peace that acknowledged the independence and sovereignty of these United States ; an act extorted from a sovereign, which made *him* more than sovereign, — the *pater patriæ* of a country peopled with sovereigns. Then he became Benjamin Franklin *plus* the Constitution of the United States.

What growth was here ! what excelsior strivings and triumphs from day to day ! what ascension from glory to glory ! not to cease even with death ; for in all Christendom there is not now, nor ever hereafter will be, a child born of woman, who has not and will not have more of well-being and less of ill-being on earth because Benjamin Franklin lived ; that is, because of his industry, fidelity, and temperance when he was a boy ; because of his integrity, wisdom, and philanthropy when a man.

Now, each class and profession of men has a different stand-point from which it surveys the world, and to which, in its peculiar position, the world presents its immense variety of aspects. To a hack-driver, the living freight which a steamboat or railroad-train pours into a city are worth twenty-five or fifty cents apiece. The barber feels ties of brotherhood, and the gates of his soul open with welcome, towards that part of the human race that shaves. The manufacturer of playing-cards thinks it terrible Puritanism to condemn what Burns calls the "Devil's pictured buiks ;" and the printer of Bibles is a most zealous member of the Bible Society. When a shoemaker is requested to fit a tiny pair of shoes to an infant's feet, he sees a row of prospective and gradually enlarging shoes stretching out into futurity. So the tailor sees a lengthening vista of coats, and the hatter of hats, for all their customers. All these are seen as clearly as Æneas saw Marcellus far away in the coming generations.

So it is easy to take an ancestor who lived a thousand years ago, and see his lineal descendants diverging and radiating from him, children and grandchildren, — each line or lineage reaching in solid rank and file down to the present time ; one branch honorable, another proud, another base. These are realities.

But in view of this law of growth, and of the rapidity of its increments, no less real to me is the spectacle presented by every young man, especially by every young man who receives the nutriment and invigoration of a college-life. Radiating from every such young man as from a central point, I seem to see long-extended lines of the forms of men, — such forms as he may enter and occupy, and so become the men they represent. It is as though these lines shot out from him as from a centre to a circumference; only there is no circumference, for the lines lengthen outward into endless perspective. Stand up, young man, and let us behold the forms of men, noble or ignoble, lofty or mean, saintly or satanic, which beleaguer you, and into which your soul enters as you pass on in your life, from glory to glory, or from shame to shame ! Here, shooting out in one direction, I see an ascending series, an upward gradation of noble forms, figures of lofty stature and mien. Health and strength are in all their limbs ; fire, ardor, aspiration, gleam from every eye ; the light of virtue shines from every face ; each life is pure. What a throne for majesty is every brow ! Beneficence is in every hand. See how each individual in that long-extended rank excels the last, as it rises and towers, and is lost at last to our view, but lost only where earth meets heaven !

But what do I see on the other side ? Another line, compact like the former, shooting outward from the same centre, but stamped and branded with all those types of infamy that can be developed from the appetites, — gluttony, intemperance, sensuality, debauchery, agony and ignominy unspeakable. O God ! I rejoice that I can see no farther into the perdition beyond. These, *these*, young man, are the forms which you may grow into and become. Choose to-day whether you will pass through this succession to honor and bliss, or this to shame and despair.

This young man proposes to be a lawyer. Shooting outwards from him on either hand are compact files of those who disgrace or those who honor the noble profession of the law. This line begins with a pettifogger, a chicaner, a picaroon, — one whose study and life it is to throw the cloak of truth over the body of a lie, like that lawyer of whom a malefactor said, " I have counted the chances, and concluded to commit the crime, for I know *he* can get me off;" and it ends in an Old-Bailey or Five-Points solicitor, sold to the service of Satan, content to take half his pay in money, and the rest in pleasure of wickedness, — like the man who was a great lover of swine's flesh, who said he wished he were a Jew, that he might have the pleasure of eating pork and committing a sin at the same time.   Another radiating file begins with examples of honor, equity, truth-loving, and ends in a chief justice such as Holt or Marshall or Shaw.

Another means to be a public man.   His first transformation may be into a demagogue, half-sycophant, half-libeller, a pimp and pander of power, a peculator, an embezzler, a robber of mails or mints, a polyglot liar; or he may pass into those types whose systems of political economy have humanity for their end, and wealth for their means only; who know no castes or classes or nobility, excepting those who bear God's patent of intelligence and virtue.

This young man looks to the sacred desk.   Next to him, on one side, stands the chameleon preacher, the color of whatever he touches.   His soul is a religious *camera-obscura*, reflecting back only the souls of those who pay his salary.   He cannot preach against the crimes of to-day, — the crimes that flout heaven, the crimes that crush life out of the human heart.   He can only preach against the " exceeding sinfulness of sin," — now and then hurling a terrific bolt at Jeroboam or Judas.   *They* are personages not very likely to disturb the sacred quiet of *his* parish.   But what a glorious column of the forms of men stands on the other side ! — true disciples of Jesus Christ, constituted of piety, philanthropy, and wisdom, — men who, for truth's sake, can bear revilings and a crown of thorns, can look without shrinking upon the cross, nay, can die upon the cross if need be.   But, oh! when the sanctifying hour of death has passed, then the revilings become world-wide homages; the crown of thorns, a crown of amaranth, blossoming forever in the air of heaven : even the accursed cross is made sacred in the eyes of men.

Thus it ever is when men make sacrifices in the cause of duty. First comes the temptation; which if resisted, the transfiguration follows. The stern fulfilment of duty enrages the wicked, and they execute crucifixion; and then comes the ever-glorious ascension: and even the memory of the Joseph of Arimathea who cared for the dead body of the martyr is gratefully and forever embalmed in the hearts of men.

Crowding thick around you, my young friends who go forth from here to-day, I see these various classes and characters of men whom I have attempted to portray. Select which you please. Transmigrate through the forms of one class into ever-increasing nobleness and dignity, ascending to all temporal honor and renown, to end in the glories of immortality; or plunge through the other, from degradation to degradation, to a perdition that is bottomless.

I need not carry out the parallel with regard to the young ladies who are before me, and who are candidates for graduation to-day. For them, if they will have the courage to lift themselves out of the frivolities of a fashionable and a selfish life, each one, in her own sphere and in her own way, may become another Isabella, securing an outfit for another Columbus for the discovery of another hemisphere wherewith to bless mankind, — more honorable to the queenly helper than to the bold navigator. . . .

The last words I have to say to you, my young friends, are these : —

You are in the kingdom of a Divine Majesty who governs his realms according to law. By his laws, it is no more certain that fire will consume, or that water will drown, than that sin will damn. Nor is it more sure that flame will mount, or the magnetic needle point to the pole, than it is that a righteous man will ascend along a path of honor to glory and beatitude. These laws of God pervade all things, and they operate with omnipotent force. Our free agency consists merely in the choice we make to put ourselves under the action of one or another of these laws. Then the law seizes us, and sweeps us upward or downward with resistless power. If you stand on the great table-land of North America, you can launch your boat on the head waters of the Columbia, or the Mackenzie, or the St. Lawrence, or the Mississippi; but the boat, once launched, will be borne *towards* the selected one of the four points of the compass, and *from* all the others. If you place your bark in the Gulf Stream, it will bear you northward, and not southward ; or though that stream is as large as three thousand Mississippis, yet you can steer your bark across it, and pass into the region of the variable or the trade winds beyond, to be borne by them.

If you seek suicide from a precipice, you have only to lose your balance over its edge, and gravitation takes care of the rest. So you have only to set your head right by knowledge, and your heart right by obedience, and forces stronger than streams or winds or gravitation will bear you up to celestial blessedness, Elijah-like, by means as visible and palpable as though they were horses of fire and chariots of fire.

Take heed to this, therefore, that the law of God is the supreme law. The judge may condemn an innocent man ; but posterity will condemn the judge. The United States are mighty ; but they are not almighty. How sad and how true what Kossuth said, that there had never yet been a Christian government on earth ! Before there can be a Christian government, there must be Christian men and women. Be you these men and women ! An unjust government is only a great bully ; and though it should wield the navy in one fist and the army in the other, though it should array every gun in the armories of Springfield and Harper's Ferry into one battery, and make you their target, the righteous soul is as secure from them as is the sun at its zenith height.

While, to a certain extent, you are to live for yourselves in this life, to a greater extent you are to live for others. Great boons, such as can only be won by great labors, are to be secured ; great evils are to be vanquished. Nothing to-day prevents this earth from being a paradise but error and sin. These errors, these sins, you must assail. The disabilities of poverty ; the pains of disease ; the enervations and folly of fashionable life ; the brutishness of appetite, and the demonisms of passion ; the crowded vices of cities, thicker than their inhabitants ; the retinue of calamities that come through ignorance ; the physical and moral havoc of war ; the woes of intemperance ; the wickedness of oppression, whether of the body or of the soul ; the Godlessness and Christlessness of bigotry, —

these are the hosts against which a war of extermination is to be waged, and you are to be the warriors. Never shrink, never retreat, because of danger: go into the strife with your epaulettes on.

At the terrible battle of Trafalgar, when Lord Nelson, on board the "Victory," the old flag-ship of Keppel and of Jervis, bore down upon the combined fleets of France and of Spain, he appeared upon the quarter-deck with his breast all blazing with gems and gold, the insignia of the " stars " and " orders " he had received. His officers, each a hero, besought him not thus to present himself a shining mark for the sharpshooters of the enemy, but to conceal or doff the tokens of his rank. " No," replied Nelson : " in honor I won them, and in honor I'll wear them ! " He dashed at the French line, and grappled with the "Redoubtable" in the embrace of death. But, when the battle had raged for an hour, a musket-ball, shot from the mizzen-top of the enemy, struck his left epaulette, and, crashing down through muscle and bone and artery, lodged in his spine. He knew the blow to be fatal ; but as he lay writhing in mortal agony, as the smoke of battle at intervals cleared away, and the news was brought to him that one after another of the enemy's ships — the " Redoubtable," the " Bucentaur," the "Santa Anna," the " Neptune," the " Fougueux " — had struck their colors, his death-pangs were quelled, joy illumined his face, and for four hours the energy of his will sustained his vitality; and he did not yield to death until the fleets had yielded to him.

So, in the infinitely nobler battle in which you are engaged against error and wrong, if ever repulsed or stricken down, may you always be solaced and cheered by the exulting cry of triumph over some abuse in Church or State, some vice or folly in society, some false opinion or cruelty or guilt which you have overcome ! And I beseech you to treasure up in your hearts these my parting words : *Be ashamed to die until you have won some victory for humanity.*

APPENDIX.

A.

PROCEEDINGS OF THE BOSTON COMMITTEE.

A YEAR after Mr. Mann had been elected to Congress, and while he was absent at Washington, some friends of the cause of education in the Legislature of Massachusetts, who were not before particularly acquainted with the pecuniary sacrifices which he had made for it, (among whom was the Hon. Charles W. Upham of Salem, the Chairman of the Joint Committee on Education), became apprised of the extraordinary devotion of his means, as well as of himself, to the cause that had been intrusted to him; and through their agency this committee was instructed " to ascertain what sums, if any, were paid by the late Secretary of the Board of Education, out of his private means, for the erection of Normal schoolhouses, and for other purposes of a public nature, with power to send for persons and papers."

In March following, the committee made their report, which consisted mainly of statements, made by various individuals, of such facts as they personally knew concerning the pecuniary contributions made by Mr. Mann out of his own private means to carry forward the

37   577

public work with which he had been charged. From this report, and the statements it contains, we shall quote largely. Biographies are rarely swelled by any great accumulation of similar details.

The committee first introduce a letter from Mr. Mann himself, dated Washington, Feb. 9, 1849, from which we make the following extracts:—

"The order empowers the committee to send for persons and papers. You are pleased to put your requisition upon me in the imperative mood; though doubtless for no other reason than that of overcoming a repugnance I might be supposed to feel against speaking upon the subject. . . .

"You must permit me to say, in the first place, that, until the receipt of your letter, I was entirely ignorant that any such movement had been made, or was contemplated, by any one. I could never have brought myself to ask, nor even to ask a friend to ask, any remuneration for the sacrifices made or the expenses incurred in promoting the objects of my office. However much it may prejudice the end you have in view, I must, nevertheless, say that those sacrifices and expenses were incurred without any expectation of re-imbursement. When I left a lucrative profession for the Secretaryship, I cheerfully surrendered all hopes of wealth or promotion; and, from the day when I accepted that office, I held myself personally responsible for the success of the enterprise; and though it might cost me my means, my health, my life, or a hundred lives, if I had them, I held the triumph of the cause to be paramount to them all.

"On entering upon the office, it is well known that numerous and in some cases heavy expenses were connected with it, such as never had been contemplated either by the framers of the law or by myself. Not a cent has ever been allowed me for clerk-hire or office-rent. At first, no provision was made for postages or stationery. Since provision was made for these latter items, I have never charged half their cost, lest the expenses of the office might excite opposition against it. Whatever books I needed, either in our own or other languages, I have been obliged to purchase and pay for myself. For other expenses incurred in travelling over the State for the first five years, — occupying about four months each year, — no allowance has ever been made me.

"What I have paid for clerk-hire must, of course, be known to those who have received it; and what I have spent for educational works and documents to be distributed over the State must be known to those who have furnished and who have received them. If there have been still other expenses, perhaps they had better come under the rule of not letting the left hand know what the right hand doeth. . . .

"In what I have already said, although said at your request, I may be thought by some to be treading on delicate ground. This movement did not originate with me. I cannot present myself in the form of a petitioner, asking for a return of what was voluntarily given. I must take care of my honor. The State is the proper judge of its own. If the State chooses to consider any part of the sums I have paid as paid on its account, — as paid for property of which it now has the benefit, or now enjoys the actual use and possession, — it will be gratefully received, both as a token of its approbation, and as the refunding of moneys I must otherwise lose. But, let what will come, no poverty, and no estimate of my services, however low, can ever make me repine that I have sought, with all the means and the talents at my command, to lay broader and deeper the foundations of the prosperity of our Commonwealth, and to elevate its social and moral character among its confederate States and in the eyes of the world.

"With the most respectful regards for yourself and your colleagues on the committee, and with an earnest request, that, in whatever you may deem it right to do in relation to this movement, you will take care of my honor, whatever may become of my purse,

"I remain, &c."

The Hon. A. Hale, then a member of Congress, in whose place of residence — Bridgewater — one of the Normal schoolhouses had been erected, made, among other things, the following statement : —

"The Board then advertised for proposals for the erection of the [Normal-school] buildings according to the plans and specifications which had been furnished by the Board.

"The proposals being very much above the amount at the disposal of the Board for that object, alterations were made in the plans and specifications, reducing the expense of the buildings very considerably ; but still the Board could not find any person to erect the buildings for the sum in their hands, and it seemed that the enterprise must be abandoned. Under these circumstances, Mr. Mann came forward, and gave his private obligation to pay the excess of the cost of the buildings over and above the amount at the disposal of the Board. With this indemnity, the Board caused the buildings to be erected ; and, on a settlement of the bills, it was found that the excess amounted to about seven hundred and forty dollars, of which an individual of the town of Bridgewater paid a hundred dollars, and Mr. Mann the residue."

The following facts were detailed by the Hon. Josiah Quincy, jun., then Mayor of Boston : —

" I cannot withhold my testimony as to the disinterested liberality with which Mr. Mann has endeavored to forward the great cause of public education.

" I shall confine myself to pecuniary sacrifices on advances made by him of a comparatively large amount.

" Five or six years ago, Mr. Mann applied to me for a loan, on his law-library, of some five or six hundred dollars, for the purpose of furnishing the lodging-house of the Normal School at Lexington. Knowing his circumstances, I endeavored to dissuade him from giving so much to the public, and refused, on that ground, to lend him the money. The result was, he sold his library, and furnished the house ; losing, I have no doubt, in the result, the whole amount.

" Shortly after this, the land and schoolhouse at West Newton were given to the public,* with the understanding that the citizens of that place and the friends of education would fit up the building in the most approved style.

" Some months after the building was completed, I learned accidentally that the necessary funds had not been raised, and that Mr. Mann and Mr. Pierce had expended and paid a large amount of their own money (a thousand three hundred dollars) for the repairs. A meeting of friends of the cause was immediately called at my house, without the knowledge of either of the gentlemen, to provide means for its payment. . . .

" Massachusetts owes the existence of two of her Normal-school buildings to the advances made by two gentlemen to complete the first.

" After the erection of the schools at Westfield and Bridgewater, Mr. Mann applied to me for a loan of two thousand dollars. On inquiry, I found that the appropriations for these buildings fell short of the contract prices ; and, rather than run the risk of losing them, Mr. Mann had made himself personally liable for the difference. He insisted on borrowing the money, and giving security for it ; and forbade my applying to any individuals or to the State on the subject. As it was a business transaction, I have never mentioned it ; and should not have done it now, except at the order of the State. He gave as security almost, I believe, all his personal property, and still owes the debt."

---

* This donation was made by Mr. Quincy himself ; though, from his letter, one would never surmise it.

Mr. George B. Emerson enumerated various items, varying from forty to six hundred and forty dollars at a time, of whose payment by Mr. Mann from time to time, for the promotion of the cause, he happened to be personally cognizant; and then adds : —

"The expenses of printing the papers he has written in defence of the cause of the Massachusetts Board of Education fell principally upon him, and must have amounted to a very large sum. . . .

"It has always seemed to me, that giving, as he did, his life to this work, and having made a very great personal sacrifice, in a pecuniary point, by accepting the office of Secretary to the Board of Education, he was less bound than any other individual to contribute towards these objects from his private purse. But he was in the habit of doing, at his own expense, what he saw was necessary for the cause, whenever no one else came forward to do it."

Messrs. Dutton & Wentworth, printers to the State, volunteered to send the chairman of the committee the following letter : —

"DEAR SIR, — Learning that a movement is about to be made in the Legislature to make some remuneration to the Hon. Horace Mann, late Secretary of the Board of Education, for personal and other expenses incurred during his term of office, we beg leave to volunteer in his behalf. During the twelve years of his term of office, all the reports of the Board and its Secretary have been printed by us. In regard to the printing he has ordered, he has always had it done in the most economical manner; and we wish to bear our testimony to the fact. Whenever he has wanted, for distribution, extra copies of his reports, he has ordered them printed on his private account, and paid for them himself: we are unable to state the exact amount he has paid us for these documents, but should say it must have been seventy-five or a hundred dollars. The documents he has purchased of us were his *own reports*, school-abstracts, lectures, &c., besides circulars he has issued for teachers' meetings, where addresses were to be delivered by himself and others. The amount stated above, we are aware, is not large; but the *spirit* of the transaction is more than the amount. He never would take a sheet or a copy, belonging to the State, at any time. If he wanted copies for distribution, he has ordered them, and paid for them out of his own purse. In the matter of postages, he has also not been less scrupulous and conscientious; having always paid the expresses for letters and proof-sheets to and from himself when he was in the country while his reports were printing. In every thing in relation to the duties of his office, he has always been very exact; scrupulous and uniform in the discharge of his duties, so far as the matter of printing is concerned. We believe the State owes Mr. Mann a great debt; and, if the simple facts here stated will help his cause, we feel we are only doing an act of justice to him as an officer of the strictest integrity.

" With sentiments of respect and esteem,

" Your obedient servants,

" DUTTON & WENTWORTH,

" *State Printers.*"

On this letter the Report remarks: —

" The letter from Messrs. Dutton & Wentworth is quite remarkable, as proving the scrupulous sense of justice and honor that has marked Mr. Mann's discharge of his late office. To use an expression which bears the stamp of his own peculiar richness of illustration, he has been careful 'to shake the gold-dust from his garments whenever he has had occasion to go into the public mint.' " *

William B. Fowle, Esq., bookseller, and publisher of the " Common-school Journal " during the last six years of the time that Mr. Mann was its editor, being called upon for information by the committee, attested as follows: —

" It always appeared to me that Mr. Mann had set his heart upon the great work of resuscitating the school-system, at any sacrifice to himself of ease or property. I never knew what resources he had; but I often wondered at the liberality, or what to me seemed the prodigality, of his donations; and yet the expenditure of his money must have been to him a trifle, compared with the outlay of strength which I often witnessed. I often warned him of his danger when I saw him suffering from an overworked brain: but he never desisted, though he admitted the danger; for the work was to be done, and if neglected, though beyond human strength, the community, not knowing this, would consider him unfaithful. This was his greatest sacrifice in the cause of education; but, as no pecuniary estimate can be set upon this, perhaps I should not have alluded to it. I have known him for weeks

---

* While Mr. Mann was a candidate for the office of Governor of Massachusetts (as before mentioned), he was informed that an emissary of one of the political parties opposed to him had been at the State House for three days, overhauling the accounts and official records made by him while Secretary of the Board of Education, in hopes to find or create some pretext for impeaching his conduct. " Let him get a microscope," said Mr. Mann, " and blind himself with looking. He will not only find no stain in my official conduct, but I hope the examination of it will make him an honester man."

to be unable to sleep. When Mr. Mann entered upon his duties, it was evident that his efforts would be very restricted if he did not contrive to scatter the information he collected. Indeed, the law required that he should both collect and distribute; but the State made no provision for the distribution! As the most popular and economical method of complying with the requirements of the law, Mr. Mann commenced the 'Common-school Journal.' At the end of the fourth year, when I became the publisher, the receipts had fallen short of the expenditures. Since that time, viz. for six years, the loss has not fallen upon Mr. Mann; but he has continued to edit the 'Journal,' because he considered it essential to the success of the great cause.

"The volumes contain many valuable documents which it was important to scatter widely over the State. It was Mr. Mann's custom to print extra numbers of these, and distribute them gratuitously to the schools. I recollect three or four cases in which he sent a copy to every district, of which there must have been three or four thousand. . . .

"Probably each of these donations cost him seventy-five dollars. Many single volumes of the 'Journal,' and sometimes whole sets, were given away for the general good; but of this I have no record, though I know the volumes amounted to hundreds.

"The compilation of the volume of abstracts was a heavy task: but, besides making this, he actually paid for the making of the index; which, I know (for I made one of them), is no slight affair. . . .

"Two other items have occurred to me; and they should be mentioned, as helping to illustrate the perfect forgetfulness of self which marked the official course of Mr. Mann.

"Three or four years ago, when outline maps began to be used in schools, it became proper that the pupils of the Normal schools should be taught how to use them. As the Board of Education had no funds, Mr. Mann paid for three sets, one for each school. The price is twenty-five dollars a set.

"Before Mr. Mann went to Europe, I had frequent conversations with him on the subject of European schools; and he regretted that he had not that personal knowledge which would enable him to compare them with our own, and to propose such improvements as would really advance our own. I think this was his only motive in going; for he visited nothing but schools, and returned as soon as possible. The expenses of his visit must have exceeded his salary ten or fifteen hundred dollars; and, on his return, I proposed to him to put his notes into the form of a book, and let me publish them, assuring him that the copyright would produce more than he had expended beyond his salary. His reply was, that he was a public officer, and went for the public, and the public were entitled to the information, free of any such tax. His remarks, therefore, were thrown into his Seventh Annual Report, and *given* to the State."

After paying a merited tribute of respect to the Hon. Edmund Dwight for his well-known liberality in the same cause, the committee close their report with the following paragraph, and with a resolve for paying out of the treasury of the Commonwealth " the sum of two thousand dollars in favor of Horace Mann, late Secretary of the Board of Education : " —

" The committee do not propose, as they feel confident that it would not be agreeable to Mr. Mann, to make out an exact account of what the State may owe him in dollars and cents. He does not desire, and would not be willing, to be fully re-imbursed ; but, before all money that the treasury of the Commonwealth contains, he prefers to cherish the happy and noble thought, that he has labored and suffered in her behalf. He asks for nothing, and has had no voluntary agency in this movement. Nothing would be more repugnant to his well-known sensibilities than to have a claim urged upon the State for an exact settlement of his accounts with it upon mere business principles. What he has done, he meant, at the time, for a gift ; and the committee do not propose to deprive him of the title of a benefactor. They do not propose to *pay him off ;* but, under the circumstances, they are of opinion that the passage of the following resolve, although not amounting by half to what, upon a strict computation, is equitably due to him, would be more agreeable to his feelings than a more precise remuneration."

From authentic information, we are able to say that this sum was but a very small part of what had been paid by Mr. Mann from his own pocket, in furtherance of the cause of education, while he was Secretary of the Board ; but, inadequate as a remuneration though it was, it was in the highest degree honorable both to giver and receiver. Before any one complains of Massachusetts for not doing more, let him point to a single State in our Union, or to a single government in the world, which under such circumstances, and *for such a class of services,* would have done as much. We believe the resolve was passed in both Houses without a dissenting vote.

B.

"CODE OF HONOR," FALSELY SO CALLED.

At a convention composed of delegates from colleges in the State of Ohio, assembled at Columbus, Dec. 29, 1856, the following resolutions, designed to promote the internal tranquillity, the literary progress, and the exemplary conduct, of students, were unanimously adopted; and a committee, consisting of the Hon. Horace Mann, President of Antioch College, the Rev. Jeremiah Hall, President of Denison University, and the Rev. Dr. Solomon Howard, President of Ohio University, were appointed to prepare an address to the faculties of colleges in the State of Ohio, setting forth more fully and argumentatively the subject-matter of the resolutions, and to cause the same to be printed and distributed : —

Whereas a sentiment very generally prevails in colleges and schools, that students ought, as far as possible, to withhold all information, respecting the misconduct of their fellow-students, from faculty and teachers;

And whereas this sentiment is often embodied in what is called a *code of honor*, by whose unwritten, and therefore uncertain provisions, students are often tempted or constrained, under fear of ridicule or contempt or violence, to connive at the offences of their fellow-students beforehand, or to screen them from punishment afterwards;

And whereas a bounty is thus offered for the commission of wrong, in the impunity which is secured to the wrong-doer: therefore

Resolved, That a college or school is a community, which, as an essential condition of its prosperity, must, like any other community, be governed by wise and wholesome laws faithfully administered.

And further resolved, That as he is a good citizen, and in the highest degree worthy of the gratitude of the community where he dwells, who knowing that an offence is about to be committed, promptly interposes to prevent it; and as he is a bad citizen, and worthy the condemnation of all good men, who, knowing that an offence has been committed, withholds testimony or suborns witnesses to shield the culprit from the consequences of his crime: so, in a college or in a school, he is a good student, and a true friend of all other students, who by any personal influence which he can exert, or by any information which he can impart, prevents the commission of offences that are meditated, or helps to redress the wrongs already committed; and that he is a bad student, who, by withholding evidence, or by false and evasive testimony, protects offenders, and thereby encourages the repetition of offences; and further, that as civil society cannot attain those ends of peace and prosperity for which it was constituted if it should suffer accomplices in crime or accessories, either before or after the fact, to remain or go at large among its members: so no college or school can ever reach the noble purposes of its institution should it permit confederates or accessories in vice or crime to remain enrolled among its members.

And whereas one great object of penal discipline is the reformation of the offender : therefore

Resolved, That just in proportion as the students of any institution will co-operate with its government in maintaining order and good morals, just in the same proportion should the government of such institution become more lenient and parental, substituting private expostulation for public censure, and healing counsel for wounding punishments.

The committee appointed at the convention above named, to prepare an address to the faculties of the colleges above referred to, have attended to the duty assigned them, and submit the following

REPORT.

Unhappily, no person needs to be informed that a feeling of antagonism towards teachers often exists among students. The hostile relation of distrust and disobedience supplants the filial one of trust and obedience. Such a relation necessitates more or less of coercive discipline ; and discipline, unless when administered in the highest spirit of wisdom and love, alienates rather than attaches. Though it may subdue opposition, it fails to conciliate the affections.

A moment's consideration must convince the most simple-minded that the idea of a natural hostility between teachers and pupils is not merely wrong, but ruinous. Without sympathy, without mutual affection, between instructors and instructed, many of the noblest purposes of education are wholly baffled and lost. No student can ever learn even the most abstract science from a teacher whom he dislikes as well as from one whom he loves. Affection is an element in which all the faculties of the mind as well as all the virtues of the heart flourish.

Springing from this deplorable sentiment of a natural antagonism between teachers and students, an actual belligerent condition ensues between them. One party promulgates laws : the other disobeys them when it dares ; or, what is an evil only one degree less in magnitude than actual disobedience, it renders but a formal or compulsory compliance, — there being, in strictness, no obedience but that of the heart. One party enjoins duties : the other evades or grudgingly performs them. Prohibitions are clandestinely violated. A rivalry grows up between the skill and vigilance that would detect, and the skill and vigilance that would evade detection. Authority on the one side, and fear on the other, usurp the place of love. Aggression and counter-aggression, not friendship and co-operation, become the motives of conduct ; and the college or the school is a house divided against itself.

We gladly acknowledge that there are practical limits both on the side of faculties and of students to these deplorable results. Still, students do bear about a vast amount of suppressed and latent opposition against faculties and teachers, which, though never developing itself in overt acts of mutiny or indignity, yet mars the harmony, and subtracts from the usefulness, of all our educational institutions.

Though all students do not partake of this feeling of hostility towards teachers, or in the practice of disobedience to their requirements, yet, as a matter of fact, the wrong-doers have inspired the right-doers with something of their sentiments, and coerced them as auxiliaries into their service. A feeling almost universally prevails throughout the colleges and schools of our country, that the students in each institution constitute of themselves a kind of corporation, and that this corporation is bound to protect and defend, with the united force of the whole body, any individual member who may be in peril of discipline, although that peril may have been incurred by his own misconduct. If, then, there is a corporation bound together by supposed collective interests, it is certain that this body will have its laws; and, as laws will be inefficacious without penalties, it will have its penalties also. These laws, by those who are proud to uphold and prompt to vindicate them, are called the *code of honor*, — a name which at once arouses the attention and attracts the sympathies of ardent and ingenuous youth. Being unwritten laws, with undefined penalties, both law and penalty will, at all times, be just what their framers and executors choose to make them. But unwritten laws and undefined penalties are of the very essence of despotism; and hence the sanctions for violating this code of honor, so called, are often terrible, — so unrelenting and inexorable, that few, even of the most talented and virtuous members of our literary institutions, dare to confront and brave them. Often they are the very reverse of the old Roman decree of banishment; for that only deprived a citizen of fire and water, whereas these burn or drown him. They often render it impossible for any supposed offender to remain among the students whose vengeance he has incurred.

The requisitions of this code are different in different places and at different times. Sometimes they are simply negative, demanding that a student shall take care to be absent when any thing culpable is to be committed, or silent when called on as a witness for its exposure. Sometimes they go farther, and demand evasion, misrepresentation, or even falsehood, in order to screen a fellow-student or a fellow-conspirator from the consequences of his misconduct; and sometimes any one who exposes not merely a violator of college regulations, but an offender against the laws of morality and religion, in order that he may be checked in his vicious and criminal career, is stigmatized as an "informer," is pursued with the shafts of ridicule or the hisses of contempt, or even visited with some form of wild and savage vengeance.

It is impossible not to see, that, when such a sentiment becomes the "common law" of a literary institution, offenders will be freed from all salutary fear of detection and punishment. Where witnesses will not testify, or will testify falsely, of course the culprit escapes. This security from exposure becomes a premium on transgression. Lawlessness runs riot when the preventive police of virtuous sentiment and of allegiance to order is blinded and muzzled. Thus, at the very outset, this code of honor inaugurates the reign of dishonor and shame. Judged, then, by its fruits, what condemnation of such a code can be too severe?

But, in the outset, we desire to allow to this feeling, as we usually find it, all that it can possibly claim under any semblance of justice or generosity. When, as doubtless it sometimes happens, one student reports the omissions or commissions of another to a college faculty from motives of private ill-will or malice; or when one competitor in the race for college honors, convinced that he will be outstripped by his rival unless he can fasten upon that rival some weight of suspicion or odium, seeks to disparage his character instead of surpassing his scholarship; or when any mere tattling is done for any mean or low purpose whatever, — in all such cases, every one must acknowledge that the conduct is reprehensible and the motive dishonoring. No student can gain any advantage with any honorable teacher by such a course. The existence of any such case supplies an occasion for admonition which no faithful teacher will fail to improve. Here, as in all other cases, we stand upon the axiomatic truth, that the moral quality of an action is determined by the motive that prompts it.

But suppose, on the other hand, that the opportunities of the diligent for study are destroyed by the disorderly, or that public or private property is wantonly sacrificed or destroyed by the maliciously mischievous; suppose that indignities and insults are heaped upon officers, upon fellow-students, or upon neighboring citizens; suppose the laws of the land or the higher law of God is broken, — in these cases, and in cases kindred to these, may a diligent and exemplary student, after finding that he cannot arrest the delinquent by his own friendly counsel or remonstrance, go to the faculty, give them information respecting the case, and cause the offender to be brought to an account? or, if called before the faculty as a witness, may he testify fully and frankly to all he knows? Or in other words, when a young man, sent to college for the highest of all earthly purposes, — that of preparing himself for usefulness and honor, — is wasting time, health, and character in wanton mischief, in dissipation, or in profligacy, is it dishonorable in a fellow-student to give information to the proper authorities, and thus set a new instrumentality in motion, with a fair chance of redeeming the offender from ruin? This is the question. Let us examine it.

As set forth in the resolutions, a college is a community. Like other communities, it has its objects, which are among the noblest: it has its laws indispensable for accomplishing those objects; and these laws, as usually framed, are salutary and impartial. The laws are for the benefit of the community to be governed by them; and without the laws, and without a general observance of them, this community, like any other, would accomplish its ends imperfectly, — perhaps come to ruin.

Now, in any civil community, what class of persons is it which arrays itself in opposition to wise and salutary laws? Of course, it never is the honest, the virtuous, the exemplary. They regard good laws as friends and protectors. But horse-thieves, counterfeiters, defrauders of the custom-house or post-office, — these, in their several departments, league together, and form conspiracies to commit crimes beforehand, and to protect each other from punishment afterwards. But honest farmers, faithful mechanics, upright merchants, the high-toned professional man, — these have no occasion for plots and perjuries; for they have no offences to hide, and no punishments to fear. The first aspect of the case, then, shows the paternity of this false idea of "honor" among students. It was borrowed from rogues and knaves and peculators and scoundrels generally, and not from men of honor, rectitude, and purity. As it regards students, does not the analogy hold true to the letter?

When incendiaries or burglars, or the meaner gangs of pickpockets, are abroad, is not he by whose vigilance and skill the perpetrators can be arrested, and their depredations stopped, considered a public benefactor? And if we had been the victim of arson, housebreaking, or pocket-picking, what should we think of a witness, who, on being summoned into court, should refuse to give the testimony that would convict the offender? Could we think any thing better of such a dumb witness than that he was an accomplice, and sympathized with the villany? To meet such cases, all our courts are invested with power to deal with such contumacious witnesses in a summary manner. Refusing to testify, they are adjudged guilty of one of the grossest offences a man can commit; and they are forthwith imprisoned, even without trial by jury. No community could subsist for a month, if everybody, at his own pleasure, could refuse to give evidence in court. It is equally certain that no college could subsist as a place for the growth of morality, and not for its extirpation, if its students should act, or were allowed to act, on the principle of giving or withholding testimony at their own option. The same principle, therefore, which justifies courts in cutting off recusant witnesses from society, would seem to justify a college faculty in cutting off recusant students from a college.

Courts, also, are armed with power to punish perjury; and the law justly regards this offence as one of the greatest that can be committed. Following close after the offence of perjury in the courts is the offence of prevarication or falsehood in shielding a fellow-student or accomplice from the consequences of his misconduct; for, as the moral growth keeps pace with the natural, there is infinite danger that the youth who tells falsehoods will grow into the man who commits perjuries.

So a student who means to conceal the offence of a fellow-student, or to divert investigation from the right track, though he may not tell an absolute lie, yet is *in a lying state of mind*, than which many a sudden, unpremeditated lie, struck out by the force of a vehement temptation, is far less injurious to character. A lying state of mind in youth has its natural culmination in the falsehoods and perjuries of manhood.

When students enter college, they not only continue their civil relations, as men, to the officers of the college, but they come under new and special obligations to them. Teachers assume much of the parental relation towards students, and students much of the filial relation towards teachers. A student, then, is bound to assist and defend a teacher as a parent, and a teacher is bound to assist and defend a student as a child. The true relation between a college faculty and college students is that which existed between Lord Nelson and his sailors: he did his uttermost for them, and they did their uttermost for him.

Now, suppose a student should see an incendiary, with torch in hand, ready to set fire to the dwelling in which any one of us and his family are lying in unconscious slumber: ought he not, as a man, to say nothing of his duty as a student, to give an alarm, that we may arouse and escape? Might we not put this question to anybody but the incendiary himself, and expect an affirmative answer? But if vices and crimes should become the regular programme, the practical order of exercises, in a college, as they would to a great extent do if the vicious and profligate could secure impunity through the falsehoods or the voluntary dumbness of fellow-students; then, surely, all that is most valuable and precious in a college would be destroyed in the most deplorable way; and who of us would not a hundred times rather have an incendiary set fire to his house while he was asleep, than to bear the shame of the downfall of an institution under his charge through the misconduct of its students? And, in the eyes of all right-minded men, it is a far lighter offence to destroy a mere material dwelling of wood or stone than to destroy that moral fabric which is implied by the very name of an educational institution.

The student who would inform me if he saw a cut-purse purloining the money from my pocket, is bound, by reasons still more cogent, to inform me if he sees any culprit or felon destroying that capital, that stock-in-trade, which consists in the fair name or reputation of the college over which I preside.

And what is the true relation which the protecting student holds to the protected offender? Is it that of a real friend, or that of the worst enemy? An offender tempted onward by the hope of impunity is almost certain to repeat his offence. If repeated, it becomes habitual, and will be repeated, not only with aggravation in character, but with rapidity of iteration; unless, indeed, it be abandoned for other offences of a higher type. A college-life filled with the meannesses of clandestine arts, first spotted, and then made black all over with omissions and commissions, spent in shameful escapes from duty, and in enterprises of positive wrong still more shameful, is not likely to culminate in a replenished, dignified, and honorable manhood. Look for such wayward students after twenty years, and you would not go to the high places of society to find them, but to the gaming-house or prison, or some place of infamous resort; or if reformation has intervened, and an honorable life falsifies the auguries of a dishonorable youth, nowhere will you hear the voice of repentance and sorrow more sad or more sincere than from the lips of the moral wanderer himself. Now, let us ask what kind of a friend is he to another, who, when he sees him just entering on the high road to destruction, instead of summoning natural or official guardians to save him, refuses to give the alarm, and thus clears away all the obstacles, and supplies all the facilities, for his speedy passage to ruin?

If one student sees another just stepping into deceitful waters where he will probably be drowned, or proceeding along a pathway which has a pitfall in its track or a precipice at its end, is it not the impulse of friendship to shout his danger in his ear? Or if I am nearer than he, or can for any reason more probably rescue the imperilled from his danger, ought he not to shout to me? But a student just entering the outer verge of the whirlpool of temptation, whose narrowing circle and accelerating current will soon ingulf him in the vortex of sin, is in direr peril than any danger of drowning, of pitfall, or of precipice; because the spiritual life is more precious than the bodily. It is a small thing to die, but a great one to be depraved. If a student will allow me to co-operate with him to save a fellow-student from death, why not from calamities which are worse than death? He who saves one's character is a greater benefactor than he who saves his life. Who, then, is the true friend, — he who supplies the immunity which a bad student *desires*, or the saving warning or coercion which he *needs?*

But young men are afraid of being ridiculed if they openly espouse the side of progress, and of good order as one of the essentials to progress. But which is the greater evil, — the ridicule of the wicked, or the condemnation of the wise?

> "Ask you why Warton broke through every rule?
> *'Twas all for fear that knaves would call him fool."*

But the student says, " Suppose I had been the wrong-doer, and my character and fortunes were in the hands of a fellow-student: I should not like to have him make report or give evidence against me; *and I must do as I would be done by."* How short-sighted and one-sided is this view! Suppose you had been made, or were about to be made, the innocent victim of wrong-doing, would you not then wish to have the past injustice redressed, or the future injustice averted? Towards whom, then, should your Golden Rule be practised, — towards the offender, or towards the party offended? Where a wrong is done, everybody is injured, — the immediate object of the wrong directly, everybody else indirectly; for every wrong invades the rights and the sense of safety which every individual, community, or body politic, has a right to enjoy. Therefore, doing as we would be done by to the offender, in such a case, is doing as we would *not* be done by to everybody else. Nay, if we look beyond the present deed and the present hour, the kindest office we can perform for the offender himself is to expose and thereby arrest him. With such arrest, there is great chance that he will be saved; without it, there is little.

Does any one still insist upon certain supposed evils incident to the practice, should students give information of each other's misconduct, we reply, that the practice itself would save nine-tenths of the occasions for informing, and thus the evils alleged to belong to the practice would be almost wholly prevented by it. And how much better is antidote than remedy!

But again : look at the parties that constitute a college. A faculty is selected from the community at large for their supposed competency for teaching and training youth. Youth are committed to their care to be taught and trained. The two parties are now together, face to face,— the one ready and anxious to impart and to mould, the other in a receptive and growing condition. A case of offence, a case of moral delinquency, — no matter what, — occurs. It is the very point, the very juncture, where the wisdom, the experience, the parental regard, of the one, should be brought, with all their healing influences, to bear upon the indiscretion, the rashness, or the wantonness of the other. The parties were brought into proximity for this identical purpose. Here is the *casus fœderis*. Why does not one of them supply the affectionate counsel, the preventive admonition, the heart-emanating and heart-penetrating reproof, perhaps even the salutary fear, which the other so much needs? — needs now, needs to-day, needs at this very moment, — needs as much as the fainting man needs a cordial, or a suffocating man air, or a drowning man a life-preserver. Why is not the anodyne, or the restorative, or the support, given? Skilful physician and desperate patient are close together. Why, then, at this most critical juncture, does not the living rescue the dying? Because a *friend*, a pretended FRIEND, holds it as a point of honor, that, when *his* friend is sick, — sick with a soul-disease, now curable, but in danger of soon becoming incurable, — he ought to cover up his malady, and keep the ethical healer blind and far away! When Cain said, " Am I my brother's keeper? " it was a confession of his own crime. But even that crime, great as it was, fell short of encouraging Abel to do wrong, and then protecting the criminal that he might repeat his crime.

> " When we disavow
> Being keeper to our brother, we're *his* Cain."

Such is the whole philosophy of that miserable and wicked doctrine, that it is a *point of honor* not to " report " — though from the most humane and Christian motives — the misconduct of a fellow-student to the faculty that has legitimate jurisdiction over the case, and is bound by every obligation of affection, of honor, and of religion, to exercise that jurisdiction with a single eye to the good of the offender and of the community over which it presides. It is a foul doctrine. It is a doctrine which every parent ought to denounce wherever he hears it advanced, — at his table, his fireside, or in public. It is a doctrine which every community of students ought, for their own peace, safety, and moral progress, to abolish. It is a doctrine which every college faculty ought to banish from its halls, — first by extracting it from its possessor, and expelling it alone; or, if that severance be impossible, by expelling the possessor with it.

The practicability of carrying out the views above presented is not an untried experiment. In an institution with which one of your committee is officially connected (Antioch College), the doctrines above set forth were announced at its opening, and have now been practised upon for a period of more than three years; and they have been attended with the happiest results. Such a degree of order, of regularity, and of exemplariness of conduct, has been secured, that for more than fourteen months last past, and with between three and four hundred students in attendance, not a single serious case for discipline has occurred.

In some respects, the experiment here referred to has been tried under more than an average of favoring circumstances; in other respects, under less. The institution was new. There was no traditionary sentiment in regard to the so-called code of honor to break down. In that organism the distemper was not chronic. And further: a large portion of its early members were of mature age, — persons who *came* to college instead of being *sent* there, — whose head and hands were alike unsullied by idea or implement of rowdyism, and who looked with a high-minded disdain upon all those brainless exploits which cluster under the name of college "pranks" or "tricks" or "practical jokes." We call them *brainless*, because there has scarcely been a new one for centuries; the professors in these arts being compelled to imitate, because they have too little genius to invent. Indeed, their best palliation is that they are too witless to know better, or that they suffer under the misfortune of having silly fathers and silly mothers, who have permitted their minds to remain in that *simia* stage of development through which they were passing up towards manhood; for, at this stage, *quadrumana* and *bimana* will act alike.

Another point in which the college referred to has enjoyed a great advantage, in regard to the motive-power actuating its students, has been the presence of both sexes. Each sex has exercised a salutary influence upon the other. Intellectually they have stimulated, morally they have restrained, one another; and it is the opinion of those who have administered the institution, that no other influence could, in so short a time, have produced so beneficial an effect. To this, perhaps, it should also be added, that this college discards all artificial systems of emulation by prizes, parts, or honors, as they are called; so that one of the most powerful temptations to degrade the standing of a fellow-student, in the hope of advancing one's own, is removed.

But, on the other hand, it is obvious that an attempt by a single college to revolutionize a public sentiment so wide-spread, so deep-seated, and so fortified by wicked purposes acting under the disguises of honor and magnanimity, must be an arduous and a perilous enterprise. So true is this, that a hundred individual attempts successively made, though followed by a hundred discomfitures, would supply no argument against the triumphant success of a combined and simultaneous assault, by all our literary institutions, upon the flagitious doctrines of the "code of honor." For while the virus of the code exists in other seminaries, and in the public mind generally, every new student must be placed, as it were, *in quarantine;* and even this could afford no adequate security that he would not introduce the contagion. It is only when moral health prevails in the place from which he comes that we can be sure of maintaining it in the place he enters.

In the experiment here spoken of, the general doctrines set forth in the resolutions, though announced and vindicated on all proper occasions, were not incorporated into the college statutes, nor were they presented to new students for signature or pledge; but, when any student fell under censure, he was then required, under penalty of dismission, to yield an affirmative acquiescence to the soundness of these doctrines, and to make an express promise to abide by them. Only a single case of contumacy under this requirement has occurred for more than three years; and, so far as known, not a case of non-fulfilment of the promise. Indeed, but few cases are left for the promise to act upon.

In conclusion, the committee would express a confident opinion that the proposed revolution in public sentiment is entirely practicable. The evil to be abolished is an enormous one. The reform would be not only relatively, but positively, beneficent. The precedent already established, if it does not enforce conviction, at least affords encouragement. The committee, therefore, recommend the doctrines set forth in the above resolutions to the faculties of all colleges, — especially to those in the State of Ohio, whom they more particularly represent, — for practical and immediate application.

On behalf of the committee,

HORACE MANN.

The same convention, at the same meeting, also unanimously adopted the following resolutions : —

Whereas, Vicious and criminal men become more potent for mischief in proportion to the education they receive ;

And whereas, If a man will be a malefactor, it is better that he should be an ignorant one than a learned one : therefore

Resolved, That it be recommended to all the colleges in the State of Ohio summarily to dismiss or expel students, who, without the permission of their respective teachers, use any kind of intoxicating beverages.

Resolved, That it be recommended to all the colleges in the State of Ohio to prevent, by the most efficacious means within their power, the kindred, ungentlemanly, and foul-mouthed vices of uttering profanity and using tobacco.

C.

INTEMPERANCE, PROFANITY, TOBACCO.

At a meeting of the Ohio State Teachers' Association, held at Columbus, Dec. 27, 1856, a committee — consisting of the Hon. Horace Mann, H. H. Barney, Esq., Prof. Marsh, Prof. Young, and G. E. Howe, Esq. — was appointed to recommend some action respecting the use of intoxicating liquors, profane swearing, and tobacco, in the schools and colleges of the State.

The committee afterwards submitted the following

REPORT AND RESOLUTIONS.

Within the crowded hours of the association, it is impossible for your committee to make an extended report. Nor is it necessary for them to do so. On the first point, particularly, — that of using intoxicating liquors, — what occasion have they to dwell? It is not any far-off calamity, removed to the other side of the globe, or hidden in the recesses of antiquity, escaping assault and overtasking description ; but it is among us and of us, a present, embodied, demoniac reality, smiting as no pestilence ever smote, and torturing as fire cannot torture, destroying alike both body and soul. It invades all ranks and conditions of men, and its retinue consists of every form of human misery. In all the land, there is scarcely a family, there is not one social circle, from which it has not snatched a victim : alas, from many, how many ! No other vice marshals and heralds such hosts to perdition. It besieges and makes captive the representatives of the people in legislative halls, and there gets its plans organized into law, where, first and chiefest, they should be annihilated. It usurps the bench, and there, under the guise of the sacred ermine, it suborns the judiciary to deny the eternal maxims and verities of jurisprudence and ethics, and to hold those prohibitions to be unconstitutional, and invasive of natural rights, which only conflict with their own artificial constitution and acquired daily habits ; and it ascends the sacred altar, and when the ambassador of God should speak like one of the prophets of old, or like an inspired apostle, against drunkenness and drunkards, it lays the finger of one hand upon his lips, with the other it points to some wealthy, somnolent inebriate below, and the ambassador forgets his embassy, and is silent. No other vice known upon earth has such potency to turn heavenly blessings into hellish ruins. It is no extravagance to say, that the sum-total of prudence, of wisdom, of comfort, of exemplary conduct, and of virtue, would have been to-day sevenfold what they are throughout the world but for the existence of intoxicating beverages among men : and that the sum-total of poverty, of wretchedness, of crime, and of sorrow, would not be one-tenth part to-day what they now are but for the same prolific, ever-flowing, overflowing fountain of evil. Youth, health, strength, beauty, talent, genius, and all the susceptibilities of virtue in the human heart, alike perish before it. Its history is a vast record, which, like the roll seen in the vision of the prophet, is written within and without, full of lamentation and mourning and woe.

No one can deny that intemperance carries ruin everywhere. It reduces the fertile farm to barrenness. It suspends industry in the shop of the mechanic. It banishes skill from the cunning hand of the artisan and artist. It dashes to pieces the locomotive of the engineer. It sinks the ship of the mariner. It spreads sudden night over the solar splendors of genius at its full-orbed, meridian glory. But nowhere is it so ruinous, so direful, so eliminating and expulsive of all good, so expletive and redundant of all evil, as in the school and the college, as upon the person and character of the student himself. Creator of evil, destroyer of good ! — among youth, it invests its votaries with the fulness of both prerogatives, and sends them out on the career of life to suffer where they should have rejoiced, to curse where they should have blessed.

Nor do the committee feel called upon to make any extended remarks upon the vice of using profane language. It is an offence emphatically without temptation and without reward. It helps not to feed a man, nor to clothe him, nor to shelter him. It is not wit, it is not music, it is not eloquence, it is not poetry ; but, of each of these, it is the opposite. Let a man swear ever so laboriously all his life, will it add a feather to the softness of his dying bed ? will it give one solace to the recollections of his dying hour ? No ; but even the most reckless man will acknowledge that it will add bitterness and anguish unspeakable. Were profanity as poisonous to the tongue as it is to the soul, did it blacken and deform the lips as it does the character, what a ghastly spectacle would a profane man exhibit! Yet to the eye of purity and innocence, to the moral vision of every sensible and right-minded man, lips, tongue, and heart of every profane swearer do look ghastly and deformed as disease and impiety can make them. How must they look to the infinite purity of God!

What an ungrateful, unmanly, and ignoble requital do we make to God, who gave us these marvellous powers of speech wherewith to honor and adore, when we pervert the selfsame powers to dishonor and blaspheme the name of the Giver! Perhaps the most beautiful and effective compliment anywhere to be found in the whole circle of ancient or modern literature is that which was paid by Cicero to the poet Archias, in the exordium of the celebrated defence which he made on the trial of that client. In brief paraphrase, as cited from recollection, it was something like this: If, says he, there is in me any talent, if I have any faculty or power of eloquence, if I have made aught of proficiency in those liberal and scholarly studies which at all times of my life have been so grateful to me, this Archias, my client, has a right to the command of them all; for he it was who taught them to me: he first inspired me with the ambition of being an advocate, and he imbued me with whatever gifts of oratory I may possess. It is his right, then, to command the tribute of my services.

If the great Cicero, standing in the presence of all the dignitaries of Rome, felt bound to acknowledge his obligations to the man who had instructed his youth, and helped to adorn the riper periods of his life, only in a single department, how much more imperative the obligation upon every ingenuous and noble soul to praise and honor that great Being who has endowed us with all we possess, and made possible whatever we can rightfully hope for!

There are certain situations where none but the lowest and most scandalous of men ever suffer themselves to swear. Amongst all people claiming any semblance to decent behavior, the presence of ladies or the presence of clergymen bans profanity. How distorted and abnormal is that state of mind in which the presence of man can suppress a criminal oath, but not the omnipresence of God! A Christian should be afraid to swear; a gentleman should be ashamed to. Every pupil, as he approaches the captivating confines of manhood, should propose to himself as a distinct object to be a gentleman, as much as to be a learned man; otherwise he is unworthy the sacred prerogatives of learning.

Your committee have but brief space and time for the consideration of the remaining topic.

Among the reasons against the use of tobacco, they submit the following: —

1. Tobacco is highly injurious to health; being pronounced by all physiologists and toxicologists to be among the most active and virulent of vegetable poisons. That consumers of tobacco sometimes live many years does not disprove the strength of its poison, but only proves the strength of the constitution that resists it; and that strength, instead of

being wasted in resisting the poison, might be expended in making the life of its possessor longer and more useful.

2. It is very expensive. The average cost of supplying a tobacco-user for life would be sufficient to purchase a good farm, or to build a beautiful and commodious house, or to buy a fine library of books. Which course of life best comports with the dignity of a rational being, —to puff and spit this value away, or to change it into garden and cultivated fields, into a nice dwelling, or into the embalmed and glorified forms of genius? What a difference it would make to the United States and to the world, if the four hundred thousand acres, now planted with tobacco within their limits, were planted to corn or wheat!

3. Tobacco-users bequeath weakened brains, irritable nerves, and other forms of physical degeneracy, to their children. The factitious pleasures of the parent inflict real pains upon his offspring. The indulgences of the one must be atoned for by the sufferings of the other; the innocent expiating the offences of the guilty. Nor, in regard to these personal and hereditary injuries to the mind, would the committee stand merely upon the principle laid down by the physician, who, when asked if tobacco injured the brain, replied promptly in the negative; for, said he, people who have brains never touch it.

4. Tobacco-users are always filthy; and we read of an infinitely desirable kingdom into which no unclean thing can ever enter.

5. Tobacco-users are always unjust towards others. They pollute the atmosphere which other men desire to breathe and have a right to breathe in its purity. A smoker or chewer may have a right to a limited circle of the atmosphere around his own person: but he has no right to stench the air for a rod around him, and half a mile behind him; he has no right to attempt a geographical reproduction of river and lake by the artificial pools and streams he makes in steamboat and car.

6. A tobacco-user is the common enemy of decency and good taste. His mouth and teeth, which should be the cleanest, he makes the foulest part of him. When one sees a plug of nasty, coarse, liver-colored tobacco, he pities the mouth it is destined to enter; but, when one sees the mouth, he pities the tobacco.

7. The old monks used to prove the pollutions of tobacco from Scripture; for, said they, it is that which cometh out of the mouth that defileth a man.

8. It has been argued that the adaptation of means to ends, which characterizes all the works of creation, intimates that snuff should never be taken; for, had such been the design of Nature, the nose would have been turned the other end up.

9. It may be fairly claimed, that, if Nature had ever designed that man should chew or smoke or snuff, she would have provided some place where the disgusting process could be performed systematically, and with appropriate accompaniments; but no such place or accompaniments have ever yet been discovered. Tobacco is unfit for the parlor; for that is the resort of ladies, and should therefore be free from inspissated saliva and putrefied odors. It is not befitting the dining-room, where its effluvia may be absorbed or its excretions be mingled with viand and beverage. Still less does it befit the kitchen, where

those culinary processes are performed which give savor and flavor to all the preparations that grace the generous board. It should not be carried into the stable; for that is the residence of *neat* cattle. And the occupants of the sty itself would indignantly quit their premises, should one more lost to decency than themselves come to befume or bespatter or besnuff them. There is no spot or place among animals or men which the common uses of tobacco would not sink to a lower defœdation.

10. Swiftly tending to destruction as is the use of intoxicating beverages; vulgar, ungentlemanly, and sinful as are all the varieties of profanity; unjust and unclean as are the effusions and exhalations of tobacco, — yet their separate and distinctive evils are aggravated tenfold when combined and co-operating. How abhorrent to the senses and the heart of a pure and upright man is the wretch who abandons himself to them all! Physiology teaches us, that, as soon as alcohol is taken into the stomach, Nature plies all her enginery to expel the invader of her peace. She does not wait to digest it and pass it away, as is done with the other contents of the stomach; but she opens all her doors, and summons all her forces, to banish it from the realm. She expels it through the lungs, through the mouth and nose, through the eyes even, and through the seven million pores of the skin. So let tobacco be taken into the mouth, or drawn up, water-spout fashion, into the nose, and firemen never worked more vehemently at a fire, nor soldiers fought more desperately in a battle, than every muscle and membrane, every gland and emunctory, now struggles to wash away the impurity. Every organ, maxillary, lingual, labial, nasal, even the lachrymal, pour out their detergent fluids to sweep the nuisance away. Not a fibre or cellule, not a pore or sluiceway, but battles as for life to extrude the foul and fetid intruder. Hence expectoration, salivation, the anile tears of the drunkard, and the idiot drool of the tobacco-user, all attest the desperation of the efforts which Nature is making to defecate herself of the impurity. When people first begin to drink or chew or smoke, outraged Nature, as we all know, often goes into spasms and convulsions through the vehemence of her conflict for escape. Finally she succumbs, and all that constitutes the life of a man dies before death.

The apostle enjoins his disciples to keep their bodies pure *as a temple of the Holy Ghost.* But, in such a body, what spot is there, what space so large as a mathematical point, which the Holy Ghost, descending from the purity and sanctity of heaven, could abide in for a moment? Surely, when a man reaches the natural consummation to which these habits legitimately tend; when his whole commerce with the world consists in his pouring alcohol in and pouring the impieties of profanity and the vilenesses of tobacco out, — gurgitation and regurgitation, the systole and diastole of his being, — he presents a spectacle not to be paralleled in the brute's kingdom or in the Devil's kingdom, on the earth or " elsewhere."

Your committee submit the following resolutions: —

Resolved, That school-examiners ought never, under any circumstances, to give a certificate of qualification to teach school to any person who habitually uses any kind of intoxicating liquors; and that school-officers, when other things are equal, should systematically give the preference to the total-abstinent candidate.

Resolved, That all school-teachers should use their utmost influence to suppress the kindred, ungentlemanly, and foul-mouthed vices of uttering profane language and using tobacco.

On behalf of the committee,

HORACE MANN.

D.

LETTER FROM MR. COMBE.

The following extracts from a letter of Mr. George Combe to the Hon. Horace Mann and Dr. Samuel G. Howe show in what a sweet spirit he received friendly criticisms: —

GORGIE COTTAGE, SLATEFORD, Dec. 31, 1840.

MY VERY DEAR FRIENDS, — I have received your letters of the 28th and 29th November, and esteem them as the highest and purest marks of friendship which you could have bestowed on me. Receive my cordial thanks, and rest assured, that, painful as these communications were, they have bound both of you to my affections with cords of double strength. It is only a real friend who will tell one disagreeable truths; and I know well how to appreciate such sincerity. I have written and printed an Introduction, which I send to you partly as an answer to your letter. And now for the remainder of the answer, which I could not put in types, being private in its nature. I sent your two letters and my first volume to my brother, Dr. Andrew Combe. He is a *severe* judge in relation to my works, because he values my reputation highly, and he condemns freely. He had read all the proofs; but I solicited a reperusal of the volume under the new lights communicated by you : and I told him that I was ready to burn the whole impression (the cost of which was at that time $1,250), but that I could *not* write a better work ; and asked his opinion, first, whether the work would *do good* in Britain ; and secondly, whether it would damage my reputation here. He gave the whole a serious consideration, and expressed his opinion, that it would *prove useful* here, and that it would *not* damage my reputation, although it would not advance it. He regarded it as just such a book as a person acquainted with my mind would expect from me in the circumstances in which I was placed. Here, then, I have great authorities on opposite sides; and, as my own country naturally claims a preference, I have decided to proceed with the publication, and to sustain meekly all the chastisement which will be inflicted on me on your side of the Atlantic. In this view, your corrections are highly valuable; and I have written to Dr. Bell to give effect to them all, except the remark about the license law, page 88. I got that from a Boston lawyer, a member of the Legislature, and a very able and excellent man; and I am bound to state both sides. I shall now answer the only points that seem to me to require notice; keeping in view that Dr. Bell will give effect to *all* your corrections, except that relative to page 88. . . .

The Introduction will stand in types here until you answer this letter, and I shall be happy to introduce all amendments and additions that you may suggest. I solicit your future corrections and remarks as freely as you like, and that you will send them to Dr. Bell. He will omit whatever you desire. And now, my very valued and dear friends, accept of the best wishes and grateful thanks of

Yours most sincerely,

GEO. COMBE.

Gorgie Cottage, Slateford, Dec. 31, 1840.

To the Hon. Horace Mann.

My much-valued Friend. — The prefixed is an epistle for you and Dr. Howe jointly; and now let me thank you personally and individually for your truly friendly letter. The only point for which I blame you is for not seeing what I told you personally, that, *in hoc statu*, I am not capable of writing a better book. My mind was constantly occupied by phrenology. My individuality is small, and my mental processes are performed slowly. Hence I could do no more than I have done. I could not devote two years to study and to sending my manuscripts to America, because in June I go to Germany in the great cause; and, as soon as this journal is completed, I shall commence a serious study of German, with a view to lecture in that language next winter. This brooks no delay; for the brain at fifty-two is stiff, and every year renders it less capable of receiving new impressions.

INDEX.